Banshee's Honor

Banshee's Honor

Shaylynn Rose

P.D. Publishing, Inc.
Clayton, North Carolina

ISBN-13: 978-1-933720-11-1
ISBN-10: 1-933720-11-5

9 8 7 6 5 4 3 2 1

Published by:

P.D. Publishing, Inc.
P.O. Box 70
Clayton, NC 27528

http://www.pdpublishing.com

Acknowledgements and Dedication:

What you hold in your hands, gentle reader, is a culmination of years of sweat and labor by many folks, including myself. I wish to tender my thanks, firstly for your purchase of this book (may you enjoy it immensely!) and secondly, to everyone who has encouraged me along the way.

To my mother, who has stood by my side and let me run when I should have crawled, thank you. I love you. You are the bestest.

And finally. This is for Koko, my beautiful baby who gave me ten years of his furry life. May you find peace with Bast, my handsome man.

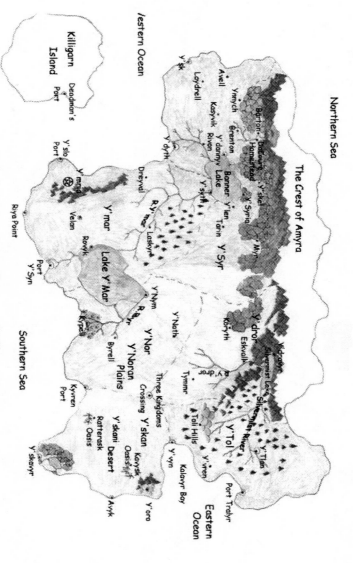

The Seven Kingdoms of Y'myran

Northern Sea

The Crest of Amyra

Jestern Ocean

Killigarn
Island

Decadnon's
Port

Y'sk

Loydrell

Avell

Yimrych

Brenton

Kasyvik

Y'danny Lake

Raven

Borton

Dadcara

Homestead

Y'skal

Y'syria

Myn

Banner

Y'len

Tarin

Y'Syr

Y'dyth

Dreydal

R. Y'mar

Y'syfa

Y'slo
Port

Y'mia

Velan

Y'mar

Laskyvik

Lake Y'Mar

Riya Point

Rovik

Port
Y'Syn

Y'Nym

R. Byr.

Byrell

Kyrell

Y'Nath

Y'Nar

Y'Noran
Plains

Y'droi

Eskvall

Koryth

Kyvren
Port

Crossing Y'skan

Three Kingdoms

Tymme

Y'dror

Silvermist River

Y'dror

Vidrayor

Y'Tal

Y'Tlan

Toli Hills

Y'yn

Kaysk
Oasis

Y'skani Desert

Ratterask
Oasis

Y'shayyr

Avyk

Y'oro

Port Trahyr

Kalavyr Bay

Y'rren

Eastern
Ocean

Southern Sea

map by sHaYcH (c) 2002

Long before the Firstlanders came to dwell upon the fair land of Aldyran, a dark vision haunted the sages of the elves. This nightmare warned of a time when war and strife would beset all the peoples of the land.

A millennia old prophecy foretold: "The breaking is at hand. The Blade, the Heart, and the Pawn shall meet, and on that day the sun will stand still and the stars will no longer spin with time. The Beast will rise to seek his place among mortals. Stand well against the storm, and sages shall sing of thy glory into the mists of Eternity. Fall, and all shall blacken and fade."

Their dreams filled with darkness and death, the ancient seers kept faithful records of their visions. Lesser divinations told that one would come who would seek to shatter the locks that bound the most terrible of all demonkind to the dark abyss of hell.

Laws more ancient than even the immortal elves prevented the gods of Aldyran from interfering with the prophecy. Instead, wise Astarus and his beloved sister Astariu kept watch, waiting for the ones who would come to battle the darkness.

In the fullness of time, the Firstlander humans came to Aldyran and claimed it for their own, giving to it the name of Y'Myran. During the wars that followed, nearly all of the elves' ancient knowledge was lost.

Peace was achieved. Kingdoms rose and flourished. The peoples of Y'Myran forgot the past and strove toward a future of prosperity.

Deep within the halls of hell one remembered and waited patiently. His time would come.

A tall, dark-haired man stared across the green-topped forests of Y'Dan and cursed his fate. *I was so close.* The thought trickled through his mind as he glared at the trees. All of his carefully wrought plans had been destroyed.

He should have known that Istaffryn, the shadowy leader of the Cabal, a loose-knit criminal organization, was cannier than he appeared. He had seen through the charms and charades of the young assassin Keskyn Nightblade and had banished him from the guild.

Angered that anyone would dare dictate the path of his life, Keskyn had changed his name and his occupation. An old, wizened sorcerer had eagerly taken on the young man as an apprentice and instructed him in the dark ways of using pain and fear to make magick. From the ashes of the man that had been Keskyn came Kasyrin Darkchilde. The young sorcerer quickly attempted to use his newfound powers to take control of the Cabal.

He had failed, again. With seeming ease, Istaffryn had foiled plot after plot of Kasyrin's. Darkchilde's final defeat came at the hands of a complete outsider to the Cabal, the Y'Dani warleader, Rhu'len DaCoure. Drawn into a web of lies and death, Rhu'len had sworn to slay Kasyrin or die trying.

Pain lanced through Kasyrin's side and he swore again. Rhu'len DaCoure's sword had been sharp enough to split him from stem to stern.

The only reason Kasyrin was alive now was due to his loyal servant, Por-thyros Omal. After watching his master duel Rhu'len DaCoure and lose, the rat-like little man had waited until sundown and then stolen out to the field and filched his master's body.

An old witch had been threatened into making Kasyrin well enough to travel, allowing him to flee northward. Now, here he was in the mountains above Y'Dan, with nothing more than the clothes on his back and a dagger in his belt.

Prior to the duel, he had been banished — cast out of the kingdoms and branded an oath-breaker. No matter where he went in Y'Myran, he would always be on the run. With nowhere else to go, Kasyrin decided to head north to the lands held by the barbarians of Amyra. There, he would rest, heal and think. A plan. He needed a plan, if he was to have his revenge.

The need for retribution consumed Kasyrin. If it was the last thing he did, he would have his vengeance. All who had stolen the power and glory that should be his would die. One pale hand closed into a fist so tightly that the nails cut into the flesh of his palm. Blood dripped onto the snow as a whispered word was stolen by the wind. "Revenge."

"Revenge." The echo awoke the sleeper from his slumber. His eyes opened and he blinked. It had been a long time since mortal speech had been heard in this place. Puzzled, he breathed a word of power. Nearby, a mirror shimmered to life, revealing a snow-covered mountain scene. Out-lined in the glow of the morning sun was a man whose face was carved into the hardened planes of one who has made an unbreakable vow.

::So it hath come to pass.:: The demon rubbed his jaw thoughtfully. As he stroked, his eyes closed and a smile creased his features into an expression of pure satisfaction. The sudden, sharp bark of his laughter echoed around the chamber. ::Excellent.:: Rising from his throne, Ecarthus strode out into his domain and began giving orders.

::Go, my slaves. Fly amongst the mortals and study their wretched lives. It is upon me to learn of those who would seek to thwart my destiny.::

The demon moved in front of the mirror once again. Extending one clawed finger, he delicately slit the palm of his hand and allowed three drops of his black blood to mar the mirror's surface. Eldritch power rippled the silvered glass. Golden light suffused it briefly and then it cleared. Ecarthus' lip curved into a snarl. Picturing the face of the greatest enemy of his children, the demon whispered a name.

::DaCoure.::

A shirtless man appeared in the middle of a forest glade. In his hands was an axe, which he was applying with vigor to a pile of wood. It was easy to imagine the same hands wielding a sword.

Ecarthus growled. Too many of his precious spawn had been slain by this mortal. He was dangerous. Rhu'len DaCoure would be among the first to block any of the demon's plans. Something would have to be done to stop him.

An idea began to glimmer in the demon's mind. It was only the barest seed of a plan, but brought to fruition, it would yield a bloody harvest. To that end, he sent more of his servants into the realms above to wait and watch. Soon they would act, and in that action, bring about his greatest desire.

::*I will be free.*::

Chapter One

Leaning heavily on makeshift crutches, a rag-covered figure slowly hobbled down the road. Muddy snow hindered the traveler's progress as she struggled to drag her splinted right leg through the thick slurry.

Home. The word drew the traveler along the road like a harlot's call.

A light sleet fell, churning into the grimy road dirt and forcing the transient to fight for every step through the slick, slippery morass. Muffled imprecations peppered the air each time she stopped to pull her twisted leg from the muck. Coming almost too late, the thundering of hoof beats caused the figure to bite off one sharp curse.

Throwing herself into a mound of snow that bordered the roadway, Azhani Rhu'len silently insulted the rider's ancestry back to his Firstlander mother's choice of footwear.

As she watched the horse gallop by, Azhani pushed greasy black braids away from her face. Her eyes narrowed dangerously when she noted who was perched upon the horse's back.

In one hand, a dark-cloaked man clutched the reins of his mount. His other arm was wrapped tightly about an unconscious, scarlet-robed body draped haphazardly across the horse's neck. The rich crimson color of the velvet robes, coupled with a flash of teardrop-shaped tattoos on a pale, bruised face, told Azhani that the man had just broken one of the most sacred of Y'Myrani laws. Frustrated by her injury, the former soldier pushed herself up and considered her options.

That was a stardancer. I'd recognize those robes anywhere. I have to help. The burn scoring the warrior's face coupled with shooting pains in her leg begged her to reconsider her thoughts. Who was she to involve herself in Y'Myrani affairs, anyway? The border was so close that she might have already crossed it. She was outside the realm of man's law — this was the borderlands where nothing was sacred.

Nothing but your oaths, warrior.

Once, she had been the warleader to the kingdom of Y'Dan. Now, Azhani was an exile. Yet though she no longer served a king or his people, the oaths of loyalty she had taken ran too deep to break. She could not allow the rider to succeed in his crime, not while she still drew breath.

Sparing a prayer to the goddess Astariu, Azhani tossed one of her makeshift crutches aside and stripped the other down, revealing an ash longbow. Under the layers of her rags was a quiver of steel-tipped arrows.

She took a deep breath and then plunged into the thicket at the side of the road. This section of the forest was familiar to her and she hoped that she remembered the trails correctly. It had been many years since Azhani had traveled its green depths, but her memory served her well. A shortcut was hidden just behind some trees on her left.

Ignoring the pain that ignited as soon as she put pressure on her bad leg, the warrior loped across the snow-covered ground. A quarter candlemark later, she broke free of the forest ahead of the horseman, but not by much.

It took only heartbeats to string her bow and nock an arrow. Quietly, she waited, breathing shallowly to control the agony shooting up her leg in fiery waves. They were close; she could feel the thud of the horse's hooves in the balls of her feet. One breath, two, and then the stale, acrid stench of sweat tickled her nostrils.

Rounding the bend in the road at a gallop, the horse thundered past the spot where Azhani was hidden. The rider cracked a stick against the animal's heaving flanks, attempting to inspire more speed. Sweat mottled the horse's light brown hide and its eyes were starting to roll in panic. The rider turned his head to scan the road behind him and Azhani made her move.

A single arrow hissed through the air, striking the man in the shoulder with enough force to knock him and his hostage off the horse. Screaming in fear, the animal reared and then galloped off down the road. Azhani ignored it, hobbling up to the kidnapper with another arrow readied in her bow. Struggling to sit, the man cursed loudly and reached for the arrow that had knocked him from his mount. Not far away, his victim lay in the dirt, moaning softly.

"Don't move, lawbreaker!" Azhani said evenly. The irony of the situation did not escape the exiled soldier as she watched the kidnapper. Out of the corner of her eye, she quickly glanced over to where the stardancer had landed. *Is that a woman? Yes, I think so. She's breathing, but I'll lay odds that her skull will ache like a beast later.*

On hearing her voice, the man looked up and swore vehemently. Five feet away, the rag-covered, bow-wielding figure looked more like a crazed wild woman than a serious warrior. Yet her aim had been perfect, stopping his flight with one shot. Anger twisted his features and he reached for his dagger.

As soon as she saw his face, Azhani growled. Branded deeply into his left cheek was the mark of the Cabal. Long-nurtured hate for the clan of villains, murderers and thieves bubbled up inside her. As he went for his weapon, she loosed the second arrow, pinning his other shoulder to the ground. With a wild shout, Azhani twisted the bow around and smashed it into the kidnapper's knees. The sickening crunch of bone, followed by a tortured scream of pain, was music to her ears.

Placing the tip of the bow against his temple, she angrily demanded, "Who are you, lawbreaker? Why have you harmed one of Astariu's chosen?"

He mumbled a reply and she frowned, then tapped her bow against his head none too gently. "Speak up, scum."

Hate-filled brown eyes looked up into hers and he smiled mirthlessly. "Dance in hell, bitch." Dark blood bubbled up and spilled over his lips. His eyelids fluttered shut and he went limp.

"Astarus' balls!" Azhani dropped her bow aside and reached for his collar. Ripping open the tunic she was just able to see a light burn mark where one of the Cabal's coin-sized amulets had rested. The mumbling had been the trigger spell to release the poison into the man's bloodstream. She was too late.

Growling, Azhani stood and counted to ten. When that did not bring relief from her rapidly growing anger, she kicked the kidnapper's body, forgetting about her injuries for just the briefest moment. The pain was like a blast of icy water in the face, and she collapsed, whimpering brokenly. Fresh blood seeped through the rags binding her leg, staining the snow. Black spots obscured her vision as she panted, trying to will the pain away.

"Shyvot!" Azhani spat, and then picked up her bow and shook it angrily. "Twins cursed mace-wielding wet-nosed excuses for pathetic soldiers!" she shouted at the uncaring trees. She forced herself to roll over, pounding the ground with a fist as fresh pain brought tears to her eyes.

The warrior searched for something to distract her from the pain. Glancing over at the stardancer, she was heartened to see that the woman was still breathing.

"Though she's not likely to be grateful for that," Azhani muttered, noting the way the woman's body was heaped on the ground. "I'm betting that whatever rescue she prayed for, it was not by an oath-breaker." *She probably didn't think she'd be kidnapped, either, warrior. This is one of the goddess' favored servants, not some fluff-headed princess.*

Azhani gritted her teeth and slowly, one inch at a time, crawled over to the body of the kidnapper. Without regard for the still-warm skin under her fingers, she ruthlessly searched the corpse, seeking clues to explain why he had broken the kingdoms' oldest laws. Those who served the Twain, stardancers and starseekers, were deemed sacrosanct by noble and peasant alike. To even consider harming one of the gods' own made the former warleader's stomach twist into painful knots.

Finding nothing but a bag of mixed coins, a vial of poison and two knives, the warrior pulled her arrows free and stowed them back in the quiver.

She kept the plain dagger but left the wicked, hook-bladed knife that was the signature weapon of a Cabal assassin on the body. For a long moment, Azhani considered the vial of poison. One drink and she could finally be out of pain. It was tempting. Too tempting. With a determined grunt, she smashed the vial against a protruding tree root. As she watched the toxic liquid sink into the earth, she secreted the pouch of gold under her rags.

Even though the kidnapper's clothes were cleaner than hers, nothing in creation would convince her to don the garb of an assassin. She had no desire to come under the scrutiny of the dark gods who favored those who slunk in the shadows and preyed upon society. That baleful gaze had already wreaked too much pain and havoc in her life. Using the body to push herself upright, Azhani stood and hobbled toward the softly groaning stardancer.

A soft whicker from behind caused Azhani to turn. The horse had returned and was standing only a few feet away, sides heaving from exertion. Limping slowly toward him, Azhani spoke soothingly while reaching for the horse's bridle.

"That's a good lad," she whispered. Her hands came into contact with the slick leather and she reached up, scratching his head. Nodding in pleasure, the horse sighed. Upon his bridle were the starburst markings of Astariu's healer aspect, which led Azhani to surmise that the animal belonged to the unconscious priest.

"All right lad, let's see if you were trained properly," she said warmly.

"Support." The horse immediately lowered his head, making it easy to grasp his mane tightly. "Easy," she said, and took a step forward, toward the stardancer. With the aid of the horse, she crossed the road to the fallen woman. Upon reaching the priest, the warrior calmly said, "Kneel." The horse went down on its front legs, waiting for the next command. "Steady," she said, and steeled herself against the torture she knew was coming. As carefully as she was able, Azhani lifted the dead weight of the stardancer's body to the horse's back.

Before the pain could overwhelm her, Azhani dragged herself up behind the priest. The added complication of the splint made finding an easy way to mount impossible. By the time she was situated, she had nearly blacked out from the pain. Throughout the ordeal, the horse placidly knelt, waiting for her next command.

Taking a deep breath to quell rising nausea, Azhani wrapped her arms around the young woman, taking care not to tangle her hands in the strap of the stardancer's haversack. The priest's head lolled to the side, revealing her face. Alabaster skin covered an angular bone structure. A mottled bruise shadowed the edge of her jaw, causing Azhani to wince in sympathy. Thick, wavy amber curls framed the woman's delicate features and brushed the tops of her shoulders. Tiny, graceful points topped her ears, proclaiming her half-elven heritage. *She's beautiful,* the warrior thought as she juggled the priest around until she was safely tucked against her body.

Fighting off dizziness, Azhani willed her stomach to settle. Once she could see clearly, she took the reins and directed the gelding to stand and head for the road.

Kyrian slowly fought her way to consciousness. Her first impression was of warmth, then movement and finally the coppery tang of blood. Shaking her head to try and rid it of the foggy sensation that kept her from comprehending her surroundings, the stardancer groaned. Her mouth was coated with a sharp-tasting slime and her head felt as though she had been drinking for a week.

Astariu, remind me not to drink the ale in Kellerdon again, she thought muzzily, bringing up a hand to scrub at her face. To her surprise, she realized that she was on horseback, but another held the reins. She was also nowhere near Kellerdon. Instead, she seemed to be facing a small homestead in the forest. Just in front of the horse was a broken down fence line that ended in a gate. An overgrown path led to a cottage that would have been welcoming were it not for obvious signs of disrepair.

"What happened?" she muttered, reaching for her baton. The two-foot length of tempered steel still rode at her hip, carefully stowed in its dark leather sheath.

"Easy," said a deep, rumbling voice from behind her, while a large, calloused hand covered hers.

Kyrian craned her head around, meeting the hooded face of a dirty, rag-covered woman. Tightening her grip around her weapon, she barked, "Who are you and what are you doing on my horse?" Inside, she rapidly quelled a sense of rising panic. *Oh goddess, what have I done? I'm not that lonely, am I?*

A quick smile flashed across Azhani's grimy face. *She's spirited, I'll grant her that. Not many would take that tone with me.* Azhani dropped the reins into the startled hands of the stardancer and then tossed her bow to the snowy ground.

Dismounting, she nearly bit through her lip when her legs hit the ground. Grabbing for the support of the old fence, Azhani took several deep breaths, hoping the starbursts in her eyes would clear quickly. *Home.* She had ridden the horse, cradling the unconscious priest until they had reached the gates of a ramshackle, sprawling homestead.

A broken wall of stone encircled the deserted property. Upon seeing the obvious state of abandonment, Azhani said a silent prayer of thanks. Her entire journey north had been laced with the hope that nothing had happened to the place.

"Who are you?" Kyrian asked again.

"I am no one, my lady." Azhani sketched a curt bow and reached for her longbow. Grasping it tightly, she turned to hobble inside. "Thank you for the ride. Astariu guide your journey."

Totally confused, Kyrian called out, "Wait!" She let go of the baton's hilt. "You're injured. I'm a healer, let me help you."

Azhani glanced over her shoulder at the young woman. "It is not necessary, my lady, the injury is nothing that time will not mend."

"Time may do, stranger, but my hands and skill are keener than it will ever be," the stardancer said as she dismounted. "Besides, you owe me the tale of how we came to be doubling on poor Arun's back. I'm certain that you were not among those sharing mugs of Gregor's finest last night at his daughter's handfasting!"

Azhani closed her eyes, reached up to pull back her tattered hood, and revealed her face. Looking up into the stardancer's almond-shaped green eyes, she grimly asked, "Would you give aid to an oath-breaker, healer?"

Kyrian hissed and drew back in fearful confusion.

Harsh, angular cheekbones prominently defined the hawk-like face. Her eyes were so blue that they contrasted sharply with the earthy duskiness of her skin. It was those eyes that caught and held Kyrian's attention, for they held the look of a warrior. Endlessly flicking from sight to sight, the woman's eyes captured everything from the flutter of a bird's wings to the rustle of grass as the horse browsed, searching for something to eat.

Thick, grimy hair clumped around the warrior's face and vanished into the folds of her cloak. Telltale pointed ears marked the woman as having elven ancestry, though she was not fully of the race. Below the corner of the stranger's right eye was a thick patch of dark scar tissue that stood out starkly against her brown skin.

Unconsciously, Kyrian's hand rose to touch the tattoo on her own face, as if seeking reassurance of its existence. Oath-breaker, the stranger had named herself. The horrible, puckered wound where once a noble mark of rank had rested gave credence to her words.

"Who are you stranger, that you bear the brand of an oath-breaker?" the stardancer asked in wonder.

It only took a moment's thought for the warrior to answer. There was nothing to lose, because a stardancer would not kill in cold blood. "I am Azhani Rhu'len," she said, bowing exaggeratedly. "At your service, my lady."

Kyrian's hand touched her chest as she stepped backward with a gasp. *I could kill her right now, and no one would care.* She had heard of Azhani Rhu'len, the Banshee of Banner Lake and former warleader of Y'Dan. For years, tales of the warrior's courage and skill in battle had spread throughout the kingdoms of Y'Myran. Now those stories went untold, replaced by the whispered horrors of her actions three months ago.

Y'Dan's king, Thodan the Peacemaker, had died in his sleep, and his son, Prince Arris, had inherited the throne. Rather than swear allegiance to the new king, Azhani had plotted to overthrow him. It was said that the young prince had stood before the Council awaiting his confirmation when the crazed warrior attempted to kill him. Arris had defended himself and had Azhani arrested. An investigation revealed the extent of her plan, and treason was only the beginning of her crimes. The Y'Dani warleader sought not only the new king's death, but his throne, as well.

King Arris had only one choice: sentence Azhani to death. But she had not gone to the gallows lightly. Choosing defiance to the last, she broke free of her jailor's bonds and attacked and killed Ylera Kelani, the elven ambassador. Compounding her crimes, Azhani demanded the rite of the gauntlet. The ancient custom allowed the warrior to face any who chose to pit their weapons against hers, until only one person was left standing.

The banks of Banner Lake were drenched with blood by the time Azhani had won her freedom. With no other option, King Arris declared the former warleader an outlaw, branded her an oath-breaker and drove her from his city. There was now a bounty on Azhani's head. If the ragged, beaten and lamed woman before Kyrian truly was Azhani Rhu'len, then no one would condemn her for walking away.

Except for Ylera. She would have wanted me to help her, Kyrian thought sadly. *Goddess bless you, Ylera, your heart was so full of forgiveness.* Ambassador Ylera Kelani, of the elven kingdom of Y'Syr, had been a good friend of the stardancer while she was still an acolyte. Though they had not seen each other for many years, Kyrian still fondly remembered their long nights spent studying by the light of a shared fire.

When she had heard of her friend's murder, Kyrian had raged in helpless anger. She had been in western Y'Dan when Azhani's treachery had taken place. Kyrian found it a beautiful irony that she had been unable to save Ylera, but now had the chance to exact a fitting revenge.

Her hand strayed toward the baton once again. Kyrian struggled to push her anger aside, to see beyond the red haze that clouded her vision and into the heart of the woman standing next to the gate. Her hand flexed as she fought the desire to exact retribution on the person who had taken her one friend from the world.

It would be easy, a sibilant inner voice coaxed. *She's already weak and barely able to stand. Just one or two well-placed blows and the bitch would be deader than last year's leaves.*

Kyrian's hand wavered as her muscles twitched painfully. She closed her eyes.

Blood dripped from the end of her baton. Bits of bone and brain spattered the front of her robes and in the distance she could hear the sound of someone crying.

Nausea washed over her and she drew in a shuddering breath, forcing the terrible memories to fade. Her lips shaped the word *no.*

Azhani sneered as she watched the play of emotion that flickered across the stardancer's face. "Go, healer, and give your skills to someone who is worthy of their learning," she said harshly, and then limped away.

Opening her eyes, Kyrian watched as Azhani struggled to cross the yard, falling every few steps. Doggedly, the warrior would pull herself up and continue to hobble toward the door of the cottage.

She's in pain, Kyrian thought. *I have to help her. She's in pain. The goddess teaches that those in pain deserve our care, even if they are guilty of terrible crimes. It is not for me to judge. That is Astariu's duty. I am her servant, and my duty is to heal.*

Wincing at the onerous direction her thoughts had taken, Kyrian was surprised by a burning ache that thudded dully in her jaw. She reached up and probed the skin, hissing at the tenderness. *What the...?* she thought curiously, reaching into the pouch at her side to withdraw a small silver mirror. A dark purple bruise covered one side of her face. *Ah goddess, how did that happen?* She frowned and searched her memories for clues.

The ale was cold, spiced with a hint of nutmeg and it tasted good on Kyrian's dry tongue. The last of the prayers for the handfasting ceremony had been spoken and she was thirsty enough to drink from a bog. Smiling at the sight of the newly 'fasted couple dancing in the center of the inn, Kyrian wandered outside with her drink and breathed deeply of the cool night air. A man who walked with an oddly unbalanced gait neared her and she reached out to assist him.

That's when she noticed the slightly strange taste of the brew, a hint of something that the nutmeg and alcohol could not disguise. Cursing softly, she tossed aside the mug and was shoving her fingers down her throat when a large fist came from nowhere and knocked her unconscious.

Kyrian rubbed her jaw again. *All right, so how did I get from there to here?* she wondered. Azhani had not been her attacker. She had caught just enough of a glimpse of the person's face to know that she had not been one of the oath-breaker's victims. Another memory intruded, this time of falling through the air and hitting the ground hard. Kyrian struggled to grasp it, to seize any details that her addled brain had saved. As she fell, she had seen a monstrous, bow-wielding form howl ferociously and leap on the man who had held her captive.

Looking across the yard to where the warrior was still struggling to reach the cabin, Kyrian realized that the bowman had been Azhani. There was a mystery here. Why would a woman branded as a traitor risk herself to save someone? Yes, that someone was a stardancer, one of the few whose gifts were so great that Astariu empowered them with the magickal ability to heal, but why should Azhani care? It obviously hadn't been to beg succor for her injuries, since she had scorned Kyrian's offer of aid.

Unless she's a really good liar. Again, anger rose.

She killed Ylera! The mental scream caused Kyrian to scowl fiercely. *She's evil. It's a trick. She saved you just so you would feel indebted to her.*

Unable to reach a decision, she stood unmoving as Azhani stumbled and crawled her way across the snow-strewn yard. The sheer amount of determination that it took to ignore what must be excruciating pain forced Kyrian to study her memories as closely as she could. Never, in all the tales she had heard about the near legendary warleader, had she heard a whisper of Azhani acting without honor.

What she could remember of the warrior's most recent actions agreed with the older tales, flying in the face of every rumor and story she had heard of the events of Banner Lake. Was this woman a monster, or was she a hero? Kyrian bit her lip, helplessly indecisive.

Azhani fell again, this time a tiny cry of pain forcing the stardancer to take a half step forward.

Help her, an inner voice urged Kyrian. *You swore never to kill another thinking being. If you don't help Azhani now, you will surely break that vow!*

Kyrian's resistance crumbled. Whatever Azhani had done in the past, she wasn't going to do harm now, not as weakened as she was.

I have to do this. I will not wash more blood from my baton.

"Guard," she whispered, knowing the horse would raise the alarm if something bigger than a rabbit came near the gate. Striding quickly to Azhani's side, she declared, "I don't care if you're a rimerbeast's mutant spawn, I'm going to help you." She knelt by the warrior's injured side, offering her shoulder for support.

Azhani looked up at the stardancer, disbelief clearly written on her harsh features. "Is this a trick? Are you going to stab me just as soon as I turn my back? You could, you know." The warrior's harsh bark of laughter made Kyrian regret her earlier thoughts. "I'm as weak as a kitten."

Taking the initiative, Kyrian wrapped one arm around Azhani's waist and waited for her to grab hold. "You are injured and I am a healer. It is my sworn oath to offer aid to those in need. You would not have *me* be an oath-breaker, would you?"

Coldly, Azhani looked up, meeting the open gaze of the stardancer. All uncertainty was gone and what remained on Kyrian's face was gentle concern. The acidic comment on the warrior's tongue dissolved unspoken. Looking down at the snow, she mumbled no and settled her arm on Kyrian's shoulder.

The stardancer was surprisingly strong. Beneath the slight appearance was a compactly muscled body and she easily lifted the heavier, taller woman, standing steady until Azhani had found her balance. The pair began to take slow, steady steps toward the cottage.

"I would not dishonor you so, my lady," Azhani added softly, after catching her breath.

"Good. Now, is that a door, or do I need to have Arun kick in the window?" Kyrian asked, nodding toward the front of the house.

Despite herself, Azhani laughed. "It's a door." Reaching up, she fished around the doorframe until she found a loosened bit of wood. After a gentle tug, it came free, revealing a rusty key. "This is my home, such as it is." The warrior took the key and began to fumble with the lock.

"Home? I thought you lived in Y'Dannyv," Kyrian said.

"I did. This is my father's homestead. I grew up here in the borderlands." Nodding to the north, she added, "Ride about five days travel that way and you'll hit the foothills of the Crest of Amyra. If you go that way," she indicated the other direction, "you'll end up back in Y'Dan. Satisfied? No laws to break here, because there aren't any."

With a sudden rusty screech, the lock popped open. Kyrian took the handle and gave it a good turn, opening the door. Seasons worth of dirt and dust exploded outward, causing the stardancer to cough and fan the air in front of her face. Kyrian blinked several times, trying to see into the dimly lit room.

Debris littered the floor; not an item of whole furniture remained. A musty odor clung heavily to the room, and Kyrian recognized a variety of animal prints in the thick dust. Dirty cobwebs stretched across the ceiling, draping down into their faces as they slowly entered the cabin.

"I thought you said that you lived here," Kyrian said uncertainly as she helped the injured warrior into the room.

Azhani used her bow to push some of the larger clumps of debris out of her way. "I do. Now."

"Why is there nothing here?" Kyrian gestured around the room at the mess. "All that remains is garbage," she finished, shrugging curiously.

"After my father died, raiders took everything that wasn't nailed down," Azhani said as Kyrian lowered her to the ground near the hearth. "The last time I was here, I locked up to keep the larger animals from making this place uninhabitable."

Kyrian smirked as she looked around at piles of rodent droppings. "I suppose it worked to some extent."

"It was all I could do at the time," Azhani murmured.

"It will do," the stardancer said. Carefully, she inspected the fireplace, seeking any blockages in the flue. "May I borrow that?" she asked, pointing at the longbow.

Azhani wordlessly handed over the unstrung bow, wincing as the stardancer used it to poke and prod at the chimney until several ancient nests fell into the hearth, sending clouds of dust and soot flying.

Coughing and wheezing, the warrior snatched her bow back when Kyrian offered it to her with a sheepish grin.

"Sorry," the stardancer said as she gathered piles of broken twigs to lay out a fire. She gave the debris a considering glance. Most of the trash would burn and the rest would go into the middens. Clean up would be easy. *Is it too much to hope that there's a broom around here somewhere?*

Once there was a small fire going in the hearth, Kyrian knelt next to the warrior and said, "Now, let me look at that leg."

Azhani had drifted off into a light doze, but came awake quickly when the stardancer spoke. She attempted to swing her legs around toward Kyrian, but her badly damaged leg had frozen in place. "I might need a little help," she admitted gruffly, trying to force her legs to move.

Gently, Kyrian helped her to reposition herself so that her legs were stretched out. Tiny gasps and mews of pain escaped as Azhani moved, but she did it, collapsing to the floor when Kyrian signaled she could stop.

The stardancer eyed the haphazard bandages critically. Calmly, she reached into her haversack and withdrew a small knife and began to cut away the cloth that held the battered splints in place. When the wood and rags had fallen away, she sucked in a breath at the revealed wound. A mottling of bruises covered Azhani's entire leg from the knee down. Thick yellow pus oozed from torn putrefied flesh and white ends of damaged bone thrust up through the wound. Large knots of torn muscle indicated that the bones had been broken more than once.

"Wasn't this set?" Kyrian asked in indignation as she began pulling out the tools of her trade.

"Didn't have," Azhani gasped, "much time." The whisper-light touch of the stardancer's warm fingers had sent daggers of pain up her leg. "I was in something of a hurry to leave Y'Dannyv."

"So it's true then, what they say?" Kyrian asked conversationally, as she ground several herbs together.

Azhani didn't answer.

Kyrian looked up and stared at the warrior, but Azhani wouldn't meet her gaze.

"Why?" Kyrian whispered. "Ambassador Kelani and the soldiers — you killed them. Why, Azhani?"

Still no answer came.

Sighing sadly, Kyrian stood and walked to the door. Arun amiably cantered over when she called out to him. When the gelding poked his nose through the doorway, he got a snootful of dust and sneezed loudly, causing her to softly chuckle. She removed her saddlebags, bedroll and extra blankets, and thanked the gods that her nameless kidnapper had thought to steal her horse too.

She dug out a pot, scooped up some snow and set it on the fire to melt. "I'm going to have to set your leg. It will cause you a great deal of pain." Her voice was tinged with regret.

"I know," the warrior replied dazedly. Lurid red spots flickered in front of her eyes as waves of pain and nausea threatened to render her unconscious while cold chills wracked her body.

Kyrian noticed Azhani's hands opening and closing spastically and made a soothing noise. "Not much longer now. Once this steeps, I'll put you to sleep and you can rest."

"No. I'll stay awake," Azhani said weakly. "Don't waste your magick on me, healer."

Kyrian poured the herbs into the pot of water and stirred them with her knife. "It's my decision to make, warrior. The magick is yours whether you will it or no." She propped her bedroll behind Azhani's head. "Close your eyes and try to rest. I'm almost ready."

While Azhani relaxed into the softness of the woolen blankets, the stardancer briskly set to work. Quickly, she searched the bottom floor of the small house. In the storage area, she found a battered broom hiding in a darkened corner. Smiling as she claimed her prize, she returned to the main room.

"Looks like the bandits forgot something!" She triumphantly displayed the ratty broom for the warrior.

Azhani grunted in amusement. "Trust a stardancer to make a treasure out of a broom."

Kyrian shot her a bright smile, and then dropped the broom to hurry over to her pot, which was boiling rapidly. "My apologies, but this is going to taste like the bottom of a chamber pot." She made a sour face as she used a piece of clean linen from her haversack to filter the steaming drink into a mug. "On the bright side, you'll feel much better."

Azhani sat up and sipped at the tea, gagging at the extremely bitter taste. "You don't honey coat the truth, do you?" she asked while coughing and gasping.

"Why should I? If I had said that it tasted like ambrosia, would you have believed me?" Kyrian asked, raising one eyebrow in curiosity. "Beyond that, after tasting such a brew, would you trust my skills as a healer?"

The warrior chuckled ruefully. "No, I would not, to both questions. I have dealt with my share of chirurgeons, my lady." She blinked her eyes. As she had suspected, there was something in the drink to make her drowsy. "I said I wanted to stay awake," she said in protest as the herbs took effect.

Kyrian caught the mug before it slipped from nerveless fingers. "I know, warrior. But I need you still to work this healing," she whispered as Azhani drifted off into the dream realms. "And I'm afraid that there'd be no keeping you steady once I set that first break."

The surgery on Azhani's leg took several candlemarks. Kyrian was appalled at the extensive damage and knew that she would have to spend at least one session using Astariu's gift to repair the bones. Otherwise, the warrior would never walk properly again.

Kyrian's hard work had not gone unrewarded, though. With the necrotic tissue cut away, the angry red lines of infection were slowly receding and allowing good blood to flow through the leg. Kyrian was quite pleased. The warrior's leg had an excellent chance of survival.

While Azhani rested peacefully, Kyrian kept busy by cleaning the small cabin.

The interior's a wreck, but at least the structure seems solid. It's cold today, and winter has barely settled on the mountains, Kyrian mused silently as she cleaned.

The cabin had three rooms. There was the hearth room where Azhani slept, a loft and a storage room. A door led from the storage area to the back of the house.

Wondering what was outside, Kyrian opened the door and looked. Not more than fifty paces away stood a small stable and paddock. She wandered out to the stable and opened the door, smiling when she saw that the inside was perfect for Arun.

The stable was not as dirty as the house, and it only took her a few minutes to clear out a stall for her horse.

"Here you go, Arun," Kyrian murmured as she led the horse through the door. As the day had passed, it had grown bitterly cold and she could tell that Arun was grateful to be out of the chill. There was a small hearth, which the stardancer cleared. Then she set a well-banked fire so that the horse would be warm all night.

Finally she curried Arun until his hide glimmered in the waning sunlight. Leaving him with a bag filled with oats, she brushed her hands off and muttered, "Now, what else can I find?"

She yawned and almost missed the outhouse. Further away from the house than the stable, the ramshackle building squatted between two trees. "I should have found this earlier," Kyrian said as she opened the door.

The stale scent of animal habitation greeted her and she wrinkled her nose.

"Oh that's wretched. This will never do." Even though it was late, she hurriedly returned to the cabin. Fetching the broom and a lantern, Kyrian went back to the privy to clean it. While she worked, the stardancer realized that she was going about her chores haphazardly. Laughing, she shrugged. Who would know if she didn't follow perfect protocol? The work was getting done, and that was what mattered.

Privy cleaned, she scrubbed her hands with snow and went back to the cabin. In the rear was a fenced off section which held a garden and a well. The broom handle doubled as a spade and she dug up a small bounty of vegetables. The well held clear potable water. Next to the well was a broken bucket in which she cleaned the vegetables.

"Thank you, Astariu," Kyrian whispered as she dried the last potato on her robe.

With her treasures in hand, she returned to the cabin. Inside, the firelight illuminated the stairs leading to the loft.

Her patient was still asleep, so Kyrian set the food near the hearth and headed upstairs. There she found the bedroom. Two pallets were built into the floor and a woodstove stood in the corner by a window. She strode over to the window to close the shutters and was surprised to find that the floor was not very stable.

I guess no one's been up here in a long time. I'd better be careful. In one section, Kyrian had to avoid a fist-sized hole where the wood had rotted through. She closed the window and quickly checked the stove. It was functional. Curiosity satisfied, she hastily made for the stairs.

"Don't need to add myself to the injured list," she muttered softly as she gingerly avoided the unstable floorboards.

Near the hearth, Azhani still slept peacefully so Kyrian decided to go check on her horse. Though she had given him grain earlier, it would not be enough to last through the night. Gorse grasses grew near the fence line and Arun was happy to eat everything she gave him.

While he ate, she searched the stable for more treasures. From time to time, the horse would look in his empty trough and then stare hopefully at his mistress, but nothing more was forthcoming.

Laughing, Kyrian shook a finger at the gelding. "Sorry boy, there isn't much to eat. We have to ration for a while."

Arun flicked an ear and huffed noisily.

"I know. But you'll survive," Kyrian said, smiling at the horse's antics. Arun was a good friend, smarter than most horses, and it showed in the way he responded her statements and actions. "I should go back to the cabin. Azhani will be waking soon." There was just one last section of the stable to explore and Kyrian decided to examine it first.

One corner of the building was piled almost waist high with bits and pieces of wood. The heap appeared to be the discard pile for a carpenter and Kyrian almost dismissed it as simply a great source of firewood until she caught a glimpse of something metallic.

Now what have we here? Curiosity outweighed any desire to head back inside and Kyrian pushed up her sleeves and began to move the wood around. In short order, she had uncovered an old trunk. Brass fittings gleamed dully.

Kyrian whistled in appreciation at the ornate carvings that adorned the lid of the box.

There was no lock, so she lifted the top and peered inside. A cloud of dust rose and caused her to sneeze repeatedly. When she was able to control herself, Kyrian smiled at the sight that greeted her. Folded neatly and wrapped in decaying parchment was a surprising wealth of blankets and clothing.

At the very bottom of the trunk, under the clothes, she found a final prize; a long, thin package shrouded in ancient silk. With a deft twist of her wrist, Kyrian flicked away the silken covering and stared at the naked blade of a finely crafted elven longsword.

Her vision blurred and for a moment, she could almost see blood dripping down the steel and puddling at her feet. Disgusted, she swallowed heavily. *I should just drop this into the well.* Kyrian closed her eyes to block out the memories. *I can't. I can't throw away a perfectly good weapon. Just because I don't use blades doesn't mean that Azhani will never want to swing a sword again.*

Thoughts of the warrior reminded Kyrian that she needed to check on her patient. Quickly, she rewrapped the blade and gathered the textiles into a bundle. For now, she would keep the sword. There was no need to hand it over to the injured woman right away.

Stardancers used no edged weapons other than the small knives made for eating, healing and other mundane tasks. As servants of Astariu's healer aspect, they carried batons, long stout rods crafted of highly flexible steel. The weapons were just as deadly as swords, but in the hands of a master, they could be used to disable instead of kill. The order firmly believed that death in the name of justice was the province of kings, not priests.

Kyrian had taken a life once, and that burden wore heavily upon her conscience. Seeing the sword reminded her of her oath and of why she had spent the last two years of her life moving from place to place, wearing herself out by trying to heal enough people to atone for the life she had ended.

Stopping to pat Arun one more time, Kyrian left the stable. The sun had long since vanished and a chilly, biting wind whipped her robes about her body as she hurried to the small house. She dropped her booty near the sleeping warrior and set her lantern in the center of the room.

Scavenged wood fed the fire, filling the room with warmth. A meager handful of jerked beef joined the vegetables in a pot of water that she hung from a hook over the fire. From her pack Kyrian took out a loaf of black bread and the remains of a crock of butter.

The loaf was a bit smashed and there was a crack in the jar, but it was intact enough to eat the contents. "Well, it's not a dwarven banquet, but this should make a tasty feast."

Soon, the aroma of food filled the room, chasing out the last remnants of decay and dust.

Chapter Two

Azhani woke to the scent of soup. *Mm, food...that smells...* Her stomach churned with nausea momentarily and then as the smells registered as good, growled hungrily. *Wonderful. I'm hungry.* She blinked her eyes open slowly, surprised when she wasn't immediately assaulted by a wave of pain.

The warrior lifted her head and looked down at her leg, which was wrapped tightly in bandages and bore a brand new splint. *She did it,* she thought with wonder. *The stardancer saved my leg.*

"Thank you," she croaked.

Surprised, Kyrian nearly dropped her bowl. She shot the warrior a vexed grin. "You're welcome, warrior. Are you hungry? There's soup."

"Does it also taste like yesterday's chamber pot?" Azhani asked, pulling herself up into a sitting position. She winced as her bladder woke.

"No!" Kyrian replied, laughing at the warrior's joke. "But I could add some bitterroot, if that would make you happy," she added slyly. Kyrian watched the warrior fidget for a moment, and then covered a chuckle. *She's doing the privy dance rather quietly. I'd be demanding an escort by now.* "I bet you'd like to take a walk, wouldn't you?" she asked delicately. Standing, she reached out a hand to the warrior.

Azhani made a face. "I can do this myself," she said before the stardancer could speak. The warrior took hold of her bow and used it to lever herself to a standing position, then took one feeble step forward while Kyrian stood off to the side, abortively reaching out to steady her.

"Be careful, warrior. Just because you can stand does not mean that you are ready to run races," Kyrian said.

Azhani grimaced as she put pressure on the leg. A quick burst of pain rippled from the newly mended injuries, causing the warrior to hiss. "I am discovering this." Slowly, dragging her splinted leg with every agonizing step, she worked her way to the back door of the cabin.

"You're quite a stubborn one, aren't you, Azhani Rhu'len?" Kyrian whispered, as rising fascination forced her to watch the warrior's retreating back. Despite the woman's violent past, something about her indomitable will enticed Kyrian to learn more. There was something that called out to the healer and begged her to give Azhani the chance to prove herself.

Azhani stepped out into the cold night and took in a deep breath, nearly weeping with the effort of staying upright. If her bladder weren't telling her with every heartbeat that she was about to embarrass herself, she would have collapsed into a heap right there. Instead, she reached down into the well of strength that seemed to be growing steadily emptier and pushed on until she reached the privy.

When she finally made it back into the house, Kyrian had set up two pallets near the fire. Next to one of the pallets was a bowl of thick savory soup, a half round of dark peasant bread and cup of lightly steaming tea. The stardancer was lying in the other, apparently asleep.

Azhani lowered herself to the ground and let out a soft groan of weariness. Quietly, she began to eat. In between spoonfuls, she said, "Not bad," and went back to shoveling down the food. She set her empty bowl down and tore into the rich nutty bread. "Better than bugs and roots."

Kyrian rolled over and stared at the warrior. "Why do I think you would say that about food served at King Arris' table?"

Azhani's face darkened. "I wouldn't. Anything served in that castle would taste like ashes to me." The warrior's voice was low and harsh. Her appetite gone, she laid the last portion of her bread in her empty bowl and picked up her tea. Azhani knew she would need the painkillers that the pungent herbal odor of the drink promised.

Not knowing how to respond to the warrior's statement, Kyrian held her tongue.

Azhani's voice was bleak as she said, "You can leave tomorrow. About a day and a half to the north, you'll find Barton. It's a mining and trading town. You can winter there. In spring, you'll be able to continue to wherever it was you were headed before you were abducted."

Kyrian looked around at the sad state of the cottage. Though her efforts had done much to create a homey cheer, there was still a sense of bleak emptiness that called out for a loving hand. It was the healer in her that spoke, though. "I'd like to stay and treat your wounds." At the very least, the warrior's leg would require several more days of the stardancer's care.

Azhani felt her jaw tighten. Didn't the healer get it? Didn't she understand that she was trying to give her a chance to get away? Azhani knew Arris would never let her escape. This was the stardancer's only chance to flee before the boy king's troops rooted them out and murdered them in their beds. "I don't need your help," she said brusquely, lying down and pulling one of the woolen blankets over her.

"I didn't say you did," Kyrian said affably. "I offered it. There is a difference, warrior."

"Stop calling me that," Azhani muttered darkly. "My days of fighting are over. I am a simple woman of the forest now, nothing more."

"Warrior or not, you will need someone to help you make this place livable. Winter is upon us, and it will be many weeks before your leg can bear your full weight. You may wish me to leave you here to rot, but my oaths as a healer will keep me glued to your side. I will be here tomorrow, and the days after that, until I've decided that you are able to care for yourself." Kyrian spoke firmly, letting the warrior know that she would not be swayed. "Besides," she added lightly, "you still haven't told me why you saved me, and I want to hear the story." Gingerly, she settled into her pallet, trying not to dislodge the hidden bundle of the sword.

"I'm no tale-spinner, healer. The facts are simple enough. I saw one of Astariu's Own in trouble and I had the means to act. Anyone who had sworn the vows I have would have done the same thing."

"What care does an oath-breaker have of allegiances?" Kyrian asked glibly.

"Perhaps none, but I'll not be damned for spite," Azhani retorted.

"Still, I sense a deeper cause. Even if you threaten to run me off with your bow, I will stay," Kyrian said resolutely. *I would regret breaking your hand, warrior, but I would still stay.* In healing her, Kyrian had touched the aura of the Banshee of Banner Lake, and that had driven away her misgivings about helping Azhani. No one could be as evil as the stories claimed the woman was and carry as much pain and grief as Azhani did. Kyrian could no more fight the need to help her than she could raise the dead. As surely as a flame melted the day candle's wax, Kyrian was drawn to aid the warrior.

The stardancer wanted to hate Azhani for the crimes she had committed, but her curiosity had been aroused. Why would a warrior of impeccable virtue turn against everything she had fought so hard to uphold? Kyrian found this fascinating. Pursuing this question would keep her from having to mull over her own past, something she desperately tried to avoid.

From the other pallet, Azhani's half-asleep voice floated over to the stardancer. "Stay then, healer. I will not refuse you shelter. Whatever else you require you will have to provide on your own."

Thinking of the soup she had made, Kyrian chuckled lightly and said, "Agreed." In the morning, she would see what other bounty the cottage and its environs had to offer. If she found nothing, she had a small supply of trail rations, including Arun's oats, and the gelding never minded sharing.

Newly formed icicles glittered from the branches of a gnarled tree. Kyrian stared at the strange beauty, and then began to pick her way up the trunk, looking for any sign of a nest. A pile of twigs bore some promise, but, to her immense disappointment, yielded nothing more than some ancient feathers.

Grumbling softly, she began to climb down. By chance, she spotted a large growth of mushrooms speckling the other side of the tree. Sparing a brief prayer of thanks, she hurried down and examined the fungi. They were edible.

Carefully, she harvested the mushrooms and put them in a pouch. Laying the pouch on a warped shelf tacked to the side of the cabin, Kyrian wandered to another tree, smiling when she caught sight of several small, reddish-yellow fruits. Opening her haversack, the stardancer culled a dozen of the tart but tasty crabapples. Her hands were aching with the chill by the time she was done gathering the fruit. There was a bite to the air that spoke of the weather to come, and she realized that the meager supplies in her saddlebags would not last the winter. They would have to find more food to set aside or they would starve.

I wonder if Azhani will have any ideas. She mentioned a trading post not too far from here; maybe I should ride up there tomorrow. Kyrian decided to talk to her patient about it when she woke. *Patient? I guess that's what she is, though she'd stubbornly deny it. Then again, she'd just as soon skewer me as speak to me.*

A search through the overgrown garden turned up a few more withered vegetables and some wild herbs. As she gathered the vegetation, she spotted a rabbit. The animal was rooting through the snow not far from where she knelt. Blessing her fortune, Kyrian whispered a prayer to its spirit and killed it quickly.

Azhani was just waking when Kyrian poked her head inside the room.

"Morning, warrior," she said cheerfully. The stardancer set aside her bounty, warmed her hands at the hearth and then walked over and gently touched the warrior's cheek. No fever today, unlike the day before, when the dark brown skin had been like touching Astariu's fires. Today it was cool, bearing only the slight heat of sleep.

"Stardancer," Azhani greeted warily as Kyrian reached over and drew a pot of tea off the hearth and poured out a measure of the warm liquid. The warrior accepted the cup, suspiciously poking her tongue into the liquid before drinking. Her actions caused the stardancer to chuckle, but Azhani did not care. Relieved that it did not carry the bitter flavor of medicine, she drank the soothing liquid. "Not trying to poison me today, hmm?" she asked.

A surprised smile lit up Kyrian's elven features. "No, not today, warrior. Today, you get willow bark and boneset, to help you mend. I added a touch of wild mint to ease the flavor."

Azhani struggled to sit, waving away the stardancer's hands when she tried to help. Grunting with the exertion, the warrior cradled the warm tea, taking a moment to relish being alive. *I won, you bastard. I made it across the border and now I have every right to skewer your black heart if you even think to attack me!* Her mood swiftly changed. *Ah gods, Ylera, I miss you so much...*

"If you're comfortable, I'd like to look at your leg now," Kyrian said after the warrior had settled.

"Fine," Azhani said, still concentrating on the tea. It was cold in the room and the warrior realized that she would have to insulate the cottage better or they would freeze.

Kyrian's nimble fingers made short work of the bandages around Azhani's foot. The sight of the battered, grimy foot caused the stardancer to hiss in sympathetic pain. The warrior wore no shoes. Her feet were covered in layers of rags that were held together by bits of rope.

Shaking her head, Kyrian muttered, "This will not do." Standing, she went outside and fetched the battered bucket that she had been using to wash vegetables. Though not in very good condition, the pail was whole enough to hold a larger amount of water than the pot she used for cooking. Returning with it, she set it down next to Azhani and resumed her place by the warrior's leg.

Azhani watched with curiosity as Kyrian unwrapped the other foot. As the stardancer dipped a soft bit of cotton into the water, the warrior growled, "What are you doing?"

"Washing your feet. They're disgusting and need tending," Kyrian said absently as she delicately scrubbed the layers of grime away from the warrior's skin.

When the icy water touched her flesh, Azhani scooted backward and hissed, "That's cold!"

Kyrian shot the warrior an arch look and said, "Did you expect it to be otherwise? Now hush and let me work, warrior."

Azhani grumbled, but did as she was asked. Gratitude welled up inside her. She hated being dirty and having her feet cleaned was a step toward being able to hobble out to the well to wash the rest of her filthy body. There was a small pile of clothes on the floor by her pallet. *She must've found them in the stable. Father always was a pack rat, although I never thought the day would come when his hoarding was necessary.* It would be nice to trade her ragged clothes for the simple peasant garb.

Mindful of the splints, Kyrian gently washed the warrior's feet. Afterward, she rubbed in a soothing salve to help heal the tiny cuts and abrasions that decorated the callused skin.

"When did you lose your boots?" The rags were put aside to be burned later.

"King Arris preferred me to go to the gallows on bare feet," Azhani said curtly. Her gaze was fixed on the boards of the loft floor. She was afraid to look at the serene face of the stardancer with so much ugliness playing havoc in her mind.

It would be too easy to like that face and to allow Kyrian's vivid smiles to shatter the shields the warrior had carefully placed around her heart. Azhani could not allow anyone to get that close again. It would be nice, though, to make a friend. Without meaning to, she lowered her gaze and studied the stardancer.

She had a nice face — full of innocence, joy and the beginnings of wary trust. Barely concealed mischief danced in her pine green eyes and a smile always seemed to hover about her soft full lips.

Meeting the stardancer's gaze, Azhani was amazed to discover that instead of contempt, a confused and weary sadness greeted her.

"They took your boots?" Kyrian whispered, aghast. She had never considered how devastating the oath-breaker punishment was. To be so stripped, not just of pride and honor, but also of the very basic necessities of survival, was terribly harsh. *Blessed Astariu, how can we be so cruel, even to those who do not earn mercy?*

"To teach me 'humility'," Azhani said distantly. She had turned her eyes to the fire and was seeing the past. The visions must have been horrible, because the naked anguish written on the warrior's face spoke more eloquently than any ten bards.

Kyrian let loose a breath as the knots that bound her remaining anger broke and fell away. All of the pent up anguish she had carried because of the actions of this woman, the rage of grief and loss she felt when she had heard of the death of Ylera and the massacre of the king's men, vanished. Within the eyes of her patient was not the glee of a murderer, but instead the broken soul of a woman shattered by terrible loss.

"Will you tell me what happened?" She moved to the warrior's injured leg and unwrapped the bandages. Carefully, she laid aside the splint and then used the damp rag to sponge the leg clean.

"I don't want to talk about it," Azhani growled, shaking her head vehemently. In one long swallow, she finished the dregs of her tea and fell into a brooding silence.

Kyrian accepted the warrior's decision for now. She would continue to ask until Azhani relented and related her side of the events of Banner Lake. There had to be more than the bard's tales of what had happened at autumn's end. For now, she would hold her peace.

The wound still wept a little pus so she called on the gift that marked her as one of Astariu's Own. As her power gathered, she began to sing a soft lullaby. The words shaped the force that directed the goddess' healing fire.

As she sang, a golden aura limned her hands. Delicately, Kyrian stroked her fingers over the broken skin of Azhani's leg. Where her fingers touched, the flesh knitted together and returned to a natural healthy tone.

Watching in awe, Azhani was impressed at how easily Kyrian controlled the magick. Astariu's fire came easily to the young stardancer's call and though the strange aura outlining Kyrian's fingers flickered like flames, her touch did not burn. Instead, it was warm and soothing. The shards of pain that had been a part of Azhani's daily life vanished under the stardancer's gentle care.

Gratitude sat heavily on Azhani's shoulders. Not many would risk the wrath of a king to aid an oath-breaker. The warrior knew that she would owe much to this stubborn woman who had healed her.

Her faith is truer than her politics, the warrior thought. Azhani had gone to a small chirurgeons' school only to be turned away by healers too afraid to practice their skills upon an exile. Only the generosity of an old blind woman had allowed the warrior to survive as long as she had.

Delirious with fever, Azhani raced through the docks of Y'Dannyv looking for a place to hide, anywhere would do, even a midden heap, but she had to rest. Her shattered leg bled profusely and left a trail that an idiot could follow. Suddenly, out of the darkness, a withered hand grasped Azhani's belt and pulled her into a shadowy doorway.

"Here, warrior. Rest, I'll take the dogs off ye while ye bind yer wounds."

Too much in pain to do anything other than nod gratefully, Azhani accepted a lump of rags that the beggar handed her and set to staunching the flow of blood from her leg. The last three men she had fought had maces, and she had been too tired to dodge several nasty blows to her right shin.

But I won, she thought numbly. Her feet were soaked with blood, hers, theirs, it was impossible to tell. The clothes she wore were caked with a sickening mix of death and sweat.

Suddenly unable to stand them any longer, the warrior stripped out of the ruined garb and dressed herself in the rags the beggar had left. At least the dirt on them was honest grime and not the lives of Y'Dan's best soldiers.

"Psst, warrior, follow me!" The old woman was back. She led Azhani on a twisting, turning route through Y'Dannyv's warehouse district until they reached a shanty town of box dwelling transients. "Here, sleep. I'll take yer weapons and get ye summat that'll let ye walk the roads easy."

Wordlessly, Azhani handed over her sword and axe. She didn't want them. They were battle finds that had come to her hand from the bodies of slain soldiers.

While the old woman was out, Azhani slept. When the old woman returned, she had a bow and arrows. "Bow'll work as crutch, c'n hunt, too. Now, ye leaves by midnight watch, out the postern gate. Be quick 'bout it, ye will, whiles I distracts the guard!"

"Aye, granther, I hear. Bless you." Tears choked Azhani's voice. "Will you be all right? By law, what you do is a crime."

"Nay, bless me not, warrior. 'Tis a hard road ye've ahead of ye, and I've nothing to fear from the boy king."

Azhani nodded, accepting that the old woman could take care of her-

self.

The warrior felt compelled to spare a moment's prayer in thanks for the old woman's help, as well as the generous gift of healing she was being given by the stardancer. For the rest of her life, Azhani would be in debt to the young healer, because she had saved the warrior's leg.

With the use of that leg, Azhani could extract the revenge she so deeply desired. Bloody visions danced through her mind. She imagined Arris flayed alive and smiled wickedly. He would answer for his wrongs. The boy king was not worthy to wear the crown. Even his father had seen it, for Thodan had called Azhani to his deathbed and made her swear to keep Arris from the throne.

"My friend, my regrets in life are few, but of them, I hold my son as my deepest. I was not a good father to Arris, and I fear that my ineptitude has left him weak minded and malleable to the darker side of his nature. I beg of you, Azhani, do not allow my mistake to harm the people of Y'Dan. Keep my dreams alive!" Thodan was caught by wracking coughs. Azhani helped him to sit. He took her hands in his and sighed heavily. *"Arris must not rule, Azhani. It shall be you who cares for my land when I am gone. I have done what I can and now it is you who shall reap the harvest of my sowing. I know that she will thrive under your care."*

He pressed a scroll into her hands.

"What's this?"

"Bear this to the Council upon my death, old friend. I have given Y'Dan to you. Swear upon your oath as a warleader that you will keep her safe!" There was a shadow of Thodan's legendary fierceness in his tired eyes as he spoke.

"I swear, My King," Azhani said, as tears crept down her cheeks. *Ylera would be so proud...*

Azhani shied away from the painful memories. All of Thodan's plans had been for naught, as Arris and his followers had successfully hidden the great king's wishes. *And all that I loved was taken from me.*

To divert her thoughts from the dark path they were traveling, Azhani looked down at the stardancer, who was nearly finished with her work. She wiggled her toes and a delighted grin flashed across her face when there was no accompanying flare of pain.

Azhani's body began to hum with joy. She would be able to walk, run, and even ride normally again. *Arris, you are doomed. You should have killed me that first night, when I didn't care about my life. Now, I will see you in hell!*

Azhani opened her mouth to thank the stardancer and realized that she didn't even know the woman's name. Furrowing her brow, she thought, *Who is this person, and why the hell are the Cabal so interested in her? Or was the abduction personal, for pleasure, rather than planned?* Suspicion brewed deep within her heart. *Maybe it's all a trick. Maybe she was sent by Arris to get my guard down...* The warrior had seen posters promising a reward for her head in every town and village she had crept through on her journey north. Ten gold marks seemed a small price for her life, but perhaps Arris was only testing the waters. After all, how many bounty hunters would choose to chase the Banshee of Banner Lake?

"Who are you, healer?" she abruptly asked as the song trickled away. The injury was gone, leaving behind thin scars as a reminder of the pain she had suffered. Only a slight dull ache remained, but the warrior knew it would fade in time.

Kyrian took a deep breath, releasing it slowly as she began to arrange the splints and straps around Azhani's leg.

Reaching down, the warrior stilled the priest's hands. Startled, Kyrian looked up, meeting Azhani's steely blue gaze. "Leave off, healer. Answer me. Who are you?"

"My name is Kyrian. I am a stardancer and I serve the Healer," was the priest's simple reply.

"What are you, then? What makes you the target of the Cabal? Who is your family? What have you done that someone would pay a heavy blood price for you?" Azhani asked, grabbing the startled woman by her shoulders and shaking her fiercely.

Fear lashed through Kyrian and she whimpered brokenly as slashes of memory, painted a dusky crimson by time, began to fill her mind. Lurid images of a bloody face taunted her and she fought to push the nauseating thoughts away. *No...* Struggling, she cried out, "Let me go, warrior!" When Azhani's grip only became stronger, she growled, "I'm nobody, I swear. Now let go of me!"

Azhani searched the woman's face, seeking a sign, some indication that Kyrian was more than she appeared. There was nothing, only fear and rising anger flushing the pale skin. Abruptly, she released the stardancer. *I'm a fool. She's not my enemy.*

"My apologies," she rumbled contritely.

Straightening her rumpled robes, Kyrian sat quietly, shivering slightly.

Azhani bowed her head, ashamed. "You can leave any time you want, I'll not stop you."

Kyrian's eyes narrowed at the warrior's words. "You keep trying to get rid of me, warrior. Do I stink?"

Confused, Azhani shook her head. "No, you... I just..." Her voice trickled away as she searched for what to say.

Kyrian resumed her spot next to the warrior's newly healed leg. She watched as the warrior looked away and realized that Azhani was ashamed of her actions. The fear that had so rapidly risen just as quickly fled, leaving Kyrian strangely peaceful.

"Azhani," she said, the word rolling strangely off her tongue. It was the first time she had spoken the warrior's name.

It was like magick. Suddenly the warrior under her hands was no longer a patient, or a killer, but just a woman who had risked death to save a stardancer's life. Words began to spill out, tumbling past her lips before she could rein them in and examine them closely. "Why does it matter who I am? Why do you say that the Cabal took me? I only remember bits and pieces about that day. There was wine, dancing, and lots of good food and I had just taken a mug of cool ale. It didn't taste right and I was about to toss it out when something, or someone, hit me." She spread her hands helplessly. "So please, tell me what it is that you want, because I don't know."

Azhani pursed her lips, considering, and then said, "Fine. About a half-day's journey south along the road, you will find the corpse of a Cabal assassin rotting in the woods. It was he who kidnapped you — you who claim to be a simple stardancer." Could a goddess-sworn priest be lured by the bright promise of gold? Ten marks was a large sum for someone who lived on a small stipend. "The answers to your questions lie with the Cabal. Go and seek them if you will. If you are wise, you will turn east and not look back."

"I'm not going anywhere until you're well," Kyrian said as she ran her hand through her short amber curls in exasperation. "I am what you see — a stardancer who has no idea of how she ended up on the northern road. Please believe me, Azhani. I have no wish to see you harmed." As the words tumbled from her lips, Kyrian realized that they were true. Her curiosity about the dark woman was rushing to overwhelm her anger. *Forgive me, Ylera, but I don't know if she's truly guilty. What if she's not?*

"Forgive me, stardancer. I am a woman hunted. Yesterday, I killed a man of the Cabal. I would have expected him to be after me, and yet it was you he held captive. I do not know why." Azhani lay back against the rolled blanket and closed her eyes against the shock scrolling across the stardancer's face.

How can she speak so casually of killing? Kyrian wondered, her gaze falling upon the pile of bloody rags she had yet to burn. *How could she ignore her wounds to save me? I'm not worth that kind of agony.* All the stories she had ever heard about Azhani Rhu'len, the finest warrior in Y'Dan, crowded into her brain, clamoring for attention. The woman had been a hero and the leader of King Thodan's armies, famed for more than one kingdom-saving battle. Ignoring pain would be second nature.

"You stopped him, you rescued me and brought me here?" Kyrian asked, groping for something to say that would encourage the warrior to tell of what must have been a spectacular event.

Azhani grunted an affirmative. "Not much of a hero, am I?" she asked dryly, indicating the rags that made up her clothes and the fading bruises on her leg.

Kyrian began to sense that the official version of the events of Banner Lake had no actual bearing on the truth. *I hope I'm right about this,* she thought, as she reached out and placed a hand on Azhani's bare knee.

Bewildered eyes opened and found her gaze. "Enough of one for me," the stardancer said, her voice softened by gratitude. Smiling, she said, "How about I repay you by heating some water so you can wash?" Kyrian looked at the neatly folded pile of clothes lying next to the pallet. "We can wait to splint your leg."

A pathetic sense of gratitude overcame the warrior, followed by annoyance. Shrugging, Azhani said, "I don't care what you do with your time."

Kyrian clucked her tongue in mild irritation. "Appreciation like that could give a snake hives," she muttered as she stood. Leaving the cabin, she returned shortly, lugging a large rusty pot. "Found this in the stable. Apparently there are things even raiders won't take." It took some time to clean and fill the pot, but soon it hung over the fire.

While the bath water warmed, Kyrian cooked. The stardancer

hummed as she worked and Azhani found that she liked listening to Kyrian's voice. Sitting up, the warrior spotted the rabbit carcass.

"I'll clean the rabbit," she offered, needing to contribute, even if it meant getting dirtier. Kyrian's willingness to do something nice even though she had been rude made her feel like a churl.

Kyrian almost shrugged off the warrior's offer, but then realized that the woman was shamefacedly fidgeting. "All right, but try not to damage the hide, I'd like to make something of it."

Azhani nodded and began to meticulously skin and bone the animal. When she was done, she traded the fur-wrapped bundle of meat for a plate of vegetables and a mug of fresh tea.

Kyrian took the meat and added it to the dregs of the previous night's stew. More vegetables, water and spices went into the pot, which she then hung over the fire to simmer. The room was filled with the small sounds of chewing as the two women ate.

"I'll hunt for more food later," she said, unhooking the large pot of hot water and setting it on the hearth. "For now, let's see about getting you clean."

Reluctantly, Azhani allowed Kyrian to wash her. The stardancer had made it clear that she was not to move her leg, making it impossible for her to clean herself. She was able to attend to her more private areas, but only after Kyrian made her promise not to jar her leg.

While Azhani washed, Kyrian cut the leg off a pair of homespun breeches to make it easier to care for the warrior's injury. To keep the fabric from raveling, she hemmed the edges.

After the warrior was dressed, Kyrian used the remaining water to bathe and then exchanged her crimson robes for a set of the same simple garb the warrior wore. Without the heavy velvet robes, the only mark of the stardancer's rank were the three small teardrop shaped tattoos that dappled the skin below the corner of her left eye.

Belying the youth of her face, the marks had faded to a soft charcoal that blended seamlessly with the half-elven woman's profile. Kyrian had served Astariu for most of her lifetime.

Once, Azhani's face had borne a tattoo, but it was gone now, replaced by a dark, thickly ridged scar. Kyrian wondered what mark denoted the conundrum the warrior had become. Cleaned up, Azhani was striking. She was not beautiful, but Kyrian doubted she would ever forget the face that was now revealed. Intense and grave, it was carved with an expression that she could only call desolation.

"I'm going to exercise Arun, can you manage here by yourself?" Kyrian asked after she had finished changing.

"I'll be fine," Azhani said remotely as she practiced using her longbow as a crutch to hobble. She wanted to look over the homestead and get a feel for what needed to be done before the winter settled in and closed her off from the nearby trader's village of Barton.

Bemused by the warrior's stubbornness, Kyrian gathered her haversack and headed out to the stable.

"Hey boy," she called out to the horse in greeting, as she opened the door to the stable. The sturdy brown gelding immediately came to her side, snuffling her hair and lipping her shoulder gently. Patting his side affectionately, Kyrian said, "Hungry, are you? Come on, let's get you saddled up and go see what we can forage." They exited through the ruined front gate and headed into the forest.

It felt good to ride through the overgrown forest and breathe the cool clean air. After a while, Kyrian dismounted and let Arun wander while she searched for food.

She found many varieties of winter plants that would make excellent teas, and a welcome abundance of an herb that was highly effective against lung inflammations. A cold, wet winter could bring at least one case of the coughing sickness and it was best to be prepared.

Kyrian didn't question the notion that she would spend the winter with Azhani. Years of experience had taught her that an injury like the warrior's would not heal overnight. Azhani would require assistance if she were to live through the season to come.

Arun huffed excitedly, causing Kyrian to go and investigate what he had found. A small, fast-moving stream cut through the forest floor. Around the rivulet grew armfuls of wild grass and vegetation.

"By the blessed Twain, thank you," Kyrian whispered as she pulled grass and loaded it into a sack. There was enough here to feed the horse for several days. As she worked, she noticed the sparkle of scales in the water. *Guess I'd better learn how to fish.*

By the time she was ready to return, her haversack was bulging with soaproot bulbs, wild parsnips, sweet onions and four large potatoes. On the way, she found a small bush bursting with tart purple berries.

While Arun bore their bounty home, Kyrian gathered an armload of deadfall to add to their growing woodpile.

After Kyrian left, Azhani put aside her bow and hobbled around the cottage, cleaning up after herself. She made her pallet and tossed the dirty rags that had been her clothes into the fire and then took stock of her father's old home.

All in all, she was satisfied with the condition of the cabin. The roof appeared to be sturdy, though there were small holes where the thatching had fallen through. Up in the loft, she discovered that the floor needed reinforcing, but the walls were sound.

All of the shutters needed work. Some were stuck shut while others flew open at the slightest breeze. Above the storage room, the roof had partially caved in and all manner of debris had gathered on the floor.

Kyrian had made large inroads into the piles of trash, seeking fuel for their constant fire, but it would take a concentrated effort to return the cabin to the warm home Azhani remembered from her childhood.

The stable and outhouse had fared the best; both were in solid condition and ready to withstand another northern winter.

The coins in the assassin's pouch would go far, but Azhani was worried that there wouldn't be enough to cover all the expenses. There would be no frivolities; only the most important supplies would be purchased. *Unless I can convince Kyrian to stay in Barton. My costs would be nearly halved, then. I could even pay her for healing me.*

Barton, the out-kingdom trading village, was just a short journey away. To get there in that time she would need to make a real crutch and return the bow to its proper use as a hunting implement.

Thinking of the longbow reminded her to whisper a prayer in the name of the blind beggar who had sheltered her. Her original arms, the sword she had crafted with her own hands and the armor her father had given her, had been destroyed three months ago.

"Let the citizens of Y'Dan take note: On this day, six hundred and thir-teen years from the time our forefathers first set foot upon this golden land, Arris Thodan, rightful king of Y'Dan, has declared Azhani, daughter of Rhu'len, scion of DaCoure, an oath-breaker. On pain of death, let none give shelter, aid or sustenance!" The herald's voice carried across the gathered crowd. *"Azhani Rhu'len, you have been found guilty of treason and murder. For these crimes you are sentenced to death. May the stain of the beloved Ambassador Ylera Kelani's blood never wash from your soul."*

As he spoke her lover's name, Azhani wanted to cry out, *"But I did not kill her! I loved her!"* She was silenced by a wad of cloth that Arris had forced into her mouth before the ceremony.

"Let there be no false protestations of your innocence to confuse the sheep, bitch." The words still rang in her mind as she watched Arris take his father's crown from an Astariun priest and set it upon his brow.

Bound as well as gagged, Azhani could only glare at the king's boots. She had then been tossed up onto the stage and forced to kneel while the herald announced the decision. Above her, Arris smirked, though there was a tiny hint of unease playing about the corners of his eyes.

The herald continued his announcement. *"In lieu of our glorious king's generous offer of a painless death, the cursed oath-breaker has requested the rite of the gauntlet. Let those who would be the hand of justice step forth and receive your king's blessing!"*

Even as she was dragged to her feet, the battered warrior exuded a dangerous presence. Her bonds were cut, and she was finally able to spit out the gag and massage her wrists until she could feel the tips of her fingers tingle painfully. Cracking her knuckles she gazed out at the crowd of soldiers and citizens, daring one to challenge her.

No one moved. Flashing a smile, she began to walk away, sure she was a free woman. Plans were already formulating. She would go south, to Ysradan, and beg for an audience. Thodan's old friend would surely hear her pleas.

From behind her, Arris snarled, *"Oath-breaker!"*

Azhani turned just in time to see her beautiful sword thrown into a bon-fire, forever robbing it of its temper. As it heated, a blacksmith pounded the metal until it cracked and broke, shattering into pieces.

Tears stung her eyes, but she refused to allow her emotions to show and arrogantly firmed her jaw, ready to take whatever punishment the boy king would deal out next. In quiet anguish, she watched as Arris' men broke her armor, burned her possessions and destroyed everything that had been precious to her. Only her dagger remained untouched. One of the guards walked over, bowed mockingly and offered the blade to her. As she moved to take it, he dropped it, forcing her to bend over to retrieve it. He would be the first to die, she decided as he walked away laughing.

"Again, herald, tell them again!" Arris commanded impatiently.

"The oath-breaker has claimed the rite of the gauntlet. Will any step forth to face her? Her only armament is a dagger," he added quickly, when Arris glared at the empty field in front of Azhani.

From the crowd came a shout, *"One thousand gold coins to the man who slays the oath-breaker! My word on it!"*

The crowd gasped. That amount of money would make a pauper into a prince. Several soldiers, none of whom had ever served with the war-leader, surged forward, each trying to be the first to claim the reward.

Gripping the dagger tightly, the warrior readied herself. There would be no easy escapes this day.

Azhani shook herself from the reverie. *Let it go. Wallow later. It is time to prepare for the future.* Stowing the assassin's gold, she hobbled outside to search for a straight stout piece of wood to fashion into a crutch.

Behind the stable, under a rotting pile of leaves and debris, she found an abandoned wheelbarrow arm. It would serve. In the stable she found an old beaver pelt that would work to pad the brace.

Taking her finds into the cottage, she built up the dwindling fire, stirred the soup and then sat on her pallet. Using the assassin's dagger, she began to carve the wooden shaft.

Kyrian returned at nightfall. Azhani had already lit the lantern and was seated on her pallet, working on a crutch.

"You've been busy, I see," the stardancer commented, bending over to stir the pot that had simmered all day. "Mm, almost done," she said, smiling at the delicious smell of the meal. Her day in the forest had left her with an appetite.

"So have you," Azhani replied, not bothering to look up at the stardancer. She was at a delicate junction and trying to remove a bit of wood around the handle of the crutch.

Yawning, Kyrian said, "Yes, I found a stream not too far from here. There're fish in it, but I've never been very successful at catching them, so instead we get to eat the scrawny bunny I caught this morning."

"I can fish. I'll go tomorrow," Azhani said, turning the crutch in her hand and smoothing any rough spots with her dagger.

"You should wait another day before putting a lot of stress on your leg, Azhani. We can live without fish that long," Kyrian said reasonably. She was getting tired of fighting the warrior for every concession.

Azhani looked up at the young woman and bit back a sharp retort. Kyrian was a stardancer. It was her duty to advise her patient, just as it was once Azhani's duty to counsel her king.

"When can I travel?" she asked calmly.

"To the stream and back? Two, maybe three days at least," said Kyrian decisively. A stray curl fell into her eyes and she absently brushed it away. *Yes! Maybe I'm finally getting somewhere. Now, what can I do to reward that...hmm, oh yes, that would work.* "Unless you ride Arun — then, further and sooner. Why, was there somewhere you needed to go?"

Azhani set the crutch aside, pointed at the squeaking shutters, the thatched roof and the unstable loft floor and said, "Place needs fixing."

Retrieving the hidden pouch, she dumped its contents onto her blankets. "The Cabal was kind enough to provide the means to do the work." She looked at Kyrian, a challenge in her eyes. "Barton's a day and a half to the north. It'd be a good place to find supplies. They don't mind outlaws." A bleak smile curved her lips.

"All right, we'll leave in two days." Kyrian held up a hand to forestall any protest. "My horse is perfectly capable of carrying both of us and I can walk if necessary. Unless you're planning to buy an ox to plow the garden, Arun can bring us and our supplies home."

"Would you use a feather to plug a dam?" Azhani retorted. She had lost another battle with the stardancer. *How is it that she so easily disarms me? I try not to like her, but by the beast's bones, it gets harder each time!*

Kyrian chuckled dryly. "I'd use whatever tool came to hand. After all, it's not the shape so much as the will behind the instrument that decides the action, right?" She gave the warrior a pointed glance.

Azhani's face split into a smile that put fire in her eyes and changed her harsh features into a beauty worthy of a bard's song. "So they don't stuff your head with cotton in those monasteries after all," she said, laughing lightly.

"No, we save the cotton for cranky old warriors with head injuries. The material swells nicely. It helps the codgers feel like they're kids again," Kyrian said in rejoinder, merriment sparkling in her eyes. *Gods, I've missed bantering with someone who can count higher than ten without taking off their shoes first.* Growing up in the monastery, there had always been someone to trade jibes with, either an older teacher or a fellow student.

Outside the temple grounds, Kyrian found it difficult to connect with people who were more concerned about crops and children than about the latest cure for boils, leaving her lonely and longing for friends. With Azhani, there was a sense of understanding that slipped beyond daily impedimenta.

As a village healer, Kyrian had turned inward for solace but Azhani's words had sparked a surge of hope. Maybe she would find a friend in the taciturn warrior. *Wait, what am I thinking? Can I befriend a murderer?*

She doesn't act like a murderer, Kyr. Look at her. She's just as leery of you as you are of her. You've already forgiven her, and you're beginning to like her. Take a chance. Forget what you've heard and let her tell her side of the story. You might be surprised.

Kyrian had to admit that when Azhani wasn't grumpy, she was pleasant to be around. At least she treated the stardancer as a person and not like the physical embodiment of Astariu herself. The last time she had felt that way was when she lived in the elven village of Myr.

Though not known for their tolerance of half-breeds, the elders of Myr had nonetheless welcomed her into their community. They trusted her to care for their ills and teach their children.

For several years, Kyrian lived in peace. Each day was a dream come true, allowing her to practice her gift as well as inspire hungry minds to explore the world around them. In the spring of her fourth year, the dream became a nightmare.

The warm day had been perfect for swimming lessons. Now that the sun had gone down, it was cool and Kyrian hurried the children through the woods toward home. Keeping close to their teacher, the students chattered animatedly and bragged of their aquatic feats.

The whispery sound of booted feet came too late to warn of the approaching danger. Kyrian spun when the children screamed in fright. Stumbling onto the path was a disheveled human male armed with a sword and a coil of rope.

Her eyes met the bandit's. The ragamuffin smiled wickedly. "It must be my lucky day," he said. His voice was a horrible whisper that sent chills down Kyrian's spine. He licked his lips. "I think you and you," he pointed to two of the elven children, "will do just fine." The rope flicked out and locked around the ones he had indicated. Quick as lightning, he reeled them in as they kicked and screamed.

Rigid with fear, Kyrian watched helplessly as the bandit bound each child tightly. While he was distracted, all but two of the children ran into the forest. As paralyzed by fear as their teacher, the pair stood dumbstruck by the sight of the horrible man and his leering grin.

Again, the lasso flickered and the other two children were drawn to his side. They fought their captor, but were no match for the man's brutal strength. Again, he tightly bound each child. Finished, he considered the stardancer. "Fagh. Too old for the customers." He started to turn away, but stopped and fondled himself. "But just right for old Barrig."

Still held in the grip of fear, Kyrian's eyes filled with tears as the man first checked the bonds of his young captives then advanced on her.

Just as he was about to lay a hand on her, one of the children cried out, "Leave her alone, you monster!"

Barrig jumped and turned with a growl. "Shut up!"

"No! Go 'way you mud sucking pig swill!" the brave child retorted as she struggled to free herself.

The bandit's face screwed up in anger. Striding quickly to the girl's side, he raised his arm and smashed her in the face with the hilt of his sword. She staggered back and he followed the first blow with a solid kick to the girl's side. He spat on her and growled, "Beasts and bones, brat, I should cut off your head right now. Don't need the money so badly that I'm willin' to listen to yer lip, so shut up!" He raised his sword threateningly.

"I wouldn't," Kyrian's voice was deathly calm. The moment he had struck Patrys, the stardancer's fear had melted, leaving her filled with a cold anger.

Barrig turned to face the young woman. "You think you can stop me?" Lazily, he twirled his sword, demonstrating his proficiency with the blade.

"No," Kyrian replied, which elicited a nasty grin from Barrig. "I know I can," she added, stepping out of the shadows and into the bright glare of moonlight.

Barrig blinked as her robes went from shadow-shaded black to crimson red. The silvery light of the moon reflected off the Astariun symbol embroidered on the front and caused him to curse vehemently.

"Let them go, and you can walk away," Kyrian offered in a calm tone.

Barrig glanced back and forth between the children and the stardancer. His face was a study of conflicting emotions. Kyrian knew he was weighing the odds of his winning a fight with her before the elders of the village arrived. If he were caught attempting to kill her, it would mean his life. Y'Myrani law held that assaulting one of Astariu's Own was a crime punishable by death.

Suddenly, the bandit laughed. "I don't think so, little priest," he said, moving closer and weaving his blade in a deadly arc around him. "I've danced the gallows and walked free before. Don't see no reason why I shouldn't again." His whispery voice gave credence to his statement.

Kyrian shivered but held her ground. "Let the children go, Barrig," she said. Her hand hovered over her baton.

His only answer was to slash at her ribs. She easily avoided his attack. When he struck again, she parried with her baton. Spittle flew as he leaped at her and brought his sword down in a blow intended to cleave her in two.

Kyrian deflected it and kicked him in the shin. Barrig howled in pain and danced backward, but not before dealing her a vicious jab with his free hand that left her gasping for breath. Twirling her baton distractingly, she stepped in and punched him solidly in the face. Bones crunched loudly and the bandit groaned.

Barrig shook his head, spitting blood and teeth. "Bitch," he growled and rushed her, slashing with the sword. Kyrian tried to spin away but the tip caught her shoulder and deeply scored the muscle.

"You bleed," the bandit chortled and pressed his attack.

Round and round they fought, evenly matched. Before long, both were covered in numerous wounds. Blood flowed freely from his broken nose and she had several cuts across her arms and legs as well as one long slash along her abdomen.

Kyrian panted heavily. Fatigue was the second enemy facing her in this fight. Barrig also showed signs of the strain as his earlier expertise rapidly vanished.

The children were not idle. The little girl had managed to free one hand and was quickly working on the other. With a cry of victory, she freed her other hand and launched herself at the bandit's back.

"Y'Dani scum!" she shouted, as she pummeled his head with her tiny fists.

Roaring, Barrig threw the child off him. She landed on the ground with a sickening crunch. With a negligent flick of his wrist, he slashed downward and cut the child open from neck to hip. Blood spurted, coating his face and chest. The girl shrieked and the other children screamed in terror as he advanced on them.

"I'll kill you all!" he shouted, raising his bloody sword.

"No!"

Fear and fury blended, overwhelming her. Kyrian's baton was a blur as it descended, colliding with the bandit's flesh and shattering the bones of his arm. As he reeled back, she punched him in the throat, crushing his windpipe. He staggered around, gagging and choking helplessly. Wildly, he swung his blade, trying to stave off the suddenly crazed stardancer.

Blinded by rage, Kyrian struck the bandit again and again until his head exploded in a shower of blood and gore. His lifeless body crumpled to the ground, leaving Kyrian standing in the moonlight, panting with exertion.

As though under a spell, the stardancer turned and began administering aid to the girl. Soft words of comfort tumbled from her lips as she bandaged the child.

"It'll be all right, Patrys. You were such a brave one. Shh, sit still now." The child's crying dwindled as the healer's tone calmed her.

When the girl's wounds were bound, Kyrian turned and started to perform the death rites for the bandit. It was then that the reality of what she had done crashed into her, driving her to her knees.

I killed him. I took his life. I made myself into his goddess, and decided his fate. I am a taker of lives now. This will always be a part of me. He will live inside and remind me of my act of vengeance. I am tainted. I am not meant to be one of Astariu's Own. I should be struck down where I stand!

Wracked by terrible sobs, she threw her head back and let out a long, keening wail. Clutching her hair, she cried out, "Oh goddess, I'm sorry!"

She collapsed, weeping uncontrollably.

Later, elven scouts found her standing over the body of the slain raider, her weapon dangling uselessly by her side. Her wounds were untended and her attention seemed to be riveted on the broken wreck that had been the bandit's head.

She could hear blood slip down her baton and drip onto the grass. The sound was deafeningly loud.

"Stardancer Kyrian?" Her name, quietly spoken, broke her gaze from the corpse. Looking up, she saw one of the village elders break through the trees and head for her.

The ground rose up quickly as her sight and consciousness faded away.

Within the week, Kyrian had left peaceful Myr behind. She could no longer live where the ghost of the man she had slain haunted her nightmares.

Azhani's voice broke the spell of the past.

"Stardancer? Are you all right?" Surprised by the worry she felt when Kyrian's vibrant green eyes suddenly fixed on a point somewhere in the distance, Azhani finally spoke and brought the priest back to the here and now.

The stardancer shook her head, rubbed her eyes and surreptitiously brushed away tears. "Ancient history, it is of no matter," she muttered, turning back to finish preparing their supper.

Knowing quite a bit about history, Azhani let the stardancer keep her secrets and went back to working on the crutch.

Ecstasy laced with a sharp edge of pain rippled through the sorcerer. This was how his master came and left him, whimpering for release all while begging for more of the sweet torture. Wet tracks on his face showed where his tears had trickled. Ecarthus' love was both awesome and terrifying, and always worth the anguish his body suffered.

The waves of pleasure that coursed through his body were part of a reward for a job done well. The demon was pleased with his efforts in the mortal realms.

With the cursed DaCoure family out of the picture, sowing the seeds of hatred, dissent and bloodshed would be simplicity in itself. His servant in the capital would see to that. For only one moment, he regretted the loss of the fierce-tempered warrior woman. Had he been able to make her his, she would have been a powerful weapon.

It was not fate's plan that she serve him. The scion of DaCoure was marked by the gods as one true and unshakable to her oaths. She would never turn her back on the peoples of Y'Myran, nor would she step from the light of the Twain. Ecarthus could not take her as he had Darkchilde. Her soul was forever barred to him. Because of that, she was dangerous. Properly forged, she could be a weapon against all of their carefully laid plans.

Now that she was branded an oath-breaker, Kasyrin gloried in his freedom to act unfettered in Y'Dan. It was sweet revenge that Rhu'len's child had been marred by the same infamy that her father had forced upon the sorcerer.

Darkchilde opened his eyes and smiled. Ecarthus' final words of instruction echoed powerfully in his soul.

::Send me rivers of mortal blood, my slave. Only in a flood of crimson rain shall I gain the power to break the locks that bind me in hell.::

Kasyrin would send oceans of blood to free his master. He would reap the reward Ecarthus promised for his freedom and claim the revenge that festered in his soul.

"It shall be so, my Master. I will begin immediately."

::My work begins as well, my slave.:: Visions came to Darkchilde then, images of chaos and confusion lying like a blanket over the eyes of the land. The tendrils of Ecarthus' power reached out and touched the minds of the demon's servants and they, too, awoke and did their master's bidding.

Kasyrin woke from his trance. It was time to start the next phase of the plan. Rising, the sorcerer whispered a word of power and lit a nearby oil lamp.

On a table near the fire sat a chessboard. As he scooped up a piece, he muttered the spell that would send it to his agent in Y'Dannyv. Porthyros would understand and act accordingly.

Clutching a tiny chessman sculpted from obsidian, Porthyros Omal scurried through the corridors of Y'Dannoch castle. It had arrived earlier, and its appearance indicated that it was time to open the tube of scrolls that had long been prepared for this day.

Reaching his chambers, the little scholar hurried to his fireplace. There, at the base, was a loose brick. Removing it revealed a small cubbyhole in which was a tube filled with a thick wad of papers that bore the seal of the master merchant, Kesryn Oswyne, who was also the sorcerer Kasyrin Darkchilde. Taking the first few layers, Porthyros tucked the rest back into the tube and replaced it behind the brick.

He rolled up the papers and put them in his satchel, where they would remain until such time as he could present them to the king.

Young Arris trusted his scholarly mentor and would no doubt be easily distracted into signing the new laws that would allow Porthyros' master to execute his plans unhindered. Fear was about to make a home in Y'Dan, and with it would come the rewards to be reaped from such an atmosphere.

With a furtive grin, Porthyros placed the chess piece on his mantle. The polished surface of the tiny pawn caught the light and it gleamed darkly from its new home.

~ Chapter Three ~

"How cold will it get here?" Kyrian asked as Azhani handed her another sack of trash. The gods had seen fit to dump several inches of fresh snow on the northern wilds of Y'Myran over the last two days. It was not enough to hamper their cleaning efforts, but it did make the stardancer worry about the winter.

"Cold," Azhani replied tersely. She waited for the priest to dump the garbage into the middens and return for a refill. "I've seen men who've frozen overnight because they weren't properly prepared."

"Brr. That won't happen to us, will it?" Smiling sheepishly, Kyrian added, "I grew up in southern Y'Syr. Snow was a rarity. Mostly, it rained in the winter." Her smile grew wry. "I know I sound like a tyro, but I'd really like to help around here and I can't do that without asking questions."

Azhani nodded absently. "Better you ask now than be unaware of danger later. You shouldn't worry, though. We will not freeze. The cabin will be warm enough to accommodate us all, including the horse if necessary. Barton will have what we need to weather the season." She handed up the bag again and stood. Looking around the room, the warrior smiled in satisfaction. It had taken most of the morning to clean up and the floor was finally clear.

Kyrian returned and picked up the broom. Making shooing motions with her hand, she waited until Azhani went into the main part of the cottage and then briskly swept the room. Once that was finished, she looked for Azhani to see what task was next on the list. She was outside, sitting on the low wall that surrounded the property and weaving a basket from grass. Leaving her be, Kyrian returned to the house and set to shaking out their bedding.

The ordinary task of weaving relaxed Azhani and allowed her to soak in the peace of her surroundings. A thicket of berries rambled along the other side of the wall and she had hopes of finding fruit that the birds had missed.

The stardancer was capable of turning even the simple peasant's meal of oatmeal into something special with just a few nuts and berries. Azhani licked her lips, remembering how good their breakfast had tasted. *Maybe she'll make something even better with the berries.* It seemed strange to expend energy on her stomach when Ylera was gone, but Azhani knew that to survive long enough to get her revenge, she would have to eat.

Ylera would not want you to forget how to live, a quiet voice insisted, and Azhani tried to ignore it.

Working with the stardancer to clean the cottage had forced Azhani to call a truce with Kyrian. It seemed foolish to eschew the help of the healer if the woman was so determined to offer it. Grudgingly, she admitted that she enjoyed having the younger woman around. It made the ache in her soul burn a little less painfully.

Tucking the last few strands of grass into the rim of the basket, Azhani limped over to the other side of the fence and found a convenient boulder to perch on while she gathered berries. Thorny, dry brambles tumbled along the stones and provided an excellent natural barrier to attack. Within the vines a tiny brown bird hopped from branch to branch pecking at a few of the dark fruits. Azhani allowed the sparrow to eat its fill and then began her own search for the treats.

One candlemark and several puncture wounds later, she had a full basket. She stood to head back to the cottage and spotted the wriggling tail of a rabbit as it scurried for the forest. A sharp piercing scream was the only sound the animal made as it died. Azhani's hastily thrown dagger had found its mark. She smiled. It felt good to contribute to the small cache of supplies that they shared.

Kyrian rolled the last blanket tightly and set it at the head of her bed. The lump of silk-wrapped sword was hardly visible under the pile of bedding that she used as a pallet. Azhani's bed was neatly made and the clothes that they shared were folded and stacked against one wall of the room.

Standing, she surveyed the changes she had made. Their pallets had been moved so that the fire would warm them both. The old trunk that had been in the stable made an excellent woodbin and a crate unearthed in the storage room acted as a rough table.

Kyrian had worked hard to find things to occupy her time so that Azhani could have some time alone. She itched to go out and find her so that they could talk. The stardancer was full of questions she wanted to ask Azhani, not the least of which still was the warrior's version of the events of Banner Lake.

The priest was rapidly coming to the conclusion that the quiet, unassuming woman she was treating and the arrogant, traitorous villain of the tales were not the same person.

Patience will yield the story. It is in that telling that I will learn the answers I seek. The truth of a person's nature is revealed in the fullness of time, so says the goddess. I just wish that time would hurry up!

Kyrian knew the legends of Azhani Rhu'len. She had listened to Laric Talespinner maunder on and on about the "Heroine of Pine Ridge." More recently, the horrific tales of Azhani's betrayal had been made public by every would-be bard and minstrel throughout the kingdom.

Since the day that King Arris' heralds had gone from town to town, announcing Azhani's crimes and the resulting punishment, the warrior's heroic tales had gone unsung. Whispered, hair-raising stories arose, naming her the Banshee of Banner Lake.

"I tell you true, my friends, 'twas a cruel day when our warleader rose against her land, cast down her oaths and spat in the face of Astariu the warrior." The craggy voice filled the tavern and drew in the crowd of listeners. *"Like a banshee she was, sent by demons to steal the souls of good King Arris' men."*

Kyrian turned away from the bar and cocked her head to take note of what the bard was saying.

"Listen, and hear of the fall of the scion of DaCoure." The skilled bard held his crowd lightly, raising his voice from the softest whisper to the bold-

est shouts to depict the battlefield at Banner Lake. Vividly, he described the vision of a woman filled with traitorous villainy. Drunk on power, she carved a bloody swath through hundreds of innocent men and women.

Pacing back and forth, the storyteller's hands wove wild patterns, casting dancing shadows on the wall behind him. Everyone was glued to his performance, sitting on the edge of their seats while he pantomimed the battles.

"No soldier born could best the witch; no plea for mercy was heard," he whispered, bringing his tale to a close. "From the first death, that of Princess Ylera Kelani, Y'Syr's beloved ambassador, to the last, Joshua Toryn, who was barely eighteen summers old, she murdered them all, screaming her victory with every blow." The bard was on his knees now, mimicking the fallen soldier's family.

"So heed my words, good friends, and take ye home carefully. For if you forsake your oaths then madness shall be your reward."

Therein lay the conundrum, she decided. Not that Azhani had broken her oaths, but that she had supposedly forsaken Astariu. Kyrian was terribly confused by this. How could a woman who had accepted the mark of Astariu the Warrior kill in cold blood? It went against every basic tenant preached by Astariuns since the world was first created.

The twin gods Astariu and Astarus had created the universe and all within it. The people of Y'Myran loved the siblings and worshipped them equally. Older gods that belonged to the era when the kingdoms were known as Aldyran appeared only in legends.

Astariu called to her side special mages and healers and gave to them the skills of starseeker and stardancer. To Astarus came the scholars, and to them he gave the gift of long life so that they could preserve the knowledge of the world and keep it safe for all to enjoy. Those who used guile and cunning also found Astarus a generous god, for the brother sibling had a strong sense of humor.

Astarus was generally viewed as the god of mages who did not wear the blue of a starseeker while Astariu was most often called upon by those whose hearts were given to the care of others. Healers, doctors and surgeons often carried small tokens blessed in Astariu's name when they saw to their patients. From these she would extend her hand and call stardancers to her service.

Starseekers were mages whose powers came from intense prayer rather than the study of spells and grimoires. Stardancers were healers of both body and mind and consequently were the most visible of Astariu's servants. It was the duty of a stardancer to go from place to place and heal the sick. Starseekers were usually sedentary and given to protecting an area against the servants of the evil.

Astariu loved her followers equally, except for those who chose her rarest aspect — that of the warrior. Those who chose this life were honored with the greatest burden, for they were the law keepers and protectors of the innocent. The goddess asked nothing less of them than the swearing of mighty oaths that made it nearly impossible for one of her warriors to betray her wishes. To be her warrior was to declare oneself a servant of the land and people. If Azhani had truly forsworn this vow, then why had she bothered to rescue Kyrian? This was what had the stardancer's stomach in knots and her head throbbing with unanswered questions in the middle of the night.

Three days in her company and I'm already going insane, Kyrian thought, morbidly amused. *This bodes well for the rest of the winter, I'm sure.*

"It looks nice in here, Kyrian." Azhani's softly spoken words caused the stardancer to jump. Giving the young woman an odd look, Azhani limped past her and laid a basket of berries and the carcass of a rabbit on the hearth. "Found some stuff out there, thought it'd be useful," she said gruffly.

Surprise caught the stardancer unawares. "Oh, you didn't have to," she blurted, and then clapped her hand over her mouth. "My apologies. Forget I said that," she said a moment later. "Thank you, it's nice to have someone around who doesn't find foraging for food an unpleasant task." She smiled sadly, remembering how Ylera had hated doing anything that resembled a chore.

Azhani shook her head, unable to fathom Kyrian's moods. "Good...I'm going to look for a flexible branch to make a fishing pole."

"May I help?"

I don't need your help, hovered on Azhani's tongue, but she held it back. *Work with her, not against her, warrior. You decided to give her a chance.* Instead, she said, "Sure, just look for anything that's about an inch thick and flexible enough that a solid blow won't snap it."

Kyrian nodded and chose to search the ground outside the front of the cottage. Arun whickered a greeting as she passed him. The horse wouldn't wander off without her, so she had felt safe in allowing him free run of the homestead. Newly pruned bushes showed the path of his wanderings and Kyrian decided to examine the ground that her horse had explored.

Azhani watched the stardancer exit the cabin and sighed. In the three days that they had been together, she had already figured out that Kyrian was naturally exuberant. She was constantly asking questions — about the area, about the weather, about anything that seemed to be on her active mind. It was only a matter of time before she started asking about Banner Lake.

What will I tell her? The truth? I'm sure she's heard all manner of stories. That was fear that I saw in her eyes when I told her my name. Yet she's still here. What does that mean? Can I trust her? Do I want to trust her? As the questions filled her mind, memories bearing the images of every warm smile, every candlemark of gentle care and every moment of pleasant conversation danced in her head. *Ah goddess, I do. I want to like her.* Closing her eyes, she thought, *I want her to like me. It would be nice to have a friend.*

With a snort of laughter, Azhani shook her head. Muttering, "You've yet to master the ability to be truly nasty, haven't you, warrior?" Azhani adjusted her crutch and headed to the rear of the property.

She found Kyrian kneeling in the mud, admiring a spread of tiny, bright yellow flowers. They had grown up from the cracks in the stones of the wall that encircled the property. The stardancer was gently stroking the petals, a smile of such wonder on her face that Azhani had to grin in response.

"Demon's blood," Azhani said, startling the stardancer.

Kyrian looked up at her and frowned in confusion. "Why are they called that?"

Limping to the stardancer's side, Azhani leaned against the wall and replied, "Because legend says that they grow where rimerbeasts have died."

"You don't strike me as someone who believes in folktales," Kyrian said as she stood and brushed her knees off. "They are pretty though."

Azhani grinned. "No, I'm not much for make-believe. I find the truth refreshing. My father used to pick the flowers and crush them to make dye. They give an amazing saffron color."

Volunteered information! Astariu, I may faint! "I'll have to give it a try," Kyrian said, smiling brightly. "Though I'm not sure what I'd do with saffron colored things, since I usually wear stardancer scarlet."

"It would suit you," said Azhani without thinking, and then wished she hadn't.

Kyrian's ears turned bright red. "Thanks for noticing," she mumbled, as she gathered flowers.

To Azhani, the stardancer's words were like an echo of the past. Visions of a woman who seemed to be equal parts of silver and gold languished in Azhani's memory.

Ylera Kelani's laugh was a musical sound that filled the stone chamber and warmed it far beyond the ability of the fire in the hearth. Standing next to her king, guarding his side as was her right and duty, Warleader Azhani Rhu'len tried not to stare openly at the elven ambassador.

King Thodan was gravely ill, but before he journeyed to the blessed lands, he was determined to end centuries of strife along the border of Y'Dan and Y'Syr. The monarch had made it plain to his court that they would hammer out an agreement that was mutually beneficial to the elves and the humans.

Peace would bring trade, allowing both kingdoms to prosper. Everyone agreed that this was desirable, but convincing some of the Y'Dani border lords to give up the "sport" of elf hunting was taking some time. By contrast, the Y'Syran nobles were more than willing to accept peace, as long as the Y'Danis returned the lands they had stolen over the years.

Ambassador Kelani and her twin, the Y'Syran queen, Lyssera, were both bright and young enough to find value in cooperating with King Thodan's efforts towards achieving a lasting peace. The Y'Dani monarch's efforts had the blessing of Y'Myran's high king, Ysradan. He had sent word to both kingdoms stating that he would be very pleased if the treaty were ratified, which gave both sides even more reason to negotiate. Being in the high king's good graces could lead to grants of royal aid for public works.

As high king, Ysradan could easily order the kingdoms to make peace, but he preferred to let the junior kings make the decisions that affected their individual kingdoms, keeping just the larger issues to decide himself. Major laws, such as those dealing with murder, were the purview of the high king, but lesser troubles, including border disputes, were better dealt with by those who were chiefly affected.

King Thodan had poured twenty years of his life into the plan, sacrificing everything to see that his people would inherit peace. There were those who were against the treaty, so Azhani kept close to her king.

Ambassador Kelani accepted a glass of wine from a page and toasted Arris, Thodan's son and heir. It was the boy's sixteenth birthday and Thodan had hosted a party in his honor. Presents from all of the courtiers were stacked high on a table behind the boy's chair, and Azhani watched in mild amusement as he squirmed in his seat and tried not to stare at the steadily growing pile.

Sitting next to the prince was the slight figure of Porthyros Omal, Arris' teacher and guardian. The scholar leaned over and whispered to the prince, causing him to still in his seat. His youthful face turned grave, and he lifted his own goblet to accept the ambassador's toast.

Thodan observed his son, a wistful expression on his face. Azhani wondered if she should have fought harder to support the king's desire that the boy be educated in the elven city of Y'Len. The youth's sharp-featured face was pinched and drawn, and his black eyes were glassy from lack of sleep. Rumor had it that Porthyros was an exacting master, sometimes forcing Arris to stay up all night working on a math problem. Arris met his father's gaze and flushed, brushing his overlong black hair away from his face.

"Happy birthday, my son," Thodan rumbled, and then coughed softly. Azhani handed him his drink, and after sipping at the mulled wine, the king added, "I hope you've enjoyed your party."

"Oh yes, Father, thank you very much," Arris said beaming happily. He craned his head to glance at the gifts and then looked to the courtiers seated at the other tables. "Thank you, my Lords and Ladies. It has been a true delight to spend the evening with you."

Glasses were raised in a polite toast, but the diners soon returned to eating and discussing the kingdom, leaving Arris to once again fidget in his chair. He looked over at the warleader and sighed.

"Y'Dan's warleader gathers gazes like a child gathers flowers," Ambassador Kelani said, causing the warrior to smile.

"You flatter me," Azhani murmured as a blush colored her ears.

"Come on, my prince, we must finish your studies," Porthyros said quietly. "I'll make you some of your favorite tea to help you concentrate."

Hanging his head, Arris rose from his seat. "Father, thank you again for a wonderful birthday. I must return to my studies." He bowed to the king and then to the courtiers and left the hall.

Azhani and Ylera watched them go. The ambassador sighed, and shook her head slightly.

"Is there something wrong?" Azhani asked.

"No, I don't think so," Ylera replied. She turned to look at her, and shrugged. "I find that I am uncomfortable in the presence of your prince — perhaps it is jealousy?" She finished her statement with a smile.

Azhani frowned in confusion. Why should the beautiful ambassador envy the boy? He was harmless. Porthyros Omal, on the other hand, was as slimy as a man could be and not ooze on the stone floors of Thodan's keep.

Not a day had gone by when the irritating little man had not found some excuse to press his suit on the elven ambassador.

"There's nothing to be jealous over," Azhani replied absently.

Ylera's smile dazzled Azhani.

They had become quick friends, Ylera and Azhani, and whenever Thodan wasn't monopolizing Azhani's time, they would spend time in the city.

At first, Azhani had been worried that the elven woman would have a problem with her heritage. Y'Dani blood was normally disdained by Y'Syrans, but Ylera had assured her that she held no such prejudice. She had even gone so far as to indicate that their blossoming friendship was what the treaty was really about — building a lasting peace between everyone of Y'Dani and Y'Syran descent.

For her part, Azhani was just happy to have someone who appreciated her mercurial nature. Her emotions would often run close to the surface, though she kept her deepest feelings hidden.

Right now, she was engrossed in thoughts of Ylera and how she seemed eager to learn what made Azhani tick.

Azhani met Ylera's gaze and smiled. She made the warrior's stomach turn flip-flops and caused her breath to come in short, painful gasps, but she couldn't stay away. She had to be near her.

Thodan poked Azhani in the leg and grumbled, "Go ask her to dance. I'll be fine."

Minstrels were playing in an alcove off to the side of the hall. Couples filled the empty spaces of the floor, moving in ancient, well-known steps. Swallowing, Azhani bowed her head to the king and approached Ylera.

"Ah-um, Ambassador, would you li-like to dance?" she mumbled, staring at her feet.

Standing gracefully, Ylera took Azhani's hand and said, "I'd love to." Together, they glided onto the floor.

"Your dress is very beautiful," Azhani whispered shyly as they danced.

Ylera's eyes sparkled warmly. "My maids would thank you for noticing," she said, laughing brightly.

That night began the first of many nights of love and laughter.

Azhani remembered every moment of her time spent bathed in the light of Ylera Kelani's desire. Amber eyes, honey-colored hair, the scent of wildflowers and a silky smooth voice that cried out her name in the throes of passion while spring rains drenched the city filled her memories. Every long, lazy night tucked against Ylera's side while making promises to the unpredictable future was crystallized in her mind.

Brilliant mornings spent laughing, dancing around each other in the practice ring while the warleader's men stood by, delighted by the commander's antics, painted the color of their summer. The days melted away to an autumn full of loving all night while spending their days working feverishly to finalize a peace that would be accepted by the nobles on both sides of the border. These were the precious candlemarks that now stood sentinel against the terrors that besieged her dreams.

Azhani had never seen the cold eyes that burned in the shadows. There was no warning that her fragile peace was not to last.

Three weeks before winter solstice, the day she planned to ask Ylera to marry, their idyll came to a crashing halt. King Thodan the Peacemaker died in his sleep. The ink on the treaty was still wet, but it had been signed into law.

The day after the king was laid to rest, Azhani stood before the Council, hating the news she bore, yet honor bound to carry out Thodan's last wishes. Facing the councilors, as well as the heir apparent, she unleashed the storm.

"It was King Thodan's wish that his son not rule after him," she said, her voice quiet. The warleader passed a sealed scroll to Derkus Glinholt, the Lord High Councilor.

Shocked silence echoed through the chamber, perforated only by Arris' quickly indrawn breath.

"Nonsense!" the prince declared, not even deigning to read the document that was handed around the room. He jumped up and loudly declaimed, "My father loved and trusted me. There is no possible reason why he would not want me to take up the mantle of Y'Dan and wear it proudly." Arris scanned the room and saw only approving nods.

Azhani's heart dropped at the prince's reaction. Arris' words were too practiced to be improvised. Only foreknowledge of the king's actions could have given the young man time to prepare. Arris must have bribed a servant to spy on his father. Her spirits were further dampened by how quickly the Council turned to listen to the young prince.

"I think," he stepped away from his chair and padded slowly up to her, "that you are trying something terrible, Warleader." Again, he looked at the old men he had spent his entire life fawning up to and saw only approval.

Azhani's stomach churned. She knew that the fact that she was a half-breed made her suspect to the full-blooded humans, but she never expected that they would give more credence to the words of a snot-nosed brat than to the will of their beloved king. The warleader had not made many friends among the merchants and nobles. Politics was a game of checks and balances that she had never enjoyed playing.

Like wolves scenting fresh meat, the soft men and women who had long been a thorn in Azhani's side came racing to the hunt, eager for a kill.

"I think, Warleader," Arris spat, turning the title into an epithet, "that you are trying to incite a civil war. I think that you are lying and attempting to seize control of the throne."

Gasps echoed around the chamber, and Azhani raised one dark eyebrow. He's bluffing, she told herself. "And your proof of this accusation is?" He has no proof of this ridiculous charge.

A cruel smile edged its way onto Arris' face. "Why, I have heard it from the mouth of your whore, oath-breaker," he said, tarring her with the label that would be hers to wear for the rest of her life. The prince nodded to one of his personal guards and the man vanished out a door, returning shortly with the battered body of the elven ambassador. Unceremoniously, Arris' guardsman tossed the lifeless husk of the elven woman to the floor. The wet smack of the body hitting the ground echoed in the council chamber. Blood and gore leaked from the numerous wounds that covered Ylera's body.

"See here the proof of the warleader's treason," Arris cried gleefully,

pulling a scroll from his belt and throwing it to High Councilor Glinholt.

Azhani paid no attention to the scroll. She only had eyes for her lover, lying broken and bleeding at her feet. Ylera's golden eyes were closed, blackened by several blows to her face. Once soft lips were now cracked and bloodied. Her heart shattered when she saw the telltale cant to the elven woman's neck. She's dead. Desolate rage left her motionless for the prince's next words.

"By the solemn oath of Ambassador Ylera Kelani, I declare you a traitor, Azhani Rhu'len. You are guilty of crimes against the Crown of Y'Dan, you are guilty of plotting to rise above your goddess-chosen station and you are guilty of breaking your sworn vows to the people of Y'Dan to be its champion.

"Furthermore, I hold you responsible for the death of Ambassador Kelani, for certainly had you not lured her into your wicked plan, she would be alive this day! Guilty, I say. You are guilty."

"I second that statement," Councilor Glinholt cried eagerly, earning a grateful smile from Arris. Others of the Council joined in, and before she could stop it, Azhani was taken prisoner.

She didn't care. Her life lay in the pool of blood that surrounded Ylera's lifeless body.

Blinking away tears, Azhani firmed her jaw. No, she couldn't allow Kyrian the chance to be burned by the flame of her life. A few smiles and a pair of gentle hands would not buy her friendship. Azhani waited for the rage in her belly to boil over, filling her heart. The dark emotion overwhelmed the tiny bubbles of tender sentiment that the stardancer's presence had engendered. Standing, she turned away from Kyrian and walked away, once again the hard, bitter warrior with a battered soul and scarred face.

Azhani's retreating back set off a flurry of questions in Kyrian's mind. Something had changed. It was evident in the way that Azhani tossed her crutch aside and forced her leg to bear her weight. Even Arun got treated to the sharpness of the warrior's temper when he tried to cadge a cuddle and got a cold shoulder instead.

Kyrian sighed and wandered toward the gate, stopping when she saw the tip of a branch sticking out from under a pile of rocks. Clearing the stones away, she pulled the stick out and was rewarded with a long, one-inch thick shaft of wood. Covered in moss and spiderwebs, the branch nonetheless flexed easily and snapped back to its shape without breaking.

"Will this do?" she called out, holding up the branch for Azhani's inspection.

Striding over, her eyes agate hard and her face closed to all but the most cursory of expressions, Azhani took the limb and examined it. "Yes. Thank you." She took out her knife and without saying another word, walked away, stripping bark as she went.

"Shyvot," Kyrian whispered, reaching up to absently pat the horse. "How am I supposed to deal with this, Arun?" she asked the horse as she scratched his ears.

The gelding whickered and blew in her ear.

"Thanks, but I don't think she'll respond to that," Kyrian said, chuckling softly. "I like you, Azhani Rhu'len. You are not the monster they say you are, and I'm going to prove it." Arun whickered at her words and she gave him a final pat before leading him back to the stable. She had dinner to prepare.

Later, while readying for bed, Azhani looked up and tersely said, "Be ready to leave at dawn."

Unsure whether the appropriate response was to salute or sigh, Kyrian closed her eyes and turned away from the brooding warrior.

Chapter Four

The morning was tinged with the scent of ice and snow. Icicles decorated the eaves of the cottage. Sun shone down on the two women while
they readied for their journey, but there was no heat in the light. Autumn
was rapidly losing the battle to winter.

Kyrian locked the door while Azhani mounted the horse. As soon as
the warrior was settled, the stardancer pulled herself up to ride pillion. Surreptitiously, she settled the sword strapped under her clothes against her
back and prayed that Azhani didn't pay too much attention to the odd lumps
under the bright red robes.

"It'll snow before week's end," Azhani commented as Kyrian found her
balance. The warrior took Arun's reins and guided him toward the road.

"I suppose that was all the break we'll get," Kyrian said, looking at the
melted puddles of slush that were all that was left of the snowstorm that
had blanketed the forest over a week ago.

"Let's hope it lasts a little longer," Azhani said curtly. She turned
around and looked pointedly at Kyrian. "You could stay in Barton. There's
a hospice there, and they wouldn't turn away a stardancer."

Patting the warrior's heavily clad thigh, Kyrian shook her head. "No.
I'm staying with you, Azhani. You're stuck with me, so get used to it."

Both women were dressed warmly. Kyrian wore her thick velvet robes
while Azhani was dressed in layers. The cold managed to penetrate their
garments, though, and Kyrian shivered. Warmer clothes were the first thing
on her list to buy in Barton. A better variety of food was a close second,
followed by the materials needed to fix their roof. Having a fat glob of
slushy snow drop onto her face as a wake up call had not been amusing,
even though Azhani had smiled when it had happened.

Azhani kept her eyes on the road and ignored the woman behind her.
She refused to acknowledge that she wanted the younger woman to stay.
She needed the stardancer's able body and agile mind. Madness loomed
at the other end of a lonely winter. *I just don't know how I can live with her
and not become her friend. I hate to admit that I'm grateful for her stubborn
streak.* The stardancer would need that obstinacy to put up with Azhani's
moods.

Determination seemed to be an inherent talent in stardancers. All of
them she had worked with over the years bore a stubborn streak a mile
wide. Even the wizened 'dancer who had come to attempt to heal King
Thodan had persisted until he had dropped from exhaustion. Sadly, he had
been unable to halt the strange wasting disease that had withered Thodan
from a robust man to a mere husk.

Warm smiles were apparently another part of the 'dancer's repertoire,
for Corellus' ancient face was always crinkled in merriment whenever he
saw her. The tattoo that marked his calling would vanish into the folds
around his eyes, his smile was so great.

Azhani's own tattoo, a single sword inked diagonally along her cheek-
bone, with its blade pointed toward the sky-dwelling Twins, had graced her

face for many years before Arris had cut and burned it away. She still remembered how the crazed prince had reached out to run his fingers along her cheek, caressing her almost lovingly, before taking a sharp knife and driving it into the skin.

The scarred flesh ached fiercely in the morning air.

The sound of Arun's hooves on the road broke the stillness of the forest as they rode. As the sun rose higher and the day warmed, Kyrian forced herself to pull away from Azhani's stiffened body. It was far too easy to want to snuggle against her.

Whether or not Azhani was a criminal had no bearing on the lonely stardancer's need for companionship. Her instincts screamed that the stories were false and that there was a connection forming in the fragmentary moments when the warrior let her guard down.

The wind changed and Kyrian frowned, realizing that they were both rather ripe. *Next item on the list — a real tub!*

"Azhani?"

The warrior grunted.

"Does Barton have a bath house?"

The plaintive question elicited a chuckle from the dour warrior. "There's one at the inn. We'll be able to clean up there. If they let us in, that is." She made a show of taking a deep breath. "We are a little on the pungent side."

Kyrian laughed in response. Things were strained, but there were cracks in the wall the warrior had erected between them. The stardancer wanted the chance to hear Azhani's side of the story, if for no other reason than to ask why she had killed Ylera.

All right, Kyr. Think about something else, or you'll go crazy. Pushing her thoughts away from that subject, Kyrian tried to condense her memories of the kingdom where she had lived for the last two years.

Y'Dan was a place of simple tastes and even simpler people. Populated mostly by humans, racial tensions were harshest along the Y'Syran border where the citizens had lived in a near constant state of war for hundreds of years. Only in recent times had peace reigned.

King Thodan had been a man of subtle action. During his rule, the liveried soldiers of the Y'Dani army had rarely been seen. Arris, the new king, was the opposite of his father, preferring to fill the towns and villages of the kingdom with a visible force.

The tiniest of communities were beginning to boast small garrisons. In the larger cities and towns, whole detachments of the Y'Dani army were encamped in the farmers' fallow fields. The changes made for tense situations which caused Kyrian some discomfort as she traveled from place to place.

Each time she entered a town, she had to provide proof of who she was and why she had come. It caused her pain to see the land she had come to love under such a harsh rule, but the citizens seemed unperturbed by the new procedures. Unable to articulate why this bothered her, Kyrian had accepted the new ways as a part of the inevitable shift in policy that followed any regime change.

She still wondered what threat was so great that the king felt the need to form such a large military force. *Maybe he was just looking for Azhani,* Kyrian snorted softly. *Surely one lone, injured woman was not a threat to his kingdom.*

The young king's actions had more of the flavor of a ruler who was unsure of his command than of one acting to protect his people. Aside from the added soldiers, the other thing that had changed in Y'Dan was the speed and severity of justice. Under Thodan, criminals were treated with a level of mercy. Arris' hand was just, but lacked the tempering of mercy that his father's had held.

In one town, she had seen a man hung for the crime of stealing food from the house of a wealthy man. Normally, this would have been punishable by lashing and service in one of the king's work gangs, but because the nobleman had been injured, the thief's life was forfeit.

Had Azhani, like the hapless thief, committed a lesser crime that under the new king's justice carried a stiff penalty? Had she killed all those soldiers, or was that fanciful embellishment on the part of overeager bards? Could Arris' fanatic devotion to ancient law blind him to the truth and make him see Azhani as something she was not? What could she have done to warrant the charge of treason?

It had been years since Kyrian had studied the history of Y'Dan, but after some thought, she could not come up with any laws, Y'Dani or otherwise, that required a man's death for causing a stubbed toe. Azhani Rhu'len had been accused of much, much worse and yet, what if those accusations weren't true? What if she had been a victim of circumstance? What if she had acted as she had under Thodan's rule and had unknowingly broken some ancient law that Arris had resurrected?

The Y'Dani warleader was known for her unflinching bravery and unbreakable honor. Even the high king had come to commend her for defending the seven kingdoms. As far as Kyrian knew, Azhani had never accepted any reward save gratitude.

How did this woman of honor become an oath-breaker? The need to know made her want to grab Azhani and shake her until she agreed to talk. *Argh! I'm doing it again!* Kyrian reached up and rubbed her face. *I'm too preoccupied with this. I've got to talk to her or I'm going to go insane!*

A frigid blast of wind ruffled her hair. She shivered and leaned closer. Azhani seemed able to ignore the temperature and Kyrian knew she would have to make sure that the warrior didn't deny herself the necessity of warm clothes.

"Cold?" Azhani asked, her voice a dry rumble. She felt the stardancer's arms tighten around her waist and she suppressed the desire to push the woman off the horse. It would be cruel not to share her body's warmth with the other woman.

"A little," Kyrian admitted shyly.

Azhani looked at the road, noting old landmarks. "We'll be in Barton by sundown tomorrow."

As she warmed, Kyrian nodded muzzily. Arun's comfortable pace lulled her toward sleep.

"Rest, healer," the warrior said. "I will not let you fall," she added in a whisper, closing one hand over Kyrian's clasped wrists.

Those are not the words of an evil, oath-breaking traitor, Kyrian thought sleepily as her head dropped against Azhani's shoulder.

Kyrian awoke to the sun high in the sky. They were stopped by the side of the road and Azhani was shaking her roughly. Rubbing her eyes, the stardancer slid off the horse and then reached up to help Azhani dismount.

With a glare, Azhani grudgingly accepted the hand. When she reached the ground, she turned and gave Arun a pat.

"Arun needs to rest. We should eat," said Azhani as she pulled her bow from the saddle.

"Oh." Sleep still fogged the stardancer's mind, making it difficult for her to concentrate.

"Check his shoes. I think he's picked up a stone. I'm going to find our lunch." The warrior strung her bow and limped determinedly into the forest.

Kyrian watched her go, realizing that Azhani's gait was getting better. *She's really tall,* she thought amusedly. *Taller than I imagined, anyway.*

The human side of Azhani's lineage was clearly evident in her height, as she topped the compact stardancer by almost a head. Kyrian wasn't short by Y'Syran standards, where most of the population were elven and not likely to grow more than five and a half feet tall. Topping that by seven inches, Azhani outstripped Kyrian's generous height.

Arun let out a whicker of happiness when the stardancer walked up to him and scratched his ears before pulling out his feed bag. Lashed to the horse's saddle was the crutch. Azhani's stubbornness made Kyrian smile fondly. She removed the wooden shaft and went in search of the warrior. The trail led to a stream where Azhani was perched on the bank, looking over the rushing water. An arrow was nocked in her bow and her gaze was fixed on a point somewhere below. Her shoulders tensed and she fired. The arrow pierced the surface of the water soundlessly. As soon as the shaft had left the bow, Azhani laid the weapon aside and began gathering in a thin bit of twine. At the end of the twine was the arrow, which had pierced a small fish.

"By Astariu, that was an amazing shot, Azhani," Kyrian said. She hopped over a few stones to stand next to the warrior. Holding out the crutch, she smiled and said, "You forgot something."

With a smirk, Azhani pulled the flopping fish off the arrow and whacked it against a tree trunk. She held the fish out to Kyrian and drawled, "Don't need it right now," then nocked another arrow and aimed it at the stream.

Kyrian shrugged, leaned the crutch against a tree and knelt to gut the fish. By the time she was done, Azhani had caught three more.

"Lunch," she said, as she bent to help clean the trout.

Kyrian looked up and gave her a quick smile. "That was really quite something, Azhani. I've never seen anyone fish that way."

"My father taught me," Azhani said as she dug a hole to bury the offal.

"Oh," Kyrian said, not knowing how to answer that. The half-elven stardancer was an orphan, having been left on the monastery steps as a newborn. "Boiled or fried?" she asked as she took the fish over to an area where she could build a cook fire.

Azhani carefully stood, brushed off her trews and ran a hand through her wild hair. It was so terribly tangled that she would probably have to cut it off after bathing. Very little pain remained in her leg, which was a testament to the stardancer's skill at healing. Azhani found it ironic that the goddess who had abandoned her to Arris' treachery had allowed Kyrian to heal her.

"Fried, I suppose," she said as she hobbled to Arun's side. In honor of the stardancer's kindness, Azhani used the crutch. While Kyrian cooked, Azhani led the horse to the stream so he could drink his fill.

"Fried it is," Kyrian said as she built a fire and then began to cook.

Azhani leaned on a tree and watched the gelding drink, absently reaching down and scratching her bared knee. The skin was chilled and she tugged ineffectively on the cut-off bottom of the pant leg. She looked forward to reaching the trader's village. A hot bath, a good meal and a decent bed were the first things on her list. Then she would take care of purchasing the goods they needed for a wintering over at the cottage.

I need armor and a weapon other than the bow, too, she reminded herself, feeling naked without the constant weight of chainmail on her shoulders and the slight thump of a sword against her thigh. *I wonder if Kyrian would help me cut my hair?* Azhani thought as a matted lock dropped into her eyes again. She fidgeted with it and thought about what Ylera would say about her appearance. *Probably that I needed a bath and a haircut, because I look like a pig in a wallow, that's what!* The warrior snorted, causing Arun to gaze at her quizzically.

Azhani raised one eyebrow and snorted again. Arun shook his head, spattering her with water. A wicked grin edged onto her face and she reached out with her bow and lightly poked the gelding in the side. He sidestepped, and then deliberately turned away and stuck his muzzle back into the stream.

The warrior chuckled to herself. It felt good to play, even with a horse. She turned to watch the young stardancer, who was busy frying fish. With unconscious grace, Kyrian sliced vegetables into a pan, dusted herbs on top and added a dab of lard to help the food cook faster.

I like her; she's an especially good cook. We need rice. Maybe some flour. Flour, for bread...I'll wager that she can make a decent loaf or two of that... Azhani considered, closing her eyes and sliding down the side of the tree.

She woke at the touch of a hand on her shoulder.

"Azhani? Wake up, lunch is ready," Kyrian said, trying hard not to smile at the sleep-fogged expression on the other woman's face. She held out a plate full of food, enticing her with the scent.

Azhani groaned. *Wha-? I can't believe I fell asleep. Cursed body; heal faster!* Without a word she took the plate and began to shovel the food in as fast as she could, slowing only to blow on the hotter bits.

Finding a log, Kyrian sat and ate, watching the warrior tuck into her food as though she hadn't eaten in weeks. Coupled with Azhani's confusion over her unscheduled nap, she concluded that the consequences of magickal healing were finally catching up to the warrior. *It's about time she felt it!* She stifled a chuckle. For a while, Kyrian thought that she would be the only one to suffer the after effects of the goddess' fire. *Now I don't feel like such a lazy piggy.*

With lunch finished, they resumed their trek to Barton. As the day passed, it grew chillier and Azhani was grateful for the stardancer's warmth at her back. By sunset, she was more than ready to make camp.

Rousing Kyrian, the two women worked quickly to make a fire and set a meal out to cook. While the stardancer dealt with Arun, Azhani wove a pallet of fallen branches and blankets for them to share. She was not entirely at ease with the idea, but they would take chill if they slept apart.

Kyrian returned to the fireside, yawning and rubbing her eyes. "I can't believe I'm so tired. I must have slept most of the day."

A smile edged the corners of Azhani's mouth. "It's the cold. Takes all you've got just to stay warm."

Shaking her head incredulously, Kyrian said, "I guess I'm just more used to rain."

"There will be plenty of that, mixed with the snow. It gets quite messy."

"Sounds joyful. Here, eat some of this while I try not to shiver my teeth out."

They ate quickly, cleaned up and dove into their bedding. Uncomfortably huddling together, neither could find words to break the growing silence. Finally, they drifted off to sleep.

In the morning, they got to a quick start, eating and packing up their camp as the sun rose. The second day's travel was much like the first, with a stop to forage for food while Arun browsed among the scrub for his own sustenance. As evening crept over the mountains, the scent of refuse came wafting to them.

"By the Twain, that's foul. What is it?" Kyrian's voice was thick with distaste.

"Barton," Azhani replied.

They crested a hill, and the haphazard sprawl of the outkingdom traders' community was revealed. Jagged streets flowed away from the main road, creating a river of homes, businesses and ramshackle shanties that dotted the landscape. Smoke wreathed from chimneys and cook fires, carrying with it the scent of charred meat, wood and coal.

Azhani pulled Arun to a stop.

"Is something wrong?" Kyrian asked apprehensively.

"I'm a little too well known here. I'd rather not have every copper-heeled bounty hunter after my head," said Azhani as she pulled the hood of her cloak up over her head and fastened it tightly.

Kyrian tried to peer around the warrior's shoulder, but could only see a swath of dark wool. Making a face, she said, "Well, I guess you could pass for a frozen, just-off-the-road traveler." She shook her head. "I thought Barton was a free town — not bound by kingdom law."

"It is. Doesn't mean the bounty hunters won't come here to look," the warrior said.

"Oh, as you say."

Guiding Arun down the center of the roadway, Azhani deftly avoided the odiferous contents of several chamber pots.

"'Ware the road," came a distant shout. Kyrian looked up in time to see a woman dump a container of noxious fluid.

Shivering in repressed disgust, the priest turned away and peered over Azhani's shoulder to see what lay ahead. Cobblestones peeked out from under layers of rubbish. Buildings were constructed of everything from fieldstone to whitewashed timbers. Here and there was a canvas tent, speaking of the transitory nature of Barton's populace.

Townspeople moved to and fro along wood-planked sidewalks. Shop-keepers stood outside their doors, sweeping their stoops or engaging in conversation with customers. Garbed in unadorned fur and leather, the residents of Barton were obviously used to winter's chill. The roofs of the buildings particularly fascinated Kyrian. Shaped like an inverted V, they looked as though a giant had come along and pushed the eaves down until they nearly touched the ground.

A boy on stilts walked along, opened the lampposts, refueled the res-ervoirs, trimmed the wicks and then sparked them to life. The streetlights glowed softly in the gathering gloom.

In the distance, a man cried, "Five marks past high sun and all's quiet."

The women rounded a corner and stopped in front of a three-story inn. Dismounting stiffly, they took a few wobbly steps to work out the soreness of their muscles. Kyrian then retrieved Azhani's crutch and handed it to her while a stable boy took Arun's reins.

Tossing the saddlebags over her shoulder, Azhani flipped a small coin to the stable boy and said, "See that he gets a good rubdown."

The boy caught the coin and nodded. "Aye, ma'am. He'll be pam-pered right proper." He led the horse toward the stables at the rear of the inn.

Azhani yawned and led Kyrian up to the door of the inn. Tacked near the wall was a wooden sign that read, "Barton Inn." From within the lamplit interior, they could hear the patrons laughing and singing along with a rowdy song. She pushed open the door and allowed Kyrian to step inside before following her. The conversation ebbed and the stardancer glanced around the room nervously as Azhani hobbled to the bar.

While the warrior paid for a room, Kyrian studied the patrons. People of all the various races of Y'Myran dotted the tables. Dirt-encrusted humans sat alongside finely dressed elves while a group of half-elves traded stories with a burly dwarf. At the front of the room was a hearth that gave forth welcome heat. Near the fire sat a minstrel and his instruments.

Kyrian's gaze met that of the minstrel and they shared a smile. Pick-ing up a drum, the man began to beat out the cadence of a familiar drinking song.

Shortly, Azhani rejoined her. The warrior held two wooden placards with keys attached to them. Handing one to Kyrian, she nodded toward a set of stairs at the side of the taproom. They made their way to the second floor where the numbers on their placards matched numbers painted on two separate doors.

"This is your room. I've paid for three days. After that..."

"We'll be on our way back to the cabin," Kyrian interjected brightly as she unlocked her door.

Hooded blue eyes regarded her. "Right," Azhani replied.

"Meet you downstairs for dinner," Kyrian said as she took her pack and bedroll and vanished into the room.

You could have asked if I wanted to eat in the common room. The warrior had hoped to stay in her room, but if Kyrian wanted to enjoy the tap-room's atmosphere, she would join her. The populace of Barton was more than a little rough around the edges and Kyrian was pretty enough to attract the wrong kind of attention. Out of duty to the friendship that was growing between them, Azhani would stay by Kyrian's side. *You saved my leg, Kyrian. That gives you the right to a free warrior bodyguard.*

Leaning heavily on her crutch, she opened the door and limped inside the room. Everything ached and she longed for a bath.

At least when I hurt, I can't think. Pain was preferable to the night-mare visions of blood and death that had plagued her since Banner Lake.

Closing her eyes, Azhani took a deep breath and enjoyed the clean scent of the room. Unbidden, Kyrian's face appeared in her mind's eye. Wearing her customary smile, the stardancer's expression was one of friendly welcome.

Azhani scowled and tossed the saddlebags onto the bed. *I do not like her. She is not my friend. She is my doctor. She cares for me out of sacred duty, not because she sees me as worth knowing. I am protective of her because my oath to the goddess compels me so.*

A tiny corner of her heart spared a moment to wish that duty and honor would take a long voyage on a small boat. *It would be nice to have a friend to share my burden.*

Her stomach growled. Outside, the opening and closing of a door reminded her that it was time to honor her oaths. Steeling herself against whatever the night would bring, Azhani schooled her face into an impassive mask and went to join the stardancer.

The common room was full of patrons when Kyrian stepped off the stairs to look for a table. There were a few spots left in the middle of the room and she started to head for one, but then she spied a booth near the kitchen door. *Well, it might be chilly in the corner, but I'll bet that my broody companion would prefer a quiet seat to a warm one.*

A strong beat played on a hand drum accompanied the poem the min-strel on the stage was reciting. A serving wench took Kyrian's order for two meals.

Looking around the room, the stardancer took in the inn's rustic atmo-sphere with mild interest. Though different from the taverns she was used to, there was enough familiarity to the place that she felt comfortable.

The town drunk slumped off a chair at the end of the bar, a petty thief slithered up and down the tables seeking an easy pouch to lift, while a pretty light-skirt dimpled and smiled at passersby.

Filling the rest of the inn was a mish-mash of trappers, miners and merchants. The minstrel seemed to have a never-ending repertoire of bawdy songs. Though on the surface he was not overtly striking, when he performed, it became very obvious why his tip hat was always full. The voice that filled the room with stories and songs was mellifluous and easily carried the thirty feet to Kyrian's table.

The drum suddenly stilled, as he spoke the last lines of his poem.
Azhani Rhu'len, the bitch with the sword,
was never a lady, and never a lord.
She's the old king's warleader

and your life she will take,
if you dare cross her—
the Banshee of Banner Lake!

The stardancer's lips pressed together thinly and she hoped that Azhani had not heard the song. Looking up at the stairway, she saw that her wish was in vain. Leaning heavily on her crutch, Azhani's face was tensed in an expression of stoic calm.

She hobbled off the last step, looked around the room and spotted Kyrian immediately. The minstrel's words rippled around the room and caused a bleak look to settle in Azhani's eyes. She made her way to the table and arrived at the same time as dinner.

Chilled to the bone by the minstrel's chant, Azhani stared down at the meal. The food looked wonderful but she had no appetite. All she wanted to do was flee back to her room.

"It's pretty good." A soft, low voice reached across the table and tore her attention away from the churning in her stomach. Azhani looked up to see Kyrian tear off a chunk of the bread and dip it into her bowl.

Their eyes met and Azhani unconsciously took a spoonful of the stew and lifted it to her lips. The smell of well-cooked food overrode the nausea and she opened her mouth quickly. The rich, gamy taste of venison hit her tongue and she gulped it down, amazed when it didn't immediately return.

Ignoring the other patrons in favor of their meal, the pair ate quickly. When she was finished, Azhani pushed the bowl away and tried to relax. The bard started another tune — this one about a young farmer boy who joined the army only to die at Banner Lake.

Swallowing heavily, Azhani stood. "I'll go see about baths for us." She hobbled over to the bar and quietly conversed with the innkeeper. The man nodded and handed her a key. She limped back to the table and presented the key to Kyrian.

"Your bath, my lady," she said, and headed for a door at the back of the inn.

Aware of how uncomfortable Azhani was in the common room, Kyrian raced upstairs to her room. Quickly, she gathered a pair of clean, faded acolyte's robes. One for her and one for Azhani — their clothes were filthy and the robes were the only thing Kyrian owned that was large enough to fit the warrior.

Azhani was waiting for her downstairs, an amused smirk twitching at the corners of her mouth. Kyrian held up the robes and said, "Now you won't have to put your dirty clothes back on."

"Thank you," the warrior said sincerely. "We can wash our things in the water when we're done. They should dry overnight."

The baths were surprisingly well appointed, allowing them to spend time soaking their sore muscles. Afterward, they retired to their rooms.

As she drifted off, Azhani was plagued by conflicting emotions. *Kyrian seems so unafraid of me. How do I close my heart to the gift she freely offers? What price am I willing to pay to keep my distance? Can I have friends?* There were no easy answers to the warrior's questions. *I have to try. Because soon I'll have to trust that those I ask to back me against Arris won't betray me. I know that a stardancer would never turn on me — even one who believes I'm a murderer.*

Other questions bothered Azhani as well. During their bath, she had noticed scars on Kyrian's body. The wounds had obviously been made by a sword. Surprised at how angry she was to see the old injuries, Azhani was overwhelmed with an urge to protect the priest.

Chapter Five

Early the next morning, Azhani rose to find her clothes still damp. Knowing that they would dry while she wore them, she dressed quickly. Before turning in for the night, Kyrian had told her that she did not have to wear the splint anymore so this morning she happily left the bundle of sticks and rags at the foot of her bed. When she was ready, she limped over to the stardancer's room. Raising a fist to knock, she stopped when her acute hearing picked up the soft sound of movement behind the door. The knob turned her under hand when she twisted it. *I'd better warn her to lock it tonight. Otherwise a drunken stranger might wander in and get a stardancer surprise.*

Sunlight streamed in through the open shutters. In the center of the room, Kyrian was involved in a complicated series of exercises. Clad only in a short, pale green tunic, the stardancer's pale skin rippled over lean muscles as she practiced movements that looked to be a combination of dance and meditation.

Azhani recognized the ritual. As a youth, she had spent time studying with the Astariuns at Y'Len. Called the Goddess Dance, the exercises were actually a part of the training that all 'dancers and 'seekers received as part of their education. Used in battle, it was a highly effective way of defeating an opponent without killing them.

Kyrian was obviously a master at the dance. Azhani was mesmerized by the young woman's movements and watched in awe as she executed a flawless spinning kick that would have knocked a real enemy through the window.

I wonder if I remember any of the counter moves? Azhani leaned her crutch against the stardancer's bed, turned and threw her arm out in a standard Dance block. Kyrian stopped the exercise and frowned.

"I'm not sure that you should be doing this," the stardancer said hesitantly.

"I'll be fine. I've done this before."

Doubtful, but willing to let Azhani test herself, Kyrian nodded. "It's your body." She started the workout again, this time adjusting her speed and skill to accommodate the warrior's weak leg.

As they trained, the lack of ambient noise allowed each woman to concentrate on her opponent. The exercise went well until Azhani attempted some fancy footwork, lost her balance and fell.

"Ouch. Shyvot." She reached down and rubbed her leg. "Guess I should have put on that splint after all." The muscles, unused to so much stress, spasmed painfully.

Kyrian knelt to examine the leg for any new damage. "Sorry about that," she said, wincing at a rapidly purpling bruise on Azhani's ankle. She began to hum and her hands flared with a soft yellow glow.

"You don't have to do that," Azhani said gruffly. "I can handle a sprained ankle."

"I've no doubt of that, but I'd like to get you fully healed before you start adding new bruises to your collection," Kyrian replied.

Azhani shook her head ruefully. "Why are you doing this, Kyrian? Why are you helping a murderer?"

Abruptly, the song ceased. Kyrian looked up and met the warrior's hard eyes and said, "Because you are not a murderer, Azhani. A killer, yes — I know you've killed. Defending the realm and yourself, I'm sure you've taken lives. What I cannot accept is that the woman who rescued me, who treats me with such respect and deference could have killed in cold blood! So whatever your story is, warrior, you're stuck with me!" She stood and rubbed her hands on her thighs. Sighing, she said, "I'd like to be your friend, Azhani." Tentatively, she extended her hand.

Azhani looked up into Kyrian's face. Seeing only a gentle, welcoming smile, she took the other woman's hand, allowing the stardancer to help her to stand. "All right, we'll give it a try," she said. "I should warn you that I'm not an easy person to like, Kyrian. I can't always promise—"

"I don't need any promises, Azhani. I just want us to stop crashing heads. Here, you'll need this." Kyrian bent to retrieve Azhani's crutch. Stepping close to offer it, she smiled as the warrior took it and shoved it under her arm, obviously grateful for its support. She then turned to close the window.

"Thanks," Azhani muttered, nostrils flaring as the stardancer brushed against her. Nerves that had been dormant since Ylera's death flashed into life, causing the blood to pound heavily in her stomach. Almost simultaneously, memories of her beloved Ylera crashed over her. It was like being doused with a basin of icy cold water.

The heady burst of attraction faded instantly and was replaced by a blast of the dark, fiery anger that burned unceasingly in her soul. Tears welled up in her eyes and she reeled away from Kyrian. Arris had laughed at Azhani's tears as he watched her from outside the cell door. Her nightmares were filled with his insane giggles and his taunting mockery of her weakness. Her hands fisted as hatred swelled. Quickly, she clamped down on the rogue emotion, refusing to let her newfound friend see the darkness.

Unaware of the rapid emotions streaming across Azhani's face, Kyrian said, "We need to make sure we buy extra clothes so that we won't have to wear wet ones." Wrinkling her nose as she exchanged her tunic for the warmer crimson robes and brown leather boots, she added, "You know how to fight like one trained to the Dance. Did you study at Y'Len?"

"A lifetime ago," Azhani replied, shaken from her dark reverie. Gripping the crutch, she said, "Come, we've a long day ahead of us."

By midmorning, Azhani's bartering skills had bought them a rickety cart and half the supplies they would need to survive the winter. The gold from the kidnapper had covered most, but not all, of their expenses. Wondering if Kyrian would forgive her for getting hurt again, Azhani started to head toward the rowdier side of town. There were always those willing to test their skills for the price of a drink. Friendly wagering went hand in hand with these contests and Azhani planned to spend what remained of her coin on a few bruises and the hope of winning a large bet.

"Azhani, where are you going?" Kyrian asked, halting the warrior in her tracks.

"I—"

The stardancer had been contemplating the Barton hospice when she noticed Azhani begin to limp off toward the seedier section of town. "Wait here. I think they're associated with my temple." She indicated the building. "Now don't wander off on me, please." This last was said with a mock stern glare.

"As you request," said the warrior meekly. Kyrian smiled and went into the hospice. *I wonder what she's after?* Shrugging, she wandered over to Arun and began to pet the horse. He had been hitched to the wagon and was still getting used to pulling the extra weight.

"Maybe she's decided she likes it here, hey boy?" she muttered as Arun nosed her hands for attention. "Well, if that's the case, at least I won't have to get my face bloodied. I can live off what's in the cart." *The cart! Demon's blood! How the hell am I going to get that home? Arun belongs to Kyrian, and he'd be staying with her...Astarus' balls! Some demented looking donkey I'd be, pulling this wagon down the road!* Arun shoved his nose toward her pouch, hunting for treats. Laughing, she pulled out a carrot and fed the friendly animal.

A quarter candlemark passed. Azhani began to pace back and forth along the sidewalk. Another quarter candlemark burned by while she knocked stones into the street with her crutch. Finally, she sat down and brooded sullenly.

Senses honed by years of battle caught the fine crunch of booted feet on gravel, followed by the whoosh of air broken by a flying object. Thrusting out her hand, she neatly caught a small, solid ball of canvas. A pouch, heavy with coin, fit snugly in her palm. She looked up to see a grinning stardancer jog across the street.

Slung from Kyrian's left shoulder was a bulging haversack while on the other, a roll of crimson fabric fluttered in the breeze.

"Did you find what you were looking for?" Azhani asked curiously.

"I did. Did you know that the hospice is run by a couple of doctors from Y'Skan?" Kyrian asked.

"Yes. I remember that they saved many people from the coughing sickness when they first arrived in Barton."

"They're not stardancers, but there's a starseeker in residence. I was able to get my stipend." She nodded at the pouch in Azhani's hand and chuckled ruefully. "Starseeker Olise was not eager to part with so much coin. There's enough there to purchase the rest of our supplies. Arun's oats wouldn't make the most appetizing of meals."

Azhani hefted the pouch again. Even if the coins were just copper, there had to be six months worth of wages in her hand. "I can't—"

A warm finger brushed over her lips. "Yes, you can. I pay my own way, warrior. Next stop is the smithy. If I remember correctly, we needed nails and brackets."

Azhani nodded dumbly, unable to come up with a reason why she could not accept the money. As they walked toward the sound of ringing metal, she realized that she no longer even wanted to. Kyrian was staying.

By the breath of the Twain, I think I like that.

I didn't get my sword, but at least we have warm clothes. The thought trickled through Azhani's mind as she curled up to sleep. With all their shopping done, they could leave Barton in the morning. Then it would be a race to see if they could fix up the cottage before the weather forced the women inside for the duration.

At least I have some armor. I'd hate to run into bandits while wearing nothing but a tunic. Outlined in moonlight was her new studded leather coat. It was why she hadn't been able to afford a sword.

The fine jacket had been hanging on the blacksmith's wall, gathering dust. It was a beautiful piece of work. Covered in burnished steel disks that glowed like tiny silver plates, she had considered offering the smith her first born child in exchange for the coat.

Kyrian had noticed how Azhani lingered over the armor and had quietly spoken to the smith about its price. They listened while the blacksmith sadly explained that the armor had been made for his son, but earlier that summer, the young man had been gored by a wild boar and was bedridden, dying of festering wounds. Not even the Y'Skani doctors could cure the infection slowly devouring the boy's body.

As soon as she heard about the injury, Kyrian asked to see the young man. The blacksmith was more than willing to let the stardancer treat his son. Six candlemarks later, the boy's wounds were healed to such a degree that he would walk by spring.

Grateful beyond words, the smith freely offered the armor to the warrior. Neither woman was willing to accept the armor without paying for it, so a nominal fee was set. The final amount was more than what Azhani felt they had to spare, but Kyrian amiably handed over the gold.

When Azhani went to protest, the stardancer shook her head. "Take it as a token to mark the beginning of our friendship."

For a first gift, it was a strange one. Yet it felt nice that Kyrian cared enough to make sure that Azhani's back was well protected. A smiled creased the corners of her mouth as she snuggled into her blankets. There was another tiny chip in the shields around her heart.

Once winter passed, Azhani planned to say her goodbyes to her new friend and travel to Y'Syr. Originally, she had thought to go to Y'Mar, but the elven kingdom was closer. There were people there who had once called her friend, and a woman who was owed the truth of her sister's passing.

There was an herbalist named Tellyn Jarelle who lived in Y'Syria who might allow her to stay while she dealt with Lyssera. Thinking of the elven queen brought memories of Ylera.

"Am I the first elven woman you've known, Azhani?" her beautiful lover asked as she stroked the warrior's face tenderly.

"No — my father took me to Y'Syr whenever he would visit."

"Then you have many friends among my people?"

Azhani laughed. "I would not say that, my love. But there are a few who would not turn me away."

"Would I know any of them?" Jealousy colored her lover's voice.

"Maybe — Tellyn Jarelle lives in Y'Syria," Azhani replied absently as she kissed Ylera's shoulder.

Ylera smiled. "Ah. Good. Mistress Jarelle is a good friend to have."

"And there's you," Azhani said, and then kissed Ylera passionately.

"Unless you plan to leave me once the treaty is signed."

There was a flash of desperate emotion in Ylera's eyes but it was quickly replaced by love. "No, heartling, I have no plans of going anywhere. By the blessed trees of my forbearers, I swear that I am yours for life."

"And I am yours, Ylera Kelani, for so long as I draw breath, my heart beats for you."

Ylera pulled Azhani to her and kissed her with fierce passion. That night, they made love with a kind of wild desperation that only time would underscore.

Hot tears pricked at Azhani's eyes and she angrily dashed them away. *My love, I pray that one set of eyes in the city of trees will not look upon me with hatred.* The empty space at her back silently mocked her with its chill.

Lying in bed, staring at the darkened ceiling, Kyrian sighed and rolled fretfully onto her side. She couldn't sleep. Over the last three days, the edgy truce between Azhani and her had matured into a friendship. In the morning, they would leave Barton and return to the DaCoure homestead, where they would spend the winter, alone, together.

The situation verged on the romantic, and Kyrian looked forward to the solitude with an eagerness that shocked her. *Romance. Goddess, Kyr, this is not a bedroll game. Azhani's a friend, not some pretty wench you can charm for a night or two of pleasure!*

She blushed, thinking of the invitations she had received from two of the barmaids. Without a second thought, she had gently refused their offers. Only later did she realize why she had done so.

In Azhani Rhu'len she saw a kindred spirit. The soul-deep agony that echoed in every gesture she made touched Kyrian in a way that left simple beauty to pale in comparison. The woman's steadfast sense of honor and blazing intelligence only added to the longing and sang a siren's call of desire in the stardancer.

Like iron to lodestone, Kyrian was drawn to Azhani. In idle moments, she wondered what kissing her would be like.

"Oh gods, this isn't fair," Kyrian whispered in consternation. "I'm not supposed to think about my patients this way!" Complaining about her feelings would not cure what ailed her.

Neither would giving the pretty tavern wenches a quick tumble, Kyrian thought bitterly. Not that a pleasant evening with a willing partner was necessarily bad — the gods knew that she was not a chaste woman — the problem was that Kyrian had no desire for anyone else.

"I don't want this," she hissed. "She's my *friend*."

She closed her eyes and began counting backward from one hundred. As reality slipped away, she felt a sense of peace ease through her mind and she began to breathe deeply.

The idea of using meditation had come to her earlier, and the relaxation techniques that had been part and parcel of her education since she was a child seemed to shave the edge off her unwanted desire.

The strategy had limited success. As they wished each other a good night, Azhani had given the stardancer one of her rare smiles. Instead of leaving her breathless with desire, Kyrian felt as though she had been given a beautiful gift.

Deep within her trance, she strove to find her balance. She had to allow the blossoming friendship between them a chance to grow.

Lust is a pale cousin to love, my friend. It masquerades as a true emotion but is a thing only of air and shadows. Do not be so quick to allow it to control your feelings. The words were Ylera's. They belonged to a memory that went back to their days as fellow students, when the young princess had broken another acolyte's heart.

The reminiscence triggered something within, allowing her to let go of her petty desires. Kyrian took a deep breath and visualized Azhani's nude form standing in the room. There was a tremble of desire, but it was nothing more than an appreciation for a beautiful woman and not the overwhelming need that had gripped her thoughts.

If she were anyone else, I'd gladly find a hay barn and spend several candlemarks exploring her body! Azhani's low, rumbly voice, smooth brown skin, summer-blue eyes and midnight-black hair all blended to create a woman of unique and memorable beauty.

A twinge of desire threaded through her as she thought of the warrior. "Be her friend, Kyr. She doesn't seem to have many of those."

The words quelled the latent desire more effectively than a thousand silent remonstrances had. Azhani's friendship was worth more than the tawdry gilt of loveless sex. She still felt a mild attraction to the striking woman, but unless the warrior offered more, Kyrian would be content to remain friends.

"I can do this," she said, turning over once more and pulling the blankets up to her chin. "I will be her friend." *Friends, yes, I like that. I haven't had a friend since Ylera...goddess, Ylera...I still need to know... Did you kill her, Azhani? I don't think I could forgive you if you did...* With that troubling thought, Kyrian drifted off to sleep.

~ Chapter Six ~

Bleak skies marked their departure from Barton. Dark clouds heavy with moisture rolled ominously overhead and the air was thick with the promise of snow. Atop the driver's seat of their wagon, Kyrian sipped from a skin of warm tea and was grateful that the trip home would be relatively short.

In the back of the wagon, Azhani dozed on a bed made of their supplies. The warrior reluctantly agreed to relax and enjoy the trip home because her leg still bothered her.

Wind ruffled the edges of Kyrian's cloak. She shivered and reached under the seat for her new fur-lined gloves and slipped them on with a sigh of pleasure. They had been a last minute gift from Azhani, given just as they exited Barton.

I wonder if she gave up a sword so that I could have these gloves? Guilt made Kyrian feel uneasy about not giving the warrior the blade she had found in the stable.

At the time, keeping the sword had seemed like a good idea. It had been all too easy for Kyrian to imagine Azhani taking the blade and carving a path of blood back to Y'Dannyv to wreak a terrible revenge on Arris. Even worse, the woman who wore despair like a second tunic might have used the blade to end her own life. As guilty as she felt now, her culpability then would have led Kyrian to a dark place no stardancer should go.

It's too late to go back and change it now. I don't know how Azhani didn't notice it. I'm just glad that it wasn't a dwarven blade — those are so much heavier than those made by the elves.

The sword now rode under the driver's seat. She almost presented it to Azhani as they left, but knew that it would be far too difficult to explain its origin. After all, the warrior was quite well aware of how much money they had.

Time will allow me to reveal the blade in the best possible manner. It's not going anywhere for now.

Comfortably seated in the bed of the cart, Azhani napped, lulled by the steady, even pace of the gelding. Kyrian had a gentle touch on the reins, and kept Arun from the larger ruts and stones.

Azhani woke midmorning. The deep ache in her bones told her that it would snow by late evening. She yawned, but stayed wrapped in the warm blankets.

The even beat of Arun's hooves clip-clopping on the dry ground mixed pleasantly with the rustle of animals and birds in the trees and bushes. An eagle spiraled overhead. From the front of the wagon came the mild scent of sandalwood. She smiled, recalling the bath that she and Kyrian had shared.

Friendship was a magickal talisman freely offered by the priest and Azhani greedily accepted it. *I can only hope that the coming season will allow us to temper this into a relationship that Kyrian is proud to have.*

It was going to be difficult to trust Kyrian. The very thought of talking about the past made Azhani feel queasy, but she knew that at some point she was going to have to tell her side of the story. She was afraid to face the dark swell of emotion that would come when old wounds were bared.

The banshee dwelling within the warrior's soul screamed to be free. It demanded the chance to sow the fields of Y'Dan with the blood of Arris and his toadies. Keeping that demon locked within a dark cell in her soul was a daily battle that Azhani dared not lose. If she failed even once and the darkness managed to escape, nothing in her path would be safe — not even the young stardancer.

The wise course would be to spend the winter in the company of the stardancer and enjoy the peace her presence brought. In spring, she should encourage Kyrian to seek another's company. This would be the most honorable choice, for to allow the younger woman to stay longer would needlessly expose her to danger. Resolution crystallized within the warrior.

She would allow herself the balm of Kyrian's friendship for the winter. When the warm weather of spring freed the passes to Y'Syr, she would escort the young woman to the nearest Astariun temple and continue on her way to Y'Syr.

This was the wisest choice. At the end of this road, she would be able to set her feet on the path to vengeance and claim her pound of Arris' flesh. It was right. Almost imperceptibly, a tiny ache threaded through Azhani's stomach, making her nauseous. *It's nothing — just the greasy bacon I had for breakfast,* she told herself firmly.

Unwilling to consider another cause, Azhani curled up to sleep once more.

Kyrian soothed her chapped lips with a drink from her waterskin. Road grit stung her eyes as she rubbed them clean. Five candlemarks into their day found the sun peeking through the clouds. Rumbling in the stardancer's stomach reminded her that lunchtime neared. As soon as she found a likely spot, she would stop the cart and wake Azhani. She looked over her shoulder at the sleeping warrior and smiled at the childlike peace in her slumbering face.

Kyrian was glad that she had taken the time to talk to Paul, the innkeeper of the Barton Inn. The garrulous Y'Tolian had been happy to share news with her. While Azhani bought more supplies, the stardancer had sat at the bar and spent a few coins on ale and gossip.

According to the innkeeper, life in Y'Dan was much the same as it had been when the stardancer had lived in Kellerdon. Arris had increased the boundaries of the law by introducing new sanctions and restrictions that at face value appeared to benefit the populace.

As the innkeeper listed each new law, Kyrian grew more disgusted. A disturbing trend rose from Arris' changes — the Y'Dani king was actively isolating his nonhuman citizens. Dwarves and elves who had been residents of Y'Dan for years were suddenly forced to pay extra taxes, or buy special permits allowing them to reside in their homes. Nonhuman goods that came into the kingdom were subjected to more inspection, import fees and taxation. To top that off, those nonhumans who made their living as merchants could only sell their products on certain days of the week. This had created an aura of fear and distrust as humans stopped frequenting the business of the nonhumans who had to charge twice as much as their human counterparts for similar goods.

Many nonhumans were leaving Y'Dan in droves — it was cheaper to live in friendly kingdoms such as Y'Syr, Y'Nor and Y'Mar. Some had even taken to the Crest of Amyra in search of the fabled barbarian tribes said to be living in the steppes.

The hardest hit among Y'Dan's nonhuman populace was the half-elves. Not only did they have higher taxes and housing restrictions, but those who had held jobs within the government found themselves unemployed. The new atmosphere made it difficult to find jobs, since no one wanted to hire a person who had been so publicly scorned.

Paul had mentioned that he expected the half-elves to be the next group to leave Y'Dan in numbers and that thought sent a chill up Kyrian's spine. Why did Arris want to live in a kingdom peopled only by humans? What was it about the other races that he feared?

The innkeeper also had his opinions about Azhani and her role in the massacre at Banner Lake.

"They say that Azhani killed the elven ambassador when she went 'n lost her mind at Banner Lake, but I'm a thinkin' that mebbe there's less truth an' more tale to that story. T'ain't no one was there that can 'member the lady's face among the dead. I lets ol' Takk tell his bloody poems cuz the customers like him, but I knew Azhi as a child and well remember when her da would bring her with him to trade furs. An' lemme tell you, Star-dancer, I don' believe Rhu'len DaCoure's little girl is the monster in them fancy tales!"

Kyrian nodded solemnly. "I've been with her for a few days, and I haven't seen any signs of the demon your Takk speaks of."

"'N you won't, neither! Azhani's a good girl." Paul beamed happily as he wiped out a glass and filled it with a draft of cool ale and then set it on the bar in front of her. *"Best you mind your speech, though, youngling. There be unfriendly ears in Barton. The girl's in no shape ta be lashing about at ev'ry would-be bounty collector."*

Kyrian had stifled a giggle over the description of Azhani as a girl, but there had been genuine affection in the old innkeeper's voice when he spoke of her. *She's worth knowing, if she's touched that old reprobate's heart.* Paul was one of the Y'Tolians who had come west to escape the hangman's noose, or so she'd discovered when she had asked him.

Hearing the rumor that Ylera had not been present at Banner Lake had sent a ribbon of hope through the stardancer's heart. If the elven ambassador had not been there, then Azhani could not have murdered her alongside the soldiers that had stepped up to challenge her.

It might mean that the warrior had killed the elven woman beforehand, and the stories had become muddled in the retelling. *Or it might mean she's innocent, and if she didn't kill Ylera, then maybe she's not guilty of treason, either. Face it; you want her to be the wronged party. You like the woman, and you are having a difficult time seeing your heroic rescuer as an evil, murdering traitor.*

Now more than ever, she wanted to hear Azhani's side of the story. *I'll just have to earn her trust.* Her stomach rumbled again.

"Lunchtime," she muttered and guided the wagon off the road.

Azhani came awake as Arun's pace changed. Rubbing her eyes sleepily, she judged that she had slept longer than she had planned. As she was stretching muscles cramped by sleep, a flash of light in the forest caught her attention. Standing, she strung her bow and nocked an arrow, scanning the trees intently.

Kyrian felt Azhani's sudden movement and pulled Arun to a full stop. Turning around, she found the warrior in a militant stance. Nervously, she reached for her baton. *I can do this...*

The air around Azhani crackled with tension as she scrutinized the forest. A muscle in the woman's cheek twitched as she spotted her target. The twang of the bowstring echoed around them as the arrow sped away.

There was a muffled scream, and then the body of a man fell from a tree across the road. A second arrow followed on the heels of the first and another shriek of pain marked its target.

A swarm of ragged bandits emerged from the trees and bushes. Armed with a variety of weapons, the men raced toward the wagon with grim determination. Azhani's hands blurred as arrows were nocked and loosed in quick succession. Two more men fell, clutching feathered shafts that protruded from their throats. Then, the bandits were upon them.

Azhani jumped from the cart, stifling a groan of pain when she landed. While stabbing one man in the eye with an arrow, she parried another's sword thrust with her bow.

"C'mon you beast lovers," she growled, and advanced on the bandits.

Paralyzed by fear, Kyrian could only watch as the bandits circled the warrior. The bow was not meant for use as a staff, but Azhani seemed not to notice as she blocked attack after attack. A bandit's sword came down and cut the bowstring. The resultant snap caused a tiny trickle of blood to appear on Azhani's cheek.

"Ow." Azhani grinned wickedly and slammed the end of the bow into the man's groin. He doubled over, gagging in pain.

"Hello, pretty one. Why don't you come on down? I've got a use for you." A voice broke through Kyrian's confusion and she blinked owlishly at the bandit who was approaching the front of the wagon.

Cold dread clutched at Kyrian's guts and the weight of her baton seemed to double as she sat, dumbstruck. Dirty fingers brushed the hem of her robe, reaching under layers of fabric to stroke her leg.

"Mm, nice." The man licked his lips, tightening his grasp.

Panicked revulsion sent her scrambling back on the seat. The baton fell to the floor. The shattered remains of Barrig's face blended with the bandit's and grinned up at her tauntingly.

"No," she whispered hoarsely. She flailed about, trying to throw off the haze that fogged her mind and cut her off from reality. The cold hard shape of her baton broke through the fear. Grasping it, she blindly struck out and scored a soft hit on the bandit's shoulder.

He shook himself and backed away. "Got claws, do you? Well then, let's see how you like this!" The bandit uncoiled a whip and struck, hitting her in the throat with the spiked tip of the weapon.

Azhani spun when she heard the strangled yelp of pain. She spotted the bandit attacking Kyrian and thought fast. *Shyvot! I'm out of arrows! Gonna have to improvise.* She kicked her current opponent in the knee and then punched him when he doubled over. Yelling, "Run, Kyrian!" she threw her bow at the man attacking the stardancer.

It wobbled as it flew, but struck him squarely in the eye. As the weapon clattered to the ground, the bandit staggered away from the cart, spitting curses and clutching at his face. The eye dangled uselessly and blood streamed freely from the socket.

Azhani's shout snapped Kyrian from her daze. Running sounded like a very good idea. Killing a man once had ripped a ragged hole into her soul and she was too scared to defend herself now. She should leave because her presence put Azhani in danger.

The stardancer sheathed her baton, took up Arun's reins and prepared to urge him on when one of the bandits threw a dagger at Azhani. She easily dodged the blade, but took a hard blow to her kidneys in exchange. Without a weapon, Azhani had to use her hands and feet to fight off the attacking ruffians.

When she didn't hear the cart moving behind her, Azhani yelled, "Kyrian — go! Run to Barton!" Her warning earned her another blow from a club-wielding man.

Sound evaporated, leaving Kyrian in a vacuum of timelessness. Everything around her seemed to move as though it were underwater. Azhani ducked a blow, spun and kicked a bandit in the stomach.

Move. The thought trickled into Kyrian's awareness. *Run.*

In slow motion, a sword sliced through the air and cut deeply into Azhani's shoulder.

Kyrian, move. Now.

"I can't leave her," she whispered. Furiously tearing away the strands of fear that had held her paralyzed, Kyrian reached under the seat and grabbed for the silk-shrouded sword. Shucking the ancient fabric, she shouted, "Azhani!" and tossed the weapon high into the air.

The newly freed sword tumbled end over end.

Kyrian silently counted, *One heartbeat, two heartbeats, three heartbeats.*

Flashing in the sunlight, the blade seemed to blaze with fire as it arced across the clearing. Combat ceased as the warriors were blinded.

Four heartbeats, five heartbeats...

Metal slapped flesh and laughter rippled across the road. An eerie, bone-chilling wail erupted from Azhani's throat. Arun started, neighing in fright. The hairs on Kyrian's neck stiffened at the hollow, keening sound.

So this is why they called her the banshee... she thought, as a chill of not quite fear crawled down her back.

Unaffected by the cry, the bandits resumed their attack.

"Care to dance with me, boys? I could use some new partners!" Azhani shouted. Brash laughter peppered the air as she effortlessly dodged their best swings. The blade in her hands spun in tightly controlled arcs and when she struck, it bit deep into grimy flesh.

Blood sprayed from the wounds and dappled her face and clothing.

More laughter bubbled out of her; she threw her head back and let out another one of her terrifying screams.

With a shudder, Kyrian turned away, unable to watch the ensuing carnage. In that moment, she understood why Azhani had been called a demon at Banner Lake. The warrior who faced the scruffy bandits with such gleeful abandon could easily take on hundreds of soldiers. This woman would glory in the bloodshed, bathing in it as she danced from death to death.

Kyrian heard the sound of bones breaking and swallowed, sickened. This Azhani was gloriously awesome and fearsomely terrible all at once.

A scream of pure agony forced the stardancer to turn and view the battle. The warrior casually pulled her sword from a bandit's belly, flicked the blood and gore from her blade and then beheaded another attacker in a series of fluid moves that would have been beautiful had they not been so deadly.

The separated head landed in the cart at Kyrian's feet.

As her gorge rose, Kyrian kicked the head away from her, drew her baton and jumped off the wagon. The whip-wielding bandit had recovered enough from his injuries to come at her. Braided leather flicked out and wrapped around the baton. With a powerful yank, the bandit pulled Kyrian close and punched her in the jaw.

Stars flashed before Kyrian's eyes and she spat blood. Shaking off the blow, she struck back, hitting him in the solar plexus with her free hand. The whip slackened; she danced backward and kicked him in the shin. He roared in pain and charged her. Spinning away, she delivered a solid rap to the back of his head with her baton. He dropped like a sack of stones.

The stardancer quickly knelt and searched for a pulse, breathing a sigh of relief at the steady thrum that fluttered under her questing fingers. This time, she had not taken a life. Reaching into her pouch, she pulled out a length of strong twine and bound the bandit's hands. This was the way she had been trained to deal with criminals.

When Kyrian was done, she stood in time to see Azhani dart around the wild swings of the remaining bandit's club and then cleave him in half with one stroke of the sword.

The warrior stepped back and watched the man topple over, the pieces of his body falling apart as they hit the ground. A primal snarl twisted Azhani's face as she looked up at Kyrian.

Kyrian staggered back under the force of the powerful gaze. Slowly, she sheathed her baton. Raising empty hands, she held them out to the warrior.

"Azhani?" she called. "It's over, my friend," she added soothingly.

The one bandit remaining conscious grabbed his bound buddy and dragged him off, running toward the forest in an attempt to flee the blood-maddened warrior. Kyrian let them go. It was more important to break through the warrior's battle fever.

Keeping her eyes locked with Azhani's, Kyrian moved closer until the other woman blinked and let her sword droop to the ground. As soon as she was sure that the warrior was in control, Kyrian raced to the other side of the road and began violently vomiting.

With a bemused expression on her face, Azhani watched Kyrian go.

The coppery tang of blood speckled the air around her and she looked down to see that her new clothes were liberally spattered with it. She wiped her face and was stunned to realize that it was coated in gore. Quickly checking herself, she found that other than the flow from a small gash on her shoulder, most of the thick, rapidly congealing fluid was not hers. A tiny cut on her face was the only other injury she had sustained. Both wounds were small enough that they would heal in days.

Disgust washed over her. *I slaughtered them like pigs,* she thought as she bent to clean her blade in the grass. *I guess I'll find out if Kyrian's really my friend, now. I didn't earn the name Banshee because I enjoyed crying at funerals.* Her ribs creaked and she winced, grateful once more for the coat of armor that she had bought. It was all that had stood between her and a mace. Though they would ache for a while, her ribs were intact.

She straightened and tried to sheathe the sword, only realizing at the last moment that she didn't have a sheath. *Where'd this come from? Somehow I can't imagine Kyrian taking this from the hand of a dead man.* Curious, she examined the blade. There was something familiar about the whorls of folded metal...

"My father's sword," she whispered haltingly, "It has to be. I'd know this rune anywhere." Etched into the blade just above the guard was a tiny mark that Rhu'len had long used to sign his letters and documents.

"Kyrian, where'd you—" The words dried on Azhani's lips the moment she saw that the stardancer was incapacitated. She took a few steps toward her friend and the realized that the last thing Kyrian needed was to see her blood-drenched body. The weapon in her hands suddenly became a hateful weight.

She almost tossed it into the woods. Instead, she gripped it tighter, letting the wire-wrapped hilt bite deeply into her palm. This weapon was her father's legacy, and with it she would take her revenge on Arris. Carefully, she slid the sword into her belt. Then she began to methodically search the bodies of their attackers.

None of the men were familiar, but she knew the type well. She had chased this same kind of scum from Y'Dan years ago. Then, she had been at the head of a large patrol of soldiers. Now, she needed to move fast in case there were others lurking in the forest.

There was not much to be had from the bandits; a few coins and their weapons were all that she took. The coins would go into a poorbox at the next Astariun temple she visited. On the other hand, the weapons could be repurposed into an assortment of useful objects. Arrowheads, snares and nails were just a few of the things that could be made out of the melted-down metal. If there happened to be a weapon of quality among the blades, then Azhani would add it to her personal arsenal.

By the time she had finished searching the bodies, Kyrian had returned to the wagon.

"Wh-what will we do with them?" she asked, after swishing her mouth out with some water. The stardancer was still a little green around the edges. She had been exposed to death before, but not on such a violent scale. Even when she had slain Barrig, there had only been one body and the sight of so many dead made her sicker by the candledrip.

Azhani gave the corpses a considering glance. Usually, she would leave the bodies on the side of the road as warning to other bandits. This was not Y'Dan, and playing forest patrol would likely earn her enemies she did not need.

"There's a spade in the wagon. It shouldn't take me long to bury them," said the warrior laconically. Truthfully, it would take candlemarks to inter the bodies into the frozen earth, but the relieved look on Kyrian's face was all that Azhani needed to see to know that she had made the right decision.

"If I can, I'll help," Kyrian offered bravely. "Were you injured? I'll get bandages—"

"I'm fine, healer. Took a few cuts and bruises — they'll keep until later. Let me get started on them. You should see to Arun." A thin line of blood marred the horse's flank. Amazingly, the horse had not bolted when the whip had struck him, but his ears were twitching and he seemed to have trouble standing still.

"Oh!" Kyrian ran to her horse's side and quickly began to pet and praise him, all while inspecting the injury.

Chuckling at the display, Azhani stripped off her filthy armor and then dug out the spade. It took four candlemarks to bury all of the bodies. By the time she was done, her aches had aches. *Oh goddess, I hope I can make it to the cabin before I pass out.*

However, a quick survey of the newly turned earth left her filled with a sense of peace that had often been absent after a battle. For each man they buried, Kyrian had offered a small prayer, and now she walked from grave to grave sprinkling handfuls of seeds over each mound. Her lips moved in the prayer that would guide the souls of the dead to the afterlife.

How strange it is to see her act as a priest. I have grown used to her as a healer, but I must not forget that she is a mender of souls as well as bodies. Azhani bowed her head sorrowfully. *Will her prayers come as easily for me, I wonder?*

The stardancer finished the ritual by anointing herself and Azhani with a few drops of fragrant oil and then pouring a libation of water over the graves.

Kyrian's eyes fluttered shut and she exhaled slowly. It was difficult to put into prayer the hope that these men who had tried to kill them be granted passage to the blessed kingdoms. She had done it, though, and as she composed herself to sing the closing chant, she felt the sense of peace that often accompanied her work as a stardancer.

The soft, simple melody was recognizable to every person of Y'Myran who had lost a loved one. This part of the ritual was not for those who had gone on, but for those left behind. It was meant to comfort as well as give closure to the rite of burial.

Azhani's eyes closed as she listened to Kyrian sing. The familiar chant called a hoard of memories to mind. The faces, voices, laughter and tears of the men and women who had fought and died under her command came drifting in, carried on the strains of the song.

Of those ghosts that haunted her, three stood clearer than the rest. Her father, Rhu'len, had been killed three years ago in these very mountains. It was a beast year, and the ice demons had burst onto a small community to the west with a ferocity that surprised even the battle hardened.

King Thodan and his armies were too thinly spread to do much more than chase each pack of demons down and slaughter them when they could. Azhani and her father each had command of several platoons of soldiers. While she was leading a cave raid to destroy rimerbeast eggs, Rhu'len had led his men to the village under attack.

Toward dawn that fatal day, she had felt a burning need to be at her father's side. She ran two horses to death trying to get to him in time, but failed. He died saving a child from the clutches of a rimerbeast. She arrived as the soldiers were carrying his body off the battlefield. The child solemnly led the sad procession, her tear-streaked face blanked by the shock of her rescuer's violent death.

Later, Azhani learned that the girl had been kidnapped from her home and left out for the beasts to consume. When she had questioned the girl, she recognized the description of the child's abductor — Kasyrin Darkchilde, a sorcerer who had clashed with her father many years ago.

She had meant to make finding him a priority, but then Thodan had made her warleader and her duties kept her from seeking the evil mage. *I haven't thought about that piece of scum in years.*

The second ghost was her mother, Ashiani Oakleaf. Born of Y'Syr, the elven woman had met Rhu'len DaCoure on a trade road and had fallen in love. The two had shared an illicit affair, which ended when Ashiani's parents discovered them. She had died bearing Azhani, and the elven merchants who were the half-elf's maternal grandparents had sent the child to live with her father.

Finally, there was her beloved, Ylera. There had been no priest to sing the ambassador to the blessed kingdoms. Arris had mocked Azhani by telling her that her lover was going to be cursed to wander the mortal realms in ghostly form as a punishment.

"You should have married me, warrior. Now, your whore will pay the price of your arrogance!"

"No! She will find her way, Arris, I swear it!" croaked the warrior brokenly. She had wept nonstop since the prince's men had arrested her. Now her voice held but a shadow of its normal fullness.

"How?" He sneered. "Will you sing the wayfinder, Azhani the tuneless? She'd never find her way to the kingdoms with that voice to guide her."

"Better a broken road than none at all, you murdering pig," Azhani growled from between clenched teeth.

"Ah, I see that your temper has not been blunted by your fall, my dear Warleader. Never fear, Azhani — those claws will be cut to the quick soon enough." Laughing maniacally, he strode away, leaving her alone. All that night, her broken voice filled the dungeons as she sang her lover to the blessed kingdoms.

Blinking back tears, Azhani turned away from the graves. Drained and saddened by the memories, she was ready to head home.

A hand on her back caused her to turn and be enveloped in a warm hug. Awkwardly, she returned Kyrian's embrace, fighting to keep a hold on her tears. The stardancer was shaking. The tiny tremors were the leftover fears stemming from the horrors of the day.

"You saved my life," Kyrian whispered as she clung to Azhani. "Thank you."

It took all of five heartbeats for the warrior to decide that she deeply enjoyed Kyrian's hugs. *Ah goddess...it's been far too long...* The last time anyone had touched her with anything other than contempt had been...*Ylera*. It was like poking an infected wound. The pain blossomed fresh each time she prodded it. Azhani swallowed heavily, pushing the anguished thoughts away with a massive force of will. Now was not the time to mourn. Later, when they were safely locked behind the doors of her father's cabin, she would grieve. She would tell Kyrian the story she seemed so eager to hear and hope that the priest would see the truth in the words.

It felt so good to be held that Kyrian did not want to let go. Too many months had passed without enjoying the contact of another's touch, and that fact was made painfully clear by how nice it felt to be in Azhani's arms. *I feel safe here.* Reluctantly, she pulled away. Taking a deep, calming breath, she said, "Sorry. I'm not usually so clingy."

Azhani shrugged. "It was just a hug — I'm not going to cut your throat over it."

Startled, Kyrian stopped in midstride and stared at her.

"Don't look so amazed. Even banshees enjoy a hug every now and again."

"Uh, sure, I just thought—"

"You thought that since I've proven that all the stories about what a great killer I am are true that something as gentle as a hug would be against my faith."

"Well..." Kyrian floundered helplessly.

The warrior gave the stardancer her meanest, harshest glare. Kyrian gulped audibly. Stepping close enough to Kyrian to smell the sandalwood perfume in her hair, Azhani growled, "You were wrong. I like hugs. Romantic ideals are what make me glad that I am the warrior the bards sing of, because I am the one who makes it possible for ordinary people to dream of the future. So I'll say this once — I am not a monster. No matter what you've heard, Kyrian, I feel. I hurt. I love. Hugs are quite," she let a small smile break through the anger, "acceptable. After all, we *are* trying to be friends, aren't we?"

Completely astounded by the scathing tone of Azhani's statement, Kyrian could only nod.

Azhani turned away and strode over to the wagon and climbed up onto the driver's seat. Kyrian followed, absently settling into the passenger side while the warrior took up the reins and started Arun down the road toward home.

Half a candlemark passed before Kyrian spoke. "I'm sorry. I shouldn't have tarred and feathered you like that."

Azhani cocked her head toward Kyrian and smiled slightly. "You're right, you shouldn't have. But it is past. I have forgiven you."

How ironic that she can forgive me, when I still don't know if I can absolve her of Ylera's death! "Thank you."

"It is my turn to apologize," Azhani said.

"For what?" Kyrian sounded surprised.

"Putting you in danger — if I'd known that there were bandits in the area I'd have asked you to stay in Barton."

"I wouldn't have, so don't flog yourself for it, Azhani. I wish I'd been more help in the fight, but I was so scared—" Her cheeks flamed red in shame.

"It's all right, Kyrian. You're no warrior. You may know the Dance, but your heart is more healer than killer."

Kyrian laughed, amazed at how with just a few words, Azhani made her feel so much better. "You've done this for a long time, haven't you?"

"What? Fought off half-trained, unwashed ruffians who've nothing better to do in a day than to make some poor traveler wish he'd never set foot outside the door? Yes, I have. It was all I ever wanted to do. My father served King Thodan with honor and nothing could have stopped me from following in his footsteps." *I'm good at it, too. I've a knack for killing and have never frozen in a fight.* Out of the corner of her eye, she glanced at the young woman beside her. *Why didn't you run, 'Dancer? What caused you to turn into a statue when that piece of beast's dung attacked you?* To think that the stardancer — a woman who had been brave enough to stand up to her almost legendary temper — was a coward made Azhani feel lost and confused. *I've seen stardancers fight. The goddess doesn't prevent them from protecting themselves.* She almost asked Kyrian the questions that fluttered about in her mind, but realized that she was not ready to return like with like. The stardancer's story, like the warrior's own, would come when Kyrian was ready to trust her with it, and no sooner. *If it becomes a problem in the future, then I'll ask her about it, but not before.*

Azhani's nose wrinkled. Her new clothes now smelled horrible. Blood, sweat and dirt mingled to create a miasma of death that was all too familiar. It was both comforting and disturbing. Part of her exulted in it and reveled in the knowledge that she still had the skills to be a good soldier, and part of her watched another piece of her soul slip away, given to the service of the sword.

The sword! Azhani glanced down at the blade stuck into her belt. The weapon had been a bride gift from her mother to her father. She remembered wrapping it in silk and locking it away after her father's death.

"Kyrian, where did you get this sword?" she asked, touching the hilt.

There was no response.

Azhani sighed softly. Trust came at such a high price, and she had yet to pay it.

"I — it was in a trunk in the stable. All the clothes were on top of it. I thought, I mean, I didn't—" The response came in a low whisper that Azhani had to strain to hear.

"You didn't want the Banshee of Banner Lake to run you through in your sleep. How prudent of you."

The words struck like hammer blows.

Kyrian shook momentarily at the iciness in Azhani's voice. Steadying her nerves, she replied, "No. I kept the sword because I didn't want to see you throw away your life. How was I supposed to know what you would do?"

"Did you think I was going to run right out and kill everyone in Y'Dan?

Or were you hoping I'd do the honorable thing and fall on the sword once you'd got me all nice and healed?" The tension in the air between the two women was thick with anger.

"No." Kyrian locked her gaze with Azhani's. The warrior pulled Arun to the side of the road and put her forehead against Kyrian's.

"Aren't you afraid of me, Stardancer?" she whispered in a deathly calm voice.

Kyrian smiled and closed her eyes. "No, Azhani. You do not scare me. I have touched your aura — there is no monster inside you."

"How can you say that, knowing what you do of my history?" Slivers of the warrior's voice broke away and crackled in the air between them.

Kyrian covered Azhani's hands with her own. "Because I have learned that what is spoken and what is truth can have as much in common as a dog and an onion. I don't know what your history is, Azhani — I only know that a person burdened with the evil deeds that have been laid at your door would not have bothered to save my life. Maybe the first time could be explained, because you required healing, but certainly not the second, when my death would have freed you from having to fake a friendship. So I must conclude that there is more to the tales than death and betrayal."

Azhani pulled away and took up the reins again. Setting Arun on the road, she sighed. "You have a point. I will tell you my story, Stardancer, but in my time. Now, are there any more secrets, or can I trust that there will be no more pieces of my past hitting me in the face?"

Tell her about Ylera.

No! I can't! I don't know if she killed her...if she did, then — I don't know, but I can't deal with it now.

"No, the sword's it. Now can we go home? I'm cold, tired and hungry."

"That's where we're headed. Why don't you rest? I won't let you fall off the wagon." Azhani lifted one arm and Kyrian cautiously slid closer to her.

The warrior was warm, and she had a spicy scent that overrode the faint tinge of blood that clung to her clothes. It didn't take long for the star-dancer to fall asleep.

She woke when Azhani pulled the wagon to the roadside.

"Camp?" she mumbled sleepily.

"Yes. If you gather wood, I'll take care of Arun."

Kyrian nodded her assent, jumped down and began to search for deadfall. Supplies made them much better prepared for the rigors of winter travel and as a consequence, they spent time talking quietly and enjoying the warmth of their fire.

It was late afternoon the next day when Azhani turned Arun up the path that would take them to her cottage.

"Stay here," she whispered. "I'll be right back."

Kyrian nodded.

Azhani ran a quick patrol around and through the cabin to make sure that the homestead had remained unmolested in their absence. Once she ascertained that it was safe, she returned to the wagon. "Take it in, it's clear."

The stardancer clicked her tongue and guided the weary horse into the yard. Together, they unhitched Arun and led him to the stable where he was fed and groomed. Afterward, they unloaded the food and clothing into the storeroom.

Stifling a yawn, Azhani draped a tarp over the back of the wagon. "Let's go in. The rest will keep until tomorrow."

Azhani thrashed to wakefulness. Hot tears scorched her cheeks and she angrily dashed them away. Nightmares had been her constant companion since Ylera's death and this one had been particularly brutal.

Watching her through partially closed eyes, Kyrian was overwhelmed by the extent of the warrior's grief. She had wakened to Azhani's ragged cries of, "Ylera, goddess, no, Ylera!" and had lain on her pallet, listening to the warrior sob brokenly.

She cries out Ylera's name with the voice of a lover, Kyrian realized sadly.

Azhani's anguish deeply moved the priest. She rolled from her bed and crawled to the warrior's side.

"Azhani?" she whispered, tentatively putting a hand on the woman's arm. Azhani flinched, but did not immediately pull away.

"She's gone," the warrior whispered hoarsely, covering her face with her hands. "She's gone and it's my fault. I killed her. Oh goddess, she's dead!" A wail of such grief as Kyrian had never heard erupted from Azhani then.

Oh goddess...she killed Ylera...Astariu, please, give me strength...let me see this through, Kyrian prayed.

"*Words spoken in grief do not always hold the golden gleam of truth.*" The maxim taught by Starseeker Golyma, an ancient, careworn teacher at Y'Len bubbled up from memory. "*My students, you must remember that the guilt-locked will often take burdens upon their souls that are not theirs to carry. It is the way of the bereaved to assign blame as part of the path to healing. Your job, as stardancers, is to see behind the words to the truth of the soul behind their speaking. Do not be quick to judge, for innocence can be clad in the garments of grief.*"

The old starseeker's words gave Kyrian hope. The answers to Kyrian's questions would come. She had to believe that the reason for Ylera's death was among those answers.

Gently, she pulled Azhani into her arms. She struggled, pulling away.

"Shh," Kyrian crooned. "You can't hurt me, Azhani. It's all right." The calmly spoken words broke the warrior's resistance and she collapsed into Kyrian's arms, sobbing uncontrollably.

Chapter Seven

Daylight hours grew fewer each day. Snow flurried lightly, piling up as the two women worked feverishly to restore the cottage. The pace was exhausting, but both women knew they were in a race with nature.

The cabin and stable had their roofs fixed first. Over many days, Azhani's leg slowly regained its strength as she crawled around on top of the cabin and tied bundles of thatch in place. Inside, Kyrian laid heavy reed mats on the floor and made curtains for the windows.

Candlemarks flowed into days as they replaced rusted hardware on the doors and shutters with newly cast pieces. Chinks in the walls were filled with a mixture of mud and grass. In the stable, they swept the floor clean and laid down a layer of fresh straw.

A table, some chairs and two rope beds changed the hearthroom from a cold, dank environment into a place of warmth and hominess. The upstairs loft was ignored — there wasn't enough time to fix the bad flooring. Only the window was attended to, as the shutters were broken.

Each day, Azhani used the crutch a little less. Mornings found both women practicing the Goddess Dance. The exercises allowed tired and achy muscles a chance to relax and limber up for the day's work.

In the storeroom, new shelves were built to hold their foodstuffs. They installed blown glass lamps to illuminate the rooms. At night, the cottage glowed with welcoming warmth. Similar lanterns were placed outside the stable and the privy, giving the women a beacon to guide them from the cottage to the jakes and back.

Cords of firewood were stacked near the rear of the cottage. Feeling inventive, Azhani designed and built a covered walkway from the cabin to the privy. Constructed of wood and canvas, it would only last a few seasons, but it would make their winter that much more pleasant.

When the structure was finally completed, she stepped back to view it while a grin of pure satisfaction danced on her striking features. "There. Now there will be no more getting soaked to the skin while answering the call of the wild."

Kyrian laughed brightly and enjoyed basking in the warrior's sense of accomplishment. With her spirit unbound, Azhani's personality soared skyward, carrying with it a smile of such fierce gladness that Kyrian's heart skipped several beats.

It's easy to forget that pain was not always her constant burden. Only in unguarded moments am I allowed a glimpse of the woman she was before Banner Lake, she thought as they began cleaning up the remains of Azhani's little building project.

As they worked, they talked, telling each other the little things that made up the bits and pieces of their lives.

The one topic not explored was Banner Lake. Though not intentionally taboo, there never seemed to be a moment when the time was right to unburden her soul, and Azhani found it easier and easier to let the stardancer feast on the crumbs of her life, rather than serving the whole meal.

Nightmares continued to harrow Azhani's slumber and each time, Kyrian was there to hold her. Humming soft lullabies until she drifted back to sleep, the stardancer never failed to slip into Azhani's bed and soothe away her tears with touch and song until the dreams faded away. These moments were always held in cherished silence, untouched by conversation.

The final repairs were made to the fence and gate. They finished on the eve of the first heavy snow. While Azhani brought in wood, Kyrian watched in amazement as, in under a candlemark, the forest was cloaked in a thick, white blanket.

"It's beautiful," she whispered, reaching out to catch a handful of snow.

"It is a deadly beauty," Azhani said from inside the cabin. "Close the shutters, Kyrian. You'll catch a chill, otherwise."

On mornings when no snow fell, Azhani could be found by the stream, chopping holes in the thick ice to fish for the lazy trout that populated the waters. Other days, she and Kyrian would trade off teaching each other what they knew of herbalism by wandering the area around the cabin and searching for elusive winter plants.

The day that Kyrian pronounced Azhani "fit as a hunting cat" was the best day of the winter so far. They had held a ceremonial crutch burning and then the warrior had run off for the forest, needing to spend some time using the leg to really believe it was finally healed.

Whistling a merry tune, Azhani loped toward the cabin at a good pace. It felt so good to run! She came around the path and stopped to admire the snow-covered warmth of her home. So much had been accomplished in such a short time, and she felt no little pride over the improvements.

Smoke wreathed from the chimney. Arun's head poked out from the window of the stable. There was a patch of red on the rooftop.

Splat! A handful of cold snow smacked her in the face and dribbled down the front of her sweater. Anger scorched through her veins like lava, and then she heard the bright, infectious laughter of her friend.

Kyrian was on the roof of the cottage, retying thatch that had come loose during the last storm. A large chunk of snow was conspicuously missing from the drift covering the roof. Azhani's eyes narrowed as she scooped up a large handful of snow. Gauging the distance, she drew back her arm and let the snowball fly. Calmly, she watched as the missile hit its target and sent Kyrian sprawling down the angular slope of the roof.

"Oof!" Kyrian grabbed for a support and kept herself from falling through the rushes by the barest of inches. Her foot slipped though and for one, terrifying moment, she felt her body angling inward. *This is going to hurt,* she thought as she fought for a stronger hold on the cross beam.

Azhani watched the stardancer struggle and felt her heart slam down to the ground. *Now you've done it, you big idiot! You could have killed her!* "Hang on, Kyrian!" She ran for the ladder and was on the roof before the stardancer had taken more than two breaths. Locking her foot around the top rung, Azhani reached for her friend. Kyrian struggled to hold on; her feet slipped on wet thatch.

"I'm going to fall," she said calmly.

"No," said Azhani as she grabbed Kyrian's belt and pulled her close. "You're not. I will never let you fall, Kyrian. Now relax." Kyrian went limp and clung to the warrior's neck. Twisting, Azhani leaped away from the roof. They spun through the air once and landed in front of the cabin with a heavy thump.

Kyrian had frozen in place when Azhani grabbed her, but as she had been pulled against a warm body, she relaxed. It had been quite a shock to feel the warrior leap off the roof, but she trusted her enough to mold her body to Azhani's, curling when she curled and stretching when she stretched.

Now that they were on solid ground, Kyrian laughed and said, "That was fun! Can we do it again?"

Gaping in shock, Azhani blurted, "Again? I almost kill you and you want to do it again? Are you insane?"

Kyrian's laughter echoed around the homestead. "I was never in danger, Azhani. I trust you because I know you wouldn't hurt me."

The warrior's jaw worked soundlessly while her face turned several different colors.

Rolling her eyes, Kyrian bent and scooped up a handful of snow and then smashed it into Azhani's face.

Azhani spluttered and looked at Kyrian, who slowly and precisely stuck her tongue out and wiggled her eyebrows mockingly. The warrior made a face, spit out snow and then smiled wickedly. *She wants to play warrior. You can do that.* The banshee's call was strong.

Grabbing snow, she tackled Kyrian, dragging her to the ground. Roughly, she ground the icy stuff into the stardancer's face while laughing cruelly. She scooped up more snow and was about to assault the priest again when she felt the barest flick of fingers against her stomach.

The tickle sent the darkness reeling from her, and she choked back a giggle. Below her, Kyrian smiled and wiggled her fingers again. Letting out a sound that was somewhere between a laugh and a sob, Azhani let the snow in her hand fall back to the ground.

Come on, warrior, let it out, she silently coaxed, knowing that laughter was the best medicine. Comically wrinkling her nose, Kyrian tickled Azhani again.

A tiny chuckle escaped.

The stardancer added her second hand and mercilessly tickled Azhani's other side.

That was the final straw. Unable to stop it, a full-throated laugh took Azhani by storm, leaving her lying on her back in the snow, gasping for breath and giggling uncontrollably while Kyrian continued to tickle her.

Fighting fire with fire, she gave as good as she got and sent Kyrian squealing away. She jumped up and gave chase.

For almost two candlemarks, they laughed and played in the snow. They ended up collapsing in the stable on a pile of hay, breathless but happy.

"Oh goddess, I haven't played like that since I was a child," Kyrian exclaimed, her voice cracking from exertion.

"Here." Azhani unhitched a wineskin, took a quick swig and tossed it to the stardancer. "I can't remember ever playing like that, Kyrian. Not even as a child." She took several long breaths and wondered if Ylera would have enjoyed the snow. She thought perhaps not. Her elven lover's taste ran to plays, music and other artistic endeavors. *I liked the magick shows best, even if most of it was illusion and sleight of hand. What made it special was spending time with Ylera.*

Strangely, Azhani felt a measure of the same contentment in the simple pleasure of laughing with her new friend.

"Ugh, I need a bath," Kyrian muttered, wrinkling her nose as she caught a whiff of herself.

"If you start the fire, I'll drag the tub into the storeroom." Azhani's offer was immediate.

"You have a deal. If you'd like, I'll even attempt to tame that beast you call hair. Or is it some strange form of warrior penance?" Kyrian stood and offered her a hand.

Chuckling wryly, Azhani said, "If this is a penance, I'd hate to hear what you thought of my clothes when we first met."

Kyrian blinked innocently. "Clothes? You mean you weren't on a pilgrimage to the ancient temple of Refuse, the holy father of garbage? I'm stunned." *I can't believe we're standing here, joking with each other after playing in the snow all morning!*

Both of Azhani's dark eyebrows shot up at the statement. Then, slowly, she stuck her tongue out, mimicking the stardancer's earlier gesture.

Kyrian's eyes went wide and she shook her head slowly. "You have utterly amazed me, warrior. I think I like you."

Clear blue eyes searched a dirt covered face briefly before Azhani softly replied, "I think I like you too, healer."

"Friends?" Kyrian offered her hand and was gratified when the warrior took it and clasped it gently.

"Friends," said Azhani, inclining her head in agreement. Her low voice held a note of amazed disbelief. Smiling brightly, Kyrian squeezed Azhani's hand tightly, releasing it only when the warrior hesitantly returned the gesture.

"**Ouch,**" Azhani murmured as Kyrian tugged on another clump of matted hair.

"Oh hush. I can't believe you let it get this bad, Azhani," said Kyrian as she carefully worked the comb through the section.

"It wasn't like I had the time to stop and primp, healer."

"You couldn't have tried braiding it more often?" the stardancer teased.

"Maybe I should just shave it off and start over."

She was seated on the floor in front of the fire while the stardancer sat on the bed behind her, patiently combing and braiding Azhani's thick hair. Kyrian finished off another small braid with a bit of waxed cord and then set to detangling another section.

"We're almost a quarter of the way through. Don't give up so fast. If we get tired, we'll work on it tomorrow."

Azhani tilted her head to look up at her friend. "I just don't want to take you away from something more important."

With a perfectly straight face, Kyrian asked, "What could be more important than making sure you don't frighten Arun?"

"Funny, healer, very funny," Azhani growled, as she tipped her head forward so that Kyrian could get to a particularly nasty snarl.

"So," Kyrian asked after a while of silent combing, "who took care of your hair as a child? Or did you run around like a wild thing?"

"My father kept it short when I was young, and later, when I studied with Master Delaye, it was shaved off." Shrugging, Azhani added, "I let it grow out of vanity."

"I once saw the master give a performance in Y'Len," Kyrian said, her voice touched with awe. Master Delaye Kelani was one of Y'Syr's finest swordsmen and only took those he deemed to have talent as his students. The old master was a cousin to the royal family. Knowing who Azhani's teacher was explained much about her style. "No wonder you're so good."

Azhani inclined her head and allowed the ghost of a smile to play about the corners of her mouth. She was good; Master Delaye would have expected no less of her.

Kyrian yawned and set the comb aside. Standing, she tottered to the hearth and refilled her mug. After adding a healthy dollop of honey, she took a long drink.

Azhani raised an eyebrow and pointedly looked at the honey pot.

Kyrian grinned. "It's not medicine — it doesn't have to taste awful."

Azhani laughed. Rising fluidly, she bounced on the balls of her feet, gratified to feel the return of her old flexibility. "You know, I never thought I'd see another day where my leg didn't hurt like it was caught in a bear trap. Thank you."

Kyrian smiled. "You're welcome. Sit and I'll give it a final examination."

"All right." Azhani sat on the bed while Kyrian grabbed a chair.

Taking the warrior's leg onto her lap, Kyrian pushed up the breech leg and began to examine the limb in question. Gently, she ran her fingers over the smooth, dark brown skin, feeling for any residual knotting of the muscles. Although the leg was slightly underdeveloped, there appeared to be no serious atrophy. Thin scars puckered the skin where the bones had broken through, but no sores remained. Lastly, Kyrian laid her hand upon the section of bone that had bourn the brunt of damage and chanted the prayers that would open her mind to the vista of Azhani's life energy.

Slowly, the image of healthy tissue and bone filled her inner vision. A healthy, white gold aura limned the warrior's body. Beneath the surface, a storm of anger and depression roiled, untouched by the stardancer's power. Sadly, she could do nothing for this wound, as Astariu's fire could only heal the body, not the soul.

Singing the closing notes to the prayer, Kyrian stroked her fingers down Azhani's leg, removing the tension gained from the day's exercise.

"Well, that's the last of it. It's good as new." She looked up and smiled at Azhani and was rewarded with an answering grin that made her heart stutter. Gently, she patted the warrior's leg and then tugged the breech leg down.

Azhani slid down to her knees and bowed her head. Placing her hands together, she touched the tips of her fingers against her brow and said, "Thank you, healer. You honor me with your gift — may Astariu bless you."

Kyrian put her hands on Azhani's shoulder and replied, "You are welcome, warrior, and may the goddess always guide your hand to honor."

Looking up at the stardancer, Azhani could feel the tears burning in her eyes. "You are special, Kyrian. Not many would have risked exile to aid such as me. It will never be forgotten."

Kyrian's face lit with a gentle smile and she leaned forward, brushing a brief kiss on the warrior's forehead. "A poor representative of Astariu would I be, warrior, if I could not fathom the truth of your soul. Regardless of what is said, I have found your honor to be above reproach." She sat back and captured Azhani's callused hand in hers. "My friend, will you at last share your story with me? Allow me to sift the strands of truth from the fabric of lies that have been spread by well-meaning tale weavers."

Azhani glanced down at their joined hands. Firelight glinted off their flesh; darkness and light twined together in a gentle grip. *She deserves to know the truth.* Kyrian's pale skin reminded the warrior of another woman's alabaster flesh. *Ylera's story should be known — not hidden within the tapestry of deceit woven by Arris' heralds.*

"Yes, I will tell my tale. Perhaps you will be able to find the truth where others failed."

"Thank you for your trust. Please, sit by the hearth. I can finish your hair while you speak." It was a chance for Azhani to face away from Kyrian, so that the hard words could be more easily spoken.

"All right," said the warrior as she settled back on the floor.

Kyrian sat on the bed behind Azhani and took up her comb once more as Azhani spoke.

"This will not be an easy thing to tell, healer. Harder will it be to hear, for some of what Arris spreads is truth. It is bent to his desires, yes, but at its root, it is still fact."

"This is often so, with stories. Tell yours and allow me to decide what to believe."

"Then my tale's beginning, such as I have pieced together, starts thusly." Speaking softly but clearly, Azhani began, "Three winters ago, after successfully defeating the rimerbeasts for another year, I returned to Y'Dannyv. The army had been decimated and I had lost my father to the beasts, but we prevailed. King Thodan immediately turned his attention to his life long dream — peace between Y'Dan and Y'Syr.

"High King Ysradan was pleased by his friend's decision to end the centuries-long enmity and came to give his blessing to Thodan's efforts.

"By order of Thodan, I attended every meeting between the Y'Syran and Y'Dani delegations, though his son, Prince Arris, did not. Thodan's reason to sue for peace was simple — our two kingdoms could not continue to bicker like children and successfully ward off the ice demons during a beast year. Nor could we truly enjoy wealth and prosperity as the southern and eastern kingdoms did. Rimerbeasts had made living near the Crest of Amyra expensive, and Thodan knew that only by combining our efforts to destroy them could elf, dwarf and man prosper.

"King Thodan was well known to the people of Y'Syria, for he had often traveled to the city of trees as a youth. So, too was my father, for as Thodan's envoy, he would spend weeks in Lyssera's court. Because of this, I was chosen to go to the queen and ask for peace.

"Lyssera Kelani, who has held her throne for over three hundred years, saw the wisdom of peace. Putting aside the years of enmity, she sent her sister, Ylera, to act as her ambassador.

"Thodan and Ylera became fast friends. It seemed that Thodan had been acquainted with Ylera's half sister Alynna, which gave them common ground.

"Constructing the peace treaty took very little time. It was structuring it to satisfy the nobles on both sides of the border that consumed months.

"Thodan fell ill. Nothing any doctor or stardancer did cured the mysterious malady that affected my king. Day by day, he wasted away, slowly losing ground to the disease that was going to kill him.

"Still, each day he would rise, stand before the Council and argue for peace. Finally, at autumn's dawning, he was granted his wish — the treaty was ratified. In Y'Syr, Lyssera's nobles accepted the terms and suddenly the strife between our lands was over.

"Of course, this was not completely true. Ylera and I both traveled extensively, speaking to the peoples of Y'Dan and Y'Syr and encouraging them to befriend one another.

"In our absence, Thodan's illness progressed to such a degree that I was called home to stand by his side as the goddess took him home. Ylera accompanied me, for we had grown close.

"On the night he died, I was summoned to his chamber, where he named me as his heir. Thodan did not believe his son was suited to rule and made me promise to shepherd the kingdom he loved. As warleader, it is my duty to obey my king, so I agreed to rule, though I am not suited to politics." Azhani paused to wet her dry throat.

She and Ylera were close. Kyrian nibbled on her lip. *What does that mean? Were they friends or lovers? Should I tell her how close I was to the princess? She was my friend, too. Would that make a difference to the friendship that is building between Azhani and me? Or would she think that I can only hate her?*

Unable to decide, Kyrian quietly whispered, "Go on. I'm listening, my friend."

The simple use of the word "friend" sent tears streaming down Azhani's cheeks. Not since Thodan had any dared to grant her the appellation. *I only hope that she does not retract it when I am done with my story.*

"After Thodan's death, I went to the Council with the papers proving my inheritance. Instead of supporting me, however, they were tricked by Arris. Somehow, the boy that Thodan had depicted as a weak-minded fool managed to gain enough power to turn the Council against the sworn word of their warleader.

"Earlier that day, I had gone to pay my respects to Thodan's tomb and while I was gone, Arris had my — had Ylera arrested." Azhani's voice broke and she sobbed.

Kyrian gathered her into her arms and held her while she cried.

"She loved me, Kyrian. She loved me and he killed her."

In between sobs, Azhani told of how Arris had tortured Ylera, and forced her to sign a statement accusing Azhani of treachery. Then, he had killed her.

"Oh, goddess, what he did to her...I will never forget what he did to her, Kyrian." A beautiful face, marred beyond all recognition by blood and gore, swam in Azhani's vision.

"You loved her," Kyrian whispered fiercely. "And she loved you. You have to hold to that. She died loving *you*, Azhani."

The relief that flowed through the stardancer knew no bounds. Azhani had not slain her best friend. Nothing else about the tale mattered as much as this one, salient point. Kyrian could forgive Azhani any crime but that — and now she could counsel her with a clear and open heart.

Now that she knew that Azhani had not killed Ylera, she could allow the shock and anger she had felt over her friend's death to color her perception of Azhani's tale. Arris Thodan sounded like an evil that did not need to be unleashed upon the kingdoms.

Abruptly, Azhani pulled away from Kyrian. "After Ylera's death, I lost all hope. Arris arrested, tried and convicted me. I was to be hung at Banner Lake, but I knew of the rite of the guantlet, the old tradition where an accused could fight for their freedom.

"My choice was easy. It was better to die defending my honor than to stand silent and appear guilty. Also, it was in my mind that maybe my men would see through his pretty lies and come to my rescue, but those who had served under me had been sent to the borders. Only green recruits and Arris' personal guard remained in Y'Dannyv.

"Still, I requested the rite and he had to allow for my choice. The bards do not embellish much on this point, for I killed many soldiers that day. It was a slaughter. I lost count after twenty." She bent her head and sighed sadly.

In Barton, the women had learned the toll that Azhani's defiance had cost. One hundred and six men and women had fallen.

"I had to get away from Arris and his lies. I thought that if I could make it to Y'Mar, Ysradan would hear me and believe my tale. Of course, that was not what happened. When I did escape, Arris sent his men after me and I had to give up on going south. Instead, I went north. You can guess the rest."

"You are safe now, Azhani." Kyrian stood and stretched. Daylight streamed in through the shutters, announcing the dawn. The warrior's tear-stained face was stony in its silence. "And I believe what you say. Arris' actions are evil, and he must be held accountable. What will you do?" She pitched her voice sharply enough to hit Azhani like a slap.

"Do?" Azhani repeated dumbly. Did she want to trust Kyrian? Lay out her plans for revenge like so many counters on the sand table? No. She could not afford to trust anyone, no matter how innocuous they seemed. "I thought I'd head east and offer my services as a mercenary."

Kyrian snorted and began gathering the ingredients to make their breakfast. "Don't take me for a fool, Azhani. You reek of revenge. So tell me, what will you do to stop the spread of Arris' evil?"

The warrior shot up as though she had been burned. "Why should I trust you?" she hissed. Pacing around the room, she gesticulated wildly. "You claim to be my friend, you listen to my story, and yet the first thing you want to know is what I'm going to do? You're insane, Kyrian. I'm not going to do anything right now. I can't."

They faced each other and Azhani gazed bleakly into Kyrian's face.

"It hurts too much. Arris took a piece of me and fed it to the rimer-beasts. Yes, he is evil. Yes, he must pay for his actions. But I must find my own path to justice — I cannot just declare that I'm going to rip his testicles off and feed them to a snake!" *Though it's a great idea — if he even has any balls.*

"But you do want justice, Azhani, and so do I. The people of Y'Dan deserve to know the truth, so wherever your quest takes you, I will be at your side." *I hope that didn't sound as weak as I think it did. Goddess forgive me, but I do this for Ylera and not for Y'Dan.*

"No. I can't allow you to tie your life to mine, Kyrian," Azhani said in a deathly calm voice.

"You can say that, Azhani, but I will stand with you." Her face was schooled to a seriousness that she rarely exposed. "I swore friendship to you, Azhani. It is an oath that I do not take lightly. Please do not let what I offer be meaningless. Don't stand alone before the storm — not when I would gladly share the rain."

Absolutely dumbfounded at the ferocity of her friend's attitude, Azhani could only stare, mouth hanging open, as Kyrian made their breakfast.

"Here, stick something in that mouth before a fly decides it looks like a good cave," Kyrian said, handing her a bowl of thick, sweet cereal.

"I...but...by the blessed Twain, Kyrian, am I ever going to win an argument with you?" Azhani finally sputtered out.

Grinning hugely, the stardancer said, "Sure. You will always win the argument that says that it's your turn to clean the stable. In fact, I'll be more than happy to let you win. Otherwise...you've got your work cut out for you, warrior."

Shaking her head, Azhani said, "Oh no you don't, healer, you aren't getting out of your chores this time. It's your turn to muck Arun's stall. I did it yesterday. As for sharing my travels..." She closed her eyes and sighed. A good warrior knew when to make a strategic retreat. "I wouldn't have it any other way. I need you, Kyrian. You're the only friend I've got."

"And you'll always have me," Kyrian promised.

After breakfast, they sought their beds. Before sleeping, they reached out and put their hands together, palms up and shared a smile.

"Good rest, Azhani."

"Good rest, Kyrian."

Chapter Eight

Arris Thodan, king of Y'Dan and master of all he surveyed, knew how to throw an excellent temper tantrum.

"But I don't want to bed the scrawny chambermaid, 'Thyro! Bring me someone important!" he shouted petulantly as he threw his mug across the room. Smiling in wicked satisfaction as the scholar ducked to avoid the missile, he added, "I'm the king. I shouldn't have to choose from the nobles' leftovers."

The scholar thought quickly, reviewing the faces of all the noblewomen currently housed in Castle Y'Dannoch. Just as quickly, he disregarded all who were aged, blonde or under the age of fourteen. Arris had a taste for dark, older women and it was difficult to fill those needs when many of the nobles were either younger or light haired.

However...*Elisira Glinholt! Of course, Lord Derkus would be only too pleased to send his daughter to the king's bedchamber, especially if I hint that the king was seeking a bride.* Decision made, Porthyros coughed gently to interrupt the boy's raging.

Using a tone that had always calmed the boy, he soothingly said, "Your Majesty, what of the Lady Elisira? She is certainly beautiful — one of the finest flowers to blossom in this court. I could ask her to join you for tea?"

"Tea with Lady Elisira?" Arris grasped the name with childlike enthusiasm. Vaguely, he recalled the noblewoman. *She's Derkus' get. She'll be tall, with dark hair, and blue eyes...yes, she'll do.* "Yes, please, ask the lady to join me."

Lady Glinholt was not of the breed of noblewoman whose skirts were easily lifted. She would be a challenge for Porthyros, and the scholar did not look forward to the promises he would have to make in order to secure the woman's cooperation. Do it he would, because keeping Arris occupied with whatever wench took his fancy was part and parcel of his master's plan. If the boy was too busy bedding, then he wouldn't care to examine the suggestions his beloved mentor fed him.

In the months since gaining the throne, Arris had not been shy about accepting the women Porthyros threw at him. Elisira would be one more link on a chain that kept the boy from truly ruling his kingdom.

The drawback was that Arris quickly tired of his toys. None of the women would replace the one he really wanted in his bed. Azhani Rhu'len had been too dangerous to allow the boy to keep her. Porthyros could have found ways to keep the former warleader docile, but something about the woman's eyes warned him that her spirit was too wild to tame.

Too bad the bitch couldn't just die quietly, he thought snidely. He had regretted killing the elven ambassador, too. She would have been such a lovely addition to his chambers, but the master's plans called for Azhani to be removed from power in Y'Dan. To keep from causing a civil war, treason had been the only way to handle it.

With the populace tricked into believing that their beloved warleader had betrayed them, it was simplicity itself to install Arris on the throne as the rightful king. Now all he had to do was control the boy long enough for his master's plan to come to fruition.

Arris had been under Porthyros' care for most of his life and he trusted the scholar implicitly. Which is why, when the older man handed the boy a cup of tea, he did not sniff it suspiciously. Nor did he notice the strange taste — to him, this special brew had always tasted this way, and it was a flavor he had grown to welcome.

Porthyros watched as the boy greedily drank his tea and then held out his mug for more. "I will extend the invitation, Your Majesty. Will tomorrow be soon enough?" He refilled the mug and offered it to the king.

The second cup went down slower than the first. "A flower, you name her? Then yes, I believe that will do nicely. Besides, you've always told me that a man should often admire the flowers that bloom in his kingdom."

"Wisely spoken, Your Majesty," Porthyros murmured. "Now if you are ready, we should begin to go over these new documents that Lord Kesryn has asked you to examine. I think you will agree with his ideas."

Arris nodded vaguely. "If you think they're good, 'Thyro, then I'll sign them. Just give me a pen."

Porthyros dipped a quill in ink and gave it to the young king. "Your Majesty is truly a wise and beneficent king," he said soothingly, as Arris scrawled his name at the bottoms of several documents.

Lord Kesryn would be most pleased.

"Good evening, Porthyros. How goes our little project?" asked a voice that resonated deeply through the room.

Porthyros Omal, a small, undistinguished human of middling height and weight and thinning sandy-blond hair, knelt before an ornately carved chair and shuddered delicately. Seated in the chair, a well-dressed human of urbane good looks was messily enjoying a dish of bloody, uncooked chicken hearts.

"It goes well, Master. There have been no reports of the hated one for several weeks now. I believe she is either dead or fled, and in any case, no threat to you." Bowing his head deeply, Porthyros waited.

The urbane man, a dealer in rare gems, bestowed a beatific smile on his servant. Taking on the life of a merchant had been the most brilliant plan! Kasyrin Darkchilde gave a silent cheer.

Thirty years had passed since his first defeat at the hands of Istaffryn and Rhu'len DaCoure, and it would be sweet satisfaction to finally have his revenge. By selling his soul to a demon of the darkest origins, the man who had been born Keskyn Nightblade would someday rule the world as Kasyrin Darkchilde, the right hand of Ecarthus, the Eater of Souls.

For now, he wore the name of a humble merchant, Lord Kesryn Oswyne, and involved himself in the affairs of Y'Myran as a concerned citizen. The man sniveling on the floor below him was the only other mortal aware of his true origins, and the wretch would never betray him. Darkchilde owned the keys to his soul. Porthyros had a weakness for gold, and the sorcerer had access to limitless amounts of it.

Kasyrin had molded Porthyros into the tool he needed to bring about his vengeance. This included turning the former apothecary into a scholar learned enough to gain employment as a mentor for a prince. Hired by

King Thodan of Y'Dan to school his only son, Porthyros quickly earned the trust of both monarch and heir.

Time had not diminished Porthyros Omal's lust for gold, and Kasyrin gladly fueled those fires. Over the next several years, money would appear in a specially made box that Porthyros kept in his possession. With that money came the instructions on how he was to proceed.

While instructing little Arris in the subjects every good prince should know, Porthyros adapted to the luxurious life of a respected nobleman's tutor and learned how to move about without anyone giving him a second glance.

Arris' education included exposure to a drug known as krile. The substance had many effects, including hallucinations, euphoria and eventually, death. Those addicted to the drug were highly susceptible to suggestion, which made it perfect for use on the prince. As a former apothecary, Porthyros was intimately familiar with the proper dosages of the powerful toxin for keeping a person alive and tractable. Disguising the drug as a special tea, the scholar shaped the boy's thoughts as easily as a potter shapes clay. Over time, Arris grew into a weak-willed young man whose thoughts were controlled by his beloved mentor. No one suspected that Arris was anything other than what he seemed — a rather callow young man.

No one, that is, but Thodan, Arris' father. Porthyros had discovered just how little the king thought of his son when he found a document in the monarch's desk. Awaiting Thodan's signature, the scroll named Azhani Rhu'len as the heir apparent.

It had taken some quick thinking to stop Thodan's plan. Using his master's gold, influence and a little blackmail, he had bought the loyalty of the majority of the Council. When Thodan died and Azhani presented her claim, she was charged with treason and sentenced to death.

Though she escaped the fate they had planned for her, both Kasyrin and Porthyros felt comfortable with furthering their plans. The warrior was out of the picture and would trouble them no further.

If she returned, they would deal with her. Nothing would keep Kasyrin from his goal.

"I'm pleased with your success, my servant. How is my favorite king-let?" The sorcerer stroked the gemstone tattoo that was his mark of place within the merchant's guild.

"Arris is well, My Lord. He delights in his powers as king. He especially," the scholar coughed, "enjoys the sports of the bedchamber. Though I believe he pines for your nemesis, I have managed to distract him with suitable alternatives."

In only one area did Arris ever defy his mentor. At an early age, the boy had developed an unhealthy fixation on Azhani Rhu'len and had dreamed of one day marrying her. The young man somehow had believed that doing this would make his father inordinately proud of him, and no matter what Porthyros did, nothing could sway that desire. It was only when the extent of Thodan's contempt for his child was revealed that Arris accepted the scholar's advice.

The merchant-sorcerer chuckled. "I trust that there will be no unwanted complications?"

Porthyros' lips twisted into a grimace. "No, My Lord. I have made certain that those with any measure of power are rewarded for their sacrifice. The others are mere chambermaids, and of no consequence."

"Ah yes, pity the plight of the poor chamber maid — to be routinely despoiled and yet still have to scrub the floors!"

"His eye has fallen upon one whose favor we could use — Lord Derkus' daughter, Elisira, has captured the king's attention."

"Your suggestion, no doubt."

Porthyros inclined his head. "I aim to bring about my master's wishes in all things."

"Of course you do. Go ahead and allow the boy his fun with the woman. It should keep Derkus on a tight leash, and we could use his support in the Council. There have been some objections to the new taxes."

"On the subject of taxes, My Lord, I have these to deliver." Reaching into a pouch, Porthyros withdrew a roll of papers and offered them to Kasyrin. "As you commanded, the king has signed these."

The merchant accepted the papers, glancing over them quickly before tossing them onto a nearby table. "Good. These should force even the most miserly of elves to forfeit their property to the crown. The old temple of Seledine will belong to Ecarthus in no time." The old building, though worn with use, was still one of the most impressive structures in Y'Dannyv. It stood nearly five stories tall and occupied much of a city street. What drew the merchant-sorcerer to the building was its obelisk shape. The towering structure would be a perfect place to build an altar for gathering magickal energy.

"You've done well, my servant. Here is a token of my appreciation." He tossed the pouch of gold at the groveling man's side. "Continue to please me, Porthyros. I know you have waited long to spend the coin you have so assiduously earned, but I need you now more than ever. The time approaches when all that we have worked for will yield a perfect harvest."

"I understand, Master. I will do as you command."

"Good. You may go." Waving his hand, he dismissed the scholar, savoring his triumph.

When Porthyros left, Kasyrin rose from his chair and paced the room, staring at the luxuriant finery that he had surrounded himself with over the years. Treasures from every Y'Myrani kingdom glittered in every corner. He fingered a tapestry woven by the desert nomads of Y'Skan and smiled, recalling the long journey that had brought him much prestige and honor when he was just a young man. The smile turned vicious as the memories hazed over with the crimson hue of blood. The small band of nomads had thought to stop him. *Nothing can stop me.* His gaze went to the corner, where he could still see rust red stains that marked where the last man had fallen, clutching feebly at his throat.

Those days were long past. When he spilled blood now, it was for a purpose. A dark, evil grin spread across his saturnine face. His master had shown him the true way. Blood was power and as he well knew, power was everything.

"You thought you had destroyed me, Rhu'len DaCoure, but you freed me instead," he whispered, turning to grasp a piece of broken metal. Dried blood still decorated the shard and Kesryn could almost taste the pain that had accompanied the blow that had shattered the blade.

Soon, he would begin the rites that would break the locks binding Ecarthus to the abyss. On that day, all of Kasyrin's dreams would be fulfilled. The demon had promised him vengeance, and he intended to collect on that oath.

Istaffryn and the Cabal would be among the first to feel his ire. Then he would eviscerate every pathetic mortal who had ever thought to cross him.

There was only one break in the road to victory. Auguries cast by Ecarthus' best oracle demons named the DaCoure family as their greatest enemy. With Rhu'len dead, that left only one person to bar his success.

"Azhani Rhu'len must not be allowed to interfere." His soft voice filled the room with harsh echoes.

Chilled by the waters of Banner Lake, wind whipped through the city of Y'Dannyv, forcing the king's woodsmen to work harder so that the castle fires would keep their monarch warm. Arris Thodan leisurely strolled up the dark red carpet that ran from the archway of the grand hall to the foot of his family's ancestral seat of power, the Granite Throne.

Guardsmen stood at intervals along the carpet and each man made a point of nodding or bowing to his king. He seated himself and looked out on his domain. To Arris' left sat the members of his Council and their staff and to the right stood a smattering of townsfolk. Hanging from the upper archways were a number of Y'Noran banners. Arris yawned.

So Cousin Padreg's here to pay his respects; how perfectly pleasant. Arris was dismissive of the Y'Noran chieftain. *I wonder if one of those ignorant barbarians will do something funny and make me laugh. I'm bored.*

Seated below and to the right of the throne was Lady Elisira Glinholt, his current favorite among the noblewomen who peppered the court like giant flowers. Arris had no queen and therefore the competition for his attention was fierce.

Elisira favored the king with a vapid, ghostly smile that sent pleasant sensations coursing through the young man's body.

Tonight, he promised himself solemnly. *Tonight, you will be mine, lady-dove. 'Thyro will see to it.*

"Good morning, Your Majesty," the lady in question said demurely.

Arris studied the lady's full, wavy black tresses, her icy blue eyes and creamy complexion. He especially enjoyed her skin — it was alabaster pure. The cut of her décolletage was especially daring today, skimming into a wide curve that perfectly displayed the peach-like flesh of her breasts.

The king's eyes lingered on the lady's most precious fruit. Yes, this was exactly what he liked about her. Elisira was a beauty and she was exactly what Azhani was not — his.

"Good morning to you, My Lady." He inclined his head politely and then turned to face her father, the Lord High Councilor Derkus Glinholt. His chief advisor stood before the throne, head bowed, a scroll of state tightly clenched in one hand. "Good morning, Councilor. What news, My Lord?"

Hidden behind the blocky construction of the throne sat Porthyros Omal, listening avidly. In his role as Arris' spy, the scholar had secreted himself in the concealed place since the day the boy had taken the crown.

Arris believed that his servant chose to sit in the cramped space to better listen for whispered secrets among the couriers, but Porthyros had another reason.

Hidden under the scholar's robes was a special mirror that his master had given him long ago. Out of long habit, he withdrew the silvery object and a small, sharp knife. With a quick flick of his wrist, Porthyros pricked his thumb and let three small drops of blood drip onto the mirror.

Very softly, he chanted a spell. The mirror shimmered and vanished. The conversations of the king and his immediate courtiers would be recorded by his master's spell. At a later date, the information garnered would be sifted and examined to be used to his master's benefit.

The gossip included the rumors of four different cases of adultery, two of suspected graft and one wonderfully shocking tale of murder. He heard nothing that his master should know immediately, so quickly ignored the speakers in favor of watching the interplay between Elisira and her maids.

The younger women fluttered around their lady, offering sweets, wine and tittering conversation that consisted of, "Oh, isn't he handsome?" and "My, he's so wise." He wondered if the lady were as bored by the chatter as he was.

Porthyros was more than a little irritated with the prissy little noblewoman. He had gone to some lengths to ensure that the king would notice her among all of the women that populated the castle, and so far she seemed unaware of Arris' interest. No matter how many times Porthyros had hinted that Arris was enchanted by their lady, no perfumed note begging an audience with the king came.

If she doesn't send one soon, I shall have to speak to her father. He will be quite wroth with her. A grin shaped the little man's narrow mouth. *I should like to see her strapped for her insolence!*

The king murmured something that caused Elisira to laugh and Porthyros narrowed his eyes thoughtfully. Perhaps it was not the lady's fault that no note had been sent. After all, her maids weren't the brightest lamps in the castle. *It may be that I must be more direct,* he decided.

As soon as one of the king's pages appeared with a pitcher of chilled wine for him, Porthyros waved the boy down and whispered instructions to him. Nodding, the boy left the drink and dashed to the side of Elisira's chief maid. Speaking quickly, the boy imparted his message and scurried back to the kitchens.

Shortly thereafter, the maid sought out Porthyros. He had moved to a cul-de-sac formed by one of the hall's many archways.

"You wished to speak to me, Master Omal?" She curtsied prettily, fluttering her eyelashes and gazing adoringly at his feet.

"Yes. I have an invitation from King Arris to the lady Elisira. He would be most pleased if she would join him for an evening stroll after nine marks this night."

A smile flashed across the maid's face. She knew the dance of man and mistress well, having followed its steps many times in her life. "I shall convey His Majesty's wishes immediately, My Lord." Curtsying again, she returned to Elisira's side.

Porthyros watched as she leaned over and whispered something into the lady's ear. He nodded in satisfaction when she looked up at her king, blushed and then began speaking quietly to the maid. Now, if only the girl would cooperate and bed the king, he could get some real work done.

"**Of course I'm** ready to greet my royal cousin from Y'Nor! Please, show him in!" Arris declared loudly.

Porthyros sneered in distaste. Once again in his spot behind the throne, the scholar was grateful that he did not have to stand beside the king at this moment. The stench that emanated from Y'Noran herdsman was worse than that of the castle middens on a summer's day. He thanked the gods it was winter, otherwise the hall would have reeked unbearably. The diminutive man peered around Arris' throne to watch the hereditary ruler of Y'Nor, the chief of all clan chieftains, enter. The Y'Noran's heavy boots thudded dully against the carpeted floor, and Porthyros wondered if the giant leading the small entourage would shake the castle from its very foundations.

Clan chieftain Padreg Keelan was a huge bear of a man, with long, flowing brown hair. His eyes were agate green, and he smiled readily. Like all of his countrymen, he was clean-shaven and his skin was deeply tanned.

Dressed in leather garments that clung to his body like a second skin, Padreg cut an exotic figure among the silks and velvets of the Y'Dani court. Each piece of his outfit was dyed a different shade of green or brown, so that when he moved he mimicked the look of grass waving in the wind. Fantastic designs picked out in careful embroidery rimmed the neck and cuffs of his tunic.

His clan mark, a black horseshoe tattooed on his left collarbone, was proudly displayed. Around his forehead he wore a simple coronet of woven gold and freshwater pearls. His stride was that of a man used to long hours on horseback, and the dagger at his belt was more functional than ceremonial. Behind him trailed two similarly attired guards.

"Hail to thee, King Arris of Y'Dan," the tall man boomed out, in a thickly accented but strangely musical voice.

"And hail to thee, my cousin, Chief Padreg of Y'Nor." Arris returned the greeting with false sincerity. Rising from his throne, he waited for the man to draw even with him.

Padreg inclined his head and then the two men clasped arms. "I have brought you a gift, my cousin. Come and you shall see what it means to be chief of all the Y'Noran clans!"

Puzzled but intrigued, Arris followed the herdsman out into the courtyard. Porthyros scurried along after his king, eager to see what riches the Y'Noran had added to the kingdom's coffers. Standing on the cobblestones, caparisoned in the finest tack, was a beautiful stallion. A black mane and tail highlighted the ochre red of his coat and he was unusually marked by a white star that his forelock just barely concealed.

Arris' jaw dropped. "Cousin! This is a horse truly fit for a king!" Inside, he seethed, for if this horse was the one that Padreg offered, then surely, the Y'Noran mount would be even *more* spectacular. The young man decided right then that he would have 'Thyro keep a close eye on the visiting monarch. If he should happen to break one of the laws of Y'Dan, then Arris would seek reparation and the horse would be a splendid start.

"He's a handsome lad, isn't he?" Padreg crowed, patting the horse's flank lovingly. "Saddle up, cousin. We will explore your fine countryside."

Lord High Councilor Glinholt, who had accompanied his king to the courtyard, clapped his hands imperiously, and quickly a unit of guards rushed off to the stables. In minutes, the two monarchs were mounted.

I was right. His mount is far finer! Arris thought jealously as he surreptitiously stole glances at Padreg's horse, a butternut yellow mare with a pale beige mane and tail. She had a sweet gait that kept her positioned right next to Arris' new stallion, whom he had named Tyrre.

By the time both horses were ready to travel, Porthyros and Lady Elisira had decided to join the party. The former went because he could not afford to let the Y'Noran's ways destroy his careful grooming of the king and the latter because she adored horseback riding.

The horses trotted through the wooded area outside the city. To the horror of the Y'Danis, Padreg delighted in examining icicle-covered trees and romping through the piles of snow that bordered the roadside. Even his men seemed off put by their chieftain's actions, but Lady Elisira laughed outright when Padreg dismounted to gather up handfuls of the snow and pelt them until their armor gleamed wetly.

Y'Dani guardsmen fanned out on either side of the party and kept a protective barrier between the king and the tame forest. At the back of the group and barely able to hide his disdain of the barbaric Y'Norans, Porthyros rode in surly silence.

Clear skies blessed the outing. In the harbor, the Y'Noran ships rested at anchor. Pennants snapped gaily in the breeze and sailors could be seen darting about in the rigging like strange squirrels in a forest of rope.

The cold weather was quite startling to the castlebound nobles, but the Y'Norans seemed to relish the chill. They were everywhere on the road, looking at plants and trees as well as pointing out the occasional jackrabbit.

As they rode, Lady Elisira entertained Porthyros with pointless blather and obsequious fawning while Arris and Padreg traded witticisms and commentary about their respective kingdoms.

"Your country is a marvel of the Twain's creation, cousin," said Padreg as he gestured to the woodland around them. The massive trees were part of the same forest that extended into Y'Syr.

Arris smiled tightly. "It's nice." He barely glanced at the foliage. The young king despised the out of doors. There were bugs, it was cold, and his bottom was growing numb from sitting on an unfamiliar saddle. Padreg's enthusiasm for nature was a mystery to him. What was so special about a tree? Arris tried to see what it was that inspired the Y'Noran, but there was nothing of interest.

A burst of bright laughter trickled up from the rear of the party. Turning, he caught sight of the Lady Elisira as she threw back her head and laughed prettily. This was infinitely more interesting! Slowing his horse, he waited for the lady to meet up with him.

Smiling, he said, "Ah, My Lady, your presence on this day is truly welcome, but I see the cold has chafed your lovely cheeks. Perhaps it is time to return to our warm halls for a cup of mulled wine?"

Elisira tittered vapidly. "If that is what you wish, Your Majesty," she demurred, blushing and batting her eyelashes coyly.

Arris preened under her fawning gaze. He wondered if she would blush like that tonight, when he intended to bed her repeatedly.

Lady Elisira Glinholt observed the countryside around her with a sigh. It was far too cold to be riding in nothing but the courtly wardrobe her father insisted she wear in the capital. The fine silks and velvets might look beautiful by lantern light, but were no defense against the weather.

She wondered if she could get away with strangling Porthyros. The king's callow scholar had attached himself to her like a leech and she was tiring of his none-too-subtle attempts to woo her on the king's behalf.

She did not wish to bed Arris or anyone else. However, for her father's sake, she played the game of courtly politics. Instead of directly refusing Porthyros' offers, she put on the airs of one whose head is full of fluff. Maybe if he thought she was a boring, vapid cow, he would seek another's charms for the king.

Unfortunately, I cannot kill him. He is Arris' creature to the core. I could not survive the rite of the gauntlet and it would be unseemly to hang for smashing an ant.

The thought brought a flood of longing for her friend, Azhani Rhu'len. The cheerful warleader and her lover, Ylera Kelani, had always managed to make Elisira feel welcome at Y'Dannoch. Sadly, Ylera was dead and Azhani exiled and branded an oath-breaker. The noblewoman's heart ached each time she thought of the lovers and their tragic separation. Elisira knew the terrible truth behind the official lies. There was evil lurking in the heart of Y'Dan's king, and that knowledge chilled her to the bone.

She shivered and drew the light velvet cloak about her tightly. The only reason she had hurried to join this little charade of pleasure was to spend more time in the presence of the intriguing Y'Noran monarch. From the moment his bootsteps had echoed through the great hall, she had been drawn to Padreg Keelan. The man from the plains exuded a force of personality that both overwhelmed and welcomed her — much like her friend Azhani. Only she had never felt like swooning into the former warleader's arms like a lovesick maiden.

She looked over at the man and their eyes met. A jolt of pure excitement flashed through her, leaving her tingling and shaking. Suddenly shy, she looked away, but not before noticing that the Y'Noran's green eyes held a similarly shocked expression.

Have I been bespelled? she wondered. *I am not given to fall for handsome faces.*

"My Lady, I am so pleased that you will attend our king this evening for a late tea." Porthyros interrupted her thoughts with his oily voice.

Tittering lightly, Elisira replied, "Why I was truly delighted to receive the invitation, My Lord. To have personal conversation with the king — however shall I prepare?"

In truth, Elisira despised the idea. Her father, Lord Derkus, would gladly see her become Arris' bride, but it galled Elisira that she was viewed as nothing more than a token in the game of courtly maneuvering.

I wish that someone like Padreg would just take me away from here, she thought wistfully. She listened as the Y'Noran queried Porthyros on the nature of the flora and fauna in the woodlands around Y'Dannyv.

He's intelligent, charming and curious about the world around him. This is a man who would enjoy spending a night discussing the patterns of the stars, or an evening of pleasant music, or even a rousing argument on the nature of the Twins' teachings. She turned to look at the skyline of Y'Dannyv and sighed again. *I hate that city, I hate this kingdom and I most assuredly hate that man!* She glared briefly at the scholar beside her, who was nattering about the virtues of the regional bush that had so intrigued Padreg.

Clanchief Padreg, the hereditary monarch of Y'Nor, listened to the weasel-faced scholar with half an ear. Most of his attention was focused squarely on Lady Elisira. That she had forsaken the warmth of the castle to join them fascinated Padreg. He had thought that all city dwellers hated the out of doors. He was not at all dissuaded by the fact that King Arris was as attracted to the beautiful noblewoman as he was.

The lady was everything he found beautiful. Tall and proud but not overly thin, with a finely sculpted face that featured a pair of blue eyes that looked as though they had been chipped from the morning sky, Elisira carried herself with a self-effacing demeanor. Entranced, Padreg found his heart filling with strange, wonderful emotions as he gazed at her.

He was further impressed by her ability to handle her mount. Astride a high strung, dapple gray stallion with a penchant for biting, Elisira capably demonstrated her knowledge as a rider. No delicate court flower was she — easily controlling the horse with knee and rein. Thoroughly intrigued, Padreg made himself a promise to get to know the young noblewoman before leaving Y'Dan.

He looked over at the lady in question and was pleased to see her glance his way. Their eyes met for a bare instant, but in that breath, Padreg felt his heart expand to fill his chest. Time stilled and became meaningless. On the brink between one heartbeat and the next, Padreg felt his soul vibrate with a single, powerful note. *Wind on the plains! She's the one!*

As soon as it came, the thought vanished, leaving behind an echo of the intense emotions that had just overwhelmed him. Ancient sages, wise in the ways of the barbarian peoples who had populated the land of Y'Myran before the Firstlanders came told stories of the *korethkyu*, the soul's perfect mate, but he had never given credence to their tales.

He took another unguarded look at Elisira and began to question his doubts. *How is it that with one smile, she can rip the breath from my chest? I feel like an unsuckled foal, wobble-legged and fumbling.*

Elisira tried very hard not to return the Y'Noran monarch's stare, but couldn't help flashing the handsome man a smile. He answered her silent greeting with a brilliant grin that left Elisira feeling as though she had just attempted to break every practice pell in the armory.

Simultaneously disturbed and thrilled, Elisira kept her gaze from landing on Padreg. She wasn't ready to face the eyes that beckoned to her like a warm pool calls to a weary soldier. Within that green gaze, she knew that her masks would be useless, and she wasn't yet ready to forgo their safety.

Ignorant of the interplay between Padreg and Elisira, King Arris continued to plan his conquest of the noblewoman's maidenhead. Marriage was not something Arris was looking forward to, so he had told Porthyros that he would rather wait until later before choosing a brood mare. It would have to be someone who was properly docile, and yet exciting enough that he would enjoy bedding her. Until then, he was perfectly happy to sample the wares. Elisira Glinholt was a perfect example of the goods he wished to try.

As they approached the gates of Y'Dannoch, both Padreg and Arris spoke at the same time.

"Elisira—" Arris crooned smoothly.

"My Lady," Padreg boomed.

Caught between the gentlemen, Elisira fought back a laugh and put on a simple welcoming smile.

"Please, my cousin, you are the visitor, state your desire," Arris said lightly, his voice betraying no hint of his annoyance.

"Nay, cousin, this is your home, please, say what you will." There was no hint of anything but polite courtesy in the Y'Noran's tone.

The bumpkin has the manners of one court bred! Porthyros silently observed as the two men verbally dueled over who would get to speak to Elisira first. He knew that Arris would take the opportunity that Padreg had presented, because he had taught the king to ignore the social niceties when he wanted something badly enough.

As he suspected, the king asked the lady to join him for the afternoon meal. However, the lady surprised everyone by inviting Padreg to accompany her. Arris looked ready to chew nails.

Deciding that he had better interrupt before the boy king did something foolish, Porthyros smoothly said, "My Lady, I'm sure that Clanchief Padreg has matters of his own that require attending."

Padreg took the hint and said, "Aye, Master Omal, you are right to remind me of my duties." He dismounted his horse and began to murmur softly to her.

The burly man knelt at the mare's front leg and coaxed her to lift it. Using a small knife, he poked at the shoe and shook his head. "Go easy on her," he said to the stable boy standing nearby. "She's taken a stone."

"Aye, My Lord," the boy said, bobbing his head and leading the mare away.

Turning to face Arris and Elisira, Padreg said, "My Lord, My Lady, I would gladly join you for a meal, but duty calls. I shall see you both anon. The gods be with you." He gave a little bow and strode off in the direction of the guest's quarters.

Arris' face twisted into a facsimile of a pleasant grin. "My Lady, would you allow me?" He leapt nimbly from his horse and hurried over to her, holding up his hand solicitously.

Elisira watched Padreg briefly as he vanished into the castle and then turned to Arris' waiting hand. Sighing softly, she allowed her king to assist as she dismounted.

"I believe I should be truly honored to dine with you, Your Majesty," she murmured blandly as she tucked her arm into Arris'. *Oh yes, I'm so delighted to be spending the afternoon with My Lord Loose Breeches. Now, how am I going to play this? Perhaps the stupid, not-quite-bright-enough-to-be-your-favorite-lap-dog routine will cool his ardor.* She stifled a sigh. *I wonder what Padreg was going to ask me?*

The garden was silent, stripped bare of its usual floral brilliance by winter's chill. Drawn to the calm, sheltered space, Elisira daily sought the outdoor courtyard hidden within the center of Y'Dannoch castle. It was her sanctuary.

To ward off the weather, she wore a heavy fur cloak. She sat picking leaves and debris from an empty fountain in the center of the garden. Rising from the fountain was a statue of Y'Dan's founder, Prince Ysradaran.

Elisira glanced up at the ancestor of the kingdom's present monarch and shook her head sadly. She felt sure that Ysradaran would not approve of his descendant's recent actions.

Arris had not desisted in his efforts to woo her. Every night for the past two weeks, she had sat through meals and late teas and used every bit of her skill with courtly manners to avoid his thinly veiled hints.

Soon the hints would turn to commands, and she knew that her father would rather see her as the king's paramour than one of the other noblemen's daughters. Sharing Arris' bed would be one step closer to sharing his throne, and that was all that mattered to an ambitious man like Derkus Glinholt.

Unhappily, Elisira frowned. *By the Twain, why can't Arris be more like Padreg? If that were the case, then I would happily go to His Majesty's bed.* But the two monarchs could not be more unalike.

Arris was small, sickly and given to violent outbursts while Padreg was tall, exotically handsome and had nothing but kind words for even the lowest scullery maid. The servants assigned to the Y'Noran delegation were full of tales of how the plainsfolk were so chary of their services that they even bathed themselves! That much self dependence among nobility was almost unheard of in Y'Dan.

A tiny smile crept across Elisira's face as she thought of Padreg and his people. In such a short time, the man had made himself a permanent fixture in her musings. It was hard to recall a time when she did not laugh at his wry, clever jokes. Hardly a day had dawned since their introduction when she did not seek his gentle company.

In fact, he would be joining her shortly. Padreg had invited her to share a meal and had asked if she knew of a place out of the view of the gossip mongers of Arris' court. The king had heard tales of her blossoming friendship with the Y'Noran, and had done all he could to keep her attentions for himself.

How unusual that a man who lives without servants so easily understands their failings, Elisira thought, smiling. Not that she would wish to do without her ladies — *Blessed Twain, no! I'd lose myself in the folds and crinkles of my court finery in half a mark!* She also had to admit that she would not be half as successful at keeping her facade in place without the gossip of her servants.

Lord Derkus Glinholt had not been pleased with his daughter's choice of friends and had made his displeasure known, loudly and clearly. *"Barbarians!"* he hissed, shaking a finger at his daughter's face. *"They're all dirt-grubbing, horse-loving, uncivilized nomads!"* The words dripped with disgust. *"I will not have my daughter consorting with such men,"* he thundered. *"I can only imagine what horrors would come to you, my darling daughter. You are better off seeking the company of our gentle king, my dear."*

Elisira snorted in disgust. There was a crowned barbarian in this castle all right, but he did not wear a coronet of braided gold.

A breeze blew through the garden, rifling leaves and causing Elisira to shiver uncontrollably. She cursed softly at the cold, but firmed her jaw. She would not be chased from her place by an errant sprite of winter.

The soft clunk of a closing door made her look up and peer across the garden. Carrying a blanket and a large basket, Padreg Keelan stepped from the shadows. As he approached Elisira, he scanned the area for unwanted listeners.

"Good day to you, My Lady," he called out quietly.

"And to you, My Lord," Elisira replied. Smiling as she rose, she went to him and brushed a light kiss across his smooth cheek. *Yet another reason to like this man,* she thought, lingering a bit longer than was proper. *He shaves.* Arris, like his father before him, had taken to wearing a beard, attempting to take on at least the appearance of manhood. To Elisira's eyes, the Y'Dani king's newly grown facial hair only made him look unkempt and scurrilous.

Padreg joyfully accepted Elisira's embrace, clasping her close and breathing in the scent of her hair. The large man's heart hammered painfully in his chest as he held her.

"I am pleased, My Lady, that it is with glad eyes and open arms that you greet me," he murmured.

Elisira stepped away to allow him to spread the blanket over the cold marble bench.

"And I, My Lord, am most overjoyed to have my greetings so gladly returned," she answered demurely.

They traded knowing glances and shared a chuckle.

"I hope that you are hungry, My Lady, for the bounty of this city is as endless as my appetite!" He demonstrated his hunger by removing the lid of the basket and laying out several covered dishes of food.

"With you, My Lord, my hunger knows no end," Elisira said as she sat and quietly accepted a plate from Padreg.

As he mopped up the last drippings from his plate, Padreg said, "So, shall we continue our discussion? I believe that we were discussing duty versus honor?"

Chapter Nine

"You wished to see me, Your Majesty?"

Standing before the visiting monarch of Y'Nor was the Lord High Councilor, Derkus Glinholt. The nobleman wore an expression of bored interest as he waited to hear what Padreg had to say.

Padreg regarded the man who had fathered his beloved Elisira. With nothing more than the semblance of a placid smile on his face, none of the thoughts whirling in the monarch's mind were available for the nobleman to see. Padreg had learned the lessons of courtly wiles long ago. Though he had little call to make use of the skills gained as a fosterling in the high king's court, the education was one he never forgot.

"I am glad to see you prosper, My Lord," Padreg said solicitously.

Derkus bowed. "My thanks, Your Majesty. How may I serve you?" *What game does this barbarian play?*

"Shall I be blunt, then?" Padreg smiled at the look that flashed over Derkus' face. "Ah, yes. It is bluntness you seek and expect from me. Very well, I shall dispense with the frivolities of politeness."

Derkus returned the smile. "Indeed. In times past I too have found candor to be refreshing."

Nodding, Padreg said, "Then plainly, I have an offer for you to consider." He allowed some of the turmoil he felt to show on his face.

Derkus' eyes opened wide as he quickly glanced around the room, seeking out the tiny spy holes he knew were drilled into the walls of the guest quarters. Was there someone waiting for him to betray his king? He felt a trickle of fear chase up his back, and he had to forcibly restrain himself from rushing out of Padreg's rooms in abject terror.

Glinholt's loyalty to King Arris was bought and paid for by Porthyros Omal. Any offer the barbarian monarch made would surely be of interest to the king's shadow.

Gaping only momentarily, Derkus babbled, "Yes, well, please, go ahead." He would pretend to acquiesce to whatever harebrained scheme Padreg had concocted. Once he had enough information, he would bring it to the attention of Scholar Omal. He might even be rewarded by the king for his service. Derkus felt his chest puff out as he imagined the accolades he would earn.

When there was no immediate answer, Derkus said, "Let us share a drink, My Lord. Perhaps a little of this excellent Y'Tolian wine?" A page appeared and silently poured two glasses of the dark purple eastern wine. Another servant brought a chair and Glinholt sat, nursing the wine and waiting for Padreg to speak.

"Your daughter is a beautiful woman," the Y'Noran king finally said, setting his goblet aside.

Derkus quickly suppressed his surprise. *My daughter? What does she have to do with anything?* "I like to think she takes after her mother," the councilor replied, injecting a curious tone to his statement.

Padreg nodded sagely. "She must have been a woman of precious beauty to have given you such a daughter."

"She was my greatest joy," replied the councilor.

Padreg frowned. "I am a simple man, My Lord. It pains me that I cannot make pretty phrases to express what lies within my heart." He looked into Glinholt's face and shrugged. "I am prepared to offer whatever dowry you deem worthy for your daughter's hand in marriage."

Derkus gasped in honest shock. His heart hammered heavily in his chest as his mind caught fire. *What? No! This, this isn't, this is...* The mental gibbering stole away his power of speech.

Padreg smiled broadly, misinterpreting the other man's silence as shocked pleasure. "Mind you," the Y'Noran said expansively, "I'll not be giving you the entire contents of my treasury — surely you understand that those monies are not wholly mine. Whatever of my personal fortunes you deem a fair bride price, though, I will gladly pay."

Still not quite able to form the clever words that would deny the hulking barbarian anything but the swiftest kick in the shins, Derkus finally spluttered, "Your Majesty, I am, of course, honored and overwhelmed by your generosity, but—"

"But you must speak to your daughter first and ascertain whether she is open to my courtship?"

Derkus leaped on the offering like a drowning man. "Yes! Yes! I must, I must go and speak to my daughter. I could not force her to marry..." The councilor's voice drifted away as Padreg nodded knowingly.

"Then, if you please, convey to her my warmest regards as well as my fondest desires. I will await her answer most impatiently."

As soon as Padreg finished speaking, Derkus fled the room.

Once he was gone, Padreg stared down at the wine in his goblet and then drank it all in one gulp. It was done. He had made his offer, and now he could only hope that the lady in question found it fair. Never had he felt the need for anything the way he desired this woman.

Softly, he prayed to Astariu that the lady's soul would answer his and that together, their song would outlast even the brightest stars.

The old tales came to him then, warning him that the cost of *korethka*, the love of the spirit, was often high. In his land, *korethka* was a word used to describe those whose love was so deep, it transcended the ordinary.

Padreg felt his eyes moisten and his heart skip beats, knowing without a doubt that he had been taken. *Twins bless me, for I am a man lost.*

A gentle, airy laugh flittered through the room. "You flatter me shamelessly, Your Majesty," Lady Elisira murmured, looking up at King Arris through fluttering eyelashes.

The king and the lady were comfortably ensconced in the young monarch's sitting room, sharing a tray of food and a bottle of chilled wine. In an effort to create a romantic mood, Arris had tried to feed the lady with his own hands. Demurely, Elisira had avoided his attempts, feigning a lack of appetite.

Instead, she delicately sipped her wine and let Arris carry the conversation. He tried to get her drunk, but even here she would not cooperate, hardly taking more than a sip of her drink so that after many candlemarks, her glass was barely emptied.

Arris was terribly frustrated. *Why won't the bitch just get in my bed and be done with it? I've never had this much trouble with a woman.*

For two weeks, there had been a constant battle between Arris and Elisira. He would invite her to dinner and try to impress upon her how attractive he found her, and she would smile and laugh and still end up leaving without even kissing him goodnight! It was all very proper, and there was nothing he could claim offense at, for she was a noblewoman, and he had not offered to marry her. It was extremely frustrating though, and he was becoming mildly obsessed with her.

The last straw came when he discovered that she had been spending time with that oaf, Padreg. Why any woman would want to spend time with a smelly, loud, obnoxious Y'Noran was beyond Arris, but the fact that it was Elisira who was interested made the young king furious. It didn't help that Padreg seemed quite affable about spending time with the brainless bitch.

Perhaps the idiot had promised to marry her. Arris almost snorted. He didn't want a wife; he wanted a woman in his bed, every night. The woman he wanted just wasn't cooperating. That would change. Tonight she would be his, or he would throw her in the dungeon.

Arris sipped from the cup of tea that his mentor had prepared for him. He had even offered to share some of the special brew with Elisira, but she had wrinkled her nose and claimed that it smelled funny. What did she know? It was fine. Finishing it in one gulp, he steeled himself to deliver his ultimatum.

"Your pardon, Your Majesty, but Scholar Porthyros has sent me with an urgent message!" A page, full of the exuberance of youth, burst into the chamber. He bowed deeply to the king and then turned to Elisira, and said, "My Lady."

Hiding a smile at the interruption, the lady covered her relief by taking a larger sip of her wine than she had previously allowed.

Arris nearly struck the boy. With pained delicacy, he accepted the scroll. Quickly scanning the contents, he said, "You did well, lad. Go tell the cook to allot you an extra ration of cocoa in the morning."

Smiling, the page raced off.

Pushing aside his anger, Arris turned to Elisira and said, "My Lady, much as it pains me to cut short our dalliance, I fear pressing matters of state have raised their ugly heads. I beg your leave, and ask that you join me on the morrow."

Elisira lowered her eyes and nodded her acquiescence. Inwardly, she sighed, hoping that Arris would weary of the game and turn his attentions elsewhere. She really was tired of being the subject of every hushed giggle, every polite glare and every secret whisper of the court. There was no fun in being the king's doxie when it wasn't true.

"No need for apologies, Your Majesty." She giggled brainlessly. "You must attend to the kingdom."

The king led her to his door and then ordered one of his soldiers to escort her to her chambers.

Once they were gone, Arris left to join his mentor.

Elisira hated being escorted to her chambers. The guardsman who walked beside her was one of Arris' creatures and would never deviate from his king's orders. She had hoped to slip away and see Padreg, but her shadow would prevent that.

Resigned to an evening of light reading, Elisira prepared herself to pass by *that* door. Once it led to Ambassador Ylera Kelani's quarters, but now the rooms were used for storage.

What made the door difficult to pass was its nearness to her suite, for early one morning she had been awakened by the sound of Ylera's strident voice as she demanded to know what was happening. Peering through a crack in her door, Elisira had watched as men liveried in the colors of Prince Arris had dragged Ylera from her chambers.

It was just after King Thodan had died, and the kingdom was still in mourning. Curious as to why an ally would be treated to such rough handling, Elisira had slipped into a secret passageway and followed the prince's men to an unused section of the castle.

From behind a wall, she had watched as Ylera was brutally tortured and, finally, murdered by Arris and his men. The memories still gave her nightmares.

That will be me, if I don't think of a way to divert Arris' attention soon. There was no way she could allow herself to be used by such a man, even to save her life. She would rather die than to be the object of the madman's lust.

The drab stone walls of Y'Dannoch held no answers. She and the guard reached her rooms and she thanked him for his escort. He bowed and she went into her chambers.

She sat in front of her dressing table and brushed her hair.

I wish I had been born a peasant — free to turn my head away from the machinations of kings. If I could, I'd throw off my silks and laces and run away to become a pirate or a simple shepherd in the fields of Padreg's Y'Nor.

She had been quite taken with Padreg's descriptions of his homeland. A land filled with rolling, swaying waves of tall grass as far as the eye could see called to her like a green ocean.

But she was not the commander of her destiny. Her mother was dead, and her father held an important position on Arris' Council. She was an asset to be bought and sold like a piece of particularly desirable land and she would never be free to make her own choices.

Suddenly overwhelmed with grief and exhaustion, Elisira undressed, climbed into bed and cried herself to sleep.

"All right, Porthyros, what's so important that you had to interrupt my evening?" asked Arris as he breezed into the council chamber.

Porthyros was seated at one of the tables while Councilor Glinholt circled the oratory stage like a caged animal. His hair was in disarray and he was muttering to himself. At the sound of Arris' voice, he jumped and looked around as if expecting a platoon of guards to burst into the room. When none appeared, he threw himself at the king's feet and began babbling.

"I swear, Your Majesty, it was not my idea! I am loyal to you, always!" wailed the older man.

Arris' lips twitched into a nasty grin before he shoved the groveling man off his boot and snarled, "What are you prattling about, old man?"

Still on the ground, Derkus fearfully replied, "King Padreg asked to speak with me, sire."

"And? I still don't see the problem here, Glinholt," Arris said. Sauntering to his throne, Arris lazily seated himself and waited for Derkus to speak. Porthyros stood and moved to his king's side.

Crawling over to kneel at the foot of the carved granite monstrosity, the councilor whispered, "He asked about Elisira."

Intrigued, Arris wondered, *What would a barbarian from Y'Nor want with a useless slip of a girl like Elisira?* A lascivious smile brightened his face. *Other than the obvious, that is.* His mind drifted off to pleasant thoughts of ravishing the nobleman's daughter.

"He wishes to marry her, My Lord!" Derkus whined, bashing his head against the stone floor.

Breaking his silence, Porthyros softly said, "What nerve he has, Your Majesty!" The scholar was furious. He had finally found someone who kept the king fully distracted and she was about to be stolen away by some featherheaded barbarian. That must not happen. Examining and discarding options, he added, "You've given him nothing but hospitality and he thinks to take what you have marked as yours."

Arris sneered. "I should like to have him horsewhipped for his insolence." *Elisira is mine to use!* His frustration blended with his anger and he shook his head, "No, I will have him hung!"

"If it pleases you, Your Majesty, I did not give him an answer. He believes that I wish to consult my daughter first," Derkus whispered.

Porthyros almost laughed. "Perhaps we can just send him on his way with a simple no, Your Majesty."

"But he has insulted me," Arris whined petulantly. "I want revenge."

Porthyros sighed. Arris would be difficult and intractable until he was pacified. He could drug him into insensibility, but he needed the king aware and alert for an important vote in the next few days. How should he handle this?

Derkus kept quiet. So far, the king had not accused him of anything, but that could change in an instant. Arris temper was growing to be a legend, and he had no wish to end up like Azhani Rhu'len.

"You will have your revenge, My King," Porthyros stated softly. "This is what we shall do." And he began to outline a plan.

I must be a fool, Padreg thought to himself as he stared into the fire. Yet, what else could he do? He was a man of action and sitting around waiting for the gods to dump a solution on his lap was not the answer to his predicament.

He was certain that Lady Elisira's feelings for him were as strong as his were for her. Padreg Keelan was an honorable man, and there was no other course but to forge ahead and seek her hand in marriage.

Aden Varice, Padreg's most trusted companion, might have goaded him into action with the information that King Arris was wooing the lady as well, but the Y'Noran monarch knew in his heart that he was doing the right thing.

A light tap at the door sent him from his chair. Opening the door, he was greeted by the sight of one of the ubiquitous pages that served the Y'Dani court. The boy bore no message tube, but his face held a look of sheer terror.

"Yes, what is it lad?" he asked gently, purposefully keeping his voice low and even so as not to startle the coltish youth.

Devon Imry looked up at King Padreg's six-and-a-half foot frame and gulped audibly. "Y-Your Majesty," he stuttered, darting his eyes from side to side. He was terrified. At only fourteen winters, he knew that his words carried less weight than even the lowest soldier, but his father had raised him to know right from wrong.

Polis Imry had served the old king for many years before succumbing to the coughing sickness the previous winter. Always, he had encouraged Devon to do the right thing, even if it meant facing that which frightened him. Not even Devon's first attempt at conjuring fire scared him as much as facing the bear-like Y'Noran king.

"Well, come on lad, don't be standing there letting out all the heat, come in or speak, but be quick about it!" Padreg said, standing aside to let the boy enter.

The boy looked familiar. He had seen the narrow-featured face a few times. All the servants of Y'Dannoch castle wore green and black tabards, so the boy's livery was no clue to his origins. Devon bit his lip, and in that gesture, Padreg recognized him.

Elisira had called him one of her father's shadows, explaining that each of the councilors had special pages that served them exclusively. Looking the boy over with more interest, the Y'Noran waited for him to make his decision. The king's heart pounded as he imagined, *Perhaps he is here with an answer to my proposal. Perhaps she has said yes!*

Heart sinking rapidly, he realized that if that was the case, it was likely a denial, rather than the joyful acceptance his heart prayed for. Padreg couldn't imagine sending a page to deliver anything but sad news.

Devon looked around once more and then slipped inside the clan-chief's chambers. "Your Majesty," he whispered and then swallowed again. Screwing up his face tightly, he gathered his courage. "Your Majesty, you're in danger!" he finally blurted, and then looked around the room as if he expected rimerbeasts to leap from the corners to rend his flesh from his bones.

One dark eyebrow lifted as Padreg regarded the boy curiously. Surely he could not be serious. "Oh, am I now? And would you be the one sent to rescue me, then?" The boy flinched and Padreg felt bad. "My apologies, lad. Speak, and fear me not."

Devon stared at him for a moment and then the words came tumbling out of his mouth. "I was in the council chambers, preparing for the session in the morning — I have to make sure there's a fresh supply of pens and ink and that there's enough paper because sometimes the scribes don't always replace what they use." He took a breath and went on. "Anyway, I was in the scribe's box when I heard Councilor Derkus come in and he was pacing and walking and mumbling something about having his," the boy blushed, "privates in a crushed codpiece and then King Arris and Scholar Porthyros came in and they started talking and, My Lord, did you really ask for Lady Elisira's hand in marriage?"

Nodding, Padreg said, "Yes, I did." He studied the boy, whose face had gone white at his confirmation. "Did I ruffle a few feathers? Was she already promised to someone else?" he asked weakly. "To Arris?" he added, almost too softly for Devon to hear him.

"No, Your Majesty," the boy squeaked. Since Padreg had not made a move to hurt him, nor had he called out for the guards to come haul him away, he bravely continued. "They talked about you and the lady. They said some very bad things that my father would have switched them for, and then they decided to use her to get you to break kingdom law." The page's hands twisted his tabard into knots. "Your Majesty, you must flee. They mean to kill you!" Very quickly, the boy outlined the plan that would involve framing Padreg for kidnapping a noblewoman, a crime that carried the death penalty in Y'Dan.

The fire popped loudly, startling them.

"Lad, you've made a very serious accusation," Padreg said carefully, searching the boy's face for any sign of trickery. Finding none, he shook his head sadly. He should have spent more time among the people of the kingdom, instead of rushing to confirm Arris' inheritance. If what the boy said was true, and Arris was plotting to kill him, then the situation in Y'Dan was grave indeed. The high king would need to be informed. Only Ysradan had the power to remove one of the lesser kings, and only if that king was such a danger to his people that they could not survive a generation of his rule.

Padreg stroked his chin thoughtfully and then called out to the two men who had served him for years. Both had been stationed within ear-shot, though out of sight.

"What think you? Do the boy's words match what you know of the men he claims spoke them?"

Aden Varice spoke first. "I do believe the lad's a fair speaker, Paddy. There be a scent hereabouts that reeks of rot and it is not the kitchen mid-dens."

Thomas Gould was next. "Aye. Aden speaks it well, My Lord. The servants are all a'feared of their masters and the people are tighter lipped than a trout pullin' bait."

"And the others, have they found it the same?" Padreg asked, knowing that the men and women who served him would have done their homework, even if he had not.

Two slow nods.

"All right, then this is what we will do," he said, and slowly began to devise a plan of escape.

Eyes widening, Devon listened in rapt awe, realizing that he was the cornerstone of Padreg's plan. There was no question that he would help the Y'Norans. Not only was it the right thing to do, it was the good thing to do.

Still, if it succeeded, he would be taken far away from the only home he had ever known. *Papa,* he prayed silently, *let me make you proud!*

"I really don't want to kill him, 'Thyro. He gave me a nice horse," Arris mumbled sleepily as Porthyros helped him undress and slide into his linen bedding. The scholar had expected this. It was what happened when krile began to wear off. He was prepared for this moment.

"But Your Majesty, no one should be allowed to touch that which belongs to you. The lady Elisira is yours is she not?" he suavely asked as he tucked the sheets around his monarch, fondly brushing a strand of limp black hair out of the king's eyes.

Arris considered the question muzzily, his face losing the cruel edge it always held when he was in public, becoming that of a very young man. At Porthyros' words, his face hardened again. "You're right. No man will be allowed to make a fool of me. Carry on with our plan, 'Thyro."

"As you wish, sire."

"Thank you, 'Thyro."

"Of course, Your Majesty," Porthyros crooned gently. Arris' eyes fluttered and he yawned again. *So trusting, so easy to control...that's my boy,* the scholar smiled as he reached over to a tray and removed a steaming cup.

"Is zat m'tea?" Arris asked thickly, drowsiness slurring his speech.

"Yes, My King. I made it for you, as always," Porthyros said, handing over the cup and watching as the king greedily sucked the liquid down.

"Mm. No one else makes tea like you, 'Thyro. You gon' teach m'wife t'make it, too?" he asked.

I doubt she'll add the special ingredients I do, boy. "Of course, My King," he said reassuringly.

Arris smiled sweetly. "Good ol' 'Thyro. Always so good to me." Arris yawned again and closed his eyes, surrendering to sleep.

"Sweet dreams, My King," Porthyros whispered, stroking the young man's face once more before tearing his hand away and exiting the king's chambers. He had plans to make.

Elisira Glinholt woke up in shock at the feeling of a heavy hand on her mouth. Fear caused her to thrash about wildly. *They've come for me! I'm to be murdered!*

"Shh, My Lady, do not be troubled, you are in no danger," said a low, lightly accented voice she recognized as Padreg's.

Calming, Elisira nodded. It was still dark, yet she could see by the flickering candlelight that she was not alone. Padreg, one of her father's pages, and two manservants dressed in Y'Noran livery were in the room with her. The Y'Noran took his hand away from Elisira's mouth and she inhaled deeply.

"My Lord, what brings you to visit?" she asked with as much aplomb as she could muster, swaddled as she was in the silks and velvets of her bedclothes.

Padreg smiled in approval at the young woman's spirit. "There is trouble, My Lady. This lad here has brought me a tale of treachery and deceit. I fear I must depart your fair city. Before I leave, I have a question to ask of you."

"Ask it," Elisira said, fear clutching her heart. *Leaving? No, please, Astariu no, he can't go...*

"Elisira, in you I have found a woman without equal. Among my people, we would call what you are to me *korethkyu* — you are my soul's match. I must know do you feel the same of me?" The plainsman's face was filled with hope.

Elisira looked around the room, anywhere but into the eyes of the man to whom she felt so drawn. Though their interaction had been limited, Elisira could not deny the tangible attraction she felt for this man. Finally, she met his eyes and saw only gentleness and patience there.

Swallowing, Elisira said, "If my life were my own, My Lord, I would give it to you." The words felt incredibly strange, even foreign on her tongue. Though she had often prayed for a chance to know love, to actually speak of it made her feel as though she were breaking some unknown taboo.

Her words generated the most amazingly vulnerable expression on Padreg's face. They gazed into each other's eyes for a long moment. "You deserve to know why I must leave, My Lady." He turned to the page and said, "Speak, lad. Tell the Lady Glinholt what you discovered."

The boy stepped into the light and Elisira recognized him as Devon Imry. Her father's "shadow" quickly related a tale of intrigue and murder that had her clutching her blankets in fear by the time he had finished. She was afraid that it was happening again. Arris was going to murder another innocent person to attain whatever evil goals he desired.

"That slimy bilge snake!" she growled, and then laughed at the stunned look on Devon's face. "I'm sorry, Devon. Forgive my outburst."

Recognizing that he was among friends, Devon smiled shyly. For the first time since Warleader Azhani had been exiled, he felt safe.

"So Arris wanted to frame you for kidnapping me, and then turn around and make me his willing bedflower? How did he think he would get away with that?"

Padreg's cheeks flushed. "I believe he intended to lead me astray by insinuating that you wished to meet me some night for a private assignation. He would have succeeded easily, for I would have gone and willingly."

Elisira smiled. "You are a dear man, Padreg, but I am not worth your life." The dejected look on his face prompted her to add, "I thank you, though, for your chivalry." She reached up and laid a gentle hand against his face.

Capturing it and pressing a kiss to her palm, he said, "My Lady, I must leave tonight. It is unseemly of me to make such a demand of you, but I would know — will you come with me? Will you take my journey knowing that at the end of our road, I would seek to court you?"

This is it. This is my opportunity. Fear of the unknown held her tongue fast. The effort to encompass the meaning of his offer made Elisira's heart beat so fast that she thought it would burst from her chest. *I can be free!* "My Lord, your words have wrought a mighty blow to my heart. I am befuddled and tongue broke by their import."

Pain filled Padreg's eyes. "I am sorry, My Lady," he whispered, and started to rise.

"Nay! Stay the course, My Lord. I shall find my way through the words in time." Elisira gripped his hand tightly. "There is evil rising in Y'Dan. It infects the root and branch of my kingdom. What will we do, My Lord, to heal this wound?"

Stayed by her touch, Padreg laughed and said, "You have much spirit, My Lady. My thoughts this mark have only been upon escape — will it suffice if I say that I promise to lend what aid I can?"

"Shall it be war, then?" Elisira asked softly.

"It will be what it is," Padreg replied.

"Then I must avail myself of your offer, for I would not be at logger-heads with you, My Lord." Rising from her bed, she showed no discomfi-ture in standing in only her bedclothes before the assembled party. Stepping close to Padreg, she tilted her head and said, "Padreg, you are a plainly spoken man, so forthwith, I choose to eschew the language of court and say what rides so heavily on my heart."

"I should be pleased to hear it, My Lady."

She smiled and whispered, "Embrace me, My Lord, for I would know the kiss of the man I will marry."

Gently, as if he were touching the most delicate spun glass, Padreg took Elisira into his arms. His heart seemed to stop beating as he placed his lips over hers in a chaste kiss that held the promise of a life to come.

A light cough from Aden Varice broke the lovers apart.

"Paddy, Thomas and I have worked out something of a plan."

"Aye, Aden. Let us seek seats while the lady dresses."

They adjourned to the outer room while Elisira quickly changed her clothes. With Devon's help, she was able to locate the trunk containing her old riding leathers as well as more practical traveling garb.

Blushing furiously, Devon averted his eyes whenever he was not needed to assist Lady Elisira with her clothes. Into a set of saddlebags brought in case the lady had agreed to accompany them he packed as much of her clothing as he could. By the time he was done packing her things, she had given herself the appearance of a beardless boy.

Devon grinned at her transformation. "Da told me how you used to sneak off with Azhani and practice your sword work. He said you were the prettiest boy with whom he'd ever crossed a blade."

"Your father was quite the scamp and I believe you will follow in his footsteps, young man," Elisira said, laughing fondly and reaching out to tousle Devon's hair.

Her heavy velvet cloak was draped over a chair, but she left it there. Instead, she chose a lighter wool cloak from her wardrobe. A garment of rich fabric would draw unwanted attention.

Devon shouldered the saddlebags and they left the bedroom.

As she joined the others, Padreg said, "My Lady, the lads have informed me that there are two routes from which to choose. After we've won free of the castle, we can either head south to Y'Mar or east, across the lake to Y'Nor. Either course will have its dangers."

"Your plans are sound, gentlemen." The lady smiled at each of the men in turn.

"Then we will go east — to Y'Nor. I can always send a delegation to Ysradan once I am safe within the boundaries of my kingdom," Padreg said, earning nods of approval from each of his men.

"The direction of escape is not my concern — what I wish to know is how you planned to escape detection by Arris' guardsmen." Elisira's words caused the room to go silent.

"Shyvot!" Devon blurted, and then quickly covered his mouth.

Padreg raised an eyebrow in the boy's direction and then laughed. "Have you got an answer to the question, My Lady, or were you hoping to hear more colorful language first?"

Elisira chuckled and replied, "This castle has a wealth of secret passageways. Some are in frequent use; others have not seen the passage of feet for many years. Most are well known to the pages," she fastened an eye on Devon, who smirked and looked at his shoes. "They are known to me, as well. In fact, I would hazard that I know of a few that young Devon here, has not yet discovered."

Devon's head came up as he shot her a surprised look.

"How do you think I snuck away those many times, youngling? 'Twas not through the front gate, I'll grant you that," Elisira said wryly.

Everyone chuckled at that.

"I think if you were to send your men to the kitchen to fetch enough provisions for a picnic, you will find the cook quite willing to be generous. We can meet by the eastern gate and decide our trail from there."

There were nods all around, and Aden sent men off to do as Elisira suggested.

Padreg took Elisira's things from Devon and asked, "Is there anything else you require, My Lady?"

Elisira looked around her quarters and then nodded. Taking a rucksack from a cupboard, she filled it with her jewelry and a few personal things. Lastly, she pulled up a loose floorboard, revealing a hidey from which she took a curved saber. She belted the sword on, giving the men a look that dared them to say anything.

Once she was ready, Elisira led them to a hidden door in her wardrobe. One by one, they slipped through and made their way down a dark, cramped passageway.

With only one candle to guide them, it was slow going. Practically fused to the lady's back, Devon silently worried that they would be captured and put to death. He was as excited as he was afraid — for if they made it, he would finally be able to study magick in peace! As a page, he was not allowed much free time, so finding a quiet moment to learn the spells in his grimoire was always difficult. In Devon's mind, visions of becoming a great mage warred with grim images of dying a horrific death. Every step he took became fraught with a double dose of excitement and danger.

Padreg brought up the rear. Dagger clenched tightly in his fist, he was ready to maim or kill any who barred their way. He was a little worried that his people might find his actions rash. He knew that they would stand by him, but would they trust him in the future? The thought gave him a moment's pause.

I could always tell them it was korethka, he mused, halting his steps just before running into the young page's back. *No one would argue with a man who has been snared by spirit love.*

They came to a wall where Elisira paused and ran her fingers over the stone and mortar until she found the hidden catch. With a gentle push, a section of the wall moved away and another passage was revealed. It led past the main hall. As they traveled along the passage, Padreg noticed eyeholes set at regular intervals on the wall. He stopped to look at them. Giggling softly, Devon leaned forward and peered through one of the holes.

"They spy on the court?" Padreg asked, dumbfounded by the concept of paying someone to listen to courtiers gossip.

Devon nodded. "All the time, My Lord. I have often brought food and drink to the official court spies as they recorded the various goings on there in the hall."

"*Official* spies?" Padreg choked out, while Elisira covered up a laugh, continuing to lead the way.

"Oh yes. It's a good job, especially for a small page with sharp ears." Something about the way Devon spoke the words made Padreg think that the boy had probably served as a spy a time or two in the past.

Closing his eyes briefly, the Y'Noran king sent up a prayer to the gods asking that he be allowed to escape this kingdom and its strange ways. All he wanted was to return to his lands with his life, and the lives of his friends, intact.

Chapter Ten

Emerging in predawn, the small party broke away from the keep and sprinted across the common without being noticed. There had been many close calls as they had skulked through Y'Dannoch's hidden passages, but between Devon and Elisira, the group had avoided detection. Twice, Padreg was filled with fear that he would have to cause harm to a child, since it was a page who would have discovered them. He was relieved when they finally were able to leave the darkened halls behind.

Tall and broad shouldered, Padreg was happy to once again be in the open and unhampered by narrow walls that forced him to walk in a back-wrenching crouch. The passages had been designed for secrecy and not comfort, and he had fought down a severe sense of claustrophobia several times before they found the exit.

At the stables, they found Padreg's men waiting for them with the horses saddled and ready to go. Hazy blues and grays painted the horizon with the fingers of dawn. The horses were restless and eager to be off.

As quietly as a group of thirty could, they mounted, moving toward the gate of the outer bailey. The guards, sleepy-eyed and surly from a long night's watch, let them through without a word.

Fog hung low over Y'Dannyv, obscuring the harbor from view. The party passed a few early risers, but traveled in near silence. As they rode, the sky grew lighter and the sound of lake birds calling heralded the dawn. The scent of rain was heavy on the air. Fishermen on their way to the docks called out cheerful hellos.

Through the haze, the eastern gate came into view. There, they met Aden and Thomas. Their faces grim, they explained that escape from the city by ship would be impossible. The night before, Arris had ordered an "honor guard" to board the Y'Noran vessels and stand watch.

The two men had revised the plan. Each rider was given a bag with several days' worth of food; their escape would be made by land, rather than sea.

No one at the gate bothered to stop them. Traffic at this hour was hectic, as farmers and workers from outside of the city crowded through to get to their daily business. There was a palpable air of suspense hanging above the group — everyone knew that it was only a matter of time before their absence was discovered.

Elisira was miserable. The fog was cold. It seeped through the travelers' clothes and settled into their bones. Breath frosted in front of horses and riders as they carefully picked their way along the lake's edge. Drawing her cloak tightly about her shoulders, she wished that she had taken the velvet cloak anyway.

Noticing his lady's discomfort, Padreg fell back and drew even with her. "Are you cold, My Lady?"

A brief nod answered him.

"I've a heavy tunic in my pack, if you'd like to borrow it?" he offered. Much of their gear had been left behind in the castle, but he always kept spare clothes in his saddlebags.

Opening her mouth to answer, she was silenced by a shrill whistle. They turned and spotted one of Padreg's scouts moving swiftly toward them.

"We're being followed," the scout said before she dropped from her mount. The animal stood with sides heaving and the scout began to walk the horse until it calmed.

Padreg voiced a few soft orders and the group vanished into the thickets at the side of the road. Less than a quarter candlemark later, a small party of guardsman wearing the livery of King Arris stopped in the roadway. It was led by Porthyros Omal.

"Hurry, men. These scoundrels have kidnapped Lady Elisira and her life may be in danger! King Arris wants them alive so we cannot let them escape!" The scholar's thin, reedy voice encouraged the soldiers to dismount and search the area for clues.

Elisira tensed when one of the guards came within inches of Devon's hiding place. She gathered her courage and was about to reveal herself when a man appeared on the road. Dressed in the purple robes of an Astarun brother, he was leading a heavily laden donkey and singing a jaunty song. He stopped when he saw the king's men beating the bushes with their swords.

The man looked straight at where Padreg was hidden and winked. Then, in a loud voice he said, "Good morrow, your lordship! Have you lost something?"

In a pained voice, Porthyros said, "Good morrow, Brother Jalen. We are looking for Lady Elisira Glinholt. She has been kidnapped by that Y'Noran dog, Padreg Keelan!"

The priest nodded sagely. "How horrible! May I be of assistance?"

The edge of fear that had been cutting into Elisira's nerves for the entire journey suddenly slashed deep and she bit her lip. The priest had seen Padreg, and if he revealed their position, they were all dead. She tensed and—

"Nay, My Lady, bide a while," a ghostly whisper made her look up into Padreg's calm green eyes.

Reluctantly, Elisira settled against the large man. He pulled his cloak over her to share his warmth.

"Have you seen any Y'Norans?" Porthyros asked the priest.

The priest closed his eyes and chanted softly. A ball of white, glowing energy formed in his hand and then lifted off and shot like an arrow toward Y'Dannoch castle. Jalen's eyes opened and he said, "There, the finder spell should lead you right to them."

Porthyros gave the priest a suspicious glare and then called to the guards, "Mount up and follow the priest's guide!"

The men did as ordered, thundering off back toward the castle.

"This trick had better work, priest, or the king will know why!" With that, Porthyros wheeled his horse around and galloped off to catch up to the guards.

Once the guards were out of sight, Jalen softly called out, "You may continue on your way, my friends. Goddess bless your journey." He then took hold of his donkey's reins and walked away.

They emerged and Elisira asked, "How did he do that?"

Padreg shrugged and replied, "I have friends in many places."

She smiled. "No, I meant the spell. He wasn't a starseeker. He wore the robes of a follower of Astarus."

"It wasn't a spell," said Devon as he crawled out from his hiding place.

Turning surprised faces on the page, Padreg and Elisira waited for an explanation.

Suddenly bashful, Devon murmured, "About six months ago, I found a book in one of the castle halls. It was an old apprentice's grimoire — I tried one of the spells and it worked! But then my father died and..." He went on to tell them how his guardian, the master of pages, hadn't cared about the boy's magickal abilities. "So I've been reading when I can. Anyway, there's a sort of sound, which I can hear whenever there's a spell being cast near me."

Padreg clapped the boy on the shoulder approvingly. "Lad, you're proving to have some good paces in you. I'm pleased. Is there ought else we should know?"

Grinning proudly, Devon shook his head. "Well, I brought the book with me — I thought that it might prove handy." He looked up at Padreg hopefully.

"Good lad, study hard. When we get to Y'Nor, I know someone that will be very interested to meet you."

For three days the party tried to head eastward, but was repeatedly blocked by patrols led by Arris' guardsmen. Traveling by night, they avoided the major roadways. On the second day, they ran into a group of tinkers' wagons and managed to buy more supplies. Everyone was now dressed for the weather.

At dawn on day four, they stopped in a copse of trees not far from a small fishing village. Water for tea was heated on a small, smokeless fire while the tents were erected. Near the fire, Padreg and one of his lieutenants, Stefan Payle, conversed quietly.

"My Lord, we're not getting anywhere. King Arris' men have barred the way home to us."

Padreg fumed in frustration. "I know, it just seems fruitless to travel north — we are not prepared to weather the passes in the Crest!"

Stefan nodded. "Agreed. Perhaps we should turn west?"

Sitting on a log next to the Y'Noran monarch, Elisira asked, "May I suggest something?"

"Of course, My Lady. I welcome your counsel," said Padreg warmly.

"Send the main portion of your entourage east or south, it matters not, for it is but a diversion. The rest send north. There, we will seek—" she broke off, and shrugged, "a friend of mine. If she lives, I believe that she will be glad to assist our cause."

Padreg put two and two together and came up with allies. "You think to find Warleader Rhu'len."

Elisira nodded. "She is no more guilty of treason and murder than you are of kidnapping, My Lord. Of that, I am certain."

"All right. What if we do not find her? It is winter, and it does snow quite heavily in the mountains."

Stefan smiled. "You've survived winters before, Paddy. Besides, aren't you the one who has always bragged about surviving the desert in summer, the plains in spring and the sea in fall? Surely you'd jump at the chance to add the Crest in winter!"

Padreg glared at his old friend for a moment and then laughed. Pounding the man on the shoulder, he said, "By the Twins, man, we'll do it! We'll ride north!"

To better their chances of survival, the diversionary force was split in two. Stefan led one group east while the others were told to make as many false trails southward as they could. Those traveling alone or in pairs said their goodbyes and made their way from camp.

When it was time for Stefan to leave, Padreg gave him a rough hug and said, "Go with the gods, my old friend. I want to see you hale and hearty at the spring foaling."

Elisira was impressed with the Y'Noran monarch. He had spoken with and embraced each of the men before they left, giving them a moment of personal time with their leader. By the way each man or woman reacted, the noblewoman knew that this was why his people loved him.

Padreg watched his people ride away until they were distant shapes on the horizon. Standing beside him, Elisira could see how dark and clouded with emotion his eyes were.

"May the Twins preserve them," she said softly.

"Aye, My Lady." He put his arm about her shoulders and she clung to him.

"You should rest, My Lord. You too, My Lady," Aden Varice said, as he approached.

Padreg looked at the trail made by his departing men once more and then nodded. "You are right, Aden. Come, My Lady. Our bedrolls await."

Porthyros hurried through the streets of Y'Dannyv. Praying that his master would not demand his life for the trouble with the Y'Norans, he made his way to the merchant-sorcerer's home. Arris was losing interest in the game of cat and mouse that Porthyros had convinced him to play with Padreg's people, and the ladies of the court no longer held any glamour for a man who had used most of them.

Most of the important votes had passed. Lord Kesryn Oswyne now owned the ancient temple of Seledine. Porthyros sensed that things were going to start changing at a more rapid pace, and he hoped that his master would allow him to see it through to the bitter end. A small part of the scholar feared that Padreg and his people might somehow find the Rhu'len woman and join forces, but even that didn't scare him as much as displeasing his master.

Arriving at the residence, he rang the bell and was admitted.

"Oh do stop that groveling, you pathetic fool. I don't give a rat's ass about the Y'Norans, or that little light skirt Derkus calls a daughter! So they ran off. Good for them — it means fewer idiots in my hair." Kasyrin punctuated his remarks with wild gesticulations of his hands.

Flinching each time one of those hands came near him, Porthyros waited until his master had finished speaking. "But Master, what shall I do to distract the king?"

The scholar's nasal voice grated on the merchant-sorcerer's nerves. For a moment, he entertained thoughts of killing the bastard. It would be so easy to gut the man where he stood. If he angled the blow just right, he could produce enough agony to fuel a month's worth of household spells.

He shook his head. No, killing the scholar now would be pointless. Arris trusted him, and the merchant-sorcerer still needed to control the king. Porthyros would live, for now. But someday, someday, the sniveling little scholar would bleed.

"Give him a larger dose of krile, if you have to. Otherwise, find him a girl — or better yet, introduce him to the game of chess. I'm sure he'll find it quite interesting."

"As you command, My Lord." Porthyros bowed.

"Now, I want you to tell good Councilor Derkus that every effort is being made to find his daughter, and remind him that it is important that he not let himself be distracted. Tell him that soon he will reap the benefits of alliance with me."

"Yes, Master."

Kasyrin smiled wickedly. "Oh, and you might want to bone up on your theology, Porthyros. Temple bells will soon be calling the faithful to worship."

Inwardly, the scholar quailed, but he let none of his fear show. "Yes, Master. I shall endeavor to perform as you expect."

"Excellent. Do not fail me, Porthyros. I would regret having you drawn and quartered." He tossed the man a pouch of silver. It was enough of a reward this time.

In his throne room, Arris Thodan sat tiredly, staring at the empty hall. He had never considered how difficult being king was. The heavily carved and ornamented granite chair he sat upon was hard, and the decorations poked him uncomfortably. The gold crown that he wore upon his brow was so heavy and so tight that it was like wearing a band of lead. Removing it, he rubbed his head. The metal had worn away his flesh, leaving a thin but painful line of sores across his forehead.

"I hate this thing," he groaned wearily.

"Ah, but My Lord, the weight of the crown is a burden given only to those chosen by the gods," Porthyros said as he entered the room from behind the throne.

Arris sighed. "I'm tired. Can I go to bed now?"

"Soon, Your Majesty," crooned the scholar. "First, you must sign these documents. They are to formally accuse Padreg of kidnapping the Lady Elisira."

"Oh, all right." Arris yawned. "Just have them killed or something." He waved his hand nonchalantly. "I did enjoy that new game you taught me. Will there be someone to play with tomorrow?"

"Of course, My Liege," Porthyros said, smiling as Arris signed a dozen different documents without bothering to read them. The first three were about the Y'Norans, but the rest were the first steps his master had instructed him to take. In a very short time, the Y'Dani populace was going to have a new god to worship.

"Good. Today, Lord Cathemon spoke of a merchant who was a master at this game — I should like to meet him."

"Name him, and I shall extend him an invitation to join you for an afternoon."

Arris stood and stretched. "Lord Kesryn Oswyne, I think he said. Have I met him?"

Porthyros smiled broadly. "Indeed you have, Your Majesty. He is one of the architects of our policies that have restored a sense of law and order to Y'Dan." *Master Kasyrin will be so pleased.*

"Then I shall be doubly pleased to engage his agile mind in this game of shrewd thinkers. Do you think I'll best him?"

The scholar tried hard not to laugh. "Surely, Your Majesty, anything is possible."

The king smiled while Porthyros gathered the signed documents.

"Now, I shall go prepare your tea. Why don't you take the time to enjoy a bath? I'll send a doctor up to put some salve on your head."

"That sounds good, 'Thyro." Arris shuffled off to his chambers.

A manservant would bathe him while the chambermaids prepared his bed. With any luck, the king would be distracted by the woman Porthyros had chosen to warm the king's sheets. With the added presence of the doctor, he calculated that he would have just enough time to send his master the newly signed documents.

Chapter Eleven

"I can't believe we're finally finished" Kyrian said as she huddled closer to the fire and sipped mulled cider.

Azhani shrugged. "We worked hard, and the place is small. I'm glad we were able to clean out the stable for Arun. I thought he was going to do tricks when I opened his new stall."

Kyrian chuckled at the image of her gelding acting like a circus acrobat. In truth, the horse had all but danced a jig as Azhani had led him into his new home. Now that everything was as done as it was going to be – the main room was a cozy place to sleep, cook and sit – Kyrian was grateful for the comfort, for the snow was waist deep and thickening.

Azhani continued to provide fresh food by trapping and fishing. Recently, she had brought in the carcass of a bear. Woken early from its hibernation, it had attacked her while she was fishing. It had taken several candlemarks to prepare the meat for curing, but it and the hide were now in the storeroom.

Leaning forward, the stardancer stirred the pot of bear stew bubbling on the fire. "You know, you shouldn't have to go out for a few days, since we have all that meat now."

"No, I suppose not," mused the warrior, but Kyrian heard the hesitation in her voice.

"But you will anyway, won't you?" She turned and grinned at her friend. Azhani looked away. "Oh come on, I know you by now. You love going out there in that awful weather and slogging through piles of snow! You're as bad as a child, Azhani Rhu'len!" Kyrian said gently.

When the warrior didn't reply, Kyrian sighed softly. She had pushed too hard again. This happened occasionally. Their personalities, while mostly compatible, could run afoul of each other at the oddest of moments, leaving the air between them colder than a mountain blizzard. Opening her mouth to apologize, she was forestalled by Azhani's voice.

"Yes, I do like being out there. It reminds me of the years I spent patrolling the kingdom. I'd rather be outside, riding under the open sky, than cooped up in a tiny cottage," she said quietly.

Kyrian nodded, accepting the tiny gem of information about her friend silently.

Azhani stood and paced around the room then reached for one of the practice blades that lined the wall by the door. "Spar with me?"

It had become habit to work out with each other. From Azhani, Kyrian learned how to counter and defeat a number of melee weapons while Kyrian taught Azhani how to master elements of the Dance.

"You bet!" Kyrian said. She shrugged out of her robes and took up the padded rod that represented her baton and met Azhani in the center of the room.

The exercise went well and left both women tired enough to sleep the night through.

Wiping her face, Kyrian looked up at Arun and said, "Sweet goddess, but I wish you wouldn't eat so much!" Today was her day to muck out the gelding's stall and she had been hard at work most of the afternoon. She thought of the job that Azhani had taken, shoveling pathways around the homestead, and realized that she probably had the easier assignment.

The steady, even crunching of a shovel hitting the snow trickled in to the stable. Looking out of the window, she could see Azhani's progress. The work must have been enough to keep her warm, for she was clad in a sleeveless tunic and a pair of breeches. Muscles stood out in relief against the dark skin of Azhani's arms and a thin band of sweat stained the back of her tunic.

The braids that Kyrian had painstakingly twisted the warrior's hair into were tied back with a thick leather thong. Kyrian sighed and muttered, "You know, Arun, it's a damn shame she's so beautiful."

The horse looked at her.

Kyrian chuckled. "I know — don't get a crush on your dead best friend's lover." She shook her head. *Well, Ylera, I don't have to ask what you saw in her — she's quite a person. Being friends with her is wonderful, but a part of me wishes that I had a chance for more.*

Azhani finished another path and stuck her shovel into the snow. Drinking deeply from a waterskin, she reached for her sword and took a few practice runs, twirling the blade about her as if she faced a multitude of foes. In the middle of this exercise, she traded the sword for the shovel and finished her practice with the unconventional weapon.

Transfixed by the display, Kyrian sighed heavily.

Arun lipped Kyrian's hair.

Kyrian laughed. "All right, I'll find you a treat." She produced a carrot and fed it to the horse. Soon, she could hear the sound of Azhani working again.

"I like her, Arun. She's a good friend."

The horse snorted.

"You're a good friend too, boy, but she's special. She makes me feel...like I'm normal — like my robes are nothing more than something I put on in the morning, rather than some goddess-given shroud of all knowing authority."

Blowing air through his lips, Arun nosed her, searching for another treat.

"Piggy," Kyrian said with a chuckle. The horse turned sad eyes on her and she capitulated. "Oh, all right. Here, this is my last one." She gave him another carrot.

With one last glance at Azhani, she returned to her work. "I'm so glad there's only one of you, Arun," she muttered as she cleaned.

Fouled straw was sifted and replaced with fresh. The remaining dirty straw was shoveled into the compost heap. Dusk had turned the sky indigo by the time she was finished. She was about to stick her pitchfork into a bale of hay when Arun whinnied loudly and shoved her against the wall of the stable.

This was the horse's signal that something dangerous was near. Cocking her head, Kyrian listened to the sounds filtering in from outside. The regular crunch of Azhani's shovel had ceased. She heard night birds, the stream, and then, a crackle of breaking branches.

Fearful now, she crept toward the door and peered out, searching for the source of the sound. Nothing but snow and the dark bulk of the out-house met her gaze. *Must've been the wind. Arun's jumping at shadows.* Driving the pitchfork into a bale, she reached for her robe.

As her hand touched the crimson fabric, she was grabbed from behind. Massive, fur-covered arms were wrapped around her body, crushing her slowly. There was an odor of pungent foulness that made her dizzy. Color-ful spots began to flash before her eyes as she fought to breathe. With all her strength focused in one blow, she kicked backwards, striking her assail-ant in the knee. It roared and loosened its grip, allowing Kyrian to gulp in air.

She screamed, "Azhani!"

Roaring again, it shook her roughly. She head-butted its chest and struggled to get free, kicking it in the shin. It barked in pain and partially lost its hold on her. Tearing herself free, she jumped back and grabbed the pitchfork. Brandishing it, she again called out for Azhani.

Facing her attacker, she was shocked to be confronted by a monster straight out of a bard's nightmare — a rimerbeast! Ugly yellow eyes gazed out from a body sculpted to terrify. Thick, gray fur curled and tufted around a pig-like snout. Hunched, it stood well over six feet tall. At the ends of its gnarled paws, three-inch claws gleamed wetly in the lamplight. It growled and lunged for her.

Yelling, Kyrian swung wildly and scored a glancing blow on the rimer-beast's head.

Arun, eyes rolling in terror, rushed from the stable and nearly bowled Azhani over. Azhani heard the sounds of a fight and raced toward the sta-ble at full speed fearing that Kyrian was in danger. Azhani leaped away from the charging horse and continued toward the building.

The monster rushed the stardancer. Using hay bales as a bridge, Kyr-ian jumped up and ran over the straw toward the doorway while the crea-ture flailed about in its attempt to grab her.

She had almost made it to the door when a hairy paw wrapped around her ankle and pulled her down. Dragging her further back inside the shed, the creature crooned its pleasure while she ineffectually beat at it with the pitchfork. The monster's gray fur was soon dappled with yellow ichor as wounds appeared in its thick, tough hide.

She tried to escape, but her efforts were for naught. The beast's grip was too tight. Inexorably, it dragged her toward its dripping maw, sharp teeth glistened with saliva. Kyrian began to sob uncontrollably.

Then, a piercing wail filled the shed and the priest went limp with relief. There had never been a more beautiful sound.

Shouting, "Hang on, Kyrian!" Azhani raced through the door. Her sword flashed – the creature roared in pain and Kyrian fell to the ground.

Freed, Kyrian scrambled backwards to cower in a corner of the stall, shaking uncontrollably. Sobbing, Kyrian flung the monster's severed paw away and tried to pretend that she was somewhere else.

"Come on you Twins-forsaken piece of shyvot, come and get me!" Azhani yelled, as she slashed at the beast. An ear went flying, spattering the wall of the shed with steaming blood.

Pain maddened, the rimerbeast threw back its head, let out a chilling cry and then plowed into Azhani, knocking her down. Rearing up, he smacked her in the head, tearing deep gashes down the side of her face and neck. Azhani shouted and kicked upward, driving her heel into the creature's gut. Carrion-scented air exploded around her as the monster choked.

"No! Get off her!" Startled from her paralytic fear, Kyrian surged up, grabbed the discarded pitchfork and swung it in a double-handed arc. The weapon, driven by fear and anger, penetrated deep into the monster's back. Viciously, she twisted the tool in an attempt to push the monster away from her friend.

Without the weight of the demon, Azhani was able to roll away. Bouncing up, she beheaded the beast with an arcing cut that sent its head flying. Not pausing to watch the beast's dying moments, she darted outside and began to search the grounds for more of the monsters. When none appeared, she returned to check on Kyrian.

She found her vomiting in the snow just outside the stable door. Driving her sword into the ground, the warrior knelt next to her friend and rubbed Kyrian's back until she caught her breath. Kyrian was trembling violently, and her face was streaked with tears. Azhani was deeply concerned for her friend, but knew that they had to get out of their bloodstained clothes quickly.

Already she could feel the caustic effects of the sickly yellow blood as it burned into her skin. Scooping up handfuls of snow, she began to wash as much of the ichor away as she could. Weakly, Kyrian tried to help her, but her efforts were ineffectual.

The attack deeply affected Kyrian. The raiders had been evil, but the monster was a creature driven by a hunger that seemed unstoppable. The terrified stardancer could not erase the image of the beast's gaping maw from her mind.

"Wa-was that a-a...?" she finally croaked.

"Rimerbeast," Azhani tersely replied. "All right, healer, we need to get out of these clothes. They're useless now. Come on, stand up." Keeping her voice firm but gentle, she coaxed Kyrian to stand.

Like a newborn kitten, the stardancer blindly allowed Azhani to strip the clothes from her body. Chilled to the bone, Kyrian began to feel better once the sticky reminder of the monster was gone. "Thanks," she murmured through chattering teeth.

"Now, go into the house and bandage your leg. I will take care of the body," Azhani said in a tone that brooked no argument.

Kyrian nodded and ran to the cottage.

Whistling sharply, the warrior waited for Arun to appear. Shortly, the frightened horse trotted up the road and leaped over the low fence. He came within five feet of her before shying away.

"I know, boy. Stinks like death over here. You just wait there; I've got a job for you," she said soothingly.

The horse's ears flicked, but he stood and watched her.

Quickly, Azhani ducked into the shed and grabbed a large piece of canvas. She pulled the pitchfork from the carcass of the rimerbeast and tossed it aside. Using the canvas, she gathered the beast's severed parts and tied them into a bundle.

Returning outside, she saddled Arun and took the end of the rope. She buried the demon in the forest, far away from the homestead. When she returned, she found Kyrian cleaning the stable.

The stardancer took charge of her horse while Azhani burned the fouled straw and clothing.

"You're hurt," Kyrian said as they watched the flames consume the evidence of the battle.

"Yep. Feels like it tried to rip my head off," Azhani said, wincing as the stardancer reached up and began probing the wounds.

"I need to get you inside and bandage that. C'mon." Kyrian tugged on Azhani's hand.

Suddenly, Azhani pulled the stardancer close, crushing her against her chest. Kyrian's breath whooshed out in a gasp, but she gladly accepted the embrace, wrapping her arms around Azhani's waist and clinging tightly.

"Thought I'd lost you," Azhani murmured brokenly, shuddering as hot tears dripped into the stardancer's hair. "I don't think I'd like that too much."

"It's all right, Azhani. I'm not going anywhere," Kyrian said gently. *I'm never going anywhere that doesn't keep me by your side.* "I'm so glad you were here. You saved my life – again."

Azhani laughed, releasing her. "And you saved mine! It was a very impressive move, my friend. The beast never saw it coming." Dropping her arm around Kyrian's shoulders, she started walking toward the cabin. "Now, you mentioned something about fixing my face? Because it hurts like beasts."

"Yes, come on. I've got medicine waiting inside," Kyrian said as they walked. "You know, I never thought I'd ever use that charcoal-colored paste that the Y'Skani doctors gave me, but they really pressed how important it was to use it on any wounds received from an ice demon. Now that I've seen what kind of damage they do, I understand why." She looked up at Azhani, who nodded.

"Infection. The claws are poisonous. I've lost too many men that way," Azhani said through gritted teeth. The adrenalin rush was wearing off and now the pain was eating into her, making her feel as though someone was pouring streams of hot lava down the side of her head.

Hearing the agony in her friend's voice, Kyrian increased her pace. *I'll take care of you, Azhani, just like you took care of me.*

Thick, driving rain snuck into the nooks and crannies of Elisira's clothes, causing her to shiver. She wished again that they had been able to stay in a town. When posters announcing a bounty on their heads had appeared on walls in the towns and villages, they had returned to the chilly embrace of the wilderness. They rode north, sticking to trade routes. It had been a week since they had seen anything besides an occasional rabbit.

Barton was their goal — a tiny pinpoint on a crude map that an innkeeper had made for them. If anyone in the north had seen Azhani, it would be the lawless folk of the free town. The innkeeper had spoken of the people of Barton in hushed, fearful tones, and Elisira had been reluctant to go to a place that inspired such trepidation. The achingly cold weather had erased any fears. She dreamed of the day she would sup with the scoundrels of the kingdoms, for then she would at least be warm.

Two of Padreg's men had taken ill during the journey. One man had died in his sleep, his body unable to fight off the horrible coughing sickness. Another, a woman named Syrah Jessup, was still fighting, but was very weak and would probably not live out the week. Their party was down to a mere handful, which did not afford the noblewoman much sleep.

Strange noises flitted around the camp, scaring the city-bred noblewoman to stiffness. Barely warm nights were broken by bone-shattering mornings of cold so intense that everyone's face was bright red within marks of waking.

In one of the towns they had stopped at, Kellerdon, Padreg had purchased extra equipment. Had he not done so, they would all be dead. He had bought them new tents that clung to the ground and bent the arctic winds over the sleepers, creating a tunnel of comfort. Even the horses were sheltered within the tube.

Elisira was almost used to the scent of wet horse. It wasn't as fuggy as the musty scent of wet dog, or as pleasant as the smell of dew-spattered grass. Still, she supposed life could be worse. Instead of spending her time in the company of people she liked, she could be stuck in Y'Dannyv, living a life as King Arris' doxie.

Padreg made her feel lightheaded, breathless and free. Arris had left her frightened, dirty and nauseated. As uncomfortable as her current life was, it was eminently preferable to what she had left behind. Elisira wiped her nose and sighed. If only it wasn't so damnably cold.

Rain gave way to sleet and then to snow as they picked their way northward. Elisira peered down the road, seeking Padreg's scouts. The men were about a half-mile away, and, with any luck, still following the right trail. Not one of the Y'Norans had ever been so far north, and finding the path through the storms had been part luck and part skill.

Food was the one resource that they needed. Their supplies were almost gone. Hunting supplemented their meager stores, but the further they traveled, the less game there was.

With less than a pound of dried meat and a few handfuls of rice, everything growing was tested for edibility. They discovered that some of the trees had parts that could be boiled into a thick, bitter broth that tasted horrible but was filling.

Elisira looked at Devon and was surprised to see the light down of a first beard hugging his narrow boned chin. *He's grown so much...* In the weeks since leaving Y'Dannyv, the gawky boy had sprouted almost two inches, now meeting her eye to eye. His voice was also undergoing the painfully embarrassing tonal changes of puberty. One moment, she would hear the enthusiastic boy and the next, the ghost of the man he would become echoed from his mouth. She was uncertain of his progress in his skills as a mage, but as a sling user, he was top notch. Many of their evening meals were provided by his quickness with the shepherd's weapon.

For Devon's sake, as well as their own, Elisira prayed that they were as near to Barton as the map promised. She was coming to realize that distances in the Y'Dani woods were deceiving and could mean candlemarks or days. Unfortunately, they did not have days.

Freeing a hand to brush accumulated snow away from her face, she looked for Padreg and found him conferring with Aden. The tall king gestured and Aden shook his head. Padreg gestured again, furiously, and again, Aden's response was negative. The young noblewoman clicked to her horse, encouraging him to join Padreg and his liegeman.

"My Lord, is there something amiss?" she called out softly as she drew closer.

Smiling unconsciously at her approach, Padreg turned to greet her. "Nay, My Lady, it is nothing to disturb yourself with," he replied.

She raised an elegant eyebrow. "Your man looks fair ready to burst, Paddy. Please, do not think to protect me by hiding ill winds from my knowledge. They will still blow fetid and rank."

"Aptly put, My Lady," Aden whispered, hiding a smirk.

Padreg sighed in resignation. "As you will, My Lady. Aden brings word that we are being tracked by something other than bounty hunters. He claims that rimberbeasts hunt the snows, though he has yet to see the creatures."

Elisira felt her heartbeat treble. "Ice demons, Aden? You are certain?"

The man nodded warily. "As certain as I can be, with only fire tales and book learning to guide me. I've never faced one of the beasts, but the histories are fairly clear on the signs — shadows in the wind, the scent of rot, and of course, the ochre slime of their waste. Look here." He held up a leather-wrapped dagger that was coated in yellowish goo. "I found this not more than a candlemark ago."

The foul substance steamed and bubbled as it ate through the knife blade and left behind blackened pits. Elisira paled.

"We must seek shelter, My Lord. Your man is correct in his tracking. Demons hunt this land," Elisira said firmly, turning to scan the road ahead. "If they have our scent, it will not be long ere they feast on our entrails."

Padreg reached out a hand to reassure the lady, but quickly withdrew it at the steely look of determination that settled on Elisira's face.

"I will require a bow, My Lord, and sturdily tipped arrows."

"Of course. We have an extra," Padreg nodded at Aden and the scout hurried off to retrieve the bow.

The group was tense. An attack was coming and everyone knew it. The uncertainty made each person twitch with nervous energy.

Astariu grant me the skill to use these weapons, and the courage to draw them under fire, prayed Elisira silently.

Mercifully, it had stopped snowing at dusk. She prayed that this was an omen — she could almost taste the comfort warm food would bring. A fat, wet gob of snow plopped onto her nose.

Her horse suddenly reared, nearly throwing her to the ground. Elisira grabbed the reins, quickly getting the horse under control. "Easy boy," she muttered, using her knees to direct the suddenly recalcitrant stallion. Behind her, Padreg's men were muttering as wind began to shake the branches of the trees.

"Rimerbeasts!" A high-pitched yell broke through the unnerving sound. Elisira's gaze snapped to Devon. He was pointing to a patch of snow that seemed just a bit grayer than the rest. The shifting wind brought the faintest hint of something putrid, causing the hairs on the back of the lady's neck to rise.

"Light the torches, men!" Padreg yelled. Each of his men carried a torch, as fire was the one known bane of the ice demons. Elisira pulled out her own torch and fumbled with her flint and striker, cursing the cold that made her hands clumsy.

The smell grew stronger as the wind increased. Large, shaggy masses of teeth and claws rose out of the snowy ground and a low, thrumming hum joined with the whistle of the wind to create an eerie chorus. The horses sidled, nervously shaking their heads and taking uncertain, frightened steps backward.

"Get those torches up, now!" Padreg's fear-tinged voice pierced the hum of the rimerbeasts. One by one, the creatures advanced on the party.

Devon, who was having difficulty lighting his own torch, suddenly shouted, "By the blood and bones of the beast, light!"

The torches all lit with an explosive burst.

"Circle up and protect the lady," Padreg ordered, as he pulled close to Elisira. His face was a mask of stoic determination. "We will not die today."

Bows were nocked and then strings twanged. There was a moment of absolute stillness as the arrows sliced through the air and then, as they struck their targets, chaos erupted. Roars of pain and fury meshed with the wind as bows were dropped and blades drawn.

Elisira struck out at anything she could, praying that her blade bit deeply into the hides of foes, not friends. Bedlam danced madly around the party. Gray-furred death reached out for the lives of Padreg's men, carving pieces away from the group one by one. The screams of horse and man blended with the grunts and growls of the demons.

Blood and ichor puddled in the snow, vivid splashes of crimson and yellow that fanned out around the raging battle. Viscous slurry made footing traitorous for the horses and the weather turned even worse. Fighting blind, the Y'Noran party tightened formation and made a knot around their chieftain and his lady.

A bloody, razor-taloned paw came out of the white haze and slashed at Elisira. She ducked, swinging her blade wildly. The sickening sensation of metal slicing through fur and flesh reverberated up her arm and she just barely kept herself from vomiting. She turned her head in time to see one of Padreg's men dragged from his horse and carried off into the woods. Grimly, she maneuvered into his spot, and faced the next rimerbeast.

Chapter Twelve

Azhani hunted. Her prey was the elusive rimerbeasts. Three days had passed since the ice demon had attacked her and Kyrian, and she was determined that no other dangers would come from the winter-cloaked woods around her home.

The former warleader was both frustrated and curious. It was not a beast year — she should not have to be out in the cold, searching for the shyvot-sucking monsters! Everyone knew that the beasts only came out of their northern fastness once every five years. It had only been three years since their last invasion. Not even breeders, the fully grown spawners that peppered the mountain caves with their eggs, would normally be seen this early.

The demon that attacked them could have been a stray. It was possible that a straggler might have escaped the Y'Dani patrols, but if that was the case, why hadn't Barton been overwhelmed with spawning demons? It only took one of the monsters to make more.

If there were more rimerbeasts in the mountains, then all of Azhani's plans would have to be changed. Nothing was more important than defending the kingdoms from their depredations. Not even her revenge was worth the lives of thousands.

Though what I would do about it remains to be determined. I am only one woman — it takes an army to defeat the beasts. She concentrated on her scouting. One lone rimerbeast did not mean thousands, but if there were more, she needed to know.

Fearsome to battle as adults, rimerbeasts were particularly vulnerable as nestlings. The egg shells were easily cracked and fire would cleanse the foulness of the dying embryos from the rock. Prayers sung by starseekers would keep the evil beasts from nesting in the same cave for at least another five years. It was only when they hatched that they became the demonic whirlwind of teeth and claws that had shredded armies to ribbons.

Fire and sunlight were the creature's bane. It was this knowledge that kept Azhani in the cold long past sunset. Her cheek ached. Three new scars marred the skin of her face.

Once more, Kyrian had given freely of her gifts, healing Azhani with judicious use of the goddess' fire. She was glad that her friend was safely tucked away in the cabin. If she did come across another rimerbeast, the priest's battle hesitancy might command too high a cost.

The day after the attack, Azhani had scoured the woods to make sure there were no other demons nearby. Once she was satisfied that Kyrian would be safe, she packed her bedroll and set out on foot. Before leaving, they discussed her eventual return.

"Promise me you'll be safe out there, Azhani," Kyrian said, *pleading with her eyes.*

"I cannot make that promise, but I will return."

Kyrian accepted the compromise. *"All right. How will I know you're* back? How will you get in if the door is locked and I have the key?"

Azhani whistled piercingly, a long, four-note burst that echoed through the cabin.

"Oh," Kyrian said, nodding wisely. "I see. Yes, I think I'd be able to hear that even in the middle of a good dream."

Grinning, Azhani said, "And if I'm not alone, you'll hear this." She added a trill. Patiently, Azhani taught the stardancer how to recognize whistle combinations for danger, friend, and injury. When she was certain the priest had memorized them, she rose to go.

Kyrian stood with her. Hugging her friend tightly, Kyrian said, "Come back soon, Azhani. Else I will be forced to talk to Arun."

Azhani sighed as she petted Kyrian's soft, curly tangle of hair. It had grown out since they had met, and now the amber locks cloaked the stardancer's shoulders. "Well, I hope poor Arun doesn't get too bored listening to your addle-pated ideas," she said teasingly.

"Azhani!" Kyrian squawked, and pulled away. "Be kind!" She smacked the warrior's shoulder, and then winced in pain. "Ow, armor — I forgot that you were wearing it."

"Here, let me see." Azhani took the stardancer's hand and turned it up, seeking signs of injury. A faint red mark marred the pale skin of her friend's palm. "Mm, this looks bad. I think I'm going to have to use one of my father's favorite remedies." A twinkle of mischief sparkled in her eyes. She looked into Kyrian's open face and said, "Now, just close your eyes, Kyrian, and count to ten, and by the time you're done, the pain will be all gone."

Gamely, Kyrian closed her eyes. Her palm really wasn't badly injured, but Azhani was enjoying the chance to let out her playful side. The stardancer started to count, "One, two, three..."

As Kyrian counted, Azhani brought the stardancer's hand up to her lips and waited.

"Ten," whispered Kyrian.

Azhani tenderly brushed her lips over the mark. "There now, all better?"

"Oh! Yes, fine, thank you! That is quite a wonderful trick there, Azhani," Kyrian babbled, suddenly eager to reclaim her hand.

"Good. I have to go," Azhani turned and gathered up her heavy cloak, wrapping its furry warmth around her like an extra suit of armor. "Stay safe, I'll be back." With those words, she left to begin her search.

The memory dissipated, leaving a smile on Azhani's face. Looking around, she found what she had hoped not to see — fresh rimerbeast spoor. She squatted and studied the substance with a practiced eye. The very sight of the foul stuff made her teeth ache. *It's too soon. There shouldn't be any sign of the damned beasts for another two years.* Poking at the goo with an arrow, she was rewarded with the hissing and spitting sound of metal being eaten by acid.

Well, now I have evidence of more of the shyvot eaters. Now what? Obviously, the one she had killed had not been a leftover. The patch of acidic slime taunted her with its existence. A gear inside her clicked, and suddenly, everything around her had a sharper smell, a brighter color and a louder sound.

The *other-sense* was part of the reason she was called Banshee. Her war cry, coupled with the fact that when she appeared on the battlefield death was sure to follow, were the other reasons why she had been given the honorific.

It was both a gift and a curse, for the heightened senses came from her elven ancestry while her ability with a blade came from her purely human father. Neither had made her friends with either race, but she had learned to use and adapt her abilities and it was never a good day when she had to rely on those skills.

The air was fetid with the stink of rimerbeast. Azhani hated the smell, but the banshee in her welcomed it. The scent meant combat, in which the dark side of her soul exulted. Nerves thrumming with excitement, she began to jog. There were demons in the forest, and she intended to locate and exterminate them.

She could not allow them to find caves. If they did, they would spawn, and the following winter the mountains would be crawling with rimerbeasts. That was what made battling the monsters so difficult, for they only attacked in coldest months.

Which was why, every five years, the armies of Y'Dan, Y'Syr and Y'Dror combined and systematically searched every cave in the Crest. This expedition lasted from spring to spring and almost always involved a winter filled with combat.

Azhani cursed. She was only one woman — she could not search the entire Crest of Amyra for signs of demonspawning. *What am I going to do?*

You'll make your home safe. In the spring, you will do whatever it takes to warn the kingdoms. The idea was a start. It wasn't enough, but it would sooth her conscience.

She stopped to catch her breath beside a burned-out tree trunk. Lining the interior was a patch of thick, dark mushrooms. Knowing that Kyrian would adore the treat, she harvested them and put them in her haversack.

Kyrian was fast becoming an indispensable part of Azhani's life. The priest's natural enthusiasm had made each day seem a little lighter. When Azhani's grief took away her cheer, Kyrian was there to hold her. The stardancer even understood her need for space, and on those days when she felt the darkness creep in, Kyrian would go and spend time with Arun while the warrior methodically destroyed another pell. There was no pressure in the relationship — just an open friendliness that made Azhani feel good.

The friendship was a gift from the gods, and was one that she intended never to lose. *Which is why I'm out here, freezing my tits off.*

The wind suddenly shifted, carrying the sounds of combat to her ears. "So you weren't alone. Let's go see who you're having for dinner tonight," she whispered as she drew her blade and began to run into the woods.

Blinking through the blood trickling into her eyes, Elisira desperately tried to hold back the demon that was attacking her. Rimerbeasts howled around her, their teeth and claws shredding into flesh and throwing out bright crimson fans of blood. She tried to break free by heading for a break in the trees, but the demon jumped up in front of her and scared her horse into rearing.

Pulling back, she returned to the huddled circle of her party and did her best to keep the beasts at bay. Her lips were curled in a feral snarl. She hated being trapped. It didn't matter if her cage was a circle of hell-born beasts or a beautifully appointed chamber in a castle, she still hated the feeling. Anger and frustration roiled in her belly.

It was too much. Suddenly, Elisira shouted, "Everyone, concentrate on breaking free! If we can get them to fall back, we can run!"

A smile sprang to Padreg's grime-coated face. "She's right, lads! Press on!"

Renewing the fight, they strove to throw off the demon onslaught. Wildly yelling, laying about them with new vigor, the Y'Norans drove the rimerbeasts back. The tightly pressed circle of horses expanded and gave them more room to fight.

Devon went down, pulled from his saddle by one of the demons.

"Devon!" Elisira yelled, as she tried to break away and ride to his defense. The beast in front of her cut her off, swiping at her horse's head.

A sound heard in the nightmares of many, the dreams of few and the prayers of one, burst into the clearing. Somersaulting into the fray was a blue and white clad figure bearing a sword that flashed with deadly accuracy. The rimerbeast that had attacked Devon lost its head.

The newly arrived warrior let out another ear splitting wail and sprang over the falling demon's body to skewer the one facing Elisira. She barely had time to see a flash of indigo blue eyes and dusky brown skin before the warrior was gone, running toward the remaining demons.

Elisira watched in awe as the stranger easily dispatched the monsters that had been, up until now, making mincemeat of the party. With a ferocity shown by few, the warrior engaged the rimerbeasts, ripping chunks of fur and flesh from their bodies.

The noblewoman rode over to Devon and pulled him up behind her.

"It's Azhani, isn't it?" he asked excitedly.

"I don't know, Dev. But I hope so."

"Me too."

The unknown warrior moved from demon to demon, never spending more than a few breaths on their deaths. The creatures seemed to sense that this new warrior was one who they could not defeat and began to back away from the newly energized party.

"Your bows, men! Feather their hides!" Padreg shouted, lifting his own short bow and quickly firing off two arrows, hitting one of the rimerbeasts in the flank. The demon howled and made to attack the Y'Noran king but was quickly brought down by a hail of arrows from the other men.

From behind Elisira came a flung stone that struck one of the beasts in the skull, stunning it enough that one of the Y'Norans was able to disembowel it.

"Good shot, Devon!" She turned to see the boy load another stone in his sling.

He nodded and let fly.

The stone connected with another of the beasts. Arrows pierced its flesh, killing it. With the same ease displayed upon arrival, the strange warrior dispatched the final two rimerbeasts.

Two of Padreg's men were dead, torn to ribbons by the rimerbeast's claws. Four of the horses were also gone, leaving the party short by two mounts. No one, man or beast, was spared injury.

Elisira felt her sword arm begin to tremble in exhaustion and was about to drop her blade when Azhani's voice echoed in her mind, *"Never drop a weapon. The minute you do, you're dead. Your blade is the one thing standing between you and whatever is trying to kill you. It is a part of you and should never be forsaken."* Her slackening grip tightened automatically and she laid the blade across the pommel of the saddle.

After a few breaths of the rank, coppery air, she felt queasy. Breathing shallowly, she turned her gaze on the person who had rescued them. It had to be Azhani. No other warrior fought as though their feet had wings.

The stranger was going from corpse to corpse, neatly beheading each of the rimerbeasts. *It has to be her. Making sure the beasts are truly dead is something she would do.*

Elisira guided her shaking horse over to the warrior. "Thank you for the rescue, stranger."

The warrior looked up and revealed a heartbreakingly familiar face.

"Azhani?" Elisira whispered. She tumbled off her horse and reached for the woman. "Azhi? Goddess, please, is that you?"

Azhani stared at the party, bemused by the circumstances. *I never thought to see Eli leave the city.* Her gaze fell upon the boy who had ridden behind the noblewoman. *Is that Polis' boy? He's grown so much...*

"Is she right, stranger, are you the one called Azhani Rhu'len?" Padreg asked.

"That's what my father named me," she replied with a smile.

In the next moment, her arms were full of a crying noblewoman.

"Azhani!" Devon crowed, leaping down from the horse's back and racing to enfold her in a massive hug. "Father always said you had more lives than a cat!" He sighed. "I missed you."

She ruffled his hair affectionately. "And I, you, youngling." She brushed a kiss against Elisira's forehead. "Elisira. It has been too long, my friend."

Gruffly, Padreg said, "Glad I am that you found us, warrior. We have much to discuss. I am considering hiring you."

Azhani broke her embrace with her friends and looked at Padreg as if he were slightly daft. The boy went to his horse and mounted while the lady cleaned her weapon with snow.

Elisira frowned at the pits eaten into the blade by the caustic blood, but sheathed the weapon anyway. Nothing could be done for it now. Turning to Azhani, she dropped to one knee and waited for Azhani to notice her. "Master, I have not lost your lessons."

The warrior looked down and noted that the noblewoman had cleaned and sheathed her blade. What impressed Azhani was how calm Elisira remained, even after the danger had passed.

"Then my teaching was not in vain. I am grateful," Azhani replied in a solemn tone, reaching out to touch Elisira on the shoulder. "You are injured, my friend. Let me tend your wounds."

The lady scuffed her knuckles across the slash on her head, wincing when they came away bloody. "I'll be all right. There are others who need your skills more."

Azhani nodded. "Devon, find bandages."

"Yes, Master Azhani," the boy replied and began digging through his packs.

"So, plainsman, why do you seek me? Who are you?"

Padreg bowed and said, "I am Padreg Keelan, chieftain of Y'Nor. I sought you at the suggestion of my lady." He indicated Elisira. "She had some idea that you would be interested in assisting a quest to bring the plight of Y'Dan to High King Ysradan's court."

Azhani snorted. "I doubt you'd get far with an oath-breaker at your side, Chief Padreg."

"As far as any other outlaw," he said with a wry smile.

One dark eyebrow rose, telegraphing Azhani's curiosity. "How does one monarch become an outlaw in another king's land?"

"With *korethka,* all things are possible," he replied. Looking at Elisira, he smiled as she helped Devon rip up tunics for bandages. As quickly as he could, he related the story of how they had arrived in the mountains.

When he was finished, Azhani shook her head and frowned. "You and your men are welcome to winter with me, My Lord. Any enemy of Arris is a friend of mine. My question to you is simple: do you trust me?"

Padreg shrugged. "In my travels, I have had much time to think. It seems to me that young Arris is fond of labeling those who do not agree with him traitors, outlaws and rebels; it seems possible that you are also among those so unjustly branded. Then, too, my lady has vouchsafed your innocence and her word I trust above all others."

Azhani grunted. "I am not wholly free of guilt, My Lord. I killed many innocent men in my bid to escape Arris' justice, but I will go to my grave knowing that I did not commit treason against my people, or my love. Draw your own conclusions."

"A man such as Arris would not know true justice if it bit him on his arse. Upon this day, in the sight of the Twins, and for naught but the sake of what was good and right, you have shown your honor. This speaks loudly of your innocence, Azhani. You are a true servant of Astariu. I would be proud to have you at my back." Padreg offered her his arm.

Hesitantly, she clasped it, grunting at the surprising firmness of the man's grip. "Thank you, Your Majesty," she murmured, granting him the respect of his title.

"Padreg'll do, warrior. I'm not one to stand on ceremony, especially when I'm freezing my manhood off in the middle of a snowdrift the size of an Y'Skani sand dune."

A genuine smile creased her face. "Follow me then, Padreg. The shelter I have is small, and already shared, but you are welcome to join us."

"Shared?" Elisira asked with some surprise.

"I am wintering with someone I met on the road — an Y'Syran star-dancer named Kyrian," Azhani said, grinning brightly. "She saved my leg with her care." Lowering her voice for Elisira's ears only, she whispered, "And her friendship has rescued my soul."

The depth of pain in the warrior's crystal blue eyes was visible for the briefest of moments, vanishing quickly to be replaced by a hard calm that sent a chill down the other woman's spine.

"If you would, warrior, lead us on to this place of refuge," Padreg said and then turned to give his remaining warriors orders to gather the slain. "I like it not to leave good Y'Noran blood to teeth and fang. We'll build a cairn some ways from here, if that be all right with you, warrior?"

"Call me Azhani. Yes, I have no issue with honoring your dead. We can leave the demons — if anything out here is willing to stomach them, they're welcome to the remains," she replied absently. Mentally, she mapped out the route they would take back to her father's homestead. She knew just the place where they could find a nice, open area with plenty of rock and debris suitable to build graves for the fallen.

With Azhani to guide them, the party no longer felt as though they were hunting blind for half-remembered landmarks. The Kellerdon inn-keeper had been a good source of information, but it was difficult to find every tree stump, mossy boulder and streamlet he had described as road-way markers. After a candlemark of travel, they stopped and buried the bodies of Padreg's men.

Azhani liked the Y'Norans. They were quiet, polite and friendly. Unlike the boisterous, rude and often times arrogant Y'Dani, the plainsmen followed orders without hesitation.

Before the stones bearing the graven names of the dead were laid over the cairns, Padreg said a few words in honor of them. Elisira, Azhani and Devon then sang the pathsong to lead the spirits of the dead to the blessed kingdoms.

Moonrise had silvered the land by the time the party reached Azhani's homestead. The warrior trilled the whistle that meant she was home and with wounded friends.

A light blossomed near the front window and the door opened. Dressed in full stardancer regalia, which included her baton and her Twins token, the pendant bearing the curving, stylized rune that marked her as a servant to Astariu, Kyrian stepped out onto the porch.

"I'm home," said Azhani.

"And you've brought company," replied Kyrian, with a welcoming smile. "Hello, I am Kyrian. I give you welcome in the name of the goddess. Enter in peace." The priest's natural charm quietly threaded through the group and put to rest any trepidation that may have remained. This was not the hideout of a known fugitive. Instead, it was the sanctuary of a stardancer, one of Astariu's most beloved servants.

Syrah and Thomas were led into the cottage by Kyrian who dictated a list of supplies she needed to a bewildered Devon.

Outside, Azhani said, "You can put the horses in the stable. It is small, but if we move a few things, it should suffice for tonight. We will have to enlarge it before long, though."

Padreg nodded, but both he and Elisira were more interested in watching Kyrian, whose efficiency was impressive.

"She's quite practiced, for one so young," said Elisira.

"She does all right," Azhani said, shrugging nonchalantly.

The horses were stabled and fed and before long everyone was ensconced in the living area. Because the house was so full, Kyrian reluctantly turned the most stable portion of the upstairs loft into an impromptu infirmary. Below, the walking wounded huddled around the fire and drank mugs of hot willow tea.

Azhani gave what aid she could to the injured while upstairs Kyrian and Elisira dealt with the severely wounded.

The creaking of the floorboards above made her extremely nervous. Nothing had been done for the rotting timbers and neither she nor Kyrian had visited the loft since it had been closed off for the winter.

They can't stay up there. Maybe I can turn the storage area into a bedroom and move our supplies outside. I'll need to go back to Barton and buy some building materials...

A sharp crack startled everyone.

"Look out!" Azhani yelled. Grabbing Devon, she rolled away from the hearth as the floorboards in the loft splintered. Wood, dust and cobwebs rained down upon the occupants of the first floor. There was a muffled oath and when the dust cleared, everyone could clearly see a leg sticking out of the ceiling.

Silence settled over the cottage. Then, bright laughter echoed down from the loft. "By all that's bright and holy — wouldn't you know that I would recall the weak spot just as I put my foot in it?" Kyrian called down between gales of laughter.

"Azhi, I believe we're in need of your warrior brawn. Could you please come up and assist a lady?" Elisira yelled.

"Yes, it's time for you to be a hero and rescue me again, my friend," Kyrian added between giggles.

Rolling her eyes, Azhani let Devon go and headed upstairs. Padreg was right behind her.

"Azhi? Is that her nickname? I like it," Kyrian said softly.

Elisira nodded. "I wouldn't use it until you're certain that she loves you, though. It was her father's nickname for her." The noblewoman's whispered comment was so fleeting that Kyrian had to wonder if she had really heard it.

Upon spotting Azhani's form at the top of the stairs, Kyrian waved and said, "Hey there, stranger, do you think you could give me a lift?" She wiggled her eyebrows comically, raised her arms up and then smiled beseechingly.

Syrah laughed uproariously, and then was consumed by wracking coughs. Leaving Kyrian to deal with Azhani on her own, Elisira went to the sick woman's side and helped her drink a soothing tea.

Between them, Azhani and Padreg were able to lift the stardancer out of the hole. The extraction was not without its casualties, as Kyrian's pants ripped loudly, to the amusement of those below. Setting her gently on an undamaged section of floor, Azhani winced when she noticed three angry red scratches on the stardancer's leg.

Kyrian sighed and said, "Somehow I do not believe that your father's admittedly excellent remedy will be sufficient to heal this wound, Azhani." She started to stand, but stopped when the floor ominously creaked. "Oh, shyvot! We need to get Syrah and Thomas downstairs — is there room in the pantry?"

"Is that room large enough?" asked Elisira curiously.

Azhani made a face. "It will have to be. This floor is too dangerous. I'd just as soon not have someone roll over and land on me when I'm asleep."

Elisira chuckled. "That would not be an entertaining alarm."

"No. Padreg, if you'll take Thomas, I'll get Syrah and we can—" she broke off as Devon appeared at the top of the stairs.

"Devon, what is it?" Elisira asked gently.

The young man smiled and proffered his grimoire. "I found a spell for mending things. Could I try it?"

At the word *spell*, Azhani shivered as though covered by thousands of spiders. Stardancer magick was something she was prepared to accept as holy and coming from a divine source, but magery created by someone chanting arcane phrases written in a dusty old book made her skin crawl.

"I am not entirely comfortable with that idea," she said, attempting to keep her voice calm and regular.

Startled by Azhani's attitude, Kyrian shot her friend a curious look, but did not receive any explanation. Shrugging, she said, "Well, it couldn't hurt to try."

Nodding, Elisira said, "I agree with Kyrian. It would save Syrah and Thomas unnecessary pain and discomfort if they were able to remain here."

The grinding of the warrior's teeth was audible. She turned her gaze on Elisira, her eyes diamond hard. "You, of all people, should understand my objections," she said softly, her voice tinged with pain.

Elisira winced. Her old friend was right. She knew why Azhani hated magick. As a lawkeeper, Rhu'len DaCoure had spent much of his life fighting practitioners of the dark arts. Of those sorcerers, the worst of the breed was Kasyrin Darkchilde. The sorcerer had held a vendetta against the Cabal, which Rhu'len would not have involved himself in but for the fact that Kasyrin had murdered an entire Y'Dani village in his eagerness to kill a man of the criminal organization.

This event led to years of trouble between Kasyrin and Rhu'len, culminating in a duel between the two men. Rhu'len had won, but before he could make sure that Kasyrin was dead, one of the man's servants had stolen the sorcerer's body. After that, Rhu'len had a healthy disdain for all but divine magick and had instilled this same aversion in his daughter.

Regardless of this, Elisira felt that she had to try to sway her friend's mind. Rising, she went to Azhani's side and put a hand on her arm. "I know that you hold no love for the arcane, my friend, but Devon is not Darkchilde. There is no evil within him, only the desire to aid."

Azhani looked away and met Kyrian's sad, curious gaze. Feeling slightly betrayed, the warrior muttered, "Fine. Do what you must."

"Thank you," murmured Elisira.

Without a backward glance, Azhani bent, scooped up the injured stardancer and began to head downstairs.

Squawking, Kyrian cried, "Azhani, what are you doing?"

"Can't let you put weight on that leg. Might've strained something," she replied gruffly.

"But I'm fi—" Kyrian broke off, noticing the bleak expression on her friend's face. *Oh, I understand. She just needs something to do. I think I can let her be the tough warrior for now.* Ceasing her struggles, Kyrian relaxed in Azhani's arms.

Once below, Azhani settled the stardancer in her bed with the command, "Wait here," and then went to make her a cup of tea.

Upstairs, Kyrian could hear the soft sounds of chanting. In moments, the gentle prickle of magickal forces in use caused her skin to tingle pleasantly. Looking up, she watched as bluish-gold threads of energy crept across the wood above her head. Everywhere the magick touched, the structure was completely repaired. Soon, the entire ceiling glowed with the force of Devon's magick.

"Blessed goddess," she whispered in awe.

In an attempt to ignore the goings-on above, Azhani made a plate of stew for her friend. Even though she tried not to, it was difficult to avoid noticing the threads of magickal energy that rippled across the ceiling. Shivering, she tried not to think about it.

"Here." She thrust the plate at Kyrian. "Eat."

Taking the food, Kyrian smiled her appreciation. "Thank you. This was very kind of you. Sit with me?" She patted her bed softly.

The winsome expression worn by the stardancer was impossible to deny. Keeping a mask of rigid neutrality, Azhani sat. Soon, the soft conversation between Kyrian and Aden had lulled her to sleep.

Chapter Thirteen

Azhani woke during the night to find that she had become a pillow for Kyrian. All was quiet in the house. The day candle burned, puddling hours on its pedestal without event. The arcane doings of the previous evening left no imprint other than a repaired ceiling. In the other bed, Padreg lay sleeping soundly, while Devon and Aden had spread pallets on the floor near the hearth. Upstairs, Azhani could make out the sounds of someone moving about and she deduced that Elisira had taken the morning shift of patient care.

Kyrian sighed and changed her position. Feeling tenderly protective, Azhani cradled her friend and enjoyed the peace the stardancer's presence bought. Sleep nearly claimed her again, but she forced herself to wake. It was two marks before dawn by the day candle, and there was work to be done.

Extricating herself from under Kyrian's deeply sleeping form, Azhani padded to the hearth, stirred up the fire and hung a pot of water to boil. Once she had a pot of tea made, she took a mugful and headed up to the loft to check on the patients.

Upstairs, Elisira was tending to Syrah Jessup. She was applying a poultice to the woman's chest when Azhani arrived.

"Need anything?" she asked without preamble.

Elisira sighed, and accepted the tea. Rubbing the bridge of her nose, she said, "About ten ounces of an herb that Kyrian doesn't have."

"Bad?"

The noblewoman nodded sadly. "It's deep in her lungs. There's blood in her phlegm and Kyrian thinks that she'll have to use Astariu's gift just to stabilize her."

"Will she live?"

"I don't know." Elisira shivered. "Could you bring me my cloak? I'm cold."

"Of course." Azhani quickly retrieved the garment and returned with an armload of wood as well.

"Thanks, Azhi." Elisira wrapped herself in the warm fabric while the warrior got a fire going in the woodstove. Shortly, the loft began to warm.

"I'll talk to Kyrian and find out about that herb. I may be able to get some in Barton," Azhani said as she headed downstairs.

Elisira nodded absently while she changed Thomas' bandages.

The rest of the morning was filled with feeding and caring for the horses. After they had eaten, she let them out to wander the grounds while she cleaned out the stalls. *I need to go to Barton. This stable is too small for all the horses, but if I get some lumber, we could expand it enough to last the winter.* Azhani began to make a mental list of supplies while she worked.

The silence of the morning was both restful and melancholy. Horse sounds blended with the rest of the usual sounds and passed over her senses without notice.

Thoughts of Ylera were never far from Azhani's mind, but this morning the peacefulness of the day had made them particularly strong. Never again would she wake to find Ylera by her side. Nor would she ever creep down to the kitchens to filch supplies for a meal and steal away from the castle for a day of laughter and play in the countryside around Y'Dannyv. The very normalcy of the day was like a bucket of cold water. It should have been raining, or at least gray and dark, but instead it was nice, and that forced Azhani to accept that the world had moved on without Ylera. Anguish crept up and struck the warrior's heart with a fatal blow.

Tears burned tracks in her cheeks as she worked. Her breath came in soft gasps and one name echoed in her mind. *Ylera...* If she closed her eyes, she could almost touch her. She reached out, but there was nothing there. *Ah gods, when will this nightmare end?*

"Azhani?" Kyrian stepped into the stable. In her hands was a cup of steaming tea. "I thought you might be chilled." Seeing the distress her friend was in, she set the drink aside and reached out for her.

For a moment, Azhani denied herself the relief freely offered, but then, with a soft cry, she fell into Kyrian's arms. The stardancer drew them down to a hay bale and held on until the tears ebbed.

"Thank you," Azhani said, rising and retrieving the cup of tea. "I was chilled." No mention was made of her tears.

Kyrian smiled and stood. "I'm going to make breakfast. Any requests?"

"Flatcakes? With honey and nuts?" Azhani suggested brightly.

"Flatcakes it is," Kyrian said, smiling fondly. Kyrian returned to the house, leaving Azhani to finish cleaning the stable.

Watching from the loft window, Elisira saw the stardancer go to the warrior and hold her through her grief. A thread of jealously formed, but was quickly quashed. She liked Kyrian and knew that Azhani needed the touch of the stardancer's art to find her healing.

Azhani needed to plan. Her grief subsided as she pondered the future. First, there would be a trip to Barton to purchase supplies. Then, come spring, she would help Padreg get his people across the mountains and through Y'Syr. She owed him that much for getting Elisira away from Lord Loose Breeches, as the noblewoman had christened Arris. After that, she would try to see Lyssera. If the elven queen were at all like her twin, it was possible that she would be willing to hear Azhani's story before she had her beheaded.

If she did listen, then Azhani would tell her about the rimerbeasts. If not, well, then as the headsman led her to the block, she would beg the queen for a boon — elves were notoriously sticky about honor — and then she would still inform the Y'Syrans of the danger. The only difference in the plan would be whether or not she lived.

The appearance of the rimerbeasts upset her more than she showed — the sudden unpredictability of the monsters, after centuries of regularity, made her stomach twist in knots. If they could appear out of sequence, could they appear out of season, as well? *Best not to go borrowing trouble,* she thought.

It was a shame that no one knew the origins of the beasts. Elven legend held that they were the remnants of a prehistoric mage war — possibly the same war that made the desert of Y'Skan.

Even though she was no longer Y'Dan's warleader, Azhani still was compelled by her oaths to defend the kingdom. It was an ingrained trait. Her father had been as oath-bound and driven to fulfill those vows as she.

Visions of gathering an army to drive out the beasts played in the warrior's head. Where such a force would come from, she knew not, but the thought was delicious.

The daydream expanded. Why just defeat the rimerbeasts when she could turn that same battle-hardened army on Arris' bullies? How hard would it be to slaughter the Y'Dani soldiers and get to the sniveling king? Who would stop her from exacting a painful and bloody revenge on the man who had slain her beloved? Then she would be queen, as Thodan had wished.

Could she do it? Would she be able to take up the crown and rule with the same ability as King Thodan? Did she have the wisdom to keep the Y'Dani people safe, sound and happy? Made restless by her thoughts, she wandered to the wall bordering the property and climbed it. Using its width to practice her balance, she closed her eyes and tried to trust her instincts.

One step. She was a warrior, not a politician. Two steps. Her oaths demanded she protect the people against those who would do them harm. Three steps. Life as a queen would demand her to do things that went counter to those oaths. She knew it; she'd seen Thodan wrestle with his conscience almost daily. Four steps and a slight falter. Ylera hated her royal status, often referring to it as the curse of birth. At the fifth step, Azhani stopped and covered her face. She did not wish to be queen. Nor did she wish to lead an army against a people she had sworn to protect with her life.

She took a new step; one filled with confidence. The rimerbeasts would be her first priority. She began to take quicker steps, almost running along the wall. All else would have to fall in line after that.

With one last step, Azhani leaped into the air, somersaulted and landed in front of the door. Opening her eyes, she grinned. She had made the right decision.

"I can't fight who I am," she said, lifting her head and gazing up into the clear, blue sky. Another road would have to be found, another path to vengeance taken — one where her honor and her oaths were not compromised.

Kyrian's heart was still full from holding her friend. It was so strange how she could find such comfort in giving it, but the more time she spent with Azhani, the easier it was to say goodbye to Ylera. *Grief shared is grief halved, I suppose,* the stardancer thought, repeating an ancient maxim of the Astariuns. *Even if she isn't aware that we share the same loss.* Guilt played merry havoc in her heart momentarily, but she pushed it aside. *This is not the right time to tell her. There's too much going on, and that would just add to her distress.* To take her mind from her thoughts, Kyrian made breakfast and was just finishing her plate when Azhani appeared.

"Here, warrior, I saved you some," Kyrian said, handing Azhani her plate.

"Thanks. I'm surprised to find you awake. I'd have expected a lack-a-bed such as yourself to have tumbled back to the sheets by now." The warrior shot a teasing wink to the stardancer.

Kyrian chuckled. "How could you expect to me to sleep when you'd stolen all the covers?"

Mock innocent, Azhani exclaimed, "I? You have surely wronged me for I would never stoop to such light-fingered lowness as the thievery of mere blankets!"

Aden and Devon looked at the two women as if they had lost their wits. The jokes continued until Padreg and Elisira appeared at the stairwell.

"Kyrian, Syrah's worse," Elisira said softly.

"I'll be up at once," the stardancer said as she reached for her medicine pouch. Padreg headed outside with his men while Azhani and Elisira enjoyed the fire.

"You're very fond of her, I see," Elisira said.

"She's a gift," Azhani replied.

Nodding, the noblewoman asked, "So how are the horses? If I remember you aright, you'll have spent the morning with them."

"They'll heal fine. I expect Padreg and his men tended to their hurts last night." Azhani shrugged. "I'm sure that Kyrian will check them later. If necessary, she and Padreg can put their heads together and cook up some noxious potions." She laughed and added, "I almost feel sorry for the horses. Kyrian's opinion about medicine is that it has to taste awful to be effective."

Elisira breathed a sharp sigh of relief. Traveling with the Y'Norans had taught her how much the plainsmen valued their four-legged friends. Horses were accepted as members of the family, and that kinship was beginning to wear off on her. The trip had allowed her to have a kinship with her stallion that she had never experienced with another horse, and she was as afraid for his health as she was for Syrah's and Thomas'.

"Looks like you've been infected with a plainsman's horse-love, my friend." Azhani grinned and wrinkled up her nose, making a silly face.

Elisira looked away, flushing slightly. "There is much to admire about those of the plains," she said softly.

Azhani's smile twisted rakishly. "Oh aye, I can see that, my old friend. I'd say that your admiration extends to one tall and handsome clanchief, as well."

"Your barbs are, as always, on the mark, my friend," Elisira replied with a deeper flush.

Shrugging, Azhani said, "It's hard not to miss such a large target." Setting her plate to the side, her jovial demeanor vanished. "I've much to do. Please, enjoy some breakfast. Kyrian is a good cook as well as a good healer." With that, she left to continue her chores.

Curse you to the endless hells, Arris! Elisira thought sadly. *You killed the best part of my friend's heart when you murdered Ylera.* From upstairs, there came the gentle strains of a healing chant. *But perhaps it can be resurrected.* Outside, she could hear Padreg and his men as they greeted Azhani. Her reply was terse, but friendly. *Perhaps you are not lost to the dark completely, my old friend. With the love of friends, is it possible that you can let go of the hurt?*

Elisira spared a moment to wonder how she would feel if it were

Padreg who had been slaughtered. Pain blossomed in her gut and her heart nearly failed to its beat. Tears pricked the corners of her eyes and her throat closed. *Oh gods, I am so lost to him!* she thought with a sad happiness that left her wondering if anything could heal a wound so great as Azhani's. *We have to try,* she thought. Or *else Arris and his cronies will ruin Y'Dan.*

The presence of out-of-season rimerbeasts in the wilderness did nothing to calm her rising nerves, either. *The other kingdoms need to know. Azhani is the best to carry the tale. Surely they will listen to the woman who has successfully driven back two invasions of the monsters.*

Shaking her head, Elisira let out a chirrup of laughter. "I'll send myself to the moon before I'll have all the answers. 'Tis a topic best saved for later, for I am hungry. I wonder what's for breakfast."

The magick helped Syrah, but her body was still afflicted with the sickness filling her lungs with fluid.

"I'm going to die," the Y'Noran warrior croaked.

"Not if I have anything to say about it," Kyrian said firmly as she moved to work on Thomas.

"You're a good 'un, 'Dancer. Tell me true — will I see foaling?"

Kyrian turned to look into Syrah's harsh featured face. "Syrah, I won't lie. We do not have the medicine you need. However, I have every reason to believe that Astariu's gift will heal you. It will just take longer." Astariu's fire wasn't a perfect panacea. It had its limitations and disease was one of them. The spell was meant more for curing grievous wounds, such as the damage Azhani had sustained to her leg. This was why stardancers were healers as well as priests; they had to know herb healing and surgical techniques in order to supplement the gift of the goddess.

"I believe you," said Syrah, comforted by the words.

Kyrian smiled and turned to Thomas.

"Good morrow, Stardancer," the young man whispered as she knelt beside his pallet.

"Good morning, Thomas. I'd like to wash off some of that dried blood so that I can see the wound better. Do you mind?" Kyrian dipped the rag into the soapy water and wrung it out slowly.

"Not at all. It would be nice to be clean," he said wistfully.

She smiled at him and pulled back his covers. Removing the blood-soaked bandage, she cleaned the wound. The blond warrior grunted a few times when she rubbed too hard, but otherwise remained quiet while she worked.

"Good morning, Stardancer. I've got breakfast for Thomas and Syrah," came a gentle boy's tenor. "If I can, I'd like to help you," he added.

Kyrian looked up to see Devon standing at the top of the steps. Floating in the air in front of him was a tray with two bowls on it. The boy's face was a mask of concentration and his fingers wove delicate patterns in the air.

"Thank you, Devon. I'd appreciate the assistance. You can start by helping Syrah eat."

"Of course, Stardancer." He allowed the tray to settle on the floor next to Syrah and then helped her to sit. Once she was comfortable, he began to feed her small bites of the warm cereal.

Between each bite, Devon watched Kyrian work on Thomas. A blend of curiosity and awe filled him as the stardancer gently soothed the injured warrior when his pain became too great.

With the wound cleared of grime, Kyrian was able to see the extent of the damage. Lifting a lamp overhead, she spent some time studying the shape and depth of the gashes in Thomas' chest and planned how best to tackle the problem.

Suddenly, the room was filled with a bright, clear light. Startled, she looked over at Devon, who was softly chanting phrases from his grimoire.

Watching the boy, Syrah had a smile of pure delight on her face. "Boy's got the gift, he does," she murmured, noticing Kyrian's stare.

Kyrian nodded. "Thank you, Devon."

"You're welcome, Stardancer," the young man replied after the final incantation had been read. "Your pardon, Syrah; I thought the extra light would be helpful."

"Rein your cares boy, I was nearly full. I'd like a few more bites and then I'll sleep." Obligingly, Devon spooned up the cereal.

"Thomas, I know you're hurting, so close your eyes and think of a peaceful place," Kyrian said softly as she turned her attention back to the wounded man.

Tensely, he nodded. When he had first woken, his chest ached with a dull throb, but as she had cleaned his wounds, the skin seemed to spark to life and roar with a fiery intensity that had tears leaking from his eyes, no matter how much he tried to stop them. "All right," he whispered through clenched teeth.

The stardancer laid her hands over Thomas's chest, bowed her hands and began to sing a child's lullaby. The words reached out and wrapped around him. Agony dissipated as he drifted away to a safe, peaceful place where pain was as foreign as death.

From his place beside Syrah, Devon watched as Kyrian's hands were encased in an aura of yellow-orange flames. The magickal energy leaped from her grasp and sunk into Thomas' body. The lullaby was replaced by a prayer chant that filled Devon's soul with a lightness that he had not experienced since going to worship with his father. Before his eyes, Thomas' wounds pulsed with a dark red light, and black, putrid smoke puffed away from the skin, leaving behind healthy pink flesh.

"Amazing," the boy whispered. His face was flushed and his eyes sparkled with wonder. This was why he burned to learn to use the power that coursed within his veins. Magick was a gift given by the gods to help, not hurt the peoples of Y'Myran. The grimoire he held was filled with cantrips, but nothing inscribed on its ancient vellum pages carried the power of what he had just witnessed.

Sweat-soaked ringlets of hair clung limply to Kyrian's face as she worked. Her cotton tunic was damp and her breath came in heavy, deep gasps. Without surcease, she gave of her powers to heal Thomas until only pink scar tissue remained on the man's chest.

When she was finished, she slumped away from the bed, exhausted. She drank deeply of a waterskin, but did not move.

Thomas woke and sat, touching his chest in relieved wonder. Holding back tears, he said, "My children thank you, Chosen. I'll not forget this blessing." He yawned, and his stomach growled.

"You are welcome, Thomas. Eat and then sleep. The goddess' fire is draining to both 'dancer and patient." Kyrian finally found the energy to stand. Handing the Y'Noran his breakfast, she said, "You're next, Syrah."

Shaking her head, Syrah said, "Nay, 'Dancer. I'll keep. You need rest, and food, else you'll do nobody good, reeling from drain-shock."

Kyrian started and the other woman grinned.

"My gram's a 'dancer. Go," she made shooing motions. "My cuts are not as bad as Thom's and I'm finally sleepy enough to rest." She yawned. "If you must see me coddled, send the lady up to poultice my arm — it's the only wound I took from those cursed beasts." A wracking cough took her by surprise, and flecks of blood stained her lips before the seizure was over.

Closing her eyes, Kyrian sighed. "I wish the lungwort hadn't rotted. All right, Syrah. I know that your injury isn't as bad as Thom's — so I'll let you rest. But you will be visited by Lady Elisira, as you suggested. There's no reason why your wounds should go untreated, even if I cannot help your illness."

"I'll go and ask Lady Elisira to come up, then," Devon said, leaping up quickly. Gathering the empty dishes, he dashed downstairs.

Kyrian swayed on her feet. She needed to rest, and she would after instructing Elisira on Syrah's care. After that, she would talk to Azhani and learn her plans. *I hope she's making a shopping list.* With their guests, there would not be enough food to last the winter. They would have to send someone to Barton.

Bearing a fresh supply of bandages, Elisira arrived and said, "Devon tells me that you need help?"

"Yes, I'd like you to change Syrah's bandage, but first, let me show you how to make this poultice." It took only a few moments to explain what she wanted before Elisira nodded her head in understanding.

"That sounds simple enough. Is there anything else I should do?"

Kyrian chuckled. "Sure, toss all the dirty bandages in the fire; they'll not be useful again. Rimerbeasts, I've discovered, secrete enough inimical substances to completely ruin everything they touch, including cloth."

"Oh aye, well do I know that! Our weavers go into paroxysms of ecstasy after a beast year, for their profits fly!"

The women shared a laugh.

Under Kyrian's watchful eye, Elisira felt more than a little self conscious as she changed Syrah's bandage. Making an attempt at small talk, she said, "You saved Azhani's life. Thank you."

"It is what the goddess called me to do," Kyrian said.

"I'm delighted that she found you, Kyrian. She needed a friend out here."

Smiling shyly, Kyrian said, "I only hope that she's as glad of me as you are."

"She is." Elisira finished the bandage and then rose to toss the soiled fabric into the fire. As a fuggy, cloying scent filled the air, she said, "The towns and villages were filled with gossip about Arris' laws. I was glad to leave the kingdom."

Kyrian nodded. "I've heard tales. The king appears to have taken issue with nonhumans."

"Aye, though I know not its origin, for before his father's death, he was filled with longing for Azhani. There were those among the nobility who felt that the prince craved the warleader for his bride."

Oh, that must have been ugly. I wonder if that is part of the root of the troubles between Arris and Azhani. Surely, if he knew about Ylera, his jealousy would have been overwhelming. Kyrian pondered the information, and then yawned.

"My apologies, the fire is draining," she said.

"Then you should rest, Stardancer. I'll stay with them." Elisira indicated the sleeping patients. "We can talk later."

"I'd like that," Kyrian said.

Elisira went to the priest and held out her hands. Kyrian took them, and the noblewoman drew her in for a quick hug. "We will be good friends, I think."

Stepping back, Kyrian smiled. "You honor me. I would be pleased to be your friend."

After a nap, Kyrian returned to the loft with lunch.

"How are they?" she asked as Elisira rose to take the tray of food from her.

"Sleeping," the noblewoman replied succinctly. "As you should be, Kyr, my friend."

I like how she calls me Kyr. Perhaps others will choose to use it too. Her thoughts drifted to Azhani. *I wonder if she would let me call her Azhi, like Elisira does?*

"I have difficulty resting when I have patients."

Elisira smiled. "Ah, well, sit with me while we eat."

They picked up their earlier conversation, and shared how each had found her way to the northern wilderness.

"King Arris sounds like a man I'd not like to meet," Kyrian said with a distasteful grimace.

"Lord Loose Breeches is a man every woman should steer clear of; though the way he would have it, it would be disloyal to the crown to avoid his attentions."

"And you're not among the crown's loyal followers, I take it?"

Elisira snorted. "Oh, I'm loyal enough to the crown — King Thodan was an amazing man, who was filled with a depth of passion for the kingdom that made it a pleasure to be a part of his court. Arris, on the other hand, is an uncouth bastard who deserves to be horsewhipped!"

Waking at just that moment, Thomas let out a bark of laughter and said, "Nay, my Lady, tell us how you truly feel!"

Elisira shrugged sheepishly while Kyrian stood and went to the Y'Noran's side.

"Good afternoon, Thom. Did you sleep well? Are you hungry?" Kyrian asked.

"Afternoon, Stardancer. I did sleep well, and I am hungry." He sat up and stretched, smiling when the action did not cause pain.

Handing him a plate of food, Kyrian said, "Here, try this. I suspect you will tire rather quickly after eating — don't fight it. It's all a part of the recovery process. The fire may have healed your wounds, but your body is still adjusting to the shock of injury."

Over on the other pallet, Syrah's breathing changed as she began to gasp for breath. Elisira moved her, and Syrah began to breathe easier.

Kyrian sighed and ran a hand through her hair. "I should go check to see if there's any lungwort I overlooked."

"There isn't; I checked." Frowning, Elisira said, "Though I am surprised, because it grows wild hereabouts."

"Yes, it does, but what we had rotted. I felt terrible when it happened, and I didn't get anymore because I wasn't expecting company. My apologies, Eli." Kyrian smiled shyly, hoping that the noblewoman would allow her the honor of using the shortened version of her name.

Returning Kyrian's smile, Elisira said, "Be at ease. Cotton would rot in this weather."

"I'll use Astariu's gift again. Twice in one day should be enough to slow down the sickness until more of the herb can be found." Kyrian licked her lips and sighed. "Listen, I'm going to be exhausted by the time I'm finished. Could you see that a blanket and pillow are brought? I'd rather not wake up freezing." She knelt next to Syrah and closed her eyes in concentration.

"You do your robe much honor, Kyrian," Elisira said as she added wood to the stove.

Kyrian looked up and smiled. "I don't do this for honor, Elisira." She stretched her hands out over Syrah's chest. The magick seemed eager to attack its foe, for without even the presence of song, Elisira could see the blazing aura that marked Astariu's fire. Proudly, Kyrian said, "I do this because she has given me this gift, and it must not go unshared." So saying, she began to sing and the flames erupted, spreading from the stardancer to envelop Syrah's body.

"She may be one of the last in these parts who honors her vows," Thomas whispered sadly.

"Oh?" Elisira asked, turning to face the man.

"Aye. I doubt that Paddy knows, but the rest of us heard tales of how black-robed healers arrived in Y'Dannyv and began charging for the privilege of being healed. Seems that they've a new religion to spread, and the king's given 'em the right to take the place of 'dancers and regular healers."

Elisira tried to fathom how anyone who practiced medicine could do it only for money. "Darkness spreads over my land," she said sadly.

"It gets worse, My Lady. Do you recall the shrines we passed on our journey? They were empty, but they should not have been, not with winter lying heavy on the people. Sickness spreads too fast for a healer from Y'Dannyv to reach a village so far north. I fear that the Astariuns left with the elves." Thomas' eyes were sorrowful.

"Azhani needs to hear this. I'm going to tell her. I wonder if the Cabal had anything to do with the absence of the priests?" she muttered, recalling what Kyrian had said of her encounter with the kidnapper.

"Go, My Lady. I think I shall do as the stardancer suggested, and sleep again." Lying back on his pallet, Thomas was soon snoring softly.

Three candlemarks later, Thomas staggered downstairs, his ruined breeches clinging in tatters to his still bruised body. "Healer's down," he said groggily. "And I need something to wear that doesn't smell like dead demon."

Padreg leapt up to assist his man to a chair.

"A bath might be prudent, as well," Padreg said as he patted Thomas on the back.

"Aye," agreed Thomas sleepily.

Azhani sprinted upstairs and retrieved the unconscious stardancer. Gently, she tucked her friend into bed. She was unhappy to note the deep lines of weariness etched into Kyrian's face. *She can't do that again tomorrow. I need to get that damned herb, or she's going to kill herself to save Syrah.*

A hand on her shoulder made her turn. "Don't be alarmed. She warned us that this would happen. Let her rest, Azhani, and she'll be fine," Elisira said.

Sitting beside the stardancer, Azhani watched her until sleep smoothed away the lines in her face. Idly, she reached out and brushed a lock of Kyrian's hair from her face.

"I need to go to Barton." Elisira's information about the loss of healers and priests in Y'Dan had made her realize just how lucky she was to have met Kyrian. She was also forced to wonder if the noblewoman was correct in her assumption that the Cabal may have had something to do with that loss. It would explain why Kyrian had been kidnapped.

"Will you go to Barton for supplies?" Elisira asked softly.

"Aye. We'll not last the winter on what is stored here."

Elisira nodded. "Well, unless you've turned to banditry, or Kyrian's richer than she lets on, you'll need money. I've some jewelry that you can use for trade."

"Thank you, my friend. I will try to get the best value from your generous offer." She rose and they shared a brief hug. "I need to find Padreg and let him know. If the weather holds, I'll leave tomorrow."

She found him outside, staring up at the clear winter sky. His breath clouded around his face, and through the thin mist the warrior could clearly see the signs of weeping. Sorrow swept through her. Well she knew the ache of lost companions, for it had been her sad honor in times past to weep for the dead.

Slowly, she sidled up to him and laid a hand on his shoulder. "There was nothing you could have done," she murmured.

"Aye. That knowledge is sure here," he replied, tapping his temple. "But rests heavily here." His fingers slipped down the side of his face to land upon his chest, above his heart.

They shared a long moment, staring at the winking stars that lit the night sky.

"Are they always so deuced hard to slay?" he finally asked.

Azhani nodded. "They're at their meanest when they're adults. Best to get 'em young, in the caves. Eggs can't fight back, though the slime is still caustic. Killing rimerbeasts is mucky, numbing work."

"I thought they only attacked every fifth year."

"So did I. Their appearance now is just as much of a shock to me as to you. It's too soon."

Padreg's gaze snapped to Azhani's face. "Too soon?" He spat out an oath. "And we are stuck here, with no one the wiser?"

Azhani's eyes seemed to burn as she replied, "Yes."

Another oath. "What now?"

"Now, I go to Barton, for supplies and news."

"And in the spring?" he pushed.

"We tell the northern kingdoms to prepare for war."

~ Chapter Fourteen ~

Kyrian fell out of bed at midnight. Literally fell, since she was in the midst of a running dream, where she felt like the spirit of the man she had killed was chasing her through the snow covered forest and she had just tripped over Azhani's dead body and — whump! She was on the floor, staring at a dust ball the size of a child's fist.

"Bleh." The stardancer rolled over onto her back and poked her tongue out between her lips. Her mouth felt like the Y'Skani desert at high noon on midsummer's day. Gradually, she sat up, weakly running her hands through her tangled hair. Her jaw popped noisily when she yawned. Blinking sleep from her eyes, she noticed that Padreg and Elisira were sharing Azhani's bed. On the floor just a few feet from where she had landed, Aden and Devon had pallets next to the hearth.

Hmm...where's Azhi? Swiveling her head around to look at her own bed, she peered hopefully up into the covers. *Not there...then...hmm...drink. Thirsty.*

Kyrian stood and shuffled down the three small steps in the storeroom to dip a cup of very cold water. "Ah goddess that's good," she muttered, and dipped another cupful. Thirst assuaged, she wandered back into the main room, seeking dinner. On the hearth was a pot containing shepherd's pie. She ate swiftly.

Full, she went upstairs to check on her patients. Both were asleep. Azhani was propped in a chair with a light blanket covering her while she dozed. Kyrian wandered to the warrior's side and touched her shoulder.

Azhani woke instantly. Rubbing her face, she asked, "Trouble?"

"No, no trouble, Azhani. You just looked uncomfortable. Why don't you go sleep downstairs? I'm awake." Checking on the stove, she stirred the coals and refreshed her tea from the pot sitting on top.

"I'm leaving for Barton later. Make a list of what you need," Azhani said, as she stood and folded the blanket over the back of the chair.

"I will," the stardancer replied. Kneeling between the pallets, she extended both her arms outward over Thomas and Syrah, the palms hovering just inches over their sleeping forms. "Catch me if I tumble?" she queried, smiling up at her friend.

"Always," Azhani replied, as she went to stand in front of her. "Go ahead and make your magick, healer."

Nodding, Kyrian closed her eyes and began to hum. Her entire body was slowly enveloped in a pale yellow glow. The aura faded quickly, and true to her prediction, she pitched forward, to be gently caught in Azhani's strong arms.

Azhani held her friend up, as the stardancer began to shake and shudder. "You can't keep doing this, Kyrian," she whispered, running nervous fingers through the stardancer's sweat-dampened hair. "You're no good as a healer if you kill yourself."

"Had...to," Kyrian managed to get out between shudders. "Needed to know...how healed they were."

Understanding, but not liking it, Azhani nodded. "And?"

"Thomas will be fine with a few days' rest and some willow tea. Syrah still needs lungwort." She sighed and yawned. "I shouldn't be so tired — I just woke up."

"Yes, but you're going right back to bed. Thom and Syrah will be fine for the night," the warrior reassured her, standing up easily. Juggling Kyrian lightly to settle her against her chest, Azhani headed for the stairs.

"Whoa! Has anyone ever told you that you are far too strong?" Kyrian asked between yawns.

"A few people, yes, but I never listen," Azhani said, her tone light but soft.

"Right, can't let everyone know that you're aware of the secret," Kyrian retorted, breathing in the sweet scent that seemed to cling to Azhani like honey.

"Of course not. It ruins the mystique." They reached the bed and Azhani gently lowered Kyrian down, pulling the covers up and tucking them around her.

"Stay. You can sleep here," Kyrian murmured, patting the empty side of the bed. "I promise not to kick."

Azhani's lips twitched into a wry grin. The bed did look inviting, and she knew from experience that Kyrian was a pleasant companion, even in the most honorably platonic sense. *Ah gods, Kyrian. It's getting very hard to resist you. You're looking for the route to my heart, and you're very close to finding it.*

"Azhani?" the stardancer burred sleepily. "Woudja get me some water 'fore you come to bed?"

"Of course." Azhani brushed her knuckles against Kyrian's face and stood. Quietly, she found a cup and filled it. When she returned, Kyrian was fast asleep. Setting the cup down on the floor, the warrior kicked off her boots and climbed over the sleeping woman. "Sleep well, Kyr," she whispered, and then pulled the extra blanket up over her shoulder. It didn't take long for her to fall asleep.

After Kyrian had handed over her carefully prepared list, she went outside to look over the horses. Padreg, Aden and Devon were already in the yard; chasing each other and throwing snowballs like children. Laughing, the stardancer entered the shed and greeted the horses.

"Good morning, my siblings. I am Kyrian, and I am here to care for you," she whispered in the elven tongue, knowing that all of them would understand her. Arun's ears twitched at the sound of his mistress' voice and he whickered excitedly.

Caring for him first, Kyrian spoiled him with love and carrots, which were his favorite treats. Next, she checked and filled feed buckets and the water trough. Finally, she approached the worst of the injured horses, Padreg's beautiful yellow mare, who tossed her head and shied away from the red-robed stardancer as she approached her wounded side.

"Be at ease, fleet-footed sister. I offer no harm, only aid," Kyrian murmured, using the same language. Settling immediately, the horse's ears only flicked forward in annoyance when she began to peel away the bandages covering a large area of stitches.

"You speak the language of the horse-kin as though you were born to it," came Padreg's admiring voice. His elven was slightly accented, but perfectly understandable.

Kyrian tilted her head to the side, allowing the curls of her amber-hued hair to fall away and reveal the slight points to her ears. "I was," she replied in the lilting language of the Y'Syran people.

"So you were," he said, with a smile. "I have heard that nonhumans have trouble in Y'Dan, is this true?"

"I have not seen it with my own eyes, but rumors of the king's new laws have spread to Barton."

"They are recent, then?" Padreg asked curiously.

"I imagine so, since Y'Dan was where I served, My Lord." She spoke as she worked, cleaning each wound with careful efficiency.

Padreg let out a huge sigh of relief. "I had hoped the blasted rules were a sign of Arris' unfitness to rule and not of a cankered mentality in the moral heart of Y'Dan. I am reassured that my late esteemed cousin Thodan was not the cause of these blasphemous changes!"

"Thodan was a good man," Kyrian said softly. "Though, I am sure that Azhani would be a better person to tell his tale."

Padreg smiled and said, "Ah, but a good clanleader hears the words of all and judges them equally. So speak what you would; I am eager to hear your words."

Swallowing several times, Kyrian spent several moments just staring at the bandages in her hand. She knew that the monarch was attempting to make plans for the future, and to know that what she had to say might affect lives...it made her sick to think she might make the wrong choices.

"I think that Y'Dan can survive a bad king," she finally said. "What it will not outlast is an invasion of rimerbeasts. I have seen one, and they are fearsome creatures. Having also seen what are considered mild injuries inflicted by one of the monsters, I confess to fearing them more than any mortal man. Were I given to command, I would seek to destroy the demons before attempting to unseat Arris."

Grinning broadly, he clapped his hand on her shoulder, staggering her. "I knew that you wouldn't shoe the horse with wooden nails, Stardancer!"

Perplexed, she said, "Pardon, My Lord?"

"You have captured my thoughts and made them heel, Stardancer."

"Kyrian, please, My Lord."

"Kyrian," he agreed. "I am Paddy, or Padreg, to my friends." They clasped hands.

"It's good to see that we are all becoming acquainted," Azhani said as she entered the stable. "I'm ready to leave for Barton," she added.

"Are you sure you'll not take Aden with you, Azhani?" Padreg asked. The pair had spent candlemarks speaking of the upcoming trip, and he was still uncertain it was safe for her to travel alone.

"I'll be fine, Padreg. It's a short trip and I know the way. You forget I spent my childhood in these mountains."

"As you will, Warleader," he muttered.

Her eyes flashed. "Don't call me that," she growled.

Padreg looked as though he was going to argue, but Kyrian rested a hand on his arm. "Padreg, could you help me with Eli's gray? He's a little more spirited than I'm used to."

Distracted, he turned away from the warrior. "Of course, I'd be happy to assist you."

Azhani sighed. Another reason to appreciate her friend's presence had just made itself known. *Don't give me titles I can't wear, King.* She thought sadly. Her scar ached.

Taking a pair of sleigh runners from the wall of the stable, Azhani exited the building silently.

With the runners attached to the wagon turning it into a makeshift sleigh, Azhani was ready to depart. Between Elisira and Kyrian, she had enough food to last a week. Barring a mishap, she would not have to hunt or forage on either leg of her journey.

The group had gathered outside to see her off. The injured soldiers leaned on Devon and Padreg for support as her two friends fussed over her. Weapons were secreted everywhere possible on the sleigh and a blanket was left on the driver's seat.

"There, now your legs won't get chilled," Kyrian said with finality.

"Hurry back, my friend. I've just found you again and I'd rather not lose you so soon," Elisira said, stepping forward to hug Azhani briefly.

Azhani flashed a reckless grin and said, "Don't worry. I'm like a bad cold. It takes forever to get rid of me."

Kyrian looked up and said, "That makes you one disease I'm not eager to cure, then."

Everyone laughed as Azhani shook hands and exchanged hugs and wishes for good luck.

She made good time, even though Arun had to get used to pulling the sleigh. The waxed runners fairly flew over the packed snow, and she had to fight to keep the horse from going too fast.

Because of the temperamental weather, she forced herself to stop before sunset. Under a stand of bare trees, she pitched a tent for Arun and then laid her bedroll on the bed of the wagon. A piece of canvas stretched over the top made it a cozy crawl space. After a meal, she threw a blanket over the horse and climbed into her cocoon and forced herself to sleep.

She woke to find the world cloaked in an icy shroud that turned the forest into a crystalline palace. Climbing from her bed, she took care of Arun, feeding him before finding something to eat for herself.

Stretching while she ate, she absorbed the magickal beauty of the forest. The morning sun refracting off the ice sent rainbows glittering around the clearing, nearly blinding Azhani with the beauty of the simple scenery.

Moved, Azhani found herself kneeling in the snow and speaking a simple prayer. "I know lately I've been remiss in thanking you for my life, goddess, but today, in the shadow of your glory, I do. Thank you, Astariu, for letting me live to see this day. Today, I believe in miracles."

::Why?:: The word was filled with an unearthly music that echoed around her.

In an instant, Azhani's blade was in her hand. Spinning about, she scanned the clearing for whoever had spoken.

::Here, warrior. It is I that thou seekest. Put up thy weapon, my

daughter.::

Azhani gaped as light filled the clearing, forming a glowing pool of water. Flowing, silvery ripples appeared on the surface of the pond. Suddenly, two watery tentacles shot from the pool, twined together, and in a burst of shimmery light, formed the shape of an armored woman. Bearing a bladeless sword, the apparition rising from the pond was instantly recognizable to every child of Y'Myran.

"Astariu," Azhani whispered with hushed awe.

::That is the name I wear, warrior.:: A smile flickered across the exotic, yet beautiful features of the goddess.

The blade in Azhani's hand suddenly felt as though it weighed thousands of pounds. Turning her face from the goddess, Azhani sheathed the sword and prostrated herself.

::Rise, my warrior.::

"I cannot," she said. Every hair on her body crackled with the presence of the goddess. The pit of her stomach burned white hot with the intensity of the sensation, and Azhani didn't know whether to laugh, cry or rage at the deity before her. All her life she had served Astariu faithfully and yet she chose to appear now, when she had been branded an oathbreaker.

::Thou art no oath-breaker, Azhani Rhu'len. Rise, and let thy goddess behold she who has set the minions of the dark to scuttling about like crabs after the tide.::

Azhani slowly stood, warily eyeing the goddess. The figure's hands reached out, and without meaning to, she took them and was drawn into an embrace. As consciousness slipped away, she realized that the goddess was rising to hover above the forest floor. She thought that she should be afraid, but then Astariu's grip shifted and Azhani was being cradled as though she were a child. Their eyes met, and Azhani looked into the streams of time.

::Relax, and allow me to enter thy mind, my daughter.::

"All that I am, all that I have been, and all that I will be is in your hands, Lady of the Sword," Azhani mumbled, unconsciously repeating the oath she had sworn as a teen. The scar on her face ached with remembered fire, and she slept.

Astariu touched every one of the warrior's memories, seeking the reason why Ecarthus had chosen to vent his ire on her family. When she found what she sought, she smiled and laid Azhani into her bed.

::Thou wilt do, my warrior. Thou art not ready, but thou wilt be. Rest now, and forget. I will come again.:: She placed a gentle kiss upon the warrior's brow and brushed her fingers over the terrible scar that held the place where Her mark had been. *::This is wrong.::* Yet she could not repair the damage, for that would give alert to the enemy. *::Peace will find thee, Azhani, child of Rhu'len. Thou hast my word on it.::*

The goddess vanished in a shower of bright sparks, leaving nothing of her presence behind.

Chapter Fifteen

The sun was high overhead when Azhani dragged herself awake. Shivering, she slid out of her bed and looked around. Her sword had left a deep impression on her hip where she had rolled over on it.

"Must have been more tired than I thought," she muttered as she went to feed Arun. The horse was out of his tent and lazily browsing among the scattered bushes.

By the position of the sun it was nearly noon. *I need to remember to tell Kyrian not to use whatever she put in the pastries — it leaves me wool-yheaded.* She hitched Arun to the sleigh, cleared her camp and was on her way.

It was nightfall when she reached the outskirts of Barton. As she guided Arun down the main street, her every instinct was on high alert. The town, though not the size of Y'Dannyv, was large enough to support a decent nightlife even in the middle of winter; yet, stifling quiet cloaked the darkened streets.

None of the lamps had been lit nor were there any drunks stumbling from tavern to tavern. No whores blithely hawked their wares from the second story windows of red light houses and there were none of the usual taciturn miners and trappers conducting business with the townsfolk. Everything was shut up tight and lightless.

Cautiously, Azhani slowly headed for the inn. It was the only bastion of man-made light in the town. The soft yellow glow of torches threw a small circle of brightness that illuminated the snow outside the door. All was eerily quiet.

Reaching the inn, she halted the sleigh, and dismounted. There was no one to greet her. The door to the inn was locked. Hand on her sword hilt, she knocked.

It seemed like a lifetime before the bolt was slid back and the door cautiously opened.

"Paul?" she said, shocked by her old friend's appearance. A makeshift patch covered an angry wound that wrapped around the innkeeper's head. The wound had taken his eye and cut into his nose and cheek.

"Oh, thank the Twins, you're alive, Azhani! Come in, come in! You'll not find much comfort in Barton, but what I've got, I'll gladly share." The innkeeper stepped away from the door and waved her in.

Azhani stepped into the well-lit inn and blinked. The room was crowded with children and the aged. Paul's wife, Orra, was distributing bowls of stew while old Takk served drinks.

"Paul, what happened?" Azhani asked as she took in the bleak stares of the townspeople.

"Rimerbeasts." The innkeeper spat out the word. "Swept through town like hell's own fury. Killed and ate 'til they couldn't find no more t' kill."

"How did you..." Her voice was harsh with suppressed anger.

"Survive? Ran like a chicken on feast day 'n grabbed anyone that'd run with me. Locked ourselves inna basements. Come out when the screamin' stopped. Waited two more days 'n then searched the town for survivors. Found them kids inna basement of the temple with th' old priest. Priest been gnawed on though 'n didn't make it." Paul's simple, dry retelling of the decimation of Barton made Azhani's heart drop into her stomach. "Others hereabouts hid as best as could, and now we all stick together like ticks on a sheep's ass. T' rest of us be inna houses roundabouts, or keepin' track o' the forest for more o' them monsters."

"When did this happen?" she asked even as she thought, *I should have been here! I should have come and made certain that they were safe. Arris was right to take my title.*

Paul put a hand on her shoulder. "There weren't nothin' you coulda done, Warleader. They came so fast. Like a wind from hell, they were."

"When?" Azhani's voice grated on the word.

The innkeeper sighed heavily. "Five, mebbe six days, I think. Got my days 'n nights a little mixed." He gestured to his face.

The warrior nodded in sympathy. "What can I do to help?" she asked bleakly.

Paul looked at her, a gentle expression of understanding warming his blue eye before he said, "Well, we ain't been eatin' too good. Think you could help Tim and Mac get up enough food for us all? We was lookin' to eat light tonight, but with you here, mebbe it's worth the risk ta go outside. Mebbe check the houses that're further out. See what's left 'n all." The innkeeper quickly explained that there wasn't enough food in the surrounding houses to feed the survivors, who were mostly children and the elderly, so every few days, some of the stronger residents would run to the abandoned houses and search for supplies. They only went during the day, and only then to those homes that were easily reached on foot.

When he was done, Azhani said, "I've got a sleigh. I'll go out to the places beyond your limit. Just show me where, and I can do it alone."

A dozen protests were raised, but Azhani's stern face quelled them. "Yer a good woman, Azhani. Don' matter none what King Arseface says," Paul said, his rough voice softened by emotion. "G'wan up to the Bakers' 'n see what's left there. Gotta warn ya though, we weren't able to do much cleanin' up after them demons left. Ground's too cold ta dig, 'n there ain't enough firewood hereabouts to waste."

"I understand," the warrior said grimly, slipping out the door. Arun whickered she patted his head. "Hard times, boy. I'll rub you down and make you a mash when we're done. How's that sound, hmm?"

The horse's ears flicked at the word *mash* and Azhani took that to mean he was agreeing with her. Taking her seat on the driver's bench again, she slowly made her way through town, paying careful attention to the snow for signs of tracks.

Even though she was only half-elven, she still had enough of the ancient race's gift of night vision to be able to see clearly. No other tracks marred the snow beyond the circle of the townsfolk's perimeter. Cocking her head, she tried listening for the telltale baying of rimerbeasts on the hunt, but heard only the rustling sounds of a rodent. Maybe the danger was over. Maybe the beasts had gone to their caves.

"Or maybe they're having an Arris picnic. I'd be happy to provide the wine and cheese." She chuckled at her own bad joke. Arun stopped about ten feet in front of the Bakers' house, refusing to go any further.

The cold weather could not completely stall the effects of time on the dead. Wrinkling her nose at the scent of rot, Azhani dismounted and approached the home.

The walls were painted a bright blue, which stood out under a thick coat of snow and ice. Dominating one wall, a large brick oven confirmed that this was the home of the Bakers. Azhani crept up to the door, and willed her other senses to seek any out of place elements.

A light wind rustled the limbs of bare trees. An owl hooted from the roof of a nearby home and the slight crunching sound of tiny animals scurrying through the snow was all that she could hear. Carefully, she reached out and put a hand on the door, noting the absence of a handle. The brass hardware had been torn away. Slowly, she pushed open the door. The carnage within made her reel back, and she cursed softly.

The moon's pale glow illuminated the room, giving evidence to the utter surprise that the rimerbeast's attack must have been to the residents of Barton. Rust colored stains sprayed the walls, furniture lay in chaotic piles, and there were bodies everywhere. Blood and gore congealed in frozen piles that made Azhani's stomach turn.

One of the bodies was that of a rimerbeast. Not far from the carcass was a heavy marble rolling pin that was coated with frozen ichor, proof that at least one of the Bakers had defended their home.

Azhani closed her eyes and whispered a brief prayer for the souls of the Bakers, and then stepped inside. The bitter cold had only forestalled the inevitable. Before the bodies had frozen, hardy bugs and desperate scavengers had found their way into the house and to the remains inside. Partial decomposition had begun, giving the remains an even more horrific appearance.

Twins honor you, I would have been proud to stand by your side, she thought sadly. The demon's victim lay on the stairwell. It was a woman. A few feet away from her lay the body of a child.

Azhani's head began to pound. Turning away from the carnage, she made for the kitchen.

Memory hit, overtaking her with the force of a hurricane. Whirling, chaotic images of blood and death replaced the destroyed living room. Whimpers, moans and screams drowned out the unnatural silence. Azhani froze in place, caught in the maelstrom.

They came. Faster than she could breathe, they came. A boy's head wobbled out into the crowd, and a woman in patched chainmail surged forward, screaming for her blood. Azhani sidestepped and brought up the sword she couldn't remember picking up to block the furious blows of her opponent. Calmly, the former warleader dodged every attempt the other woman made at striking her. The woman grew angrier and angrier, finally shouting, "Die, you oath-breaking bitch!"

She lowered her sword and charged, managing to surprise Azhani with her audacity. Barely able to turn aside the blow, she ended up taking a shallow cut along her ribs. It was the first time someone had got through her defenses. The crowd cheered, howling for her blood.

Emboldened, the woman turned and tried to charge again, but Azhani wasn't going to allow it to work a second time. Neatly stepping away, she flicked her wrist casually and gutted her opponent. The woman's eyes registered shock even as her mouth dropped open, spilling blood on the already crimson snow.

Azhani turned away, ready to meet her next attacker.

Sound fractured the memory. Azhani whirled, drew her blade and charged through the doorway into the kitchen, sweeping the sword in an arc in front of her. She blinked in the sudden darkness. Moonlight leaked through the shutters, and gave the room just enough light for her to see several large, dark shapes. There was a heartbeat of silence and then...

"Mew."

Azhani's gaze snapped to the corner of the room where a smallish lump twitched and then rolled aside to reveal the dim form of a kitten. Shaking her head, she looked again, just to be certain her eyes weren't deceiving her. Slowly, she reached into a pouch for a candle and a box of matches. Fumbling slightly, she managed to set the candle on a nearby table and strike the match. The candle flared, brightening the darkness.

"Mew," the kitten cried again, jumping from the floor to the table and cautiously approaching her.

"Greetings, little cat," Azhani said, sheathing her sword and reaching out to lift up the scrawny feline. A bone-jarring purr vibrated her hand as she tucked the kit into her vest. "Let me take you to a safer place." The rest of the litter, as well as the mother, had frozen to death.

Quickly, Azhani searched the kitchen. No one had been in the kitchen when the rimerbeasts attacked, so the room was relatively undisturbed. Soon, she had filled the back of the sleigh with goods from the Bakers' larder.

Tomorrow, she would return to the houses on the outskirts of town and bring back all that she could. In return, she would take from her findings the supplies her friends would require to last the winter. To pay for the goods, she would leave Elisira's jewels with Paul. The innkeeper would use them to rebuild the town.

The kitten had curled up and was sound asleep by the time Azhani returned to the inn. When Paul and Orra saw what she had brought, they immediately called for several of the younger men to help carry the items into the inn. When they were done, they led Arun to the stable, gave him a rub down and then a hot meal.

Azhani wearily went inside and sat, not noticing how quickly a spot was cleared for her. Carefully, she brought the sleeping kitten out and laid it on the table, stroking its soft fur lightly.

The kit was orange and white striped, with whorls of a deeper orange, almost reddish tone that streaked down its body and ended with a white tip on the tail. There was also a white patch on the kitten's face, giving it a somewhat comical expression.

It woke and looked up with Azhani with liquid, golden eyes. "Mew."

Azhani's heart melted. "Oh goddess, what am I going to do with you? I can't put down a rimerbeast rising with a kitten in my pocket."

One tiny paw reached out and rested against Azhani's hand, claws extending and kneading the battle-toughened skin.

"Ouch!" Azhani jerked her hand away. "You've got needles on that thing," she said, reaching out and tapping the paw in question.

The kitten thought this was an invitation to play and hunched up, hissing slightly and batting at her hand. Azhani amused herself by playing "catch the mouse" with the kitten until she realized that she had quite an audience.

The table was surrounded by at least two dozen children, all staring at the kitten with needy eyes. One brave child lifted her gaze from the kitten to Azhani's face and said, "Do you think I could give him this?" In her hand was a piece of cooked chicken. Before Azhani could answer, tiny whiskers twitched curiously. Then, the kitten leaped across the table, landed in front of the child and delicately accepted her gift. When it had finished eating, it started to wash.

The action was an invitation to the children. One by one, they each produced a treat until the kitten was full. The bravest of them petted the sated animal and were rewarded with a purr. Soon, it was asleep. There was a collective sigh of disappointment, but the children withdrew, leaving only the brave little girl behind.

"What's his name?" she asked, hiking up onto a chair so she could watch the kitten sleep.

"I don't really know," Azhani said as she stared at the sleeping feline. "I wasn't even aware he was a he."

The little girl gave the warrior a look like she was the dumbest creature in the world. "Of course he's a he! He's orange! Only boy cats are orange!" she said, as if that explained it all.

Azhani nodded sagely and said, "Well then, I think since you know so much about orange boy cats, you should name him."

The girl's eyes became tiny saucers. "Really?" she asked incredulously.

Azhani smiled and said, "Yes, really. Go ahead. In fact," she leaned toward the girl conspiratorially, "why don't you keep him? He needs a good home."

She squealed, waking the kitten and attracting the attention of the others who still sat in the taproom. Quickly, before the warrior could change her mind, the girl scooped up the bleary-eyed kitten and crooned, "It's all right, Toby, everything'll be fine now."

The kitten, a little disconcerted at first, settled down and began purring as the little girl petted him.

Orra came to the table with a plate of food and a mug of ale balanced on one arm. "Looks like you got yourself a little friend there, Mattie."

"Oh yes, Auntie Orra, this is Toby and we're gonna be friends forever!" crowed the child happily.

A look of profound sadness washed over the older woman's face, as she said, "Why don't you take Toby upstairs and get some sleep, honey. It's very late."

Mattie looked up at her aunt and sighed. "Aye, Auntie, good night." She turned to Azhani, who smiled gently at her. "Thank you."

"I am Azhani, Mattie," the warrior said.

"Oh! Uncle Paul talks about you all the time! Thank you so much, Azhani, I'll never forget this! Ever!" The little girl bounced out of her chair and raced up the stairs, the kitten firmly tucked against her chest.

Tears glistened wetly in the barmaid's eyes. Setting the food down, she said, "That was a good thing you did, warrior. Rimerbeasts took her brother. His name was Toby."

In the morning, Azhani gathered several wagonloads of supplies from the outlying homes. By afternoon, she had found something that would make the coming of spring much easier for the people of Barton.

At the outskirts of town was a single cabin. There, with the help of the remaining townsfolk, Azhani carried the bodies of Barton's dead. When every building in the town had been cleared, casks of whiskey were poured over the walls of the cabin.

A fire was built not far from the cabin, and the survivors gathered. Paul stepped forward and began to speak.

"Ain't no use 'n tryin' ta blame the Twins for our sadness," he said, his rough voice carrying across the crowd. "'Tis the gods who we should be a-turnin' to now, thankin' 'em for givin' our families a place to go that's safe and beautiful. 'Tis the work of the demons that we hate, not the acts of our beloved gods. I say, Astarus and Astariu, bless my kin, take 'em home and let 'em know the peace of your valleys."

At those words, just as the sun dipped behind a mountain, Azhani lifted her bow and fired two flaming arrows. They hit solidly and within moments, the cabin was ablaze. As the cabin burned, the remaining townsfolk began to sing the ancient pathsong.

> *Bright sun has gone*
> *and the pale moon comes.*
> *Lift up high*
> *Reach the sky*
> *and my family will go home.*
>
> *Earth and air*
> *Fire and water*
> *bind us all*
> *Father and son*
> *Mother and daughter.*
>
> *Bright sun has gone*
> *and the pale moon comes.*
> *See up high*
> *in the sky*
> *my family is home.*

Unbidden, tears dripped down Azhani's face as the heat of the fire burnished her skin to a ruddy brown.

The next day, after several forceful suggestions from Azhani, the people of Barton built a wall around their sanctuary. Using rocks, snow and anything not already tagged for something else, the townsfolk began to erect a berm large enough to dissuade anything short of an invading army.

In gratitude, the citizens generously gave Azhani all that she could carry in her sleigh, plus two more horses to pull it. One of the horses, a smoky gray warhorse named Kushyra, was a personal gift to Azhani from the hostler. Most of his family had been slain in the attack, and her arrival had allowed him to bury his dead.

Kushyra and Azhani bonded instantly. The two warriors knew that they had found kindred spirits. *I've gone mad with Padreg's horse-love,* Azhani thought as she stroked her mare's velvety soft nose.

"Sorry Arun," Azhani called out to the patently jealous gelding. "When we get home, Kyrian will pamper you silly."

The other horse was a sturdy brown gelding of Arun's breed, who immediately decided that Arun was his long lost brother. Happy with her finds, Azhani prepared to return home.

Paul helped her get the horses into the sleigh's harness and then reached out to take her hand.

"Ye've done naught but good by us, Warleader," he said, giving the warrior her former honorific. "I thank ye. Someday, the gods'll repay your kindness. I knows it."

She shook the innkeeper's hand firmly and said, "I have done what any decent person would do, Paul. Stay safe. I'll see you this spring."

Paul nodded and stepped back while Azhani climbed up into the sleigh. Orra ran out of the inn just then, holding out a burlap wrapped package.

"Here, take this, warrior, with our thanks," said the innkeeper's wife.

Azhani accepted the package, smiling when the scent of pasties wafted up to her. The inn door opened once more and a small figure with an oddly orange lump on her right shoulder picked her way across the yard to the sleigh.

"Toby wants to say goodbye," Mattie explained, a cheeky smile working its way across her freckled face. "And so do I," she added defiantly, one hand reaching up to steady the kitten, who was starting to wobble.

Azhani smiled and petted the kitten before ruffling the child's flaming orange curls. "Be good, both of you," she counseled sternly, "and mind your aunt and uncle."

Bright green eyes sparkled as a freckled nose crinkled into a mischievous smile. "I'll try," Mattie said, sticking her tongue out at the warrior when Azhani frowned in mock anger.

Lifting her arm to wave, Azhani clicked her tongue at the horses and slapped the reins gently. The sleigh slowly began to glide away from the inn, cutting deep runnels in the snow.

She looked back once as she left. Men and women scurried about, working feverishly to construct the temporary wall. Nodding in approval, she turned her eyes toward home.

Chapter Sixteen

A faint vibration caused Kyrian to look up from helping Syrah Jessup into a bath.

The Y'Noran smiled. "Warleader's back. I feel the horses."

"I don't know, Syrah. She only had Arun."

"It's Azhani, Kyrian. You knows it, you've touched her aura — you'd know her if she were in the next kingdom."

Kyrian blinked in surprise at the other woman. Syrah smiled. "I told you, my gram was a 'dancer. You get the knack of it ev'ry time you use the fire."

Kyrian had known this, but she was amazed by how insightful the taciturn warrior was. "You must have spent a lot of time with your grandmother."

"Aye. She raised me," Syrah said as she sank into the warm tub. "Ah bods and bodkins but this feels wonderful." She laid her head along the rim and sighed. "Now, get you to the outside and help your friend. I'll not relax so much that I forget that I'm not a fish." Kyrian nodded and headed outside.

Elisira was there as well. "Are you excited to see Azhani?" the noblewoman asked.

"Yes. I've missed her."

They shared a bench on the porch while they waited for the warrior to arrive. *I'll wager she missed you too, Stardancer,* Elisira thought. The sensation of hoof beats soon changed from something felt to something heard. When Azhani pulled into her home, she was greeted by the smiling faces of her friends.

As they unpacked, Azhani quietly described the devastation she had seen in Barton.

"I should go...maybe I can help," Kyrian said, turning to head for the cabin.

Azhani's hand on her arm stopped her. Shaking her head, she said, "No, those that are left are well cared for by the Y'Skani."

"But I can't just sit here and do nothing!" the stardancer said.

"Pray, Stardancer. Pray for the souls of those who are left, so that they make it through the winter." Her dark eyes were saddened, but her voice was hard.

Biting back a retort, Kyrian nodded.

Very softly, Azhani said, "I'm sorry." Stepping away, she lifted up a crate of goods and carried it into the cabin.

"When does spring come to the mountains?" Padreg asked as he and Aden led the horses into the cramped stable.

"I'd say we'll be looking at the first thaw in about six weeks. However, we'll have to wait at least a week after the snow melts to avoid avalanche conditions," Azhani said as she and Thomas hauled the sleigh behind the cabin. "We should talk about our destination. I found a map of Y'Myran in

Barton."

The plainsman nodded. "I am not a man of the north, but it likes me not to ignore the troubles facing those who claim these lands as their home."

"So what will we do, Paddy?" Aden asked.

"I do not yet have the meat of a plan, Aden. It troubles me that a kingdom suddenly saddled with an unfit leader has also been subject to attacks by an enemy too early come. I should like to hear what Ysradan has to say of Arris' actions, and what the other kings think, as well."

"As would I," said Azhani. "Ysradan should know of Arris' actions — only he can legally remove a lesser king from power. Why he has not attempted to investigate bothers me, as does the apparent involvement of the Cabal." Briefly, she outlined her encounter with Kyrian's kidnapper.

"What a bale of broken straws that was! I too shall inquire into their doings within my borders." The monarch frowned. "It likes me not to think that such scum could somehow be involved with the troubles facing Y'Dan. Let us go to Y'Nor, my friend. I will give you the resources to seek out these answers," Padreg said.

Azhani shook her head. "No, it will be up to you to learn what you can in Y'Nor, my friend. My honor compels me to seek another's counsel before I can make further promises."

He looked at her curiously.

Softly, she said, "I will go to Y'Syr, My Lord. You must return home, where you will have access to better resources."

Padreg exchanged glances with his men. In her absence, Elisira had told everyone what she knew of the events that led to Banner Lake, including the death of Ylera Kelani. Facing a vengeance-filled queen would not be easy. Azhani might not live to help them save the kingdoms from the rimerbeasts.

The Y'Noran monarch put his hand out and Azhani clasped it. "You have great honor, Azhani Rhu'len," he said. "But your brains have leaked out of your arse! You'll die!"

Azhani's face darkened. "That may be. I'm prepared to accept that eventuality." Proudly, she held her head up and met the clan chief's gaze. "Lyssera will know of Ylera's last days from me, My Lord. If my life is forfeit, then so be it."

"What of the stardancer?" Thomas asked softly. "Will you condemn her to your fate, as well?"

"She is innocent. Queen Lyssera is not cut from the same cruel cloth that Arris rotted, and she will not clothe her in the garments of my wrongdoings. Besides, Kyrian may choose to accompany you to Y'Nor."

Aden, Padreg and Thomas all tried desperately not to fall down as their laughter echoed around the cabin.

"Would you make me a cup?" A deep, warm voice purred into Kyrian's ear, causing her to jump and almost spill the hot water she was pouring into a mug for tea.

"Ahh!" she choked out before the warrior's hand covered her mouth.

"Let's not wake everyone. It's far too early for some of them to even consider it," Azhani said as Kyrian pulled away, glaring at her.

The night before had been spent talking with Padreg and his men and there had been a keg of very good ale that had made its way around the small circle many times, causing Kyrian to glare at her more than once. Azhani had said nothing, though, deciding that if the Y'Norans got sick from too much drink, they shouldn't expect sympathy in the morning. For her own part, the warrior stuck to tea or water, needing a clear head to examine the map of the kingdoms.

Kyrian, Elisira and Devon also stayed away from the ale, needing to be on constant guard of Syrah. The lungwort Azhani had brought was doing its job, but she still needed to be watched, to make sure that she didn't stop breathing.

By the time Azhani had crawled into bed, there was a plan in place. Come spring, they would go through Y'Syr to the Y'Noran border. There, Padreg would take his people and go home while Azhani and Kyrian would turn northwest to Y'Syria. Once there, Azhani would seek her friend Tellyn Jarelle and ask that she allow Kyrian to stay with her while she went to present her case before the queen. Azhani had privately hoped that Kyrian would decide to go with Padreg, rather than follow her to the uncertain safety of Y'Syr. When she had mentioned it, the stardancer had firmly closed the door on that idea.

"No, Azhani, I don't want to go to Y'Nor — no offense, Your Majesty — I want to go with you. I swore that I would stand by your side, and I will!" Kyrian's face was flushed with indignation.

"I might be going to my death," Azhani pointed out rationally.

"Not if I have anything to say about it," the stardancer muttered. "Look, Azhani, I know you think you're doing the right thing, and maybe you are, but," she frowned, "I'm still not going to let you do it alone. You're my friend."

"And if the queen decides that my head on a pike is what she wants?" Azhani drawled.

Kyrian firmed her gaze and said, "That won't happen." She seemed poised to make a binding declaration that Azhani could not allow her to make.

"Fine, I won't stop you but—"

"I won't get in your way, Azhani. I'm your friend, not your pell," Kyrian inserted, which caused the warrior to smile wryly.

"Aye, you are my friend." They clasped hands, and all was forgiven.

"You scared about three years off me, warrior," Kyrian quietly said.

"Sorry," Azhani replied in mock contrition. "But I still want some tea."

"Well here, then," she said with playful aggravation. Handing Azhani the cup she had just finished stirring, she pulled out another mug for herself.

"So, what do you want for breakfast, Azhi?" *Please let me be right. Prove that you care about me, Azhani.*

"Um." Momentarily flummoxed by the stardancer's use of her nickname, Azhani stood there with the cup of tea held up to her lips. *Do I want her to take that liberty?* she wondered silently. Her eyes sought the stardancer's face and saw the hopeful gaze. *I do,* she decided. "Whatever you'd like to make is fine with me, Kyr."

The prettiest smile transfigured Kyrian's face. "How about something simple, like fruit and toast?" *Blessed Twain be thanked!* Inwardly, she did a jig. Outwardly, she maintained a friendly demeanor.

"That's fine with me."

After breakfast, they resumed their habit of sparring. There was a thick blanket of snow on the ground, but that didn't stop either woman from changing into more practical clothing and meeting each other in the yard.

Kyrian attacked with an open handed swipe at Azhani's shoulder, but she countered and scored a light tap on the stardancer's stomach.

"Point, warrior," Kyrian said. Her gaze never left the center of her opponent's chest as she watched for the motions that would indicate the warrior's next move.

"I always get the first point," Azhani noted, studying her opponent casually.

Kyrian's eyes crinkled as she smiled. "Yes, but I usually get the last," she taunted.

Leaping, Azhani grunted as she attempted a half speed spin kick, which Kyrian easily deflected. She was also able to score a tap just above the warrior's knee.

"Point, Stardancer."

They began to circle each other. Now that they had proven the other's alertness, it was time to play.

The day candle burned as they traded blows and blocks until Kyrian's natural impatience ended the match. Lowering her head, the stardancer charged and knocked a surprised Azhani into the snow.

She jumped back, laughing, "Hah! Point. I win!"

Azhani scowled indignantly, but stood and brushed herself off. "All right. Again."

"Go!" Kyrian cried as she danced away.

The warrior cracked her neck then shook her shoulders and watched the stardancer. Not moving, she just followed Kyrian's movements with her eyes until her friend noticed.

"Well, are you going to stand there all day, or what?" Kyrian asked, putting her hands on her hips.

Allowing nothing to give away her plan, Azhani casually began to turn aside and then somersaulted up and behind her. In a blur of motion, she hooked a foot around Kyrian's knee, and pushed her to the ground. Falling with her, she quickly sat and straddled the stardancer. With the point of her elbow touching the nape of Kyrian's neck, she asked, "Do you yield?"

Kyrian tried to buck her off, but Azhani's greater weight gave her an advantage. She attempted to twist away, but the warrior clamped her legs shut, holding her in place. Turning her head slightly, Kyrian blew out a mouthful of snow. "Cold," she murmured.

"What's that? Did you say, 'I yield, Azhani, because you are the almighty great and powerful one'?"

"No, I do not yield," the stardancer said through clenched teeth. Without warning, she pushed up and got one hand underneath her.

Azhani immediately wrapped her arm around the stardancer's throat and locked her head in place. Ignoring it, Kyrian reached her other hand back and casually tickled the warrior's knee.   The action so surprised Azhani that she jumped, loosening her hold.   Swift as a fish, Kyrian squirmed away.

Jumping up, she easily deflected Azhani's punch, and the battle was joined once more.   Grabbing Azhani's arm as she let go of a punch, she used the warrior's weight to throw her and as soon as she hit the ground, the stardancer put her foot on the warrior's neck.

"Do you yield?" Kyrian's face was flushed with exertion.

"I yield," Azhani said.   As soon as her friend's foot was removed, she bounced up and said, "Round three?"

Kyrian was tiring, but she knew the warrior wanted a chance to beat her, so she nodded her assent.

As soon as the stardancer agreed, Azhani rushed with a series of punches.   Hard pressed to block or avoid the blows, Kyrian ended up pinned against the side of the cabin.

"Do you surrender?" Azhani growled, as she leaned into the smaller woman.

Kyrian's already reddened cheeks flamed even brighter as the weight of Azhani's body enflamed a desire she had thought buried.   Swallowing hard, she looked up into the warrior's intense blue eyes and projected a calm that she did not feel.   *Surrender?   Yes, freely and completely,* she thought, but said nothing.

Kyrian wriggled, attempting to push her away, but Azhani only pressed closer, slipping her leg between the stardancer's.   Warm breath mingled, filling the space between them with white puffs of air.

Leaning in closer, Azhani whispered, "Do...you...yield?"

Kyrian held the warrior's gaze, battling for the right to claim victory. Frustrated, she banged her head against the wall, but she did not answer. A grin slipped across Azhani's face; she knew she was going to win.   Then, just as she thought the stardancer was going to say the words that would signal the end of the match, she got a face full of snow.

"Never!" Kyrian said, and laughed as the warrior reeled back, spluttering.

Azhani watched Kyrian ease away from the wall, still laughing, and felt her own temper begin to fray.   Hands clenching and leg muscles tensing, she stood there panting, as if readying for combat.   *Whoa there, warrior. She's just playing with you.   Don't lose your head over this!* Her inner voice grabbed her temper by its reins and hauled it up short.

Still chuckling, Kyrian left the wall to drink from the waterskin they had left on a barrel.

Azhani's temper demanded some form of retribution.   Quietly, so as not to alert the stardancer to her intentions, she gathered a large ball of snow, snuck around her and dumped the frozen glob down the back of Kyrian's tunic.

"Gah!" she shrieked as the cold snow slid down the center of her back. "Azhani!   That's not fair!"

Azhani smirked, crossing her arms and giving the stardancer a raised eyebrow.   "What ails?   Shoe not fit so well on that other foot?"

"Ooooo!   You big oaf!   I didn't shove it down your gambeson!" Kyrian retorted as she shook her tunic out.   *If I were going to shove anything down your gambeson right now, Azhi, it wouldn't be snow!*

Azhani stuck her tongue out. "So hire a barrister and sue me." *She is quite adorable when she is angry.* The thought came as a complete surprise to her.

Kyrian was enjoying the playful side of her friend. Smiling, she said, "Nah, barristers cost too much for a poor little priest like me. I'll have to handle this case myself." Scooping up a handful of snow, she rolled it up and tossed it, scoring a direct hit on the warrior's thigh.

Watching as it melted, Azhani felt a band around her chest loosen. She gathered a handful of snow and let a smile trickle across her face. "You have 'til three to run, Kyrian."

Eventually, the others found them and joined in the fun.

The stable was enlarged to accommodate the influx of horses. New beds were added to the upstairs loft as well as to the main floor of the cabin. Elisira and Padreg kept sharing their sleeping space, as did Azhani and Kyrian. One couple did it for the closeness that it engendered while the other stayed together because it made more sense to leave some open space in the overcrowded cabin.

On clear days, Azhani took to training those well enough to practice. Everyone pitched in to educate Devon in all the matters a young man should learn.

It rained; it snowed; there were blizzards that would last for days on end. The mood in the cabin became strained. Azhani installed a pell in the storeroom so that angry words could be deflected by the opportunity to exercise.

Syrah continued to thrive; her lungs got better every day. Soon, she was able to spend most evenings by the fire with her friends. At night, Thomas would escort her upstairs and sing her to sleep.

Everyone was aware of the time and how it passed. Each knew that the passing of days brought them closer to spring and a future that would be filled with war.

Chapter Seventeen

Hardag the fruit seller scurried through the streets of Y'Dannyv as sleet flurried lightly around him. Pulling his cloak closer to his body to ward off the chill, the older man prayed to the Twain that he would make it home before *they* came out. *They* were the black robes – men and, it was whispered even women, who had given their lives to the service of a new and terrible god. That they were allowed to roam the kingdom's streets after dark was an innovation of the king, Arris. *They* had arrived with winter's snow, posing as mendicant doctors, but now, everyone knew their horrible secret.

For these terrible, frightening and new priests needed sacrifices for their god. So far, only those who were condemned criminals had gone to feed their bloody fires, but just that day, Hardag had seen one of the desert folk, a morgedraal slave, taken from its owner in broad daylight.

If he closed his eyes, he could still hear the poor thing's screams. Hardag shuddered and hurried on through the night.

"You have beaten it, my friend," Kyrian said as she came out of her healing trance.

Syrah smiled. "So you promised." She looked down at her loosely fitting clothes and laughed. "I guess I'll be eating seconds of your meals, Kyrian. I'm a wraith!"

"Like eating her cooking is such a chore, Syr," Thomas said with a teasing grin.

Syrah made a face. "Well, what I've been allowed to have has been all right, though I've got a complaint to lodge with the cook about the tea."

Kyrian chuckled. "I promise no more foul brews — from here on, honey and cinnamon is the order of the day." She left to let the Y'Noran finish dressing.

The stardancer moved stiffly since she had injured her ribs sparring with Azhani the previous day. That left her sitting on the sidelines while everyone else geared up for practice. The mountains had been snow free for almost a week, and everyone was excited by the prospect of leaving. Every day they waited for the snow to melt, they packed their things and prepared for their trip. When that was done, their time was spent in weapons practice.

Outside, Padreg watched as Azhani put Devon and Aden through their paces. The monarch was impressed with the way the warrior handled her charges by giving equal amounts of praise and criticism, never fawning or berating them too harshly. Padreg's soldiers had taken to calling Azhani by her former title of warleader.

At first, it had bothered Azhani to be accorded a title she no longer held, but then Kyrian had explained it was a way for the Y'Norans to accord her a respect that they felt she deserved. Even the stardancer had started to use the term, albeit when she did, it was usually was in jest. Everyone worked hard to hone their skills, even Elisira and young Devon, but it was

Padreg and his warriors who routinely were chased around the field by an exuberant Azhani.

Inside, Kyrian was making a final check of the cabin. In the morning, they were leaving the homestead, and that meant that everything had to be packed, because no one knew when or if they would return. The horses were fit. The wagon had been refitted with wheels and it was ready. Azhani was so eager to leave that she visibly twitched whenever anyone spoke of the coming morning. The Y'Norans could talk of nothing but home; Devon was excited because Padreg had promised to introduce him to a mage who was a teacher of apprentice mages. Even Elisira had caught the fever of seeing the plains.

Kyrian felt a tiny twinge of anxiety. Here, they were safe. The cabin had become something of a cocoon for her. Insulated from the world, she had felt safe for the first time since that horrible day in Myr. Now, that safety was about to vanish, and she was afraid of how she would react. If battle came, would she be ready to fight?

Then, there was the issue of the Cabal. What would they discover about the criminal organization? Who had gone to such lengths to kidnap her? As much as she welcomed the spring, the stardancer wished that she could unburn the time candle.

Azhani's dark moods had almost completely vanished. She smiled often, and though her eyes were always haunted by pain, that ache did not seem to rule her slumber as much as before. Kyrian hoped that she had been a part of what made those nights easier. Sharing the bed had, at first, been difficult, especially since her body seemed to think of Azhani as a child's stuffed toy, but she never appeared to mind the affection. In fact, it was often the warrior who would open her arms to Kyrian when the lights were put out at night.

A yell of frustration sent her to the window to see what was amiss. Devon looked up from his reading, curious as well, and joined her.

Outside, Elisira rubbed her forearm. Leaning the bow against her hip, she said, "That's it. I'm finished. Would you be so kind as to stick this someplace where I won't see it for at least a week? Otherwise, I'll be forced to shove it up our esteemed warleader's arse."

"My Lady," Aden said in a tone meant to calm, but was interrupted by a hand on his shoulder.

"Well, well, what have we here? Throwing a tantrum all proper and lady-like, now, Elisira? Do you think that just because I'm all the way across the yard that you can get out of target practice, hmm?" Azhani's amused voice caused Elisira to roll her eyes and sigh.

Turning, Elisira gave her old friend a long look of severe irritation before putting her hands on her hips. "Well, *Warleader,* if you would deign to instruct me on how to fill that," she nodded toward the straw target, "with blunted arrows without turning my arm into meatloaf, I'd be forever in your debt." A syrupy smile ended her statement.

"Tcha, you've been sharpening your tongue when you should have been honing your aim, my friend," Azhani replied, casually taking the bow from Aden. He backed away, content to allow the warleader to handle the touchy noblewoman. "Now, let's see what we can do about that meatloaf problem, hmm? This is an Y'Noran bow, which you will have noticed has a heavier draw than your typical Y'Dani bow..."

Kyrian watched as Azhani handed the bow back to Elisira and then wrapped her arms around the lady. A sharp jab of jealousy cut through her and she angrily pushed it aside. *Stop that! You've got no right to be feeling the way you do, knowing how she felt about Ylera.* The seldom spoken of but often felt presence of Azhani's lost lover was palpable even to someone as sense blind as Aden. Once, when Elisira had made the mistake of asking about that particular subject, *everyone* had felt the anguish that bled out of Azhani's eyes. Even though her answer had been curt, they had all got the message that the subject was to be forgotten.

This was one of the reasons that Kyrian wanted to be by Azhani's side. For only with the stardancer did the warrior allow herself to grieve, even a little bit. Kyrian would not deny her that comfort, even if it meant that she would have to forgo her baser desires. Azhani needed her friend.

Though the insight proves painful, you are right, Kyrian. Azhani may be your new friend, but Ylera was a friend too. Would you dishonor her memory by luring her lover to your bed before she was ready to open her heart again? Azhani deserves the chance to grieve. Best you remember that. Closing her eyes, Kyrian pushed away the unwanted emotions, freeing them to drift away on the next breeze.

When she opened her eyes, Azhani had stepped away from Elisira and was encouraging her to shoot. The snap of the bowstring was audible across the yard, and so was the cheer of joy that Elisira let out when her arrow hit the target. Kyrian smiled at her friend's victory and pushed away from the window to fetch her medical bag. She had just the right thing for that nasty bruise.

The day of departure was nearly perfect. Sunlight gleamed off a snow-free wilderness while the horses were so eager to travel that they seemed to bounce with energy. Standing outside her door, Azhani placed her fingers against the worn wood and whispered, "I'll make you proud, Papa. This land will be whole again, I swear it."

She turned and studied the area, taking in the scenery. Snow was melting, giving way to patches of dark earth. The sky was a clear, sapphire blue chased with thin trails of clouds and the white-capped mountains seemed to reach high up into the heavens. All around her, the land was coming alive with the sounds of birds and beasts. Even the insects were waking from their winter nap.

Azhani shaded her eyes with a hand as she memorized the sight. She would return. This land was her home, and nothing would stand in her way, not even the enmity of a king. Nodding slightly, she lowered her hand and headed to Kushyra's side.

The horse sidled nervously as she approached. Taking the reins, she whispered soothingly to the mare until she calmed. Slowly, Azhani put her foot in the stirrup and pulled herself into the saddle, speaking softly and scratching the short, stiff hair continuously. Once she was settled, the horse reacted to her rider by pulling against the reins, almost as if saying, "Let's run!" Azhani smiled and allowed the horse her will. Using her knees and legs to signal the warhorse, she directed her up and over the fence in a smooth jump.

Looking back at the others who were watching their antics with amusement, she asked, "Well, shall we?"

Devon was the first of the group to join the warleader, guiding his smaller gelding to the gate and leaning down to open it. He smiled shyly at Azhani, who grinned in return.

"Good to see you've got some of your father's spirit, Devon," she said, moving her mount aside so that the others could join them.

He shrugged and said, "Well, Da always said that a man could only eat three feet of sword once before he learned how to get out of the way. I never quite understood him, but I always took it to mean that you had to be prepared to take chances."

Azhani nodded sagely. "That's as good an interpretation as I would give, lad. So tell me, how go your studies?"

Having spent most of his winter either burying his nose in a book or learning herb lore with Kyrian, Devon had needed considerable prodding to take up weapons practice. The call of magick was stronger in his blood than the call of the blade, but the boy strove to impress all of his teachers.

"Eh, well, you know I'm having troubles with the sword; Syrah thinks I'll never be a decent wrestler; Thomas says I could burn water and My Lord Padreg thinks my horsemanship to be passable. However, I can knock the knot off a tree at seventy paces." The young man grinned. He was proud of his ability with the sling.

Azhani eyed the boy's slight form, noting the way he held himself in the saddle. "You'll do better once you've got your height. As for the sword — well, a mage doesn't have to be a swordsman. Would you rather concentrate on the staff?"

Devon thought about it. Finally, he said, "Well, I'd like to have some knowledge of all weapons, so that I know how to counter them in battle. However, I am better at staff and sling than I am at the sword. I think that I'd like to continue to practice with all three, but concentrate on the weapons that are best suited to my abilities."

"Good choice, Devon," said Azhani. "Now, tell me what you've learned from Kyrian and Elisira."

They took their time. A day and a half later, they were in Barton. Radically changing, the once thriving town was now a shell of its former self. Several buildings had suffered damage in the winter storms and were being demolished. The foundation of a defensive wall was being laid out — no more would Barton be a place where a traveler could arrive at any time of the day or night.

There was much activity, but little of it was frivolous. Few children filled Barton's streets — there was too much work to be done. Recently arrived traders had set up down alleyways and were doing a brisk business.

They bought supplies. Azhani spent some time with Paul and Orra, discussing the plans for the town and giving them the benefit of her tactical advice.

Though the innkeepers invited them to stay, the party decided that it was early enough in the day that they could still travel a few miles closer to Y'Syr. They were passing a building undergoing renovation when they heard a voice call out, "Well bless me twice Padreg!"

Padreg smiled as he recognized the speaker. "Brother Jalen! Good it is to see you, my friend." Dismounting, the monarch and the priest met at the roadside and exchanged enthusiastic hugs. Introductions were made, with those who had been beneficiaries of the brother's gentle deception in Y'Dannyv taking the time to personally thank him.

"It was nothing," he said with a twinkle of mischief in his eyes. "It gave me great pleasure to send the little toadies out searching for owldragons."

Laughter was shared all around. "So what brings you to this blighted community?" Padreg asked.

"'Twas a dream sent by Astarus, Paddy. I woke one morning and suddenly knew that I was needed in the north — and here I am!"

The Y'Noran grinned. "Well, now we know how to drag you from your dusty books and moldy parchments. Though I doubt me that we'd get the Lord of Lore to prod you from your featherbed more than once in a lifetime!"

Huffily, Jalen said, "I go where the gods direct. Can I be blamed if my directions always seem to end up in a library?"

"Oh, surely not, Brother Jalen; for who else is so eminently qualified to rate the vintage of those books?" Kyrian asked, which caused the other priest to laugh.

"Ah, Stardancer, I see that my reputation has spread. Have we met?"

"I am Kyrian, Brother Jae, and yes, we have met. You were my instructor in the preservation of ancient texts at Y'Len one semester."

He cocked his head, as if trying to place her features. "Ah yes, Kyrian. You were the one with the flair for mending torn pages, I remember. It is good to see you, child."

They clasped hands.

"It is good to see you as well. You will forgive me if I admit that I do not have any of Y'Len's wines among my packs. The winter was quite chill."

Clutching his chest as if he had been struck, Jalen said, "Perish the thought, young Kyrian. I am a man of the cloth and do not require such earthly delights as the fruit of the vine."

Padreg, Aden and Kyrian all burst out laughing. It was the stardancer who was able to speak first. "So it was not you who raided the Abbot's wine cellar?" she asked, arching an eyebrow.

"Well, ah, blast it! You've knocked the wind from my sails, Stardancer." He smiled gently. "Yes, I will admit to a fondness for spirits, but you need not worry for my lack of Y'Lennese pressings, for I happen to have a skinfull with me!"

"Then you'd be able to give a girl a taste of home?" Kyrian returned impudently. Gaping, the older priest handed over his skin. The stardancer took it, drank deeply and handed back. Wiping her mouth, she said, "Thank you."

The brother laughed and said, "Padreg, my old friend, only you would be able to find the one person in all the kingdoms that could talk me out of my wine!" He thumped the Y'Noran's back heartily. "What brings you this way? I would have wagered that you'd be home by now."

"Plans have a way of shifting like grass in the wind, old friend. After we ran into that patrol, my men and I separated so that we would all have a better chance of getting home safely." His eyes glistened as he spoke.

"Are you headed back to Y'Nor now?" the priest asked.

Padreg carefully considered his answer. Even though he trusted Brother Jalen with his life, there were many ears in the open market where they had run into the priest. "Eventually. My Lady and I — we are enjoying the mountains."

Jalen's eyebrows shot up in surprise. "Your lady? Are congratulations in order, my friend?"

Elisira interrupted then. "Not quite yet, good Brother, but goddess willing, and my lord's courage providing, I'll soon call Y'Nor home."

Jalen's booming laugh once again filled the space around the small group.

"Brother Jae! Brother Jae! Come quick! Toby's stuck in the tree again!" a small child shouted as she ran up to the group.

"Oh dear, that is a problem isn't it?" the priest said, excusing himself and racing to follow the red-headed child who scampered down the road.

Padreg looked at Azhani, who was watching the priest's progress. "Should we lend a hand? A child in trouble is never good."

Azhani shook her head. "Toby's a cat — probably gets himself into trouble once a day. I'm sure Jalen can take care of it. We should go if we want to make it to the cave before nightfall."

"Then let us be on our way," Padreg said, easily mounting his horse and heading for the other side of town.

~ Chapter Eighteen ~

What remained of winter's chill did little to mar the breathtaking reality that was the Crest of Amyra. The trail that the party followed cut through a gap between two of the shorter peaks, which meant that there was snow at the very top, but the sides were a rippling tapestry of rocks, scrub trees and rapidly growing wildflowers.

When rain came to strip away some of the good cheer brought by the sun, Azhani's party affably put up their hoods and persisted. If the storm was particularly fierce, they would huddle under whatever shelter they could find, build or borrow from an absent occupant. Every cave was thoroughly examined for traces of rimerbeast spoor, though it was not likely that they would find anything on such a well-traveled route — it would have been the first place to be cleansed during the last invasion.

By day, the sky was an ocean of blue so deep that it rivaled the color of Azhani's eyes. At night, the indigo field was broken so often by stars that the sky glittered like a black diamond.

Game was plentiful. Rare finds of tubers, nut caches and early ripened fruit provided an interesting cornucopia that added to the supplies purchased in Barton.

The long tent that the Y'Norans had purchased on their way north was broken into smaller tents and shared by the group in pairs. Padreg and Elisira shared one, Azhani and Kyrian another, with Thomas, Syrah, Devon and Aden taking the other two. The horses were loose picketed.

The tents were small, but comfortable. Most nights, the occupants had separate watches, but on the nights when sharing was unavoidable, Kyrian found that she was unable to keep from gravitating toward the warrior's warmth.

Azhani did not mind being Kyrian's rag doll. The stardancer's embrace kept her nightmares at bay, and the warrior knew that every extra moment of sleep was an extra degree of alertness the next day. She kept herself to an exacting schedule of weapons practice, often rising early to face imagined enemies while the others slept. At night, she would spar until there was no one left who wished to stand against her.

Devon devoted his time to his studies, improving his magickal skills daily. His control slipped only twice, resulting in singed eyebrows and a long lecture from Azhani and Kyrian about responsibility. His skill with the staff improved, and he became passable with the short-sword, but his best weapon was still the sling.

The group's bond that had started in the winter grew during the trip. Padreg and Azhani became good friends while Elisira and Kyrian acted like sisters. Padreg and Elisira's burgeoning romance blossomed into a love that made the Y'Norans grin and slap each other's backs. For Azhani, the depth of emotion shared between her friends was both a welcome sight and a prod to the pain she harbored in her heart. Sensing this, the two tried hard to keep their feelings contained.

Throughout, Kyrian was Azhani's rock. At night, when the tears would come, she held the mourning woman. During the day, when Azhani needed to don a mask of control, the stardancer allowed her to keep her peace.

It was at these times when Kyrian and Elisira would ride side by side, and share memories of their youth. The noblewoman willingly shared stories of Azhani, and Kyrian's favorite tales always included an awkwardly endearing portrayal of her friend.

"Did I tell you about the time Azhani and I snuck into the kitchens to snitch pastries?" At a noise from the warrior in question, she said, "Hey, I could always tell her about the fishing trip."

Rolling her eyes, Azhani turned to Kyrian and said, "I should pray that you do not see me as a complete dolt by the time she has finished destroying my perfectly honed persona."

"Your reputation is safe with me, Azhani."

"You haven't heard all my stories yet, Kyrian. Anyway, so it was late and..." By the time she had finished, both women were nearly in tears, they were laughing so hard.

"Oh gods, Azhani, you must have looked like a ghost with all that flour covering you," Kyrian said, spurring her horse up to ride beside the brooding warrior.

Azhani shrugged. "Probably. Thodan wasn't amused when he had to come down and calm down the cook. I spent three days mucking out the royal stables as penance."

Putting a hand on the warrior's arm, Kyrian quietly said, "You know, if it makes you uncomfortable for me to hear these stories, I'll ask Elisira to stop."

Oh do cease this surly behavior, warrior! Kyrian just wants to get to know you. Can you truly deny her that? Looking into the earnest eyes of her friend, she sighed. "No, it's all right, Kyrian. I just...I haven't thought of those things in a long while."

"All right, but to be fair, let me tell you some of my embarrassing stories," she offered, smiling brightly.

Azhani never turned down a chance to hear about her friend's past. "All right," she replied, a tiny smile twitching at the corners of her mouth. "But nothing to do with baking ingredients, please?"

"All right, one story, minus baking ingredients, coming up." *Victory!* Bringing out Azhani's sweet, wry smile had become one of Kyrian's daily quests. Sometimes, she would relate an anecdote from her childhood in the monastery; others, she would question the warrior about their surroundings or something she had found.

Azhani knew enough about the area to spend candlemarks talking about the rocks, trees and animals that lived in the mountains. Once she had a background, Kyrian would then spend the rest of the afternoon concocting a tale about the item and related it to the group in the evening.

One afternoon, Kyrian discovered a feather, the type of which the stardancer had never before seen. "Do you know what this is?" she asked, handing it to Azhani. It was quite large — bigger than any normal bird – though in coloration it was close to a pigeon's gray and white shadings.

"A feather," the warrior replied evenly.

Kyrian made a face. "Azhani, please. I'm uninformed, not blind. I know it's a feather. What bird is it from?"

The warrior took the feather and examined it. The plume was familiar, though it was not one she had seen recently. It was fluffy and had a musky scent.

Kyrian watched as Azhani's mind worked, and she enjoyed the peacefulness that utter concentration brought to her face. The stardancer was barely able to keep from reaching out and stroking the dark scarring that marred Azhani's cheek. Taking away the tattoo that marked her chosen path was almost as great a crime as murdering Ylera. It made Kyrian's heart ache for Azhani's loss once again.

Unconsciously, her fingers strayed to her own face, lightly brushing the tattoo that rested just below the corner of her left eye. She vividly remembered her own marking day.

At eleven summers old, Kyrian was young to be seeking her future, but like many whose blood was of hybrid descent, the goddess had woken her menses early. In honor of that, a starseeker guided her to the casting pool, where she would learn if her life had been written in the stars. Kyrian eagerly awaited the chance to look into the goddess' waters, for she had long wondered if she would be called to serve Astariu, or if her destiny was unknown.

The moon's light outlined her naked body in a pale luminescence as she walked to the pool. She could hear the wind as it caressed the trees and tossed her shoulder-length curls about her face.

White grass marked the border of the pool. Clearing her mind, she approached the water and knelt beside it and closed her eyes. She did not allow herself the time to feel fear or excitement. Carefully, she recited the prayer that would activate the magick.

> *Astariu, lady of light, hear my voice tonight*
> *Is my life thine to honor*
> *or mine to hold?*
>
> *Is the path written*
> *or shall I carve the pen?*
>
> *Astariu, lady of light, grant me sight*
> *that I may serve all my life*
> *in honor and in joy.*

Kyrian opened her eyes and stared down into the pond. Silvery ripples spread across the water, creating beautiful patterns in the dark pool. Believing it to be a trick of moonlight, she started to stand. Mist rose and coalesced into a hazy shape. Blinking, she rubbed her eyes and willed the form to clear.

Under her gaze, the amorphous shape pulsed and then dissipated, revealing a portrait of Kyrian wearing the crimson robes of a stardancer. On her left cheek glittered the distinctive, three-teardrop tattoo that marked a person as one of Astariu's Own.

"A 'dancer," she whispered, and reached up to touch her as yet unmarked cheek. Tears welled in her eyes. To be called to serve Astariu

so — it was an honor that she had never dared to imagine. Stardancers were the most revered of the priesthood, because of their ability to heal.

"Thank you, Astariu. I swear that I'll not use your gift lightly."

Kyrian turned to leave the pool, but the image hovering over the pond shifted and revealed a new scene.

A great battlefield lay before her. The dead and dying were clumped together in bloody heaps that left the child-Kyrian feeling ill. Moving among them was a red-robed figure. At each body, the figure stopped and attempted to render aid.

She could not tell where the battle was, but she had the sense that it was cold, for the stardancer in the vision was dressed in heavy velvet robes. As the unknown priest passed through the battlefield, they seemed to draw closer to the actual fighting.

The vision shifted, and now the stardancer was climbing, for there was a sense of height about the surroundings. Bodies were fewer and further between, and the battle seemed to be occurring somewhere in the distance.

It felt as though she was trying to catch up to someone — as though the stardancer was hurriedly following a trail. Kyrian was filled with an enormous sense of dread that led her to believe that if she didn't catch the person, the battle would be lost.

Willing the stardancer on, she watched as the figure reached what appeared to be a plateau. Then, the image began to flicker and grow fuzzy, and then it vanished completely.

The next thing she knew, Kyrian was standing at the edge of the path leading to the casting pool.

Kyrian shuddered as the memory faded. She had forgotten about the strange vision. It was odd that she should think of it now. Dismissively, she pushed it back into the recesses of her mind. *There's no reason to invent disaster, Kyrian.*

"I think I have it," Azhani's voice sent the remainder of Kyrian's daydream scuttling off into the ether.

"What is it?"

Grinning mischievously, Azhani said, "It's an owldragon feather." She then went on to detail the creature's habits and habitat, but during the entire recitation, she wore the same, teasing smile, leaving Kyrian to wonder if Azhani were telling the truth or a carefully constructed story.

"Is this true? You're not making this up are you, Azhi?" A mixture of wonder and hope filled the stardancer's voice.

"I swear it's true," Azhani replied innocently. "Share watch with me tonight, and I'll see if I can find him for you."

"All right, I'll do just that," Kyrian said, a challenge rising in her voice. Even if the owldragon was just a fantasy, the stardancer would not regret spending time with her friend.

For her part, Azhani knew that the time spent with Kyrian might be the opportunity she needed to find out why the stardancer had frozen in the fight with the bandits. Azhani had tried waiting to see if she would trust her enough to talk about it, but there never seemed to be enough time for the two of them to share a private moment.

"I'm going to scout ahead. Tell the others that I'll be back shortly," Azhani said, spurring her horse into a light canter.

"Certainly," Kyrian said to the warrior's departing back. Moving back, she joined Elisira and Padreg. He was attempting to instruct the noble-woman on the art of grass weaving.

"Ah, Kyr, have you come to save me from my own fumble-fingered-ness?" Elisira asked jovially.

Kyrian laughed and shook her head. "No, actually, Azhani sent me to tell you that she's gone to scout ahead."

"Ah, well you are welcome to ride with us. Aden, take point, please," the clanchief said.

Aden nodded and moved up to take the lead while Thomas dropped back to the rearguard position. Tucked between the amiably chatting trio and Thomas, Devon used his time to study his grimoire while he rode. Every so often, the young man would look up to ascertain that he was still on the trail and then go back to his studies.

"Have you seen it yet?" Kyrian whispered for the thirtieth time.

"No, I have not. Don't worry, Kyr. I'll tell you if I see it," Azhani replied. The night was cold, and the breeze had quickened into a brisk wind, which made her grateful for Kyrian's gift of a ranger's cap. Tucking the ends of the scarf portion into her cloak, Azhani continued to watch the forest around them.

The silence was restful and, before long, Kyrian had slumped over in sleep. Smiling at her friend's odd position, Azhani pulled the stardancer against her and wrapped her cloak around them both. A candlemark later, she was shaking Kyrian awake. "Wake up, Stardancer. Listen." Azhani pointed toward the sky.

Kyrian struggled to sit up while cocking her head in the direction the warrior was indicating. Slowly the ambient sounds of the night faded away until all that was left was the flutter of giant wings.

With wonder in her eyes, Kyrian whispered, "Is that the owldragon?"

They stood, listening to the far off flap of wings.

"Aye, it is."

Leaning against Azhani, Kyrian whispered, "It's wonderful. Thank you for sharing it with me."

Smirking, the warrior said, "Told you they were real."

"You did," Kyrian said agreeably. "And I think that deserves a treat."

"Treat?" Azhani sounded remarkably like a child and her face lit up eagerly. "I love treats. We haven't had treats in a long time. What'd you make?"

Kyrian chuckled. "Devon found a beehive today and somehow he managed not to get stung to death while retrieving the main ingredient for these." She walked over to the fire and uncovered a pot. Inside were several small, honey-covered seedcakes.

"Ooo," Azhani purred, reaching in and scooping out two of the sweet, gooey cakes.

"These are ours — everyone else has had theirs," Kyrian assured the warrior who was quickly demolishing the pastry.

Azhani's face split into a huge grin.

Their watch was filled with quiet conversation. Azhani tried to entice the stardancer to talk about her battle troubles, but the priest cleverly manipulated the conversation back to the warrior's past.

Silently accepting her friend's need to avoid the subject, Azhani told of her own childhood. At six, she and her father had moved from the mountains to Y'Dannyv and at twelve, she had taken the mark that would lead her to the title of warleader. During her recitation, Azhani often reached up to stroke the scarred flesh that had once held a sword-shaped tattoo.

In a burst of compassion, Kyrian reached out and covered the warrior's hand with her own. "Maybe you can have the mark reinscribed," she said as their fingers entwined.

Azhani closed her eyes. *I don't know what I did to deserve her friendship, Astariu, but I'll never stop thanking you for the chance to know her.* She didn't bother to hide the slight hitch of a sob.

Kyrian's heart hammered in her chest when she heard the soft cry. *Hug her, you dolt!* her mind screamed. Standing, she opened her arms and said, "My hugs are free, if you'd care for one."

"I would," Azhani whispered, reaching for her friend and sobbing again when the other woman enveloped her in a long, soothing hug.

Kyrian rested her cheek on the top of the warrior's head. *Feel me love you, Azhani, because I do. You are my friend, and nothing will change that.*

"I don't deserve your friendship," the warrior muttered.

"I give it freely. There's no need for you to earn it," Kyrian replied.

"How are you so able to accept me, Kyrian?" Azhani sighed. "There are times that I feel so empty and so lost — all that keeps me going is the desire to see Arris dead. Shouldn't you hate me?"

"No. It is not my place to hate, Azhani. You want justice. And even though you don't think so, I know that your honor is stronger than your need for vengeance."

Azhani tore away, shaking with anger. "No!" she hissed. "You're wrong." Her eyes stood out brightly against her dark face. "I want Arris to suffer, Kyrian. I want him to know every iota of pain he gave her."

Unmoved by the warrior's ire, Kyrian simply asked, "Then why are you more concerned about the rimerbeasts than Arris? Why are you taking the time to make sure Padreg and Elisira make it to Y'Nor safely? After all, Padreg is a more than capable warrior, and Y'Syr isn't exactly enemy territory. It would be easy enough for you to slip away and return to Y'Dan."

"And become a murderer like he is? Never!" Gape-mouthed, Azhani stared at the stardancer. After a while, her mouth snapped shut and she grunted. "Will you always be here to pierce my evil moods, healer?"

Chuckling, Kyrian opened her arms again and Azhani returned to their embrace. "I will always be here for you — evil moods or not."

A candlemark later, the rustling of bushes broke them apart. Looking up, they spotted a sleepy-eyed Elisira, stumbling off into the woods for privacy. They shared a grin at the lady's loud sigh of relief that echoed through the camp only moments later.

Kyrian reached out and silently cleared the tearstains from Azhani's face. The warrior closed her eyes, bowed her head and muttered, "Thank you."

Stumbling into the firelight, Elisira looked up, squinting at the sky. "I guess my internal day-candle is getting better. Go to bed you two, I'll go get my grumpy bear up for our watch." The noblewoman waved as her friends bade her goodnight and crawled into their tent. Smiling, she filed away the memory of their sweet embrace. "Please let them be happy," she whispered and walked over to her tent to wake Padreg.

Chapter Nineteen

After a fortnight of hard travel, they crossed into the Y'Syran forests. To celebrate their escape from the mountains, they spent the night in an old shrine, safe in the knowledge that Arris could not reach them there. The atmosphere was jubilant, filled with hope and expectation rather than fear of what lay around the next bend. A keg of ale was opened and shared around the fire, and prayers were said to thank the Twain for their blessings. They found traces of elven rangers, but managed to remain unnoticed.

The weather turned warmer. Winter garments were packed away and the Y'Norans surprised everyone by dressing in an amazing assortment of dyed leather clothing that was a panoply of color and texture.

Small villages provided the group with fresh supplies and news of Y'Myran. Rather than add to their travel time, the party eschewed the inns, preferring to camp on the road. Azhani kept to herself whenever they neared one of the towns, sometimes remaining in the forest while the rest of the group went in to trade.

The news from Y'Dan was discouraging. Arris' laws had driven all but the poorest of nonhumans from the kingdom. There were rumors of a religious cult, but they were nothing concrete. Of the Astariuns living in Y'Dan, all that was said was that they had no longer felt welcome by the monarchy. The most distressing piece of information came in the form of rimerbeast sightings. Rumors all; nonetheless, everyone felt it was even more important for them to come to their journey's end.

Two and a half weeks past the border, they left the forest and entered the Y'Syran plain.

"Is this what your homeland is like, My Lord?" Elisira asked as they stared out over a vast, green sward that bent gently under the pressure of a light breeze.

"Aye, my heart. Though Y'Nor's lands are not as level as this. Our lands roll with gentle hills that are as green as the heart of an emerald." He smiled and took her hand. "However, the land's beauty is incomplete without our herds. Picture it, My Lady, thousands upon thousands of horses ranging among the hills. They share our lives and lands. You will see, Eli. I only hope that you will love it as I do."

The lady's hand unconsciously went to the mane of her horse, Windfoot. Sifting through the thick strands of hair, she lightly scratched the stallion's neck. Suddenly, she smiled and said, "I am sure, My Lord, that with your poetic eye to guide me, that loving your home will be as easy as loving you."

The clanchief could do nothing but smile like a stunned fool.

"My Lord, I hate to interrupt, but the warleader's asking to speak to you," Aden's soft voice rumbled from behind them.

They rode to Azhani's side. "Is there something amiss?" Elisira asked.

Azhani shook her head. "No, but we're in need of supplies. Myr's that way by a day or so." She pointed eastward. "I thought that it would be best to send Kyrian and Syrah into town for supplies."

Kyrian, overhearing the name of her former home, said, "I'd rather not go, if that's all right. I-I'd like some time to study the plants that grow around here."

Azhani frowned at her friend, but Elisira asked, "Why don't we send Devon with Syrah? It would be a good experience for the lad, don't you think, Azhani?" Something about the town of Myr made Kyrian very unhappy, and the noblewoman knew that Azhani could inadvertently cause the stardancer grief, were she to insist that Kyrian go anyway.

Devon shot the warrior a hopeful look and she laughed. "Fine, yes, you can go, Devon. Just don't dally at the library. We don't have much time." *And another mysterious clue lands in my lap. Kyrian's been to Myr. I can sense the truth of that; so why does she not wish to return? It can't be because I'd be staying here.* Puzzled, Azhani added the mystery of Myr to her short list of things to discover about her friend.

"Of course, Warleader, but, could I look for a little while?" Devon asked eagerly while everyone chuckled.

While Syrah and Devon went to Myr, the rest of the party set up camp at the border between the plains and the forest. True to her word, Kyrian spent much of the first night collecting herbs and plants indigenous to the area. Tagging along behind her, Elisira tried several times to bring up the subject of Myr, but on this one issue, Kyrian was strangely mum. The night passed swiftly, and the morning was filled with sparring and joking between the friends.

Later, Padreg and Azhani sat before the small fire and shared the dregs of a wineskin. "I've a question to ask, warrior, and I lack the words to say it without causing offense, so forgive me," rumbled Padreg hesitantly.

"You want to know why I was exiled." Azhani's voice was flat.

"Aye. If Arris' version of events is ill spoken, then I would know the truth. Elisira has told what she knows, and your stardancer related the information she heard from the bards and minstrels, but I would hear your version."

Kyrian didn't tell them? She was strangely touched by her friend's reticence. *Of course, that means I have to tell it – again.* A hundred emotions flickered across her face. Sighing, she said, "Much of what you have heard about Banner Lake is true. I am guilty of slaying or maiming a total of one hundred and six soldiers beholden to the kingdom of Y'Dan. What I am not guilty of is treason, or of the death of Ambassador Kelani."

Padreg nodded. "I am aware of your innocence with regard to your beloved, Azhani. Elisira has given me that tale." The sick expression on his face sent a chill through the warrior.

"She knows what happened to Ylera?"

Padreg closed his eyes and let out a deep sigh. "Aye, and I beg of you — never ask her to relate it."

A haunted look of pain entered Azhani's eyes. "I can imagine what she must have seen."

"'Twas not a good tale in the telling," Padreg mumbled. Gently, he set a hand on her arm. "It is the accusation of treason that most concerns me. Did you try to take the throne?"

Azhani looked away. "Yes, and no — it's complicated." Slowly, she related to him the tale of Thodan's shame in his only son, and how he had made her his heir.

"Did you have proof of this anointing?" the Y'Noran monarch wanted to know.

"Yes. I had a scroll duly signed and sealed by Thodan himself. It did me no good. Somehow, Arris managed to turn the Council against me, and before I knew it I'd been arrested. Of course, I wasn't much in the mood to fight back, not after he presented what was left of," here, her voice turned so flat it was nearly toneless, "Ylera to the nobles of the Council." A muscle in Azhani's cheek twitched uncontrollably. "I was so arrogant — so sure that they would heed the word of the man who'd given them peace that I never suspected that they could be led by their coffers."

"You suspect they were bought off?"

"Yes! How else can you explain it? I did not forge the document, as Arris suggested, nor did I plan to overthrow Y'Dan and hand the kingdom over to the elves, as rumor has it." Azhani stood and began to pace.

"If Arris is dethroned, will you step in and rule in his place?"

Azhani looked at Padreg as though he was daft. Covering her face with her hands, she shook her head. "I don't want the throne, Paddy. I never did. All I wanted was to marry Ylera, teach people how to defend the kingdom and maybe raise a few kids." She looked at him with bleak eyes. "Those dreams are ashes. All I have left is hate and honor."

"And friends," he said softly.

She glanced over at Kyrian and Elisira and her expression softened. "And friends."

"As your friend, Azhani, I can say that there is no one else more qualified to rule poor Y'Dan than you," Padreg said softly.

"The Council of Nobles would say you different," she replied.

"Aye, they would. But you love your land, and the people. The nobles I saw in that muck bin wouldn't give two plugged coppers for the land unless it made them more powerful. In any event, think on it, my friend. Sooner or later, Arris will be made to pay for his crimes, and when that happens, your name will come up — and I will be the first to sing your praises to Ysradan!"

Azhani glared at him, but Padreg only smiled.

After gathering herbs, Kyrian wandered back toward the forest while the others searched for firewood. The memories came unbidden, even though she was nowhere near the empty glade where she had taken a life. Ruddy pools of blood seemed to lurk in every shadow, and finally Kyrian could stand it no more. Sinking to the ground, she gave in and cried for a man who had not earned anyone's tears.

A candlemark later, Azhani found her, sitting in the middle of a clearing, running her fingers through a patch of yellowed grass. Tears stained a face haunted by a look of sadness so infinitely regretful, that it tore at the warrior's heart.

"Kyrian?" she called out.

Startled, the stardancer leapt to her feet. "Sorry, I was just exploring the area. It's been a while since I was here and I wanted to see how it had changed," she babbled, edging away from the spot where she had been sitting.

There was a frantic, almost panicky quality to her friend's voice, so Azhani didn't press for details. "It's all right. I came to tell you that Devon and Syrah are back. We're all waiting breathlessly to try your new recipe," she said, smiling brightly.

"Oh, yes, dinner! Of course, I'll come right away," Kyrian said, the sadness vanishing so completely it was as if it never existed. Yet Azhani could see the stains on the stardancer's face, and there were shadows in her brilliant green eyes. Casually, she dropped an arm around her friend's shoulders, pulling her into a loose hug. "Thanks for cooking today. I believe that Elisira was growing tired of Aden's charred meat-on-a-stick meals."

A sweet smile was her reward. "Thanks, I know how much you like my stew."

"Hey, a person's got to have one favorite, right? Just be glad it's something simple, instead of some incredibly complex marzipan sculpture," Azhani replied teasingly. They left the clearing, but the warrior painted the details into her memory, and knew that soon she would have to seek the root of the trouble.

They returned to the camp in time to see the last of the supplies unloaded from the wagon. Nearby, two exhausted horses were being treated to a brisk rubdown while Kyrian cooked supper.

"What's the news?" asked Aden after their provisions had been put away and the meal served.

Syrah chuckled while Devon tried hard to ignore the conversation. "Well, our good warleader here is worth an astonishing amount of gold to Lyssera, for one thing."

"How much is my carcass worth?" Azhani asked lightly as she speared a piece of meat with her fork.

"Dead — nothing. Lyssera wants you alive. For that, she is willing to pay the princely sum of 25,000 goldmarks."

Low whistles echoed around the campfire.

Azhani only shrugged. "What's Arris paying?"

"He's doubled Lyssera's price, but it's not likely that any Y'Syran bounty hunter would collect. They're all up in arms over his nonhuman policies."

"So between them, I'm worth 75,000 goldmarks. That's not too bad," she said nonchalantly. "Maybe I should turn myself in and use the reward money to start up a bookbindery."

Everyone looked at Azhani as though she was daft.

"What?" The warrior returned their stares. "Am I not allowed to have a sense of humor? Please, my friends, I know I'm usually as prickly as a cactus in a windstorm, but blood and bones, I can enjoy a good joke."

Elisira was the first to speak. She looked directly at Kyrian and said, "You've got to stop mixing up your healing herbs with your cooking spices, Kyr. It's dangerous."

Kyrian made a face and said, "I don't carry herbs that could cause that type of reaction, Eli."

"All right, if you didn't do it, then," she said as she turned and mock glared at Azhani, "Padreg, hand me my sword. I do believe that we have an imposter in our midst."

Laughing and shaking her head ruefully, Azhani said, "I guess you can't change overnight, can you?" As fast as it had come, her good humor vanished, to be replaced by a frightening mask that was as dark and brooding as any she had worn in the past. "Is this any better?" she growled.

Elisira tried hard not to laugh. "Oh, yes," she said solemnly. "Much better. Now you're the sourpuss we all know and love."

"So what else did you find out?" Kyrian interjected, hoping to head off any unpleasantness. By the look in Azhani's eyes, things were about to become very unfunny.

"Well, Syrah mentioned the nonhuman policies. The elven merchants are angry enough to spread the word. Rumor has it that even some human traders are staying away from Y'Dan this season," Devon said.

"I heard that Three Kingdoms Crossing is considering a full embargo on any traders from Y'Dan," Syrah added.

"Someone on the Council must have been turned away by the border guards," Aden said. "Because the last time Crossing declined trade was when those slavers attempted to claim asylum from Y'Skan."

"Aye, well, Crossing isn't the only kingdom put out by Arris' actions. The dwarves have declared Y'Dan as a place of no fire, meaning that they will sell nothing to the kingdom until a new king sits upon the throne." Everyone grew silent at Syrah's pronouncement.

"And what of the high king?" Padreg asked.

"No word. There's a rumor he's not even in Y'Mria," Devon said.

"I'll send a messenger to Ysradan the moment I return to Y'Nym," Padreg declared.

"I would like to hear what you learn," Azhani said.

"Aye. I'll contact you in Y'Syria through one of my factors. I'm sure that my royal cousins will have an opinion on young Arris' actions as well; I'll add their observations to that report."

"Thank you," Azhani said quietly.

As the meal concluded, Padreg stood and said, "Are you sure that I cannot entice you to travel to Y'Nor, Kyrian? Your talents as a stardancer are wasted — you could be serving as a chef to kings!" His smile was openly teasing.

Laughing, Kyrian said, "As much as your flattery polishes my ego, My Lord, I'm afraid that it does not hold the same passion for me as medicine."

"'Tis a shame, Stardancer, for I was ready to offer you luxuries of the kind only found on the endless plains of my homeland."

Kyrian's bright laughter put a frown on Azhani's face.

Noticing this, Elisira put a hand on Padreg's arm and said, "My Lord, my heart doth flutter about in anxiety. Surely thou wilt not favor thy desire for a meager cook over the needs of your chosen lady?" She batted her eyes prettily.

Flummoxed, Padreg's plate slipped from his hand and crashed to the ground. Taking her hand within his, he drew the noblewoman to her feet and clasped her in a gentle embrace. "Nay, never would I say such, My Lady." He sounded broken by her words. "Forgive me."

Elisira smiled and caressed his face gently. "There is nothing to forgive you, silly oaf," she whispered for his ears alone. "I was attempting to save you from a royal thrashing by one irritated warleader. In the future, I would not suggest even jokingly that Kyrian be removed from her side by any other than the stardancer herself."

"Have I thrust my foot into my mouth and gnawed off a toe?" he whispered back as they embraced to hide their conversation.

Shaking her head slightly, Elisira said, "Nay, My Lord. You have only bitten it lightly."

"Then I shall mend it," he replied and they parted. Turning to Kyrian, he put on a mournful expression and said, "Good Stardancer, please forgive any impropriety. I meant no harm in my teasing."

By now, Kyrian had recognized that something was wrong. She looked at Azhani and caught the barest hint of her mood before she stood and strode away from the fire. "That's not necessary, Padreg. I knew that you were joking." *What's the trouble with Azhani? Surely she knew that it was a joke.*

Lowering his voice to a bare whisper, Padreg said, "But others did not."

"I'll help you wash the dishes," Elisira said. Grabbing the stunned stardancer's robe, she dragged her to the back of the wagon.

"All right, what's going on?" Kyrian asked archly.

"I think the good warleader is afraid of losing another person she cares for, Kyrian. If her eyes had been daggers, my Paddy would have been bleeding from a dozen wounds."

Kyrian's eyes grew round with wonder. A brilliant smile blazed on her face. "I thought she was indifferent to my presence. Your lord deserves my thanks," she said softly as they began to clean the dishware. *I knew you cared, Azhi. I just didn't know you were so afraid of my leaving.*

Azhani prowled the darkness. Inwardly, she berated herself for behaving like a child. *What is bothering you, warrior? Padreg was just having a little fun and there you were acting like he was trying to kidnap her. She's free to go wherever she chooses, and you know that!* Azhani kicked a loose stone and watched as it flew over the tall grass. "But I don't want her to leave me," she whispered.

Back at camp, the clean up was finished. Thomas and Aden took their places at watch while the others gathered around the fire to enjoy a cup of spiced cider. Off to one side, Devon practiced lighting and snuffing a candle while cards and dice were brought out by the others as the group paired off to enjoy a night of quiet entertainment.

Only Azhani abstained from the jovial atmosphere, for she was still at odds with her earlier behavior. On the one hand, she wanted Kyrian to be safe and happy, but on the other, she knew that it was the stardancer's gentle presence that allowed her to stay sane.

Within the warm circle of friends, Azhani's absence was keenly felt by Kyrian. However, she was unsure of how to leave without breaking up the good mood that had settled over the group.

An opportunity finally came when she drained the last of her tea and she realized that now would be a good time to locate a private bush. Politely, she excused herself, found that bush and then went off in search of the warleader.

"Bit of a chilly night to be out for a starlit stroll, don't you think, healer?" Azhani's deep voice asked from behind her.

Kyrian spun around and almost slammed into the warrior's armor-clad chest. "Oof! Astarus' breath, Azhi, don't you ever warn a body before you send 'em to the heavens?"

Azhani smirked and put a hand on Kyrian's shoulder to steady her. "No. What would be the point? Anyway, what are you doing out here? Has Padreg used a set of loaded dice and stripped you of your coppers so quickly?"

"No, I just missed you. We're enjoying ourselves and I thought that you'd like to join us."

"I have no stomach for company," Azhani said as she stepped away from her friend. "You go back and enjoy it. I'll keep an eye out for trouble — let Aden and Thom know that they can stand down for now." She vanished into the darkness.

"No, wait, please," Kyrian called out. The faint outline of the war-leader's aura was the only clue that she had been heard. *Maybe she feels pressured to perform.* "Azhani, come and join us. You don't have to play, just sit, and enjoy the camaraderie."

There was silence, followed by the rustling of an animal in the tree overhead, and then, "We used to play outside on nights like this." Azhani took a deep breath and haltingly continued. "We'd go into the garden and harp. She taught me, to keep up her own skill, she said. Though now I wonder if it was just another excuse to be near me." The thin moonlight illuminated the tears that streaked her dusky skin. Dashing them away angrily, Azhani said, "I didn't join you because I didn't want to. So please, just leave me be."

There was so much raw pain in the warrior's voice that it stopped Kyrian in her tracks. *Oh Ylera, I seem to always be chasing away your ghost.* "No," she said, stepping up to her friend's side. "I'll stay out here with you, if you won't come back with me."

"Kyr—"

"Azhi, no. You're my friend, and you need me." *Please don't make me go away.*

Their eyes met, and equal amounts of determination flashed in silent communication between them.

"Fine then, follow me and don't get lost. I don't feel like searching the entire forest for you, healer."

Kyrian only smiled and slipped up behind her friend, determined to show the prickly warrior that she was capable of walking patrol.

The absence of the high king gnawed on Padreg's thoughts like a beaver on a tree. When morning turned the sky gray, he was the first to awaken. Eager to reach Y'Nym, he was already planning which of his contacts to speak to and what he would say to the other kings. He also considered sending spies into Y'Dan to foment rebellion, but that would have to be something he discussed with his clanchiefs. War was something he wished to avoid, but if there was no other way to remove the tyrannical king, it was an option to be explored.

Before anything could be done to depose Arris, though, the north had to be made safe against the rimerbeasts. That meant waiting while diplomats and scouts did all the legwork.

It also meant waiting to see if Azhani would be successful at making peace with Lyssera. The Y'Noran monarch nearly decided to discard their original plan and go with the warrior to Y'Syria, but respect kept him from doing so. To the elves, it might appear as though Azhani only came to them because she had been forced to do so by Padreg.

Just as eager as Padreg to reach their goal, Azhani quickened their pace. There was no celebration that night, for by day's end, everyone was bone tired. Yet there was a sense of accomplishment, because the border was only a day's travel away.

It was a somber party that packed up the next morning, for all knew that their path would diverge at nightfall. Talk was purposefully light, for each knew that in their next meeting, their lives would be very different. Riding side by side, Kyrian and Elisira spoke quietly of the future.

"Are you as frightened by what looms on the horizon as I?" the noblewoman asked.

Kyrian nodded. "Yes. But only because I worry that it will cause her further harm. I wish that she would let Padreg speak for her."

"I agree, but Paddy has said that the elves might perceive it wrongly. It is best this way, though it causes those of us who love her grief."

"Yes," Kyrian said. There was something in her eyes that Elisira felt compelled to pursue. "But I belong at her side. I need to be there."

"She has taken more than your friendship, hasn't she?"

"What do you mean?" Kyrian's head snapped up and she glared at her friend.

Elisira smiled and glanced at Padreg, then back at the stardancer, understanding written on her face. "She makes your soul sing."

The statement hit Kyrian like a bag of bricks. Pulling Arun short, she gaped at Elisira and tried to find something to say that would refute the truth of it. "Eli, I—," shaking her head, she said, "Then you know why I must go."

"And now you know, as well," Elisira said softly, causing the priest to blush.

At the head of the group, Azhani and Padreg's conversation was of a much different variety.

"When I have secured quarters, I'll contact your factor," Azhani said. "We can begin a regular exchange of messages. If you don't hear from me, or of me, after a month's time, assume that I am dead and carry out whatever plans you feel are necessary to warn the north."

Padreg nodded and said, "I see now why Thodan made you warleader, Azhani. I would be a poor second if I could not match your honor with my own. Worry not, no matter what befalls you, my friend, the north shall not go unprotected."

"Thank you."

"Now, the man you need to see in Y'Syria is Brannock Maeven. He's a scurrilous sort that can usually be found lifting skirts at the local watering hole." At Azhani's raised eyebrow, Padreg chuckled and added, "Don't worry, he's trustworthy — I pay him a fortune to maintain his loyalty!"

Nodding, Azhani silently repeated the name until it was memorized.

Turning her attention to Elisira, she asked, "So when should I expect to be called to witness a wedding?"

"We've talked of having a midsummer ceremony."

Smiling, she said, "May the goddess bless your union."

With a grin of pure mischief, Padreg said, "Well, we can always wait until midwinter — perhaps you and Kyrian will join us?"

Blinking in shock, Azhani looked first at Padreg and then at the star-dancer. Her stomach was a whirl of churning emotions and her heart felt as though it would fly from her chest and explode upon contact with the air. *Kyrian? As my mate? No! I loved Ylera!* Gritting her teeth, she said, "My Lord, you see shadows of a path that is not mine to take."

Padreg nudged his horse up against Azhani's and growled, "Say what you believe, warrior, but I have felt the stirrings of *korethkyu* as it blossoms between my lady and I. The soul's love is hot, and its fire always seeks to warm others. Can you say that you do not feel it?" His voice was soft and filled with such a passion for his belief that Azhani was mesmerized. When she did not respond, he shook his head. "You are too blind to see what lives before you, warrior. Listen then, and take my words deep into your heart. As surely as you have bound yourself to the fate of Y'Myran, Kyrian has bound herself to you. That is a gift that you cannot return."

Azhani turned the statement over in her mind. *He is wrong. Kyrian is no more than a friend. I-I care about her, but I cannot love her, not as I loved Ylera.* "I cannot accept what you say, my friend," she said softly.

Padreg closed his eyes and sighed. "Then let us make a wager upon it."

"A wager?" Azhani's eyebrows shot up, conveying her interest.

"Aye. If, by midwinter, you do not see what is waiting for you to reach for it, then I shall grant you half a hundred horses and tack."

Azhani pondered the offer. "And if I lose?"

Padreg laughed. "You won't have lost, no matter who is right. But in that case, I will claim the first of Kushyra's offspring and one year of your service."

"Agreed. You'd best be prepared to lose some fine horses, Paddy," she said as they clasped hands to seal the bargain.

Padreg kept his silence.

They rode without further speech, each alone with their thoughts.

Would it be so terrible to share your life and your bed with Kyrian? The thought rose unbidden in Azhani's mind and she nearly clapped her hands to her head to drive it out. *No! I will not be unfaithful to Ylera!*

Padreg felt a great sadness well within him as he watched Azhani struggle with her emotions. He had been truthful — the *korethka* burned hotly between them. Its tether was almost palpable. He wondered if his men could sense the same connection between Elisira and him.

As if the thought of her name could conjure the lady, she rode up to him and held out her hand. Taking it, he brushed a kiss across her knuckles. "Do you hunger or thirst, My Lady?"

"Nay, My Lord, but, who is that?" she pointed toward a group of riders heading toward them. A pennant bearing the arms of Y'Nor flapped in the breeze.

It was Stefan Payle and a company of his cavaliers. Letting off a whooping shout, Padreg raced to meet them.

Standing apart from the others, Devon watched as everyone said their goodbyes to Azhani. His face was streaked with tears, and he clutched his grimoire and his pack so tightly that his arms were beginning to tingle. He couldn't stand to hear what was said because everyone had that look on their face that meant they didn't know if this was the last time they would ever see her. Azhani had grown into both the sister he'd never had and the mother he'd never known. There was a physical ache at the separation that he had not felt since the day he had lost his father.

I won't do it! Papa, I know I promised to serve Padreg, but I can't leave Azhani.

"It's hard to say goodbye to someone you love, isn't it, Dev?" Kyrian's soft voice nearly caused the boy to drop his things.

The young man turned, surprised to see the red-robed stardancer standing behind her. Beside her, his horse was saddled and waiting.

"You were about to go and beg Azhani to take you with us, weren't you?" she asked gently, smiling as consternation showed on his face.

He scuffed his foot in the grass and ducked his head. "Why shouldn't I go?" he asked sullenly. "I'm not useless. I can do spells, and cook, and catch fish, and I know three languages, and—" he impatiently listed his skills, dropping his book to the ground to tick them off on his fingers.

Kyrian reached out and closed her fingers around Devon's, drawing the young man into an embrace. He fought her briefly, and then collapsed against her, crying. "I know. It would be wonderful to have you with us, Devon. However, Elisira and Padreg need your services more than we do."

"B-but I don't want her to go away and never come back, Kyrian. I don't want to never see her ever again. I can't lose her now, not after I found her! I don't want to be alone anymore," Devon whispered brokenly, as he clung to Kyrian.

Knowing that the boy had lost both of his parents, Kyrian felt tears gather in her eyes. At fourteen summers, Devon was on the cusp of manhood and buried the pain of his past in his studies. She had forgotten that he was still young, and that it would be hard for him to relinquish even a shred of his past that linked him to his family.

"You are not alone anymore, Devon. We are all a part of you." Kyrian pulled away and placed her hand over his heart. "We are here, always."

"It's not the same," he said softly.

"I know, but I promise that we will meet again. This isn't goodbye forever, just goodbye for now."

She cupped his face, and wiped away his tears until he managed a half-hearted smile. "You mean it?" he hiccupped.

Nodding solemnly, she said, "I do. Now, go say your farewells to Azhani, and make sure she gives you a hug." Turning him around to face the warrior, she gave him a pat on the back.

He scampered across the grass and nearly flew into the other woman's surprised embrace. With a sad smile, Kyrian picked up the boy's things and put them on his horse.

Kyrian watched as Azhani spoke to Devon, saying something so serious that the boy's shoulders stiffened to soldier-like straightness. Just as she thought he would topple over from trying to imitate a statue, Azhani presented the boy with a dagger from her belt. Then, she reached out and fondly ruffled his hair.

The next morning Kyrian watched Padreg and his people ride south. Beside her, Azhani turned her eyes toward Y'Syria. Quietly, she said, "If you hurry, you can catch them."

"Why would I want to do that? I'm where I want to be."

Azhani nodded, accepting her statement. Together, they started toward the capital.

Chapter Twenty

"You're certain of this, boy?" Leaning forward, Arris glared down at the grubby messenger who knelt at the foot of his throne. Though winter still had a hard grip on the land, the youth had clearly run himself near to death to deliver his news.

"Yes, Your Majesty. The mayor of Ynnych himself gave me the message. Rimerbeasts hunt!"

At the boy's outburst, the gallery rippled with shocked mutters of, "What? Impossible!"

"This is just one more example of the false warleader's treachery," whispered Porthyros.

Arris jumped to his feet. "Here me, my people! If what this lad says is true, then we have but one more crime to lay at the feet of our most despised former warleader!" He began pacing as sullen grumbles filled the air.

"The truth must be discovered so that Y'Dan will be adequately protected against the demon menace." Again, Porthyros fed Arris enough of a goad that the young man would act.

"I will see to it that scouts are sent to verify this tale. No one in Y'Dan shall suffer for the traitor's failure!" So saying, he spun away from the hall and left the court to discuss the news.

Quickly, Porthyros followed the king. "Ably spoken, My King," he said warmly.

Arris nodded tightly. This was the moment for which he had longed! Now he would be a hero like his father to the people of Y'Dan. "Send for Captain Niemeth. I wish to hear what is to be done about this apparent threat to my kingdom."

"Of course, My Lord."

The king went to his chambers while Porthyros scuttled off to find the captain. Once the message was delivered, the scholar went directly to his chambers. There, in the special place, a note awaited. Succinct, it simply read: *Direct the boy to a winter campaign. I will come on the morrow to enact my part of the plan.*

After burning the communication, Porthyros hurriedly made a pot of tea, adding a bit more krile than normal so that Arris' compliance would be assured.

When he entered the king's chambers, he found the young man staring intently at a series of maps laid out by Captain Niemeth. Setting the tray down near the king, Porthyros bowed and said, "Your Majesty, I made you some tea. Captain, please, tell us what you know."

Arris sat and accepted a cup of the dark drink from his mentor while the soldier spoke.

"Well, you know the ritual. If demons are spotted, then we send men into the hills to search for caves. It could be weeks before anything is known."

"And if there are rimerbeasts?" The king's excitement could hardly be contained.

"Then I would hope that we would do what is always done," Niemeth said darkly.

Arris nodded, and a wicked smile flashed across his face.

"Your Majesty, perhaps you should ask the good captain to be sure that we have enough supplies for a winter campaign," Porthyros whispered.

"You are right, 'Thyro. Captain, please make certain that we are outfit-ted with the finest supplies. Should it come to a war, I would like to know that I will have all that I need to defeat the foul beasts."

"Is there anything else, Your Majesty?" Niemeth had learned quickly that his king preferred to leave matters of war to others, a policy with which the captain was content. As long as he could continue to implement the training procedures taught to him by Azhani Rhu'len, he did not care how much extra work he had to do.

"Yes, find me a decent sword teacher. That last one had no idea of how to make me into the hero I know I am," the king said dismissively.

Niemeth nodded. "Yes, Your Majesty. I'll see to it immediately."

"Thank you, Captain. Oh, and please remind your men that the laws include everyone — even the relatives of soldiers." Arris' look was a pointed reminder that some of the Y'Dani soldiers had been heard to com-plain about the new rules regarding nonhumans. Many had lost parents, spouses and siblings as the nonhumans moved away from the kingdom.

Gritting his teeth, for his wife had been one of the half-elves who had abandoned the kingdom, Niemeth said, "Yes, Your Majesty. It shall be done." He bowed and left the room.

Arris drank the rest of his tea and sighed. "I should like to be a part of the cave explorations, 'Thyro."

"I'm sure that could be arranged, Your Majesty, but, are you certain that you wish your people to see you perform such a lowly task? You are their king, not their housemaid." Porthyros shaded his statement with a tone calculated to irritate the king.

Arris' eyes narrowed. "No, I am not. Thank you for reminding me of that, old friend. I will not have the gossiping nags of the court speak of me as though I were no better than a common kitchen drudge!"

"I think, My Lord, that winter will be your time to shine. For if there are rimerbeasts rising, then that is the time when heroes will be needed to go forth and lead the army to glory." He offered another cup of tea to the king. "Now, I bring good tidings, My Lord. Lord Oswyne has returned and will attend you at chess tomorrow."

The king brightened. "Has he? He will? How wonderful! I know I can beat him this time!" He yawned. "Will he have more stories to tell of his wonderful god?"

Porthyros smiled. "I'm sure that he will, Your Majesty. After all, it is by your grace that he has finally been allowed to build the temple prophesied so long ago."

Arris sighed happily. "Will it open soon, 'Thyro? I should like to attend a ceremony that did not bore me to sleep. The Twins are a nice enough pair of gods, but their priests do natter on so."

"Soon, My Lord. I am certain that Lord Oswyne will personally invite you when it is time." Porthyros could barely keep his voice calm. His master would be pleased to bursting with this news! Everything was perfectly on schedule.

"**I am beyond** pleased with your efforts, Porthyros." A handful of gold was showered into the scholar's lap.

In the prelate's office of the newly formed Ecarthan temple, Kasyrin Darkchilde looked down at his servant and smiled. "Tomorrow, I will bring a gift for our heroic king. You are to see to it that it occupies as much of his time as possible, but do not use it yourself. I should not be responsible for the consequences if you do."

"Yes, Master. I will do as you command." More gold was added to the pile in his lap.

"Good. Now, is there any word on the whereabouts of the Rhu'len bitch?"

"Not so far, My Lord, but my spies may be hampered by the weather." Though winter was nearly over, it was having a last gasp of life over the land by dumping several inches of fresh snow on the kingdom.

"No matter, I will find her, and when I do, I will send her screaming into the pits of hell. Now, go back to Arris. See to it that he pays attention to his new weapons instructor. We want him to look inspiring enough that men would die for him."

"Yes, Master." Porthyros gathered his gold and bowed his way from the room.

Once his servant was gone, Kasyrin exited the office into a small antechamber. The floor was inscribed with a protection circle and at the center of the circle was a small, obsidian obelisk that glowed with a faintly crimson tinge. Stepping into the circle, Darkchilde chanted the harsh syllables that would link him to the demon he claimed for his god.

::*Thy efforts please me, toy. Thou art a worthy vessel.*::

Kasyrin's lips moved but the voice coming from them was like nothing in Y'Myran. It echoed around the circle and made the sorcerer's ears ring.

::*I will instruct my children to breed. They have fed well. With each passing day, the hated barrier grows thinner. Soon, I will lay my love upon this land like a lash. The sweetness of thy offerings lingers and allows me to harvest the power of their deaths. With it, I will forge the key to unlock the gates that bar me from thy world.*::

Feeling the strength of his vessel wane, the dark god gave one final order. ::*Find the child of Rhu'len. Only in her death will I know that I am truly free. Give her to me, and the power thou shalt attain will make that which thou currently own'st like unto the parlor tricks of a rank apprentice. Remember, my slave, that thy vengeance is my vengeance. The screams of the scion of DaCoure will sustain me for eons!*:: With that, he was gone.

Kasyrin exited the chamber. Plans flew in his head faster than the shuttle of a weaver's loom. He had at least one operative in every major court in the seven kingdoms. With the magicks granted by Ecarthus, Darkchilde could see to it that no one was able to stop him from freeing the demon. He took a series of scroll tubes from a desk drawer and, laying them out, examined each for blemishes or cracks. Assured of their wholeness, he read the messages contained within and then returned them to the desk drawer.

A faint scream echoed in the room and the sorcerer smiled. The sacrifices were getting better. His handpicked cadre of priests were growing to crave the power that fear gave them, which in turn led them to be more and more creative with each of their victims. Never before had Kasyrin seen so many men dedicated to the art of torture, and it gave him a heady sense of accomplishment to know that even now one of his priests was carefully carving tiny strips of flesh from the body of a sacrifice while the others watched, awaiting their fate. The power generated by that one act alone would go a long way toward furthering his master's goals. But there must be more and it was death that engendered the greatest amount of magick. To this end, Kasyrin had instructed his priests to gather followers.

He was pleased with how the temple had grown in his absence. The merchant-sorcerer had recently visited each of the different kingdoms with the purpose of leaving behind special talismans. Each of these amulets was charged with a spell that unleashed a specific doom upon the land in which it was left. All of his little presents were working their magick. Come spring, the kingdoms wouldn't know what had hit them. By next winter, Y'Dan would stand alone against the rimerbeast threat, leaving him free to harness the power of death and fear to release his master from his bondage.

His agents had orders to watch for Azhani Rhu'len. If she appeared in any of the kingdoms, he wanted to know. Alongside those instructions, he made it clear that his people were to continue their activities against the Cabal. Istaffryn would suffer as he had.

His revenge was within his grasp, and he would allow nothing to take it from him. A particularly powerful scream rippled through the room. The sound made him throb with ecstatic memory.

Huddling next to a hibernating bear inside a tiny cave was not Kasyrin's ideal way to spend a winter afternoon, but he was not going to complain. A blizzard had come from nowhere and turned the world into a white hell that threatened to steal the remaining life in his body.

With the shreds of his power, Kasyrin made the cave as livable as he could. For days he had existed on a diet of insects and melted snow, and he knew that soon he would have to kill the bear in order to live.

Yet for all his knowledge of man-slaying, Kasyrin was at a loss as to how to do away with the gigantic mountain of fur that shared the cave. His only weapon, a broken dagger, would never pierce the hide deeply enough to kill, and his magick was at its lowest ebb ever.

Frustrated beyond the ability to think, Kasyrin decided that he would risk his own death to harness enough power to slay the bear. Standing in the center of the cave, he placed the dagger against his chest and began to chant.

*::**Put thy toy away, mortal.**:: The words filled his mind, sending him reeling to the floor, clutching at the sides of his head.*

"Who?" he croaked. "Who are you?"

*::**I am thy master, Kasyrin. Serve me and thou wilt be rewarded with thy heart's desire and more.**::*

Again, the voice caused white-hot lances of pain to ricochet in the sor-

cerer's brain. This time, however, they were followed by the vision of men on their knees chanting, "All hail Istaffryn Darkchilde, Lord of the Cabal." On the wall behind his worshippers the bodies of his enemies were displayed for all to see. The image changed, and now he sat at the feet of the most beautiful man he had ever seen. Around his head he could feel the weight of a crown. Thousands of kneeling people surrounded them, chanting, "Long live the king of Y'Myran! Glory to Ecarthus forever!" Kasyrin gasped. It was a dream that he had never dared to risk. Could it be true?

::It will be, if thy service is true, my slave.::

Again, pain lashed over him, but his body responded to it as though it were the touch of a lover's hand. "What must I do, Master?" he asked eagerly.

The pleasure in the speaker's voice was evident with his next words. ::Thou art worthy of my attentions, Kasyrin Darkchilde. I am Ecarthus. From this moment on, thou wilt know the hand of no other god, for thy destiny is to break the locks that bar me from the love of all who trod the mortal realm.::

A sudden burst of knowledge filled Kasyrin's mind, a mélange of images that laid out a plan so daring, so terrible, that he felt exalted above all others to be chosen the god's hand. With the instructions came a warning — no child of Rhu'len DaCoure must be allowed to interfere, for they were fated to stand against any who wished to foil the plans of the Twin gods.

Having already been a victim of one DaCoure's attention, Kasyrin was doubly glad to serve Ecarthus. "My vengeance is yours, Master," he said, knowing that the demon would rip the memories from his head. The almost-hoped-for pain came, and while he shed tears of agony, he shivered in release. Ecarthus now knew every shade of his servant's soul.

Gasping for air, Kasyrin turned his mind toward planning the future. To gather the men and women needed for such an undertaking, he would have to seek the darkest parts of Y'Myran, for there would not be many who would willingly serve a demon. Yet there were always those who existed only for the pleasure that power and money could bring. As for the DaCoures — seeing to their downfall would go a long way toward mending the pride that Istaffryn had stolen with his machinations.

"It will be done, my Master," he promised.

::Thou pleasest me, Kasyrin. This is thy reward.:: Power flooded into Kasyrin, mending his hurts and giving him the strength to face the winter.

"Thank you, Master."

As the memory faded, Kasyrin licked his lips and exercised a thread of his power. A cup of restorative wine flickered into existence and he consumed it with relish. Once he was finished, he crushed the vessel and tossed it into the fire. Standing, he strode out into the temple proper. It was time for his underlings to view the master at work.

Hardag the fruit seller loaded the last of his belongings onto a cart. Throughout the winter he and his wife had sold off most of their things, and what they took now was but a fraction of their life's accumulations. It did not matter, though; Hardag would have left it all behind if it were necessary. With the closing of the last temple to the Twain in Y'Dannyv, he knew it was time to leave. The black-robed priests who called themselves Ecarthans ruled the city with an iron vise of fear.

So far, he had managed to avoid their notice, but he knew that it would not always be so. Someone would remember that Hardag's grandsire had been elven, and then the black robes would come and drag him away... Fear drove his hands to move faster as they tied down the last package. He prayed that Ysradan had not caught the madness that filled Y'Dan's king, for the trip south would be long and arduous. He prayed that the Twain had not forsaken the whole of Y'Myran, as they had Y'Dan.

Chapter Twenty-One

Kneeling before his king, Derkus Glinholt pleaded with all his considerable skill. "Please, my glorious liege, I beg of you. Lend me the men to go to Y'Nor and fetch my daughter." With his head nearly pasted on the ground, the councilor waited for Arris' answer.

The king's attention was completely focused on a new gift. Just weeks ago, Lord Kesryn Oswyne had delivered a magickal chessboard to the king, and it now consumed his every spare moment.

The pieces moved by themselves. Different commands would allow the king to play against an invisible opponent, or two such bodiless spirits could play at his order. The game was infinitely more interesting than the plight of his advisor, especially since he no longer wished to bed the idiot's cow of a daughter.

And this new religion — I am so excited that I was chosen to be Ecarthus' first king! Lord Oswyne's priest friend was so ecstatic to see me! Me! Hah! Take that, Azhani! The king imagined the former warleader's face when she heard that the boy she had snubbed was Ecarthus' favorite. She would be green with envy. She would come to him and throw herself at him, and he would graciously allow her to crawl behind him as his personal body slave.

"His Majesty will take your request under advisement, My Lord. For now, be contented with the knowledge that King Padreg has made no move to defile her soul," Porthyros smoothly said.

"Yes, it is of much comfort to me that the barbarian has only stolen her body," Derkus said bitterly. As much as he loved his king, the Ecarthan religion that was gaining favor among the court dandies left a bad taste on his tongue.

Porthyros frowned. The nobleman's tone bordered on being insolent, and yet it held just enough grief and outrage that the insult, if there was one, could be ignored. However, he would keep a closer eye on the advisor, knowing that without his daughter as a hostage, Glinholt could easily be lost to their cause.

"Go now, Lord Glinholt, and see to your duties. I shall send word, if there is any news," Porthyros said dismissively.

The nobleman rose, nodding his head at the king's mouthpiece and then bowing deeply before the king. "Thank you, Lord Porthyros."

Porthyros watched him leave and then turned his attention to Arris. The Y'Dani monarch intently watched as the king piece strode across the chessboard, drew his sword, and bloodily skewered a rimerbeast pawn.

A smile of pure glee lit up the king's face. "I'm going to do that," he whispered. "I'm going to kill them all. One by one, they will die, until there are no more threats to my people." He gulped down a mug of tea. The king's eyes glazed over momentarily and then cleared. He set the mug down and watched as the demon rook moved into a position that his king could easily take. "And once I'm done with them, I'm coming for you." His gaze fell on the opposing queen, a mounted figure that bore a strong resemblance to Azhani Rhu'len.

Porthyros allowed a small smile to cross his face as his king continued to lose himself in the game. His master's gift was having the desired effect. Now, he no longer even bothered to tell the king anything about the documents he signed — he just slipped piles of parchment under the young man's hand and he automatically scrawled his name on them.

An unexpected side effect of the king's new ability to concentrate came when he took up the sword. True to his word, Captain Niemeth sent a swordmaster up to the castle every day, and Arris dutifully practiced. The clumsy boy was becoming moderately competent in the weapon, which made him even easier to control, for all Porthyros had to do was to schedule Arris' day in such a way that he had no time to spare. Arris had done as the scholar had hoped and had ennobled him to such a point that most of the court's daily business was now in his hands, or in the control of trusted underlings.

The king looked up from his game and said, "You know, 'Thyro, when I'm done with saving my kingdom, I think I'll go to Y'Nor and kill Padreg. He really shouldn't have kidnapped Elisira. She was mine." The boy's eyes were completely unfocused, and his expression was filled with such cruelty that Porthyros felt a tiny quaver of fear.

Too much that last time. I'd best lower the dosage, the scholar thought. "If that is Your Majesty's will, then it will be done," he murmured.

The king did not reply. His gaze had once again returned to his game.

After the first, gentle blush, spring slapped Y'Syr with a vengeance. Heavy, cold rains drenched the land and the two travelers as they made their way to the capital.

Only two days from the Y'Noran border, Azhani called an early halt at an abandoned barn. The roof was only partially intact, which made for a dry, but not very warm, campsite.

"Good old soggy Y'Syr. I did not miss this part of my homeland," Kyrian said as she wrung out her soaked robes.

Azhani grunted. She was currently hunched over a meager stack of wood, attempting to get a fire going.

"Have you decided upon a plan when we reach Y'Syria?" Kyrian asked softly as she draped her soaked clothes over a stall to dry.

Azhani looked up. A contemplative expression settled on her angular face as she regarded Kyrian. Then she looked away and struck her flint against the blade of her dagger with more force than was necessary. Within moments a small but merry blaze was furiously consuming the dry tinder.

"I have a friend we can stay with until we are sure of the queen's mood," she muttered.

"All right," Kyrian said as she hunched near the fire. "If you'd like, I can go to Lyssera and petition her alone."

"No!" the warrior barked, scaring Kyrian. "I will present myself to Lyssera. She will know that I go of my own will."

Kyrian cursed softly. "Stubborn warrior pride." She crossed her arms and said, "I won't let you leave me out of this, Azhani. I pledged my help and you will get it."

Azhani closed her eyes, and hated what she was about to do. "Fine, I'll take you with me."

Kyrian met the warrior's hard gaze and nodded. "Thank you. Just remember I didn't save your life so that you could throw it away."

Azhani smiled. "I know," she said gently. "Trust me to be chary of your gift, Stardancer."

Though wide open, the gates of Y'Syria had never seemed so foreboding. Side by side, the women rode into the city at sundown amongst the last of the merchant caravans arriving from the east. Overhead, gulls flew in formation, seeking shelter. Kyrian glanced around the capital of her homeland and beheld the wonders of her forbears' magicks. The city built on Banner Lake existed within the trees of the great forest. Giant trees so ancient that their seedlings had sprouted at the dawn of the world gave shelter to hundreds of thousands.

However, their massive boughs did not shade the homes and business of the citizens; rather, the people lived in the trees. Long ago, the elves had moved their homes up into the trees, creating a maze of bridges, walkways and buildings that were now as much a part of the forest as the trees themselves.

Over the years, a secondary city had grown around the bases of the massive trees, but their construction always echoed the arboreal nature of the original city. The docks, situated approximately a mile from the city proper, even held a trace of the natural, with their sinuous, almost aquatic shapes.

To Azhani, these sights were familiar, for she had been to Y'Syria many times in service to King Thodan. She was able to guide them through the streets to an inn near the shore. After a meal, they made their way into the city proper, where the herbalist Tellyn Jarelle resided.

The residential shop was located at the base of a massive aspen. Tiny mage lights illuminated the way the home of the herbalist wound up the side of the tree like a giant vine. The fragrant scent of herbs wafted about the area, causing Kyrian's nostrils to twitch. They dismounted and tied their horses to a hitch.

The door was answered on the first knock. A boy with a mop of curly black hair and the typically narrow-featured face of an elf peered out at them. "Yes, may I be of assistance?" he asked politely.

"I would like to see Tellyn Jarelle," Azhani said and gave the boy a look that should have sent him scurrying into the house as though the ground scorched his feet.

He shrugged. "She's busy, come back tomorrow." The door closed.

Azhani knocked again and waited until it was opened.

The boy's head poked out and when he saw who it was, he said, "I told you, she's busy. Go away."

Before he could close the door this time, Azhani wedged her foot against the doorjamb, and said, "I think you had better get your mistress," she allowed a bit of menace to creep into her voice, "now."

Kyrian reached out and put a hand on Azhani's arm. "Azhani," she said soothingly. "We can come back."

Tensing, the warrior shrugged off her friend's hand. "You're welcome to go back to the inn," she said distantly.

Stung, Kyrian stepped away and watched as Azhani's will slowly dominated the stubborn young man in the doorway.

"Gyp, what's going on, boy? You're letting out all the warm air," a cantankerous, but affectionate-sounding voice called out.

"Visitors, Mistress Tell. They won't go away like you told me to say," the boy yelled as he pulled his head from the doorway.

"Well then let them in, if they're so intent on interrupting an old woman," Tellyn replied.

Shrugging, the boy threw open the door and snidely said, "Please come in and be welcome in Mistress Tellyn's house."

Azhani smirked and walked in. Meekly, Kyrian followed her, turning to the boy and whispering, "Sorry to disturb you."

"Tell that to her," the boy said, jerking his chin in the direction of an elderly elven woman who was busily scrubbing a pile of clothes.

"Tellyn," Azhani said cautiously, stepping into the building.

"Azhani Rhu'len." The name came out sounding halfway between a blessing and a curse. "Always said you had plenty of courage. Come in, and be welcome. My home is your haven," the old woman said gruffly.

Slowly, Azhani and Kyrian made their way into the wisewoman's domain.

"Come, come, you're letting out the heat, and it's perilously cold today." Tellyn bustled into a sitting room where a large fire burned in the hearth. Adding another log to the already toasty blaze, she held her age-withered, gnarled hands out and sighed happily. When her hands had warmed to her satisfaction, she turned back to her guests. "So you've come to Y'Syria, Azhani. Have you been to see the queen?"

"No, I needed to ask a favor of you first."

Tellyn's eyebrows rose. "I won't hide you from her, Azhani. I am loyal to my queen."

Azhani shook her head. "I would never ask you to compromise your honor, Tellyn." She stepped aside to reveal Kyrian. "This is my friend Kyrian. We'd like to stay until I've seen Lyssera."

The old woman held Azhani's eyes with her gaze. A moment passed between them and she knew that the old herbalist had understood her true request. Nodding, Tellyn said, "A stardancer. You are welcome in my home, Beloved One."

Smiling warmly, Kyrian reached her hand out to the old woman. "Thank you. Please, call me Kyrian, Mistress Jarelle."

The herbalist clasped the stardancer's hand and then returned to her gruff manner. "Right. Well, you may have the room behind that door." She indicated a door that was stained a dark purple. "I have customers six days of the week. On the seventh, I clean. I don't wear mystical robes and I can't stand the stench of dead plants." The old woman limped over to a kettle containing the laundry. Lifting a tunic from the soapy water, she began to scrub.

Kyrian looked around the cozy dwelling and noted that it was scented with the sweetness of cinnamon and nutmeg rather than the musty odor of lungwort and cow's ear. In front of the fireplace, comfortable chairs squatted invitingly and the walls held a mixture of knick-knacks, paintings and curio shelves. Kyrian hefted her pack. "Let's put our things away, Azhani."

The warrior nodded. "I'll help you get things settled and then go get the horses."

"You might want to pick up some supper, as well. I had planned on a light meal tonight," Tellyn said as the two younger women carried their things into the back room.

"All right. Anything else?" Azhani said gamely.

"Well, since you're offering..." The herbalist went on to list an enormous number of goods she suddenly decided needed to be bought and carried to the house that day.

Azhani patiently waited for Tellyn to finish her list and then said, "Tell, you haven't changed a bit. I'll borrow Gyp if you don't mind. He'll be handy, I'm sure."

"Certainly, take the boy. He could use some exercise," the herbalist said absently.

Azhani poked her head into the room that she and Kyrian had been given. "I'm going out. Can I get you anything?"

Kyrian looked up from where she was hanging her robes. "Nothing that won't wait until we can go together," she said, with a slight edge to her voice.

Azhani nodded and left. *Please don't let her leave me,* she prayed silently. The next few days would be the proving ground of their friendship. She only hoped that they could make their way past the giant rimerbeast in the ring.

I am going to spank her. It was the first thing that came to Kyrian's mind when she woke that morning. From there on, her thoughts dove into a cesspool of rage that nearly had her take Gyp's head off when he came in to offer a cup of tea.

For three days, Azhani and Kyrian had left the herbalist's house and prowled the city. The warrior never spoke of what she learned, except for once, to say that no one had heard of a Cabal contract on any stardancers, let alone one on Kyrian herself. They agreed that the man who had taken her had probably done so for his own pleasure, rather than at the whim of another.

Then, on the fourth day, Kyrian woke to find Azhani absent. Only a note on the desk gave some clue as to where she had gone.

~Kyrian. Please forgive me. I could not allow you to face the wrath that is rightfully mine. Whatever happens, I will find a way to return and explain everything. Azhani~

I'm going kick her. How could she do this? How could she turn my friendship into a joke? Tears burned Kyrian's cheeks as she angrily tore up the note and tossed it into the fire.

Twelve candlemarks passed without word. A full day later and Kyrian was ready to seek Azhani on her own.

"Don't do what you're thinking, child. It'll do no good and only get you grief. She's got a head like a mule, that one." Tellyn handed the stardancer a bunch of dried herbs to grind.

Driving the pestle into the greenery, Kyrian said, "I can pull a mule to water."

Tellyn laughed. "Aye, you can, but child listen. Azhani is cut from a different cloth than you or I, and Lyssera will see that. Trust in our queen, for she is wise with her years."

The stardancer's shoulders slumped. "I just feel so useless. Like all I'd pledged meant nothing to her."

"Oh, Kyrian, don't say that. It would strike her to the core to hear it."

The priest harrumphed and poured the herbs into a bowl.

"Take heart in the fact that you are here, youngling. Mulish as that one is, it would surprise me not to have learned that she sent you to the other side of the kingdoms."

Kyrian blinked. She remembered how vehement Azhani had been about her going to Y'Nor. "How do you know Azhani anyway?"

"Ah, now there is a tale to tell. Come, we will have tea and I will tell you about a child named Azhani and how she fell into Banner Lake."

Leaving their work, the women settled on the comfortable chairs and Tellyn related the story of Azhani as a child. Kyrian found herself smiling at the story that featured a seven year old Azhani on her first trip to Y'Syria.

Seated on a pile of soft carpets, surrounded by the familiar scents of grass, horse and cooking meat, Padreg Keelan sipped at his cup of dark tea and looked at his companion curiously. Aden Varice, his oldest, most trusted friend, had just returned from Y'Nym, the plains people's largest city. Built on the edge of Lake Y'Mar, Y'Nym was one of the major trading sites for horses, which was largely what Y'Nor exported.

"Sea monsters? Aden, are you sure?" Padreg asked. "It's not like Ysradan to go haring off after a myth." Outside, he could see his mother showing Elisira how to cut and fashion a plains-style saddle.

"Yes, Paddy, I'm certain. Had it from Cragus One-Eye himself. Nearly two months ago, the old man took his best men, boarded ship and headed out to hunt down sea serpents. The beasts had sunk four merchant vessels and the nobles were beginning to get restless. Since then, there have only been two more ships lost, but the carcasses of the critters are littering the shores of Y'Mar," Aden replied. He leaned back and puffed deeply on his pipe, waiting for his chieftain's response.

Shock colored Padreg's face. "Sea monsters? I thought they didn't exist."

"Apparently, there's some truth to the old sailor's yarns," Aden said gruffly, hiding a chuckle at his chieftain's surprise. "Word is that there are hundreds of the beasts, all large enough to wrap 'round a ship thrice and swallow 'em whole. If even a piece of that is true, then I'm sure Ysradan hasn't got time to deal with Y'Dan."

Shaking his head in disbelief, Padreg asked, "Who is regent? Prince Ysrallan is too young and Queen Dasia would never leave Ysradan's side, even if it meant she had to paddle after the warships in a canoe."

Aden laughed slyly. "*Korethka* at work, hey Paddy?"

"It's a powerful thing, Aden. Love like that is rare and Ysradan was right to cling to it." Soberly, Padreg asked, "If Dasia's at sea with Ysradan, is Princess Syrelle the regent?"

"No, the high council would never accept her. Count Madros was chosen to warm Ysradan's throne," Aden said, visibly bracing for the chieftain's response.

"What? How could Ysradan leave that overgrown windbag cousin of his in charge? Everyone knows that Madros is incapable of tying his own boots, much less ruling a kingdom!" The plainsman jumped up and began pacing around the tent. "The high council won't be any help, either. They're a bunch of old men who care more for gold than justice. By the hooves of my herds, Aden, the Twain have not played us easy, have they?"

Aden shrugged, as if trying to say that the reasoning of kings was beyond him. "Ysradan might not have had much choice, Paddy. If Dasia wouldn't stay behind, then who else could he trust? At least Madros is a known entity. Imagine if someone like Arris had been named? It's not out of the realm of possibility. This way, Ysradan has some assurance that his kingdom will be there when he comes home."

Padreg stroked his chin and nodded, accepting Aden's words. As boys, they, like all noble children, had been sent as fosterlings to another home. Their time had been spent in the high king's castle, as pages for Ysradan. The experience had given them insight into a monarch's duty, and just how difficult it was for one man to balance so much responsibility. Only by constructing careful alliances with the nobles and merchants in the high council was the high king able to maintain order. The greatest lesson Padreg had learned from his time in Y'Mar was to delegate power as evenly as possible. Only when it was shared was power capable of great things.

"All right, I've had news of Y'Mar. Now tell me of the rest of the kingdoms. Surely they have sensed the madness that festers in Y'Dan?"

Aden's face twisted into a wry grin. "They may have, My Lord. It does not mean that they have the wherewithal to investigate. It seems that there be a plague of monsters upon us."

"Why do I feel as though I'm not ready to hear this?" Padreg asked.

"Because you are not, my old friend. Truth to tell, this story liked my ears no better than it will yours, and I have had the facts from those who have born witness to their creation. Monsters, Paddy, monsters have risen from the hidden places and are covering our lands. I've spoken of the sea beasts that plague Y'Mar. The dwarves of Y'Dror face a dragon — a fire breathing, gem-scaled, straight from a minstrel's tale, dragon. I've seen a man who was caught in the beast's breath and I'm no weak man, but I'd rather face the rimerbeasts than the creature the dwarves fight."

Padreg shook his head sadly. "Can we send aid? Do they need aught of Y'Nor's people?"

"Stefan Payle sent a dozen of our finest horsemen to aid the dwarves, much more we cannot spare."

Nodding, the chieftain asked, "And what of Y'Skan? Or Y'Tol? How do they fare?"

"Gigantic beasties from the darkest of a man's nightmares plague their lands, my friend. Beetles the size of birds have decimated King Naral's crops in Y'Tol and in Y'Skan, massive scorpions have forced the clans to Ratterask Oasis."

"We stand alone, with Y'Syr, against mad King Arris, then?" Padreg asked sharply.

"Aye. And Y'Syr is not assured — unless you've had word from Azhani?"

"No, I have not. But it is far too soon. So then, let us speak with Stefan and the others. Perhaps we can spare some more of our riders to assist Naral and the dwarves."

Suddenly, from outside the plainsman's tent, came a shout. "Ogres! Ogres attack Y'Nym!"

Chapter Twenty-Two

It was deep into nightwatch. Standing outside a door, Azhani gathered her courage about her like a shield. *This is it, warrior. This is what you came here to do. She's here, you can smell her perfume.* Azhani wished that Kyrian were here, beside her, a quiet presence that could bolster her confidence. *But she's not here, warrior. She's not here because* you *didn't want her to be here. She's safe, free of any association with the murderous Azhani Rhu'len. Now take your bitter drink, warrior. It's time to face your past.*

Taking a deep breath to calm her nerves, Azhani quietly stepped into the lantern-lit room. Though her boots made barely a whisper on the carpeted floor, the figure seated at an ornately carved desk ceased reading and turned to face the intruder. Clear gray eyes blinked in surprised recognition. A whispered oath was followed by a harsh question. "Give me one good reason why I shouldn't call out to my guards, oath-breaker."

Azhani Rhu'len, former warleader of Y'Dan and beloved of Princess Ylera Kelani gave no spoken answer. Laying her sword at the feet of the woman behind the desk, she knelt before Queen Lyssera Kelani, Ylera's sister. The elven women had been twins, though Lyssera was the elder. That accident of birth made her the ruler of Y'Syr, and brought her sister to Y'Dan and into Azhani's life.

Contemptuously, Lyssera ignored the blade. Leaning back in her chair, she crossed her legs and curiously considered the top of the warrior's head. *What does she want? Is she here to taunt me, to drive the wedge of pain deeper into my heart? Or am I to believe the words of spirits?*

"So you're the reason why Ylera was killed. Strange, you don't look much like the vaunted Banshee of Banner Lake. In truth," gray eyes flicked over Azhani's body, observing the woman's general appearance, "I would hazard to say that you should be better known as Farmer Francis' Crowscare."

It had been several years since Lyssera had seen Azhani, and the woman kneeling before her now bore no resemblance to the happy, healthy warrior she remembered. This Azhani was leaner, sadder and carried an infinitely greater burden than Thodan's warleader ever bore.

"I am whatever Your Majesty wishes," Azhani said, her voice devoid of emotion.

A cruel smile blazed across Lyssera's face. "What I wish is for my sister's killer to be flayed alive, and packed in sea salt, but I'll have to settle for having you hung in the public square. That is how we punish murderers here in Y'Syr, or have you forgotten the law altogether?"

Having visited Y'Syr many times, Azhani remembered. "I remember that your justice is merciful, Your Majesty. I also remember that the accused was innocent until proven guilty."

The elven woman's relaxed posture dropped away, leaving behind the regal presence of the queen. "Are you claiming innocence?" she asked, cocking her head and watching the warrior's body language. *Oh Ylera, did you really come back? Were the words I heard the truth? Are you blameless in my sister's death, Azhani Rhu'len? I hope it is so.*

Azhani looked up, her face a studied mask of calm, even as tears pooled in her eyes. "I am, Your Majesty. I did not kill Ylera. She was," her voice broke. Taking a shuddering breath, Azhani said, "She was my heart and soul, My Queen."

Lyssera stood and paced around the room, circling the still-kneeling warrior. "Am I to trust your word just because you profess your love? I have documents which prove your guilt, warrior." She stopped in front of Azhani. Tonelessly, she asked, "Do you know what those documents say, warrior?"

"I can guess," Azhani muttered.

"They say you are traitor! They say that you used," she ground the word, "my twin as a shield against the guardsmen who tried to arrest you. They say, murderer, that you cut her throat when the guards would not back away." The words were bitten off, filled with anger and hate. Grabbing Azhani's face in her hand, she ruthlessly turned it up and exposed the dark scar to the light. "Tell me," Lyssera hissed, "How am I supposed to believe a branded oath-breaker?"

Azhani's hands balled into fists, but she made no move to fight back. All of the rumors she had heard now paid off. Firming her jaw, she only asked, "How's the trade with Y'Dan, these days, My Queen? Are your merchants profiting? Have they sold silks and spices by the crateful in the streets of Y'Dannyv this year? Do your nobles still vacation in Y'Dyth?" Lyssera's hand dropped away as if burned.

Blue eyes flashing, Azhani stood and calmly asked, "When was the last time an Y'Syran child was fostered in an Y'Dani home? When was the last time Y'Syran gold bought the same amount of wheat as Y'Dani? Tell me, Your Majesty; have you seen the Writ of Behavior? Could you follow all of its laws? Will you implement them here, so as to make Arris feel more comfortable, if he should visit? Have you ejected your stardancers in favor of black-robed doctors? Do you follow that new religion?"

Lyssera winced and Azhani knew her words had penetrated the queen's anger. Kneeling once more, she reached for her sword and offered it to the woman who so closely resembled her lost love.

"I am not guilty of murdering Ylera. I am, however, responsible for her death. To that end, I offer you what should have been hers — my sword and body are yours to command, My Queen. Do with me what you will. I will undertake any task you set me."

The elven woman snorted and asked, "What if I ordered you to fall on your sword? What then?"

"I shall fall upon my sword, and you will have to order your servants to mop up my blood," the warrior replied evenly, though a tiny smile tweaked the corners of her mouth.

Lyssera closed her eyes. "By the First Tree, Azhani, can't I win just one argument with you?" she asked plaintively. *She never changes. All the years I've known her and she's just as stubborn and honorable as ever. Ylera must have fallen hard enough to forget the stars.*

Suddenly, the queen was kneeling next to the warrior, reaching for her as tears ran hotly down her face. "I don't want your life, Azhani. I don't want your sword. I know you're innocent. Starseeker Vashyra was able to briefly contact Ylera. Her spirit told us everything we needed to know about Arris' treachery. The last thing she said, before reaching the kingdoms, was that she had loved you."

Azhani sobbed, and the two women held each other and shared their grief.

"Will you seek to depose Arris?" Queen Lyssera had listened to the tale of the Y'Dani's betrayal and the subsequent travails that Azhani had undergone. The remains of a midnight snack lay between them as they conversed near the hearth.

"I had thought of it, but then I ran into the rimerbeasts." Azhani quickly described the events in the mountains, ending with, "I beg of you to send your rangers out tomorrow. If even one cave is filled with the beasts, next winter will see the slaughter of innocents."

Lyssera nodded. "I will take your words to heart." She licked her lips thoughtfully. "I will help you with Arris, but only after the rimerbeast threat is destroyed."

"Thank you. I won't turn away a helping hand or fifty," Azhani said wryly.

Lyssera chuckled and set her cup down on the table by her chair. "Are you alone then?"

"No, not completely. I told you how I left Padreg and the others at the border, but one of my companions came with me to Y'Syria."

"The stardancer," Lyssera said succinctly. She had heard the joy in Azhani's voice when she spoke of the young woman who had saved her leg.

"You read me better than Ylera, My Queen," Azhani grumbled sullenly.

Laughing brightly, Lyssera said, "Perhaps. I freely admit to calling on all the years we've sparred together as a key to your body language."

"Master Delaye would be so proud, Lyss." Azhani stuck her tongue out at the queen. "All right, yes, Kyrian is here."

"I have heard of this Stardancer Kyrian. Those of Y'Len say that she is deeply touched by Astariu's fire. Is she within Oakheart, perhaps hiding in a closet? If so, please, go and get her, I'd like to meet her."

Azhani chuckled. "No, she's with a friend in town." She sighed. "Probably quite angry with me, for I broke my promise to bring her with me to meet you."

Lyssera shook her head. "You always were too damned honorable for your own good, Azhani. I would not have hung a stardancer, even if you had been guilty."

"But would your court have been so ready to accept her?" Azhani countered evenly.

The queen frowned. "I believe I see your path, warrior. Tomorrow, I shall take steps to keep that from ever becoming a well-trodden walkway. Meanwhile, you and she are welcome here at Oakheart."

"Please allow me some time to acquaint myself with the environs before I bring Kyrian to the manor, My Queen. I'd like to be sure that the path you spoke of is well hidden before I introduce my friend to the delights of your court." Azhani kept her tone carefully neutral.

Steepling her fingers and pressing them to her lips, Lyssera nodded. "Age has given you wisdom, warrior. All right, I agree with your assessment, but I will not cooperate with this plan for long. Now let me call for a servant to lead you to your old rooms. I have much to prepare." She grinned wickedly. "My court is going to receive a bit of a shaking on the morrow."

The queen stepped into her council chamber. Around a table sat the most important nobles of Y'Syr.

"Good morning, my friends," she said softly as she sat. Behind the queen, a hooded figure knelt next to her chair. "I have called you here this day to impart news of great import."

Lord Bethelsel grumbled, "Spit it out, Lyss. I'm tired and I'd like to crawl back to bed."

The queen turned a brilliant smile upon the elderly elven lord. "My Lords and Ladies, rejoice! I have determined the identity of Ylera's killer."

There was a collective sigh.

"But we knew that it was that damned half-breed!" groused one lady.

"Yes, Rhu'len's child was found to be at fault by her king. She was exiled," another said.

"True," Lyssera said. Laying her hands on the table, she added, "But not completely factual. Azhani is no guiltier of Ylera's death than I am. It was Arris Thodan who murdered my sister."

There were gasps around the room, followed by, "Can you prove it?"

"Yes." She turned and spoke to a page, who ran outside. Shortly, they were joined by a blue-robed starseeker. "Thank you Vashyra. Could you show them the crystal?"

"At your command, My Queen," the starseeker said as she produced a shard of clear quartz. "This is a memory crystal, My Lords and Ladies. You have all heard and seen its like. Now, behold the truth of your queen's words."

The figure kneeling on the floor next to the queen stood then, and quickly exited the room. No one noticed, however, for they were glued to the vision of Ylera who stood before them.

"Azhani Rhu'len holds no guilt for my death, Lyssera. The documents you have seen are false. Arris coerced me to sign them on pain of death. Lay your blame for my murder at his door, for his hands are ruddy with my blood." The wraith related a harrowing tale of pain and death that sickened all present. As the story concluded, she whispered, *"Please, tell Azhani that I will love her always."* The former ambassador's voice was thin and hollow, but it was clearly her. As the image vanished, someone in the room sobbed.

"Vengeance!" cried one of the nobles.

"Hold! You must hear the rest of this tale!" Lyssera shouted over the rising clamor.

Now, the hooded figure returned. Throwing her cloak aside, Azhani revealed herself to the room. "My Lords and Ladies, I have some terrible news."

The morning was spent telling and retelling the tale that had brought

Azhani to Y'Syria.

By afternoon court, the whole of Oakheart knew that Azhani had been exonerated of Ylera's murder. Only the nobles knew the actual reasons why, which left everyone to speculate, but Azhani did not care as long as she was free to roam the castle. Currently, she stood next to the elven queen and waited for her to address the court.

As talk slowed to an inaudible murmur, Queen Lyssera stood. "Good afternoon, my friends. I trust that your bellies are full and your minds are ready to ponder the fate of our lovely kingdom?"

There was a general assent and Lyssera smiled.

"Good. My first order of business is to announce that I have hired Azhani Rhu'len as personal retainer. I have given her my complete trust and faith."

With those words, Azhani knelt before the queen. "I give you my sword," the warrior said, offering the blade to the queen hilt first, "as a token of my willingness to champion your cause, My Lady."

"I accept your sword, Azhani Rhu'len," the queen said, taking the blade and touching the hilt to her breast, "and grant you permission to walk in my shadow, armed against my enemies."

The queen passed the blade back to Azhani, who stood and sheathed it in one fluid motion. The warrior turned and bowed to the court. "Ladies and gentles all, I am Azhani Rhu'len and I serve at the will of Lyssera, Queen of Y'Syr."

A collective gasp thundered through the room. The soft murmur became a roar as people began shouting, hurling questions and accusations like stones.

"I thought you were an oath-breaker?"

"Murderer!"

"How can you serve the sister of the woman you slaughtered?"

"Silence!" Lyssera bellowed. The room quieted. "It has been proven to the satisfaction of the Council of Nobles that she is free of guilt. This is all you need know. Speak with Starseeker Vashyra if our word is not honorable enough for you." Lyssera caught and held the gazes of several of the more vocal members of the court. Each one looked into their queen's eyes and then nodded, accepting her decision. "Now, I ask my herald to begin today's session, as I am certain that there are more important matters pending."

The herald stepped forward as the queen sat. Azhani tugged her hood up, settled into the shadows behind the throne, and listened to the chatter that filled the silences between petitioners.

In one afternoon, she learned several things, most of which was useless. Information such as who was cuckolding which lord, knight or lady was of less interest to her than who might wish to see her, and by extension, any of her friends, dead. Surprisingly, no one seemed particularly interested in seeing her dead, though many wondered what hold she had over Lyssera.

A niggling sense of guilt reminded her that she had left Kyrian to wait indefinitely. Surely her pride had been served by now? She had won her pardon on her own merits, and not by the honor of those who accompanied her. The thoughts sat heavily in Azhani's gut. *I miss her,* Azhani realized as she thought about Kyrian. *I'll bring her to Oakheart once I find out what Lyssera requires of me as her retainer. Please, Astariu, let Kyrian forgive me.*

Court ended. Azhani slipped out of the gallery to meet with Lyssera in the hall.

"I have an assignment for you, Azhani."

"Oh?"

"Yes, my nephew, Allyndev, he may rule one day, if I do not produce heirs, yet he has not the character of a king. I need for you to take him on as your student and teach him the ways of the blade."

"Why not have one of your swordmasters train the boy?" Azhani asked.

Lyssera made a face. "Because Allyndev is half-elven, and therefore unworthy of their attention. He is also somewhat of a dreamer, and lacks the proper adherence to his training."

"That will change," Azhani said darkly. "Or he'll find himself mucking stalls."

The queen smiled. "Let me take you to him."

"All right. I met your guard captain. He was rather irritated with me for some reason," she said, smiling with amusement.

Lyssera laughed delightedly. "That might have something to do with the four soldiers he found sleeping on the job."

Azhani shrugged. "It wasn't their fault. They had soft heads."

Still chuckling, Lyssera said, "I believe that your skills will be best used with Allyndev, rather than upon the guards. I would ask you to instruct my men on everything you know of rimerbeast lore, though."

"I will give all that I can, My Queen. Tell me about Allyndev," Azhani said as they passed through the great doors that led from Oakheart into the castle's environs.

Lyssera sighed softly. "What is there to tell? Allyndev is the son of my youngest sister, Alynna. His father was human."

"Which leaves him as neither fish nor fowl, and unable to swim or fly in the court." Azhani snorted and shook her head. "Lyss, I love the elves, but your politics are as convoluted as a sailor's knot."

The queen chuckled. "Yes, but no prince of the blood shall be unfit to defend the realm, even those that the court would prefer to see left in a closet."

The two women reached a grove of massive trees a part of the forest that made up Oakheart. High above them, bridges and branches melded together to form the pathways that linked each tree to its neighbor. A young man knelt at the base of the tree. His tunic was liberally stained with sweat while his hands and knees were so dirty that it was difficult to tell the color of either. Around him lay the fruits of his labors. The hacked up bits of choking vines spoke of a long day's work at keeping the trees healthy.

As Azhani and Lyssera came to a stop, the boy let out a string of curses and let fly with a hatchet, cutting away the last of some vines that were wrapped around the tree. The warrior was impressed with the zeal with which this young nobleman worked. In her experience, princelings avoided work, rather than reveled in it. Appraising him, Azhani took in the boy's features. Tall, like herself, thin yet muscular with shoulder length blond hair, Allyndev Kelani was an attractive young man.

"Allyn, come here please," Lyssera called out to her nephew.

He stood and wiped his hands and face. Azhani noted that the boy's eyes were nearly as green as the vines he had been industriously clearing. When he walked over to them, the warrior recognized the gait of one who had just gained their full height. Allyn was gawky and moved as though both of his legs had been affixed to his hips backwards. *Hmm, balance first and then the light sword, small shield, perhaps even two blades. He'll do. Though I wouldn't place a heavy blade in those hands — too unwieldy. I wonder if he can hit the broadside of a barn? Probably not, otherwise he'd be under the instruction of the master archer, half-elf or not.*

The boy bowed to Lyssera. "My Queen, I am honored by your company," he said warmly. A hint of a smile played about his handsome face, and Azhani observed that Lyssera's face held an answering grin. The queen embraced her nephew and then turned him to face Azhani.

"This is the boy I told you about, Azhani. He is to be your student. Allyndev, this is Master Azhani Rhu'len. It is my hope that she will be able to instill in you some sense of how to defend yourself."

Taking one more look at the boy, Azhani said, "All right. Meet me in the salle at dawn, boy, and don't be late." The warrior's tone was a hair off insulting. She turned to go, wondering if he would rise to her bait.

From behind her, a sullen voice answered, "Yes, Azhani."

Time for your first lesson, she thought. Turning, she stepped forward, grabbed the axe from his hand and thrust the boy against the huge tree behind him.

With the blade held just against the flesh of his throat, she hissed, "Master Azhani, boy. Always remember that I hold your life in my hands. Until you can walk away from a battlefield, you will call me Master Azhani."

He nodded and she stepped back, handing him the axe, hilt first. Their eyes met and he quickly looked away. The first lesson was learned.

Two more days passed. Azhani haunted the corridors and bridges of Oakheart Manor, staying out of the way of curious courtiers and listening to the gossip of the servants. She ran into an old friend, Kuwell Longhorn, a dwarven blacksmith with a huge sense of humor and an even greater sense of honor.

Now the Y'Droran ambassador, he was happy to see her. After hearing the tale of her arrival in Y'Syr, the dwarf immediately pledged to aid her cause. She left him making plans to contact his people about searching the caves near their mines. Rimerbeasts did not normally make nests near dwarven lands, but there was always a first time. He also told her what he had learned of the dragon plaguing the Y'Droran countryside.

In the afternoon, she went to meet Allyndev for another lesson. As she passed one of the struts that made up the interior structure of Oakheart, she marveled at the skill of the ancient gardeners. Everything about the elven castle, from Lyssera's throne to the windows lining the walls had been coaxed from the trees by Y'Syr's greatest mages, the Gardeners of the Elves.

Holding a position in elven society above that of even the most venerable of starseekers, a gardener's entire life was given to the care of the kingdom's massive trees. Gardeners controlled a form of magick that allowed them to touch the very essence of the earth's life force and shape it to their needs. It was a skill that could be used for great evil; therefore, only those whose souls were pure were allowed into their ranks.

Azhani felt a moment's admiration for young Allyndev, whose only wish was to be counted among their ranks. The feeling passed as she continued on her way toward the salle where the young prince waited.

The previous evening, the terms of her service had been finalized. In exchange for shelter and a stipend, Azhani agreed to act as Allyn's weapons instructor as well as a special liaison with the queen's guard. In the event that rimerbeasts were spawning, then she would take command of the Y'Syran army and keep the northern kingdoms safe from their depredations. If she should be successful, Lyssera would back her claims against Arris to Ysradan. The queen's knowledge of Y'Mar was sketchy and included rumors of sea monsters, which Azhani was hard put to believe, but her scouts had yet to return with more concrete word.

Prince Allyndev had learned his first lesson well — almost too well, for he gave the warrior a level of respect that was heavily tinged with fear. The fear, she suspected, would ease with time. What else he would learn from her remained to be seen.

Weighing heavily on Azhani's mind were thoughts of Kyrian, who languished in the care of the herbalist, Tellyn Jarelle. The queen's introduction of Azhani had quashed any daggers that might be thrown in the back of the young stardancer and the warrior knew that she was only prolonging her friend's ire by waiting to bring her to Oakheart. She had made a silent promise that she would seek out the young woman after meeting Allyndev, but now she found herself curiously reticent.

So what are you so afraid of, warrior? she thought sardonically. There was no answer forthcoming. It could not be fear that Kyrian would be made a target by Arris. By her very nature, the stardancer was opposed to all that the mad king stood for, marking her as an instant target whether or not she was friends with Azhani.

I don't want her to be angry with me. Azhani finally decided, realizing that Kyrian's friendship was more important than she cared to admit. *Tomorrow,* Azhani decided. *I will go and apologize for making her wait so long.* Tiny doubts bubbled up and pecked at her mind, which made her stomach roil uncomfortably. *I hope she's not too vexed with me.*

As full as Azhani's days were, her nights were as busy. Queen Lyssera kept the warrior by her side late into the night. The elven woman seemed to derive some comfort from her presence, and Azhani was loathe to deny her. She too found comfort in the aura of Ylera's twin, though the memories that Lyssera's face conjured were painful to experience.

Of the subjects the two women covered in their discussions the one which brought out Lyssera's effusiveness was her nephew, Allyndev. Azhani learned more about the boy's history, which gave her clues to understanding his motivations.

Allyndev was the only son of Lyssera's youngest sister, Alynna. In elven terms, he was no more than a child, having only twenty summers to his lifespan. Though his mother had been Y'Syr's warleader, Allyn had never shown any inclination toward the martial arts. He preferred the peaceful ways of the gardeners, though he lacked the gift that would have admitted him to their order. In Y'Syr, the position of warleader was heredi-tary, and it was only by luck that there was no need for such a role in the kingdom. Even though he was only half-elven, Allyn was expected to take up the mantle of his mother's office when he became of age. Yet by the time he was sixteen, he was so unskilled with any weapon other than a common spade and trowel that the Queen's Council had asked Lyssera to leave the position open.

Allyndev's human ancestry made it difficult for Lyssera to find anyone within elven society who was willing to train a student whose short lifespan would preclude them from adding any significant amount of glory to the teacher's name. By agreeing to train Allyndev, Azhani had given the queen hope that her nephew would prove his naysayers wrong.

Gossip among the servants of Lyssera's court held that Allyndev was arrogant and standoffish, which had caused Azhani to wonder if she would spend more time spanking the young man than training him. After meeting him, her impressions were revised. His aloofness was nothing more than a mask — a cover that would easily fall away under the right circumstances. Azhani was a competent teacher and had trained more than one touchy young man in her life.

In the short time they had worked together, Azhani could already see the young man's attitudes shifting. She had high hopes for him.

One evening, late, the sound of music drew Azhani to Lyssera's side. As the queen toyed with her harp strings, she said, "Tell me about Ylera's response to Y'Dani music."

Azhani's eyes moistened and her chest felt as though a hunting cat had suddenly leaped on her. "She adored it," the warrior choked out.

Lyssera nodded. "Tell me," she repeated softly.

A tear slipped free and scalded a path down Azhani's dusky cheek. "She used to make me go to these recitals — awful or artful, it didn't matter so long as there were at least a dozen different bards all vying for her attention."

Shaking her head sadly, Lyssera said, "She loved music. She loved everything to do with it — even the badly played parts."

Azhani nodded, unable to speak as memories rippled in her mind. The oil lamps in the queen's chambers gave off just enough light to obscure Lyssera's face, and for just a moment Azhani could pretend that it wasn't a stranger sitting across from her. For just that one heartbeat, Azhani could see Ylera staring out of Lyssera's eyes. Then Lyssera shifted, and her bearing was more regal and impersonal than Ylera's had ever been. The spell was broken. The woman seated across from Azhani would never be Ylera Kelani.

Wiping away the tears that had smudged her face, Azhani attempted a half smile. "You are too clever, My Queen."

Lyssera inclined her head gently. "I am discovered. Do not think harshly of me, Azhani, for it would score my heart to have you hate me. You had to see our differences to understand."

"You're not her, Lyss. I know that, and now my heart knows it."

"I miss her. Everyday, I wake knowing that half of me is gone—"

"I miss her too! Do you think I don't spend my marks wishing that it was I that Arris had slain? Do you think that I'm glad that she's dead, Lyss?"

The queen started at the vehemence in Azhani's voice. "No, of course not! But you need to know that you aren't the only one whose life was shattered!" Lyssera stood and began pacing the room. "Do you know how I found out about her death?" When Azhani indicated she did not, Lyssera continued. "He sent her to me in a box. A plain, undecorated box without even the barest of 'seeker's spells inscribed to stop the ravages of time. My sister came home as a stinking, rotting mess! As for why she was dead, well, I had to ferret that out myself. With all of the lies, truths and half-truths, I was ready to declare you an oath-breaker here, as well. It was Vashyra who stopped me, who came to me with a request that I could not deny."

Azhani had half risen to face the queen's words when Lyssera suddenly crumpled, sobbing. "My sister — our Ylera — she came, and she told me. Everything. About you, about Arris..." The queen's words became lost in her tears.

Feeling herself break, Azhani stumbled to the queen's side and fell, clutching her lover's twin close. Wax on the day candle puddled the time until with two great sniffles, the two women parted.

Wiping her face on her sleeve, Lyssera said, "If I look as bad as you do, Azhi, I'm afraid my maids are going to keel over from fright in the morning."

A half smile creased Azhani's face. "They'll survive," she said dryly.

Lyssera's answering smile was gentle and filled with the promise that their friendship was stronger than ever. The warrior stood and then helped the queen to her feet.

"I can see why Ylera fell for you, warrior," Lyssera said playfully. "Strong, smart and sensitive — who could resist?" She resumed her seat and took up the harp once more.

"Will you—," Azhani hesitated, her characteristic calm wavering. She cleared her throat and said, "Will you play for me, My Queen?"

Touched by the simple plea, Lyssera played a short chord, checking the tune of the strings. When it sang to her satisfaction, she asked, "What would you like to hear?"

"Play something she loved."

The words were spoken so softly that Lyssera had to strain to hear them. Looking up at Azhani, the elven queen stared into the warrior's fire-lit eyes for a long moment and then nodded. A liquid trill of music filled the room. The queen played, not with the consummate skill of a bard, but with the pauses and stops of one who has not practiced in many months. Yet, the notes evoked memory, surrounding both Azhani and Lyssera in a time-less place where Ylera lived, breathed, laughed and loved.

The queen's rusty fingers soon recalled their candlemarks of training, and true music rippled forth. It was a song that Azhani had not heard for a year. The tune was gentle, comforting and wonderfully, terribly familiar. But it was not what she remembered. A misplayed note here, a differently timed chord there, and, though tears trickled down her cheeks at the pain of it, Azhani knew that she would never again hear Ylera play.

As the queen played, the band around Azhani's chest broke, and she took what felt like her first real breath since that awful morning when she had been dragged away from the body of her beloved. When she exhaled, the sharp grief that had been her constant, unforgotten companion trickled away with the tears, leaving behind a muted ache. Tipping her head back, Azhani inhaled deeply, understanding that now she could heal. *Ylera is dead, but I still live. My life is not over, and I take joy in that fact. I miss you, my beloved, but my future is before me. Be happy. I love you.*

"Thank you," Azhani said, wiping her eyes.

Fingers stilling on the harp strings, Lyssera quietly said, "You are welcome, my friend. I am glad you have found a measure of peace."

Azhani smiled thoughtfully, and found that she wished Kyrian were there to share the moment.

A message from Padreg arrived the next day. Delivered by mage-courier, the thickly rolled scroll was filled with news about the high king. The report supported the rumors Azhani had heard. Dispatches from the mages of the other kingdoms also arrived, and though each of the missives bore sorrow over Azhani's situation, as well as condemnations of Arris' actions, there was precious little assistance they could offer.

King Naral of Y'Tol's letter best summed up the other kingdom's words. *"I grieve for the loss of the lovely Ylera Kelani, and it sickens me to know that one of my brother monarchs has caused this tragedy. However, my forces must concentrate upon the evil that befalls my land before I can cast a glance beyond my borders. I send then, a token of my wishes that you succeed in removing the cancer that has grown in the heart of one of Y'Myran's finest kingdoms."* Naral had sent bottles of the finest of his vineyard's wines — wines that Azhani knew would draw the attentions of some of the better mercenary groups. From the dwarves came a bundle of swords and arrowheads, forged by their finest smiths and from the desert dwellers, glass blown and ground so fine, they could be used by near-sighted scribes to magnify fading letters.

There was no note from the high king, only a brief letter from his regent, Pirellan Madros, stating that he would inform the high king of the situation. Even Padreg could not send any immediate aid, beset as he was by an invasion of ogres.

Kuwell, the Y'Droran ambassador, did have one small bit of good cheer for Azhani. He had sent word to his clan, and his cousin's clans, and over the next few weeks, those dwarves not pledged to fight for their kingdom and who were interested in following the famed warleader into battle, would be arriving in Y'Syria.

Azhani was about to leave to bring Kyrian to Oakheart when she overheard an elven scout's excited discussion with some friends.

"I swear, Rythias, it was rimerbeast spoor. Thick, viscous and acidic enough to destroy the blade of my dagger — look!" The young man withdrew a pitted and blackened knife and showed it to the other man. "They're coming, Ryth, and they're going to eat everything in their path!"

Azhani's heart hammered heavily against her chest. So they had been right. The rimerbeasts were rising early. She would have a war to attend before relieving Y'Dan of the burden of its monarch. Turning away from the rangers, she raced for the queen's chambers.

She arrived just as the master of rangers was exiting. Spotting Lyssera within, she called out, "My Queen, a word—"

"Azhani, just the warrior I wanted to see."

By the tone of Lyssera's voice, Azhani knew that the queen had just heard the news. "You've heard?"

"Yes. Since you led the last cleansing, tell me what you would do."

Stepping inside, Azhani closed the door and quickly outlined the rimer-beast lifespan — scouts, egg layers, gestation over the warm months and finally, the hatching in fall and the feeding of winter. Winding down, she said, "I suggest that you call the army in — a little prevention now will save many lives in winter. If we go into the mountains now and seek the eggs, we can thin their forces considerably."

"This method has worked in the past, so I don't see any reason to change it. I will make the arrangements. It will take time to gather my forces, for they are spread throughout the kingdom. For now, go and see to Allyndev. Afterward, I'd like to meet your stardancer."

"Yes, My Queen." Azhani bowed.

"Azhani?"

"Yes?"

"I expect you will serve Y'Syr as you have Y'Dan."

Azhani bowed deeply. "Yes, My Queen, until there is no blood left in my body."

Lyssera rose and touched the warrior's shoulder. "Nothing has changed, my friend. I will still help you to defeat Arris when the time is right."

Swallowing, Azhani covered Lyssera's hand. "By the grace of the Twain, I will be your servant."

A pall of dread had settled over Azhani as she walked through Oak-heart's halls, nodding to those she passed on her way to the castle's weapons work area. Perhaps breaking a few more practice swords would serve to lighten her mood.

Allyndev was already there and deeply engrossed in his regimen of exercises. After their initial meeting, she had thought that the prince would require careful handling, but that was not the case. Instead of acting like an arrogant nobleman, Allyn had carefully listened to her tutelage. When he surprised himself by showing real ability with the weapons she chose for him, his attitude completely melted and he became the pleasant young man that Lyssera had described.

It's a shame that he'll never garner the respect he deserves here. He could serve Y'Syr well. While Lyssera and Thodan's treaty had wrought some changes among the nobility of the elven kingdom, the attitude of the people still varied greatly. She herself was tolerated only because of her past as Y'Dan's warleader, a mixed blessing in her eyes. Very few would think to disparage her to her face, but she could feel the icy glares of those who longed for the days when Y'Dani and Y'Syran did not coexist peacefully.

Allyndev was possessed of darkly sullen moods, but those could be traced to times when he had been exposed to his peers. Determining that his behavior was linked to his sense of self-worth, Azhani was careful to give both praise and critique when working with him.

She stood in the shadow of the doorway and watched as her student exercised. As with most children whose parentage was a blend of the two kingdoms, shame had kept the name of Allyn's human parent a closely guarded secret. In the short time she had known him, Azhani had come to like the solemn young man and had added him to the steadily growing circle of people she could name as friends. His diffidence touched her, and she hoped that rising self-confidence would someday compensate for the young man's shy sullenness.

She wondered what Kyrian would have to say about the young man, when she finally met him.

Chapter Twenty-Three

"She's coming, Mistress Tellyn! The queen is coming here!" Gyp shouted over the ringing noonday bells, as he ran into the shop.

Tellyn looked up from grinding her herbs, and chuckled. "Yes child, I know. I had a visit from her page this morning."

Biting her tongue at the news, Kyrian asked, "Is there a reason why she comes, Tellyn?"

"Lyssera always has more than one reason for her actions, Kyrian. Her page informed me that she wished to purchase some of my restorative teas, but I believe she is using this as an excuse to meet you. It could also be that a certain mule-headed warrior has grown tired of playing nursemaid to the queen's nephew and has recalled that she has other duties," the herbalist said gruffly, laying aside her mortar and pestle. With a rustle of skirts, the old woman moved across the room and began gathering a sampling of her unguents and potions, packaging them for transport.

Kyrian was silent, absorbing the information. She had not seen Azhani for a full week, and the only word of the absent warrior had been that she was now in the employ of the queen, much to the surprise of the court. It hurt her deeply that Azhani had yet to come back for her. She hadn't even sent a note. What news Kyrian had heard came from the gossip of customers.

Upset by the warrior's continued absence and lack of communication, the stardancer's gut churned painfully. Once again, she considered packing up and leaving. Y'Len wasn't far, and she knew that Tellyn would be happy to provide her and Arun with supplies. While she was staying with the herbalist, Kyrian had gladly given of her healing knowledge, teaching Gyp how to bind wounds while Tellyn dealt with the business.

Only her oath of friendship kept her from fleeing. Heart hammering in her chest, Kyrian took several deep breaths to calm down. The hurt flowed out of her, leaving behind the sharp sting of anger. She would stay in Y'Syria and help Azhani, even if all she could do was instruct boys in the proper way to bind a splint.

Angry, healer? a tiny mental voice asked.

Just a touch, she answered, sighing. *Lyssera is Ylera's twin sister. There's no mystery in why Azhani would choose to spend her time with the queen.* The "rather than with me" was left out of the thought, but deeply felt.

The muffled thudding of mail-covered fists knocking on the front door filtered into the room. Tellyn barely twitched an eyebrow as Gyp raced out of the stillroom to greet their visitors.

Gyp's breathless voice announced the arrival of their expected royal guest. "Mistress Tellyn, Lyssera of House Kelani is here to see you." The boy's shrill impersonation of a court herald caused Tellyn to wince.

Shaking her head ruefully, she looked at Kyrian. "Never stuff your patient's heads with false praise, even by virtue of your respect, Stardancer. Treat all equally and leave the poppycock to those who have the taste for it!" said the herbalist grumpily as she scooped up her skirts and made her way into the foyer.

Kyrian chuckled and began grinding another bunch of herbs.

Lyssera beamed in pleasure, even though her old friend looked as cantankerous as ever. "Mistress Tellyn, it has been far too long," she said, taking the old woman's hands in hers and brushing a fond kiss on her wrinkled cheek.

"If those idiots in the high court would get their heads out of their asses, you'd have more time to visit, Lyss," Tellyn griped, returning the queen's embrace brusquely.

Lyssera's tinkling laughter filled the room as Tellyn turned to greet the others who had accompanied the queen.

"Allyndev! Astariu's tits, boy, you look well! You're not hunched like an old man! Is it a miracle? Has someone shown you that there is more to life than weeding the garden that is Y'Syria?" the old woman asked incredulously as he embraced her.

Allyn blushed, his tanned cheeks flaming a deep scarlet. "Nah, nah, gram, I've been tutoring under Master Azhani. It has been a most illuminating experience. I have never felt so invigorated!" He spotted Gyp and let go of Tellyn, flashing a brief look at Lyssera before running over to the herbalist's assistant. "Gyp! I have to show you this thing Master Azhani taught me." The two young men immediately exited out a door that led to the rear of the house.

"Mind the plants, boys!" Tellyn called after them, as the door slammed shut on their excited babbling.

Standing but a pace behind the queen was Azhani, who searched the room eagerly, anxious to greet the priest. When she did not see her she asked, "Where is Kyrian?"

Tellyn's eyebrows rose as a disapproving grimace perched on her lips. "Hello to you too, warrior. Your *friend*," she emphasized the word, "is working in the stillroom." The herbalist lifted the flap to a belt pouch and removed several packets, handing them to the queen. "I believe this is what you've come for. If you'd care to stay a bit, I'll find something in the kitchen for us to drink while Azhani visits Kyrian. In fact, why don't you tell your men to come in too — they're probably cluttering up my porch with their armor."

Gamely, Lyssera opened the door and motioned to the guards who had accompanied them. The men entered the herbalist's house respectfully and stood at attention against the walls. Tellyn vanished into the kitchen, where much clattering and banging of pots could be heard.

Squaring her shoulders, Azhani took a deep breath, steeled her courage and went to face Kyrian. *Now remember, warrior, this isn't a fight. Don't attack; let her lead the discussion. Be honest. You've lied to her once; she'll be expecting you to do it again. Show her that your intentions were to keep her safe.* She silently coached herself as she headed for the stillroom.

A myriad of herbal scents swirled around the warrior as she entered the room, the most pungent being freshly ground mint leaf. Kyrian's back was to the door, and she took a moment to admire the stardancer's well-developed arms as she stirred a large, bubbling cauldron.

Right, warrior, now open your mouth and say something. You can do it, just don't shove your foot in too deeply. Azhani searched for something to say, stalling for time. She continued to stare at her friend's back, hoping for inspiration. Wavy locks of Kyrian's reddish gold hair escaped a loosely tied ponytail, curling up and brushing her jaw. Perspiration soaked the fabric of her short-sleeved tunic, and as Azhani watched, Kyrian reached up and wiped her face with the back of her arm.

Here goes nothing... "Try this. It might help." Azhani offered quietly, hanging a skin full of cool wine over the stardancer's shoulder.

"Thanks," Kyrian replied absently, taking the skin and drinking deeply before handing it back.

Well, I didn't get it dumped on my head. That's a good start, right? Azhani thought as she hung the skin on her belt.

Licking her lips, Kyrian said, "That stuff's pretty good. They must treat you pretty well in the dungeon." She looked up and over her shoulder at the warrior.

Though lacking any rancor, there was a hard edge to the words that matched a similar gleam in her eyes. Azhani's stomach clenched painfully and she winced. *Ouch. I deserved that. All right, don't say anything yet. Let her keep talking.* Azhani silently coached herself.

Laughter breezed in from the reception room and Kyrian raised an eyebrow, listening as the queen and the herbalist exchanged bawdy jokes. "You must be here to say goodbye before she has you hung."

Again, the words were free of anger, yet they struck Azhani like the sharpest blades. *Well, I suppose that she's more than just a little upset with me. Blessed Astariu, how do I repair this? I don't want her to hate me. I don't know what I would do if she hated me...* "Kyrian, I—" The words stuck in her throat and she looked at her friend helplessly.

"Hmm?" Kyrian turned around fully, facing Azhani for the first time since she had entered the room. "You what? Are you here for some other reason? Are you telling me that you weren't a prisoner; that wild dogs weren't keeping you from visiting? That your hands weren't broken beyond repair? Because that's exactly what I've been thinking, even, goddess forbid, hoping had happened." Now, acid etched the words as deep green eyes began to glisten wetly. Stubbornly, Kyrian held the tears back, clamping her jaw shut and gazing into Azhani's face.

What? Flash fire anger sang in the warrior's veins. *To the middens with this. I'm leaving.* It was on the tip of her tongue to scathingly tell the stardancer to take her accusing looks, her teary eyes and wild speculations and feed them to a rimerbeast. *To hell with friends. Friends are for...* But the thought faded away when Azhani saw the minute quavering of Kyrian's pale, pressed lips. The tiny flicker of hurt that had manifested as flippant anger broke through Azhani's defenses, drenching her ire. *Astarus' balls, have I buried us in a pile of shyvot? I need to say something, anything...*

"You lied to me, Azhani. You promised me that I would be with you, and you left me. How could you do that?" The pain that sang from Kyrian's words was like a dagger in the warrior's heart.

"Kyrian. Oh Kyrian, gods, I'm sorry. I didn't mean to mislead you. You were with me, all the time, in here." She put a hand over her heart.

"But I had to face Lyssera alone — please understand."

"But you never gave me the chance to stay behind. If you had tried to explain—"

"I did try, and you refused to listen," Azhani said softly. She looked away. "I don't want to fight with you, Kyrian."

Kyrian's anger was still hot. "Well I want to fight with you! I swore my friendship to you, Azhani Rhu'len — and my oaths do not come lightly! I thought you had returned that vow, but perhaps I shouldn't have expected so much of an oath-breaker."

Flinching at the bitter words, Azhani said, "I may deserve that. If that is how you truly feel, then I cannot change your mind. Be well, Kyrian. Lyssera will see that you have the supplies to return to Y'Len." Holding back tears, she turned to go.

"Azhani." The word came out as a half growl, half cry.

Azhani looked back to see tears streaming down Kyrian's face. With an inarticulate sob, she reached for her friend. Kyrian flew into Azhani's arms.

"You did not imagine my friendship, Kyrian," the warrior whispered. "You are my friend — truly, there is no other that I want by my side but—," she sighed. "There is nothing that I can say that will repair the damage I've caused, but I do not regret my decision. I needed to do it for me, not for you, or for Padreg, or anyone else — for me. I regret that what I did hurt you, but please forgive me. Give me the chance to mend the pain between us."

Sobbing against the warrior's chest, Kyrian did not reply.

Commandingly, Azhani spoke. "Kyrian."

The stardancer looked up into eyes so blue, they were almost purple.

"Please, I need you. I don't want to go back to Oakheart without you."

Timeless seconds passed as the two friends shared their gaze, each trying to read the other's soul.

Astariu, if ever there was a time for me to pray to you, it's now. Please don't let her leave.

"I'm still angry with you," Kyrian said softly, cracking a tiny smile.

"I accept that," Azhani replied, a grin breaking out over her face and lighting her eyes. *Thank the Twins! I wonder if I should do a dance of victory?*

"I reserve the right to chase you around the practice field every morning," the stardancer added.

Maybe not. Ah gods, it feels good to know she's coming home with me. "I'm all yours," the warrior said. "Perhaps you can even run my student around the practice ring a time or two."

"Student?" She let go of the warrior and gave her a look of infinite curiosity. "You've got some stories to tell, I'll wager. Now, why don't you introduce me to this woman you charmed into keeping you alive."

Linking their arms, Azhani turned to head into the reception room. "Well, I didn't exactly charm her..."

As Kyrian prowled her new room, Azhani stifled a grin. The stardancer's face was a wash of pleasure and consternation. *She looks so adorable!* The thought fluttered through her consciousness before she could stop it. *Blessed Twain, why did I think that?*

"But...this is just so huge, Azhi! I don't need this much space, I—"

"Am grateful to the queen for her generosity?" Azhani interrupted when Lyssera opened her mouth to suggest a new placement. She gently enforced her statement by stepping on the priest's toes. *Come on, my friend, please don't offend the elven queen in her own home on the first day.*

The quarters Lyssera had chosen for Kyrian were near Azhani's rooms, and she was pleased with the thought that her friend would be so close. At night, she could pretend to hear the stardancer's soft snores, and that thought comforted her. *It's a nice room, Kyr. Please like it.*

Closing her mouth, Kyrian nodded in agreement.

"All right, if it is acceptable, I'll leave you to unpack. Afternoon court begins shortly and it would set a bad example if the queen were tardy," Lyssera said, winking at Azhani. "You, on the other hand, have the freedom to stay and help your friend introduce herself to Oakheart."

Azhani sketched a short bow. "As Your Majesty commands," she said, smiling wryly.

Light, airy laughter followed the queen out of the room.

Alone with her friend, Kyrian continued to look around the chamber, amazed at the simple beauty of its construction. Grown from oak, the wood held a pale amber hue. Tapestries decorated the walls. Brilliantly colored Y'Skani rugs padded the floors and gave the stardancer the impression that she stood in a field of wildflowers.

Her quarters were a suite of three smaller chambers linked by short halls. She shared a covered balcony and private garden with Azhani's suite, but had her own bathing area and bedroom. Stepping outside, Kyrian inhaled the fragrance of the flowers and smiled.

"It's magickal," she said as she felt her friend's presence behind her. "This place, this city — it's nothing at all like I imagined it to be." Kyrian strode to a balcony and looked out to the lake. Two ships passed as she watched, their bright white sails catching the wind that would take them to new ports. "Y'Len is not of the trees. Not like it is here."

Azhani joined Kyrian at the balcony rail. "I remember. There are more ground dwellings there and places where there are no stairs at all," she said, smiling at the memory.

"The temple was like that. All one story, so that the acolytes could dash to wherever the masters needed them to be," Kyrian said, with a far away look in her eyes. "Invariably, your classes would end up on opposite ends of the school."

Azhani chuckled lightly. "Do you miss it? Do you want to go home?" she asked. *Please say you want to stay. I need you, Kyr.*

Kyrian turned and looked up at the warrior's face. Shadowed by the balcony overhang, Azhani's eyes glittered brightly as she stepped into the light.

"I do miss the school," Kyrian said as she maintained eye contact.

Opening her mouth to speak, Azhani found herself silenced by the stardancer's fingertips on her lips.

"But I don't want to go back there, Azhani. I'm where I want to be."

"Bu—" Azhani's voice burred against Kyrian's fingertips.

The stardancer giggled over the sensation. Lowering her hand, she twined her fingers with Azhani's. "When are you going to accept that we are friends, Azhani Rhu'len?" Kyrian asked, a tinge of exasperation coloring her voice.

Shaking her head, Azhani shrugged and replied, "I don't know, Kyrian. With all that has happened I'm amazed that anyone would want to share my company."

"Well, I do. You're not the plague, Azhani. Now please, just throw away your fears. I'm not leaving." Raising her eyebrows, the stardancer shook her finger to emphasize her point.

Azhani's eyes sparkled, and she snapped her teeth at the offending digit teasingly. "Yes, Kyr," she said, when she'd caught the tip of the stardancer's finger between her teeth.

Kyrian laughed and gently withdrew her finger from Azhani's mouth. Inwardly, she trembled, and hoped that her feelings weren't visible. *Ah gods, I started this, now how do I finish it?* "Shall we unpack my things? I'd like to see the rest of the castle." Kyrian headed back inside.

The ancestral home of the elven monarchy, Oakheart Manor was an astonishingly beautiful place, filled with the greatest treasures of the seven kingdoms. Unfortunately, it was also crawling with the hoards of individuals who ran the bureaucracy of Y'Syr.

Maybe I should have stayed with Tellyn, Kyrian thought as she struggled to keep up with Azhani. She was overwhelmed by the sheer mass of population that moved through Oakheart's halls. At any given time of the day, the manor housed an amalgam of noble and servant that flowed in an ever-changing, amorphous dance. For a person used to the politics of small towns and villages, it was utter chaos.

Various factions controlled the members of the Queen's Council, a group of men and women who had been chosen to represent the towns and villages of Y'Syr. Each councilor was convinced that their district was of utmost import to the kingdom and each was equally convinced that their neighbor was a hindrance to their growth. Loud arguments between the differing groups often peppered the halls as delegations jockeyed and parlayed for audience with their representatives or even, the queen.

As a member of Lyssera's retinue, Azhani had full access to Oakheart and took pains to show Kyrian the easiest routes through the massive structure. For three days, they roamed the castle, venturing out at all candlemarks while Azhani gave a running commentary about the different wings of the manor.

Built thousands of years before the Firstlanders divided the land into seven kingdoms, Oakheart Manor was a staggering complex of buildings and bridges that were constructed in and around fifty massive oak trees. The highest levels of the castle were reserved for the monarch and their family, but the lower halls teemed with races from every corner of the kingdoms.

They passed an alcove where dwarves diced desert men for bags of gold and sand. In another, Y'Tolian lutenists played merry tunes with Y'Noran pipers. Y'Maran docksider cant burred throughout, weaving a harmony of culture that made Kyrian gape with wonder.

Currently, they were headed to the kitchen to cadge a meal from the cooks. Kyrian could barely hear Azhani's directions of which hall went where. Instead, she began to memorize the mosaics that marked each major hallway. The unique pieces of art had long since become the preferred method of navigating the manor's maze-like interior.

Entering the Hall of Trees, Kyrian noted the mosaic that featured an array of trees, birds and animals. Set against this background was a small, but functional, fountain. In front of the fountain, seated on a bench, was Prince Allyndev.

He rose as the women approached. "Master Azhani, Stardancer Kyrian, did you hear? Ambassador Kuwell has just challenged Ambassador Iften to a duel!"

Azhani groaned and bit off a curse.

Frowning, Kyrian tried to place faces to the names. She recognized the name of the dwarven ambassador, but not the other.

Changing direction in mid-stride, Azhani began fighting her way through the stream of people toward the courtyards. Though dueling was legal, the queen frowned upon such actions, preferring diplomacy to swordplay. Allyn easily kept up, leaving Kyrian to once more duck and dodge her way down the hall.

"Do you think they'll kill each other?" The young man seemed to relish the thought of bloodshed. "Will there be a lot of blood?"

"Not if I can help it," Azhani growled.

Many members of Queen Lyssera's court were scandalized by the unseemly haste with which the three half-elves took themselves through Oakheart's halls. Finally, they reached the great hall and burst out the doors and into the main courtyard. A crowd had gathered, surrounding the two men who were loudly shouting epithets at each other.

"You dirt-grubbing mole! I'm going to take a strip of your flesh for every one of these fake stones you tried to pass off on me!" Ambassador Iften's menacing shout could be easily heard above the noise of the gathering courtiers. An ominous shattering sound echoed in the courtyard.

"Lies! You're the thief, Iften! You stole the gems and switched 'em out for glass. Just like a sand-eating desert raider to try and pawn his fakes off on a good, honest dwarf. Put your tail between your legs and run home to your masters, for I'm about to whip you like a dog," the dwarf growled menacingly.

Screaming incoherently, the desert man charged him.

Before he could reach him, Azhani leaped over the crowd and landed in front of the dwarven ambassador. The thud of creaking armor was almost deafening as Iften ricocheted off the warrior's body. Dazed, he staggered back, shaking his head woozily.

"Is there a problem here?" Azhani drawled, turning to wink at Kuwell.

"Well," Kuwell replied, hooking this thumbs in his belt and peering around her elbow at the still-stumbling desert man. "Not so's you'd notice, m'friend. Though, that gentlemen there's gonna need a 'dancer soon, or like as not, he'll be making an intimate acquaintance with them there cobbles."

"Trouble always finds you, doesn't it, Ku?" Azhani said aggrievedly. Catching the staggering desert man, she led him to a bench and sat him down. Kyrian arrived and began examining him for injury.

Singing softly, Kyrian scanned the Y'Skani's aura to look for an explanation for his behavior. She expected to find that he was intoxicated, but
there was no resonance of alcohol on the surface of his aura. A black
shadow beckoned to her though, and she followed it.

Tracing its pathway from the ambassador's abdominal area to his
brain, the brackish substance emanated an evil that was difficult for her to
recognize. Other, older hurts attempted to call her attention, but she
pushed them away and concentrated on the darkness that was coiled within
the desert man's brain.

She quickly saw how the invader had wrapped itself around the por-
tions of Iften's brain that controlled reasoning. Suspicious now, Kyrian
checked areas that correlated to sight and touch and saw that they, too,
were overwhelmed. Sure of her findings, she withdrew from her scan and
shook her head sorrowfully. "Azhani," she said softly.

"Yes?"

"I need my herb bag and a flask of brandy. This man is under the influence of krile."

Azhani's eyes narrowed. Krile was a powerful narcotic that Ysradan
had made illegal to own, use or possess within all seven kingdoms. "Damn
krile heads. I'll call the guard." She started to stand.

Kyrian's hand stopped her. "No, I think this is a poisoning. His nails
aren't stained." She lifted the ambassador's hand. He grinned and began
to giggle when she showed Azhani his fingernails.

"I see two pretty birds fluttering around my head. The elves are nice,
but I don't like sand anymore. Scorpions are ugly only when they're pink,"
he babbled complacently.

"All right. I'll send Allyndev." Azhani spoke to the young man briefly
and then turned to the dwarven ambassador.

"Gone to get the guard?"

"Medicines. The ambassador is not well," Azhani's curtly replied.

The crowd thickened, and people began to mutter questions about
what was happening.

Out of breath, Allyn returned with the items Kyrian requested. Quickly,
she chose a potent combination of herbs, crushed them into the brandy and
then coaxed the Y'Skani ambassador to drink.

Almost immediately after the last swallow, he passed out. The crowd
surged forward but was halted by the stardancer's voice. "Wait! Listen! I
am Stardancer Kyrian of Y'Len and I have news about Ambassador Iften's
condition." She waited for the crowd to settle.

"Good day, Stardancer Kyrian. I am Ambassador Kuwell Longhorn of
Shale Valley. Can you tell us what is wrong with Y'Skani?" the dwarf asked.

"The good ambassador is sick. His fever is high, which caused him to
experience a form of dementia. With care, he will be fine."

"Is it contagious?" One bystander wanted to know.

"No, it is not. Please, everyone, go back to your day. Let us take care
of Ambassador Windstorm."

"So what's really wrong with him," muttered Kuwell to Azhani as the
crowd dispersed.

"Krile," she said in a soft voice.

The dwarf snorted. "Damn. Never took 'im for an addict."

"Kyrian thinks it's not a voluntary ingestion."

This caused the dwarf to snort. "Desert men are notorious for doing strange things, Azhani."

Allyndev, overhearing their conversation, hissed, "Are you accusing the ambassador of being a krile addict?"

"Enough!" Azhani growled. "Allyndev, get Lyssera and ask her to join us in the swan garden," she ordered quietly, her tone brooking no argument. The young prince's lips twisted to argue and then he visibly took hold of his temper, stiffly turning and walking back toward the manor.

Pointing to one of the many lurking pages, she said, "Go to the kitchens and bring refreshments for," she mentally tallied who would be there, "six. Take them to the swan garden."

The boy nodded and said, "Aye, Master, 'twill be done as you say," and then ran off.

By this time, Iften's personnel had arrived and Kyrian was directing them to carry their master back to his quarters. She followed, conversing quietly with a concerned-looking Y'Skani man.

The swan garden was situated in the center of the Kelani residence, and therefore, private. Azhani and Kuwell made their way to the upper levels of Oakheart. A quarter of a candlemark later, a winded Kyrian and an Y'Skani gentleman joined them. Azhani knocked on the door and they were admitted by Lyssera's chamberlain.

The queen and her nephew were waiting for them in the garden. A myriad of swan decorations mixed with the foliage, giving the greenhouse its name. Lyssera's chair was the most elaborate of these ornaments. Made from white ash, it curved up behind the queen, and cradled her in a cloak of painstakingly carved wings.

A page, liveried in Lyssera's personal colors, pulled out chairs for the arriving group of people, waiting patiently as each of them sat. When they had all arranged themselves comfortably, the young man turned to a cart and began serving drinks. Once he was finished, he left the group to their discussion.

As introductions were made, the desert man who had accompanied Kyrian stood and bowed. "I am Vice Ambassador Kirthos. I serve Y'Skan in the absence of Iften Windstorm."

"Welcome, Kirthos. Now, someone please tell me what has happened in my halls," Lyssera said.

Kyrian stood and calmly explained what she had found when she examined the desert man. "I believe his exposure is recent, for he showed no signs of long term addiction. That he was unable to control his temper speaks to his lack of experience with the drug, as well. Most krile users are adept at hiding their addiction. Lastly, Ambassador Iften woke briefly and mentioned something about his meals tasting strange."

Kirthos nodded. "Yes, yes, Master Windstorm has complained about the food. We thought that it was just a desert walker's inexperience with Y'Syran spices." The Y'Skani's accent was thick, and it took a moment for them to ponder his words.

"Our food is terribly bland compared to that of you fire eaters," Lyssera said, smiling genially at the desert man. "Who would wish to cause Iften harm?"

"Any who wished to create chaos in your court, My Queen," stated Azhani flatly.

Lyssera looked at the warrior and raised her eyebrows. "Yes, I gathered that, Azhani. What I wish to know is who, among my people, would be so disloyal as to bring krile into Oakheart?"

"I'm sure Captain Evern'll discover it," Azhani said dismissively. "Kyrian, will Iften be all right?"

Sitting, the stardancer said, "Yes, I gave him an antidote. With continued treatment and a monitoring of his food, he should recover in a few weeks."

Kuwell sneered. "I still think the old snake snorted it for pleasure."

"No!" Kirthos slammed his hand down on the tabletop, revealing a portion of a snake tattoo on his hand. "Krile dust is anathema to those who follow the Serpent — we would rather eat glass!"

It was true. The followers of the Serpent, a group of desert dwellers who practiced a religion based on an ancient snake god, eschewed all forms of intoxicants save those which came from the venom of their deity.

Kuwell looked belligerent enough to challenge the Y'Skani, until Azhani said, "Old friend, he speaks the truth."

Grumbling, the dwarf sat back and turned his gaze on Lyssera. "What do you intend to do, Your Majesty? If there be a poisoner hereabouts, then perhaps you should alert the other delegations?"

Kyrian paled. "That might cause a widespread panic. People would get hurt—"

"I will not allow my home to become a haven for poisoners. Azhani, normally Captain Evern would be in charge of this investigation, but I do not wish this information to spread. You will find this person who has harmed our friend from Y'Skan and you will bring him to me!"

Azhani stood and bowed. "Yes, Your Majesty."

"Please, everyone, keep this information quiet until Azhani has found the scoundrel. Kyrian, I want you to be in charge of Iften's care. Allyndev, you are to make yourself useful in whatever way you can to them. No more gardening until this is settled."

"Yes, My Queen," Allyn mumbled sullenly.

"Ambassador Kuwell, Vice Ambassador Kirthos, I realize that I have no authority over you both, but please consider the implications if word of this spreads."

Kirthos nodded. "My people will say nothing, Your Majesty. We will aid Master Azhani and Stardancer Kyrian in whatever way they require."

"Aye, and I'll second that. Count me in on this one, Azhani. Whatever you need, just ask," said the dwarf.

"Good, go to work, my friends." Lyssera stood, and everyone else rose and bowed to the queen. "Stardancer Kyrian, before you attend to the ambassador, will you join me? I would converse with you."

"Of course, My Queen," Kyrian said.

As Azhani exited the Kelani quarters, she pondered the suspects. Kuwell would never stoop to poisoning — the dwarf was of the type that would smash his troubles with an axe. Kirthos, the Y'Skani vice ambassador, was ruled out because of his faith. Lyssera was a possibility, but the idea was so ridiculous, that Azhani nearly started laughing when she considered it.

The warrior knew that she could also leave out herself and Kyrian, for the stardancer would sooner cut off her own foot than to poison someone. As for herself, well, if she couldn't believe in her own innocence, then who else would?

That left — *just about the entire city of Y'Syria. I'd better get to work. But first, food.*

"**I will try** not to keep you," Lyssera said as they sat. She closed her eyes, and sadness washed the laughter from her face. "Ylera's loss is a wound from which I will never recover, and yet I worry that Azhani has allowed her grief to set her on a course of destruction."

"She loved Ylera deeply, Your Majesty," Kyrian murmured.

"I know. She would have been helpless to do anything less. My twin's ability to inspire passion is legendary in the court. If she wanted someone, then not even altering the course of the wind would have prevented her from having them."

Kyrian sighed. "I know, My Queen. I have not told Azhani, but Ylera was once a friend of mine. We were classmates in Y'Len." She smiled wistfully.

"How is it that you have not mentioned this?"

"At first, I was too angry at her. If she had slain Ylera, I don't know what I would have done. Later, I felt that the trust building between us would be shattered by the knowledge."

"You will tell her, won't you?" Lyssera's voice was filled with the timbre of command.

"In my own time, Your Majesty, yes." Kyrian did not flinch at the queen's tone. Instead, she met Lyssera's gaze with her own, even stare.

Lyssera laughed. "You are formidable, Kyrian."

"As are you, My Queen. Though I may have the advantage. Ylera had the same aura of control that you do, and her conquests were the subject of much gossip among the acolytes." Kyrian sipped at her wine and eyed the day candle. Much time had passed, and she worried for Iften.

At this news, Lyssera sat forward, her interest in Kyrian's story plain on her face. "Were you one of the Princess' conquests, Stardancer Kyrian?"

Startled by the boldness of the queen's question, Kyrian laughed. "Nay, My Queen. I was thirteen when we were friends. It's possible that I might have developed an infatuation, but those feelings passed as we grew to know each other. It's hard to see someone as a romantic object if they snore, tell bawdy jokes and hold belching contests which they regularly win. An untouchable beauty she was not, even if others in the novitiate believed her to have hung the moon."

Lyssera smiled at this description. "You knew her well?"

"Aye, well enough. We shared a room for a couple of seasons. She worked very hard to make you proud, Your Majesty. Ylera knew that one day she would be your envoy, and she worked hard to learn all that she could about diplomacy."

Lyssera's eyes had filled with tears.   As they spilled, she said, "Please, tell me more of my sister."

Kyrian spent some time telling the queen of the various adventures that she had experienced with the princess.

Lyssera laughed along with the stories until she finally said, "You know, some of this sounds familiar. You must be the Kyr that she spoke of so fondly."

Wistfully, the stardancer said, "It's nice to know she remembered me."

The queen described a midnight venture into the woods that ended with them falling into a bog. "I'm not sure how she managed to talk me into her adventures, but we always ended up somewhere in the forest, usually covered in muck. I wonder if she dragged poor Azhani out into the rain to look at massive mushrooms and yellow mint."

Uncomfortably, Kyrian shifted in her seat mumbling, "She's never mentioned anything to me."

Lyssera nodded knowingly. "She wouldn't. Azhani has never been at ease with speaking about her losses. Even with me, she is reticent to share her life with Ylera. I hear bits and pieces, but never whole cloth. When she first appeared in my study, I thought I was going to have to kill a friend, but instead, I ended up hearing a broken tale of pain that made me fear for her sanity. I tried to help her, Kyrian. I know it was hard for her to see me."

Leaning forward, the queen took Kyrian's hand in hers and stared earnestly into the stardancer's eyes. "It was only when I saw her with you at Tellyn's that the spark of life came back to her eyes. Your presence has unlocked her heart. I'm glad that you're here."

"So am I," Kyrian whispered. "I missed her, and I worried about her."

"I worry now. She talks openly of defeating the rimerbeasts, but when it comes to Arris, she is silent. I know she craves revenge. She has mentioned presenting me with Arris' head on a platter. Such a bloody gift would not ease the loss of my sister!"

"No, it would not."

"It sickens me to think that Azhani would plan such a deed. My sister was my best advisor, and there is not a day that I do not miss her wit and intelligence." She ran a hand through her hair, disturbing the carefully coifed locks. "She would never have wanted such a bloodthirsty justice. Ylera would not want our countries to war over her death."

"She would rather Azhani dueled the king," Kyrian said softly. "It would appeal to the romantic in her."

Lyssera smiled sadly.

"What will you do?"

"I do not know. Nothing, for now. Arris is not the greatest threat — the rimerbeasts are." The queen sighed and rubbed her temples. "Tell me, Stardancer, how do I trust someone who is vengeance bound with my armies?"

"I don't believe that she would leave Y'Syr unprotected."

Lyssera snorted. "No, she would not. Her honor is too great. It is so great that when I suggested sending an assassin for Arris, she turned white. No, when she speaks of Y'Dan's king, it's always in terms of him dying on her sword."

"Wouldn't you want to be the one to deal the blow of vengeance, if it were your fiancée that were murdered?" Kyrian asked simply.

Surprise colored the queen's face. "Fiancée? No, Kyrian, I don't think their relationship would have gone that far, had Ylera lived. My sister, bless her, was far too conscious of her place in Y'Syran society. Our people would not have tolerated the marriage. The ink on Thodan's treaty was still too wet."

"Ylera may have decided to thumb her nose at society. It was within her nature," Kyrian said calmly, trying to keep from shaking Lyssera. *Azhani will never hear of this conversation. I will not be the one to tell her that the queen laughed at her love.*

"You think me unkind," Lyssera said solemnly. "Perhaps I am. I am a queen, Kyrian, and that means that I cannot forget for one moment that every word I speak, every action I take, will have infinite repercussions. This is why I must — *must* — be sure of those in whom I have placed trust. I trust you, Stardancer, because Astariu has touched your life with her fire. Because of that, I trust your wisdom with regards to Azhani. Guide me, Stardancer. Help me to see that her desire for murder is not lunacy!"

"I wish that your concerns could be eased by a few words, Your Majesty. However, I can only offer you my memories," Kyrian said as she tapped the side of her head. "Perhaps the tale of my friendship with Azhani will suffice to mellow your concerns."

Lyssera listened, avidly clinging to any clues that would give her peace. By the time the story was finished, the queen was satisfied. "You are right, Stardancer. Azhani's honor does compel her to seek the hardest road. I shall be content to know that however dark her words may be, her heart still seeks the light."

Kyrian smiled as she stood. "My Queen, I am pleased that my words have brought you comfort, but I have stayed over long. I must see to Ambassador Iften's health."

The queen waved her away. "Go, Stardancer, and take with you my thanks. We will speak again."

Chapter Twenty-Four

After tending the ambassador, Kyrian was recalled to Lyssera's side. They shared a meal and were now ensconced within the queen's study, watching a fire burn on the hearth.

"How long do you think she will be?" Kyrian asked.

"Azhani?" The queen shrugged. "Thodan said that she and Rhu'len would vanish for days at a time, when they were on the trail of a criminal."

"I wish she would have taken me with her," Kyrian said wistfully. "I hate worrying."

For several minutes, the queen was silent, contemplating her words. Fastening her gaze on the wall behind Kyrian, she said, "You love her." The statement fell out into the air between them and echoed madly in the stardancer's ears.

The room was silent as the words played over and over again in Kyrian's head. Finally, she quietly said, "How could I not? I have tasted the color of her aura and swum in the energies of her essence. More than that, I have laughed with her, cried with her, saved and been saved by her."

Her mood now somber, Lyssera's eyes closed slowly as she said, "I wonder if that's how Ylera felt? Her heart was so eager to love that she was drawn, moth to a flame, to those whose energies were strong."

"I'm sure that she felt cherished above all others," Kyrian said. "I know that when Azhani allows me to see the truth of her heart, that is how I feel."

The room grew quiet.

Lyssera closed her eyes and allowed the peacefulness of the stardancer's presence to soothe her. She was almost jealous of Azhani, for she found Kyrian to be the kind of woman with whom she would enjoy spending time.

She is not for you, the queen thought sadly. Kyrian was half-elven and the same standard that she applied to her deceased twin was hers to follow as well. Besides, today, tomorrow or ten years from now, it would be moot — destiny had bound Kyrian to Azhani and had claimed their love against all others.

Better sooner than later, though. For all involved, Lyssera thought. She allowed herself to entertain the possibility of playing matchmaker. The idea carried her into sleep. She felt nothing when Kyrian carefully lifted her up and carried her to bed.

Oily smoke from dozens of torches scattered about the large warehouse and settled around the casino's patrons. Azhani slowly worked her way through the room, losing and winning enough coin to keep the bouncer's suspicions down as she listened to the thread of conversation that flowed around her. It didn't take long to learn which of the men and women in the establishment would, for the right price, fulfill her every wicked desire.

Not that I have any wicked, wanton needs, the dark-haired warrior thought, half sorrowfully, half in amusement. Azhani's gaze flicked from whore to whore, but measured against the remembered beauty of her Ylera, they were found wanting. And when held against the bright newness of Kyrian's smile, even Ylera's splendor paled.

When she realized the truth of her thoughts, she stood stock-still, stared down at a handful of copper coins and tried not to shake. Guilt filled her throat with bile and she was tempted to throw down the money and jump off the nearest pier. Sanity in the form of a vomiting drunkard intruded at the very last moment, bringing her back to reality.

Disgusted, she pushed around the gathering crowd and headed for the back of the casino. *So she has a nice smile. Kyrian is my friend, and it is no shame for me to see her as a beautiful woman.*

Determined not to think about it, she looked around at the section devoted to pit fighting, arm wrestling and drinking competitions. Surrounded by bloodthirsty men and women who cheered every violent blow, the pit was filled with fighters who stopped at nothing to smash their opponents into the dirt. The tables were filled with drinkers, bettors and wrestlers. Azhani skirted the pit arena and slipped into a chair across from a man who could have masqueraded as a bear.

Naked from the waist up, muscles bulging and gleaming with sweat and oil, Eskyn Dowser was one of Yannev's best arm wrestlers. He was also an excellent source of information about all things illegal in Y'Syria. The wrestler was in the middle of a long, lusty kiss and paused only long enough to grunt, "Be right with ya, friend," before returning his attention to a scantily dressed woman who eagerly leaned in for more kisses.

"Don't fall in," Azhani purred, hiding a smile when Eskyn suddenly shoved the flustered girl away from him and pounded his fists on the table.

"Astarus' balls! Azhani Rhu'len!" he exclaimed loudly, a huge smile spreading across his dark-skinned face. He looked up at the woman he had been kissing and said, "Why don't you grab us a couple of beers, love? And tell Yanny that I'm off for a while — I need to refuel."

"You want something to eat, Essie?" the woman asked, running her fingers lightly over his bald head.

A deep, rumbling chuckle emerged from the man's chest and he nodded. "Yes, I think I'd like that. Breaking bread with the *former* warleader of Y'Dan isn't something I do every day."

"Bad news travels faster than Astarus' hounds, old friend," Azhani said, settling into her chair and sighing heavily.

"Ah, but good news flies on the wings of owldragons, no? Whispers come to me that our fair queen knows quality when she sees it." The big man leaned back in his chair, cracking his neck and shoulders loudly.

Shrugging nonchalantly, Azhani said, "Well, I'm not exactly claiming poverty at the moment."

"Ah, good. I am pleased to hear that." He smiled at her, then turned his brilliant white smile up at his lady friend when she delivered a large tray of food and beer. "Beautiful, my sweet. Thank you. Why don't you go and enjoy the bard, my dear?" he suggested, giving the woman a push in the direction of a shadowed stage. When she had gone, Eskyn lifted his mug of ale and said, "Now then, what is it I can do for my old friend?"

"I need to know who would be desperate enough to bring krile into

Oakheart, Eskyn," said the warrior calmly.

Surprised, the wrestler set his food down and stared at her. Shaking his head, he said, "Let's say I know the answer to this. What's in it for me?"

A pouch heavy with coin appeared on the table. Eskyn reached for it, but was stopped by a powerful hand grasping his wrist.

"This one, and two more if your information pays out," Azhani said, her voice steely with determination.

She released him and he gathered up the pouch, mentally tallying its contents. Azhani Rhu'len had yet to stiff him; he trusted her not to start now. The leather bag vanished under the table, sequestered in a specially built compartment in his chair.

"All right, this is what I know," he began carefully, telling her a story of greed, corruption and scandal.

Chapter Twenty-Five

Lyssera rubbed her eyes tiredly. The pre-dawn arrival at Oakheart of her retainer, Azhani Rhu'len, had sent the court gossips into a tither about what she could possibly be up to. The morning court had been filled with rumors about her that ranged from the ridiculous to the sublime and included such feats as howling at the moon and cuckolding a well-known nobleman.

Lyssera ignored the gossip. According to Allyndev, the warrior was sleeping. Azhani had not answered her door when the young man had knocked to inquire after her health.

Kyrian was still with Ambassador Iften, making sure that there were no other ill effects from the krile poisoning. Without any new information, Lyssera had dealt with the court's regular business, telling her people that Ambassador Iften was recovering under the stardancer's care.

The queen sighed and looked around at the men and women who jockeyed for position within the court. One of them had tried to kill someone who was a guest in her home. The thought made an icicle of rage form in Lyssera's stomach.

Oakheart was supposedly the safest place in the kingdoms to live; that someone had tried to destroy its sanctity made her sick. As her eyes flitted from person to person, she felt the suspicion build. Taking a sip of wine, the queen spared a prayer that Azhani would discover the traitor soon. If she didn't, Lyssera knew that her own paranoia would harm her subjects.

Azhani was not asleep; she was completing her mission. The information from Eskyn had led her to Baron Draygil Var, a minor nobleman who had a habit of losing a lot of money in gambling dens. But, within the last few days, Var had paid all his debts and had purchased a supply of krile from a dealer who was now cooling his heels in the jail of a city guardsman.

Azhani had a suspect; now she needed a motive. To that end, she had returned to Oakheart in the early hours and was now perched above Var's guardsmen, waiting for the baron to leave his quarters so that she could search them.

She didn't have long to wait. Giving the baron half a candlemark to be well and truly gone, Azhani dropped in on his guards.

"Hello lads," she purred, acting swiftly. Grabbing both men by the collar, she slammed their heads together with a resounding thud. *Subtlety, thy name is not Azhani Rhu'len,* she thought, grinning widely.

The men slid to the ground. Within moments, she had them both bound and dragged into the baron's rooms. Satisfied that they could cause no harm, she began to search the suite for clues.

Baron Var was as good a criminal as he was a gambler. In under a quarter candlemark, Azhani had found all the proof she needed to charge him with the Y'Skani ambassador's poisoning. Hidden under the mattress of the baron's bed, she found a half-empty vial of krile and a scroll tube. The tube bore mute testimony to the fact that Baron Var fancied himself a bit of a mage, for inscribed about the cap were a series of runes.

Frowning, Azhani went into the baron's bathroom and retrieved a bottle of bathing salt. Pouring the scented crystals over the tube, she watched as the runes vanished. "Well, you might use the language of magick, Var, but you're no mage," she muttered while opening the container.

~You are to cause a disruption, Var. Keep the elves from looking beyond their borders for as long as you can. Please me, and I will reward you handsomely.~

The note was unsigned, but Azhani was certain that it was from Arris. Who else would wish to cause such trouble in the elven court? Rage flashed within her and she nearly crushed the scroll tube before throwing it to the bed.

"What is he trying to hide?" she wondered aloud as she tucked the evidence into a belt pouch. Her mind whirling, Azhani left Var's quarters and headed for court.

The rumors were flying fast and furious when Kyrian finally made an appearance in the large chamber that served as the queen's court. Lyssera, seated in a rigidly uncomfortable position on her throne, stood and walked down to greet the red-robed stardancer.

"My posterior thanks you for your timely arrival, good Stardancer," the queen muttered as she smiled politely at the men and women lining the sides of the aisle.

"It's always a pleasure to serve, Your Majesty," Kyrian replied just as softly, smiling gently.

"And how is the good ambassador?" Lyssera asked in a normal voice.

Kyrian's smile broadened. "He is well, Your Majesty. Cranky and irritable and demanding that he be allowed to eat real cow, instead of just the drippings."

Lyssera chuckled, her merry laugh infecting the stardancer until she too, was laughing. Returning to the dais, Lyssera sat on her throne while Kyrian was provided with a low chair at her side.

"I have had a letter from King Padreg," Lyssera said conversationally.

Kyrian tilted her head interestedly.

"He and his lady send their love to you and Azhani. Padreg also wishes you to remind Azhani of their wager." The queen's dark golden eyes twinkled.

"Wager? Blessed Twain but I wish Azhani would tell me these things. What wager?" she wondered in confusion.

Shaking her head, Lyssera shrugged and said, "I don't know, but you could ask the warrior yourself; she's here."

Striding up the red carpet toward the queen's throne was Azhani, her expression portending dire news. Effortlessly sinking to one knee as she reached the foot of Lyssera's throne, Azhani announced, "I have done as you commanded, My Queen. I regret to inform you that there is a traitor in your court."

The crowd hushed as her words penetrated the fog of conversation. Stillness filled the room as everyone waited for the queen's reply.

Lyssera stood and looked out at her people. "My friends, all of you know of the illness that befell the beloved ambassador from Y'Skan; however, only a few know the extent of that illness. It pains me to tell you that he has been a victim of krile poisoning."

There was a collective inhalation at the statement.

"I set my retainer, a noted lawkeeper, Azhani Rhu'len, to the task of discovering the poisoner. She now has returned with this news. Please, listen as she reveals the name of the one who slithers in our midst and seeks to destroy the peace of Oakheart Manor."

Lyssera returned to her throne while Azhani stood. In a clear voice, she said, "After much investigation, I determined that Baron Draygil Var is guilty of attempted murder and the action of high treason against the crown of Y'Syr."

Fragile silence held the court's breath.

"Nonsense! The oath-breaker lies to gain your favor, Your Majesty. Please, do not be gulled by her deceitful ways!" The baron in question pushed his way to the throne. Bristling with indignation, he said, "I demand you arrest her for sullying my good name!"

Calmly, Azhani turned to face the small-statured elf, one eyebrow raised in curiosity. "If it is lies that I speak, My Lord Baron, tell then why it is that I discovered these in your quarters?" From the pouch at her belt, Azhani produced the vial and the note. Handing them to Lyssera, she added, "Upon examination, you will find that the vial is half empty and the note contains instructions to Var to cause harm to your court, My Queen."

The queen read the note, her eyebrows shooting up at its contents.

Baron Var went white, fear and rage flickering across his face before he sputtered, "You didn't find that in my room, you planted it! I know who the poisoner is, My Queen. It's this scum you've hired, Azhani Rhu'len!" Disgusted, he sneered, "I am shamed that you allowed such a one into your household."

The scar on Azhani's face twitched as she ground her teeth, but she maintained her silence.

Rising from her throne, Lyssera stepped onto the carpet and began to circle the baron and the warrior. The court was glued to the scene playing out before them.

"Baron Var, who I hire is none of your concern; however, your opinion is noted," she said icily. "Azhani, your service to me thus far has been unimpeachable and all know that Thodan of Y'Dan held you in the highest regard. Hence, I trust that your information is fairly gathered, but my court may not be so swayed by your reputation. Therefore, I ask, do you have any further proof of the baron's guilt?"

Turning to face the queen, Azhani started to reply, "I—"

"Why don't we ask the goddess to verify the truth?" Kyrian stepped forward, her words echoing through the room. Smiling sweetly at the fuming baron, she said, "I am sure that Starseeker Vashyra would be happy to oblige you, My Queen." The approving warmth in Azhani's eyes made every word she spoke worthwhile to Kyrian, who was beginning to shake under the scrutiny of the hundreds of nobles that were attached to Lyssera's court.

"An excellent suggestion, Stardancer Kyrian," Lyssera said. A page was dispatched to locate the starseeker. Ascending the steps to her throne, Lyssera sat and prepared to wait.

The tension in the hall rose to a fever pitch as Var stared daggers into Azhani's back. In return, the warrior maintained an expression of unconcerned boredom. Nervous chatter flitted from one end of the room to the other as the nobles began to quietly whisper.

Indifferently ignoring the fuming baron, Azhani casually bumped her elbow into Kyrian's arm. She looked up, surprised, but then smiled at her friend.

"Want to get something to eat after the manure hits the crowd?" the warrior whispered, her voice barely carrying beyond the stardancer's ears.

"Aye, and while we eat, you can tell me about the bet you made with Padreg," Kyrian whispered back.

The bet? What is she talking about? Then she remembered. *Beast's bones! What am I supposed to say? Oh, it's just this friendly little wager over whether or not you and I will fall in love? That should turn about as well as a square wheel.*

What's the matter, warrior? Scared to admit that falling in love again wouldn't be so bad? a mischievous internal voice prodded.

Azhani wanted to close her eyes and thump her head against the nearest wall, but she didn't. *No, you rutting satyr! Ylera is the only one I will ever love!* The passionate words felt strangely hollow.

At the end of the hall, the double doors opened and saved her from further internal arguments. The tall, agelessly beautiful form of Starseeker Vashyra swept down the aisle, and gathered everyone's attention.

Azhani felt her eyes drawn to the willow-thin woman. The priest's silver-touched black hair flowed down her body in graceful waves, and the ends nearly touched the floor. Azure silk robes enhanced the sense of ethereal beauty that clung to the starseeker like an aura. Emblazoned on her forehead was the star shaped tattoo that proclaimed her status for all to see. Vashyra was a hand of Astariu, and none would call her testimony into question.

As the starseeker reached the small group clustered at the edge of the dais, Vashyra bowed to the queen and said, "I understand that my skills are needed, Your Majesty?"

"Starseeker, you are welcome in my home. Thank you for joining us so quickly."

"I serve at the will of my queen," Vashyra said humbly.

Lyssera inclined her head. "There is a matter of law before the court, Vashyra. Evidence has been presented that requires additional testimony before I can render judgment. Will you aid me in determining the truth, so that the goddess' will may prevail?"

"My skills are yours to command, Your Majesty. How may I assist you?" The priest was serene as she looked from Azhani, then to Kyrian and finally to Baron Var.

The room quieted down as the nobles all strained to watch and listen. Kyrian felt sweat break out on her palms and would have turned and run from the room if Azhani had not leaned over and whispered, "Look at Var. I think he's about to piss on his fancy velvet shoes."

Covering her giggles with a sneeze, Kyrian looked at the queen and said, "I beg your pardon, My Queen."

Lyssera waved her hand as if it were nothing and said, "Starseeker, the issue is thus: Master Azhani Rhu'len has accused Baron Draygil Var of poisoning Ambassador Iften Windstorm with krile dust. To prove her claims, she has produced a half-empty bottle of poison and a letter from an unknown master ordering Var to cause chaos within my court. In return, Baron Var has denounced Master Azhani as an oath-breaker and claims that he is falsely accused of the crime. I ask that you seek the truth in these claims, Starseeker."

"It shall be as you have asked," the priest said, as she accepted the evidence from the queen.

"No! I refuse to submit to this charade! My Queen, you have been placed under a cruel spell by this vile beast! Please, cast her from your home before she does you harm!" Baron Var exclaimed, causing the crowd to murmur and mutter excitedly.

Around the room, nobles whispered, "It's true."

"Didn't she betray her own king?"

"Did we not see the bodies of the slain burn in a weeklong bonfire just on the other side of the great Banner Lake?"

"Was she not the one responsible for the death of the queen's beloved twin, Ylera?"

"Silence!" Lyssera's shout caused the entire chamber to be seized with a quiet that was almost holy. Rising, Lyssera stalked over to Baron Var. Anger poured off her in waves. "You will accept the judgment of Starseeker Vashyra, or you will be summarily exiled!"

The quiet extended until the only sound heard was the creaking of the manor's walls. Baron Var closed his mouth and backed away from the dais while Starseeker Vashyra began to chant. The evidence levitated off the starseeker's hands. Slowly, a ruddy glow enveloped the vial and the parchment.

The items hovered momentarily and then, as though shot from a long-bow, flew through the air, smacked into Var's chest and clung there as though they were fused to the fabric of his tunic.

Rage transfixed Var's already angered features. Snarling, he drew his jeweled dagger and lunged for Azhani. She had no time to react. Thrusting the blade deep into her gut, he growled, "This is your fault, you bitch."

Azhani staggered back and the blade came free. Blood spurted from her stomach and she quickly clutched at the wound.

While everyone was fixated on the warrior's actions, Var slipped his hand into a pouch and withdrew a mirror. Smearing it with the blood from his dagger, he chanted a few guttural words and then cried, "Master, attend me!" Flinging the mirror down, he smiled in satisfaction when it burst into pieces and sent a plume of noxious smoke into the air around him.

Kyrian rushed to Azhani's side and helped her to the ground. The stardancer's mind was a whirl of indecision. Should she stay and attend the bleeding warrior, or should she draw her baton and subdue the now gibbering Baron Var? The crazed nobleman still held the bloody dagger and was waving it about madly as if daring someone to attack him.

Suddenly, Var charged Queen Lyssera, but was rebuffed by a spell cast by the starseeker. In a belated move, Kyrian leaped to her feet and drew her baton. At her feet, Azhani weakly tried to sit.

The smoke from Var's spell had all but dissipated into a thin haze that drifted over the top of the muttering crowd.

Lyssera approached the man who was now bound by thin bands of magickal force. Beside her, Vashyra chanted softly, weaving the spell that prevented the baron from acting.

"Baron Draygil Var, hear now my judgment. You are hereby declared guilty of the act of poisoning a known friend of the Crown. For this act, you are sentenced to a term of no less than one hundred mortal years in prison. For the crime of collusion to create chaos and disruption among the courtiers of Oakheart, you are found guilty and are sentenced to a period of exile that shall extend the length of your natural life. In final, you are further found guilty of the crimes of attempted murder, both of the queen and of her chosen retainer. Your sentence, Baron Var, for these offenses, is death." The queen's voice, cold and harsh, echoed through the chamber.

Laughing madly, Var said, "You think I care for your judgments, Queen Listless? Your laws are nothing against the glory that is My Lord Ecarthus and the favors he has granted." Struggling against his bonds, he suddenly shouted, "Master Darkchilde, I have done it! I have struck down the one you seek!"

In an act so brutally violent that it would give all assembled nightmares for years to come, Baron Var tore his arm free from the starseeker's spell and drove the dagger into the side of his neck. As blood spurted from the mortal wound, he chanted a spell that made those closest to him physically ill to hear it.

Above the crowd, the smoke that had begun to dissipate suddenly coalesced into a silvery disk that settled to the ground behind the dying baron. Starseeker Vashyra's chant changed and the baron's spellbonds vanished. Dropping to his knees, the elven nobleman continued to chant brokenly while blood pooled around him.

Azhani dragged herself to her feet, supported by Kyrian, who had dropped her baton in order to aid the warrior. Guardsmen mounted the dais and surrounded the queen in a shield of bodies while Vashyra continued to chant.

The mirror-like magickal construct flashed with clashing energies as Var and Vashyra fought for dominance. As they fought, a face appeared in the mirror, its lips moving in silent chant. The glassy surface rippled and the shadowy figure of a black-robed man stepped from the newly created portal and into the throne room.

"Draygil, you fool!" he snarled as he viewed the assembled crowd. The sorcerer's body flickered as golden arcs of lightning coruscated around him. Spotting the starseeker, he spat a few words and pointed, sending a bolt of pure force at the priest-mage that knocked her to her knees and halted her spell.

Azhani stared at the apparition and suddenly cried, "You!" Grabbing for her sword, she staggered forward, causing fresh blood to erupt from her wound. Weakened by blood loss, she fell to her knees.

Hollow, mirthless laughter came from the sorcerer. Striding toward the fallen warrior, he said, "Daughter of Rhu'len, how nice that you remember me." His shade stopped only paces away from her. Squatting, Darkchilde hissed, "Tell me, how does it feel to grovel at my feet?"

Darkchilde could not believe his luck. The idiotic Var had actually delivered his enemy straight into his hands. He grinned wickedly — vengeance was imminent.

On her knees, Azhani shook with hatred. Digging into her well of strength, she drew herself up, keeping one hand plastered over the wound in her abdomen.

"Darkchilde," she growled, "your feet stink." Behind her, she felt Kyrian place a gentle hand against her back. Soft song and a faint yellow glow were the only clues to the fact that the stardancer was healing her.

Darkchilde cursed and said, "Demons take you, spawn of DaCoure!" He spat out the lines of a spell, thrust his arms into the air and the temperature in the room plummeted. "Die," he whispered. Wind rose, and caused the chill to increase. An eerie moan echoed through the room, followed by a growl that was filled with hate and hunger. Hideous shapes began to form around the room and people screamed in fear.

There was a stampede toward the doors, but they were sealed shut. Darkchilde laughed as men and women began to batter the doors. He looked at Azhani and said, "I'm going to enjoy watching this. Just as I enjoyed watching the rimerbeasts kill your father."

"You bastard!" Azhani shouted as she leapt. She passed right through him. His laughter grew even more mirthful.

"Comedy, Azhani? I didn't know you had a funny bone in your body."

"Sorcerer!" Starseeker Vashyra, having recovered, now stood and faced the wraith. Enveloped in a purple-hued aura, the priest-mage's tattoo began to sparkle with energy. A single amber beam of force erupted from the mark and struck the sorcerer square in the chest.

Reeling back, Darkchilde glared at the starseeker. He began to chant and his hands took on an ugly green glow. The chill in the room increased and the walls creaked as ice began to form.

"Get ye hence!" Vashyra shouted and gestured. Once more, the amber bolt of force struck the sorcerer and sent him flying toward the portal.

Darkchilde landed in a heap. Struggling to stand, he pointed at Azhani and shouted, "I will have my vengeance!" From his hand, a fireball was launched toward the warrior, only to be intercepted by Kyrian's baton. The weapon was consumed by the spell and both disappeared in a blinding flash.

"No!" Darkchilde shouted as he felt the force of Vashyra's spell push him through the portal.

With a distinctive, sucking pop, the window closed, preventing the sorcerer from unleashing further harm.

"Darkchilde! Where is he? Is he dead?" Azhani demanded fiercely as she wavered on her feet. Bleeding again, her normally dark-brown skin was turning gray from pain.

"I'm sorry, Azhani. I do not know where he went," Vashyra said as she rubbed her temples. "Nor is he dead. What we fought was only Darkchilde's image, not the man."

Kyrian asked, "So he could be anywhere? Even, not in Y'Myran at all?"

Vashyra nodded wearily.

"Blast him, bones to dust! What the hell does he have to do with everything?" Azhani growled as she slumped to the ground.

Lyssera emerged from behind her guards. "Vashyra, can you trace the sorcerer's location?"

"I—" the starseeker started to speak, then went utterly still. A preternatural calm settled over the room.

::*"The breaking is at hand. The Blade, the Heart and the Pawn shall meet, and on that day the sun will stand still and the stars will no longer spin with time. The Beast will rise to seek his place among mortals. Stand well against the storm, and sages shall sing of thy glory into the mists of Eternity. Fall, and all shall blacken and fade."*::

The voice that spoke the words had nothing of the timbre that Vashyra's did. To all assembled it was eerily familiar. For the elves, it touched upon a memory so ancient that none could grasp its origin.

The starseeker's eyes rolled back into her head, and she collapsed.

"She's got the right idea," Azhani muttered as more blood leaked from her wound. "Ow," she added as she started to topple over.

Kyrian caught her and helped her to lie down. "Rest, Azhi. I've got you," the stardancer murmured as she ran her fingers through the warrior's hair.

"All right," Azhani mumbled, smiling weakly.

Chapter Twenty-Six

Kasyrin Darkchilde stood in the center of a maelstrom. The interior of his manor house had been reduced to wreckage by the battle with the elven starseeker. Brilliant golden energy wrapped the sorcerer's body and pinned him in place.

Face contorted with rage, Kasyrin fought against the mage-priest's magick. All at once, there was a shrill keening sound as a burst of dark force shattered the magickal bonds, freeing the sorcerer from the starseeker's spell.

"No!" he shouted angrily and kicked a bit of flotsam. "You will bleed for this, Azhani Rhu'len, I swear it!" He summoned an army of invisible servants and, drained of the last of his power, he slumped against a wall, weary to the bone.

Discarding his ruined robes in favor of the clean garments fetched by his servants, the sorcerer left the wreckage of his house and went to the Ecarthan temple. Once safely ensconced in his office, he tapped into the raw power gleaned from the sacrifices to refuel his reserves. The pain-laced energy chased away his lethargy and allowed him to think clearly.

Pouring a glass of thick, amber mead, Kasyrin first went over his correspondence, finding solace in the fact that High King Ysradan had lost another ship to the sea serpents. Similar messages containing information about the loss of resources and high death tolls came from his agents in the other kingdoms.

From his priests came the news that the first openly held services had drawn a few worshippers. To entice Y'Dan's populace, Ecarthan priests promised the curious a day of pure indulgence. Darkchilde grinned at the thought of the babies who would be born as a result the services — more souls to feed the god.

Within days there would be three fully operational temples meeting the spiritual needs of the Y'Dani people. Every day, more priests were being ordained into the Ecarthan religion as converts left the main temple with zeal to serve their new god burning deep within their hearts.

From Porthyros he had the news that the Nonhuman Restriction Act was now law. Any nonhumans who wished to cross into Y'Dan must now register with a local guardhouse or face imprisonment. The dwarves and elves were of course incensed and messages indicating that they would shun the kingdom only made Kasyrin smile. *That's right, little sheep. Stay away until it's your turn to face the darkness that is my lord Ecarthus!*

Included within the missive from Porthyros was the comment that Arris was looking forward to his next visit. Kasyrin's smile grew broader. The knowledge that he had successfully converted Arris to the worship of Ecarthus made the defeat he had recently suffered easier to endure.

With Arris openly supporting the temples, the rest of Y'Dan would quickly follow. That thought gave him an idea, and he quickly dashed off a message to Porthyros. Why should he have to wait for the people to follow their king? Arris could make it law that everyone attend services.

That would mean that the sacrifice schedule could be accelerated, which would give Ecarthus and by extension, Kasyrin, more power to access.

::*Thou hast a keen mind, my servant.*:: Ecarthus came upon him suddenly, filling him with the burning lust for pain that always accompanied the demon's possession. ::*Thou hast encountered the enemy and failed. I am not pleased.*:: Kasyrin was racked by agony. ::*However, I am a forgiving god.*:: As quickly as it had come, the pain vanished and left the sorcerer feeling as though something precious had been stripped from his grasp.

"Master," he whimpered. "I'm sorry."

::*Do not fail again, Kasyrin. Azhani must not interfere. Use the boy to lure her out. Her desire for vengeance is nearly as great as thine.*:: The demon's suggestion was followed by images of dangling Arris as bait to bring Azhani out of the safety of the Y'Syran kingdom.

Kasyrin smiled. "I won't need to do that, Master. The DaCoure family is afflicted by the worst case of honor I've ever seen. Your children will be adequate enough to keep her occupied. She'll not interfere with our work here, and Arris is useful for that purpose." The sorcerer felt the demon's approval as it left him.

The rimerbeasts would keep Azhani and her allies from interfering in Kasyrin's plans. With their attention focused northward, the Ecarthan temples would spread, and he could gather power unhindered. By the time the day of the breaking arrived, Azhani would either be dead, or too busy to stop him.

Opening her eyes, Azhani groaned faintly. The pain in her side was a dull roar, and her bladder indicated that it was more than past time to seek the chamber pot. *What happened?* Yawning, she rubbed her eyes and tried to remember. *Oh, right. Traitor, stabbing, sorcerer. I'm too old for this shyvot.* "Ugh," she croaked, and tried to sit.

The motion woke Kyrian, who had been dozing in a chair near the bed. Blinking her eyes sleepily, she said, "Sorry. Must've fallen asleep."

"S'fine," muttered the warrior. "I need to use the privy," she said and yawned again. "Then you can go sleep in your own bed."

Staggering to her feet, Kyrian lifted Azhani up and helped her to stand. "As lovely as that sounds, I can't. Lyssera ordered me to stay with you."

Azhani snorted. "I can take care of myself, Kyr. I don't need a nurse — ow!" A startled oath of pain was forced from her when she tried to move too quickly toward the water closet. "Shyvot. I hate being injured," she growled.

"Will this become a routine aspect of our friendship, Azhani?" Kyrian asked as she helped the warrior. "You get broken and I fix you?"

"Hah-hah, very funny, Kyrian," she griped. "Ah gods, is there anything to drink in this room? I feel like I ate a sheep, wool and all."

Helping Azhani back to bed, Kyrian laughed. "There's plenty of water, my friend." She poured a cup and set it on the bedside table.

Relieved, Azhani lay in bed and drank the water. "Thanks. If I remember this correctly, next comes the foul-tasting, bitter brew that makes me sleep half a day, am I right?" Lines of pain shadowed her face as she spoke.

Smiling, Kyrian said, "I can add honey to the tea, but don't come crying to me if it doesn't work as well." She winked and added a dollop of honey to a gently steaming cup of tea.

Azhani drank the brew quickly, making a face when she got to the dregs. "Still tastes like the bottom of a mud pit."

"Here, suck on this." Kyrian held out the spoon she had used to stir the tea. It still had a honey residue on it, so Azhani gratefully took it and licked it clean.

"Thanks. That's better," she said. Taking another drink of water, she patted the bed beside her. "Now, since you won't go back to your room, at least share this massive bed with me."

Kyrian regarded the bed and then her friend. Pursing her lips she said, "Promise you'll wake me if you need something?"

"Promise," the warrior said sleepily.

"Then let me get you tucked in first." She helped Azhani to snuggle down, then stripped down to her under tunic and climbed onto the bed.

"Goodnight, Kyrian," Azhani mumbled, as she patted the stardancer's hip absently.

"Sweet dreams, Azhi." Within moments, she was asleep.

Lying beside her, Azhani stared at the ceiling and listened to the deep, even breathing of her friend. *Go to sleep, warrior,* she told herself, but her eyes wouldn't shut. Instead, she basked in the warmth cast by the body of her best friend. Azhani allowed herself to revel in the wonder of the stardancer's care.

Kyrian rolled over and snuggled up against Azhani's side. One pale hand was draped over the warrior's chest, and Kyrian's fingers automatically tangled themselves in Azhani's tunic.

The action caused the warrior's breath to hitch as a sudden explosion of awareness drove all thoughts of sleep from Azhani's body. Heat blossomed in her belly and she shivered. *Goddess! What is happening to me? She's my friend. Why do I suddenly find it so difficult to breathe? We've cuddled before.*

Kyrian shifted again, and now the stardancer was completely wrapped around her.

"Astariu," Azhani whispered, overwhelmed by the wave of intense desire that flooded over her. Closing her eyes, she willed a vision of Ylera's dead, battered body to appear. What came was a hazy memory, tinged with sadness and regret, but lacking the knife-like pain that usually accompanied such thoughts.

Frightened now, Azhani fought to remain calm. Every muscle in her body went taut with the strain of staying still. A part of her was shouting at her to get up and run as far away from Kyrian as she could.

She's stealing the hatred that makes you strong!

Azhani didn't move. *No, she's showing me that hatred cannot bring my Ylera back,* she thought defensively.

Don't let her take away your rage! the banshee within yelled. *You need it to defeat Arris!*

The only thing I need to defeat Arris is myself. With that thought, the banshee within vanished.

Opening her eyes, Azhani looked down at the sleeping woman and felt the fear melt away. *I will always love Ylera, and there is nothing evil in noticing that my best friend is beautiful.* Tears trickled from her eyes as she slowly draped her arm over Kyrian's shoulders. The stardancer sighed and snuggled closer.

Azhani's heart was pounding heavily in her chest. Pressing a kiss against the priest's crown of amber hair, she mused, *I thought my heart died with Ylera. Could it be that Kyrian will bring it back to life?*

Waking up wrapped in Azhani's arms was like scratching a bother-some itch for Kyrian. It felt wonderful and yet she knew there would be a painful aftermath. It was bliss to feel the softness of the warrior's breath on her neck, and at the same time it made her feel sick to know that she derived so much pleasure from the innocent contact.

Do I love her? Why yes, My Queen, I'm so in love with Azhani that I'll make do with whatever scraps of emotion she'll give me. Is that what you wanted to hear?

Kyrian wondered what the queen had truly been asking when she posed the question. Regretfully, she disengaged herself from Azhani's embrace and got out of bed. The room was temperate, but Azhani's skin burned with fever.

After stoking the fire, Kyrian headed for the kitchens. Breakfast was next on the list as she intended to expend whatever energy necessary to return the warrior to full health.

At the doorway, she paused and looked back at her sleeping friend. What she saw was a sight that would remain forever burned into her mem-ory — Azhani, tightly clutching the pillow the stardancer had so recently abandoned.

"Have you found anything?" Lyssera asked as she and Vashyra strode through the halls of Oakheart. There had been a meeting between the queen and her councilors that morning. After much shouting and demanding of answers, the starseeker had informed them that the sorcerer who had attacked Lyssera's court was not of Y'Syr.

Because they had no true idea of Darkchilde's location, they could do nothing to apprehend him. Instead, they would concentrate on protecting their borders and on the threat of a rimerbeast invasion. Messengers were leaving Oakheart now, headed for the furthest holdings to call for the armies of the land to gather in Y'Syria.

"Only bits and pieces, My Queen. The prophecy is ancient and fairly well forgotten. Give us time; something must remain in the archives," the mage-priest replied.

"Keep looking. The Twain know that a prophecy of doom is the last thing we need added to the plate of bad luck that fate has served us." The queen looked exhausted.

"Yes, My Queen. Please, go and rest. I will send a message if any-thing is discovered."

Lyssera sighed heavily. "I wish I could, old friend, but there is still much to be done."

A week passed while Azhani recovered. The stardancer was at her side constantly, only leaving to check on the care of Ambassador Windstorm. Lyssera visited briefly to discuss Vashyra's progress on tracking down any references to the strange prophecy she had uttered in the throne room. Both she and Kyrian felt that the words came from the gods, while Azhani was more skeptical. By week's end, small contingents of soldiers were arriving in Y'Syr. A colorful field of tents was beginning to blossom by Banner Lake.

The mood around Oakheart was tense. Guards were more vigilant, and everyone looked over their shoulder as they moved about their daily business. Lyssera tried to calm her people, but Darkchilde's attack had left their sense of safety bruised. Reports from the mountain villages about egg-filled caves filtered in and the energy in Y'Syria moved up another notch. Lyssera started visiting Azhani daily to take advantage of the former warleader's mind.

"You'll want to start gathering supplies now, Lyss," the warrior said as Kyrian changed her dressing. "Oh, hey, that tickled, Kyr."

The stardancer smiled and gave the warrior's belly an affectionate pat. "Tickling is good, Azhani. It means that it's healing."

Making a face, the warrior said, "Thus speaks the woman who thinks that medicine is better when it tastes horrid, when it is just as efficacious when it is pleasing to the palate."

Kyrian stuck out her tongue. "Just because you're a poor patient doesn't mean my methods don't work, Azhani. You have admitted that the tea seems stronger when I don't put honey in it."

Azhani sighed.

Lyssera laughed, enjoying the easy banter between the friends. The smiles that sprang easily to Azhani's lips made the elven queen ache with joy for her friend. *Has it really been such a short time when she came to me, filled with grief for Ylera? Astariu, you have given her a miracle.*

"All right, I promise, no more bitter tea, Azhani. You've had your last dose of herbs. For this injury, anyway."

"Thanks. I'm grateful, really. Especially for the quick heal in the throne room. I'm afraid that I'd still be kissing Darkshyvot's feet if you hadn't helped," Azhani said while Kyrian tugged the warrior's tunic back in place.

Kyrian smiled. "I'm sorry it wasn't more — what if you'd had to fight him?" The stardancer's smile changed to a worried frown.

Azhani shrugged. "I'd have thrown you at him so I could make a run for it." Though the statement was made straight faced, there was enough mischief dancing in Azhani's eyes to make the stardancer smile.

Rolling her eyes, Kyrian said, "Wonderful, leave me to do all the heavy fighting while you head for the woods like some demented rabbit. Thanks, but no thanks, Azhi."

They shared a smile. *She makes me feel good to be alive. I like being around her.* Azhani was not looking forward to sleeping alone again. Since the events in the throne room, the stardancer had spent every night wrapped in the warrior's arms. Neither woman spoke of the feelings their closeness engendered, but both knew that something was changing between them.

"I need to check on Ambassador Windstorm, if you'll excuse me, My Queen?"

The elven monarch waved her off.

"You two are quite the pair," Lyssera said without bothering to hide the mirth in her tone.

Instantly, Azhani's face was filled with a strange combination of regret, fear and hope. "She's special." Then, as if wanting the words to be unsaid, she added, "But I still love Ylera."

Lyssera inclined her head. Leaning forward in her chair, she caught the warrior's gaze and said, "Ylera is dead, Azhani. You are not. There is no shame in wanting to love again. She would not wish you to hurt forever."

Azhani looked away as tears wetted her eyes.

"Azhani, look at me," said Lyssera, a note of regal command in her tone.

The warrior faced the queen.

"Talk to me."

Azhani searched Lyssera's face. "Revenge was what motivated me into claiming the rite, Lyss. Every person who died at Banner Lake gave their life so that I could spit Arris Thodan on the end of my sword — all for Ylera." She bowed her head. "I'd have died, otherwise. How can I lose my heart so quickly? Did I truly love her?" she sobbed.

Lyssera went to the warrior's side and wrapped an arm around her shoulder. "Yes, you did, Azhani."

"Then how come I'd rather fight rimerbeasts than deal with Arris? It's certainly not due to fear of the upstart."

The queen laughed. "You're a warrior, Azhani. I'd imagine that it has something to do with risk assessment. After all, which is more dangerous – a beast season, or Arris?"

"A beast season," Azhani answered promptly.

"There you have it — you worry overmuch, my friend. Your mind knows what is best for the land, even when your heart is confused."

Azhani's face grew pensive as she considered the queen's words.

"Deep thoughts?" Lyssera asked softly.

"I'm drowning in them," Azhani replied, her face troubled.

"You should allow yourself the right to heal, Azhani."

The warrior sighed. "I keep telling myself that, Lyss. I lie here at night, and I tell myself that it's perfectly acceptable to look at another woman and see beauty, to feel desire — and it feels right." Hope graced her face, soothing the harsh lines to softness. "It's like a miracle." Then her expression shifted, once again hard and angular. "Then I remember that Ylera is dead, and I feel guilty for wanting anything when she can no longer see the sun."

"Oh Azhi. There's nothing wrong with your feelings. Life goes on, and so does the heart." Lyssera rubbed the warrior's back soothingly. "If your places had been reversed, would you wish her to weep forever?"

"No! Never! She deserved to be loved and honored," Azhani said resolutely.

"Then why do you not feel you deserve the same? You could do worse than to let someone into your life," the queen said gently.

Shocked, Azhani spluttered, "What?"

"You could do worse than to open your heart to someone like Kyrian." Lyssera held up a staying hand. "My sister would be honored to share your heart with another."

For a long moment, Azhani stared at the queen, her jaw working as words tried to form. Tears gathered in her eyes, and then vanished to be replaced by a deep confusion. Shaking her head, Azhani said, "I don't know what to say, Lyss. What I felt for Ylera was deeper than anything I had ever known before. Watching her die leeched away all the love in me. For so long, I had no emotions; they had bled away and stained the stones of Y'Dannoch castle." Wide-eyed wonder shone from her face. "I like Kyrian, Lyss. She is so much to me, and she touches me in so many ways that I can't begin to name them, but love? I don't know. I just don't know."

Lyssera took Azhani's hand in hers, cradling the warrior's calloused fingers with her own. "All I'm asking is that you allow for the possibility of love, my friend. The heart and the mind don't always speak the same language, but with love, translations aren't necessary."

"I-I'll have to think about it, Lyss." The warrior scrubbed her face. In effort to regain control, she said, "How's Allyn?"

Releasing the warrior's hand, Lyssera replied, "Anxious to have his teacher back. He won a few bouts with the guards and now struts about like a bantam cock."

"Really? I'll ask Kyrian to spar with him. She'll knock the arrogance from him quickly enough."

"The stardancer must be very good, for you to trust Allyn to her training."

"She routinely humiliates me at Dance," the warrior said. *Though she does have that rather irritating habit of avoiding direct confrontation when weapons are involved. I need to address that. I wonder if my being bedridden will get her to talk, because Astariu knows she's as close-mouthed as a monk about it otherwise.*

"This I have to see. All right, please ask her to spar with my nephew."

"You are so good to me," Ambassador Iften said, while Kyrian plumped pillows and straightened covers for him.

"Yes, and you return that kindness with your curmudgeonly ways, you know," Kyrian said, shaking her finger at him.

He chuckled. "I'm an old man, lass. I've earned the right to be grumpy."

The banter between Iften and Kyrian was natural, flowing out of a mutual admiration that had been in place since she had been caring for the old desert man. Pieces that had been missing from both of their lives were filled by each other. Kyrian had gained a grandfather and Iften a granddaughter. As a desert walker, Iften had seen many marvels and Kyrian never tired of listening to his adventures. In return, Kyrian told the old man what it was like growing up in Y'Len.

"Well, if you insist upon being grumpy, then I'll just have to give this to someone else," Kyrian said as she lifted the lid on the desert man's dinner tray.

Iften squawked in delighted surprise when he saw a steak still sizzling on a plate.

"You'll do no such thing, young lady," the ambassador said primly. Kyrian was unmoved. Plaintively, he said, "Don't make an old man beg, lass, it's unseemly."

Chuckling, she set the tray on Iften's lap. "I'd not ruin your pleasure like that, Granther. Enjoy your meal."

Greedily, he tucked into the meal. A loud moan echoed around the room, proclaiming Iften's absolute pleasure over the meal. "I take it," he said, wiping his lips, "that I'm no longer in danger of feeding the worms?"

"Yes, the krile is gone." She smiled sadly. "Though the sandlung is not."

Iften set his fork down and looked at Kyrian. "Lass, I made my peace with that long ago. Do not let the joy of today be spoiled by tomorrow's storm clouds."

"It irritates the healer in me to know that no matter what, I'm going to lose," Kyrian said softly.

The old man felt his chest ache with the sadness that was etched on her face. "You must not think on it. Come, tell me how your friend is." He forced a cheerful smile onto his face.

Kyrian took a deep breath and smiled faintly. "Azhani's fine. I'm sure she'll be up and about shortly."

"Thank the Serpent! I would not wish her death to ride on my conscience," Iften said. The desert man had been appalled to learn of Baron Var's treachery, and frightened to hear of the appearance and attack by Kasyrin Darkchilde.

"It wasn't your fault, Granther," Kyrian said. Her eyes filled with tears. "It was mine," she added softly.

"What?" Iften blurted.

"It's my fault that she was hurt. If I had moved faster— hadn't froze—" She shuddered. "I let my fear win." There was a lost and faraway look in her eyes that disturbed the Y'Skani ambassador.

"Kyrian, come here, lass," he called to her. Slowly, as though she were swimming through molasses, the priest reluctantly made her way to his side. Setting his meal on the bedside table, Iften patted the bed. "Tell me about it," he said softly.

Collapsing to the bed, she began to sob. "I-I-I freeze, in battle," she admitted.

Iften took her hand in his. "There's no shame in that, little one. I've never been much for staring certain death in the eye, either."

She sniffled and looked up at him. "But you've fought giant scorpions, and raiders, and—"

"That doesn't mean I wasn't scared spitless each time," the old man said. "What you have to remember is not that you were afraid, but that you overcame that fear — and you did beat it, lass. Else, Azhani would not be with us today. You said yourself that you sang her wound closed during the conflict."

"Yes, but—"

"Let it go, lass. Life is too short to dwell on should-have-dones," the ambassador counseled wisely.

Kyrian looked away. "At night, when she's sleeping, I look at her, to remind myself that she's alive. I watch her breathe and think about what would happen to Y'Syr if she had died, and I feel so ashamed."

"You're a good lass, Kyrian, with a gentle soul," rumbled the ambassador. "Y'Syr would have gone on without her, though."

The stardancer's eyes closed. "That's just it, Granther. I find that I care not for the kingdom, but for myself," she whispered.

"Ah, I begin to understand." The old man smiled and sighed dramatically. "I remember being young, and in love."

Kyrian froze. *Oh no. No, he can't have known. No. He'll—* "Please, don't say anything," she whispered. "She doesn't know. I'm not supposed to feel this way. She's my friend, and she loved Ylera, who was also my friend..."

Holding up a hand to halt her tumbling words, Iften said, "Don't fret yourself about it, lass. I'll not give up your secrets; they are yours to hold and yours to tell. A load heavy to bear, I am sure, but my shoulders are strong and I am willing to lend them to you." A gentle smile creased his careworn face.

Sighing, the stardancer stood and shuffled to the hearth. Adding some wood, she retrieved her tea, drinking the cool liquid absently.

Iften's offer to listen was genuine and motivated only by his care for her. Shouldn't she return that generosity by treating it as the gift that it was? Hadn't she been going in circles for weeks on her own, trying to tell herself that all she felt for Azhani Rhu'len was friendship? Didn't the warrior's face haunt her dreams, taunting her with what she would never be able to have? Iften deserved some truths from her, since he had willingly allowed her to probe every corner of his body in an attempt to cure the sandlung. Surely talking to someone about her feelings was better than brooding over them.

Of course, it doesn't make it any easier to deal with knowing that I almost got her killed. I froze again. If Lyssera hadn't thrown my baton, Azhani would be a black smear on the throne room carpet. My teachers will be so proud to learn that I've turned into a coward!

"Here now, lass, if you go falling into the quicksand of your mind, even a dust storm will seem like a blessing." He dug around under his pillow and held up a flask. "Drink," he said, holding it out to her.

Setting her tea down, she returned to his side and accepted the flask. Kyrian uncorked the bottle and drank. Almost immediately she began to choke. Coughing as the harsh liquor burned all the way down, she wheezed, "What in the name of the Twain is this?"

"Desert mead," Iften replied, winking charmingly.

Shuddering as she took another drink, Kyrian capped off the flask and handed it back. "Thanks, I think I needed that."

"Any time, lass," he replied, settling back on the bed and taking a swig of the harsh beverage.

"I fell in love with her, Granther," she whispered almost inaudibly. Shaking her head ruefully she said, "I don't know how to forget those feelings. I've tried and it's tearing me apart."

"Why are you so intent upon throwing away what the gods give?" the old man asked.

Kyrian paced about the room and then sat and buried her head in her hands. "She'll never love me. How could she? I knew Ylera and I am but a shadow when compared against her light."

"Kyrian, lass, love isn't about filling a mold. You're right. You can never be what Ylera was to her, but that doesn't mean Azhani is incapable of loving you," Iften said gently.

Hope rose thickly in Kyrian's heart, but she pushed the heady feeling away. "No. We're just friends. Ylera was special. She found the way to Azhani's heart because she was supposed to."

"Don't let the loves of the past control the future. The heart is very resilient. Azhani will love again — and you are worthy of that affection." The old Y'Skani hadn't felt so alive in years. To give such fatherly advice; he had thought his chance had died with his children.

The lost expression had returned to Kyrian's face. "I don't know, Granther," she whispered.

"Then come here, and let me comfort you," he said, opening his arms. With a small cry, Kyrian flew across the room into his embrace. Rubbing her back soothingly, he said, "I don't know what you want to hear, lass. All I can say is that love can grow from many foundations, and friendship is the best of them. Be truthful, share your honor, and let your heart be your guide and what is meant to be will follow."

Chapter Twenty-Seven

"Ecarthus frees us. Our blood is his blood and to him we gladly go," the black-robed priest chanted, while below him gray-shrouded acolytes dragged a bound and gagged prisoner up the steps to a black basalt altar. Behind the altar was a cauldron holding a fire that burned menacingly.

Watching from a balcony, Arris yawned. The ceremony had been shocking at first, but now it was commonplace. The blood that spewed forth when the sacrifice was butchered no longer sickened him nor did nightmares haunt his sleep. Instead, he felt strangely energized.

Beside him, Porthyros sat with his gaze fixed upon the scene taking place on the altar. The scholar seemed to be in a religious haze as he watched the high priest of Ecarthus bend the prisoner over the basalt table and begin to slowly eviscerate him.

Absently, he passed Arris a cup and said, "Here is your tea, My King. It should be cool enough now."

Arris took the drink silently, engrossed by the sight of the priest as he offered the sacrifice's entrails to Ecarthus. The scholar handed the young king a meatroll and it was consumed as well.

The king was gaining muscle from his training with his new swordmaster, and as a result, was always hungry. However, the lessons were paying off. Arris had successfully defended himself against a would-be attacker. The peasant's remains now decorated a spike outside the castle — a reminder to any who would seek to remove their rightful king.

The service below ended when the body of the sacrifice was unceremoniously rolled into a fire pit at the edge of the stage. Flames erupted and the air was filled with the scent of burning flesh.

Porthyros stood and inhaled deeply. "Exhilarating, isn't it, My King? Just think, that man will wake up in paradise, gifted with the eternal gratitude of Ecarthus himself!" the scholar enthused.

"The ultimate reward," the king muttered hazily. Yawning, he said, "I'd like to nap now, 'Thyro."

"Of course, My King. I'll call for your carriage."

Nightmares tainted the sleep of Arris Thodan.

Wind ruffled his shaggy, snow-coated beard. Around him, the mountains rose in sharp spires, creating a beautiful backdrop for the hellish scene at his feet. He was coated in gore. Lying in the snow were the bodies of his men, their green and black tabards shredded by the claws of the rimerbeasts that howled just beyond the edge of his vision. Waning sunlight kept the creatures at bay, but soon, they would be free to attack.

He searched for Porthyros, but his mentor did not appear to be anywhere on the battlefield. Moving from man to man, and checking for signs of life, he discovered that he was completely alone. Wrapped in a cyclone of snow and wind, he almost didn't notice the setting sun until a victorious howl sent chills down his spine.

Grimly, he gripped his sword and bravely prepared to meet his end. The snarling rimerbeasts grew close enough for him to smell their stink on the wind. Then, out of the realms of his deepest fear, came a sound that he had prayed to never hear again.

A long, piercing wail cracked through the twilight, followed by the thundering of hooves. Erupting from the swirling snow she came, mounted on a beast the color of smoke. Her blade was flaming ice, and with it she carved a swath through the rimerbeasts that circled his position.

Fear put wings on his feet and he raced away from the pursuing figure, running all the way across the mountaintop until he reached a cliff. Barely stopping himself, he watched chunks of ice and snow fall into the darkness. Turning, he faced the mounted woman, clenching his teeth to keep from screaming in terror.

The apparition thundered right through him — it was not real.

Relieved, he sank to his knees and wept in gratitude. Sharp, wrenching pain overwhelmed him then. Gaping, he looked down to see the tip of a sword explode from his chest.

"No," he gasped, as blood filled his mouth. As he toppled over, his last sight was of a pair of golden eyes that blazed with victory.

"No!" Arris bolted out of bed, grabbing his sword and slashing at the darkness. The door opened and Porthyros ran to him.

"My King, are you unwell?" he cried, turning up a lamp to chase back the shadows in the king's bedchamber.

Dressed only in a pair of light breeches, gripping his sword in both hands, Arris' body was drenched in sweat. Blinking in the sudden light, he let his sword drop and then sank into a chair, panting heavily. "It's nothing, 'Thyro, just a dream. Bring me some tea and I shall be fine," he ordered weakly.

"As you wish, My Lord," the scholar said, dashing out of the room quickly. *Too much krile last night, you almost killed him, you stupid fool!* The scholar made a cup of plain tea for the king. He would have to be careful. The poison levels in Arris' body were becoming dangerous. Better to keep the young man in a mild haze of intoxication than to kill him.

"Master will not be pleased," Porthyros muttered fearfully.

Chapter Twenty-Eight

Seated at her desk, composing a letter to Padreg, Azhani was interrupted by a timid knock at her door. "Yes?" she called as she spread a thin layer of sand over the parchment to dry the ink.

The door opened and a page entered. Bowing respectfully, he said, "Master Azhani, a man called Brannock Maeven is here to see you."

"Thank you. Please show him in."

Nodding his head, the page moved away to allow a man dressed in the colorful robes of an Y'Noran trader to enter. Doffing his ridiculously oversized hat, the man bowed deeply and said, "Thy face is a balm to my lonely heart, Lady Azhani."

He strode to her chair and knelt beside her and pressed his hat to his chest. "The days have passed ever so lengthily since the dulcet strains of thy fulsome voice hath caressed my ears."

Smirking in amusement, Azhani allowed the trader to press a florid kiss to the back of her hand. "Flattery will get you nowhere, My Lord. What can I do for you?"

Standing, he replaced his hat and grinned. "Paddy warned me that you were as dour as a maiden aunt." When she did not return his smile, he sighed and said, "From the hand of Chief Padreg of Y'Nor, I bring you tidings. Hear now his words."

From a pouch, he withdrew a scroll and began to read.

My friend,
I have heard of your encounter with the foul sorcerer. I pray that you and Kyrian both are well. Elisira is concerned for your safety, but knows that you will do all that is necessary to stay alive.

She also wishes you to know that she is happy and I must add that she has taken to the husbandry of our herds as one born to the plains.

Young Devon sends his love. With tutelage, the boy is becoming a fine mage. The rest of our party sends their greetings as well.

As you know, we are beset on all sides by fearsome catastrophe. Monsters long thought dead or myth have appeared to try the armies and navies of the kingdoms. I have had little to no success in gaining allies to stand with us against the coming beast season.

Of Ysradan, I have heard only that Regent Madros has attempted to contact him, but has had no word. I fear that the snake is lying, but I cannot prove it.

Princess Syrelle, the high king's daughter, has come to foster among my clans. I'm afraid that our lifestyle is not what she dreamed, for she often laments the lack of servants. My lady felt the same way, and the two have become friends over lace and buttons.

Azhani interrupted Maeven's easy brogue with a laugh. "I fear that the princess will scandalize the high court when she returns home. However, I am glad that Elisira has found a friend."

The trader nodded. "Oh aye, those two giggle like younglings at their first summer fair."

She smiled and indicated that Maeven should continue.

The monsters which roam our kingdoms are many, and terrible. Yet it pains me to have to relate the darkest news of all. There is no easy way to break this news, my friend — Y'Dan has fallen into the hands of a grave evil.

Arris has cast out the worship of the Twain in favor of a demonic god known as Ecarthus. My spies tell me that the Eater of Souls claims many lives in daily sacrifice and that the land you once served is now wrapped in terror.

Azhani, my friend, it is not lightly that I speak of regicide; the king who seeks to slay another can, himself, be open for the knife. My cousin is not well; his rule has poisoned the earth and caused a weeping in the land that even we of Y'Nor can sense. If ever there was doubt of Thodan's choice, it has faded into history.

Nightly, I pray that we will win victory over the rimerbeasts. We must send them screaming back to hell in a timely fashion so that our attentions may be entirely focused upon ridding the kingdoms of the scourge that is Arris and his devotions to this heinous god, Ecarthus.

To that end, my seers have urged me to send to you this gift.

With a flourish, the trader withdrew a long, leather-wrapped bundle from his cloak and presented it to Azhani. She unwrapped it, revealing an old, battle-scarred sword.

Behold, Gormerath — slayer of demons. Forged by the hand of Lyriandelle Starseeker, this blade has been a part of my family throughout the ages. I give her to you; wield her well. May she love your hand as easily as she loved the mothers of my foremothers.

I end this missive in the hope that we shall meet again soon.
Padreg

"He honors me," Azhani said softly as she looked down at the legendary blade. She, like every other goddess-trained child, had heard the tales that surrounded the mystical blade.

Crafted by Lyriandelle Starseeker, the firstborn daughter of Ymaric Firstlander, Gormerath had been instrumental in transforming the wild, monster-ridden continent into the prospering lands that now existed. The blade was forged from a chunk of ore that fell from the sky and was said to possess a host of magickal properties, not the least of which was the ability to sense the presence of demons. Ymaric's daughter took up the blade when he died, and from her, the sword passed from woman to woman until it came to the hand of the Keelan clan.

And now it's mine, Azhani thought as she looked at the sword. The ratty and battered leather sheath that housed a mud-encrusted hilt did little to impress her.

"She needs a bit of love and tenderness, I'd say," Brannock Maeven commented, tucking his hands behind his back and bending over to peer at the revealed sword.

The warrior grunted in reply. Narrowing her eyes, she said, "Are you certain that this is what Padreg sent? You didn't stop at Ironfoot's casino before coming here, did you?"

"I swear on my beloved mother's honor. I came directly from my liege's tent to this lovely home without even stopping to sample the local mead," the man assured her in a slightly hurt tone.

Accepting that the blade had come from Padreg, Azhani stood and went to her equipment trunk. From there, she took a weapon cleaning kit and began to work at removing the years of built-up grime from the artifact.

"If there's nothing else, Lady Azhani, there is a pint of mead clamoring for my attention in the lower city," Brannock said.

"No, you may go. Tell Paddy I said thanks for the gift," Azhani said absently. The trader left as flakes of dirt fell away from the sword, revealing shining metal below.

In a relatively short time, Gormerath's true beauty was revealed. A longsword, it was a true testament to its smith. Wedge-shaped, incredibly sharp, and nearly weightless, the most striking element of the sword's appearance was the rainbow-hued sheen of the blade. Wavy bands of color and shadow rippled throughout the length of the weapon, showing that the smith had folded the metal thousands of times to imbue the blade with a supernatural strength.

The hilt was a warm brass that glowed softly in the lantern light. Inset in the center of the crosspiece was a dark blue sapphire that glittered with its own life. The handle was hardwood and felt as though it had been constructed for her hand when Azhani gripped it.

Gormerath was also longer than her current blade; a difference she knew would take some time to adjust to. Unlike her shorter sword, Gormerath would have to be worn on her back.

Taking a few experimental swings, Azhani smiled with wicked glee at how perfectly balanced the massive blade was. She ran through several practice blows. By the end of her run, she was nearly laughing — Gormerath felt so wonderful in her hands! The blade seemed to sing as she moved, and it was nearly weightless in her grasp. With this weapon, she felt as though she could conquer whole armies of rimerbeasts.

Standing in the center of her room, panting from her exertions, she felt the strangest sensation of warmth creep through her hands and up her arms. She looked down and watched with amazement as a pale blue aura of power rippled down the sword and spread up her arms to envelope her body. Images hit her — faces and battles that stepped from legend to become an instant's reality. As soon as they had come, they were gone, leaving Azhani dazed.

I am Gormerath, warrior of the people. We will serve well. The thought trickled through her and was gone.

"Paddy, the next time I see you, it's going to be a tough decision of whether I will kick you or kiss you," Azhani muttered softly.

Loathe to part with the blade, she strode out of her room toward the armory. Gormerath needed a sheath, and she wasn't going to trust a page to know what she wanted.

"**He sent you** what?" Lyssera's eyes widened when Azhani revealed the blade of Gormerath.

"I was stunned as well, My Queen," Kyrian said softly. "She has not been seen for centuries."

Azhani twirled the sword around. "I like her. She's light, balanced and," she shrugged, "she feels right in my hand. Padreg's generosity will help save Y'Myran."

The two Y'Syran women nodded.

"I shall have to repay him," Lyssera said absently as she watched Azhani weave dazzling patterns of light with Gormerath's colorful blade.

"Azhani, put your toy away. You're mesmerizing the queen," Kyrian said dryly. Smiling sheepishly, Azhani sheathed the blade.

"My apologies."

"It is nothing, Azhani. I rather enjoyed the show," Lyssera said with a smile.

"I did too," Kyrian said. "If you will both excuse me, it's time for Allyndev's object lesson."

"**No, strike, block,** feint *then* disarm, Allyn. Be aggressive, but cautious — you're trying to disable your opponent, not kill him. Let's try this again," Kyrian said as she stepped back and held her staff at the ready.

The wood felt odd in her hands. The staff was not her best or even second best weapon, but her baton had been destroyed by Kasyrin Darkchilde's spell. To replace it, she would need to return to Y'Len and have a new one crafted for her hand.

Rather than subjecting Allyndev to the taunts of his peers, Kyrian chose to face him with a weapon instead of her bare hands. It would not do his fragile self confidence any good to be disarmed by an unarmed opponent.

Sighing heavily, Allyn lifted his sword and whined, "When is Master Azhani coming back?" During the week following Azhani's injury, the prince had shown several of the younger guards the effectiveness of the warrior's tutelage by soundly defeating them. It had earned him a never-before-sensed respect. However, that admiration vanished the first time that Kyrian had spent a full candlemark showing him just how little he truly knew about the art of the sword. It was humiliating and his tormentors took every opportunity to make him feel the sting of it.

"She will come when she is ready. Now, lay on!" Kyrian knew that the young man was frustrated by his seeming lack of progress, but she knew that the lessons he gained from her hands would be tempered by Azhani's hands into skills that could someday save his life.

Warily circling, Allyn searched for an opening. The skills he had learned from Azhani were exercised to their fullest as he sought to defeat the stardancer. Kyrian was a good teacher, but he missed Azhani. The stardancer had more patience than the volatile warrior, but Kyrian was less likely to pull her blows. More than once, Allyndev had gone to his rooms covered in welts and bruises earned when he didn't move fast enough to avoid one of her strikes.

His current task was to disarm the stardancer. At first, it had seemed easily done, but the priest was faster than he thought possible. Allyn's knuckles ached from repeated blows from the staff.

"Are we sparring or dancing, my prince?" Kyrian asked with some amusement.

She struck and he blocked as he had been taught. Twisting the blade, he struck back, attempting the combination move that would disarm her. With a flick of his wrist, he caught the blade under her staff, but instead of immediately pulling the weapon from her hand, he tried to get a better handle on the weapon.

Taking advantage of his hesitation, Kyrian freed her staff and delivered a smart rap to Allyn's arm that caused him to drop his sword.

Cursing under his breath, he held up his open hands in surrender. "You win. I'm done," he grumbled crossly. He sucked on his throbbing digits and sulked. Master Azhani never treated him like this. He was a prince, by the First Tree. *You'd think she'd have more respect.* Opening his mouth to complain, he was interrupted by voices calling out mockingly.

"Arris-loving half-breed!"

"Run back to your nursemaids, little princeling, and leave the war games to the real warriors."

The guardsman's jeers made him wince, but now he was far too drained to defend himself. Shoulders slumping, he turned away and headed over to the bench where his towel and waterskin rested. The jibes were nothing new. Taunts had been hurled at him nearly every day since his birth. Not even his aunt could shelter him from the venom of the more hidebound of her people.

Kyrian lowered her weapon, resigned to ending the session for the day. It was just as well — one more bout, and Allyn's anger might get the best of him, and if he attacked with true aggression, she might freeze. The guards' japes were beginning to wear on her as well. She too was half-elven, and it was hard not to retort in anger.

Watching from behind the guards, Azhani softly growled, "Ajep, Torvik, go and I'll pretend I didn't just hear you insult your prince."

Both men glared at her, but one long look into the icy calm of her eyes forced them to submit to her authority.

"Yes, Master Azhani," the two guards muttered softly while giving her a half-hearted bow.

As soon as the men were gone, Azhani stepped into the salle. "Battle conditions! Don't stop until the kill strike is made!" she called out commandingly.

Allyn spun and flung his towel at the stardancer. She batted it away with her staff and ducked the thrown waterskin as well. This gave the prince enough time to somersault over and retrieve his sword. As he came up, he slashed at Kyrian but she deflected the strike.

The fight was joined. Dancing around each other, trading faster and faster blows, the two half-elves appeared to be evenly matched until Allyn's fatigue caused him to miss a crucial opening. Stepping in, Kyrian smacked the prince on the elbow, effectively disarming him.

The practice sword clunked to the floor. Allyndev prepared himself for the stinging blow that never came.

Instead of delivering the killing blow, Kyrian had stepped back and was leaning on her staff, visibly shaking.

It's now or never. Emitting a half strangled growl of frustration, Azhani said, "Astarus' thumbs, Kyr. Knock him down!"

Jumping at the voice, Kyrian shook her head. "No," she whispered.

Azhani noted the reaction and felt her irritation double. Padreg's gift of Gormerath had driven home the imminent nature of the upcoming beast season, and she needed to know that Kyrian could defend herself. *I can't allow her to follow me if she can't hold her own. I won't have the blood of another person I care about on my hands.*

Driven to action, she grabbed a practice sword and swung, forcing the priest to defend herself. Raining blow after blow down on Kyrian, Azhani growled, "Fight me, Kyrian. You can defeat me, I know it!"

Kyrian blocked each strike, but made no move to be aggressive. This was different than their usual practice sessions. This contest felt somehow more real, more like actual combat, and that made the stardancer's blood freeze. Fear clamored in her chest and she began to make mistakes. The warrior's hits got through her defenses, marking her with sharp cracks of pain that would bruise later.

"Fight me!" Azhani yelled fiercely.

"I can't!" Kyrian wailed as she tried in vain to escape the attacks.

Grimly, Azhani drove the priest toward the wall of the salle and pinned her there with vicious, powerful blows.

Overrun with anger and fear, Kyrian leaped away from the wall and brought her staff down in a two-handed strike.

Azhani met the blow with equal force and the wooden shaft snapped in two.

Armed with two weapons now, Kyrian's face twisted as she fought in earnest. Sweat and tears poured from the stardancer's face as Azhani began to speak.

"Good, Kyrian. Fight me. Whatever is hurting you, whatever is causing you to fear battle, use me to beat it out. You can't hurt me, my friend."

Kyrian sobbed and missed a strike, which earned her a reprimanding tap on the arm.

"You can't quit — I won't allow it."

The warrior's words struck a bitter chord. "Won't allow it?" Kyrian shouted. "What are you doing to me, Azhani?"

Whatever answer Azhani may have had was lost in the flurry of blows that were exchanged as Kyrian launched herself at the warrior, her sticks moving so fast, they almost blurred.

Having gotten himself out of the way of the furious melee, Allyn watched his mentors in awe and prayed for the day when he would possess a fraction of their skills. *I'm just a scholar with a sword.* His hard earned self confidence fled. *I should go back to my stars and flowers.*

Now that Kyrian was actually fighting, Azhani calmed. As the stardancer's attacks grew more wild and frenetic, the warrior met each blow with calm resolve. "Talk to me, Kyrian. Why do you hate this?" She pressed an attack that had Kyrian backing up toward the wall once more.

"No...please, no more," Kyrian said softly. Almost automatically, she blocked the blows. "It hurts...gods, this hurts so much," she whispered.

"You've let it fester, Kyr. As a healer, you know the best thing to do is to cut the wound open and let it drain." Azhani tossed her sword toward

Allyn, who caught it easily. Stepping toward her friend, the warrior said, "You healed my wounds, Kyrian. Allow me to return the favor. Talk to me. *I don't care what it is.* I'll still be here."

"I–" Kyrian's voice broke.

Azhani placed her hands over the broken ends of Kyrian's staff and gently tugged them from her hands. Tossing them aside, she softly said, "Please, Kyrian. I need to hear this as much as you need to say it."

On the other end of the room, Allyndev silently racked the practice blades and left. His lesson was clearly over and he didn't think that his mentors would appreciate an audience.

Kyrian's gaze flicked from the departing prince to her friend. Nervously, she licked her lips.

"I'm listening," Azhani said gently.

The words shattered the walls that Kyrian had erected so long ago. Falling to her knees, she sobbed, "I killed a man." She tensed, expecting scornful laughter.

Instead, she felt a warm embrace as Azhani knelt and drew her into her arms. Knowing that no words could erase the sickness that dwelled within the healer over such an act, the warrior quietly petted her friend's sweat soaked hair and waited for her to speak.

Kyrian looked up at Azhani, her eyes oddly dry. "I've cried so much over it, that I have no more tears."

"Tell me about it?" the warrior gently asked, as she settled comfortably against the wall and pulled Kyrian's shivering body closer.

At first, the words wouldn't come, but as Azhani sat and rocked her, Kyrian found that she was able to speak. Haltingly, the story was told. Beginning with her posting in Myr, Kyrian described her duties as teacher and healer of the elven community. Eventually, she came to the day she had taken the children for a swimming lesson and had ended up killing a raider.

"In the end, as I stood there gathering my thoughts to perform the pathsong, it hit me that I had stripped that man of his life. That's when I knew that nothing I would ever do would balance the wrong I had committed." Taking a deep breath, Kyrian said, "That's why I freeze. In my mind, I always see his face and I hesitate. The conscious decision to kill leaves me so sickened that it's easier to avoid it. I fear combat more than I fear death."

"Why is that?" Azhani continued to stroke the stardancer's hair and marveled at its softness.

"I'm afraid I'm going to stop caring; that one day, there will be an enemy that it gives me pleasure to kill. From then on, I'll cease to be a healer and become a murderer." Guiltily, Kyrian leaned into the touch. Hating herself, she greedily accepted the comfort offered.

A gentle laugh burbled in the warrior's chest. "Oh, Kyrian. There's no need to berate yourself for the future. Astariu knows that your heart is bright. I doubt you'll ever go down the dark path you envision." She rested her cheek against Kyrian's head. "If you allow your fears to rule, you will always run from them. The decision to take a life is a terrible one, but often it is necessary for the good of the many. Think of it like surgery — you have to shave away the poisoned flesh in order for the body to live."

"You don't counsel fairly, Azhani," Kyrian said, as a warm sense of well being settled over her. Unwittingly, she snuggled closer. "You're using my profession against me."

"Life isn't fair. Distasteful actions are often necessary when you're a hero," Azhani said softly. The stardancer's proximity made her heart throb heavily in her chest.

"All right, I think I understand what you're saying. My fears will not be conquered in a day, but if you're around, I'll have hope."

Brushing her knuckles over Kyrian's cheek, Azhani said, "I'm not going anywhere, Kyr. You're my friend and I'm not going anywhere."

Kyrian looked up at Azhani. Their eyes met, and a flash of something profound passed between them. For Kyrian, it was enough to start a bonfire of hope within her heart. For Azhani, it set off a firestorm of feelings and fears about how her relationship with the stardancer could evolve. Closing her eyes, Kyrian covered the warrior's hand and pressed her cheek into Azhani's palm.

In that timeless moment, two heartbeats merged. Neither woman spoke. Instead, they allowed the silence to complete the comfort of their friendship.

Chapter Twenty-Nine

"Has anything been decided?" Kyrian asked as she and Azhani paddled a small boat along the edge of the lake. For the last week, Lyssera and her Council had argued over how best to approach the rimerbeast situation. After days of endless council sessions, the two friends had escaped the city to enjoy some time alone.

"No. I think Lyssera's going to have to make a monarchial decision. It's probably going to offend the councilors, but she does have the final word regarding the defense of the kingdom." The queen wanted to give the armies to Azhani; the nobles were against it.

"Will you accept command, if she hands you the army?"

"Yes," Azhani replied without hesitation. "The rimerbeasts are a horror that must not be allowed to rampage. Arris can wait. Even his new religion can't cause the harm that a dozen spawning demons can."

Kyrian shivered atavistically. Rumors of the Ecarthan sacrifices were trickling through the city and had left the stardancer feeling sullied by their very existence.

"Let's not speak of worldly matters, Kyrian. I want to spend some time in the comfort of nature before I go north to slaughter demons."

"All right." That Kyrian would follow her friend into the mountains was never in doubt. Even if it meant seeing battle, Kyrian knew that she would rather be by Azhani's side than anywhere else in the kingdoms.

They saw a shaded beach and pulled ashore. Grabbing a basket of food, Kyrian followed Azhani across the sand and into the forest. Half a candlemark later, they found a clearing bathed in sunlight. It did not take long to gather a couple of armloads of deadfall. Shortly, a small fire burned cheerily. While a pot of tea steeped, Azhani laid out a blanket and spread out their repast.

Enjoying their meal, they spoke quietly of their surroundings. The peace of the forest settled around them and held the apprehension over the coming beast season in abeyance.

Afterward, Kyrian lay back and watched the wispy clouds that skated across the sky. "What will you do about Arris?" she asked, turning to glance at Azhani.

The warrior toyed with the ties on her dagger. "I'd like to rip..." her voice trailed off as a strange expression traveled over her face. Sighing, she leaned back on her elbows and said, "I don't know. For the longest time, I wanted to skewer him on a pike and watch him dance as his entrails spilled over his feet." The sheer callousness of the statement shocked Kyrian to the core. "I was driven by blind vengeance. Now, I'd like to see justice, but I don't know how to find it."

"What changed?"

"I don't know. Maybe I did. Lyssera and I have talked of what Ylera would want and," Azhani wiped tears from her eyes, "I've come to realize that life is bigger than I thought."

Kyrian couldn't help weeping too. Softly, she said, "She would be grateful to know that you are letting go."

"What do you mean?" Azhani sat up and wrapped her arms around her knees.

Taking a deep breath, Kyrian wiped her eyes. "I knew Ylera, Azhani. She was a friend."

The enormity of the statement thundered through Azhani like a herd of Y'Noran horses. *She and Ylera were friends? And she still treated my wounds, and stood by me, without knowing the truth?*

Fear etched a path over Kyrian's face as she waited for Azhani absorb her statement.

Watching the emotions flicker in her friend's eyes, Azhani knew that she would have to tread carefully. *She trusts me not to hate her. How can I defy that faith? Isn't what we've built bigger than an omission?* "How did you know her?" It seemed a safe enough question.

Kyrian choked back a sob. "At Y'Len, we were classmates."

Ah. That makes sense. How does that make me feel? Azhani examined her conscience and found that it didn't matter. Kyrian was still the woman who had risked retaliation in order to save the life of an oathbreaker and was still her friend. *More than a friend,* Azhani thought, as she felt her heart catch when Kyrian looked away from her. "She would be glad to know that we are friends, then," Azhani said softly. "Ylera often spoke of introducing me to those important to her."

"Thank you," Kyrian whispered.

"For what?"

Turning to face her, Kyrian smiled sadly and said, "For not hating me; for not judging me when I've kept secrets."

"How could I hate you, Kyrian? You gave so much of yourself for me, even before you believed in my innocence." *Can't you see how important you've become to me?* Azhani smiled.

"It's my job to heal those in need," Kyrian replied characteristically, but she smiled as well.

"Why don't we agree that honor is served? I am grateful for the friendship we have. Let the future carry us forward."

"Agreed," Kyrian said shyly. They clasped hands. "It's been a long time since I had a good friend."

"I feel the same." Azhani stood. "It's getting late. We should return."

Kyrian nodded her agreement and began to clean up the site. After folding the blanket, she brushed crumbs from her robes and asked, "Do I have food on my face? I'd hate to walk into Oakheart with jelly on my nose."

Azhani studied the stardancer's face. "Nothing on your nose, but there's a bit of something," she reached up and gently brushed crumbs off Kyrian's lips and said breathlessly, "here."

An electric tingle passed through them as their eyes met. Everything went still as she continued to lightly stroke Kyrian's mouth. Azhani leaned forward, drawn to the lips she was caressing.

Kyrian couldn't breathe. Her lungs were screaming for air, but she dared not take a breath as the warrior moved closer, until she was almost close enough to — *Is she going to kiss me?*

For just the briefest instant, their lips touched.

"Hello? Master Azhani? Stardancer Kyrian? Are you out here?" Allyndev Kelani's voice was never more welcomed, or hated, than it was at that moment. He finally crashed into the clearing just as Azhani spun around to greet him.

"We're right here, Allyn. What is it?" she asked in concern.

Smiling sheepishly, the prince reached into his belt pouch and pulled out a scroll. "Aunt Lyss needs you back at court."

Azhani accepted the message and scanned its contents. Cursing, she crumpled the note and finished kicking dirt over their small fire.

"What is it?" Kyrian asked dazedly. Her lips still throbbed and it was hard to breathe.

"The Council has gone mad. They want Lyss to lead the army north."

"Blessed Astariu!" Kyrian gasped. Lyssera was a competent warrior, but to leave the kingdom ungoverned when a known enemy lurked near the border was unthinkable.

"Aye," Azhani said darkly. "I've got a few noble heads to break," she added.

Allyndev laughed. "They won't know what hit them, Master."

"I doubt it," she said. Her body ached from the desire to finish what she had started. *I was kissing her. It felt so right. She kissed me. Blessed Twain, I can't think about this now.*

Well, I'm glad that's straightened out, Azhani thought as she watched the councilors retreat. After returning, she had spent several candlemarks outlining in stark terms just what kind of horror the kingdom could experience if they forced Lyssera to abandon her throne.

Not even the most ignorant among the councilors had been able to ignore the fact that Y'Dan and Y'Syr had miles of a common border. In the end, they agreed that Lyssera would stay in Y'Syria, but nothing further was decided.

"I'm going to have to do something drastic," Lyssera said as she rubbed at her temples.

"I know," Azhani said. "It's going to change everything."

They shared a glance.

"Are you ready for it?" Lyssera asked.

"No. But it's not about me. It's about the lives of two kingdoms — maybe three, if they get close to Y'Dror."

Neither woman mentioned the word, but it hovered between them anyway. Warleader. It was the title that Azhani had worn proudly in Y'Dan. It was the honor that Arris had stripped from her as easily as one would peel an orange.

"I'm going to have to say something, soon. The armies are nearly assembled."

Azhani nodded. "You must do what you must for your people, My Queen."

Lyssera rose and placed her hands on Azhani's shoulders. "There is no one else I trust, Azhi. In five days, I will speak." She exited the chamber, leaving Azhani to face a torrent of thought.

Gliding from shadow to shadow, Azhani Rhu'len prowled the streets of Y'Syria. With eyesight made clear by half-elven ancestry, Azhani drank in the fog-dusted sights. The past lived before her. There, at Banner Gate, she and Thodan had come to the elven port. Twenty years had passed since they had come to sue for peace.

Memories crowded her mind.

Seeing Y'Syria without the hurt losing Ylera had burned into her soul left Azhani searching for a reason not to follow the pull that drew her inexorably toward Kyrian.

Unbidden, a smile rose to transform her harshly planed face to that of striking beauty. Feisty was the only word she could use to describe the beautiful young woman. *Astariu moves in so many ways, and most of them mysterious and cunning.*

I am in love. The thought stunned her as much as it freed her. To put a name to the emotion that had boiled in her whenever the stardancer was near was as much of a relief as it was a fright. She had thought that she would never feel again. The long night she had spent cradling Ylera's lifeless body had inured her heart to any emotion but hate. It had taken the kind perseverance of a stardancer to batter those walls aside.

Thoughts of Ylera pulled painfully on Azhani's heart, but that pain was easily soothed by the image of Kyrian's smile. *She kissed me.* The truth lay between them. She just had to find the courage to seek it. Again, Azhani turned her gaze upon the city. Perhaps she would find it somewhere within its elemental beauty.

The knock was almost soundless, yet it invaded Kyrian's dreams and woke her. Drowsily tumbling from her bed, she grabbed a robe from the back of a chair and pulled it over her arms. The material was thin and barely covered her nakedness, but was enough to satisfy the bounds of propriety.

Grumbling as she padded through the room, she opened the door expecting to find one of the queen's pages. Instead, Azhani's haggard, careworn face shocked the stardancer to full alertness.

"I need you," the warrior whispered and then stood there, unable to ask, but clearly begging to be allowed entrance.

"I am always here for you, my friend," Kyrian said as she stepped aside.

Azhani stumbled in, collapsing on Kyrian's bed as though she was severely intoxicated.

Kyrian closed the door and slowly walked over to the bed, carefully sitting next to her. "Are you drunk?" she asked, thinking over the various cures she had for hangovers and hoping one of them would work on the warrior's strong constitution.

"Haven't touched a drop in weeks," Azhani said woodenly. Suddenly, she turned, taking a long, hard look at her friend. Kyrian felt her cheeks flush as the warrior's gaze lingered over every exposed curve. Azhani's eyes reached her face, and finally matched her gaze. Like a bolt from the sky, Kyrian's memory was flooded with the sensation of their kiss.

"Azhani, wha-what is it that you need?" Kyrian forced herself to say, as she tore her eyes away from drowning in a sea of cobalt blue.

"You," Azhani whispered, one hand lifting to reach for Kyrian. "I need you, Kyrian." Her gaze shifted to the floor and she whispered, "Are you in love with me, healer?"

The question ripped through the air and into Kyrian's heart like a knife. Every shred of hope that she had bundled up and locked away in carefully constructed boxes began to rattle, screaming for release. *Oh, goddess...* "Azhi...I..." The words struggled to get out, but months of imprisoning her tongue made it difficult for them to escape.

Azhani took Kyrian's lack of response as her answer and stood to leave. "I am sorry, Kyrian, to have awakened you. I shall see you in the morning at breakfast." She turned to leave, closing her eyes against the scorn that she was sure lurked in the other woman's eyes. One step...two steps...just a few more and she would be out and away from the rejection that she could feel gathering in the room. *How could I have ever thought that someone like her would want a murderer like me?* Another step. She reached out, felt the shape of the doorknob under her fingers, gripped it firmly, and started to turn it.

"Yes! I love you!" Kyrian leaped off the bed, raced across the room and interposed herself between the warrior and the door. Putting her hands on Azhani's arms, she said, "Do you...love me?"

A slow, sweet smile drifted across Azhani's face. "Yes," she whispered. Azhani leaned into Kyrian, pressing her against the hard wooden door. The stardancer's hands slid up Azhani's arms until they cupped her cheeks. Her skin was hot.

Kyrian returned the smile with one of her own that was so heartbreakingly beautiful that Azhani had to touch it. Her dusky fingers skimmed the stardancer's pale cheeks and then stroked her lips.

Kyrian gasped as she felt an ache burn into her gut at the caress.

Azhani tipped her head down, her smile widening as Kyrian's hands slid into her hair and flexed, gripping the braids. Their lips touched, brushed, painted each other lightly, and then joined fiercely. Tentatively, Kyrian slid her tongue into Azhani's mouth, moaning when she returned the passion tenfold. The bright edge of teeth clashed as their kissing grew heated, until their ardor became almost painful.

Desire rose thickly in Azhani, forcing her to draw back and take in a ragged lungful of air. She licked her lips and tasted Kyrian's sweetness upon them. The last remnants of the numbness that had engulfed her heart melted. Eagerly, she allowed the stardancer to pull her down for another kiss. Her heartbeat trebled when Kyrian's leg wrapped around hers.

Delicately, Azhani ran her tongue over Kyrian's bottom lip, teasing the stardancer's mouth into a soft pout, then plunged in, drinking deeply of her new love's appreciative moans. Trembling wantonly, Kyrian surrendered, grinding her silk-clad hips against the warrior's thigh.

Azhani groaned appreciatively. Tracing Kyrian's lips with her tongue and then brushing a trail of kisses down her lover's face to her throat, the warrior paused to suckle at the throbbing pulse she found there. After only moments of tenderly tasting the stardancer's skin, Azhani retraced the still-wet path back to her lips, crushing her mouth into Kyrian's in a bruising, deeply passionate kiss.

Kyrian felt the change immediately. Their first kiss had been timid, with a sweetness that defied the near frantic need that she felt welling out of her as Azhani's fingers stroked her neck. This was different; this was a kiss of such awareness that Kyrian could only respond to the desire coiling around her. Fiercely, she kissed Azhani, opening herself to her passionate need, completely. She barely felt it when the warrior bit into her bottom lip, slightly piercing the skin.

A tiny whimper broke into Azhani's concentration and she stopped kissing Kyrian and pulled away. "Oh gods, I'm sorry, Kyr," she said, as she noticed a tiny trickle of blood that oozed from a cut on the stardancer's lip.

Kyrian dabbed at the wound with her fingers and shook her head. "Don't be; I'm not. Kiss me again," she whispered, pleading for more of the intoxicating touch.

"I don't," Azhani said, raining feather light kisses on the stardancer's face, "ever want to hurt you, Kyrian."

"You won't," Kyrian said as she wrapped her arms around the warrior's neck and captured her lips for a long, uninterrupted period. "Because I understand." She did. Somehow, she recognized that this was new; that the explosive emotions flooding the room were so raw and tender that they would have to tread lightly. Time would lay the ghosts and demons of the past to rest. Together, she and Azhani would slowly seek their future.

Azhani nuzzled her face against the top of Kyrian's head, breathing in her scent. "I should go," she whispered. "We...I..."

"I know, but...stay," Kyrian said, as she slipped away from Azhani. Taking her hand, she drew her toward the bed. "Hold me. Be here in the light of morning so that I know I'm not dreaming," she pleaded. "I don't kick, remember?" She smiled sweetly.

If you stay tonight, warrior, you will stay every night. There's no walking away. The thoughts raced through her mind. *Kyrian wouldn't give her heart lightly. Are you ready for forever?*

Yes.

"I remember," Azhani said. Quietly, she surrendered to both the wishes of her heart and the wishes of her beloved, allowing Kyrian to lead her to the bed. At the edge, there was some strangeness but she pushed it aside. They had been naked together before.

It was different though, now, in the dim moonlight. Kyrian's robe slithered away, revealing pale, almost colorless skin. When Azhani's clothes joined the robe in a fabric puddle, the difference between them was mutely obvious. Scars peppered her dark brown skin, standing out starkly. Years as King Thodan's warleader had left their mark on Azhani's body.

"You are so beautiful," Kyrian whispered as she gazed into Azhani's eyes. For the first time, she was able to put voice to the thought that had been with her since the very first time she saw the warrior.

"And you are a shameless flatterer who should spend more time looking into a mirror. You are the one who is beautiful, my Kyrian." Reverently, Azhani stroked Kyrian's face, stopping her fingers just above the stardancer's hammering pulse. "It's time to sleep; if that is acceptable to you?"

"Yes," Kyrian said breathlessly as Azhani slid under the twisted linens and moved over, making room for the stardancer. "It's very acceptable."

Skin on skin was a sensation that left both women fighting to cling to their unspoken agreement. Warmth cocooned around them, the covers both shielded and added to the hundreds of tiny little jolts that skittered across their skin. Soon, they found the right joining of arms and legs, heads and shoulders and lay quietly. As they cuddled close, they could hear each other's heartbeats diminish from hammer blows to gentle thuds. Rhythmically, their breath began to flow around them as sleep stole in on gossamer wings.

Daylight streamed in through the windows, flooding over the two women wrapped tightly around each other. Gazing sleepily at Kyrian, Azhani dared to touch what she was certain was a dream. Sun-warmed skin pebbled under her light caress. An almost inaudible intake of breath let her know that Kyrian was very aware of the touch. Reverently, Azhani stroked Kyrian's arm from shoulder to wrist, then continued the caress down to her hip.

Drawing her fingers back up their previous path, she nuzzled her cheek against Kyrian's hair. Azhani's heartbeat began to thunder loudly as the caress was returned. Butterfly-soft kisses fluttered against her collar-bone, creating tiny jolts of pleasure that buzzed pleasantly in her belly.

"Good morning," Azhani rumbled, her voice harsh from sleep. *I think I could wake with Kyrian at my side until the stars faded, and it would not have been enough.*

Kyrian stretched, and shivered where her body touched Azhani's. "Morning." Reaching over the warrior's shoulder, she retrieved a waterskin and drank, then offered it to Azhani. Their hands brushed, and Kyrian sighed dreamily.

After drinking, Azhani drew Kyrian in for a kiss. Mapping newly familiar territory with her lips, Azhani used her hands and fingers to explore Kyrian's body, igniting the stardancer's desire to bonfire heights. Unlike the kisses of the previous night, this kiss was neither tentative nor passionate. Aware and teasing, the embrace added yet another new facet to their burgeoning love.

Kyrian opened her eyes. Passion had darkened them to emerald fire, but they were shaded with hesitancy. Gazing into Azhani's desire tinted eyes, she sought new answers to questions that had been asked by moonlight.

For a moment, her heart froze as she waited for a response. Then, a gently crooked smile broke out over the harshly planed beauty of Azhani's face. This smile was for Kyrian alone. This warming of indigo eyes was because of the stardancer's love and touch. The ice that had rapidly formed inside Kyrian melted, leaving behind only loving warmth.

Bravely, the stardancer unwound her fingers from the warrior's hair and began to touch her, lightly caressing all of Azhani's curves. Delicately, she traced the sharply defined slope of the warrior's nose and lips, stopping to briefly slip her fingertip into the warrior's mouth. Continuing her exploration, Kyrian skimmed her fingers down Azhani's throat and over several tiny scars.

Azhani let out a soft groan of appreciation. Smiling, Kyrian leaned down and kissed her gently, and then let her fingers drift across the slope of Azhani's breast. Lovingly, she stroked the warrior's dusky nipples until they hardened.

"By the Twain, Kyrian," Azhani growled softly, causing the stardancer to smile.

Kyrian loved this. She loved the way the warrior's muscles trembled under the tips of her fingers as she touched her. It was exciting, intoxicating even, to look up and see that her desire was mirrored in Azhani's eyes. When Azhani threw her head back to moan with longing, Kyrian pressed delicate kisses along the revealed skin.

The warrior's pleasure revealed itself as a deep groan that vibrated along her entire body. "Ah goddess," she whispered, rolling onto her back and drawing the stardancer on top of her. She scraped her blunt nails lightly over Kyrian's back, stroking her soft skin gently, and then stopped to cup the firm smoothness of her lover's buttocks. The fire between the two women was rapidly blazing out of control. Kyrian nipped and sucked at every bit of exposed skin she could reach. The shadows of the past were quickly vanishing under the loving caress.

Azhani found that she wanted to lose herself in the shape and feel of Kyrian. Every new sound that Kyrian made was a gentle goad that drove the warrior to try harder.

Their breath came in broken gasps as they kissed, and both women were ignoring the ache of already bruised lips. The unspoken agreement of the night before melted away in the bright reality of waking naked in each other's arms. Bathed in sunlight, any ghosts that lingered in the room vanished, leaving them free to express their desire.

Kyrian broke the kiss first, sliding off Azhani's body and sitting up on the bed. "We should stop," she wistfully said, though she continued to stroke the warrior's abdomen. *I wish we didn't have to.* Her brow wrinkled as she sighed heavily. The very idea of pulling her hands away, of ceasing to indulge in the delightful sensation of Azhani's skin made her heart tremor painfully.

Staring up at the ceiling, Azhani laced her fingers behind her head and just let the sensations of Kyrian's gentle touch have free rein. Fleetingly, she wondered if she were crazy to allow herself to fall in love again. Common sense intruded, forcing her to realize that, where Kyrian was concerned, she had no control over her heart. From the moment they had met until this very candlemark, Azhani knew that fate had been weaving them together.

Her first impulse was to stop, and let what her body was craving slide away to be explored another day. Would setting aside the desires of their hearts be wise? Or was she only punishing herself, and worse yet, Kyrian, for falling in love? Everything about loving Kyrian felt inescapably right; turning her back on that would be a slap in destiny's face.

She closed her eyes as the stardancer's feather-light caresses returned and grew bolder, edging over the curves of her ribs and down her side, to glide over the bones of her hips. The voices of caution blew away under the loving onslaught.

"I don't want to stop," she whispered as she captured Kyrian's hand and brought it up to her lips, kissing the fingertips softly. She stopped at the stardancer's index finger and began to suck on it slowly, running her teeth over the ridges of her lover's skin. "Do you?" she asked, continuing to suckle the fingers lovingly.

"No," came the barely audible reply. Kyrian was shaking. The touch, the desire and the emotions she felt were caught up in a cyclone of sensation, and it sent her reeling.

Azhani opened her eyes to the sight of Kyrian's face tipped up and her mouth parted in rapture. The vision broke a dam inside Azhani. Driven by both love and desire, she rolled up to her knees, then leaned over and wrapped her arms around the stardancer, cradling her loosely and kissing her deeply.

"Oh goddess, I love you, my Azhani," Kyrian whispered between the gently passionate kisses. Azhani's braids tickled her face and the stardancer laughed joyfully, threaded her fingers through the warrior's ebony hair, and affectionately pushed them away.

Pulling the stardancer down to the bed, Azhani whispered back, "I love you too, Kyrian." Their legs twined as their hips arched and ground together. Soft gasps shuddered out lengthily as their fingers found sensitive spots and learned what touches caused pleasure to each other.

The sounds of their loving filled the room as their mouths and tongues retraced the paths of their fingers and hands. Sunbeams highlighted the bedding as it slipped to the floor, their warmth unable to compete with the rising tide of passion generated by two newly made lovers.

Chapter Thirty

For three days, Kyrian and Azhani luxuriated in their changed relationship. Alternately talking and loving, they forged an easy partnership. No
subject was sacred or profane, and soon there was nothing they did not
know about each other.

They were folding freshly delivered clothes when Lyssera came to
visit.

"Well, aren't you two the picture of domesticity?" the queen's amused
voice interrupted.

They turned to face her, their expressions mimicking that of a child
caught with his fingers in a pie.

Lyssera smiled, though the happiness the expression reflected did not
quite erase the worry in her eyes. *The Twain grant that they are not separated now that they have found one another.*

"My Queen," Azhani said respectfully. "What brings you to visit?"

"Arris has sent a messenger," Lyssera said solemnly.

"What did Lord Loose Breeches want?" Azhani asked flippantly.

"Among the rambling declaratives proclaiming Ecarthus as the true
god, he blithely informed me that he was leading an expedition north to
hunt for rimerbeasts this winter. He wanted to know if we could combine
forces under the guidance of his god and drive the demons from Y'Myran."
Lyssera rubbed the bridge of her nose as if attempting to stave off an
impending ache. "He has also requested that I extradite you to his cus-
tody."

Kyrian blurted a curse while Azhani glared darkly in the direction of
Y'Dan.

With a wry grin, Lyssera said, "Needless to say my reply to him contained eloquently phrased versions of 'not if you were the last warrior on
Y'Myran' and 'not a snowball's chance in Y'Skan'."

"That will earn you no points at the Y'Dani marketplace," Azhani said.

Lyssera shrugged. "I'm not interested in tainted goods. In any event,
I came to give you that news — not to interrupt your pleasure. Stay. Enjoy
this while you can; I can give you one more day of peace."

That day of peace was one the two lovers fondly remembered in the
days and weeks to come.

At midday on the fifth day after Lyssera's promise to act, the elven
queen led her court into the center of Y'Syria. A platform had been constructed and heralds had gone out to announce that the queen would be
making a statement about the rimerbeasts. The populace had gathered
around the stage. Lyssera, followed by her guards and then Azhani and
Starseeker Vashyra, mounted the platform.

"My people, you have watched as our armies have gathered around
our fair city. I tell you today that they meet in preparation for war."

A gasp of fear erupted from the populace.

"Who is our enemy?" someone shouted.

"Who will lead our armies? We have no warleader. Princess Alynna is dead!" another man called loudly.

"Your questions are well founded, citizens. Our enemy is they who have been our bane since our ancestors built our vaunted city — rimerbeasts." Lyssera's voice was strong, and carried the news to every ear.

"Rimerbeasts? How— When— Why?" The questions flittered about the crowd like butterflies in a field.

"We know not why or how, only that they are there. The mountain caves are choked with eggs. My people, I came here to announce that we will not face this danger unguided."

Vashyra and Azhani stepped forward.

"All have heard the tales of the heroic warleader, Azhani Rhu'len. All know how she served good King Thodan wisely and loyally, and how her bravery kept Y'Dan free of the rimerbeast scourge."

Mutterings of assent rippled through the crowd, though a few shouted questions regarding Azhani's innocence in Ylera's death.

"We have come to view Azhani as a friend to the crown, and therefore loyal to all that Y'Syr represents. It is with our blessing that she takes the mantle of warleader, so that our soldiers may be victorious in battle. Azhani Rhu'len, you are called to serve your queen!"

Azhani knelt in front of Lyssera.

Dipping her fingers in a bowl of blessed water, Starseeker Vashyra daubed the warrior's cheeks and said, "I cleanse you before the gods, warrior."

"I am clean in the eyes of the Twain," Azhani said solemnly.

Vashyra smiled and stepped back.

The sun crested, bathing those upon the platform in a halo of golden glory.

Lifting a sheathed blade, Lyssera held the weapon out to Azhani hilt first. In a clear, ringing voice, she said, "Azhani, daughter of Rhu'len, scion of the House DaCoure, you are found worthy by the people of Y'Syr. Our land is benighted by minions of the dark and we have no warleader. Will you take up your sword and defend us? Will you accept the burden of command and pledge your life against our honor?"

"I will," Azhani replied gravely, touching the hilt. Though the monarch offering her honors now was Lyssera, Azhani could not help but to recall a similar day from twelve seasons past.

"Astarus' thumbs, you are the best warrior I've ever had the pleasure to serve with, Azhani Rhu'len! Will you be Y'Dan's warleader?" Thodan's kindly blue eyes sparkled with amusement at the shock that was plain on the warrior's face.

Standing on a field of battle, surrounded by a swath of death that would send lesser men running, the two had emerged victorious. The bodies of rimerbeasts and Y'Myrani soldiers commingled in noxious piles of carnage. Cries and wails of the dying could be heard echoing around the mountains. The cost of life had been great, but Azhani had successfully led the combined armies of the kingdoms against the rimerbeasts, slaughtering them to the last, rescuing Thodan's small platoon.

"I don't suppose I have a choice, do I?" the bloodied, gore-spattered

warrior replied as she leaned on her sword and kept a wary eye on the piles of the dead. Until the field had been put to the torch, she would not abandon her watchfulness.

Smiling wryly, Thodan clapped her on the shoulder and said, "'Fraid not, my old friend. Come on, let's get out of here and go find some cold ale. Let the priests deal with this mess."

Together, they limped away, and headed for the king's pavilion.

"So be it. Let all hear and rejoice. Arise, Azhani Rhu'len, Warleader of Y'Syr!" Lyssera shouted, turning the sword enough to draw it and tap the rising warrior's elbows with the flat of the blade.

Viewing the sword for the first time, the people of Y'Syria reacted with suitable shock.

The elven queen's face blazed with a fierce smile as she offered the artifact to Azhani. Taking the sword, Azhani slowly raised it overhead. Sunlight struck the metal and caused it to blaze with rainbow fire.

The crowd began to cheer.

Lyssera retreated and allowed Vashyra to stand before Azhani. The warrior dropped to one knee and presented the hilt of her sword to the starseeker.

The priest-mage smiled and cupped her hands over Azhani's. "By the Twins, I charge you to live with honor." She leaned over and pressed a soft kiss to the warrior's forehead. "From this moment on, all past deeds have no meaning; by the light of the Twain, you are reborn."

"Let all stand and bear witness; the warleader is chosen, long live Azhani Rhu'len, long live the queen! Hip-hip huzzah!" cried the elven herald.

"Huzzah!" the crowd shouted back.

Looking out at the mass of people, one face stood out to the warrior's blurred vision. At the edge of the crowd, Kyrian gazed up with love and pride clear in her bright smile.

Upon hearing of Lyssera's plan to make Azhani warleader, the stardancer had been wary of the idea. Only after long consideration did she realize that Azhani needed to step into this role, and then she gave her wholehearted support. *Please don't make this the wrong choice,* she prayed as she beamed up at her lover.

Beside the priest, Prince Allyndev fairly bounced with glee over the honor his aunt had bestowed upon his mentor. In the short time as her student, he had come to cherish her terse wisdom and sharp sense of humor. He was doubly excited because as Azhani's squire, he would accompany her north to face the rimerbeasts.

"I knew you'd find a good use for that old relic!" a familiar voice boomed out over the crowd as Azhani sheathed her blade.

Striding through a rapidly opening corridor, Padreg and Elisira came to the edge of the stage and bowed first to Queen Lyssera and then to Azhani. Behind them, Devon Imry escorted a young woman wearing the colors of the high king, Ysradan.

Surprised, yet pleased that her friends had come, Azhani surveyed the group as they gathered below her.

Young Devon had sprouted like a weed over the months and a tall, fine-boned young man had replaced the gawky boy. Wavy brown locks had straightened to fall around his shoulders and gave the boy a noble appearance. His hazel eyes still held their sparkle of mischief, and the smile on his face conveyed his excitement.

Weeks in the sun had darkened Elisira's pale skin and had given her a healthy glow that sat well upon her beautiful face. Dressed in the traditional leather garments of the plains nomads, she and Padreg stood out against the Y'Syran preference for silk and velvet.

The young woman on Devon's arm was not familiar to Azhani, but the style of her dress marked her as Y'Maran. *That must be Princess Syrelle,* the warrior thought as she clasped hands with Padreg.

Lyssera descended from the platform, reaching her hands out to Padreg and embracing him warmly. "We are always pleased to greet our cousin from the south," she said cordially.

Returning the queen's greeting, Padreg said, "As I am always pleased to visit your fair city, cousin."

The visiting monarch and his entourage were escorted to the side while the ceremony concluded. Afterward, Lyssera left Azhani in charge of entertaining Padreg and his people while she returned to Oakheart to have rooms made ready for them.

"Thank you for coming," Azhani said as she and her friends strolled the streets of Y'Syria.

"Did you think I'd let you claim all the glory?" Padreg asked with a mischievous twinkle in his eyes. "I've brought a few friends to the party as well. We of Y'Nor know that it is the north who keeps our kingdoms free of rimerbeasts." He indicated a rapidly growing tent city that was forming to the south of the city.

Azhani smiled. "You are generous, my friend." She draped a casual arm around Kyrian's shoulders and received a pleased kiss.

Padreg smirked; Elisira grinned broadly.

The young woman attached to Devon's side was indeed the Princess Syrelle, Ysradan's daughter. Between Devon and Allyndev in age, she carried herself with a grace that belied her youth. Slight of stature, with a shock of curly red hair that fell to her waist, and eyes a teal blue of the deepest seas, Syrelle earned herself many appreciative stares from passersby.

"I win," Padreg murmured as they stopped at a wine seller's stand to purchase skins of chilled fruit juice. "However, since your service is given to another, I'll take two of Kushyra's offspring instead!"

"What's this about?" Kyrian asked.

Azhani's skin darkened as she flushed. Padreg laughed while Elisira shook her head ruefully. "It seems that my lord has the sense for *korethka* and when it strikes. He wagered Azhani that you and she would find the love that sat so plainly before your faces," Elisira said softly.

Kyrian's eyebrows rose. *Should I be offended?* She looked at Azhani's plainly embarrassed face and decided that she was not hurt. Rather, she found the situation adorably amusing. "Are you a sore loser, my love?" she whispered to Azhani, causing the warrior's flush to deepen. To ease Azhani's distress, she said, "It is well, love. I know that you meant no harm."

"I didn't want you to be hurt," she replied. "I—"

Kyrian kissed her.

Smiling foolishly, Azhani turned to Padreg. With a shrug, she said, "I'm not breeding Kushyra this season — but when I do, her first two are yours."

They shook on it.

Walking with them, Allyndev listened to their banter, but his gaze never left the face of Princess Syrelle. When she had first appeared, he had thought that Astariu herself had come to walk among them. *She's so beautiful.* The beauty in question laughed, a hearty, joyful sound that made Allyn's heart contract painfully. *I hope she's going north with us.* The young prince found himself composing sonnets about Syrelle's hair as they wandered the streets of his city.

Azhani and her friends continued their joyful discussion as they wandered about the city, eventually returning to Oakheart. They were greeted by Lyssera's chatelaine, who led the newcomers to their rooms.

While Azhani met with Lyssera's guard captains to discuss battle plans, Kyrian went to visit Starseeker Vashyra. Since the day that Kasyrin Darkchilde's shade had assaulted the elven throne room, the priest-mages had been busy. This was the first opportunity for the stardancer to see one of them.

"Kyrian, welcome," Vashyra said as the stardancer entered the sanctuary.

"Thank you," she said. Brushing nervous fingers down her robes, she said, "I've come to request a new baton." A stardancer's baton was made to exacting specifications, and each weapon was specially fit to the wielder.

Vashyra nodded. "I've been expecting you. I'm sorry we couldn't see you sooner. Come with me," she said. Together, they left the starseeker's office and headed for the temple armory.

Once there, they found that there were no baton blanks on hand.

Kyrian felt embarrassment creep over her. "I guess I should have been more careful with the one I had," she muttered.

Vashyra frowned. "Ah, child, you cannot fault yourself for your fears, nor should you blame the queen for her actions. She is a warrior trained, though she is rarely called upon to defend herself or her kingdom in such a personal manner. I shall have a new baton made for you, and that will be that."

"But it will take weeks to forge a new one and I—"

"You wish to accompany your lover north. I know. We'll take your measurements now, and when it is done, I will deliver it." The starseeker smiled. "I too am going north, Kyrian. It is not so hard to forge a baton on the road — just time consuming."

"I hate to be so much trouble," Kyrian said.

"Nonsense! I shall enjoy the simple task of crafting your weapon. Now, grip this," Vashyra said as she handed Kyrian a shaft of wood. By process of elimination, the length, weight and grip size for the stardancer's weapon was chosen.

"Thank you for doing this, Vashyra," Kyrian said when they were through.

"You're welcome. Now, I suggest that you choose a staff from the armory. I don't want you to be unarmed."

Kyrian shook her head. "No, I won't see combat, Vashyra. I'd rather not be encumbered by something like a staff."

"As you choose, Stardancer. Here, take this, then," the mage-priest took a box from one of the shelves and removed a pendant. It was a silver and gold representation of the Astariun rune. "Wear this. The dweomer cast upon it is small, but it should help you if you find yourself a target of attack."

Kyrian accepted the amulet. In her hands, it gave off a faint trace of magick, but she could not determine what the spell cast upon it was. "Thank you," she said as she donned it.

Vashyra smiled. "No, thank *you*. I'd not want to be the one to stand before your Azhani and inform her that you'd been hurt."

After a grand meal welcoming the Y'Noran delegation, Lyssera called them to a private meeting. Joining Padreg and Elisira were the Y'Droran and Y'Skani ambassadors. Devon and Allyndev served as pages to keep gossip at a minimum.

"It's good to see you up, Granther," Kyrian said as she went over to give Iften a kiss on his weathered cheek.

"You didn't expect me to miss out on the fun, did you?" he said with a smile. "As ambassador, I have a considerable retinue of bored warriors. I'd like to donate my men to your cause." He turned to face Azhani and said, "That is, if you'll have us, Warleader."

Azhani nodded her head in recognition of the honorific. "Of course, Iften. Your men are welcome. Please remind them that snow is cold and rain is wet."

Iften roared with laughter.

"Count me and mine in with the old snake," Kuwell Longhorn said.

As the group settled into their seats, Azhani made introductions. Soon, they were joined by Queen Lyssera, the captain of her guard and the elven scoutmaster.

"I've called us here so that everyone can be apprised of what has been discovered," Azhani said.

The scoutmaster stood and went to a map of Y'Myran that took up most of one wall.

"Here, here and here," he tapped places within the Crest of Amyra that were directly north of Y'Syria, "we have located several caves filled with rimerbeast eggs." He drew his finger west and tapped a location above Y'Dan. "We have heard of nestings here, as well."

"What of Y'Dror?" Kuwell asked. "I have heard nothing from my kin, but they live closer to Y'Tol."

The scoutmaster said, "My Lord, I have heard nothing of dwarven lands. However, knowing how these demons breed, I would not rule it out."

Kuwell looked bleak.

"They are so terrible, then?" Iften said.

"Worse than a rain of scorpions in the middle of a sandstorm, Ambassador," Azhani replied.

The old man gave a start. "By the Serpent! I had heard the tales but," he shook his head in disbelief, "how is it that we are not overrun by these creatures?"

"Planning, and the courage of many lives," Azhani said. "Thank you, scoutmaster. Captain Evern, we'd like to hear from you next."

The elf rose and bowed stiffly. He had been one of those who had protested the Y'Dani warrior's position, but he was too loyal to his queen to leave her service. "My Lords and Ladies, Your Majesty, the army has assembled. Fully ten thousand archers, five thousand rangers, fifteen thousand cavalry and thirty thousand regular infantry now fill the fields and forest outside Y'Syria. We are ready to march."

"Thank you, Evern," Lyssera said. She looked at the face of each person present and said, "I have it from Starseeker Vashyra that the mages are ready. You shall not lack for supplies." The starseekers and the mages would not only be instrumental in battle, but were the lynchpin to the army's supply lines. Without them, Azhani's quartermasters would be forced to have huge wagon trains of gear and food follow the soldiers. Instead, supplies and reinforcements would be sent through periodically opened magickal portals. "Kyrian, I'd like to ask you to be the liaison with the healers. Y'Len is sending more stardancers, but they will not arrive for another four days."

"I'd be honored to serve, My Queen," Kyrian said.

"Azhani, I understand that you have a plan," Lyssera said.

"I do. Here is what I want us to do." The warleader stood and walked to the map. There, she began to make plain how the combined troops of three kingdoms would fight off the rimerbeasts.

The discussion went late into the night as those present offered suggestions on how best to adapt each of their soldiers to unfamiliar terrain. Devon and Allyndev found themselves sent on many trips to the kitchens and the archives.

In the middle of their discussion, Starseeker Vashyra joined them. "I have news of the prophecy," she said. All in the room looked to her intently. "In a scroll nearly as old as this city, I found a line that mirrors that which was spoken in the throne room. *The beast will rise to seek his place among mortals.* The rest was gibberish."

"Thank you, Starseeker. Please, keep searching," Lyssera said. "It may be important."

"Sounds like they're talking about the rimerbeasts," Kuwell said gruffly. "'Course they'll rise and take their place among mortals. We are a buffet of delicacies to their hungry mouths."

"I'm here to see that they choke on us," Azhani said grimly. "Thank you, Vashyra. I'd like to see a copy of that scroll."

"Of course. I'll have a scribe make one immediately."

"Now, back to the Y'Droran troops. Ku, I'd like your people to fan out here. They're more likely to gain the trust of the mountain clans." Azhani indicated a ridge of mountains near the dwarven capital.

By dawn, a plan of action had been forged.

Chapter Thirty-One

Enacting the plan took time. The soldiers had to be split into units that would work both coherently as a separate unit as well as be able to fuse into a larger group when winter came.

Acting as a messenger between the various groups, Princess Syrelle became a familiar sight to those serving under Azhani's banner. Devon introduced the princess to Kyrian, and soon Syrelle could be seen spending as much time with the chirurgeons as she did with the soldiers. Wherever she went, either Devon or Allyndev were sure to be found. Whether Syrelle noticed the attentions of the two young men, she did not say. The charming young woman was far too busy learning wound care and how best to slay a rimerbeast.

Azhani was wary of instructing the high king's daughter in the art of war, but she would have no unarmed followers in her army. Rimerbeasts were not the only danger lurking in the mountains above Y'Myran.

The combined mass of military might could have posed a problem for discipline, but Azhani came up with the brilliant plan of throwing mock tournaments. Soldiers were given the opportunity to display their abilities without killing one another. By week's end, the first of several small groups headed north to establish base camps and begin the tedious process of denuding the mountains of rimerbeast eggs.

From Y'Dan, three more delegations of Ecarthan priests arrived demanding that Lyssera join her efforts to that of Arris. Each time, the queen politely heard them out, then had them escorted to their ships. Because of the dire warnings and threats the black-robed priests heaved on the elven monarch's head, Lyssera ordered her navy launched. No more ships from Y'Dan would be allowed to cross into Y'Syran waters.

Padreg sent orders to his regent and within days, Banner Lake was filled with the sails of three navies.

Devon was bored. Princess Syrelle was off running errands for Azhani, leaving him to wander the byways of Oakheart and its environs alone. Distantly, he could hear the chatter of courtiers as well as the strains of minstrels, but neither piqued his interest. As a page, he had never found much to interest him in the gossip of the nobility. He could be studying — no candlemark spent in contemplation of magickal energies and their applications was ever wasted — but the young man desired company, not the dusty realms of magickal academia.

The young mage rounded a corner and spotted a familiar face. Prince Allyndev, the queen's nephew, was out in one of the many raised courtyards that dotted Oakheart, diligently weeding a flower garden. The sight caused the former page to pause. *You'd have never caught Arris on his knees for anything — especially a weed.* Smiling, the young man stepped into the courtyard and called out to the prince.

"Ho, there, Prince! What ails the plants that you must dirty your hands so rapidly?"

Allyn jumped away from the flower pot guiltily. Hunching his shoulders, he mumbled, "'Tis nothing to concern yourself over."

Cocking his head curiously, Devon said, "That may be, but you've taken it upon yourself. Are Oakheart's gardeners so lax in their duties?"

Allyndev drew himself up, anger coloring his face. Glaring at the young mage, he said, "Oakheart boasts the finest gardeners in Y'Syr. I should strap you for suggesting otherwise."

"Hold, Prince. I meant no offense," Devon said, raising his hands in supplication.

Allyn maintained his sullen glare.

Extending his hand, the mage said, "I am Devon Imry."

It was ignored.

"Was there something you required?" Allyn muttered.

Slowly, Devon lowered his hand. "No, I suppose not," he said, turning away from the prince and leaving the young man to his weeding.

Not exactly a successful meeting, Devon thought, sighing again. "Perhaps I shall go find that book."

Azhani was busy deciding how to deploy her soldiers. Sitting at a desk, the warleader poured over scrolls and maps, marking the maps where each of her groups were and should be. She wanted to be able to find them when the time came for her to go north.

The door opened and Lyssera entered. The queen quickly sat and wasted no time in speaking. "Azhani, there's something you need to know." With an economy of words, the elven queen told the warrior a story that had her riveted.

When Lyssera finished speaking, Azhani shook her head. "That old scoundrel. I never suspected...this changes—"

"Nothing. It changes nothing," Lyssera said firmly.

Azhani's eyes hardened. "No, Lyss. It changes everything."

"It wasn't supposed to be known. I told you because—"

"Because things are different now," the warleader said. "Will you accept that I will keep the information until such time as it is needed?"

Lyssera smiled wanly. "Ever the tactician, Azhani?"

"It is my nature," she replied.

Arching an eyebrow, Lyssera said, "Then do not waste what I have told you."

The warleader gazed out of her window toward the mountains. "I shall make every effort to use it properly."

Standing, Lyssera sadly said, "You will forgive me if I say that I hope another choice presents itself."

Azhani looked at her queen. "I must do what is right, My Queen. Even if it is not the choice you would make."

"Thodan often spoke of your stubborn nature, Azhani. I see that he was not exaggerating."

The warleader smiled wistfully.

"Do as you must, Azhani, but please remember that some secrets are better left alone."

Azhani nodded. Lyssera exited, leaving the warleader to mull over what she had just learned. *I will try to keep your secrets, My Queen, but sometimes, they have a way of escaping.*

When Azhani finally left Y'Syria to go north, she went with the greater portion of the army behind her. At her right, Kyrian rode Arun while Padreg and Elisira flanked her left. Beneath her, Kushyra tossed her head and stamped proudly. The warhorse seemed thrilled to be heading off to battle. For herself, Azhani was consumed with the usual doubts and worries that always plagued her whenever she was faced by a beast season.

Men and women would die. Supplies would run out or spoil. Civilians would lose their lives, homes and families to the depredations of the rimerbeasts. It was enough to put knots in the warleader's stomach.

Kyrian reached out and ran a loving hand down her lover's arm. "Azhi, please try not to scowl so. You're scaring the birds."

Rolling her eyes, Azhani laughed. "Thank you, love. I needed to remember that the future is far ahead."

Concerned, Kyrian moved her horse closer. "Do you need to stop?"

"No. I'll be fine, love. Truly," Azhani said. Turning to look at Kyrian, she twined her fingers with the stardancer's. "Have I told you today how grateful I am to have you beside me?"

Charmed, the priest flushed. "No."

"Then let me say that you make this," with a sweep of her hand, she indicated the army, "easier to face."

"As you do for me, my heart," Kyrian said. They shared an infatuated smile.

"I may have to drink my tea plain if that is the sweetness we will be exposed to on this journey," Padreg said loudly.

As they neared the mountains, Gormerath began to softly hum. No one else seemed to notice the sword's song, but it was a constant thrum in the back of the warleader's mind.

Kyrian continued to give Syrelle and Devon lessons on herbs and medicine, while Azhani trained Allyn in the use of a variety of weapons. Others joined the classes until the warleader's camp was filled to capacity by those eager to learn. Seeking to create order from the chaos, others were recruited to teach. By day, they marched; at night, there was laughter, learning, and song.

The forest and foothills teemed with life. Azhani ordered her hunters and gatherers to judiciously cull from the local flora and fauna, but not to denude the areas through which they passed.

As they neared the northern borders, they were joined by former Y'Dani citizens who wished to do what they could to protect their new home. Many were sent back to garrison the villages from whence they came; others were given tasks and accepted into the army.

The night before they entered the foothills, Azhani sent the order for everyone to don their armor. They had traveled unencumbered by the leather and steel armaments, but the morrow would find them entering hostile territory. Out came the light chain favored by elves, the highly decorated studded leather sported by those from the plains and the scale mail that marked a desertman. Only the dwarves' armor seemed unremarkable, for it was an amalgamation of whatever bits they could shape to fit their diminutive, yet stocky, bodies.

Kyrian helped Azhani to clean the traditional armor of the Y'Syran war-leader. The mail, made of interlocking scales shaped like oak leaves, replaced the coat that had been purchased in Barton, though that one had been packed as well.

Half a day's travel into the mountains, the buzz that was Gormerath's song suddenly became a howl that was nearly painful for Azhani to hear. Wincing, the warleader reached up to pull the blade from her back and was startled to feel it tug her toward a nearby cave. Curious, she chose men to follow her as she investigated the strange tugging.

From the cave entrance came the stench of partially hardened rimer-beast eggs. Shuddering atavistically at the sight of row after row of the leathery, slimy boulders, Azhani turned to her men and said, "Follow me. Move quickly but break every shell. Do not get the yolk on your skin. If you do, leave immediately and seek a healer."

"Aye, Warleader," was the hearty reply.

"Let's get to work," the warleader said grimly as she drew Gormerath from its sheath. The cave was suddenly lit by a brilliant glow. Azhani was so surprised, she nearly dropped the blade.

Her men cheered.

Maintaining her composure, Azhani broke the first egg. Soon, the air was filled with the sound of cracking shells. Afterward, the warleader sent for a stardancer and a mage to cleanse the cave with fire, and then bless it against reinfestation.

Chapter Thirty-Two

Destroying rimerbeast hives was nasty, messy work. From sunup until sundown, Azhani and her men cut their way through the hardening sacks of goop and tried to avoid getting the acidic innards on their skin. The mountains reeked of the foul smoke from burned out caves.

The one bright spot to the drudgery for Azhani was having Kyrian by her side. Mornings were spent loving and sharing breakfast while the nights were given to teaching their willing students.

Weeks dragged on as the army searched every cave they could find for rimerbeast spawn. To spice up their daily life, they discovered a nest of hoblins, a particularly nasty humanoid monster that fed off on the flesh of others. Days were lost to chasing the beasts down to make certain that none would harry the army as it moved from mountain to mountain. The existence of the monsters was not unexpected. Such was the nature of a beast season.

Summer had come to the mountains. Rain dappled the night as Devon sat against a stack of barrels and cleaned rimerbeast slime from his boots. Giving them up as lost, he tossed them aside and lifted his head to allow the cool rain to wash the sweat from his face. He heard someone clear their throat softly and opened his eyes to see Prince Allyndev standing before him. Choking back a sigh of consternation, he raised an eyebrow in silent question to the young man he had nicknamed "Azhani's shadow".

Devon and Allyndev did not get along. They rarely, if ever, spoke. The prince was standoffish and arrogant while the mage was jealous of how Princess Syrelle always found a way to talk about the prince. Devon was quite taken with Syrelle, yet kept his affections to himself. He had learned long ago that nobles did not dally with commoners with honorable intentions. Instead, he maintained a close friendship with the princess, but he could not help but wish for more. Especially when his rival was an oafish princeling who had more kind words to say to the trees than to his fellow citizens.

Devon watched as the prince licked his lips and gaped at him. *Maybe he's just shy?* the mage thought suddenly, as Allyndev shuffled his feet and seemed ready to bolt. Standing, he offered his hand to the prince. "Hello, I'm Devon."

Cautiously, Allyn grasped it. "I know," he said. His voice held the arrogant tone of the nobility, but his face was painted with confusion. "I'm, ah, Allyndev."

"I know," Devon replied, returning the arrogance with full measure. The two young men sized each other up while maintaining the handclasp.

Allyn looked away first. "I...maybe I should go," he said. He pulled his hand away and turned.

"No, wait," Devon said. "Please...don't be shy. I won't bite."

Allyn shivered. Making friends had never been easy for him. His peers had always gone out of their way to let him know how little he meant to them.

"Are you thirsty? I have some ale," Devon said. He tried to make his voice inviting. *Kyrian says that more patients are tamed with kindness than crude words. I wonder if that applies to arrogant princes, as well?*

Allyn spun around and looked at the mage. His saffron robes were wet and liberally splattered with dirt. The hems were burned by the acidic slime from the rimerbeast eggs. He appeared weary, but there was an openness in his bearded face that enticed the prince to step nearer. "I — yes, I am thirsty."

Devon handed him an aleskin and he drank.

"How can I help you, Prince Allyndev?" the mage asked when he finished.

"Allyn. Please, call me Allyn. You...know the princess, right?"

Chuckling, Devon said, "Yes, I do." *He's really shy.* Devon felt his heart crack as he realized that this very shyness was what drew Syrelle to the prince. That same shyness called out to the mage, and he found that he was helpless to resist. "Join me?" he offered, indicating the barrels he had been using as chairs.

Hesitating only briefly, Allyn settled on a barrel. The prince pulled a distinctive purple scarf from his pouch and said, "I found this. I think it belongs to the princess, but I didn't want to bother her if it wasn't hers."

Devon recognized the scarf. It was one that Elisira had given Syrelle when the Y'Maran princess had first arrived on the plains. "Yes, it's hers. I'll return it for you, if you'd like." *This is her favorite scarf. I might earn a hug if I give it back to her.*

Torn between saying yes and wanting to say no, Allyn said, "Why don't we both take it to her?"

Thus the reason that he is the prince, and I am the mage. Politics is in his blood, Devon thought sourly. Yet the young man could not find it in him to dislike Allyn too greatly — he too was caught by the charms of the Y'Maran princess. *Be the better man, and accept what fate gives you, Dev. That's what father always said.*

"All right. I think she's eating dinner. Shall we go find her?" the mage said. Standing, the two young men went in search of the princess.

The small groups that had been sent to the mountains first began to trickle back to the army. There were a few losses due to injury, but most were elated to have done their part to cull the rimerbeast hatching.

Azhani's time grew less and less her own as the infested caves grew more frequent. She had to give up her evening classes in favor of going over the duty roster for the next day.

As the army's size grew, so too did the shape of their camp. No longer were there small encampments that dotted the mountainsides. The groups were separated in concentric circles with the most vulnerable, the chirurgeons, being housed in the center. At the outer edge of the rings was the warleader's camp. For the length of the campaign, Allyndev had taken shelter in one of the elven tents that bordered the edge of Azhani's camp and the regular army.

Devon and Syrelle shared a tent that sat nearly in the middle of the warleader's camp. The princess had moved in shortly after they had left Y'Syria, because the young mage's tent was far more comfortable than the canvas affair that had been assigned to her. The tent they shared had been a gift to Devon from Padreg. The plains people were masters at tent making, which gave the young mage a certain edge over his peers. Made of a complex weaving of fiber and fur, it was warm when it needed to be, but could also be arranged to catch the night breezes and keep the sleepers cool as well. Beyond that, it did not leak during the sudden summer showers that were frequent in the mountains. The tent was large enough to house six, or three and their gear. It didn't take long for the third person to be added.

Late one night after a long patrol, Allyn stumbled into Devon's tent behind the mage. It was raining and the prince's tent leaked persistently. The mage could not see his friend, already fighting a cold, suffer another night in the chill. One night became two, then three. On the fourth night, the two young men had returned to find a third rope bed and all of Allyn's gear set up in the empty corner of the tent. Speechless, the prince stared at the arrangement while Devon raised an eyebrow.

Syrelle shrugged. "Well, he's been here for three days and I haven't wanted to stuff a sock in his mouth. He doesn't snore nearly as loud as you do, Devvy."

"I do not snore!" the mage said, though his eyes sparkled in merriment. The contention was an old one that stemmed from their days in Y'Nor. It was one of the reasons why Devon had been given his own tent — no one else would bunk with him.

"You do snore," Allyn finally said, his voice softened by emotion. No one had ever just *invited* him in like these two crazy humans. As both a prince and a half-elf, he had grown up on the fringes of the society he called home. Any casual offer of friendship was fraught with political motivation, which left Allyndev feeling like a prized pig at a farmer's market. Blinking back tears, he swallowed the lump in his throat. *I have friends.*

"So, will you be staying with us, lad?" Devon asked, clapping a hand on his friend's shoulder, perfectly mimicking the Y'Noran monarch's voice.

Smiling openly, Allyn said, "Yes. Thank you."

"Oh good. I really didn't want to move everything around again," Syrelle said. "Those beds are a pain in the backside!"

The three friends shared a laugh.

"Prince Allyndev!" a voice called from outside.

The change over the young man was instantaneous. Gone was the easy smile and relaxed posture. Snapping erect, Allyn became every inch the prince. Stiffly, he ducked out of the tent to greet his visitor.

Outside stood Sergeant Matthias, the commander of Allyndev's unit. As soon as he spotted the prince, he adopted the air of one who had been made to wait for candlemarks. "Boy, when I call you, I expect you to appear, double-time!" he growled.

"Yes, sir," Allyn said tonelessly. Matthias was the worst of the prince's tormentors. At home in Y'Syria, the coarse commander had treated Allyn like the lowest scullery boy, and now that he was his superior officer, the treatment had worsened. No job was too terrible for the prince to tackle. More than once the young man had been stuck scrubbing beast slime from

the unit's boots for imagined infractions. "I will do better in the future, sir."
The sergeant snorted as if this were an impossibility. "So you say. This your billet, boy?" At the prince's nod, he said, "All right. Get some chow, then go to bed. You're on first patrol now." Matthias allowed himself a long look at Syrelle's cleavage before marching off.

The princess suppressed a shiver of nausea. The elven commander made her feel like a two-copper doxy. "I don't like him," she said softly.

There was a far away look in Allyn's eyes as he said, "He's the sergeant. You don't have to like him."

"You seen the landscape over at the warleader's camp, Hawkins?" a soldier grunted between bites of his trail rations. Wistful groans of assent passed from man to man as the soldiers picked up on the conversation.

For three days, they had traveled from cave to cave, breaking eggs. Sergeant Matthias had placed Allyndev with the third unit cavers — the group that went in last, before the priests and mages. Most of his clothing had been ruined by the acidic slime that invariably coated the caves.

"Hey Allyboy, why don't cha give us a *personal* run down of Princess Syrelle's attributes, since you're so close t' her highness and all," one of the men suggested.

Noticing that the sergeant's gaze was upon him, Allyn bit back a harsh retort.

"We're waiting, boy," the elf said gruffly.

Was this the way men were supposed to behave? Maybe, if he tried to fit in, he would get a little more respect. Then he might get better job assignments instead of clean up duty.

"Well, um, she's got this, uh, really nice arse, and, uh..." To his horror, he found himself hesitantly describing the princess in the crude fashion the soldiers around him seemed to relish.

Matthias moved Allyn from swab crew to spotter, the first to enter a new cave. It was the spotter's job to ascertain the hardness of the embryonic rimerbeast sacs.

"Hard boiled, Sarge," Allyn would call, if the leathery shell were stiff to the touch. This meant that the soldiers needed maces to break open the sacs. "Raw 'n ready," was when the eggs were still soft enough that a common sword could cut through the outer covering. Three more days passed as the patrol cleared its assigned section of mountains.

The prince knew that his new place had been gained by acting like a boorish cad, and that made him uncomfortable. Yet that alone was not enough to make him change his ways. He did not want to return to being just Alynna's bastard.

Mealtimes were the part of each day where soldiers could intermingle freely. During the day, food was doled out in ration packs, and at night fires dotted the hills for miles. These glowing beacons were a welcome sight to the weary patrols returning from days of slogging through caves. Azhani encouraged her people to foster a peaceful atmosphere that allowed the soldiers of three kingdoms to become a cohesive unit.

Astariun priests kept their tents open at all hours for those who sought spiritual counseling. The chirurgeons reported a rise in the requests for contraceptive teas. Occasionally, a fight would break out, but for the most part, the army bonded.

Standing on a hillside, Azhani looked out at the constellation of fires that was her army and smiled in satisfaction. She had never felt as at home as she did in the field. Beyond the administrative duties that required her to write countless reports, she enjoyed the fierce rush of excitement that poured through her veins whenever she ventured into an unexplored cave.

There were always more caves than her soldiers could clear and winter would bring rimerbeasts to fight. Though the warleader regretted that lives would be lost, the part of her that she called the banshee delighted in the coming battles.

From where she stood, Azhani could see Prince Allyndev's patrol returning from their week-long trek. Assigning him to Sergeant Matthias had not been her first choice, but none of the other elven commanders had wanted him. Allyndev needed experience in the field away from her, and this had been a chance for him to earn some self esteem.

"We got really drunk. I almost puked on the fire. But I didn't." Prince Allyndev sounded very proud of his accomplishment. "The next day, we found another cave with eggs and I got to go in first and smash the first one and it was gross." He paused to inhale half a mug of ale, belched and then continued. "I picked the biggest egg — it must have had enough goo inside to make four of them damned demons. Shyvot, but that stuff stank like a cesspool in summer."

Listening in stunned silence, Devon and Syrelle exchanged uncomfortable glances. Hearing the coarse words come from Allyn's mouth made both of his friends feel confused. When they had presented him with a suit of clothes that they had made, he hadn't even thanked them. Instead, his gaze never seemed to leave Syrelle's bosom. He was dirty, his breath stank of ale, and he was arrogant.

"Anyway, I'm gonna go get out of these damn clothes. They stink," Allyn said. He left the fireside and headed for their tent.

Syrelle watched him go, and her eyes were troubled. "I used to like him," she whispered.

Devon put a hand on her shoulder and squeezed softly. "Yeah, I did too."

"He seemed so gentle. In Y'Syr, he told me about how the gardeners are the most important people in his kingdom because it is their spells that keep the trees alive. The oaf that just left wouldn't care about a tree unless he could burn it or fornicate with it!" Syrelle said sadly.

Devon slipped his arm around the princess and hugged her gently. She sighed and rested her head on his shoulder. "Perhaps Azhani will say something to him."

Chuckling, Syrelle said, "Surely there is something more appropriate. Couldn't you turn him into a turnip? They're rather bland and inoffensive."

Devon laughed. "For you, My Lady, he shall be a turnip of grand proportions, flavored only with the finest of manures."

A candlemark later, the group was gathered around the fire, sharing a meal. Light banter flitted back and forth between the friends.

Pointing at Allyndev's grimy boots, Devon held his nose and said, "My friend, I enjoy your company, but you need to leave your lady friends in the cave when you're through with them."

Allyn's face hardened. "At least my clothes suffer from the efforts of a man's work, tailor boy."

Stung, Devon stood and left the fireside.

"That was rude," Syrelle said, casting a withering look at the older boy.

"If he can't stand the burn he shouldn't smash the eggs," Allyn grunted as he wiped his mouth on his sleeve and belched loudly.

Azhani met the gazes of the adults present. Apparently her experiment with the prince had backfired. Instead of boosting his self esteem, the trip had honed his arrogance to a jagged point.

"I hear your voice, but it is not the words of my friend that spill forth and clutter the air with their foulness. You are being mean and spiteful," Syrelle said angrily. Standing, she looked down at Allyn and said, "I do not consort with brutes or savages. When you have thrown off this terrible face and returned to the person who treats his friends with respect, then I shall hear your words. Until then, I will seek companionship elsewhere." Lifting her head high, she stalked off after Devon.

"Looks like it's time to do some serious groveling, boy," Padreg commented, as he reached over and clapped the young man's shoulder.

Allyn shrugged noncommittally. "She's just a woman," he said.

Eyes narrowing, Azhani said, "Allyndev, come with me."

The prince looked up at her, and rebellion was written cleanly on his face.

"Now." The tone brooked no argument.

Sullenly, the young man set his half-finished meal aside and joined her. Together, they walked outside the fire-lit circle to the edge of the encampment. The warleader acknowledged her sentries as they passed out of their sight and into a wooded area that lay just beyond the camp.

"Prince Allyndev, would you care to explain to me why you are behaving like a rimerbeast?"

"No," he replied sourly.

Azhani settled against a large boulder. "In the last few months, I've had the pleasure of getting to know you, boy. In all that time, I've never seen you act like such a fool. Your behavior today was unbecoming to a prince of Y'Syr and to a person I'd like to think of as one of my best students. So, you will tell me why your head has suddenly become lodged in your backside, or I will send you home in disgrace."

The facade of sullen arrogance faltered as Allyn gasped. "No," he whispered and kicked at the rocks that lined the path. "Please don't send me home." Tears welled in his eyes and he lifted his head stiffly in an attempt to deny their release.

"Give me a reason not to," Azhani said.

"I hate this," Allyn finally said as his shoulders slumped in defeat. "I hate getting up before the sun every morning just so I can slog through something I wouldn't feed a pig. I hate that I'm either cold and wet, or hot and sweaty." The prince kicked at another rock, following its trajectory as it skimmed over the grass to lodge in a bush not far away. "I hate that I'm either the prince or a pariah." In a small voice, he said, "Master, I hate wishing that I'd never been born. I thought that if I tried to fit in, maybe I could be like everyone else — and I was right." Defiantly he lifted his chin. "They respected me, once I started to act like them. I tried to tell myself that I could change back, once my patrol was over, but," his shoulders slumped, "you saw what happened. I can't seem to open my mouth without sticking my stinky foot in it."

Azhani patted the boulder she was leaning against. Reluctantly, Allyn hitched himself up next to her. "It's not all legends and tales, is it, My Prince?" she asked as she looked into his youthful face.

"No," he cried softly.

"I wish that I could tell tales of how being the hero was all glory and no pain, Allyn, but I cannot. It's dirty and disgusting, and often you have to kill to save your life or the lives of those you protect. Respect is what you earn by deed and not by accident of birth."

"But everyone loves Aunt Lyss," he said.

"Your aunt has devoted her entire life to the care of Y'Syr. Do you think that her work is any less important than mine?"

Allyndev considered that and said, "I wish they would all let me be! I didn't ask to be born a prince. I'd rather be a gardener! But I failed there, too. I do not have the gift. Aunt Lyss told me the best way to honor Y'Syr would be to become a good ruler, but if she had spent even one day listening to my instructors, she would not have said such a thing." The tears streamed freely from his eyes as he spoke.

As a half-elf in an elven society, the boy would have been tormented by those who felt they were better than he just because his blood was considered impure. Azhani had felt the arrows of the opposite end — humans who felt that her elven ancestry diminished her value as a person.

The warleader knew that she could not allow her sympathy to color her words. "Allyn, the real world does not care who you call parents. Out here, what matters is how well you face adversity. Will you run, or will you stand fast and hold the line? Once you've made that choice, you will find your place."

Daring to hope, Allyn asked, "I will?"

Azhani nodded. "And I'll help by knocking you around until you're capable of making the right decision," she said with a mock growl. Then she pushed him down.

Outraged, he stared at her.

"Are you going to sit there like a flower and eat dirt, or are you going to defend yourself?" Azhani asked as she crossed her feet and blew on her knuckles.

He wrinkled his brow in confusion.

Azhani sighed and straightened. "Wrestling or sparring — make your choice, or I make it for you."

"Wrestling!" Allyn blurted.

"Then come at me, boy," Azhani said. He lunged for her and pulled her to the ground in an attempt to pin her. Half a candlemark passed before the warleader had pinned the prince. By the time they were done, both were breathing heavily, laughing wildly and covered in debris.

"We should get back," Azhani said, looking up and noting the position of the moon, "Before they send the cavalry after us."

Allyn nodded. "I have friends that require an apology," he said ruefully.

"Aye. Don't worry. They're waiting for you," Azhani said, affectionately tousling his hair.

Chapter Thirty-Three

Leaving behind a trail of blackened rock and plumes of gray smoke streaming skyward, the army worked its way to the western sea. Days stretched out until they seemed to meld into one another. Time was not the only enemy the army fought. Weather in the mountains wildly vacillated, swinging from bitter cold to aching heat. The chirurgeons were kept busy with everything from simple colds to compound fractures. Injuries were endemic to any large force. The army soldiered on, dealing with any downed men as they happened.

Over the crest of the next mountain lay the Ystarfe pass, their halfway point, and the location of more than three hundred caves and crevices that were perfect for demon breeding.

"Stardancer Kyrian, we're ready for you," a familiar voice called from outside the tent. Today, Kyrian was one of the stardancers whose duty it was to sing the blessing chants that would prevent the rimerbeasts from reinfesting a cave.

"Thank you, Sergeant Matthias," she said politely. Secretly, she disliked the coarse soldier because she knew that he was partially responsible for the poor treatment Allyndev had received from the soldiers in his unit. After that night where both Azhani and Allyndev had come back from a long talk looking like a pair of bog creatures, the warleader had transferred the prince back to her own patrols.

Reaching the caves, Kyrian let out a sharp groan of dismay. Lengths of knotted rope hung from a cliff that was nearly a mile up the sheer side of the mountain.

Hooking his thumbs in his belt, Matthias smirked and drawled, "Sorry 'bout the inconvenience. Demon's ain't the most accommodating bunch." He looked her over disdainfully. "I could go get another 'dancer if you'd rather not do it."

"No, I can do it. Thank you, Sergeant."

By the time the caves were thoroughly blessed, Kyrian's back was in more knots than the rope she had climbed earlier. Her throat was on fire from chanting while breathing the acrid smoke.

Pain made her stomach churn. Slowly, she picked her way down from the rocks and headed toward her camp. Beside her, Sergeant Matthias ambled along, whistling a bawdy tune.

"By the Twain, Sergeant, where are your manners?" Prince Allyndev stepped out of the shadows and put a supportive arm around the flagging stardancer.

The sergeant's face reddened. Balling his hands into fists, he sneered, "Do not speak to me as if you were a better man than I, half-breed. A tainted parasite like you would have no clue about who deserves honor."

"I know more than you will ever grasp, Sergeant." Allyn's tone was frigid.

In a single motion, Matthias unsheathed his sword. "Prove your words upon my body, boy."

Allyn's jaw clenched, but his hands never left off supporting Kyrian. "I have better things to do than engage in pointless brutality, Sergeant."

Kyrian opened her mouth to intervene, but a searing burst of fire from her back turned her words into a garbled gasp of pain. The world spun dizzyingly and spots danced in her vision, causing her to forget even the most basic of pain-killing chants.

"It's all right, Allyndev, I've got her." It was Azhani. She took command of the ailing stardancer with a gentle hand. "Easy now, Kyrian," she whispered. Raising her gaze to encompass the sergeant and the prince, she said, "I'm going back to camp, gentlemen. I will see you at dinner, Allyn." Then she purposefully turned her back on the unfolding drama.

As soon as the warleader was out of sight, Matthias turned to Allyn and said, "All right, boy, I've been waiting a long time for this moment."

Allyn's blade stayed in its sheath. Open handed, Allyn viewed the elven soldier with curiosity. "Why? Will it make you feel like a real man to beat up a half-grown boy?" he asked.

Lashing out in furious rage, the sergeant flicked his sword toward Allyn, intending to slap the boy across the face with the flat of the blade. Allyn ducked away, easily avoiding the blow.

The prince did not draw his blade. He intended to defeat Matthias bare handed in order to show everyone the quality of his honor. From the corner of his eye, Allyn could see several soldiers gathering to watch the contest. He grinned. He would give them a good show.

Dropping into a crouch, he rocked from foot to foot and waited for Matthias to strike. The elf faked a blow toward Allyndev's midsection, crowing triumphantly when the prince followed the move.

Almost too late, Allyndev danced away, narrowly avoiding the strike that would have sliced open his face. He lunged for the elf's left. When Matthias blocked with his sword, Allyn kicked out and connected solidly with the sergeant's elbow. There was distinct crunch, and the elf howled in pain. Matthias' sword dropped to the ground and his arm hung uselessly at his side.

Warily, Allyn stepped back and waited for the sergeant's next move.

Behind them, the soldiers began to murmur softly.

Matthias stared at Allyndev with hatred in his eyes.

With his gaze still firmly planted on the sergeant, the prince bent and scooped up the man's sword. Offering it to him hilt first, Allyn said, "Do you yield, Sergeant?"

Respect flooded into Matthias' eyes. Allyn had fought with honor. "I yield, My Prince," he said, and went to kneel before the younger man.

"No, Sergeant. I do not require your obeisance," Allyn said softly. "Let me help you to the chirurgeon's."

"Thank you, My Prince."

Allyn closed his eyes briefly. The victory was hollow, but sweet. He opened them to look at the gathered soldiers and saw a reflection of the sergeant's respectful demeanor on the faces of many of the warriors present.

I should not have broken his arm, Allyn thought sadly as he helped the sergeant to walk to the healer's tents.

"**Oh I hurt,**" Kyrian whimpered softly.

"We're almost home, Kyrian." Azhani carefully picked her way across the camp to their tent.

"I think I pulled something in my back," Kyrian said as they entered the tent.

"I'll take care of it," Azhani said, and brushed a kiss over Kyrian's brow. She then had Kyrian remove her dirty clothes and lie down for a back massage.

"You would make a good chirurgeon, Azhani," Kyrian said as the warrior rubbed at the sore muscles. "You are very good with me."

Azhani snorted. "I love you, Kyrian."

Kyrian smiled brightly. "I love you, too, Azhani."

When she finished with the massage, Azhani shed her dirty clothes and then climbed in next to Kyrian.

"I love the way you look at me," Kyrian whispered. Reaching up she stroked her lover's cheek.

Azhani smiled. "Yes, how is that?"

"Well, it's as though the world goes away. In your regard, I feel unique, special."

Azhani leaned forward and kissed Kyrian then suckled on her bottom lip until the stardancer's hands seemingly rose of their own accord to tangle in the warrior's braids.

"That is because you are unique and special," Azhani said while brushing kisses over Kyrian's face and lips. "You reach into my heart and make my soul sing."

Kyrian groaned as Azhani's hands slipped under her shift and began to stroke her rapidly hardening nipples. "Goddess, yes," she murmured. The garment was removed and flung across the tent.

"Do I make you sing?" Azhani drawled as she traced a fiery path of nips and kisses from Kyrian's neck to her breasts.

"Yes. I long for you, my Azhani," Kyrian whispered. Azhani undulated against her, and the stardancer let out a soft mew of pain. "Gently, love. I am still tender."

Azhani pulled away. "We can stop—"

Kyrian let out a bark of laughter. "No! Love me!" Kyrian reached out and grabbed her lover's shoulders and pulled her down for a hard, passionate kiss.

Each time they made love was a gift. Kyrian sometimes wondered if Azhani felt the same depth of emotions that she did — if she truly burned as hotly as she claimed. The stardancer did not have the courage to ask. With all that faced them each day, Kyrian knew that she would wait until they had a future that was safe from monsters and madmen before she faced that demon. Until then, she would lose herself in the wonderfully loving arms of her warrior.

As summer progressed, Azhani's legend grew. Soldiers with a skill for crafting stories told of how the blade, Gormerath, seemed to know where the demon-riddled caves were. Once, the warleader even spoke of the sword's hum, which added to the blade's lengthy mythology.

Azhani ignored these tales and concentrated solely on ridding the mountains of eggs. Using the sword's powers to ferret out every last egg in their path, the warleader left a trail of smoke several miles wide behind her.

The idea of a glowing, singing magickal sword was amusing enough to Kyrian that she would occasionally tease her lover about it. At other times, the stardancer would feel overwhelmed by the sheer numbers of mages and starseekers whose magicks spun fire from the very air.

Azhani accepted her lover's levity, knowing that mirth helped Kyrian deal with her fear. Not once did she leave the safe confines of the camp as part of a patrol. If the caves were close, then Kyrian would volunteer for blessing duty, otherwise the priest kept to the chirurgeon's tents. The warleader never asked her to go — even when she herself was gone for days at a time.

At midsummer, the army celebrated the longest day of the year by spending three full days at play. Games of skill and chance, bardic competitions and feasting on sweet cakes and wine, gave the soldiers a chance to rest and briefly forget what lay ahead.

On the eve of their crossing into the Ystarfe Pass, scouts made a grim discovery. In the higher altitude caves, the eggs had hatched. Though they had yet to be attacked, Azhani ordered the guard doubled. Three groups of ten soldiers each patrolled the outskirts of the encampment at all times.

Summer flamed out and autumn blew in one night on the blustery wind of a rainstorm. Without pause, the army traded its warm weather gear for oiled wools and linens. The threat of rimerbeast attack caused those not wearing armor to trade their simple cloth robes for heavier leather coverings that were dyed to reflect their occupation.

Mages wore saffron; starseekers bright blue; stardancers scarlet and chirurgeons donned robes in varying shades of green and white. Mixed with the panoply of armors worn by the various kingdoms, the army made a colorful picture.

Kyrian absolutely loved how Azhani looked in her regalia. On top of the silvery armor she wore a tabard embroidered with the arms of Y'Syr. Against a sky-blue background, a golden crown was cradled in the branches of an ancient oak tree. An added decoration was a border of golden leaves, marking Azhani as the warleader.

Against the wishes of Padreg, Elisira donned both armor and arms, proudly bearing the device of Y'Dan. Standing alone in the Y'Noran contingent, the wheat sheaf badge seemed very lonely in the sea of gray capes emblazoned with a rearing horse.

As Elisira helped Padreg to clip his capelet to his armor, the Y'Noran king said, "I do not understand why you bear these arms, Eli."

Turning him around a few times to take in the overall effect of his look, Elisira sternly replied, "Because something of the spirit of Thodan should stand to face the rimerbeasts. I care not that Arris comes north. He does not honor the man that made his kingdom great."

"You have shamed me," Padreg said roughly.

"There is no shame to be earned, my love. I am simply giving honor where it is due." She brushed a kiss over his stubbled chin and said, "I did not forget you, either." Holding up a belt, she proudly displayed the buckle, which bore the insignia she wore upon her chest. "Wear this, My Lord, and honor those who cannot stand with us."

Solemnly, Padreg allowed her to gird his waist with the belt.

Clustered together, Allyndev, Devon and Syrelle held hands and tried not to appear frightened by the sudden changes. Soon, the two young men would join Azhani on the first patrol since hatched eggs had been discovered. The sky was darkening rapidly as the sun set, and the warleader was certain that tonight the demons would hunt.

The princess was terrified for her friends. Alternately fighting back tears and anger, she wanted to cling to both Allyn and Devon, though it was Allyndev's embrace she craved the most. After losing his false bravado, he had become everything she had dreamed — honorable, caring, and brave. The Y'Syran prince made her heart flutter with desire. The fact that he returned her feelings only made her need greater.

Only one thing kept her from singing her affections out loud, and that was Devon. The mage's feelings for her were clearly written in his eyes, though he never once spoke of them. Instead, his actions betrayed his heart, and Syrelle feared losing the friendship they had built.

Unaware of the princess' chaotic thoughts, Devon wrestled with his own emotions. He knew how deeply Allyn cared for Syrelle, just as he knew those feelings were returned by the princess. Jealousy swept through him and left him shaking with the need to scream at the unfeeling fate that had brought him to this place. Fleetingly, he considered martyring himself, but realized that his death would only cause his friends grief.

In an effort to tame his wildly careening emotions, the mage said, "Hey, stick swinger, I'll wager that I kill one before you."

"I'll take that wager, sparkle fingers," Allyn gamely shot back.

Syrelle rolled her eyes. "I will be quite happy if your night is boring and you each return in one piece."

Devon smiled and reached for his weapons. A sling, a staff and a shortsword were gathered quickly. The mage relied heavily on his spells, but if they failed, he wanted to have a fighting chance. "Don't worry, Syrelle. We'll be fine."

Taking a moment to hold the princess close, Allyn said, "He's right, Sy. Master Azhani will keep us safe."

The two young men bade their farewells and joined Azhani's patrol. Kyrian and Syrelle watched as they mounted up and rode from the camp. Kyrian had already said her goodbyes, though she had to fight the urge to race after Azhani and beg just one more kiss.

"We should go and help prepare bandages. There will be wounded," Kyrian said. Syrelle nodded, and they turned away from the sight of their departing loved ones.

~ Chapter Thirty-Four ~

Gormerath's song was a constant buzz, but Azhani had grown used to interpreting its pitch. By the strength of its current tone, the warleader knew that rimerbeasts lurked nearby.

Gripping the hilt, she scanned the area. Crackling bushes exploded outward as three dozen gray-furred bodies leaped onto the path around her patrol. An eerie croon echoed around them as the rimerbeasts circled the mounted warriors. Ochre yellow slime dripped from claws and fangs, and Azhani had to shrug off a shudder of fear.

"Fire!" she shouted. Bows twanged as arrows flew toward their attackers. Feathered shafts sprouted from demonic bodies and several dropped, gasping out their lives. Out of the corner of her eye, Azhani watched as a mage's fireball caught three of the monsters and turned them into cinders.

"Take 'em down, lads!" she called, and drew her sword. Using only her knees, Azhani drove Kushyra toward the nearest rimerbeast.

Gormerath exploded in a brilliant tongue of fire. When the blade touched the beast, its song went from a jarring buzz to an incredible song of such intensity that Azhani was compelled to match it.

The Banshee's cry echoed around the soldiers.

A ragged cheer followed it as the soldiers went to it with a will.

Azhani fell into a haze of strike, parry, dodge, kill. Kushyra's hooves and legs were soon covered in a miasma of gore. Distantly, the warleader noted the sounds of signal arrows. The high pitched shrill of the specially made missiles told her that the other patrols had also encountered the demons.

Around them, the thick, coppery scent of blood misted the air. The gurgling screams of the dying filled her ears. Unable to spare a moment to mourn her lost soldiers, Azhani pressed on, determined to wipe out every rimerbeast she saw.

There came a break in the battle when she heard the telltale sound of a dying horse. Wheeling Kushyra, Azhani caught a glimpse of Prince Allyndev as he was knocked to the ground.

She wasted no time. Spurring her warhorse, she charged the rimerbeast that loomed over her protégé. Hitting the monster at full speed sent it flying into the mountainside.

"Climb on!" she shouted as she reached for Allyn's hand.

The prince leaped up and settled with his back to hers. The position was awkward, but he was a consummate rider and this would allow him to fight unhindered.

The battles raged on through the night. False dawn sent the remaining rimerbeasts scurrying into caves to wait out the day. Demonic origins made sunlight inimical to rimerbeasts.

Of the men and women Azhani started the night with, all but three horses and one soldier returned to the camp. No one had escaped injury. Field dressings covered gaping wounds and bound broken bones, while healers and stardancers fought to keep those whose injuries were the gravest from dying.

Exhausted but proud of a good night's work, Azhani returned to her tent. The wounds she had sustained were minor by comparison with the others, so she intended to bandage them in private. Small cuts, scrapes and bruises covered the places where her armor had slipped. The worst injury was a long, shallow gash that extended from her hip to her knee on her left leg.

Filling a pot with water, she gathered the supplies necessary to make the repair. Half a candlemark later, she was discovered by Kyrian as she attempted to stitch the wound closed.

"Azhi?" she called out as she entered. "Are you in here? I didn't see you...oh goddess, Azhani, what are you doing?" Making a sound of frustration, she rushed in and knelt next to the warrior. Taking the needle, Kyrian examined the wound and clucked her tongue reproachfully.

Azhani sighed. "It's just a scratch. There were others who needed your care."

Regarding the four-inch long, one-inch deep wound, Kyrian said, "Azhani, this is not a scratch. This is a laceration." She looked up and smiled ruefully. "Did you clean it first?"

"I used some whiskey," she said. She winced when her lover prodded the wound.

Smirking, Kyrian said, "The stuff we got from Kuwell? I'm surprised you didn't scream. It's quite potent." Dwarven-brewed alcohol was fabled far and wide for its dual purposes — it could both get one incredibly intoxicated and clean the worst of wounds to perfect health.

"I was too busy staying awake," Azhani said wryly as Kyrian gently cleaned the injury.

Kyrian chuckled and dusted a layer of herbs over the wound. Azhani hissed as she felt the astringent properties of the medicine begin to draw out the poison from the rimerbeast clawmarks.

Mentally drained, Kyrian eschewed her gift in favor of surgical healing. With quick, neat stitches, she closed the wound while Azhani drifted in a doze.

"All done," she said, some time later.

"Thanks," Azhani said as she stood. They embraced and shared a moment of silent communication.

"I'm glad you're all right," the stardancer finally said.

Azhani nodded. "I have to go and meet with the other patrol leaders. Do you want to come along?"

Kyrian was tired, but she knew that Azhani counted on her support, and today she would need her lover there. The list of the dead was short, but it was still a hard reality that the warleader would face for the first time since leaving Y'Syr.

"Yes, I'll come," Kyrian said. "Let me get a cloak."

*Oh goddess, **twelve** dead, one hundred thirty-six wounded.* Azhani stared numbly down at the tally sheet in her hand. To her right, Kyrian slept quietly. Few others populated the mess tent as the other patrol leaders had gone to bed. Spread on the table was a pile of letters she was writing, one for each of the dead.

The list of casualties struck harder than the blow that had lacerated her leg. Name by name, the warleader called their faces to mind until she could associate some portion of the person with the terse letters that shaped the final moments of their lives. Ink blurred as angry tears filled her eyes. Dashing them away, she hardened her heart against the pain. Twelve had given Y'Myran the ultimate honor so that others could live in peace.

The army would stay in the area for three more days, and then move west. By day, they would search for caves. At night, patrols would circulate and destroy every rimerbeast they found.

Messengers had been sent to Y'Syr to warn the outlying communities that dotted the borderlands. Barton was not the only outkingdom trading post, and Azhani felt that they deserved a chance to flee or fortify against the coming menace. Starseeker Vashyra was off using her magick to send word to Lyssera. The queen needed to know of the night's work.

Last of Azhani's seconds to leave, Padreg had stopped to give what comfort he could to the warleader. The warmth of his hand on her shoulder still lingered, as did the gentle words. *"Grieve later, my friend. Tonight, take your lady and hold her against your heart for tomorrow we will rise and send the bastards back to the abyss."*

Wishing she could heed the Y'Noran's advice, Azhani sighed and turned her attention back to the letters. Later, when they were up to their ears in rimerbeasts, she would not have time to attend personally to honoring each of the dead. For this one moment, she wished to brand these names into her heart.

Dipping her quill into a pot of ink, she began to write. *To the family of Ariana Wintersky: I regret to inform you that your daughter has perished in battle. She gave her life courageously, defending her land from the forces of evil...*

A candlemark later, twelve scrolls lay in a pile in the center of the table. Twelve reminders of the price paid to destroy the demons. Stoically, Azhani drained the dregs of her tea and shook Kyrian.

"Kyrian, love, let's go to bed," she said. Her voice was ragged and raw. A normal occurrence after battle; the banshee cry she was famed for always left her hoarse.

Reluctantly, the stardancer woke. Rubbing sleep from her eyes, she wrapped an arm around her lover and the two women went to rest.

Prince Allyndev groaned softly as Princess Syrelle washed dried blood away from a wound in his shoulder. A careless turn had left him open to attack and a rimerbeast had taken full advantage of that mistake. "That hurts," he hissed.

"Hush! If you hadn't stopped to woolgather, we wouldn't be here!" Syrelle's voice was harsh, and she scrubbed a bit harder than she meant to in her ire. When she had first seen him, she had felt her heart stop at the sight of so much blood. Now he was on the mend, but she was still deep in the clutches of her fear.

"Wasn't woolgathering," Allyn said weakly. "Thought it was dead and—"

"Yes! I know all about it! You've said nothing else for three days,

Allyndev Kelani," Syrelle said bitterly. She packed on a new poultice and rebandaged the wound. The prince had been relegated to bed rest, and it was up to Devon and the princess to keep him from aggravating the injury.

Allyndev was restless. He longed to be out in the field, patrolling with Azhani. It was the fourth day since spotting live rimerbeasts, and the lust for battle was still strong in the young prince.

Finished with the dressing, Syrelle noticed the condition of the young man's hair. Matted and tangled with blood and ichor, she shivered and said, "I'm going to do something about your hair. It's a fright." She laid a gentle hand on his bared shoulder and said, "I'll be back shortly."

"I shall wait, My Lady," Allyn said dreamily. Her touch had driven away all thoughts of pain.

Syrelle stared down at her hand, seemingly dark against the pastiness of Allyn's skin. His color was better today than yesterday, when he had seemed so ghostly that she could see blue lines in his neck. Alternately, she wanted to shake, strangle, kiss and hug him. He was alive, but he was hurt, and that fact drove her to distraction.

"Hail my friends, I have returned!" Devon's voice broke the quiet spell in the tent. Ducking inside, the freshly washed mage tossed his damp robe onto his cot and walked over to kneel beside Syrelle. "How is he?" he asked, gently putting a hand on her knee.

The princess lifted the edge of the bandage and said, "It's a little better today. Look."

Devon tilted his head to see, and nodded. "You're right. It doesn't look as puffy. You were very lucky, my friend." He reached out and ruffled Allyn's hair. When flakes of blood and dirt fell free, the mage pulled his hand away and said, "That's disgusting. You're a mess, Allyn!"

"Enlighten me with new information, if you please?" Allyn growled impatiently. The prince didn't mind being pampered by Syrelle, but it made him feel silly when Devon did it.

"A wee bit irritable, are we?" Devon asked as Syrelle stood and exited the tent.

Allyn sighed. "I'm sorry. I just feel so useless at the moment, Devon."

Devon patted the prince's back lightly. "I understand, my friend. It's hard to rest when you want to work. The stardancers are very busy."

"I know. There are many whose injuries require stronger aid. It would be dishonorable of me to demand the goddess' touch when it is needed elsewhere."

"Nobility becomes you, Allyndev." Azhani's voice floated into the tent. The warleader stepped inside and came to kneel beside the prince's cot.

Allyn snorted derisively. "It's not nobility, it is practicality, Master. My arm is not worth the lives of the soldiers that your lady's magick can save."

"Ah, you are right, it is not nobility — it is self pity. I stand corrected," Azhani said. She stood and looked at Devon, who was massaging the prince's arm. They shared a moment of empathy, and then she said, "When you're done wallowing, Kyrian will see you in the chirurgeon's tent."

Devon was nearly thrown from the cot, Allyn stood so quickly. "I'll attend her immediately," the prince said tightly, as he reached for a clean shirt. Sprinting through the tent flap, he narrowly avoided bumping into Syrelle. The princess was carrying a heavy bucket of hot water.

"Sorry, My Lady," he said, grinning cheekily as he headed toward the tall white pavilion in the center of the camp.

"Allyn—"

"Don't bother trying, Sy," Devon said as he relieved her of her burden. "He's off to see Kyrian."

"But I was going to wash his hair!"

"I'm sure he'll appreciate that, Princess," Azhani said as she joined them. "After he's seen Kyrian."

Devon wrapped an arm around Syrelle and said, "Come on, I'll help you prepare a bath for him."

Kyrian laughed as Allyn, flushed from his run, stripped off his shirt and knelt to present his wounded shoulder to her. "You could have stopped to put shoes on, Allyn."

"I didn't want to keep you waiting, Stardancer," he murmured, as he moved his matted hair out of her way. He was both nervous and excited. Kyrian began to sing and he relaxed and drifted into a hazy place where he felt nothing but peace.

When he awoke, he was once again in his tent with his head suspended over a tub of steaming water. Devon was supporting his head while Syrelle washed his hair. Blinking, Allyn groaned and clenched his left hand. He smiled when there was no pain.

"Nice to see you back among the conscious, my friend," Devon said as he continued to support the prince's head.

"I'm starving," the prince said as he licked his lips. "And thirsty enough to drink that bathwater."

"Here, drink this. It's something Stardancer Kyrian made for you." Syrelle handed him a skin.

Gratefully, Allyn sucked cool, sweet tea from the skin. "Thank you," he said. Setting the skin down, he added, "And thank you for this." He indicated the bath. He knew that he would not be able to wash blood and gore from either of his friends so calmly.

"You are welcome," Syrelle said and Devon nodded his agreement.

When they were done, the mage said, "I'm going to get our dinner."

Allyn sighed. "I can't believe how hungry I am."

"Stardancer Kyrian says that it is typical after a healing." Syrelle motioned for Allyndev to sit so that he could towel his hair dry. He did, and she smiled when he was able to use his arm without any indication of pain.

"It didn't hurt!" he exclaimed. A bright smile blossomed on his face. He flexed his arm and then raised it above his head. "Ow." He winced. "All right, so it mostly does not hurt."

Syrelle nodded. "There are stitches — but those will come out soon." The princess sighed and looked away. "You can patrol tomorrow."

In the process of putting on his tunic, Allyn almost didn't hear the hesitation in her voice. Letting the light blue fabric settle on his shoulders, he said, "Syrelle?" He turned to look at the kneeling princess. "Don't you want me to be better?"

She stood, her face a mask of anger. "Of course I do!" she hissed. "Why would you think otherwise?"

He went to her and put his hands on her shoulders. "Because you are so angry. You didn't sound happy that I would be able to defend Y'Myran tomorrow."

A tiny noise of frustration erupted from her throat and she spun away from him. "I'm perfectly elated that you are healed, Prince Allyndev," she said bitingly. "However, do not mistake my joy in your health for pleasure at the consequences of such health!" Grabbing the bucket of dirty water, she exited the tent.

"Syrelle, wait!" Allyn scrambled to chase after her, but dressed only in a tunic and breechclout, he could not follow her into the rocky wilderness. Confused, he dejectedly returned to the tent.

From his vantage point on the path leading from the mess tent, Devon sighed. The mage wasn't sure which irritated him more — the fact that he was as smitten by Syrelle as Allyn, or that the prince was oblivious to the princess' interest. Either way, it was painful to experience. It was the tiny hope that Syrelle might suddenly decide that he was her true love that kept him from turning his back on the nobles altogether.

Pasting a cheerful smile on his face, he made his way to their tent. "Dinnertime," he sang out enthusiastically as he juggled three bowls of stew.

Allyn relieved him of a bowl and sat on the edge of his bed. Eating mechanically, the prince barely bothered to grunt a thank you.

Is there a way out of this without pain? the mage wondered as he ate.

Chapter Thirty-Five

The army of Y'Dan was on the march. For three months, Arris had waited while his men had cleared cave after cave of demon eggs. Finally, at the beginning of autumn, Porthyros had encouraged him to join them.

The work of egg smashing was foul, but rewarding. Never before had the young king felt as alive as when crushing the shell of one of the demons that had plagued his lands for eons.

Arris was just sitting down to a meal when a soldier burst into his encampment.

"My King! I bring news!" Heading pell-mell for Arris, the young man slid to his knees, bashed his head against the ground and blurted, "I hail thee, Arris Demonslayer, overlord of Y'Dan."

"Speak, man!" Porthyros commanded. The scholar suspected that he knew the content of the soldier's report, but it would do morale good to see that the forms were followed.

"Rimerbeasts attack, Your Majesty! Hundreds of the foul beasts have flanked our eastern divisions."

Arris leaped from his chair. "Wonderful! I mean, terrible, this is terrible news! We must defend our people at once!" Pacing to and fro erratically, the king babbled on about destiny for nearly a quarter candlemark. Suddenly, he stopped, grabbed the messenger and shook him. "More! Tell me more!" There was a wild, fey look to the king's eyes.

Swallowing fearfully, the soldier stammered out the tale he had heard from a half-dead scout. When he was finished, he handed over an ichor-stained, broken swordblade.

Nearly shaking with glee, Arris clutched the sword as though it were magickal. "Rimerbeasts," he whispered. Reverently, he dipped his fingers into the ichor, and then cursed when the fluid burned him.

"Shall I call the squad leaders, Your Majesty?" Porthyros asked. The scholar was pleased. The hatching of the rimerbeasts signaled that the final stage of Kasyrin's plan was in place. *And his royal bratness will shut up about the damn demons.* For weeks, Arris had pestered the scholar with his desire to slay one of the legendary beasts.

"Yes! At once! And make me some more tea — I'm parched!"

Of course you are. It's the last stage of your addiction, you pompous ass! Porthyros bowed and left to do his king's bidding.

The king turned his attention back to the messenger. "I will save you all, boy. Remember that."

"Yes, Your Majesty," the soldier said. He would not disagree with the king. Those who disagreed with the king quickly found themselves as the centerpiece for the nightly Ecarthan rituals.

A piercing scream ricocheted through the night, followed by a loud gong.

Arris smiled and bowed northward. "Ecarthus frees me. My blood is his blood and to him I gladly go," the king chanted brokenly.

The soldier echoed his leader, though his pronouncements weren't quite as fervent as Arris'.

After three weeks, the Y'Syran army left the Ystarfe Pass behind. Three patrols stayed behind to mop up any remaining rimerbeasts while the bulk of the army continued westward.

As the weather changed, so too did Azhani's strategy. No longer were there egg-laden caves to seek. Instead, patrols worked night and day to kill the newly hatched rimerbeasts. By day, they raided the places where the beasts slept, and by night they roved the mountain passes and met them head to head.

Two thousand men and women died in the first month of full combat. Each loss scarred Azhani's heart. Pyre watch was a time of solemn sadness. Every soldier was honored by the pathsong, and no one forgot the gift that had been given to their land. For days following a funeral, all watched in awe as their warleader fought with a fury that seemed almost otherworldly.

Tales of Azhani's prowess spread, invoking a devotion to duty never before seen by the Y'Syran people. Elves who would never have followed a half-elven leader now gave freely of themselves because of the honor that Azhani gave them in her fierceness. There wasn't any among them who would not follow her to the abyss, if she asked it of them.

Over their cups, they told their tales of Azhani's bravery. The warleader was said to have single-handedly held back a wave of rimerbeasts when her entire patrol had gone down. They called her the whirlwind of death, and her cry had sent the demons fleeing into the night. Of the forty soldiers in the unit that night, thirty-eight survived to tell the story. A song was made, and the Banshee was metamorphosed from nightmare to hero.

Given a choice, Azhani would have preferred to let the glory fall to another. Every chance she had, she countered tales of her bravery with depictions of the heroics of others. Soon other songs permeated the camp. Minstrels honored Padreg, Allyndev and even young Devon with tunes of their deeds. There was even a song for the healers, written by the soldiers whose lives were saved by their gentle hands.

Almost everyone took a turn at riding a patrol, but thus far, Kyrian had avoided combat. Instead, she gave tirelessly of her strength to help the chirurgeons. Any free moment she could steal, she gave to her lover. So far, the warleader had not graced the bunks of the chirurgeons, and the stardancer suspected that Gormerath had something to do with it. Whatever it was that kept Azhani safe, Kyrian blessed it, for she did not think that she could handle losing her lover to fang or claw. Their loving was fierce — sometimes painful, but always precious.

Barton was no more.
A thick miasma of death shrouded the once thriving community. Nothing was left intact. Around the town, the ruins of a half-built wall bore the remains of the town's defenders. Scattered fires burned in the rubble of the houses and added a thick, oily smoke to the noxious atmosphere. Nothing moved. The streets were liberally littered with mutilated corpses. Decomposition made it difficult to ascertain which were mortal and which were rimerbeast.

Riding in horrified silence, the army viewed the destruction with sorrow. Tears stained many faces while others looked on in stoic anger.

Uncontrollably shaking, Kyrian led Arun to the center of town. There was an aura of evil that pervaded and turned what was once cheerful into a place of inky darkness. Carefully, the stardancer picked her way through the rubble to stand beside her lover.

Azhani and her seconds were gathered around the remains of a well. Not one face was dry.

Kyrian silently slipped her arm around Azhani's waist. The warleader paused in her quiet conversation to bestow a tight smile to her lover and then drape an arm around her shoulders. "Kyrian," the warleader said.

"Azhani." Kyrian looked at Padreg and the others. "What are we going to do?"

"I was about to assign men to clear and burn. This place stinks," Azhani said while tears continued to trickle down her cheeks.

At the end of town, there was a sudden commotion. Four scouts burst through the soldiers. On a stretcher, they carried a figure garbed in the purple of an Astariun brother. He was covered in gore, and blood spurted in slow arcs from a laceration in his throat.

Kyrian raced to meet them. Her hands were outstretched and limned in the pale yellow fire that was Astariu's gift. The moment she touched him, she began to sing.

The love of Astariu for her people was well known. Best of all, she loved those who sacrificed their lives to her glory. The light of Kyrian's fire suddenly blazed and enveloped both the stardancer and her patient.

When the flames died away, the terrible bleeding had ceased.

Opening his eyes, the man looked out at his rescuers and smiled. "Padreg? Is it truly you?" It was Brother Jalen.

The priest was gently laid in a cot. Another stardancer, along with Starseeker Vashyra, arrived. The priest-mage knelt next to Jalen and began to pray while the two stardancers took up another song. Their voices blended in harmony and golden light limned the prone priest.

Kneeling on the other side of the priest, Padreg took Jalen's hand and squeezed it. "Aye, 'tis me, Jae," he said roughly. The priest's wounds were terrible. Through giant rents in the fabric of his robes, the plainsman could see the pale pink of ravaged bowel and intestine.

"Couldn't stop them," Jalen said softly. Tears wetted his eyes. "They came in and destroyed everything."

A strangled howl came from Azhani and she buried her head in her hands, sobbing brokenly. Paul, Orra, Mattie — they were all dead?

Seeing that his mentor was in pain, and knowing that Kyrian could not stop to help her, Allyn pressed a skin of wine into the warleader's hands. "It's not an answer, but it may help," he murmured.

It was drained in three swallows.

"Sent the children and the noncombatants to Y'Syr three months ago, when the mines were infested with eggs. A few of us stayed behind, to tend the shrine." Jalen coughed and blood flecked his lips. "Damned Ecarthans weren't going to drive *me* from my homeland. I was determined to keep the memory of the Twain alive in Y'Dan."

"Of course, my friend," Padreg soothed. "Rest now; let the stardancers work."

The priest's eyes fluttered shut as sleep overtook him. Kyrian and the other stardancer stumbled back, panting heavily.

"We have done all we can. It's in Astariu's hands now," Kyrian said. Both of the healer-priests were wobbling on their feet from exhaustion.

Azhani stepped behind Kyrian while Allyn moved to support the other priest. The warleader was elated — her friends were alive! She sent a silent prayer of thanks to Astariu.

She and Kyrian clung to each other for a few precious moments and then the warleader passed her exhausted lover into Elisira's capable hands.

"Vashyra, take the mages and cleanse this place. Padreg, I want patrols of no less than fifteen soldiers each scouting the terrain within three miles of Barton. Allyn, take two squads and find a place for the army to camp."

"What can I do?" Syrelle asked. The Y'Maran princess was a fair shot with a bow, and had donned a light coat of leather for the ride toward the trade town.

"Find a place for central camp. We need an area for chirurgeons, the mess tents, my pavilion. Do you think you can manage this task?"

"Of course, Warleader," Syrelle said. She began pointing to several soldiers, who immediately stepped up to follow her.

"What about the shrine?" a scout said. "It's intact, upwind and has a functioning well."

"Go and inspect it," Azhani ordered, and Syrelle nodded.

Everyone scattered, leaving Azhani to begin the arduous task of searching for survivors.

Magickal energies rippled above the ruins that had once been the town of Barton. The combined forces of mage, priest and mundane manpower worked long into the night to clear away the devastation.

The glow of fires dotted the forest and hills. The soldiers who were not terribly superstitious took up residence in the newly cleansed town. At the far end of town, a bonfire burned. Those priests not needed to perform the cleansing chants knelt in prayer, singing the pathsong for the citizens who had given their lives to defend their homes.

Under the rubble, many things were found. Useful objects — furniture, clothing, linens — all were absorbed by the war machine that was Azhani's army. A large cache of food was found in the cellar of what was once the Barton Inn.

Aside from the priest, the only other living beings discovered among the wreckage were a gaunt, near-dead female hunting cat and her litter of kits. The animals were coaxed out of their hiding place and given over to a small platoon of men and women who volunteered to look after them.

The animals were a gift, for once the mother was healthy, she would be a welcome addition to the corps of hunters whose job it was to provide meat for the army's stew pots. Trained to hunt with a two legged partner, the massive felines could easily bring down a deer. The cats came from a long lineage of companion animals that had been brought to Y'Myran by the Firstlanders.

Strong, agile, and incredibly smart, Azhani knew that the kits would be a hotly contested prize among her hunters. But, it was the animals themselves who would choose the ones with whom they would bond.

The first cat to choose a human was the mother. Strangely, she did not gravitate toward a hunter, or even a soldier. Instead, she chose to shadow the footsteps of the young mage, Devon. He named her "Avisha" which meant "miracle" in the Firstlander tongue, and was charmed by her loving attention.

After two days of recovery, Avisha left camp and returned, dragging the carcass of a wild boar. All but one of her kits had gravitated toward other hunters, and each had mild to moderate success at hunting them. The remaining kit moved from fire to fire, never staying with one person for more than a night.

Because of this behavior, she was named, "Zhadosh" or "ghost."

Azhani rubbed the bridge of her nose and groaned. The area around Barton was rife with rimerbeasts. She longed to escape her duties and check on her home, but she feared what she would find. Instead, she sent Padreg to scour the southern quarter.

Earlier, Starseeker Vashyra had received word from Queen Lyssera. While the army battled rimerbeasts in the north, the combined forces of the Y'Syran navy and some vessels from Y'Nor and Y'Mar were waging a battle against an enemy fleet. Dark ships sailed by Ecarthan priests had attempted to take Y'Syria but the attack had been repulsed. Stalemate now existed. The Ecarthans could not take the city, but neither could the queen's forces defeat the priests.

In Y'Nor, black-robed priests were attacking the clans and preventing them from sending reinforcements northward. The other kingdoms still suffered from the depredations of various monsters, and no one had heard from High King Ysradan in weeks.

If he's dead, it's going to send the kingdoms into complete chaos, Azhani thought. She was already weary of battle, and she knew her future held nothing but conflict.

There was one bit of good news. Ambassador Kuwell and his men had cleared the Y'Droran mines of all traces of rimerbeasts. He and his men were marching west, and hoped to join her shortly.

Knowing that the dwarves were at her back allowed Azhani to breathe easier. But a final piece of news had been the last straw that set off her headache.

Arris was coming.

The Y'Dani king and his army were in the western ranges, cutting a jagged swath eastward. If she did not change her plans, their forces would meet somewhere in the mountains north of Ynnych. The thought was enough to make her stomach roil.

A cup of warm tea was offered to her.

Looking up, Azhani spied the smiling face of her lover and sighed. Taking the tea, she drank and said, "Thank you."

The stardancer sat next to Azhani. "You're welcome. I thought that you might need it."

Brother Jalen watched the people around him with a smile on his face.

He was still quite pale, but on the mend. "I am glad that the goddess brought you this way, Azhani," he said.

"As am I, Brother Jae," the warleader said. She looked behind the priest at the shrine that he had built. "You've done a beautiful job here."

He smiled, pleased with the compliment. "It lacked only for a pair of dedicated hands."

The interior of the temple had been graced with an altar that held two intricately carved statues. The twin gods, Astariu and Astarus, held a bowl of rock crystal from which water flowed in an ingenious waterfall. Fragrant incense burned in tiny cups and there was an oil lamp that hung from the ceiling.

Spread outward from the altar were bedrolls filled with a variety of priests and mages in the various stages of sleep. Flashes of saffron, azure and crimson fabric peeked out from under dark woolen blankets and Azhani could hear the sounds of heavy snoring.

Azhani watched as Syrelle took a bowl of stew to Allyn and then the two sat on a log to chat while they ate. Devon found a chair and took his meal nearby while Avisha lazed at his feet.

Syrelle reached out to wipe a bit of food from Allyn's face and Azhani smiled. *They're going to shake a few people up when they finally figure out their relationship,* Azhani thought smugly.

"Are you hungry, Azhani?" Kyrian asked as she stood to get her dinner.

Azhani nodded. "I'll get it. You rest, my love." The stardancer was still drained from healing Jalen.

"Gladly," Kyrian said as she returned to her seat tiredly.

After the meal, Devon wandered off to sleep while Allyn and Syrelle went to listen to a bard perform at another fire. Azhani and Kyrian busied themselves with repairs while Padreg and Elisira listened to Brother Jalen regale the group with tales of his adventures.

Kyrian wiped tears of laughter from her face. "I can't believe you snuck into the king of Y'Tol's *private cellar!*"

Jalen smiled beatifically. "I did not sneak, my dear. I was invited. He offered me a reward, and I chose to take it in three bottles of a fine vintage."

Padreg shook his head ruefully. "Remind me to hand over the keys to my cellar the next time Jae visits, will you my love?"

"Paddy, you don't have a cellar," Jalen said. "Besides, I'm not fond of ale, or mead."

The plainsman shrugged, holding out his hands as if to say, "Your loss."

The priest smiled. "So, Paddy, when is the wedding?"

"Midwinter, wasn't it?" Azhani asked pointedly.

Padreg smiled ruefully and Elisira said, "We had thought to have it then, but we have decided to wait until we have returned to Y'Nor."

"We do not wish to sully a day that should be filled with joy with the blood of war," the Y'Noran monarch added. He turned to look at Azhani and Kyrian. "What of you ladies? Will you stand before the goddess and pledge your lives together?"

Caught with a needle in her teeth, Kyrian shot a glance at Azhani, who licked her lips thoughtfully. The stardancer took the needle from her mouth and said, "I think that it is wonderful that you two have made that decision. I hope to be there on that day." With her gaze still on her lover, she added, "But I do not know if Azhani and I are ready to make that commitment."

The warleader put her gorget aside. "I am ready," she said softly. She smiled at Kyrian's startled expression. "I was ready the night I came to you." She reached out and took Kyrian's hand in hers. "My friends," she turned to look at Elisira and Padreg, "I wish that your day of bonding be as special as you are."

"Thank you," they murmured.

The warleader then rose from her seat and knelt before Kyrian. For long moments, nothing was said as the lovers stared into one another's eyes. Finally, Azhani brought Kyrian's hand to her lips, pressed several soft kisses into the palm and then cupped it against her heart.

"My beloved, not a day passes when I do not thank the gods for your presence. When darkness covered my soul, you soothed the hurts of my body and heart. I needed a friend, and you were there. It was your constant faith that called me back from the abyss and gave me the will to live again. Now you are my love — the friend of my heart, the song in my soul and the light in my life. I cannot name all that you are to me, for you are so much more than words can convey.

"I only know that there would be no greater gift, no greater honor that could come to me than to stand before the gods on winter's solstice and claim you as my wife. Kyrian, will you share my life and claim the right to cherish our love as long as the stars shall spin in the heavens?"

It began to rain.

Kyrian fell into Azhani's arms and covered her with kisses.

Looking up at the warleader, the stardancer said, "I have no words, my love." She leaned her forehead against Azhani's. "Everything and the universe; that's what I see when I look into your eyes, Azhani." She drew back and lifted her face toward the sky. Closing her eyes, she said, "I've never met anyone who could make me forget the rain." She nuzzled the warrior's chin. "But here, in the circle of your arms, the sun always shines."

They kissed.

"Yes, I will marry you," Kyrian said as they parted. They stood and went to their tent.

Padreg surreptitiously brushed tears from his eyes as he watched his friends depart.

Elisira leaned over and whispered, "That was a beautiful proposal. I doubt that you could best such lovely words. Though if you could, I'd eat my boot."

A gleam of something wicked sparkled in the Y'Noran's eyes and he whispered back, "Have you acquired a taste for old leather, My Lady?"

Startled, Elisira replied, "Nay, but—"

"An unwise wager made in haste will flatten a pouch quickly," he advised smugly, and wriggled his eyebrows.

She playfully shoved him and said, "Do you truly believe that you can outdo such eloquence?"

Shrugging, Padreg said, "Of a sureness, My Lady. T'would be of light labor."

Archly, Elisira asked, "Truly, My Lord?"

A wide grin spread across Padreg's face as he slid to his knees. "Of a certainty." Taking her hand in his, he brushed his lips over her knuckles and said, "My beautiful Elisira, in the first moment that I saw you, I knew that you were special. You spoke with educated grace and your words had more than merit — they had sense. Astride an uncommon horse, you rode with the poise of one born to the hoof. Your beauty outshone the brightest bird in Arris' unfriendly flock and when you smiled, blessed Astariu, I was truly lost!" A shy, almost wondering smile transformed his rough-hewn face. "I had to travel across the kingdoms to find you, but when I did, I knew the journey was worth the ride. It would please me, My Lady, if you would consent to wed."

Elisira's eyes glistened in the firelight. Placing her hand against Padreg's cheek, she said, "Glad I am that you did not take my wager, for I would have lost." Leaning in, she kissed him softly. "Yes, My Lord. I shall wed thee."

The Y'Noran's answering smile was nearly as bright as the noonday sun.

Good news breeds gossip, and within days of Azhani's proposal, everyone knew that their warleader was going to be married. That Clan-chief Padreg had also knelt to claim his lady only enhanced the telling of the tale. Soon, talk around the fires included varying themes on the cursed rain, the bloody rimerbeasts and the blessed events. Harvest came and went almost unnoticed as night after night, Azhani's army met and destroyed the ice demons.

Early one morning, the peace of camp was shattered by a mass tele-portation of supplies and reinforcements. For candlemarks, group after group of mage and starseeker pairs held open a rift between the mountain-side encampment and the elven supply depot in Y'Syr.

The reinforcements were particularly welcomed, for it meant that those whose injuries were too severe to recover from could be sent home. Azhani gave the new recruits a week to settle in and learn the routine before she sent them out to face the nightly horror of rimerbeast attacks.

Word trickled north of rimerbeast incursions into the outlying villages of Y'Syr and Y'Dan. Each attack left Azhani cursing bitterly at the twisted fate that had taken her from her role as Y'Dan's warleader.

Winter swept in on the wings of a bitter snowstorm. Frostbite was now as much of an enemy as the rimerbeasts. Azhani was grateful that she had kept the main body of her army quartered in and around the ruins of Barton, for the soldiers had been able to create stronger shelter against the weather.

Late one morning after a long patrol, Azhani and her lieutenants were gathered in their headquarters. All present were weary, but her scouts had just returned, and she wanted to hear their news while it was still fresh in their minds.

Tal Gwyeth, the leader of the elven scouts, stood and bowed. "Greet-ings. I know that we are all tired, so I will make this brief." Walking over to a map, he pointed to a valley three days westward. "This was the furthest point of our last mission. There are no more egg-filled caves; all that are left are the broken shells of hatched rimerbeasts."

There was a murmur and many nodding heads around the room.

"Here, here and here," he tapped the map at points near the coast and slightly further inland, "King Arris and the Y'Dani army have engaged the demons." The scout made a face. "Though they managed to drive the demons back into the mountains, Arris' tactics are unsound and will eventually cost the lives of his entire army. He wastes his soldiers without regard for their safety. Without reinforcements, he will be overrun in a month."

"Thank you, Tal," Azhani said. She stood as he resumed his seat. "The rimerbeasts will go south next. Y'Dan will fall to their hunger quickly. From there, they can move into Y'Syr, Y'Mar and Y'Nor."

The group erupted into a flurry of hurled questions and suggestions of action. Azhani listened with half an ear. She was still bemused by the idea of Arris actively fighting the rimerbeasts. The warleader remembered the king as a pale, weak youth unable to lift a shortsword, much less lead an army.

He's trying to defend his kingdom, she thought. It was crazy — the mad king who had given his people to Ecarthus was out in the snow, throwing the lives of his soldiers away in a bid to defend his land.

Back in Y'Syr, before they had gone north, when Arris had offered to join forces with Queen Lyssera, both Azhani and the queen had felt that it was nothing more than a ploy to leave Y'Syr undefended. *Was I wrong? Does Arris have enough honor to stand against the threat? Or is this just another trap — a clever construction of smoke and mirrors to capture me for the king's amusement?* The whirl of thought churned round and round in her head until one idea boiled clear. *Y'Dan is in danger. Arris will fall, and there will be no one left to save the people. Trap or not, I must not abandon my oaths.*

"Go back to your units and choose three of every ten men. In two weeks, we will ride to save the king." If any were surprised by the warleader's orders, no one voiced it.

"**I wish to** go with, when you go to rescue Arris," Kyrian said as they exited the command quarters.

Azhani stopped and gave her lover a searching glance. "Kyr, you've yet to see combat. Why expose yourself now?"

"Because you'll need me," the stardancer replied with such conviction, Azhani wondered if she were prophetic.

"What if you're attacked?" She tried to sway her lover's decision.

Kyrian squared her shoulders. "I will do all that I can to stay out of the fight, but I will be there, where you can find me, when you need me."

Azhani closed her eyes. "I always need you," she whispered.

"Then I am here," Kyrian replied and opened her arms to her lover. "I will always be here, Azhani. It is my promise to you."

Devon and his cat, Avisha raced across the camp. They were late, and their patrol was leaving soon. This would be the last night that Azhani would lead them. Tomorrow, the warleader was going to take a hand-picked platoon and head west to rescue the Y'Dani army, which was being decimated by rimerbeasts.

A flash of red hair caught his attention. Stopping, he peered into the shadows between two tents. Avisha paused beside him and sat, waiting for her partner. Partially illuminated by torchlight, Syrelle and Allyndev were engaged in a soft conversation.

Guiltily, Devon crept closer to hear them.

"Be careful," Syrelle said as she buckled Allyn's sword belt tightly. "I don't want you to get hurt again."

Allyn captured the princess' hands and brought them up to his lips, brushing a gentle kiss over her knuckles. "I will be chary of my health, My Lady, I swear."

The princess pulled her hand away. "I don't need oaths, Allyndev. I just want you..." She paused to look down and then whispered, "I just want you to come back."

"Sy—"

Devon's heart caught at the note in his friend's voice. Allyn had finally realized how the princess felt.

"Kiss me, Allyndev," Syrelle said in a soft voice of command.

The young mage felt his world shatter around him. He tried to turn, but could not look away. With tears streaming down his face, he watched as his best friend kissed the woman he loved. Angrily, he dashed away the signs of his grief and ran to where the horses were picketed. His heart hammered in his chest, yet it was not the pain he expected to feel. Rather than the void he had feared, all he felt was a deep sorrow over what never would be.

He loved Syrelle, but he could not begrudge Allyn his happiness. Smirking mirthlessly, he thought, *Maybe I'm just daft.* He found a horse marked with the saffron of a mage-trained animal and mounted. Closing his eyes, he began the calming exercises that would ready his mind for manipulating magick.

Besides, it's not like I'll never love again. Just look at Azhani. She loved Ylera so much, and yet...even her heart opened again. Feeling a false calm settle over him, he opened his eyes. Not far away, the warleader was kissing her betrothed goodbye.

"Hey, don't leave without me!"

Devon turned and saw Allyn jogging toward the horses. Shaking his head, the mage grabbed the reins to the prince's mount and asked, "Why would we do that? We'd be forever lost without your heroic magnificence."

"Funny, sparkle fingers. Real funny," Allyn retorted as he leaped onto the horse's back.

"Syrelle's waving," the mage said.

Allyn turned to return the princess' wave. A soft grin had washed over his face. "She...uh," the prince flushed, "she kissed me."

Devon gritted his teeth. "Congratulations."

Allyndev shot his friend a curious look. The mage's tone had been anything but congratulatory.

Azhani's sharp whistle cut off any response he might have had. "All right, lads and ladies, listen up. The weather watchers have said that tonight is going to be a bad one, so be on your guard. The colder, the deader isn't just a joke during beast season. The demons will be out in force." Her fierce gaze caught the eye of each of her soldiers. "Are you ready to give your lives to your kingdoms?"

"We serve for the honor of our queen!" the group shouted.

"Let's ride," Azhani said commandingly.

Heading north, they didn't have to travel long before the eerie howling of a pack of rimerbeasts raised the hair on everyone's necks. "Look sharp now," Azhani said as they slowed to a walk.

Allyn scanned the sides of the trail, searching for any hint that a demon was lurking in the bushes. Twin arcs of energy lit up the night behind him and he wheeled the horse around, ready to face whatever had caused Devon to fire off his spell.

Rimerbeasts leaped from the bushes and surrounded the patrol. The Banshee's cry split the night. Tearing his sword from its scabbard, Allyn shouted, "For Y'Syr!" and charged the pack of monsters.

Chanting at the top of his lungs, Devon fired two more lightning bolts. The mage energies unerringly hit their targets. Beside him, a mage named Jasyn was tossing fireballs at the demons. The bushes exploded and a demon leaped out, knocking Jasyn from his mount.

The mage and the monster tumbled several feet away. Jasyn tried to scramble free, but was trapped by the beast's weight. "Help!" he shouted.

The rimerbeast rose and drove its claws deep into the mage's shoulders, pinning him to the ground.

Devon spun at his friend's cry. "No!" he cried and spun to aide the other mage.

Forgetting the battle around him, Devon grabbed his sling, chanted a quick spell and let fly. The bespelled missiles flew and connected with the rimerbeast pinning Jasyn. Each hit, and with a soft pop, caused a massive explosion. The demon toppled over.

Sliding to kneel beside his friend, Devon frantically began to try and pull the dead rimerbeast's claws from Jasyn's shoulders.

"Dev," Jasyn said, choking on blood.

Devon looked up in time to see a pack of three demons converging on them.

"Run," Jasyn said. "Save yourself."

"No," Devon said. "I won't leave you. Allyndev!" he shouted.

The prince turned at his friend's yell and drove his knees into his horse's sides.

The rimerbeasts continued to advance on Devon. The mage stood and magickal energy crackled from his fingers. He knew he was staring death in the eye. *Hurry, Allyn.* He let fly with a lightning bolt and was satisfied to see one of the demons fall, its neck a smoking ruin where the head used to be.

The other two roared and charged him.

Oh, shyvot! He met them halfway.

An inhuman scream of rage filled the clearing and Avisha pounced on one of the demons, biting and clawing at it with an unholy ferocity. Devon had time to draw his sword and swing it once before the rimerbeast was upon him. He screamed in pain as the beast's jaws closed around his leg.

"Devon!" Allyn screamed as he watched the beast pick up his friend and shake him like a dog shakes a rodent. A sick tearing sound preceded the mage's body as it flew across the clearing. "Die!" Allyn shouted as he leaped from his horse's back.

The prince landed on the demon's back and drove his sword into the beast's neck with both hands. Feebly, it roared once and fell. Jumping free, Allyn raced to Devon's side. The mage's leg was a ruined mess of bone and flesh.

Ripping off his belt, the prince babbled, "Don't you die on me, you damn sparkle-fingered brat!" He pulled the belt tight around Devon's mangled leg and then scooped the unconscious mage up and carried him to his horse.

Another soldier was tending to Jasyn. The rimerbeasts were all dead. The hunting cat, Avisha, was still hissing and tearing at the demon she had killed.

Devon came to lying on a travois. Overhead, the stars spun and danced in a bright haze of speckled lights. His leg throbbed dully, and his foot itched madly. A breeze blew across his face and he shivered. He tried to speak the words of a warming spell, but the phrases lingered just out of reach. The stretcher began to move. He heard the gentle strains of a star-dancer's song and gave in to the lassitude stealing over his body.

Chapter Thirty-Six

Blood and bones! These things just won't die! Arris panted as he drove off another rimerbeast. He evaded a paw full of wickedly gleaming claws and returned the strike with a vicious slash of his blade, cutting off a chunk of flesh and fur. Cackling madly, he spurred his horse to chase the monster down and then skewered it over and over again. The beast collapsed, emitting an eerie moan before dying.

"Did you see that, Porthyros?" he called out excitedly, and then stopped and stamped his foot angrily. The scholar was still gone. No one had seen him since he had vanished from the king's encampment two days prior. Rage-tainted fear throbbed in his chest. Ire forced him to curse his oldest friend. "Damn you, 'Thyro! Why did you have to abandon me when I needed you the most?"

Because you're a murderer, son. The voice sounded uncannily like his father's.

"What, who said that?" Arris turn about seeking the speaker.

There was no response. Shaking his head, the king wheeled his horse and searched the battlefield for another demon to kill. A brief lull settled over the clearing. In the distance, he could hear the sounds of combat, but all was quiet around him. Arris rubbed his eyes wearily and then wiped the caustic blood from his blade.

Killing was tiring work; more exhausting than his instructor had ever made it seem. Washing his mouth out with some water, he then drained the skin. The liquid was warm and tasted heavily of minerals. He missed the tea that Porthyros used to make just for him. Arris experienced a wave of longing for his friend. The scholar had left without even saying goodbye.

No one wants to be around a murderer, Arris. Another voice filled his mind, only this one sounded a lot like Ambassador Kelani. Arris grabbed his head.

Without the calming influence of the special tea, he heard horrible voices in his head. Arris had attempted to replicate his mentor's recipe, but no amount of honey and cinnamon had come close to the spicy sweetness that the scholar could imbue into a simple blend of herbs.

Slinging the skin around his saddle horn, Arris kicked his horse, Tyrre, into action and rode off to find another fight. Blood would drive away the voices. Drowning himself in the fever and haze of the kill would keep them at bay for a little while longer.

Killer, the voices accused. *Killed me, killed her, killed us. You're just a murdering bastard, Arris Thodan.*

"I'm no bastard," he growled from behind gritted teeth. "I have a father."

I should have strangled you in your sleep, boy.

"But you didn't and now I'm king, father!"

A passing soldier stopped and bowed. "My King, can I help you?"

"No! Go kill some rimerbeasts, you blundering dolt!"

"Sir!" The soldier saluted and ran off.

Arris giggled madly. "See father, they obey me, now!"

Oh child. They obey a madman. See what you have done, my son?

The snow drenched forest vanished from Arris' sight, to be replaced with a memory.

He stood in a room at Y'Dannoch. Splayed at his feet was a naked woman. Her shallow breathing was interspersed with sobs of terrible pain. In his hand was a knife. The blade dripped with her blood. He could feel the rush of power that was cresting through him. He had caused this misery. The dagger clattered to the floor as he knelt next to the weeping woman.

"You can make it stop, Ylera. Sign the document. Prove to the kingdoms that Azhani is a traitor, and I promise to leave you be." He tried to sound convincing, filling his voice with pity, just as Porthyros had instructed him. He felt nothing but exhilaration, though.

"Die in the abyss," she spat weakly.

"You first," he retorted, and punched her hard enough to knock several teeth free.

She cried out and he laughed. She would die shortly. Porthyros could fake her signature and then Arris would take the bitch Azhani Rhu'len and make her beg to be his wife!

"No," Arris whispered, refusing to believe in the awful image. It was not the first time he had suffered such a terrible vision. Once before, he had been caught in a memory. Then, he had seen himself deliver a cup of poison to his father night after night until the king had died of a mysterious disease that none could cure.

Porthyros had assured him that the visions were nothing more than an evil spell sent by Azhani's elven friends to wreak havoc and force him to allow the nonhuman scum back into his pristine kingdom.

This is no spell, Arris. This is truth. It is your memories that you see, not the weavings of a mage bent on your destruction. His father's voice was terribly insistent.

"Oh gods, no."

Yes. Ylera Kelani's musical voice was a shriek of anguish that ripped the king's heart into shreds.

The boy king started to shake uncontrollably. "No!"

::Yes. It is as thou hast seen, boy king. Now, go and kill for me, for thou art mine!::

Mine...mine...mine... The words echoed in the king's ears. That voice could only belong to Ecarthus Soul-Eater. No other being could speak and cause pain with just a whisper.

"What have I done?" Tears brushed his cheeks.

It was all real. The waking nightmare that had followed him since Porthyros' abrupt departure was no dream, but the reality of his memory. Bile rose in Arris' throat and he spewed into the bushes. Shaking, he wiped his mouth and took up Tyrre's reins.

::Kill for me:: the demons' voice had commanded. Steely determination filled the boy king's eyes. He had been a pawn, he could see that now. So be it. Pawns could be powerful, if sacrificed properly.

Driving the horse toward a knot of soldiers, he yelled, "To me!"

A new wave of rimerbeasts poured into the small valley and Arris led his men toward them. With each death, he prayed that the voices in his head would be silenced.

The routine of slash, slice, dodge and run allowed the king some peace. This was what being a king was like. To stand before chaos and keep it from destroying his land was what he had been born to do — Arris was quickly realizing this. The truth that the voices revealed burned away the last of his fog and with a clarity he had never before had, Arris realized that he had failed his people.

No longer. Father, I will make you proud.

Knowing that all of his visions — the one of him delivering the fatal cup of tea to his father — the one of him killing Ambassador Kelani — even the one of him ordering Azhani Rhu'len tried for treason — were true, Arris did the one thing he knew was right. He fought. The young king drove his soldiers all night, killing wave after wave of rimerbeasts.

Ah gods, 'Thyro. You shouldn't have gone. I can't stand this hole in my head.

A horn sounded and hope flared with incandescent brightness in the king's chest. Was it Porthyros? Had he returned with reinforcements? Perhaps it had all been a bad dream. Arris grabbed on to that thought and held it tight. Turning to greet his friend, he nearly fell off his horse at the sight of who awaited him.

It was not Porthyros Omal who came to his rescue. Illuminated by magelight, Azhani Rhu'len appeared, leading an army composed of Y'Syran, Y'Noran and Y'Droran soldiers. Their banners snapped in the wind raised by the thundering of hooves along the snow. Proudly seated atop a beautiful warhorse, garbed in the traditional armor of the elven kingdom's warleader, Azhani Rhu'len, the woman he had banished — the woman whom he had framed for an innocent's murder — spared him one brief, hate-filled glance. Judgment on a horse's back had just arrived in Arris' valley.

A sense of surreality settled over Arris as he watched the warleader confidently lead her people into the thick of the rimerbeasts.

"The wounded!" he suddenly cried. "Get them out of there!"

A lieutenant heard the king's cry and raced to obey.

It began to snow. Soon, the field was slippery, and staying mounted was nearly impossible. Endlessly, the rimerbeasts charged on, pouring out of the mountains, seeming to rise up from the stone itself. The screams of the dead and dying echoed around Arris, yet he stayed still, letting the battle wash around him.

Suddenly, Tyrre went down, his throat torn out by crimson-coated claws. Time slammed into the king in a rush, snapping the sense of shocked lethargy away and replacing it with raw anger. Rolling away from the falling horse, Arris shouted in rage and charged the demon, hacking it to bits.

His vision blurred, but he continued to fight on, his sword flickering in the moonlight. Death raced beside him as he blindly carved his way through demon after demon, until he was fighting at the side of the woman he both loved and hated. He looked at her and saw nothing but determination on her dusky face. She was beautiful, terrible and everything he had dreamed. Since the moment he fell in love with her, this was the Azhani that had fueled Arris' nighttime passions.

She ignored him.

He wanted to speak, to say the words that puddled in his throat and begged to drown his tongue, but his voice had left him. What could he say? How could he defend his actions? What excuses would cause her to forgive him for stealing her life, her love and her honor?

I'm sorry. I had to do it. I had to kill your beloved and strip you of your title so that you would love only me? It was insane. She would never hear the truth behind the words, only the hurt that they had caused. He laughed brokenly.

Was he crazy? Arris couldn't grasp reality anymore. It shivered and fled his touch like a wild bird flees the falconer's jess. Without the calmative tea, he was only half there.

That cursed tea! As a child, he had refused to drink it. Porthyros had encouraged him to try it by showing the impressionable young prince how the sweet liquid brought an amazing sense of calm self discipline. Under the influence of the tea, Arris had been able to stand before his great father and not feel like a complete failure.

What was in that tea, anyway? he wondered idly. Memories bubbled up of Porthyros handing him a packet and telling him to put it into his father's wine.

Arris had tasted the grayish powder and choked. There was something so familiar about it and yet, not. Then, he had ignored it. Later, when he was king, he had asked the scholar about it.

"It was krile dust, My King," the scholar replied calmly.

"Krile? But that's poison!"

"Of course it is, My Liege. How else could you have removed such a terrible threat as Thodan the Weak?" Porthyros handed the king his tea. Out of long habit, the young man drank. The scholar continued, *"Really, Your Majesty, you saved the kingdom."*

"I did?" the king asked blearily as the tea began to take effect.

"You will be remembered for all time for your great deeds, Your Majesty."

Krile. The poison so toxic it was outlawed in all seven kingdoms. That was what he had given his father. How fitting that Porthyros had been serving it to Arris since boyhood.

I'm going to die, Arris thought calmly. It was a certainty that those addicted to krile always died horribly. *So be it. If I am to die, then it will be by my choice.*

He took one last look at the woman who had haunted his dreams forever. Cold, dark eyes met his, boring deep into him and daring him to threaten her. The boy king only smiled and saluted the warleader with his sword then turned away and slashed at another rimerbeast.

In the morning, he would deal with the arrival of Azhani Rhu'len.

Dawn's gray light touched the mix of snow, blood and gore and sent the rimerbeasts scurrying for their caves. Nearly dropping where she stood, Azhani surveyed the battlefield. A full day of riding and then fighting all night had left her drained.

Standing no more than six feet away was King Arris. He too looked exhausted. Leaning on his sword and panting with exertion, he glanced up at her and spat. Blood trickled from a scalp laceration, staining half his face in red.

"Oath-breaker," he croaked. It might have been a taunt, but it sounded more like a plea.

"We're not on Y'Dani soil," Azhani sneered weakly. "So you may take your false accusations and plant them in a privy! You're lucky I haven't got the strength to rip your intestines out and feed them to the crows."

He shook his head. "I have no more quarrels with you, Azhani. I—" He wiped his face and looked down at it. "So much blood. There's so much. Gods, how can there be so much blood?" The king broke, tortured sobs tearing out of him and wracking his entire body.

Azhani watched him, pity and hatred wrestling within her.

Kyrian walked over and handed Azhani a cup of warm tea. The star-dancer's robe was covered in gore. Her eyes held a level of weariness that the warleader had never seen before.

I should have made her stay in Barton. She should be with Devon, not here, among all this death.

Kyrian looked over at the weeping king and said, "He's hurt. Should I—"

"Leave him," Azhani said coldly. "He's not worth your time." She turned away and sipped at her drink, watching as the sun's first rays painted the horizon in pale amber hues.

Kyrian couldn't just let the man sob. Her heart broke each time Arris cried out, and she started walking toward him to try and offer some comfort.

Through his tears, Arris could see the crimson robed priest come for him. She was red — like blood — blood, the thick, coppery fluid that stained his hands and painted the altars of Ecarthus' unholy temples. He shrank back, quavering in fear. Those memories — the shockingly vivid images of the carnage that took place during the ceremonies of worship, made him whimper brokenly.

The rising sun glimmered off the silver Astariun token on Kyrian's chest, catching Arris' attention. *Goddess. Good. Astariu, blessed lady of life and healing.* The chants of childhood echoed in the king's mind, and broke through his terror.

He started to stagger toward her, intent on falling at her feet to beg for forgiveness. Out of the corner of his eye, he saw a massive, gray-furred figure leap from the bushes.

"No!" he shouted. From a place deep within him, he called upon the last dregs of his energy. Raising his sword, he pulled the stardancer behind him.

The rimerbeast hit Arris at full speed. Its skin popped and bubbled as the sun's light ate into the demonic flesh. Ignoring the acidic ooze that rapidly coated him, the king tried to push the beast off. Kyrian was trapped beneath him, and she struggled to get free.

The rimerbeast managed to bring a leg up between them and kick downward. Razor sharp claws ripped into Arris' chest and gut. Blood filled his mouth as he screamed in agony. The beast roared and tried to bat at the stardancer beneath him.

"No!" he gasped. "There will be no more blood on my hands!" Thrusting his sword upward, Arris pushed the blade through the demon's ribs and into its heart. It shuddered once, and then died.

Kyrian finally freed herself and Arris rolled his head up in time to see her scramble away. "It's...done," he wheezed, and then passed out.

Arris awoke to the sound of singing. Blinking open his eyes, he saw that the red-robed priest was kneeling over him, her hands hovering inches above his abdomen. An aura of a bright, almost painful shade of yellow limned her hands and she was chanting. The moment her hands touched him, pain unlike any he had experienced lanced through him.

"Oh gods, stop, please!" he begged as tears flowed from his eyes. The priest ceased her actions, confusion clearly marking her face. The stardancer's touch had wounded him to his very soul. The taint of Ecarthus had prevented the Astariun-born healing.

Kyrian looked up at Azhani and said, "I don't understand. I can't heal him."

Azhani stared at her lover helplessly.

"I," Arris spoke slowly, pain lacing his words. "I belong to Ecarthus now," he whispered bitterly. "The goddess cannot touch my soul. Ah gods, what have I done?" he cried. With the revelations of the past day still fresh in his mind, he looked over at Azhani. Her eyes were hard, unreadable and he sighed heavily. "You hate me. I don't blame you. I would—" he coughed and blood erupted from his mouth. "I would ask you to forgive me, but it's too late. Just...promise me, Warleader. Promise me that you'll save them. Save my kingdom, Azhani Rhu'len, I revoke the oath-breaking and call you once again, Y'Dan's warleader."

Spotting his squire, Arris lifted his head and weakly shouted. "Hear that? You're hers now, boy! All of you! Hers! I command it. Follow Azhani. She is the warleader now." He fell back, displacing a drift of crimson stained snow.

"Yes, My King!" the boy smartly saluted and ran off to tell the remaining generals.

Arris coughed, wincing at the pain in his stomach. "Damn that Porthyros to the lowest hell! I would gladly welcome his cursed tea now!"

Azhani offered him hers, but he only spat it out.

"Gah, too bitter." His eyes glazed as he stared up at the gray sky. Light snow drifted down, coating his lashes. He closed his eyes and sighed. "I can feel Ecarthus, you know," he said, his voice deepening. Arris' eyes popped open and he stared up at Kyrian, the intensity of his gaze causing her to shiver. "He's eating my soul," he whispered. He smiled beatifically. "I wonder...what it will be like..." As his voice faded off, he took one, shuddering breath and then went limp.

Sadly, Kyrian looked down at the dead king, covered him with his cloak and said, "He might have been a monster, but he saved my life."

Mixed emotions roiling in her eyes, Azhani whispered, "I know." She stood and walked away, heading toward the Y'Dani army.

"I hope you find your peace, Arris of Y'Dan," Kyrian whispered, as she stroked the fine black hair off his face. She moved to stand, but stopped when something caught her attention. Lowering herself to her knees once more, she lifted his hand and curiously inspected it.

The king's hands were coated in blood and muck, but she could clearly see that the fingernails were a ghastly shade of greenish black, one of the signs of krile poisoning.

"Oh goddess..." Kyrian whispered breathlessly, still staring at the dead man's hand. "That tea...I wonder if..." Calling upon her skills, she scanned Arris' body, seeking the hints and signs that would confirm her suspicion. It didn't take long.

The king had been krile-thralled for years. The drug had meshed completely with the young man's system, tainting every breath with its hallucinogenic poison. Wearily, the stardancer stood, letting Arris' hand fall. Looking down at the dead king, Kyrian said, "It's no wonder you were insane." She shook her head sadly. "I've got to tell Azhani. It's not an absolution, but it might help her to understand you, Arris Thodan."

Chapter Thirty-Seven

By midday, the rest of Azhani's army had caught up with her. While there was still a small garrison in the ruins of Barton, the main body had marched west. They were her back up plan, in case Arris had attempted treachery.

There wasn't enough time to combine both armies into a coherent unit, so she ordered each side to set up in a semi-circular formation. Once again, the center of camp was where the chirurgeons tents were pitched.

The wounded of the Y'Dani army were beyond grateful to see the red, white and green robes of the healers. The one remaining Ecarthan priest who had been discovered earlier dangled from a convenient tree.

There were a few complaints about Azhani's assumption of leadership. Some of the dissenters simply packed their things and left. Others had the grace to turn in their resignation before returning to the kingdoms. Azhani let them all go — they had seen enough death.

As the afternoon wore on, Azhani found herself experiencing a sense of terrible dread. While it was light out, she had yet to feel the heat of the sun. Glancing skyward, the warleader was surprised to see a shadow stretching across the daystar.

At her side, Kyrian looked up as well. "What is it?"

"I don't know, but I need some time to think. Why don't you go visit Devon?"

Kyrian raised an eyebrow. "All right, but if you need me, send someone."

"Of course." They kissed quickly and then Kyrian jogged off toward the chirurgeon's tent. She was intent on finding out how Devon was handling the loss of his leg as well as the end of his dreams of a relationship with Princess Syrelle. He had felt deeply for the Y'Maran princess, and Kyrian was concerned that the mage might succumb to his injury in order to avoid further emotional anguish.

Ducking into the tent, Kyrian spotted Allyndev and Syrelle asleep against the mage's cot.

Stifling a smile, she gently woke the sleepers and made them curl up in an empty bed. Devon watched from his bed with an openly longing expression on his face. At the foot of the mage's cot was Avisha, the hunting cat. When Kyrian approached, she raised her head and growled warningly.

"Hello, Avisha," Kyrian said in greeting.

Satisfied that it was a friend approaching her partner, the cat huffed once and went back to sleep.

"She certainly protects you well," Kyrian noted as she began to inspect Devon's bandages. "How do you feel today?"

Weakly, the mage said, "I feel like I got my leg chewed off." Kyrian said nothing and he made a face. "I'm alive. Jasyn's alive. But," he glanced at the curled forms of Allyn and Syrelle, "it hurts."

Since the mage was dosed to the gills with every pain killer that was available to the chirurgeons, Kyrian knew that he wasn't speaking about his leg. Taking a seat, she said, "Tell me."

"I'm in love with her," he said softly. "But she loves my best friend. Can I be happy for him and feel sorry for myself at the same time?"

Kyrian smiled sadly. "Yes, you can. You have a great heart, Devon. Does Allyn know how you feel?"

"No, but I think Syrelle does. She wouldn't say anything, and I don't really want Allyn to know. He might do something stupid, and go all noble on me."

Kyrian chuckled ruefully. "Yes, I agree. Honor is a strong point for him."

"So you won't say anything?"

She shook her head. "No. But if you ever need to talk, I'm here."

"Thank you." He clasped her hand in his. "You are a good friend, Kyrian."

Suddenly, his eyes rolled back in his head and he screamed in agony. His pain was echoed by every other mage in the tent.

As if from a great distance, Kyrian heard the faint echo of what sounded like thousands of dying wails. Nameless dread crept like ice over her. *Azhani!* She raced out of the tent to search the camp for her beloved.

Outside, the sky was a nasty shade of charcoal. Counting the marks on a nearby candle, she was stunned to realize that it wasn't anywhere near sundown.

Then the rimerbeasts attacked.

Swarming the guards, the beasts quickly penetrated the camp. The stardancer reached for a weapon, but remembered at the last moment that she no longer carried one. Starseeker Vashyra had yet to forge a new baton for her.

"Kyrian!"

She turned and was stunned to see Devon standing at the entrance to the pavilion. He was leaning on a chair, and his face was white with the effort it had cost him to move that far. Blood dripped from his bandages. Avisha paced back and forth in front of the tent, as if daring the rimerbeasts to cross her path.

Kyrian raced to the mage's side. "Devon, you shouldn't be up!"

"Here," he said as he held out a baton. "Vashyra and I made this for you. It was in my haversack. I meant to give it to you before you left, but I forgot."

She accepted the weapon, only deigning to glance at it when it did not feel as she expected. It was lighter, and when she touched it, the weapon tingled in her hand. "It's—"

"Magickal, I know. I told you. Vashyra and I made it for *you*, Kyrian. I can't explain everything now. You need to find Azhani. She will need you before this day is through."

Torn between the desire to find her lover and staying to help Devon, Kyrian stood staring down at the weapon in her hand. All around her, soldiers were battling the invading rimerbeasts. Death and chaos swirled through the camp. Above the shrieking of blood-maddened demons, she could hear her heart hammer like a drum in her chest.

Can I do this? She tried closing her fingers around the baton's handle and found it easier than she remembered. *I have to. There's no one else.*

Kyrian turned away from Devon and went to look for her lover.

"Go with the gods, Stardancer," Devon whispered softly. He turned and fell into the waiting arms of his friends. "Allyn, belt my leg and bring me my spellbook. Syrelle, see if you can find something that dulls pain but not wits."

The prince nodded and set the mage down in a chair while the princess raced to find a chirurgeon.

A rimerbeast thought to attack the tent and was taken down by Avisha. Another followed and was destroyed by a fireball launched by Devon.

In between chanting, Syrelle fed the mage a concoction so vile he nearly gagged. Swallowing it all, he continued to cast spell after spell, protecting the entrance.

Once he had retrieved the spellbook for Devon, Allyn took up a position at the other tent flap and fought alongside several of the walking wounded.

It was going to be a long night.

On a ridge above the camp, Azhani Rhu'len stared down at the mixed banners of four kingdoms that made up her army. Each flag marked a camp like pins in a territory map. These were her people now.

King Arris the Kinslayer was dead.

Azhani snarled in frustrated rage. She felt cheated because the young man had died heroically, instead of facing the justice he so richly deserved. Not only was he a hero — he had saved the life of her beloved. It was an irony so great, the warleader almost laughed.

A part of her wanted to kick Arris' corpse until it was a bloody smear. The rest of her felt empty; lost without the focus of her rage.

Azhani found a boulder and sat. Cradling her head in her hands, she tried to think, to plan what the future would bring. The rimerbeasts still had to be fought. Kasyrin Darkchilde was still loose. She felt his hand in the evil that was the Ecarthan priests.

Oh goddess, what if all of this was his plan? The epiphany touched off a barrage of thought. *It's certainly feasible — he was a powerful sorcerer when Father fought him, but not so powerful that he could battle a starseeker like Vashyra and escape. If he had somehow come across a key to great power, such as selling his soul to Ecarthus—*

"He would need a political foothold," she muttered softly. Lifting her head, she looked out at the Y'Dani quarter of her army. "Arris. Damn, this is not over. It hasn't even begun, has it?"

She stood and stared up at the sky, as if seeking answers in the gray heavens. "Arris is dead!" she shouted. "What will you do next, you bastard?"

Gormerath's song erupted in a blaze of sound.

Immediately, Azhani's gaze snapped back to the camp. Rimerbeasts were appearing seemingly from the air itself. Fear prickled through the warleader.

Drawing the sword, she once again turned her eyes to the sky. *The sun! Where is the sun?* The warleader knew that it was afternoon, and the daystar should be blazing in full glory. Yet what she saw was not a bright yellow orb, but a shadowed circle.

Memory, swift as eagle's wings, caressed her mind. *"The breaking is at hand. The Blade, the Heart and the Pawn shall meet and on that day, the sun will stand still and the stars will no longer spin with time."*

Wonderingly, Azhani took two steps toward camp and was jerked off her feet by Gormerath's excited pull. The blade urged her to climb. Numbly, she began to stumble up a goat trail.

She rounded a corner and the sight that greeted her spurred her into a run. On the top of a nearby mesa, a black-robed figure was outlined in a nimbus of magickal energy.

Azhani was overwhelmed by a feeling of such dread that she stopped in her tracks. *The prophecy — it's real. This is the breaking.* She spared a glance back toward the embattled army. *I love you, Kyrian. Remember that forever.*

There was a great deal of distance to cover between herself and that figure, so Azhani gripped her blade determinedly and began to ascend the mountain. Halfway up, she encountered an embattled patrol and threw herself at the rimerbeasts with unfettered glee.

In the camp below, where chaos reigned, the soldiers stopped and took heart when the sound of their Banshee's wail filled the valley.

Kyrian raced through the camp, dodging the combatants. Her robes were thick with the gore of those she had stopped to help. She heard Azhani's war cry and looked up, spotting the warrior on the ridge above her. Gormerath's flame illuminated Azhani like a torch.

"I'm coming, Azhi. Wait for me," the stardancer cried as she picked her way up the mountain.

The bodies of slain soldiers barred her way. Each time, she had to battle her fear into a corner. She would not freeze. She would not run from this fight. Azhani needed her! She ran on, cursing when her boots slipped on the wet rocks.

Ahead, she could hear the sounds of combat.

Rounding a curve, she was brought up short by the sight of Azhani and six rimerbeasts. The warleader was grinning fiercely and laughing with a joy that Kyrian had only seen once before — this was the Banshee.

Behind the warleader were the remains of a patrol. A mage and a soldier huddled against each other. The soldier had her hands pressed into a wound on the mage's chest.

Azhani was hampered by her need to protect the downed soldiers. To help, Kyrian would either have to fight, or somehow make her way to the injured mage so that the soldier could join her lover.

One of the beasts roared and charged Azhani. Grabbing her, the rimerbeast pulled her into a bearhug that could squeeze the life from a full grown horse.

The decision was simple.

Later, the watching soldier would tell her comrades that she had never seen anything like it. Kyrian burst into a run, leaped and flipped over the heads of the attacking demons and landed behind the one that was grappling with her lover.

With a deftly placed blow, the stardancer crushed its head. Dancing away, the priest delivered a series of kicks, punches and strikes to another, killing it.

Stunned momentarily, Azhani took great gulps of air, and then let out her cry. Gormerath appeared to become a brand of flame and together, Azhani and Kyrian destroyed the attacking rimerbeasts.

When it was over, Azhani and Kyrian turned and spent several heartbeats staring into each other's eyes.

Finally, Azhani broke the gaze and pointed to the mesa. "I need to be there. I love you," she grabbed Kyrian and kissed her fiercely.

"I know. I'm going with you." The stardancer then handed the soldier her haversack. "There's bandages and medicine inside." She cleaned her baton and sheathed it. "Let's go," she said to Azhani.

They shared another glance. Several heartbeats passed and then Azhani nodded. "Together, then," she said softly.

Chapter Thirty-Eight

The journey seemed to take forever. The sounds of the dead and dying had long since faded, leaving only the panting of their breath as they scrambled to the top of the mesa.

At the edge, Azhani put a hand on the stardancer's shoulder and whispered, "Wait here."

By now, fear had wound itself deeply into Kyrian's heart. She looked up at Azhani and licked her lips. "All right," the stardancer whispered. "But yell when you need me."

Azhani smiled. "I need you. I'll yell when I need help." There was no time for the kiss they both wanted.

The warrior leapt onto the top of the mesa and crept toward the figures perched near the edge. A stone obelisk rose out of the ground. Its black surface was covered in a series of faintly glowing runes.

Standing next to the artifact was a man dressed in robes so black they seemed to absorb the shadows. His arms were upraised and his lips were shaping the words of a chant. Blood coated the sorcerer's hands.

Kyrian shivered. Though she could not translate the man's speech, their evil intent was something she could plainly feel. Not far from the sorcerer was a pile of bodies. Each had been brutally slain.

The man was Kasyrin Darkchilde. She recognized him from the attack in Y'Syria. Neither he nor the smaller man beside him appeared to notice the women.

His chant came to an end. With a great cry, he thrust his hands into the obelisk. Arcane energies swirled around him and enshrouded the black stone.

There was a popping sound, and Kasyrin fell back.

"I guess even evil has taste," Azhani said grimly.

The dark mage and his assistant spun.

"You!" he spat. "Why aren't you dead?" For an instant, the sorcerer turned his fury on the man beside him. "Arris was supposed to kill her. He was my creature."

Dancing back and forth, Porthyros gibbered, "I trained him to be a good boy, Master. I swear it."

"Your pawn learned a new move, Darkchilde. He sacrificed himself to save another," Azhani said. "Maybe you shouldn't have taught him how to play so well."

Kasyrin snarled. "Then I will deal with you myself." The sorcerer chanted a string of harsh syllables that ended with the word, "Ecarthus."

The obelisk began to pulse, throbbing like a beating heart.

A terrible groan filled the air as the ground began to shake.

Suddenly, a rupture appeared in the ground in front of the obelisk. A plume of noxious smoke and ash filled the air.

Coughing, Azhani shielded her face. "Circus tricks, Darkchilde?" she asked as she waved away the smoke. "They'll do no good against my blade."

Kyrian gasped as Azhani drew the blade. The song that the warrior had spoken of — she could clearly hear it. It was so loud, that she covered her ears, though that did nothing to smother it.

"My Lord Ecarthus is no circus trick, bitch," Darkchilde said through gritted teeth. His hands were busy weaving a delicate tracery of symbols in the air. "Behold, he who comes to devour your soul."

Rising from the rift was a demon whose aura was so hideous that Azhani staggered back several steps. He was both beautiful and horrid — his body was blood red and muscular. Horns and fangs ruined the picture of comeliness that was his face.

The demon's eyes glowed green as he gazed around the mesa. Ripping his hands from the earth, he flexed his fingers. Six-inch long claws glistened with a yellowish ichor.

Still entombed in the earth from the waist down, the demon roared with frustration, *::Kasyrin!::*

Breaking off his chant, the sorcerer said, "I have brought you the mortal bitch, Azhani Rhu'len, My Lord!"

The demon ignored his servant. *::Chant, thou fool! The spell must be completed!::*

Azhani's mind gibbered in fear. She staggered back several feet. Even Gormerath's song seemed to subside under the awesome menace that Ecarthus exuded.

From her hiding place, Kyrian could sense the tide of evil that rolled off the demon. Fear held her fast. Though she had fought to stand beside her lover in this place, the brilliant aura of pain and death permeating the mesa had shattered her resolve.

She was locked in a vicious cycle of memory. In her mind's eye, she was forever seeing the bandit's blood as it dripped from her baton.

Motionless, Kyrian watched as Ecarthus rose. The sky above had gone completely black. No stars, no moon and no sun illuminated the struggle taking place. Only the obelisk gave off a ruddy glow as Darkchilde called upon his powers to break the locks binding the demon in the abyss.

Beside his master, Porthyros watched as Ecarthus rose. *I will be rich, rich, rich. Gold, jewels, everything — it will all be mine!* The little man gleefully rubbed his hands together.

He watched as Azhani struggled to overcome her fear and laughed. *I could kill her right now and she would not stop me.* The idea seemed far too good to resist. *I'll do it! I'll make Master so happy that he will shower me in gold coins for a week!*

The scholar drew his dagger and charged.

The sight of a wickedly curved dagger appearing in the hand of Kasyrin's lackey snapped Kyrian's fear. As he charged Azhani, she drew her baton. She was too far away to intercept him, and he was moving too fast for her to hit, but *Azhani needs me! It must work!*

Kyrian whispered, "Fly true," and launched her baton high into the air.

End over end, the weapon arced across the mesa. The baton shimmered and began to pick up speed. As it flew, the weapon emitted a whirring buzz that was akin to Gormerath's song.

322 ❖ *Shaylynn Rose*

Bone shattered as the baton hit its target.

Porthyros stumbled and fell to his knees; his charge abated. "Master?" he called.

Kasyrin stared dumbly as blood pumped from a gaping wound in his head. His mouth moved, but no sound came forth.

Ecarthus was outraged. *::Finish the spell, dog, and I will save thee.::* He extended a finger, and a tendril of power flowed from him to the mage. The wound in his head stopped bleeding.

"Yes, Master," Darkchilde gasped thickly. He continued to chant.

Porthyros crawled back to the sorcerer's side and stood. Gripping his dagger, he searched the mesa for the one who had dared to interfere with his quest for gold.

::Hear me, my daughter. The time has come for thee to test thy faith.:: Memory flooded over Azhani at the sound of that voice.

"Astariu," she whispered. "You came to me—"

::Yes. And as I promised, I have come again.::

"Why?"

::Dost thou trust in me?::

Once, not so long ago, she would have answered to the negative. Time and fate had conspired to untangle the warrior's hurt and give her a new view on the world. The gifts of love from Kyrian and the sacrifice of her most hated enemy had proven that there was a force beyond the evil that had destroyed her life.

"Yes."

The world went dark. She heard the far off sound of bells.

She burned. A suffusion of fire hotter than the forges that warmed the Mountains of Y'Dror rushed through her being. She was pulled, guided toward a goal that she could not see, but knew she was inevitably moving toward...

The warleader watched in fascinated detachment as her whole body was bathed in the azure aura of the goddess Astariu. She tried to blink and couldn't. Confused, she attempted to frown, but could not perform that feat either.

Suddenly, she felt dizzy.

Her vision was filled with the sight of an armored woman. The woman moved, and she was dizzy again.

I am the sword.

That didn't feel quite right.

I am the Blade.

Astariu laughed brightly. *::Yes, my child, thou art. So it was written and so it is.::*

If she had owned a body, Azhani would have nodded. "What of Kyrian?" The warrior understood that she was giving up her life to fight Ecarthus.

The goddess smiled and said, *::My stardancer loves thee deeply, warrior. She will not lightly accept thy loss.::*

The goddess' words did nothing to comfort her, but it was too late to change her mind. Resolutely, she thought, *I am ready. Strike now, My Lady, while you have the element of surprise.*

Astariu's mental laughter helped to defray some of her fear. *::Always the tactician, my warrior. Thou hast pleased me.::*

The goddess gripped her weapon and went to step toward the demon. An invisible wall blocked her way. Cursing silently, she noted the chanting sorcerer and realized that her stardancer's throw had not totally incapacitated him.

::I have come to defy thee, Soul-Eater. Thou must not enter this world unchallenged,:: the goddess yelled.

Kyrian started. It was Azhani's voice, but filled with a timbre that was so much more. Only during the most holy of ceremonies had that tone been heard. She climbed to the top of the mesa. Slowly, she approached the warrior's side.

"Astariu?" Kyrian whispered.

The effect of the voice on Ecarthus was no less stunning.

::Nay!:: he shouted. *::Thou shalt not bar me from what is rightfully mine!::* He set a demonic hand upon the shoulders of his minion. Energy rippled down the beast's arm and into the sorcerer.

Kasyrin's strange chant paused. With a negligent twist of his fingers, he said, "Hold." Shimmering bands of force coalesced and bound the warrior where she stood.

::Kill her,:: Ecarthus said.

Porthyros leaped to do the demon's bidding.

Kyrian froze. She had to do something. Azhani or Astariu — whoever she was — needed her help. She could not stand by and allow Ecarthus and his minions to succeed.

I have no weapon.

When has that ever been a problem for a stardancer?

She almost laughed. Instead, she broke into a run. Tackling the scholar in midstride, she delivered a single, forceful chop to his throat. Porthyros gagged and collapsed clutching his neck.

Kyrian danced back and swept his legs out from under him. All the while, she looked for her baton. It lay in the grass not far from Darkchilde.

Damn! I wish it would come here.

The metal rod shivered, then, slowly rose and gracefully returned to her hand. Grimacing, the stardancer struck the scholar on the back of the head, rendering him unconscious.

Very nice spell, Devon. If I live, I'll remember to tender my compliments. Now...for the sorcerer.

She began to creep across the mesa toward Darkchilde. It occurred to her that she should be absolutely terrified, but it was as if all her emotions had drained away. *I wonder if this is how Azhani deals with combat.* Kyrian knew that she would have to deal with the consequences of her actions later.

Astariu fought the spell binding her. The body she wore was strong, but the mage was stronger. Sweat stood out on her head as she struggled to move.

Satisfied that the goddess was contained, Kasyrin returned to the spell that would eventually free Ecarthus.

The demon kept his gaze pinned on the warrior. He thought nothing of the stardancer — her fear would eventually catch up and she would once again become meaningless.

::*Thy pride will be thy undoing, Astariu,*:: he said bitingly as he watched the goddess break free enough to take two steps forward. ::*Thou claimest the adulation of the mortals while granting me the leavings of their nightmares. I shall suffer no longer. Thy days of drinking the wine of faith are over. I will rise and herald a new era where fear and hatred outshine thy pathetic ideals of love and tolerance. I shall sup from the table of mortal misery and thou wilt have the dregs!*::

Astariu looked into the eyes of her enemy and said, ::*Hate and intolerance shall never gain favor among the mortals. The blessings of love and faith will always win over the nightmares thou offerest, beast of the abyss.*::

The demon snorted, raising his arms and gesturing expansively. ::*Then stop me, godling. Strike me down where I stand.*::

Kyrian took her final step. She was standing directly behind Darkchilde. *It's now or never.* Raising her arm she was assaulted by wave after wave of vision. Hatchet cut images assaulted her, filling her mind with the stuttering pictures of blood and death.

She froze.

No no no no no no... The word spun around in circles in her thoughts. Tears burned down her cheeks. *Murderer. You will be a killer forever.*

Kyrian looked at the chanting sorcerer, at the demon and at her lover-turned-goddess. Astariu's eyes met hers and in that instant, the stardancer saw a spark of her Azhani in them.

The warrior's voice cut through the visions with the sharpness of a scalpel. *"If you allow your fears to rule, you will always run from them. The decision to take a life is a terrible one, but often it is necessary for the good of the many. Think of it like surgery. You have to shave away the poisoned flesh in order for the body to live."*

"I will not be ruled by my fears anymore," Kyrian said through gritted teeth. Her arm finished its descent.

Blindly, Kasyrin chanted, "Ecarthus unbound...Ecarthus unbound...Ecarthu—"

The sorcerer's voice was abruptly cut off as Kyrian's baton shattered his skull like an overripe pumpkin.

::*As thou hast requested, so shalt thou receive,*:: Astariu said. Her face blazed with a brilliant smile as she nodded at Kyrian. The stardancer saluted her with the bloody baton.

Ecarthus gawked at the slowly crumpling body of his minion.

Astariu began to slowly walk across the mesa.

::*No!*:: Ecarthus wailed, shooting beams of energy at the lifeless body of Kasyrin. ::*Thou must not fail me, slave! Rise, and say the words to free me!*::

The mage did not move.

Kyrian looked down at her gory weapon, then up at the maddened demon. "It's been a terrible day for all concerned," she said, her voice hollow and emotionless.

Held in the magick that was the blade, Azhani could do nothing but ache for her beloved. *You will survive this, Kyrian. Be strong, my love.*

Ecarthus looked at the stardancer. ::*Thou hast breathed thy last, creature of Astariu. Prepare to pay for thy interference with thy life!*:: He blasted Kyrian across the mesa with a negligent flip of his hand. As she struggled to stand, he lifted his hand and prepared to hit her again.

Astariu screamed and leaped between them.

::*Hast thou forgotten me, spawn of slime?*:: she demanded, swatting at his hand with her blade.

He roared and batted at her futilely. Trapped as he was in the earth, he could do nothing to defend himself as the goddess dodged his blows.

::*Thou wilt pass from this place and return nevermore, Ecarthus. It is thy destiny.*:: Astariu skewered the demon in the heart.

Azhani felt herself penetrate the demon's half-solid flesh. The fire that was her essence poured from the blade and into Ecarthus. Mortality suddenly blazed into the demon, granting him the release from the abyss that he so desperately sought.

He laughed, and black blood burbled up and spilled down his chest.

In the moment of joining, Azhani learned the terrible truth — it was by Ecarthus' will that the rimerbeasts had attacked Y'Myran unceasingly. The demon had struggled for eons to be free of his jail and had done whatever he could to secure that freedom.

Upon him rested the blame for so much death that Azhani's ire ignited into a bonfire of hate. Jagged edges of pain threaded through her as she recognized the ultimate murderer of those she loved.

"*You wished to enter my realm, demon. So be it. Welcome to Y'Myran. Now die.*"

Ecarthus looked down at the sword lodged in his chest. The blade had taken on a brilliant golden glow that was slowly spreading over him.

::*No,*:: he whispered. His perfect, beautiful body began to wither.

"*Yes. You are mortal now, beast. Feel the effects of time unbound. It is my gift to you, in return for all the bitter tears you have given me.*"

The demon whimpered one last time before collapsing inward and crumbling into a pile of dust.

The silence on top of the mesa was profound.

Kyrian stepped over Darkchilde's body. She walked over to Azhani, whose body was limned in an aura of silvery blue.

"Is it over?"

Astariu turned to face her stardancer. ::*Yes, child, it is.*::

The stardancer closed her eyes and let out a long sigh of relief. With wondering eyes she looked up and met the eyes of her goddess. "You saved us all."

Astariu smiled. ::*I had help, Kyrian.*::

"Azhani?" she asked, as she looked at the warleader's body. It was so familiar and yet completely alien to her. The presence of the goddess had completely erased any sense of the woman she loved.

::*She fulfilled the prophecy, as it was written,*:: Astariu said, sorrow and pride mingling in her voice.

"The prophecy?" Kyrian asked. It didn't take much for her to recall the words that Starseeker Vashyra had spoken in the Y'Syran court. "Azhani was the Blade." Her gaze fell to the weapon that hung limply in the goddess' hand. The sword, once bright, was now blackened and dull — seeming almost brittle. Astariu lifted it and cradled it against her.

Gaping at the lifeless weapon, Kyrian whispered, "No. Damn you, no." She fell to her knees, weeping. "Damn you for taking away the one person I loved enough to fight for."

The goddess winced. She was particularly fond of Kyrian and the words hurt. *::Brother, it is thy turn.::*

There was a flash of light, a sound of a body falling, and then a man appeared on the mesa. He reached down to touch Kyrian's shoulder. "Here now, darling. Put up yer tears and have a wee drop with me." He offered her a skin, which she took.

Drinking from it, she gasped at the rawness of the liquor it held.

He pounded her back until she could breathe. "That's the spirit, lass."

Kyrian looked up at him and flinched. The newcomer was so ugly, she turned away. "Who are you?" Despite herself, she liked him.

"Don't you never mind about that, lass. I've come bearing gifts, if you but ask for them."

She stood and cocked her head. "What could you have that I would want?"

He shrugged and did a comical little dance. "Ye'll never know unless you ask. Tell me lass, if there were but one thing you could have, what would it be?"

Kyrian stared at him as if he were daft. Her gaze drifted to the prone body of Azhani and fresh tears fell. Looking up at the sky, she said, "I want my life back. I want to wake up tomorrow and be in Azhani's arms."

Mischievously, the man smiled and said, "I can do that." Flapping his arms and clucking like a chicken, he danced around her and then blew her a kiss.

Watching in amazement, Kyrian was stunned when the man's lips actually flew off his face and smacked her on the mouth. When the odd manifestation had returned to his face, the man grinned delightedly. "There ya go lass — just pass it on and all will be well."

Kyrian ran to her lover's side. Her lips tingled powerfully. Kneeling, she rolled the warrior over. Azhani's head flopped about lifelessly. Blood trickled from her eyes, ears, and nose. Cradling the warrior against her chest, Kyrian whispered, "Beloved, you can't die." Her tears mingled with the gore on the warrior's face.

The tingling in her lips grew to a buzzing sensation.

"You can't die, you can't leave me now. Not after you promised me a future. I need you with me, Azhani, and I won't let fate steal the life that we have earned," Kyrian whispered fiercely and then bent her head down to place a single, chaste kiss upon her lover's rapidly cooling lips.

Almost immediately, the tingling vanished. The lips under hers warmed and opened as a tiny gasp of air escaped. Sobbing with joy, Kyrian clutched the warrior close.

Engaging her gift, she saw that Azhani's life force was fragile at best. Closing her eyes, Kyrian touched upon her powers and gave of them unflinchingly. Her essence blended with Azhani's. Every small hurt became hers to feel.

Swiftly, she eased those tiny pains. Larger injuries demanded attention. The goddess' struggle against Kasyrin's spell had caused terrible internal trauma. Drawing energy from the earth, Kyrian focused the raw power to repair the damage that Azhani had sustained.

She worked until she was drained, until all of Azhani's physical hurts were healed. It was not enough. Deeper wounds — hurts of the soul that had been ripped open by combat with the demon — Kyrian's gift could not touch.

Kyrian tended these the only way she knew how. She loved. Opening her heart, she let every last ounce of emotion she felt for Azhani spill through her link. Without reservation, she allowed Azhani to experience the depth of love she felt.

"Come back to me, love. Come home, Azhani," she whispered.

Candlemarks passed as Kyrian sang and rocked the warrior's body. Lost in her praying, she almost didn't recognize her name. It was only when a hand cupped her cheek that she opened her eyes and looked down.

Azhani was looking up at her, a strange and peaceful smile blossoming on her face. "That's it, beloved. Let me see those pretty green eyes of yours," Azhani rasped.

Kyrian sobbed and rained kisses on the warrior's face and lips. Laughing, Azhani laced her fingers in her lover's hair and pulled her down for a long, loving kiss.

Kyrian drew herself from Azhani's arms and walked over to the strange little man who had waited while the stardancer worked her magick. "Thank you," she said and kissed his cheek.

Blushing deeply, the man said, "'Twas nothin' lass. I was honored to help."

Kyrian smiled and then sighed. "What a day," she murmured. All around her, the day's battle had left a vista of destruction. The massive obelisk was now a pile of cracked and pitted rubble. The body of Porthyros Omal lay partially buried under the wreckage, blood trickling from dozens of wounds. Of Darkchilde, all that remained was a dark smudge on the snow.

Above them, the sun glared brightly. Kyrian looked at the strange man. Winking, he nodded his head to her and then skipped over to the ruins of the obelisk. The stardancer watched as he began to sift through the wreckage.

Slowly, Azhani pushed herself to her knees. After getting her balance, she stood. Lying in the snow at her feet was a blackened hunk of metal that she belatedly realized was all that was left of Gormerath. She bent to retrieve it. The blade was shattered, but the blue gem set in the hilt still sparkled in the sun. Out of long habit, Azhani sheathed the sword.

"Azhani, I have a question," Kyrian said as she went to her lover's side and embraced her.

Azhani ran her fingers through the stardancer's hair and smiled. "What?"

"Who was the other man?" There was a heavy note of sadness in her tone.

"Porthyros Omal, Arris' mentor and guardian."

"Oh." The priest closed her eyes. In a small voice she said, "I killed them."

Azhani drew her close. "I know." Her stomach twisted into knots. Would having slain the sorcerer and his servant cause Kyrian more grief than she could handle?

"It was easy — too easy." Kyrian looked up at her lover. "Killing shouldn't be so easy."

Azhani brushed a kiss over her brow. "Unfortunately, it is."

Tears leaked from Kyrian's eyes and painted her face in glistening tracks. "Am I a murderer?"

Shaking her head, Azhani said, "No, you are a defender. You killed because you had to, not because you wanted to."

"I don't regret my actions, but I hate that I had to kill them," Kyrian said and then sobbed quietly.

Wordlessly, Azhani held her until the tears quieted.

"Don't fash yourself too long o'er the lives of those scoundrels," the strange man said as he ambled up to the two women. "'Twas the hand of fate that worked through ye to rive their worthless lives from their bodies, not the choice of thy heart, young Stardancer."

Azhani frowned. "It does not matter whose choice it was, stranger. The death was meted out by her hand."

"Aye, and sad I am that it had to be," the man said as he hooked his thumbs into his belt.

Kyrian pulled away from Azhani's embrace and looked at the man. "Who are you, anyway? How is it you speak so familiarly of fate? Where did you get the power to revive the dead?"

He chuckled. "Full of questions, aren't ye?" Shrugging he said, "P'raps ye'll best recall me thusly." He clapped his hands and in place of the ugly little man was a black-robed stranger. A death's head tattoo decorated his cheek and a wickedly curved dagger dangled loosely from one hand. "Is this better?" he whispered ominously.

Kyrian shivered. The man radiated an evil presence that touched a memory but she couldn't place why. "No, I don't think so."

"I know you," Azhani said. Her hand had dropped to the hilt of her sword. "I killed you."

The person standing before them changed yet again. This time, he was a handsome, scholarly gentleman. "Aye that you did." He rubbed his shoulder and winced. "You shoot a mean bow, warrior."

Kyrian, who had been watching the man's shapeshifting, suddenly blurted, "You're Astarus!"

He laughed and a ghostly fanfare echoed around him. *::Splendid guess, my dear.::* The god's form began to fade away.

"Wait!" Kyrian cried. "Why did you kidnap me?"

::Someone had to make sure you two met,:: came the soft answer. *::Good work, children. You have our gratitude.::* Then he was gone.

The women used the remains of the obelisk to cover Porthyros' body.

Azhani sighed and rubbed her face. "Kyrian?" she asked as she started to look for a path down from the mountaintop.

"What, love?"

"I'm tired. Let's go home."

Halfway down, they stopped to rest. Sinking onto a convenient boulder, Kyrian sighed and massaged trembling calf muscles. "Do you have anything to drink, Azhi? My flask is empty."

"No, but I think there's a waterfall over there." She hiked around a rocky outcrop.

Too tired to follow, Kyrian continued to massage her sore legs. Astariu's fire would not come to her call for many days — she was utterly drained.

The warrior returned bearing a full waterskin. "Here."

"Thank you," Kyrian said gratefully as she drank.

Azhani nodded and settled on the ground between Kyrian's legs and rested her head on her knee. Icy wind buffeted the women, causing them to shiver.

Idly stroking Kyrian's leg, Azhani said, "We can only rest a short while, love. It's only going to get colder."

"I know, but it's nice to just sit here with you, Azhani." Kyrian pulled the warrior's braids back from her face and brushed dried dirt and blood from her cheek. Azhani yawned and closed her eyes as the stardancer's gentle stroking continued. More dirt fell away and Kyrian gasped softly.

"Mm, what?" Azhani murmured sleepily. When the stardancer didn't answer right away, the warrior's eyes shot open and she leaped to her feet. "Are we being attacked? Quick, loan me your baton!"

Kyrian tried hard not to smile. "No, love. We're not under attack. I just um," she bit her lip. "Here," she said, drawing her dagger and cleaning the blade until it reflected the warrior's face. "Look for yourself."

Bewildered, Azhani took the dagger and examined her face. Bits of dirt and blood made her dusky skin appear even darker than usual. Her hair was in dire need of washing and several of her braids had come undone. On her left cheek, a thin, dark scar was all that was left of a nasty cut she had taken from a rimerbeast's razor sharp claw.

When she caught sight of her right cheek, Azhani nearly dropped the dagger. The small, disk-shaped scar that had been left after Arris had burned out her tattoo was gone. In its place was a silvery, sword-shaped mark. Azhani reached up to stroke her face disbelievingly. It was real; she could feel the raised edges of the design under her fingertips. "How?" she whispered in amazement as hot tears spilled freely.

Kyrian rose and took her dagger from Azhani's numb fingers. "Does it matter? Accept that the goddess has returned what is rightfully yours." She grasped the warrior's hand. "Come, let's head back."

Chapter Thirty-Nine

Camp was a complete mess. Exhausted teams of soldiers worked day and night to remove the bodies of the dead. Rimerbeast carcasses were burned in a mass pyre while each fallen soldier received full honors.

The one boon seemed to be that Ecarthus' death had called a halt to the attacks of the rimerbeasts. Whether the monsters had vanished along with their creator or if this season's hatching had been destroyed in the final battle remained to be seen.

The conflict on the mesa had been seen by all and its legend was already spinning out of control. Neither Kyrian nor Azhani was particularly interested in recounting the tale, though each had taken the time to tell Starseeker Vashyra their version of events. The mage-priest had used her magick to cause their words to be inscribed upon scrolls, which would be presented to Lyssera upon their return to Y'Syr.

Others came forth with their versions, and soon, Vashyra had a trunk-ful of scrolls. History would not forget what Azhani and Kyrian had done because nearly everyone had seen them strike down the Eater of Souls.

During the recovery effort, Azhani was everywhere. If she wasn't repairing a tent or carting away debris, she was leading patrols into the mountains.

Kyrian was just as relentless. Once her powers were restored, she could either be found in the chirurgeon's tents or with Starseeker Vashyra. The older priest offered what comfort she could to ease the stardancer's soul, for the deaths of Kasyrin and Porthyros weighed heavily on Kyrian's conscience.

Three days after the battle, Devon left the care of the chirurgeons. Waiting for him were Allyndev and Syrah, who gently helped him to return to his tent. The hunting cat, Avisha, was there, having already claimed her half of the mage's bed.

Chief Padreg and Elisira were both still guests of the chirurgeons, having sustained several grievous wounds while fighting the rimerbeasts. The worst of these included a broken arm for Elisira and a deep set of gashes in Padreg's side.

The army continued to work and heal. Azhani gave Allyndev more and more responsibilities that took him from Syrelle's side. Though she hated to separate the two young lovers, Azhani knew that it was important for Allyndev to learn all that she could teach. Upon her shoulders rested a heavy burden. Gods and fate willing, she would soon be able to share it.

Once everyone was able to travel, Azhani ordered the army to march south. Arris had left Y'Dan in shambles and as the acting Y'Dani war-leader, Azhani intended to drive out any remaining Ecarthan priests and make the kingdom safe for its people once more.

As they traveled, messages arrived bearing welcome news. From Lyssera, they learned that the black ships that had terrorized the waters of Banner Lake had been soundly defeated. The news from Y'Nor was that all was peaceful — the ogres and bandits that had harried the clans were gone. In Y'Dror, the dragon vanished and was seen no more. The nomads of Y'Skan reported that the giant scorpions had succumbed to the spells of their mages. King Naral of Y'Tol sent a bottle of wine with the message that the beetle infestation was destroyed and his crops were saved.

Lastly, they heard from the high king. Ysradan's message was filled with lengthy descriptions of his endeavors at sea, as well as his regret at not noticing what had taken place in Y'Dan. He condemned Arris' actions and added his voice to the growing list of those who believed Azhani to be innocent of oath-breaking. The high king promised to meet her at Y'Dannyv so that they could jointly repair the wrongs that had been done to the kingdom.

Marching through snow, even on horseback, is probably the worst way to travel that anyone has ever invented. Kyrian shivered under her cloak and leaned over to pat Arun on the head before jumping down and accepting the fresh towel from the young soldier standing at her horse's side.

The morning that Azhani had marked as their return date dawned gray and cold. By afternoon, snow was falling. Since then, thick, icy flakes had blanketed the countryside, making travel difficult. Every few miles, riders would have to dismount and rub down the legs of their horses to prevent the beasts from faltering. Travel was limited to a mere six candlemarks a day, and even then, everyone was chilled and bone weary.

Without the rimerbeasts, the army's greatest enemy was now the fevers and colds that spread from soldier to soldier like wildfire. Every chirurgeon, healer and stardancer was needed to help stave off sickness.

Not even Azhani was immune to the illness. She had been struck down by the coughing sickness after forgetting her cloak during one day's ride. Kyrian had expected a fight when she ordered her lover to ride in the wagons with the rest of the fevered soldiers, but Azhani had proven to be a better patient than anticipated. Kyrian was properly grateful, and as a reward for her lover, she tried to visit her often.

The stardancer remounted. In two days, they would be in Kellerdon. After thirteen days of cold and wet, she was looking forward to resting in the farming community. Vaguely, she recalled that there was a small guard's outpost on the outskirts of the town. Perhaps there would be enough room for everyone to sleep in comfort.

With **Padreg, Elisira** and Azhani out of action, Prince Allyndev, Princess Syrelle and the mage Devon became the faces that those in the army looked to for guidance.

From Allyn came Azhani's orders while Devon and Syrelle did their best to assist their friend. The half-elf emerged as a leader, discovering an ability to delegate responsibility while balancing the egos of the various commanders within Azhani's army.

When Padreg was well enough to leave the care of the chirurgeons, he surprised everyone by allowing Allyn to remain as Azhani's second.

Kyrian entered her tent, expecting to find Zhadosh curled up on their cot, waiting for her. What she did not expect was one fully dressed warrior, playing, "chase-the-string" with the kitten. Azhani looked up at her entry and smiled alluringly, though the effect was ruined by a bout of coughing that wracked her body.

Sighing, Kyrian dropped her mittens on a trunk and said, "You should be on the chirurgeon's wagon, planning the invalid rebellion."

"Well hello, I'm awfully glad to see you, too," Azhani said hoarsely.

"Azhani, why are you here?" Kyrian asked, coming over and putting her hand against the warrior's face. "You've a fever."

Azhani captured Kyrian's hand in hers and kissed it. "I know where I should be, but I needed to be here, with you." She pulled her lover down into her lap, cuddling her close. "Tomorrow we will reach Kellerdon. I need to present a strong front to any lingering supporters of Ecarthus."

"Not to mention you like looking heroic in front of the masses," Kyrian said, grinning at the indignation that flashed across Azhani's face. "You know, I've never seen you around normal people. Not really, anyway...I mean, there was Barton, but that was like being with your family, because they knew you so well. I've seen you with nobility, I've watched you around your soldiers, but I've never seen how you behave around simple people like farmers and blacksmiths."

"I don't eat babies for lunch, Kyrian," Azhani growled, a trace of hurt in her words. "And I don't strike off people's heads when they don't do what I want them to."

"Oh, I know that." Kyrian played with the lacing to Azhani's tunic. "What I meant was...it will be interesting to see how people who have called you both hero and murderer react, now that you're a hero again."

"I haven't thought about it," Azhani said as Kyrian stood and began peeling off her traveling clothes. "I've tried not to."

"It may be time to consider it. How do you want us to be viewed, love? Are we the usurping conquerors, or the returning heroes?"

Azhani lay back on the bed. Zhadosh took this as an invitation to come and snuggle, so she jumped up next to her and began to roughly knead Azhani's thigh.

"Hey, hey, stop that, you little monster." Azhani grabbed the kit by the scruff of her neck and sat up. Bringing the kitten up to eye level, she growled and said, "I am not your personal pincushion. Go puncture someone else!" Overcome by a fit of coughing, she dropped the kitten.

Zhadosh sought refuge behind Kyrian's legs. The stardancer rubbed the kitten's head affectionately and said, "Will you please cease trying to scare our friend away, Azhani?"

"Only if she stops trying to ventilate my extremities," the warrior said as she accepted a waterskin from the priest.

"That's a bit extreme, love. Zhadosh was just fluffing her bed before going to sleep." The stardancer busied herself by warming a pot of tea on a small brazier.

Azhani made an indignant noise in the back of her throat. "Fluffing? Kyr, I'm bleeding because of her 'fluffing'."

The stardancer briefly eyed the wound. "Those pinpricks barely qualify as scratches, much less cause for complaint, love."

Azhani pouted.

"Here, drink this," Kyrian said as she handed a steaming cup to her lover. "It will ease your cough."

"Thank you," Azhani said. "At least I still rate a cup of your best bitter brew."

Kyrian snorted. "It's neither my best, nor my bitterest, Azhani, and you know it. There's enough honey in there to fill a hive!"

Azhani grinned and her smile turned contemplative as she sipped at the tea. "We will approach Kellerdon as friends. More than half of this army is Y'Dani. If we fly the banners, but leave off the fanfare and panoply, it should make the citizens of the town stand at ease. Perhaps if they see familiar faces, they'll be more willing to accept us."

"I agree. Now, finish your tea and get some sleep, mighty hero. Tomorrow you can play peacemaker." Kyrian helped her lover undress and then tucked her into bed.

"I hope I don't have to shout. My throat still feels like I swallowed a sword blade."

"Put Allyndev in charge of negotiations."

"I might do that."

Kyrian smiled and slipped into the bed next to her lover. Shortly, they were joined by Zhadosh.

"Ow."

"Azhi, just hold still. She'll settle soon."

"Ow, damn cat. I think she's doing it on purpose."

"She's just a baby."

"She's about to be a pair of gloves."

"Azhani..."

There was no further response as Zhadosh settled comfortably between the women.

Azhani gritted her teeth as she watched young Allyndev act on her orders. Taking Kyrian's advice, she had put him in charge of negotiating with the mayor of Kellerdon for the right to camp outside his town. The outpost that Kyrian had recalled had not been adequate, and rumors of Ecarthan activities in the surrounding area meant that the army would not budge until the people were safe from the predations of the evil priests.

Though he was more than willing to welcome the natives home, the mayor was insistent that the remainder of the army continue on to Y'Dannyv. Since neither Azhani nor her lieutenants had any intention of doing that, it was turning into a nightmare of a discussion.

"Mayor Graystone, we are not here to invade. We require rest, and we are offering to help your people rid the area of the Ecarthans." Allyn's tone sounded reasonable, but Azhani could detect the edge of frustration to the words.

"Prince Allyndev, we of Kellerdon are most grateful for the offer of the Y'Syrans, but we are quite capable of protecting ourselves." The mayor's voice held just enough imperiousness to completely irritate Azhani.

She could take it no longer. "My apologies, Allyn," she said softly as she intruded. "Mr. Mayor, must I remind you that I am the acting warleader? By law, you are required to quarter any and all of my men."

The mayor blanched. "Warleader, please we cannot—"

"I know. This is why we seek only to use the fallow fields. Allow us that right, and I promise to keep my men from despoiling the lands of your farmers."

Graystone sighed. He recognized that he was outmatched. "Yes, Warleader. The south fields are fallow this year. Please try not to trample the westward ones. We hope to harvest a good crop of wheat."

"Thank you. Allyndev, take ten men and rope off the west fields. Post warn-off markers. Padreg, you and Elisira see to the deployment of camp. Devon, ask my squad to join us. I'd like to make sure that temple is out of business." The warleader pointed toward a black building that was in the center of the village. Even now, the townsfolk avoided it as though it were diseased.

"Aye, Warleader," came the chorus of replies.

Three candlemarks later, the temple was cleared and camp was bustling with activity. The townsfolk, now assured that Azhani's people were truly there to help, willingly came out to trade foodstuffs for tales as well as Y'Syran gold.

Allyn and his men had roped off a massive section of land, but there was still plenty of room for the army to spread out. Azhani was pleased with his work. In the morning, she would detail several patrols to go out and clear the surrounding lands of any Ecarthans. Briefly, she wished that she had the song of Gormerath to lead her to the evil men, but she brushed that aside.

Their stink will draw us quickly enough. Only once had they encountered the black-robed priests and at that time, the fight had been short and brutal. *This land will be safe once again.*

They were gathered outside what appeared to be an innocuous farmstead. Yet a palpable aura of wrongness clung to the small buildings. Perhaps it was the scent of burnt flesh that permeated the air; or maybe it was the fact that the farm lacked any sign of life, even though the land and buildings were in perfect repair.

Prince Allyndev felt his heart beat heavily in his chest. Licking his lips he quietly said, "All right men, let's air this place out. The stench is beginning to pall."

They dismounted and moved quickly toward the front door. Kicking it in, Allyn and three others rushed into the room with weapons drawn. The room was empty.

"Aw damn, nothing," Larrig Osten, Allyn's second, said as he sheathed his weapon.

"Belay that, Lar," Allyn said, motioning for the man to keep his weapon drawn. "Listen."

Breaths were held for long moments. Behind the noise of creaking armor and shifting feet, they could all hear quiet whimpering. Allyn's gaze was everywhere. Silently, he motioned for the soldiers to begin searching the rooms for secret doors.

In moments, a starseeker had found one. An ornamental piece of carved wood on the wall in one of the bedrooms was actually a doorknob. Swiftly, a soldier opened it, revealing a tiny chamber.

Within the room were nearly twenty men, women and children. All were in various stages of ill health. Some had terrible, festering sores that oozed blood and pus while others were beaten so badly that it was difficult to tell whether or not they were mortal. The stench was awful. None of the victims had bathed in quite some time and there was only one small chamber pot in the room. One woman, completely naked and badly emaciated, held a whimpering infant against her chest and sang tunelessly.

When they saw Allyn and his men, they drew back in abject fear.

The prince felt sick to his stomach. Pasting a gentle smile on his face, he stepped into the room and said, "Peace be with you, citizens. I am Allyndev Kelani, I am here to free you."

"Be ye a ghost, then?" One elderly man asked.

"No, Granther, I am as alive as you." Allyn sheathed his weapon and walked up to the old man. "Here," he said as he offered his hand. "Let me help you."

The old man suspiciously reached for Allyn's hand. A sudden, heart-wrenching smile broke out on his face when the prince gently helped him stand. "By the Twain," the old man whispered as tears welled in his ancient eyes. "You are real."

Others, emboldened by the prince's actions, began to filter into the room and offer assistance to the remaining prisoners.

The three chirurgeons that were with Allyn's patrol took over and began to treat the prisoners.

Sickened, Allyn said, "All right, this building is clear. Let's check the barn and move on."

Larrig nodded. "Should I leave guards?"

"Aye, pick three men to stay."

Shortly, the remainder of the group exited the house and began moving across a fallow field toward a structure that would normally be used as a hay barn. It lay some distance from the main house, and Allyndev worried that his men were vulnerable in the open. Motioning for the soldiers to move in double time, the prince prayed that there were no traps waiting to trip up the unwary.

The closer they got to the barn, the stronger the scent of death became. Two men had to stop to vomit while their partners stood guard. Finally, they reached the barn.

More silent signals sent men to scout both sides seeking other entrances. Once the layout was established, Allyn gave the go-ahead. "For the peace of Y'Dan," he said softly.

"Peace!" his men chanted as they threw themselves at the ban doors.

The wood gave way with a splintering crack.

As daylight flooded into the building, a horrific sight was revealed. Some two dozen men and boys knelt before a hideous altar. At the foot of a grotesque statue of Ecarthus, a black-robed priest had just finished butchering a woman. Her corpse lay at his feet. In his hands, he held a still throbbing heart.

"For the glory of our beloved lord, may he reign forever!" he shouted, and dropped the heart into a burning cauldron.

"Ecarthus lives!" the others replied.

"Destroy the infidels!" the priest yelled. "Feed our lord the blood of the nonbelievers!"

With a yell, the two sides rushed toward each other, weapons flashing in the torchlight.

Allyn met two gray-robed acolytes head on, knocking one dagger away with his shield while catching the shaft of a torch on the flat of his dirk. Furiously, he worked to block the knife blows while struggling to keep the flames away from his face and hair.

Sweat broke out and dripped down the center of his back and briefly, he thought, *I wish Azhani were here instead of me,* but then the man with the torch switched tactics.

Jumping back, the torch bearer kicked out, trying to trip the prince and almost succeeding, causing Allyn to stumble.

Pay attention, Allyn or you're going to feed the crows! The prince caught himself before he fell, pivoting and slashing out with his dagger. The tip caught in the fabric of a robe. Jerking his blade back, Allyn was satisfied to see the gray material shred.

The three men faced off. The man with the torn robe gripped his dagger reflexively while the torch bearer passed the flaming brand from hand to hand, hoping to mesmerize his opponent. Allyn kept his gaze moving back and forth, searching for an opening.

Around them, men were fighting and dying and pools of blood were beginning to slick the stone floor of the barn. Suddenly, the torch bearer lost his footing and slipped.

Allyn acted, stooping to stab the man in the gut and then quickly spinning around to slash at the other acolyte. The razor-sharp dirk cut deeply into the torch bearer's gut, forcing him to his knees as his entrails began to push out through the wound.

Allyn's blade now dripped with the other man's blood. Licking his lips, the man with the torn robe struck, slashing his blade in a wide arc toward him. The hook point of the dagger caught on Allyn's mailed glove as it hit, biting deeply into the prince's knuckle.

"Shyvot!" he growled and kicked the acolyte in the shin.

The other man grunted in pain. Allyn kicked him again and yanked his hand back, roaring as the blade skimmed over the mesh of his gauntlet, cutting his hand in several spots. Dancing out of the way of the now furious prince, the acolyte allowed a slow, feral smile to flicker into life.

"Ecarthus shall feast upon your soul," he said, feinting to the right.

Allyn ducked and dove for the gray-robed man. The torch bearer slashed down, cursing when the prince twisted and caught the hook point of the knife in his armor.

"Maybe," Allyndev grunted as he stabbed his opponent, driving the blade up through ribs and into the heart, "but not today."

The acolyte blinked once, then his eyes rolled back into his head as blood fountained from his mouth, coating the prince's chest.

Allyn spun away from the dying man, searching for more enemies.

The remainder of the fight was short and dirty. Three of Allyn's men would not return to Kellerdon alongside their leader, but none of the evil priests would ever cause harm to another innocent farmer.

Standing before the smashed-in doors, Allyndev stared at the carnage littering the floor and felt his gorge rise. He swallowed heavily and then said, "Burn it. Let this be their pyre."

The bodies of the dead soldiers were retrieved while oil was spilled over the corpses of the priests.

The sun was setting when Allyn accepted a torch from one of the soldiers. Taking a deep breath, he whispered, "May the gods have mercy on you," and tossed the torch into the barn.

The army bivouacked in Kellerdon for ten days. While there, Allyn led several more successful raids against Ecarthus' temples, destroying a total of ten of the heinous structures. The army was spread in thin groups across the breadth of Y'Dan as each patrol attempted to remove the scourge of the Ecarthans from the countryside.

Farmers who had gone into hiding came to Kellerdon to welcome Azhani and her army as heroes. Solemnly, the warleader accepted their praise, but made it a point to introduce them to Prince Allyndev. The shy prince was bashful about accepting admiration, but with Azhani's support, he learned how to interact with them.

Every night, a bonfire was lit in the center of town. Into those fires went the accoutrements of Ecarthan worship — robes, hangings, and daggers — whatever bore the terrible sigil of the crimson obelisk was consumed by the hungry blaze.

One evening, Allyn and his friends were quietly talking as they tossed robes into the flames.

"I wish I knew what was in Master Azhani's head," the prince said wistfully. He bundled up another robe and threw it into the fire.

"Why do you say that?" Devon asked as he dismantled a book and tossed the pages into the fire.

The prince rubbed his hands on his breeches and frowned. "All this responsibility — the patrols, this—" he indicated the massive pile of items to be destroyed. "Isn't this something that Chief Padreg should do? He's a king. Kings are supposed to be the heroes, not half-breed princelings who'll never amount to much."

Devon shifted on his crutches. Shaking his head, the mage said, "Maybe it's because you're capable of doing the work? I've never known Azhani to allow able hands to stand idle."

"I've noticed that she encourages you to choose soldiers from Y'Dan to go with your patrols. Perhaps she wishes to create a sense of pride for these people?" said Syrelle.

Allyn shrugged. "I know, but then I get treated like I'm some kind of hero." He limped over to the pile and pulled out another handful of things to burn. Earlier, he had taken a cut from an Ecarthan dagger, and the wound ached. "I'm no hero. People like Azhani, Padreg — even Elisira and Kyrian — they're the heroes." The prince glanced over at the warleader's fire where those he had named were gathered, laughing and talking among themselves. Zhadosh lounged on Kyrian's lap and the kitten was batting playfully at the stardancer's Astariun token.

"That's not true, Allyn," Devon said. He reached down to pat Avisha's head when she stretched up to butt his hip commandingly. "You were the one who kept those of us in the infirmary safe that day. You were the one who pulled one of those damn rimerbeasts off Starseeker Vashyra. You saved our lives."

The prince sighed and threw the last robe into the fire. "I'm not a hero," he said again, daring his friends to defy him.

Two arms wrapped around his waist as he stared into the flames. "Maybe not," Syrelle said as she laid her head on his shoulder.

"But you're doing a credible imitation of one," Devon finished, flashing a hearty grin at the startled look on Allyn's face.

"So what you're saying is to be quiet and take it like a man?" Allyn asked jokingly.

Syrelle smiled sweetly and looked over at Devon. "I think he's got a brain in there after all," she said, her tone full of mock surprise.

"Amazing, isn't it?" Devon replied, his grin turning cockeyed. "Allyn, you've been given an opportunity to do something wonderful for this kingdom. My father often said that there is no wine sweeter than the regard of one's peers. Drink up, my friend, for the love is flowing!"

It was on the tip of the prince's tongue to say that he didn't want to become drunk on the wine of praise, but he held it back. The fact was, he did enjoy the admiration, but more, he was coming to like the sense of pride in his actions that he felt. It was confusing and strange to think that he was capable of standing next to people like Azhani and know that he could hold his own.

I've learned how to fall, I've learned how to walk. Maybe what I'm supposed to learn now is how to run.

The last of the black robes turned to ash and blew away into the night.

Chapter Forty

On a clear, sunny morning, with her friends at her side, Azhani Rhu'len, the Banshee of Banner Lake, returned to the city of Y'Dannyv. Sparkling brilliantly, the clear waters of the Banner filled her with intense memories of a time when those waters ran red with the blood of innocents. Barely a year had passed since that horrible day, but in that span of time, harsh changes had been wrought to the city that was once her home.

Houses and buildings that had always been draped in colorful swags of cloth now only boasted somber-hued paint. Inns and taverns that usually were filled to the brim by customers from all over the kingdoms were empty — even closed for business. Those townspeople who dared to wander the streets viewed Azhani's group with haunted, fearful eyes and made the warleader tighten her grip on the hilt of her sword.

There were no children blocking the streets with their games. No beggars sought alms. Only a few folk who scurried from place to place as they conducted their daily business.

Out in force were men dressed in the green and black of Arris' personal guard. Beside them, black-robed Ecarthan priests glared as Azhani's army filled the streets with rank after rank of soldiers.

Azhani marked the placement of each of the priests. Soon, they would feel the bite of her hounds, but for now, she was content to allow them to eye her with hate and fear.

Behind her, Lady Elisira rode next to Mayor Graystone. Padreg and Allyndev rode at the head of smaller patrols, ready to halt any attempt to assassinate the warleader.

At her right rode Kyrian. The stardancer clutched her reins tightly, her knuckles white with the effort. Azhani reached over and covered her lover's hands. "Be at ease, love."

"I'm a little scared, Azhani. I'd rather not see blood shed this day."

"I cannot promise that, my heart."

Kyrian sighed and flinched when one of the Ecarthan priests hurled an epithet at them. "I know. Just be careful. I don't want to lose you, again."

Azhani squeezed the stardancer's hands. "You will not."

Riding pillion behind Kyrian, the kitten Zhadosh began to hiss comically at the black-robed priests who dared step toward her friends.

At the head of a patrol of fifty men, Prince Allyndev gawked openly at the predominantly brick and stone buildings that made up the city. The half-elf was used to towns made of trees, not stone. The smaller villages like Kellerdon had not prepared him for this massive city where buildings seemed to grow from the very earth itself.

Next to him rode Princess Syrelle. She tried hard to remember what the city had looked like when she had last visited, but found it difficult to reconcile her colorful memories with the dull reality.

At Allyn's left, Devon rode with silent tears streaming down his face. The city of his birth had become a strange place to him. Familiar landmarks were gone. The fountain he had swam in as a child, the street market where vendors hawked their wares from sunup to sundown, even the gaily dressed minstrels had vanished, leaving behind a town that he did not recognize. The hunting cat Avisha rode proudly on Devon's saddle, surveying the scene with the disinterested gaze of a feline. Unlike Zhadosh, Avisha seemed completely at ease on her perch.

The army was met in the center of the city by a group of men and women dressed in the rich garments of the King's Council. Unlike the people of Y'Dannyv, the faces of those waiting were filled with expressions of utter relief.

Lord Councilor Valdyss Cathemon waited while Azhani dismounted. Standing proudly, the nobles bore no weapons nor did they have guards to stand between them and the army.

Lord Cathemon stepped forward. Speaking in a clear, carrying voice, he said, "Welcome to Y'Dannyv, Azhani Rhu'len. In the name of the Council, I greet you as the rightful warleader of Y'Dan."

His pronouncement brought the citizenry of Y'Dannyv into the streets. Voices carrying snatches of excited conversation began to flurry around them.

"Azhani? The warleader is back? Wasn't she exiled? Oh gods, has she come to free us from the Ecarthans?"

Azhani walked up to the councilors and knelt before Cathemon. In a clear voice, she said, "I have come to challenge the ruling of King Arris. By his hand was I freed of the onus of oath-breaking. By his word have I been restored as warleader."

She held out a scroll bearing the signed and witnessed statements of several Y'Dani soldiers who had heard Arris give command of the army to Azhani. Other scrolls would be given to the Council at a later date. Among the personal effects of Porthyros Omal, journals were found. These diaries included detailed descriptions of how the scholar had, at the command of his master, Kasyrin Darkchilde, caused the prince and then king, Arris, to carry out heinous acts, including the murder of Ylera Kelani.

"Rise, Azhani Rhu'len, and be welcome. We accept the word of our king."

Azhani stood and clasped the older man's hands warmly.

Nearby, Lord High Councilor Derkus Glinholt gazed longingly at his daughter, Elisira. The nobleman seemed ready to vibrate out of his clothes, his longing to go to his daughter's side was so plainly apparent.

"I have returned to free this land from the clutches of those who would bring evil to its people," Azhani said to Cathemon. "To that end, I would declare a state of martial law while my people restore order."

Cathemon looked taken aback by the warleader's determined statement. "If that is your will, Warleader, then by all means. We shall not stop you." If he also looked at all pleased by the notion that the men and women who had made his city into a cesspit of evil were about to receive the warleader's justice, Azhani did not comment on it.

"Allyndev, Padreg, go," the warleader said succinctly. Like arrows shot from a bow, the two men kneed their horses into action. Suddenly two hundred soldiers broke ranks and began to arrest each and every person bearing the arms of Arris Thodan or the robes of an Ecarthan priest.

There were small pockets of resistance, and several attempts were made to flee, but by the end of a candlemark, there was not one Ecarthan left free in the city.

Councilor Glinholt stood quietly the entire time until Padreg rode up leading a line of several chained priests. Then he turned to his daughter and said, "I suppose he expects a medal now."

Elisira shot her father a bemused look and said, "Nay, Father, he expects naught but to have good neighbors, as would any man."

Stung, Glinholt turned away from his offspring.

It was Prince Allyndev who received the loudest cheer as his men herded a large group of black robes into the square. The prince was nursing a wounded arm, which caused the Princess Syrelle to dash off to his side. Stardancer Kyrian was not far behind her.

Along with the priests, Allyn had brought scores of men, women and children who had been freed from their prisons. Ragged, battered and in poor health, the newly liberated people nonetheless followed the prince with something akin to worship in their eyes.

"I recognize Chief Padreg, but who is the young man?" Cathemon asked softly as Azhani watched her people lead the prisoners off to the gaol.

"Prince Allyndev Kelani," Azhani said, which caused Councilor Glinholt to gasp.

"Is he Ylera's get?" the councilor blurted.

The councilor was pinned by a glare so fierce he actually felt pain from the look. "No. His mother was Alynna."

Glinholt wisely chose not to say anything more.

Cathemon cleared his throat. "Why don't we repair to the castle? It will take time to sort everything out." He looked at Azhani and smiled. "Welcome home, Warleader."

She returned his smile. "Thank you, Councilor. Though I doubt that you will continue to extend that welcome for much longer."

"Planning a disturbance, Warleader?" he asked as they began to walk toward Y'Dannoch.

"Always, Lord Cathemon."

For his role in the plan to assassinate Padreg, Derkus Glinholt was exiled to his home on the Y'Dani coast. Twelve other councilors excused themselves from service and left the city before their profiteering was discovered. The guards who bore Arris' colors quickly traded in the black and green tunics for ones bearing the Y'Dani wheat sheaf. Those who had worn the black robes of Ecarthan priests were bound over to be tried by the new ruler of Y'Dan.

Slowly, the people of Y'Dannyv began to emerge. Colorful pennants once again decorated the rooftops. The Astariun temples were once again filled to capacity by those seeking to bask in the love of the Twain. By ones and twos, the farmers of the outlying lands began to trickle in, and the market reopened. Fishermen once again sailed the lake and hauled in their daily catch.

On the tongue of nearly everyone who lived in Y'Dan rode one question: Who would take the Crown of Y'Dan?

Rumors flew concerning Azhani. Some said that she would be queen;

others said that she would choose one of the remaining councilors.

The warleader knew that the Council would gladly hand her the throne. Unfortunately for Y'Dan, Azhani did not want to rule. She no longer wished to be the kingdom's warleader, either. Leaving the kingdom had given Azhani the opportunity to see a life beyond its borders and now, because of the oath she had given to Y'Syr and because of her own desire to find a future by Kyrian's side, the warrior knew that it was time to put her time in Thodan's realm in the past. Y'Dan was home no more — all it held were shadows of old pain.

On the fourth day after their arrival, High King Ysradan made his appearance. Unlike Azhani, he did not forsake the pomp and circumstance that was due his station. The Y'Maran ruler's ship sailed into the harbor flanked by four large warships.

Azhani and her entourage hurried to greet Ysradan. It had been at least five years since she had seen him, and she found herself at odds over how she felt. *Would he agree with the Council? Would he uphold her freedom? Or would he reinstate the oath-breaking and force her to become a fugitive once more?*

Running almost as fast as Azhani was Princess Syrelle. The young woman was desperate to see her father. She had missed him and her mother terribly. She also wanted them to meet Prince Allyndev and gain their approval of the young man. When the king came into sight, the young woman raced past Azhani and flew into her father's arms. "Papa!" she crowed, obviously delighted to see him.

Ysradan caught his daughter and lifted her up, swinging her around until she laughed. "Ah, how's my beautiful angel?" he asked, bringing her down and hugging her close.

Syrelle grinned and said, "Better, now that you're here. Where's my brother, the demon?"

"Right here, fish breath!" said the high-pitched voice of a child. Behind Ysradan was the six-year-old Y'Maran heir apparent, Ysrallan. He stuck his tongue out at his sister, screwing up his face into a nasty parody of a demon's mask. Then he grinned and ran over to Syrelle's side, hugging her fiercely. "You've been gone forever and ever, Relly," he whispered, clinging tightly.

Syrelle lifted her brother, hugging him close. "I know, Rallie. I missed you too."

"Mama's hurt," Ysrallan whispered softly. His voice was filled with all the fear that he had hidden from his parents.

The princess felt her heart clutch at the news. A group of guardsman parted and revealed Queen Dasia. The high queen's head was wrapped in a bandage that covered her eyes.

Syrelle released her brother and went to the queen. "Mother," she cried softly, "what happened?" She reached for her, but stopped short, an uncertain grimace on her face.

Queen Dasia bridged the gap and embraced her daughter. "It is nothing, dear. An unfortunate encounter with the breath of a sea serpent has caused me some minor injury but I am fine, Syrelle." She held the shaking girl tightly. "I've been assured that the venom blindness will pass."

Ysradan noticed Azhani watching his family and smiled sadly. "She took a blow meant for me. I'd be paste if it weren't for her boldness."

"I thank the gods that you are both safe," Azhani said. "Y'Dan welcomes its high king joyfully." She bowed deeply.

"Thank you, Warleader Rhu'len. I have come, as you requested, to set right the pain felt so keenly by your benighted land."

Another quarter candlemark passed as Azhani and the high king exchanged formal pleasantries. Once those were out of the way, Ysradan moved on to grab Padreg and embrace him heartily. "Padreg, my gods, lad, you've grown like one of your damn weeds!"

"My King," Padreg said, bowing after Ysradan released him. "I'm afraid I'm a little taller than even the grasses of my homelands now."

Ysradan chuckled and looked up at the man he knew as a boy. "I would have to agree. But then, we always knew you were part giant." He turned to the Lady Elisira and took her hands in his. "My Lady, it does my heart good to gaze upon your beauty once more. How are you?"

Elisira leaned in for a kiss, and replied, "I am well, you old charmer. How are you?"

"Good, good," Ysradan said, moving on to Kyrian. He smiled brilliantly at her, the full force of his charm in effect. "You will perhaps pardon me, for I do not know you, but your face shall haunt my dreams until the moment I look upon the perfection that is our beloved goddess."

Kyrian looked at Azhani and whispered, "He's quite good at this, isn't he?" Looking back at Ysradan, she said, "I am Stardancer Kyrian, Your Majesty."

"Pleased I am to greet thee, revered one," he said and bowed deeply. "It is to thee that our thanks must fall for it was thy care that returned this land's beloved warleader in a timely fashion. Without thee, Y'Myran most surely would have suffered greatly. Whatever boon thou cravest, should it fall under my purview to grant, grant it I shall."

The high king's formal attitude caused Kyrian to stumble over her words. "I am pleased to meet you too, Your Majesty."

He beamed happily and moved on, greeting others of the Council that he knew.

Taking his place was Queen Dasia. Guided by the loving hand of Syrelle, the high queen stopped before Kyrian and said, "Ysra is fond of his formal speeches, young Kyrian. Do not allow his fancy words to stand in the way of our becoming friends." She smiled, and even though half of her face was covered, Kyrian could see that the queen was a woman of rare beauty.

Kyrian reached out and took the queen's hand and squeezed it warmly. "I'll try not to, Your Majesty."

After a great deal of talk, Ysradan finally returned to face Azhani once more. For long moments, the high king and the Y'Dani warleader shared a silent communion. Then, Ysradan sighed sadly and wiped his eyes. "I miss him," he said. "Thodan was a good man who fought hard to bring peace to his land. It pains me that his legacy was so terribly corrupted in such a short time."

"Those dreams may yet live, Ysradan," Azhani said softly. The warleader's gaze fell upon Prince Allyndev, who was fidgeting in place. She smiled and said, "There is much to discuss, My Lord."

Feeling very much like an outsider, Prince Allyndev stood to the side of the assembled nobles and aimlessly scratched at his jaw. Frowning, he scuffed the palm of his hand against the itchy beard stubble and sighed. A chance comment by Syrelle had kept him from shaving for the last few days. The princess had stated that she thought he looked rather rugged and handsome with the shadow of a beard, so the prince decided to leave the growth rather than shaving as he was accustomed. Unfortunately, the extra growth made his face itch terribly. *I am going to shave tomorrow. Syrelle will just have to learn to accept my face as it is.*

With her brother in tow, Syrelle left her mother's side and sidled up to the prince. "Allyn," she said, biting her lip shyly.

"Yes?" He smiled, looking into her brilliant blue eyes and seeing everything he wanted for the future shining back at him.

"I, um, this is my little brother, Ysrallan," she mumbled, thrusting the boy forward. "Rallie, this is Prince Allyndev."

Shyly, the boy prince held his hand out to the older prince. "Hello?" he smiled, his lips curling in an unconscious echo of his sister's uncertain grin.

Clasping the boy's hand warmly, Allyn took a knee and bowed his head to Ysrallan. "Good day, My Prince," he said solemnly, causing the lad to giggle. "How was your trip?"

Ysrallan's face screwed up and he rolled his eyes comically. "It was awful! I don't like boats." The young prince covered his mouth and puffed out his cheeks, managing a credible imitation of seasickness.

Allyn chuckled. "I can remember my first few times on a ship. The scenery was all water!" He winked and stood, taking Syrelle's hand in his and pressing a gentle kiss to the palm. "My Lady," he murmured.

"Allyndev," she said, and her voice dropped as her heartbeat increased, "I'd like to introduce you to my parents."

Suddenly, all of Allyn's hard-won confidence seemed to vanish and he was once again the gangly boy who was teased for his love of books. Nervously, he turned to face the high king and his queen as they approached their daughter's side.

"Mother, Father, this is Prince Allyndev Kelani. He has become a very good friend," she said shyly, looking sideways at Allyn and then back at her parents.

The high king pumped Allyn's hand. "Good to meet you, young man, very good. Heard about how you made those black-robed bastards dance. Good show, lad, excellent." Ysradan released Allyn's hand and moved on before the Y'Syran prince had a chance to respond.

High Queen Dasia took a moment longer to embrace the half-elven prince. "Hello Allyndev. Are you Alynna's child?" When the prince replied in the affirmative, she said, "I knew your mother well. She was a good friend to our family. I am pleased to learn that the same can be said of her son."

"Thank you, Your Majesty," he mumbled, unable to think of anything else to say.

She smiled. "Come, I grow weary and would seek the warmth of a fire and the comfort of a cushioned chair." Taking a firm hold of Allyn's arm, Queen Dasia indicated that the young prince should escort her to the confines of Y'Dannoch Castle.

There was a day of boring, sleep-inducing ceremonies, in which High King Ysradan confirmed Azhani's pardon. The high king's words were mere formality, but they touched off a celebration that seemed like it might never end.

Tales carried by the soldiers of Azhani's army spread like wildfire through the town, and soon all spoke of the Battle of Shield Mountain, as the struggle between Astariu and Ecarthus had become known, as if they had been there themselves.

A week passed as the citizens of Y'Dan celebrated with abandon. The last of the Ecarthan temples was razed, and the contents of Porthyros' diaries were made public. History was made when Queen Lyssera arrived from Y'Syr. For the first time in hundreds of years, an elven ruler stepped onto Y'Dani soil with peaceful intent.

A conclave had been called. A new ruler for Y'Dan would be chosen, and as Y'Dan's nearest neighbor, the Y'Syrans had a definite interest in the proceedings. As high king, Ysradan would oversee the actions taken by the Y'Dani Council to restore order to their kingdom. He also held the right of final approval of the person chosen to hold the reins of the kingdom.

Though Y'Dannyv was blanketed under several feet of snow, the council room was crowded and stuffy. Azhani stifled a yawn, glanced at the day candle and counted the remaining lines. Three days remained until winter solstice and she was deathly tired of the interminable meetings that Y'Dan's nobility held to determine who would sit upon the Granite Throne.

Nervously, she doodled on a piece of old parchment. Beside her, Kyrian placed a gentle hand on her knee and gave it a reassuring squeeze. Smiling, she left off her drawing and tried to concentrate on the proceedings. Having her lover by her side made the long sessions bearable, but only just.

The stardancer leaned over and whispered, "Do you think it will last much longer?"

Azhani listened to the latest round of arguments for a particular faction's candidate and shook her head. "Not if I have anything to say about it."

Lord Cathemon, alongside several other Y'Dani nobles, was firmly rooted in the belief that Azhani should take the crown of Y'Dan. Others weren't so keen to give the throne to the woman who had been responsible for the deaths of so many, even if she had ultimately been proven innocent.

Since Arris left no heirs, many claiming to have even a trace of royal blood came forth to press their case for the throne.

Azhani did not want the throne. She had never wanted to rule and had simply made her claim at Thodan's request. After all that had happened, her desire to rule had only diminished.

The bickering came to a head as each side screamed foul epithets proclaiming the worthlessness of the other's candidates. Rising, Azhani threw back her head and let off a shortened version of her distinctive war cry.

Stunned, the crowd fell silent.

With all eyes firmly pinned on her, Azhani raised an eyebrow and said, "Did any of you idiots think to ask me if I even *wanted* the damned crown?"

346 ❖ Shaylynn Rose

A collective gasp echoed around the room at her pronouncement. Kyrian chuckled while the high king shook his head at the histrionics that several of the Y'Dani courtiers were displaying.

Queen Lyssera and Chief Padreg exchanged similar grins while Azhani waited for the room to quiet. The Y'Syran and Y'Noran monarchs both knew that their friend was up to something, and each was interested to discover what it was.

Azhani paced about the room, finally coming to a stop in front of a page. She whispered something to the boy and he was off as though shot from a ballista. The warrior turned to the high king and said, "Your Majesty, this may take some time. Would you care to stretch your legs?"

Ysradan inclined his head. "Yes, I believe I would be delighted to regain feeling in my feet." The high king stood and offered a hand to his wife. "Come, love, let us seek fresher air."

The doors leading to a balcony that overlooked the castle gardens were thrown open. By ones and twos, the assembled nobles moved about the room and enjoyed the opportunity to refresh drinks or visit a nearby water closet. Others bent their heads together to discuss the warleader's surprising statement.

Kyrian stood and went to her lover. Embracing her, she asked, "What are you up to, Azhani?"

The warrior only smiled enigmatically and kissed the stardancer.

Prince Allyndev was wandering the halls of Y'Dannoch. In the time that they had been here, Devon had taught the prince the trick to navigating the castle's passageways and Allyn had spent much of his free time exploring the castle environs.

Y'Dannoch was nothing like Oakheart. Made entirely of stone and timber, the castle walls did not pulse with life like the massive tree that was his birthplace. Yet, there was something ineffable that called out to the young man. There was a presence in Y'Dannoch that was welcoming in a way that Oakheart had never been.

It puzzled him greatly.

The beard he wore no longer caused his face to feel as though he had slept in a patch of poison ivy. However, the castle staff now regarded him with strange looks — almost as though they had seen a ghost. Many went out of their way to serve him, which left him even more confused.

He was just passing the library when a page spotted him and called out, "Lord Allyndev, please wait!" Racing pell-mell down the hall, the boy nearly slid to a halt in front of him.

Allyn smiled and said, "Aye lad, what is it?"

Gulping air, the page said, "Warleader Azhani asks that you join her in the council chamber."

The room fell silent as Prince Allyndev entered. Milling council members turned to view the newcomer. Walking with sure, firm strides, the young man made his way through the room to Azhani's side. Dressed simply, yet elegantly, Allyndev stood out in a room filled with peacock hued garb.

Azhani spared a moment to share a proud smile with Queen Lyssera.

Each remembered the half grown boy that had been given to the war-leader's care. Months of hard work had chased away the remnants of youth and sculpted him into a fine man. The fullness of boyhood had given way to the fine, narrow features of his elven ancestry. The beard that shadowed his face only served to emphasize the duality of his nature. His hair, kept long on the elven style, framed his face in a fall of multiple braids while his eyes gazed with piercing clarity out on the world.

The prince stopped before Queen Lyssera and bowed deeply then presented himself to his mentor. Respectfully, he bowed and said, "You sent for me, Master Azhani?"

Azhani smiled. "Aye, lad."

He nodded. "What can I do for you?"

Azhani's face suddenly became very serious. "Do you trust me, Allyndev?"

The prince carefully schooled his expression to diminish the amount of surprise he displayed. Azhani's tone indicated that she was planning to do something that would have far reaching effects. He looked into her eyes and tried to gauge her intent, but could see nothing behind the icy blueness. Bowing his head he said, "Yes, I trust you, Master Azhani."

She put her hands on his shoulders and gripped them tightly. "Thank you. Please, sit down. You'll know when I need you." She smiled suddenly and said, "I'm about to tweak a few Y'Dani noses."

"Yes, Master Azhani."

Her grin twisted wryly. "You can drop the 'master', Allyn. You've earned the right to stand beside me." She released him and he stumbled to a seat.

"Yes Ma— Azhani," he whispered dazedly. The prince glanced at his mentor. *I'm her equal?* The warleader called for the councilors to return to their seats.

He remembered the first day they had met, and how Azhani had taught him a lesson in manners. Stunned was the mildest way he could think to describe how he felt at this moment. Lost in his memories, he barely noticed as Azhani brought the room to a state of calm.

"Woolgathering, boy?" A voice interrupted his thoughts.

"What? Oh, no sir!" Allyn sat at full attention as High King Ysradan chuckled and took his seat on the Granite Throne of Y'Dan. Queen Lyssera looked over at her nephew and winked, while Queen Dasia smiled serenely, waiting for the council session to begin again. The bandages had been taken off her eyes, allowing her to both see and hear the proceedings. A fine network of scars that webbed over her eyes was all that was left of a terrible injury and Allyn was once again reminded that not all of the casualties of the Ecarthan conflict were from Y'Syr and Y'Dan. All of the kingdoms had suffered because of Kasyrin Darkchilde's machinations. The half-elven prince took a breath and tried to relax.

Kyrian leaned over and whispered, "Allyndev looks as though he's been knocked in the face by a dead fish. What devilment are you at, Azhani?"

Azhani smirked and winked. "Wait and see, love."

Kyrian rolled her eyes and sighed in exasperation.

Ysradan cleared his throat. "All right ladies and gentlemen, the respite is over. Let us return to the matter at hand. Azhani, I believe that you have something to say?" There was a twinkle of merriment forming in his eyes as he turned the floor over to her. He was looking forward to what she had to say. Anyone who didn't want a crown was bound to be amusing, at the very least.

Walking to the center of the room, Azhani kept her face inscrutable. All eyes were upon her as she clasped her hands behind her back. Deftly, she bowed to the assembled monarchs and nobility.

From the corner of her eye, she caught a glance of a piece of her past that she had thought long buried. Against one wall, pushed out of the way, was the table upon which she had thrown Thodan's proclamation. Momentarily disoriented, Azhani believed she could see the spreading stain of blood on the rug below the piece of furniture.

Blinking, she tore her gaze from the table and looked into Kyrian's gentle green eyes. The stardancer smiled brightly and mouthed, "I love you."

Taking a deep breath, Azhani allowed the pain of the past to drain away. It was time to grab the future and hold on to it for all that it was worth.

"My Lords and Ladies, when I spoke earlier about not wanting the crown, I spoke truly. I have never desired to rule; not when Thodan asked it of me and most surely not now." She looked around and met several pairs of surprised eyes. Even now, there were those who felt that she had forged the proclamation. The warrior knew she had to make them believe before she could continue. "I have no desire to sit upon the Granite Throne."

She strode about the room, coming to stop before Ysradan. "Your pardon, Your Majesty," she said, bowing deeply. "But my head was not made to bear a crown."

Ysradan inclined his head fractionally. "I accept that, Warleader."

Azhani smiled.

Lord Cathemon spoke. "If Azhani will not take the crown, then who will rule Y'Dan?" A spark of something — almost greedy — flared in the nobleman's eyes.

Azhani took a deep breath. She looked at Queen Lyssera and nodded imperceptibly. The Y'Syran monarch's eyes widened and then she looked away.

Azhani smiled sadly. "Allow me to tell you a story, my Lords and Ladies." She began to move about the room again. "Twenty years ago, I was just a child. I lived here, in Y'Dannoch, serving as a page while my father worked for King Thodan as a special lawkeeper." Her face took on an expression of memory. "If there was something out of the ordinary to be done, it was my father who performed that task.

"King Thodan's greatest desire was to give his land a legacy of peace. The kingdoms of Y'Dan and Y'Syr had long been at odds as elven and human lords on either side of the border skirmished over land rights. Thodan felt that if our kingdoms could live in peace, we would know a prosperity akin to that of our eastern cousins, the Y'Tolians.

"With the high king's blessing, Thodan began the long process to bring peace to the two kingdoms. You are all aware of how long this took. I will not bore you with the details that can so easily be read in our history.

"Instead, I wish to tell you of Thodan's first visit to the beautiful city of Y'Syria, and how he met his first love among the elves."

She had the room's full attention now. Raptly, they listened as she spoke.

"I was there, my Lords and Ladies, when my father and my king were presented first to Queen Lyssera, and then to her sister, the Warleader Alynna."

Allyn and Lyssera both bowed their heads at the mention of the prince's mother.

"Afterward, my father took me to see the sights of Y'Syria while Thodan and Alynna joined Lyssera in a council for peace. What words they may have exchanged, I do not know. I only know that from that day forth, Thodan and Alynna were great friends."

She came to stand before Kyrian and Allyndev.

"I did not know how great their friendship was until recently."

The stardancer looked at her lover and then at Allyn. Her mouth opened in an "O" of understanding, and her eyes grew moist.

"You must understand Thodan loved Alynna deeply, as the elven princess greatly cared for the human king. However, the peace between our lands was tenuous at the best of times. By no means would either side tolerate a joining between the two houses." The assembled Y'Dani nobles nodded understandingly.

"Yet Thodan could no more ignore the calling of his heart than he could fly to the moon. Alynna was stronger. She saw that peace between Y'Syr and Y'Dan was the greater good, so she told Thodan a small lie. She made him believe that she did not love him as he loved her.

"Thodan left Y'Syr brokenhearted, but with a solid foundation for peace in place.

"Two years later, he met and married Queen Siobhan and to him she gave Arris. The prince was eight when his mother died in a sudden squall on Banner Lake.

"With an heir in place, Thodan eschewed the idea of marrying another, and instead threw himself into holding together the fractured peace between Y'Syrans and Y'Danis.

"By then, I was serving in his army, and we had plenty of distractions. Rimerbeasts, bandits, barbarians — for a goodly length of time, it seemed as though Y'Dan's northern border would never be safe.

"Yet Thodan would not be thwarted. He gathered his armies and we marched north, to the Ystarfe Pass. There, joined by a small force of Y'Syrans, he drove the barbarians back over the crest.

"Young Arris grew, cared for by his mentor, Porthyros Omal.

"I became warleader. Under my command, we drove the bandits from our forests and Y'Dan prospered." Azhani took a breath and looked at Allyn.

"And you, My Prince, you aged, and grew up in Y'Syr and became the man you are now. You learned your letters and your numbers. You discovered the love of the earth and its growing things. You lifted your eyes to the heavens and sought answers to age old riddles in the stars that whirl above. Yet neither gardener nor starseeker came to call.

"From your aunt, you had memories of your mother, the Princess Alynna, but never was the name of the man who sired you spoken."

Allyn looked up at his mentor with fearful eyes as her words washed over him. His heart was beating so fast, he was certain it was about to leap from his chest. He felt hot and cold at the same time.

"Never did you know of Thodan the Peacemaker, and how he had loved your mother. My story has been for you, Prince Allyndev Kelani, son of Alynna and Thodan." Ahzani's voice was soft and her gaze was fully on the young prince. She waited several heartbeats as the tension in the room grew. Then she knelt before Allyn and said, "Thodan gave me the throne because he knew Arris could not rule wisely. I say that had he known of this son — this man whom all speak of with nothing but honor — he would have joyfully named him heir."

Allyn was sure that the world had just stopped. His vision started to fade. His stomach was in a thousand knots and his tongue felt glued to the roof of his mouth. *My father was...King Thodan?* He looked everywhere but at Azhani and his aunt.

The councilors and noblemen stared at the young prince. All had heard tales of the boy's bravery — how he had defended the injured against the final rimerbeast attack and how he became one of Azhani's best patrol leaders on the journey home.

High King Ysradan stood and slowly approached the half-elven prince. "Stand up, boy, and let us look at you," he said hoarsely. The older man's eyes were wet with tears and his face was a mask of emotions.

Slowly, as if fighting his way up through water, Allyn stood.

Ysradan circled the prince. Stopping in front of him, he reached out and took Allyn's face in his hands, turning it toward the light.

"Astarus' blood, but she's right," the high king whispered. "His look is strong in you, lad. Especially with the beard — Thodan never could remember to shave." Suddenly, the older man grabbed the young prince and pulled him into a long, hard embrace.

The hug reached through the cotton that had wadded around Allyn's consciousness and he clung to Ysradan, weeping openly. He knew his father's name! He was not a result of some shameful coupling as his peers had insinuated. All of his life, he had tried to ignore the whispers, and mostly he had succeeded. Yet there was always that small voice within him that wondered, *Why am I here?*

"I know his name," Allyn whispered.

Ysradan sobbed. "Ah gods, my old friend. Would that you could see this boy, and be proud." The high king turned to Queen Lyssera and said, "Be the words of thy warleader true, Queen of the Elves? Do we behold the son of Y'Dan's king?" His words carried a formality that affected all within the chamber.

Rising, Lyssera inclined her head regally. "Aye, My King, let it be known that Allyndev, prince of our house, was sired by Thodan, of the Y'Dani people."

Ysradan nodded. "Thank you, Queen Lyssera, for your candor." He looked at Azhani and said, "And thank you, good Warleader, for discovering this most perfect solution to Y'Dan's dilemma."

Azhani bowed. There was a slight smile affixed to her face, and a measure of relief in her eyes.

The high king guided Allyndev to the center of the room and placed him in front of the throne. He then moved to stand behind him, using the throne's step to place himself above the prince. Putting a hand on each of Allyn's shoulders, Ysradan said, "Let it be known that I, Ysradan Ymyras, high king of Y'Myran, do hereby accept Prince Allyndev Kelani-Thodan as the right and true heir to Y'Dan."

There was a moment of stunned silence, and then a cheer rose from the gallery.

"Y'Dan's throne sits empty, boy, will you take it, and accept the legacy of your father?" Ysradan whispered in Allyn's ear.

Time seemed to be moving so fast. Allyndev stared at the portrait of the man named as his father and tried to imagine a connection between them. He tried to picture what it would have been like to grow up surrounded by the people of Y'Dan, to know his mad younger brother, Arris. The prince swallowed heavily. He felt fear claw its way up his throat. The muscles in his legs bunched as if getting ready to propel him as far from the council chamber as they could take him.

What right did he have to take what was offered? Who was he to think that he could be a better ruler than Azhani, or even Lord Cathemon? He was nothing, just a half-elven bastard child who would never amount to anything.

Azhani looked at her protégé and smiled. "You can do it," she mouthed silently. "I believe in you."

Allyndev swayed on his feet. Closing his eyes, he thought, *What do I want to do?* He listened to his heart beat as it slowed. In the moment between one breath and the next, he knew his answer. Turning, he knelt before Ysradan. The prince looked up into the high king's eyes and said, "I will take it, My King."

Another cheer rocked the room.

Smiling, Ysradan said, "Rise, King Allyndev. Rise and take your throne."

Allyndev stood.

Azhani knelt.

Lord Cathemon knelt.

One by one, the noblemen and women of Y'Dan dropped to their knees until only Allyndev and Ysradan remained standing.

Ysradan stepped aside and bowed.

Allyndev Kelani, king of Y'Dan, took his throne.

Y'Dannoch was overrun with pages. With a coronation and a wedding in the immediate future, none of the castle's staff got much rest. Both events had been scheduled to take place on solstice day so that the celebrations could run simultaneously. Allyndev and his advisors reasoned that Y'Dan needed to return to a sense of normalcy as soon as it possibly could.

As the ranking member of the Astariun faith, Starseeker Vashyra would perform both ceremonies. Because she was more familiar with Y'Syran tradition, she and her staff had been closeted in the library for the last few days learning about Y'Dani customs.

In a quiet ceremony attended by a very few friends, Queen Lyssera released Azhani from her oath as Y'Syran warleader. As he had yet to be formally crowned, Allyndev stood by while Lord Cathemon did the same as a representative of Y'Dan.

For the first time since she was fourteen years old, Azhani Rhu'len was free to pledge her service to any she chose. At the moment, she had no plans other than sharing time with her beloved Kyrian.

While chaos reigned around them, the two women spent quiet moments curled up on a couch in front of a fire in their room. Lounging with them was Zhadosh, the rapidly growing hunting cat. While she had not bonded to Kyrian as a true partner animal, the cat seemed to prefer her presence to that of any other. Both women had grown fond of the cat and delighted in spending candlemarks playing and petting her.

On the other hand, Avisha had fully bonded with Devon. He had discovered that this meant more than just having a pet who could hunt. Once, while wandering the streets of Y'Dannyv, he had tripped and fallen. Avisha had easily helped him retrieve his crutches and then pulled him to a position where he could stand on his own.

Princess Syrelle, when not in attendance on her mother, spent her time with Allyndev. The high king was pleased by this development, and he and his wife began to plan for the day when their daughter would become queen of Y'Dan.

Chief Padreg and Lady Elisira absented themselves from Y'Dannoch to visit Brother Jalen. There, plans were discussed for the wedding celebration that would take place in the coming summer on the plains of Y'Nor.

The day of solstice came. Nobles and commoners alike gathered in the center of Y'Dannyv to witness the crowning of a king and the marriage of a former warleader.

"Good morning, citizens of Y'Dan." Starseeker Vashyra spoke softly, but powerfully. The tall priest's voice carried out into the crowd, easily catching everyone's attention. Striding across the stage, Vashyra held her head high and looked out at the assembly. Y'Dannyv's streets were crammed with people.

Men, women and children had swollen the city's population until it nearly burst. Now, on this chilly, wet morning of winter solstice, they were jammed dozens deep, waiting to see their new king. Nearby buildings were decorated with throngs of people who clung to awnings and stood on rooftops. Windows and doorways were jammed until their frames cracked. Even the docks were crammed with full boatloads of people jockeying to see their king.

"Today is a day of celebrations," Vashyra began, schooling her face to serenity. "You, who have suffered much at the hands of darkness, are now free to walk in the light. Today is a day of remembrance, as we mourn those whose lives fell into shadow. Let us both celebrate and remember those we loved, for their lives enriched each of us immeasurably."

Vashyra bowed her head. Kyrian, leading the other stardancers, walked onto the stage, singing the pathsong.

At the end of the song, Vashyra read a list of the dead. She started with Ylera Kelani and continued until the last name echoed through the city. The sun was setting when the priest, whose voice had grown hoarse, looked up and out into the crowd. Very few eyes were dry. "And finally, let us remember Arris, son of Thodan, whose life on this earth was short and filled with pain. May he find peace in the arms of the Twain."

"Peace!" the crowd cried back thunderously.

Vashyra faced the crowd. "We have mourned, Y'Dan. Now, let us celebrate, for you will be kingless no more." Turning to look at Allyndev, she called out, "Come, Prince, let all Y'Dan greet thee."

Allyndev stepped up and slowly climbed onto the platform.

"Allyndev, Prince of the House Kelani, thou art recognized as the rightful and true ruler of this land. Dost thou solemnly swear to keep and defend her, protecting her from all that would rise against the people that love her?" Vashyra asked, taking Allyn's hand and placing it over her heart.

"I do," Allyn said clearly.

"Dost thou promise to promote law, encourage commerce and provide heirs to the throne?"

"I do."

"Then Allyndev, of the House Kelani, I bless thee in the names of Astariu and Astarus and name thee king of Y'Dan," Vashyra said and released his hand.

An acolyte offered a pillow upon which rested a coronet. Vashyra took the crown and stood. "Kneel, Allyndev, King of Y'Dan, that I might be the vessel of Astariu and place thy crown upon thy brow."

He knelt and bowed his head.

"Thy humility honors thee," the mage-priest said as she placed the crown upon his head. "Rise, and greet thy people, Your Majesty."

Allyn stood and turned to face the crowd.

The Y'Dani herald stepped forward, took a deep breath and announced, "All hail King Allyndev. Long live the king! Hip-hip—"

"Huzzah!" the crowd cheered. Fists, swords, caps, even children were hoisted high into the air, celebrating their new monarch. Many in the crowd recognized their new king as the brave young man who had brought peace back to their villages. To them, he was a hero and they loved him deeply.

The new king allowed his people to vent their happiness for several long moments. Then, he motioned for quiet. Slowly, the crowd calmed. "My friends, I am overwhelmed and honored by your welcome. Thank you."

They cheered again.

Smiling, Allyndev said, "I also know that you have stood for long candlemarks today; I ask that you have patience and stay but a while longer." He began to walk back and forth across the stage. Every so often, he would stop and make eye contact, or smile at groups of people gathered near the platform. "Autumn's harvest has left the land and led us to winter solstice, a traditional day of marriage in this great land. Today, I have the great honor of bearing witness to the joining of two of my friends. I invite you to stand with me and cheer while the gods bless the union of Azhani Rhu'len and Stardancer Kyrian. What say you? Will you stay?"

"Aye!" came the overwhelming response. Regardless of her shadowed past, the Y'Dani people loved the woman who had been responsible for the care of their lives. That she was joining to one of Astariu's Own only enhanced her legend.

Allyndev grinned and turned to motion Azhani to join him. Her elven scale mail gleamed in the scattered light of thousands of torches. Her freshly braided hair was pulled back, revealing every edge of her angular face. The silvery brand that was Astariu's mark stood out in sharp relief against the warrior's dark skin. Azhani's sword was slung across her back, it's highly decorated sheath a wedding gift from Padreg and Elisira. Proudly, Azhani joined her lover.

Kyrian wore the deep, crimson robes of her order. Around her waist, she wore a golden yellow silk belt from which hung her baton. Joining hands, the two women walked across the stage to stand before Starseeker Vashyra. King Allyndev rounded out the group, standing opposite the starseeker.

Neither Kyrian nor Azhani were particularly nervous; this day had been inevitable since the moment they declared their love. Facing each other, they shared a blazing smile as Vashyra began to speak.

"Long has it been said that the gods do not spin the wheel of fate lightly. Given that, it behooves all of us to cherish the lives we intersect. Today, we bear witness to the fruits of that maxim. Azhani, daughter of Rhu'len, do you come to ask a boon?"

Azhani nodded. "Aye, Starseeker, I do. I crave the right to walk the road of life hand in hand with my beloved, Stardancer Kyrian." Azhani's deep voice rumbled sonorously.

The priest-mage smiled. "I have heard your request. Kyrian, of Y'Len temple, do you also come to ask a boon?"

"Aye, Starseeker, I crave the right to greet the sun's rise with my beloved, Azhani Rhu'len, at my side," the stardancer replied. Her voice was high and pure, carrying across the crowd.

"I have heard your request and answer it thusly," Vashyra said as she took their joined hands and raised them up until they were parallel to the floor of the stage. As she wrapped a silver cord about their wrists, she said, "As the gods have wrought, so do I demonstrate. This cord entwines your hands as fate has woven your hearts. Azhani and Kyrian, the tapestry of your lives has begun — the future you walk will be one trod together. On your honor, do thou swear to share all that comes with humility, love and understanding?"

Bowing her head, Azhani said, "I do."

"I do." Kyrian echoed her.

"Then with gladness and joy do I proclaim thee joined as partners until death and beyond."

Azhani looked up at Kyrian and said, "My beloved." She closed her eyes and for a moment, another's face ghosted through her mind. Ylera's amber and honey visage faded in the next heartbeat and was replaced by the brilliant fire that was her Kyrian. Opening her eyes, Azhani said, "Your friendship has been my greatest gift. Your faith and strength have been the keystones of my soul. Because of you, I am alive. And more than just living, I greet each day with a lightness that comes from the knowing that I do not stand alone. I love you, my heart and the stars blazing in our heavens will fade and die long before that love fades."

Kyrian's face was wet with tears. "My beloved," she said, drawing their bound hands together and brushing her lips over Azhani's knuckles. "You are the best friend I have. Your belief in me gave me courage to stand

and face the storm. Because of you, I will no longer fear the unknown. Now, I greet each day eagerly, knowing you are there beside me. I love you, and all the mountains in all the lands will be dust before my love for you fades."

Stepping toward each other simultaneously, Azhani and Kyrian put their heads together, smiling shyly. Kyrian slowly tilted her head up, while Azhani bent hers down and their lips brushed together. Somewhere beyond the space they shared, the thundering roar of the crowd echoed.

In a place that was separate from time, the souls of two lovers joined and were reflected in a kiss that was both pure and passionate. Astariu's fire erupted from the stardancer and bathed the lovers in a golden glow.

When they parted, Kyrian and Azhani shared a soft smile then turned to face Starseeker Vashyra.

The priest-mage's face was transformed by a beatific smile. "Clearly, the gods have blessed your union," she said. She held up her hands upon which were perched two intricately woven silver bracelets. "Wear these tokens openly as a sign of your oaths. Let them remind you of this day, and how love can make miracles."

Solemnly, Azhani slid the bracelet on Kyrian's wrist and then allowed Kyrian to do the same for her.

The herald, prodded awake by the king, coughed and said, "To Azhani and Kyrian. May their love blossom anew with each passing day. Hip-hip—"

"Huzzah!"

The kingdom of Y'Dan held a celebration that would be talked about at firesides for years to come in honor of both their new king and the newly joined couple. In Y'Dannyv, it snowed, and the citizens celebrated by holding a city-wide snowball fight.

The high king and his family left after a week's visit while Queen Lyssera stayed another two days and then returned to Y'Syr. Azhani and Kyrian stayed in Y'Dannyv at King Allyndev's request. The new monarch asked his old mentor to help him settle into the task of becoming a good ruler. With the help of long time civil servants, including Lord Cathemon, Allyn quickly learned how to handle even the most truculent of people.

The new year came and went. On the eve of Padreg and Elisira's departure, the group gathered to share a meal. There was much laughter as the friends regaled each other with stories of misspent youth.

On the morrow, Padreg, Elisira and Devon would return to Y'Nor. Devon intended to continue his studies as a mage. Padreg and Elisira planned to begin preparations for their wedding in the coming summer. Princess Syrelle had remained behind and would go with the Y'Norans to complete her fostering. It was clear that in the following year, she would return to Y'Dan to marry King Allyndev.

Azhani and Kyrian discussed their plans to visit the Y'Maran seacoast.

"You will enjoy it," Elisira said brightly. "But do not linger long. I wish to have you present this summer."

"We wouldn't miss it," Kyrian said and Azhani nodded her assent.

"Good," Padreg said. "I'd hate to make it an order."

Azhani frowned, and then deliberately turned her back to the Y'Noran. "Did you hear something?" she said loudly. "Because I could have sworn that I felt a blast of hot air."

Padreg's cheeks turned red as everyone laughed.

The teasing went on late into the night until, one by one, each of the companions said their good nights and made their way to bed.

Kyrian stood on the balcony overlooking the darkened courtyard and sighed, thinking of all that had passed to bring her to this place. She thought of the men and women whose lives had been lost along the way. She thought of poor, drug-maddened Arris and wondered how different life would have been if Porthyros Omal had never come into his life. A strong northern wind skated across the city, ruffling the stardancer's hair and sending a wave of chills over her thinly clad body.

Deep thoughts are poor company, Kyrian. You should be with your partner, not standing in the frigid wind, she quietly told herself; yet, she did not move.

Sleepless eyes continued to stare, seeking hidden meanings to the sound and shadow of the darkness. Too many had paid with their blood so that she could stand here and look down upon the night-shadowed pennants that fluttered and snapped in the breeze.

She didn't know how long it was that she stood, buffeted by the wind, but suddenly, a beautifully warm body was behind her, and two long arms were wrapped lovingly around her.

"Mm, what're you doing? Looking for owldragons? They don't fly in the city," Azhani murmured sleepily, nuzzling the side of Kyrian's head gently.

Kyrian exhaled deeply, almost chuckling. "No," she whispered, not quite willing to put her thoughts into words.

Azhani's hands slipped up under Kyrian's light silk robe and began to slowly chafe the stardancer's nipples. "Oh? Then what is it?"

Kyrian's response was a staggered groan as she leaned into her lover's caress. Azhani's touch grew heated, her fingertips gliding from breast to hips and back. Head falling forward, Kyrian moaned loudly. All her dark thoughts melted away at the tender touch of her beloved.

Seizing her opportunity, Azhani quickly began covering her lover's bared neck with kisses, until finally Kyrian spun around and fiercely whispered, "Love me."

Azhani grinned joyfully, replying, "Every day, for the rest of my life."

Kyrian let out a soft sob and stepped into Azhani's kiss, nearly bowling the warrior over with the force of her embrace. Staggering backward, Azhani cradled Kyrian against her, returning her kiss eagerly and trying to guide them safely to their bed.

When dawn's golden fingers painted across the harbor, nudging the sleeping city to wakefulness, the two women, curled tightly around each other, slept on, their dreams filled with the gentleness of loving peace.

Shaylynn Rose is 30-somethingish. She has cats, tattoos and a fascination for sparkly things like beads and crystals. Crafting jewelry, crocheting this-and-that and playing dress up for the next Society for Creative Anachronism event are her hobbies. Someday, when she grows up, she wants to be a published writer. (It says so in her first ever book, written for a fifth grade class project!) Until then, she's content to sell shiny baubles and play "chase the string" with her kitties.

Printed in the United States
106165LV00003B/121/A